OLD SINS

PENNY VINCENZI

Old sins cast long shadows...

CROWN PUBLISHERS, INC.
NEW YORK

Published by Crown Publishers, Inc., 201 East 50th Street,
New York, New York 10022. Member of the Crown Publishing
Group.

Published in different form in Great Britain by Random Century
House in 1989.

CROWN is a trademark of Crown Publishers, Inc.

Manufactured in the United States of America

Book design by June Marie Bennett

Library of Congress Cataloging-in-Publication Data
Vincenzi, Penny.
  Old sins/Penny Vincenzi.—1st ed.
    I. Title.
PR6072.I525O44   1990   90-2577
823'.914—dc20   CIP

ISBN 0-517-58191-4

10 9 8 7 6 5 4 3 2 1

First American Edition

ACKNOWLEDGMENTS

◆ ◆ ◆

BOOKS ARE NEVER A SOLO PERFORMANCE; I WOULD LIKE TO THANK THE small army of people who have given their time and expertise to help me get *Old Sins* on stage:

In England, Robin Vincent, Sarah Gilbert, Nicky Lyons-Maris, and Stephen Sutton from Clarins Cosmetics, Janet Fitch, Lindy Woodhead, Sally O'Sullivan, Major Anthony Harvie MC, Minna and Peveril Bruce, Tim and Maxi Hudson, Geoff Hollows, Jo Foley, Sue Stapely, Peter Townend, Fred Perry, Caroline Richards, Penny Rossi, Vicky Carrel, James Crocker.

In the United States of America, my editor Betty A. Prashker, Brian Sharoff, Carol Schuler, Lewis Sterler, Ruth and Michael Harris, Clive and Elaine Dawson, Gabrielle Donnelly, Debra Ghali, John Hiscock, Cathy Hudson, Anita Alberts, Benjamin Urmston.

And crucially, Desmond Elliott for continuing faith and encouragement; Rosemary Cheetham for inspirational editing and knowing how the book should be; Susan Lamb for some dazzling communication; Patricia Taylor Chalmers, Julia Forrest and Charlotte Bell for administering much-needed nuts and bolts; and most importantly, my husband, Paul, and our four daughters, Polly, Sophie, Emily, and Claudia, for their unstinting, uncomplaining, and loving support through a long year.

OLD SINS

PROLOGUE

♦ ♦ ♦

ROSAMUND EMERSON LOOKED across the room at her stepmother and her father's mistress and decided he couldn't possibly have loved either of them.

Not to have subjected them to this; to have insisted that they meet under these circumstances. She found the thought comforting.

Just for a moment, just a brief moment, it was almost worth all her own pain, her sorrow that he had died, to witness theirs: and the added distress they were feeling by being forced to be in the same room, observing a degree of social nicety.

They were sitting, the two of them, on either side of the heavy marble fireplace in the first-floor boardroom of the family solicitors' office in Lincoln's Inn, both formidably quiet and still, neither looking at the other. Occasionally Camilla would shift in her chair and turn another page of the magazine she was reading. Ms., Roz noted with a stab of vicious amusement. Such inappropriate reading for a mistress, so deeply symptomatic of Camilla's earnest American feminism. Phaedria stared fixedly into the fire, almost unblinking; she seemed barely conscious.

Roz felt an almost overpowering urge to go over and wave her hand in front of her face, to say boo. This personification of grief, the latest of the many roles she had watched Phaedria play over the past two and a half years—ranging from child bride to wronged wife, via media cult figure—was probably, she thought, the most pathetic. She was doing it well, though, as she had done all of them. God in heaven, why had Roz's father not seen through her earlier? She sighed, her own unhappiness surfacing again, fiercer for the brief respite; the pain made her irritable, impatient. What the hell was going on? Why wasn't anything happening? Why had she bothered being punctual, when half the family—well, a good third of it—still hadn't arrived? And what was Henry Winterbourne doing? He was so hopelessly inefficient; just because Winterbourne and Winterbourne had looked after the family since 1847, when old Sir Gerald Winterbourne had offered his services to his friend Marcus Morell in settlement of a gambling debt, nobody ever seemed to question his tendency to behave as if Queen Victoria were still on the throne or his inability to recognize the close association between time and money. Well, Roz was about to question it, and to find herself a lawyer of her own: someone young, hungry, and who appeared to be a little more *au fait* with the existence of such late twentieth-century aids to efficiency as the word processor, the motorbike messenger and the fax machine; Roz was always mildly surprised to find Henry using a telephone and not signing his letters with a quill pen.

She walked over to the large Georgian window and looked down briefly on Lincoln's Inn in the late spring sunshine, trying to distract herself, take in what she saw, but it was all meaningless. Barristers striding about in their court robes and wigs, pink ribbon–bound papers under their arms. Why pink? she wondered idly, such a frivolous, unsuitable color. Why not black? Sober-suited solicitors making a business of hurrying, bustling along. Some ordinary people—clients, she supposed—walking more slowly. A pair of extremely elderly looking judges, heads together, in earnest discussion. All those people with happy straightforward lives, and here was hers, a complex nightmare. And quite possibly about to become more complex, more of a nightmare. She turned and looked back into the room; her husband was hovering rather helplessly in the doorway, trying to look purposeful, as if he was actually doing something.

"C.J.," she said, "would you get me a drink, please? Not coffee, something stronger. And while you're about it, could you ask Jane why we're being kept waiting like this? I have a meeting at two-thirty; I can't spend the entire day here. I do think it's too bad of Henry not to get things properly organized. And also, is there any news of the others? Have they got the wrong day or something? I just don't understand why this family can't get together without being hours late for everything."

C. J. Emerson, christened Christopher John, but nicknamed by his initials in the good old American tradition when he was only two years old, turned obediently to go in search of Jane Gould, Henry Winterbourne's secretary, and almost collided with her as she walked in with an armful of files.

"Jane," he said apologetically, "I'm sorry to bother you when you're so busy, but do you have anything stronger than coffee? My wife is feeling the strain, and I think we could all use a little something to lift our spirits."

Jane Gould looked at him with immense sympathy. She had rarely seen a man more miserable. Like a dog, she thought, who has been thoroughly whipped already and is waiting in the certain knowledge of a second onslaught. She wondered, and was not alone in wondering, why C.J. stayed with Roz, how he had ever got mixed up with her in the first place; he was so gentle, and charming, too, and so good-looking, with his brown eyes, his freckly face, his floppy hair.

"Well," she said, her usual irritation at being treated like a waitress by clients eased by her sympathy for him, "we've got some sherry. Would that do? Nothing stronger, I'm afraid."

"I'm sure sherry will be fine," said C.J., anxious to be as little trouble as possible. "Thank you very much. Oh, and Jane . . . ?"

"Yes, Mr. Emerson?"

"Jane, do you have any idea what this delay is about? Is Henry going to be much longer? Eleven, he said, and it's not like him to be late."

Jane's face went instantly and loyally blank. "I'm afraid I couldn't possibly tell you," she said. "I have no idea what can be delaying Mr. Winterbourne. But I'm sure he'll be with us as soon as he possibly can."

Roz appeared at C.J.'s side. "Jane dear, I'm afraid that isn't good enough," she said. "Just go and find Henry, will you, and tell him we need to get on. We are all—well, most of us," she added with a ferocious glance at Phaedria, "busy people. We can't afford to sit about for hours on end just because Henry hasn't prepared things properly. And is there any news of my mother and Lord Garrylaig, or Mrs. Brookes? I suppose they're all held up in the traffic?"

"I'm sorry, Mrs. Emerson," said Jane calmly. "It isn't quite hours, of course, only about twenty minutes. But I can see it's irritating for you. Mr. Winterbourne is just on the phone to New York. He really won't be very long, I'm sure. And yes, I was just coming in to tell you, Mrs. Brookes has just telephoned from her car. She is indeed in a dreadful holdup on the Embankment. No news from your mother, I'm afraid, but I expect it's the same kind of problem. Anyway, I'll get you your drink. Would Lady Morell like some sherry, do you think? And Miss North?"

"I really can't speak for them, I'm afraid," Roz said smoothly. "I suggest you ask them yourself. I daresay Lady Morell would like anything that's going. That's her usual style."

C.J. looked at her nervously. She was wearing a black crepe Jean Muir dress that skimmed over her tall, slim body; her long, long legs were encased in black tights; she wore no jewelry at all; her dark hair was cut very short. She looked dramatic, almost severe. Roz was not beautiful and certainly not pretty, and the fact caused her much anguish, and yet she was striking-looking; she turned heads, with her white skin, her very green eyes, her strong mouth, her straight if rather large nose. And men liked Roz; they were drawn to her in preference to her prettier sisters. She was better fun, she was direct, she was sharp and clever. She was also extremely sexy.

"Roz," said C.J., who spent much of his life wishing she were less direct and who did not benefit greatly from the fun, or even from the sexiness, "please don't start saying things we could all regret."

"C.J.," said Roz, with quiet savagery, "I shall say what I like about whom I like, and I have no intention of regretting any of it. I am finding it very hard to endure the sight of Phaedria sitting there like a queen of tragedy when it's patently obvious she's got exactly what she's been after ever since she married my father. All I can hope is that she will get a few unpleasant shocks when his will is read. Clearly she isn't going to be homeless or penniless—unfortunately, in my opinion—but maybe she won't get quite as much as she has clearly been hoping for. As for Camilla North, well, I really cannot— Oh, Jane dear, how kind, but I really don't like sherry. Haven't you got anything else at all?"

"I'm afraid not," Jane said, irritation breaking into her bland tones. "We don't stock a full bar. I can get you some more coffee, of course."

"Oh, forget it," said Roz, turning back into the room.

"Here, Jane, I'll have some sherry," C.J. said hastily, stifling the thought of the bourbon he had been planning to ask for. "That's very kind, very kind indeed. Would you like me to ask the others what they'd like? Save you the trouble?"

"Yes, thank you, Mr. Emerson," said Jane Gould, "that would be kind. I'll see if I can hurry Mr. Winterbourne along."

C.J. went back into the main room and across to the fireplace. "Phaedria, can I get you anything to drink? A sherry, or maybe something stronger?"

Phaedria Morell looked up at him and smiled. "That's sweet of you, C.J., but what I'd really like is something hot. Coffee or something. And C.J., could you possibly ask Jane if she could bring in a heater of some kind. It's so cold in here."

C.J. looked at her in astonishment. The temperature in the room was a good seventy-five; he had already removed his jacket and was now glowing profusely in his Brooks Brothers shirt. Phaedria, who was huddled deep in the folds of her sable coat, her hands in the pockets, was clearly, he decided, suffering from shock.

"I will if you like," he said, "but the fire is doing its best for you. Try the coffee first."

Phaedria looked in apparent surprise at the flames leaping in the gas-fired fake coal. "Good heavens," she said, "do you know I hadn't noticed it was alight? Don't worry, C.J., I'm sure the coffee will do the trick. Oh, and do we have any idea why this is taking so long? We seem to have been here forever. And where are the others?"

"I don't really know," C.J. said carefully. "Apparently Henry is on the phone to the States. And Susan, and presumably Eliza and Peveril as well, are stuck in traffic. Now, be sure to shout if the coffee doesn't warm you up. Er, Camilla, would you like anything?"

Camilla North looked up slowly from her magazine, shaking back her heavy gold-red hair, brushing a speck of dust disdainfully from her cream silk dress; she looked immaculate, cool, and in command, not in the least as if she had just made the flight from New York, and if she was fazed at being confronted by much of the Morell family, including her lover's widow, she certainly did not show it. She appeared to consider the question very carefully.

"I'd like a mineral water, C.J., if that's not too difficult. Still, not sparkling."

"Fine," said C.J. "Ice?"

Camilla looked at him in apparent astonishment. "Oh, no, thank you," she said, "no ice. Not with water." She made it sound as if ice were as unsuitable an addition to water as gravy or black treacle. "In fact, C.J., unless it's room temperature I won't have it at all, thank you."

"Why not?" said Phaedria curiously. They were the first words she had ever spoken to Camilla.

"Well," said Camilla, seriously courteous, "iced liquid of any kind is very bad for the digestion. It predisposes the system toward gallbladder disease. Or so my yoga instructor tells me."

"Good heavens," said Phaedria, "I had no idea. I love it iced. Only the sparkling sort, though."

"Well, really, you shouldn't drink that at all," said Camilla. "It is very seldom naturally sparkling, as of course you must know, and it often has a considerably higher sodium content."

"Oh, dear," said Phaedria, "well, that's a shame. I hate the still sort."

C.J. held his breath. He had been watching the two women warily all morning, half expecting them suddenly to hurl a stream of abuse at each other, fearful at the way they had settled together on either side of the fire, and here they were discussing the relative virtues of mineral waters. Deciding that the room temperature in Henry Winterbourne's boardroom had to be practically boiling—why did he have to keep that fire going almost all year round? tradition, he supposed—he moved off in search of further orders.

"Letitia," he said, crossing the room to another large wingback leather chair set at the end of the large mahogany table. "Would you like a sherry?"

Letitia Morell, Roz's grandmother and one of the few people in the family C.J. felt properly at ease with, had also been reading a magazine; it was *Tatler*, as appropriate to her tastes as *Ms.* was to Camilla's, and she was totally engrossed in the society section, her eyes moving swiftly from captions to pictures and back again. "Look," she said. "Roz's school friend Rosie Howard Johnson. Did you ever meet her, C.J.?"

"No," C.J. said, "no, I don't think so."

"Well, she's just got married. To Lord Pulgrave. I always liked her so much. Such a lovely dress. Where *is* Roz? I'd like to show her."

"I think she's in the rest room," said C.J.

"The what, darling? Oh, you mean the lavatory. Such a curious name they have for it in your country. Well, anyway, never mind. Yes, please, C.J., I'd love a drink. But not sherry; I do hate it, especially in the morning. I always think it's rather common. I don't suppose Henry has any champagne?"

"I doubt it," said C.J. "Jane said only sherry. I'm sorry, Letitia. Shall I go and see if I can find some for you?"

"Oh, good gracious, no. Sweet of you, but I wouldn't dream of it," said Letitia. "I'll have the sherry. It will be better than nothing. Oh, dear, I seem to have been drinking much too much ever since Julian died. It's the only way I can get through a lot of the time."

C.J. looked at her tenderly. She was very old, eighty-seven, but until the death of her son three weeks ago she had very rarely looked anything near that age. Suddenly now she seemed smaller, frailer than she had been, a little shaky. But she was beautifully dressed today in a vivid red suit—from Chanel, decided C.J., who was clever at such things—sheer black stockings on her still-shapely legs, black low-heeled shoes; her snowy hair was immaculate, her almost-mauve eyes surprisingly sparkly. She was courage incarnate, he thought, smiling at her with a mixture of affection and admiration.

"All right," he said, "I'll buy you some champagne at lunchtime if you like. Will that do?"

"Of course. Thank you, darling. Oh, how nice, here's Eliza. And Peveril. Oh, thank goodness. C.J., go and tell Roz her mother is here; it will calm her down a bit." C.J. thought this was very unlikely, but went off obediently in search of Roz. Letitia patted the chairs on either side of her and beamed at the new arrivals being propelled gently into the room by Jane Gould. "Come in, you two, and sit here with me. I was just telling C.J. that Rosie Howard Johnson has been married. Did you go to the wedding?"

Eliza, countess of Garrylaig, crossed the room and bent and kissed Letitia. "Hallo, Letitia darling, how are you? We've had the most dreadful journey from Claridge's, haven't we, Peveril? It took almost as long as the entire trip from Scotland. We hardly moved at all for about forty minutes. No, no, we didn't go to Rosie's wedding. Peveril doesn't like weddings, do you, darling?"

Peveril, ninth earl of Garrylaig, half bowed to Letitia, and settled down thankfully in the seat beside her.

" 'Morning, Letitia my dear. God, I hate London. Dreadful morning, dreadful. No, I don't like weddings. The service always makes me cry, and the receptions bore me to tears. Saves on handkerchiefs to stay away."

He beamed at her and patted her hand. He was tall, white-haired, charmingly courteous, and acutely vague, and only came properly to life when he was pursuing some animal, fish, or bird—and presumably, Letitia thought, his wife. He was dressed as always in extremely elderly tweeds; he looked, she thought, among the collection of people in the room, like a wise old buzzard settled briefly but very deliberately among a gathering of feckless birds of paradise. Why the dashing Eliza—then the vicomtesse du Chene, formerly Mrs. Peter Thetford, and once Mrs. Julian Morell—had married him only a few years earlier was something that probably only she herself and Letitia really understood. Even Letitia found it difficult entirely to accept; Peveril was nearer her own age than Eliza's, and they seemed to have absolutely nothing in common. But then, Eliza had always had a predilection for people considerably older than herself, and a talent for charming them, beginning with Julian Morell, so many years ago. And there was no doubt she was very fond of Peveril and was making him extremely happy. Letitia smiled at them both.

"I'm afraid the only thing on offer is sherry, but after being stuck in traffic, perhaps even that would be welcome. Or would you rather have coffee?"

"Oh, I think coffee," said Eliza. "I do hate sherry. What about you, Peveril darling?"

"What's that? Oh, no, not coffee, thank you. Dreadful stuff. I'll just have a glass of water if I may."

"I'm sure you may," said Letitia. "I'll ask Jane."

Peveril looked around the room, and his eyes rested on Phaedria. He beamed happily; he liked her.

" 'Morning, Phaedria my dear. How are you?"

Phaedria looked at him and smiled back. "I'm fine, Peveril, thank you. It's lovely to see you. And you, Eliza. I'm sorry you've had such an awful journey."

Peveril studied her more closely.

"You don't look fine, my dear, if you don't mind my saying so. You look a bit peaky."

"Oh, Peveril, don't be so tactless," said Eliza. "Of course she's looking peaky. Poor angel."

She walked over to the fireplace and kissed Phaedria. "It's lovely to see you, darling. I wish you'd come up and stay with us for a bit. It would do you so much good."

"I will," said Phaedria, clearly trying to sound enthusiastic. "I will. But not just yet. Thank you," she added dutifully.

Eliza patted her hand. "Well, when you're ready. Ah," she added, a thick ice freezing over her bright voice, "Camilla. Good morning."

"Good morning, Eliza," said Camilla, smiling calmly back at her. "How are you?"

"I'm extremely well, thank you. I don't think, Camilla, you have ever met my husband. Have you?"

"No, I don't think I have," said Camilla. Her smile became more gracious still; in deference to Peveril's age she stood up. "How do you do. I'm Camilla North."

Only Peveril, Letitia thought, watching this cameo with a sort of pained pleasure, could fail to appreciate the fine irony of this tableau: the two wives of Julian Morell grouped with the mistress who had usurped them both.

He smiled, half bowed over Camilla's outstretched hand.

"Heard a lot about you, my dear. How do you do? Nice to meet you at last."

"Peveril," said Eliza briskly, "come along. Let's go and sit down with Letitia."

"I'll sit down when I'm ready, Eliza," said Peveril firmly. "Been sitting much too long this morning as it is. Nice to stand up for a bit. Do sit down again, Miss North. You must be tired. I believe you've only flown in this morning. I expect you've got that jet jag or whatever it calls itself."

"Jet lag," said Camilla, smiling at him again, "but no, I don't suffer from that at all. I have discovered that, providing I eat only raw food and drink nothing but water, I'm perfectly all right."

"Good lord," said Peveril, "who'd have thought it? Raw food, eh?

So do you ask them to serve you your lunch uncooked? What an idea; I expect they're pretty grateful to you, aren't they? Saves them a bit of trouble. Raw food. Good heavens." He smiled at her benignly. Camilla, most unusually at a loss as to what to say, smiled back at him. Eliza turned rather irritably and looked out of the window.

Letitia smiled at Peveril and wondered if she dared make a joke about Camilla making off with Eliza's fourth husband, as well as her first. She decided it would be in too bad taste even by her standards and that Eliza would certainly not appreciate it. For want of anything else to do, she returned to her *Tatler*.

"Eliza, can I get you a sherry? And you, sir?" C.J. had come back into the room and had witnessed the tableau also. He smiled rather nervously at Eliza as she blew him a kiss; he was always rather afraid of what she might say or do. She was phenomenally tactless. And still so beautiful, he thought. What a mother-in-law to have. Poor Roz, no wonder she had all those hang-ups about her looks with a beautiful mother and grandmother. Eliza was forty-nine years old, awesomely chic—Jasper Conran, who adored dressing amusing middle-aged ladies, traveled up to Garrylaig Castle twice a year with his designs and to stay the weekend—beautifully, if a trifle heavily, made up, her silvery blond hair cut in a perfectly sculptured bob, her body as slender and supple as it had been thirty-one years ago when she had married Julian Morell.

"No, thank you, darling. Just some coffee," said Eliza. "And some water for Peveril, please. And, C.J., what on earth is going on? I thought we were late. Nobody seems to be here. Where's Henry? And what's Roz doing?"

C.J. was beginning to feel like an air steward, nursing his passengers through an incipient disaster.

"Roz is on the phone to her office. She's worried about some meeting she has this afternoon. Susan is on her way. And I don't know what's happened to Henry. I'm sure it's nothing to worry about."

"Well, let's hope not." C.J. went off again with his orders. Eliza looked after him. "Poor C.J.," she said, apparently irrelevantly.

"I do wish Susan would arrive," said Letitia fretfully. "She always makes me feel so much better. And Roz, too, which is probably more to the point."

"Where is Susan?" said Eliza.

"She's looking at houses with Richard. He has this plan to move down to the country. Wiltshire. Such a mistake, I think, when you've lived in London all your life. Of course everyone in Wiltshire is terribly nice."

"Everyone, Granny Letitia?"

It was Roz; she had come back into the room and heard her grand-mother's words. She was smiling for the first time that day. Letitia smiled back up at her.

"Why don't you come and sit here with me, darling? Yes, everyone. So many of the very best people live there."

"Granny Letitia, you're such a snob."

"I know, darling. I'm not ashamed of it. In my young day it was a virtue. It was called having standards."

"Ah. I see."

"I was just saying," Letitia said, "that I wished Susan would arrive."

"So do I. And I really don't want her to go and live in Wiltshire with the best people."

"Well," said Letitia quietly, "it will suit her. She is one of the very best. Oh, Susan darling, there you are. I was just saying you were one of the very best people."

Susan Brookes had hurried into the room. She smiled at Letitia and bent and kissed her cheek. "Not by your standards I'm not. I'm surprised at you, Letitia, saying such a thing. And me only an honorary member of this family. Sacrilege."

"Oh, Susan, don't be difficult," Roz said. "Come and sit by Granny Letitia. She's in a naughty mood. She needs keeping in order. And if I can find C.J., I'll ask for a drink for you. What would you like?"

"Tea, please," said Susan. "I haven't missed anything important, have I? And I don't suppose there's anything to eat, is there? I'm famished."

Roz looked at her and smiled again, leaned forward and kissed her gently on the cheek. Susan was a tall, thin woman with bright brown hair heavily flecked with gray; she was not classically good-looking but with a strong humorous face, clear, beautiful skin, and startlingly bright blue eyes. She was in her mid-sixties now, and in some ways she looked older, as her face tended to gauntness. But she had a style of her own: she was beautifully and very simply dressed in a navy wool suit and cream silk shirt, her only jewelry a pearl necklace and earrings, which no one, with the exception of Letitia, could ever remember seeing her without.

"Oh, Susan," said Roz, feeling much better suddenly, restored to something near normality, "can any of us think of an occasion when you didn't feel famished? I'll get C.J. to find something for you."

She walked out of the door again; Susan and Letitia looked after her.

"How is Roz, do you think?" Susan asked quietly.

"I think she's in a terrible state," said Letitia. "Eaten up with hatred of Phaedria, whom she seems to blame in some way for Julian's death, desperately unhappy, wretched that she didn't say good-bye to him. Oh, I know it was her own fault—"

"Poor Roz," said Susan. "Poor, poor Roz. I've known her all her life, and I've never felt sorrier for her than I do now. What on earth can we do to help her?"

"God knows," said Letitia with a sigh. "God knows. She will persist in making things worse for herself. She always has, of course. And I feel sorry for Phaedria too. She looks dreadful, poor child. So alone. Well, perhaps today will help in some way. Although I can't imagine how."

Absolutely on cue, Henry Winterbourne suddenly appeared in the room, followed by Jane with yet more files—I'll bet they're just for show, thought Roz—and C.J. bearing a tray and looking like a particularly inept waiter as he hurried around trying to deliver his complex order.

Henry took up his place at the head of the table, his back to the window. "Good morning," he said. "I am extremely sorry to have kept you waiting. A very tedious call from New York. Do forgive me."

He opened the top file on the table, took a large envelope out of it and set it firmly in front of him. Everyone slowly, very slowly, as if in a badly directed play, took up a new position. Phaedria got up and sat with her back to the fire at the end of the table, pulling her coat more closely around her. Peveril sat next to her, assuming an oddly protective role. Eliza settled in the chair next to him. Camilla stood up and walked around to take up the chair nearest to Henry. Letitia and Susan stopped talking. Roz took up a challenging position, standing alone by the door, every ounce of her formidable energy focused on Henry's face.

Henry smiled faintly around the room, catching everyone's eye in turn with the right amount of sadness and sympathy, bestowing a smile here, a conspiratorial look there. Smooth bastard, thought C.J., finally divesting himself of the tray and moving over to sit next to Susan.

"Lady Morell, are you all right?" C.J. said suddenly.

Everyone looked at Phaedria; she was resting her head on her hands on the table. She appeared to be about to faint.

"Phaedria, let me take you outside," said C.J.

"I'll take her," Eliza said, getting up and crossing over to Phaedria, putting her arm around her shoulders. "She needs some air."

"No, no, really, I'm all right," said Phaedria, "I'm sorry, just a bit dizzy, that's all. Perhaps I could have a glass of water."

"I'll get it," said C.J. quickly, grateful for something to do.

"C.J.," Roz said from where she was standing, "do settle down. You've been rushing 'round with drinks all morning. Jane will fetch Phaedria a glass of water, I'm sure. Jane dear," she called through the doorway, at Jane's back, "could you fetch Lady Morell a glass of water, please? The strain of the occasion is proving a little too much for her."

Roz watched Phaedria carefully as she took the glass of water, sipped at it halfheartedly, put it down, leaned back in her chair, shaking the dark waterfall of hair from her face. Looking at her, Roz did have to admit she looked ill. Her skin was starkly white, rather than its usual creamy pale, and she seemed thinner than ever, shrunk into herself. God, Roz hated her. So much Phaedria had taken from her, so much that should have been hers, and what were they all to learn now? How much more was to go Phaedria's way, away from her, Julian Morell's daughter, his only child, his rightful heir? Roz swallowed, fixed her eyes on Henry's face. She had to concentrate. The words she was to hear, had to hear, were what mattered just now, not her thoughts, her emotions. Time for them later.

"Very well," said Henry. "Perhaps I could begin. Now as you may appreciate, this is an out-of-the-ordinary occasion. These days, public readings of wills are very unusual. Although, of course, perfectly legal. And it was at Sir Julian's request that it should be conducted in this way. In the presence of you all. He particularly specified that you should all"—his gaze fell briefly, unbidden, on Camilla, then shifted hastily again—"all be here. There are of course minor beneficiaries, staff and so on, who were not required to attend. So perhaps the best thing now is just for me to read the will. If any of you have any comments or questions, perhaps you could save them to the end."

Christ, thought Roz, what on earth is the old woman going on about?

She shifted her weight slightly onto the other leg, took a sip of her drink, and fixed her eyes on Henry's face again.

Henry began to read: " 'I, Julian Morell, of Hanover Terrace, London, Company Director, hereby revoke all previous wills and testamentary dispositions. . . .' "

It began slowly, with a trickle of small bequests; it was like the start of a party, Roz thought, with only one or two guests arrived, making stiff and stilted conversation. The atmosphere was cold, tense, uncomfortable.

There were five-thousand-pound legacies for minor staff: the housekeeper and the gardener at the house in Sussex, the part-time secretary Julian had employed in Paris for ten years, and elderly Mrs. Bagnold who had directed the cleaners of the offices in Dover Street for longer than anyone could remember.

Mrs. Bagnold was also bequeathed a set of "Victorian watercolors she had once admired, to do exactly what she likes with; she may sell them tomorrow if she wishes, without fear of incurring my displeasure from wherever I may be."

As Henry read out this part of the will, Phaedria looked up and caught Letitia's eye, in a sudden flash of humor. He is still fun, that look said. He is still making life good.

" 'To Sarah Brownsmith, my patient and very loyal secretary, I bequeath ten thousand pounds, both early Hockneys, and the use of my house on Eleuthera in the Bahamas for at least one month a year, at a time mutually agreeable to her and my wife. This is in the devout hope that as she lies in the sunshine, she will think kindly of me and forgive me the many years of exasperation and overwork I have inflicted upon her.

" 'To the headwaiter at the Mirabelle Restaurant, to the chief wine waiter at the Connaught Hotel, and to my good friend Peter Langan, the sum of five thousand pounds each for the great happiness and gastronomic good fortune they have brought me.

" 'To Martin Dodsworth, my trainer, ten thousand pounds, my three Stubbses, and my brood mare Prince's Flora, and to Michael O'Leary, my jockey, five thousand pounds and a yearling of his choice from my stable. To Tony Price, my groom, the same.

" 'To Jane Gould, secretary to my solicitor, Henry Winterbourne, I bequeath my Hispano Suiza, because I know how much pleasure it will give her, and a one thousand pound a year maintenance allowance with which to care for it.' "

Jane, sitting quietly at the back of the room, beamed with pleasure. She and her husband belonged to the MG Club and were staunch followers of the London-to-Brighton rally, but the possession of such a car was quite beyond the dreams of her own personal avarice. Roz wondered briefly and rather irritably where the rest of the Morell vintage car stable would go; her father had known how much she loved them. It would be very sad if the collection was to be broken up and scattered piecemeal. If this was a taste of the rest of the will, she didn't like it at all.

" 'To my good friend Peveril, earl of Garrylaig, my Holbein and the two Rembrandts, which will hang so happily in the gallery at Garrylaig, and my grandfather's guns, which have always deserved better hands than mine to rest in.' "

"I say, how kind," murmured Peveril, flushed with pleasure, more at the contemplation of the guns than of the Rembrandts. Eliza smiled at him fondly and patted his hand.

The party had begun now; the room was humming with tension and nervous energy.

" 'To my first wife, Eliza, countess of Garrylaig, in appreciation for the gift of my daughter Rosamund, and for several interesting and entertaining years' "—Henry at this point cleared his throat, reached for a glass of water, and paused a moment—" 'I bequeath my collections of Lalique glass and Chiparus figures, and my apartment in Sutton Place, New York, all of which I know will give her immense pleasure and be put to excellent use.' "

"That's true," said Eliza.

There was a brief silence.

" 'To Camilla North, in recognition of many years of tolerance, companionship, and wisdom, I bequeath the following: my apartment in Sydney; my hunter, Rose Red; and my collection of Sydney Nolans, as a memento of the expertise and pleasure she gave me in the course of their collection.' "

That's a lot, thought Roz, illogically pleased. A lot for a mistress. Even a long-standing one. That's a smack in the eye for Phaedria. Without even realizing she was doing it, she smiled at Camilla. Watching her, Letitia reflected it was probably the first time she had ever voluntarily done such a thing, and shuddered mildly at what she could only assume was the reason.

Camilla's beautiful face was expressionless; she sat with her eyes fixed on Henry, her hands clasped loosely in her lap. No one was to know that she was concentrating with some fervor on her relaxation therapy and that if she gave up for one moment, stopped breathing deeply, chanting her mantra silently to herself, she would be in grave danger of bursting into tears, hysterical laughter, or both.

" 'To my very dear friend Susan Brookes, who has worked with me for so many years on this company, and without whom I would not be where I am today, I bequeath my house in Nice and the sum of five million pounds free of tax.' "

Good God, thought Roz. He didn't leave anyone else that sort of money. What on earth did he do that for?

Then she saw Susan looking at her, flushed, her eyes suspiciously bright. Watched as Susan unmistakably winked at her and realized why her father had been so generous: to give Susan pleasure, to be sure, but also to burden her, discomfort her in her passionate between-the-wars socialism, leave her wondering what on earth to do with all that money. They had been such good friends, such affectionate lifelong opponents, Susan and her father, and she was the one person he had never quite been able to get the better of. Until now.

Oh, well, thought Roz, no doubt the Labour party and Mother Teresa will benefit considerably from that. She was wrong.

" 'This bequest is for the sole benefit of Mrs. Brookes and is not to be passed on to anyone with the exception of Mrs. Brookes's two daughters; should the house in Nice be sold, the moneys realized should pass to her daughters also.' "

Oh, God, thought Roz. Oh, God, he was a clever, difficult bastard. She looked at Susan, smiled, and winked back. She felt briefly better.

" 'To my son-in-law Christopher John Emerson, I bequeath my two Monets, my collection of Cartier cuff links, all the shares in my property company in the Caribbean, my hotels in the Seychelles and the Bahamas, neither of which would have been so successfully built without his commercial and visual skills, the 1950 Rolls Corniche, which he has always so admired, and the entire contents of my wine cellar, in recognition of the knowledge and appreciation he will bring to it. I expect it to be added to with wines that will grace and indeed improve it.' "

Suddenly, Roz felt, her father was back with them, in the room, charming, witty, civilized. She saw him looking at her, smiling, trying to win her over, make her do what he wanted. She could hear his voice, see his graceful, deceptively relaxed figure, feel herself being pulled into the willful web he spun around everyone who was close to him. She swallowed hard, blinked away the rising tears, tried to concentrate on the present.

Phaedria was sitting very upright now, her dark eyes fixed on Henry's face. She had taken off her coat at last; she was wearing a dress of brilliant peacock blue, as bright as, brighter than Letitia's red suit, but what on Letitia looked defiant, courageous, on Phaedria seemed odd, shocking, inappropriate.

And now it was Letitia's turn: " 'To my mother, my best and dearest friend, I bequeath three million pounds free of tax from my Guernsey bank account, the whole of which may be spent at Harrods should she so wish; my hotel in Paris, in recognition of her great love for that city; and my entire collection of historic cars, with the exception of the Hispano Suiza and the Rolls Corniche already mentioned, knowing how much she will love and enjoy them. And what an adornment she will be on the occasions when she drives any of them, which I trust will be frequently. Should she wish to dispose of them for any reason, I would only request that a Motor Museum be established in my name and the entire collection should be placed within it. Also, my first edition prints of *Jungle Book*, and an oil painting of Edward Prince of Wales by Sir James Holbrooke, in acknowledgment of the important part she played in the prince's life.' "

There was a long silence. Susan reached out and took Letitia's hand; Letitia looked down into her lap. Then she smiled bravely at Henry.

"Do go on, Henry dear. Although," she added, sparkling through her tears, "as queen of England manqué, I wonder if I might ask for another small glass of sherry."

"Of course," said Henry. "Jane, would you . . . ?"

Jane did.

Henry waited until everyone was quiet again and then cleared his throat rather loudly.

" 'To my granddaughter, Miranda Emerson, I bequeath two million pounds free of tax from my Guernsey bank account, to be held in trust for her by her mother until Miranda reaches the age of twenty-one, the trust to be administered for her by my firm of solicitors, Winterbourne and Winterbourne. In recognition of her already apparent talent for horsemanship, I also bequeath her the sum of one hundred thousand pounds free of tax, to be spent entirely on horses and their upkeep, training, and any related activities she herself might wish to pursue.' "

"How old is that child?" said Letitia quietly to Susan. "Three? Well, that should buy her the odd pony."

"Er, if I might continue. 'To my beloved daughter Rosamund—' "
Again a pause. Roz tensed, closed her eyes briefly. " 'I bequeath the following: five million pounds free of tax, all of the horses in my stables at Marriotts Manor, with the exception of the aforementioned Rose Red.' " That was cruel, thought Letitia; Phaedria loved those horses. " 'And' "—Henry paused, looking at Roz carefully, for a brief second—" 'forty-nine percent of the shares in Morell Industries.' "

There was a long, hurtful silence. Roz clenched her fists, compressed her lips; whatever she did, she knew, she must not move or make a sound; otherwise everything would break out, she would scream, punch the air, Henry, Phaedria, anyone. She looked at the floor, at her feet; they suddenly looked very far away. Then she managed, with a supreme act of courage, to meet Phaedria's eyes.

The expression in them was thoughtful, concerned, almost kind; but still triumphant. I have won, that look said. I have won and you have not.

Henry paused again, then perceptibly straightened and continued reading.

" 'To my dear wife, Phaedria Morell' "—only dear wife, thought Roz savagely, her rage and misery lifting just for a moment; I was his beloved daughter, but she is only his dear wife—" 'I bequeath the following: ten million pounds free of tax, my house in Hanover Terrace, Regent's Park, London; Lower Marriotts Manor, in the county of Sussex; Turtle Cove House on the island of Eleuthera in the Bahamas; and my entire collection of paintings, with the exception of the three Stubbses, the Rembrandts, the early Hockneys, the Holbein, and the Sidney Nolans already mentioned.' "

There was yet another silence. That's funny, thought Roz, who is getting his plane? He loved that plane.

Henry looked around the room again with an expression almost impossible to interpret; there was a challenge in that look and amusement, much apprehension, a sort of triumph even, and as it brushed over Phaedria, tenderness and concern. He took a long drink of water, cleared his throat, shifted in his chair—anything, thought Roz, anything rather than continue. Finally he looked back at the document on his desk.

" 'I also bequeath to my wife Phaedria forty-nine percent of the shares in Morell Industries.' "

The mathematical implication of this bequest hit the room slowly; the silence grew heavier. Phaedria was no longer pale. She was flushed; she could feel sweat breaking out on her forehead. Roz was standing almost to attention now, her eyes very bright in her white face, her fists clenched. C.J. was looking with equal apprehension from Roz to Phaedria; Camilla was no longer relaxed but taut—tense, thought C.J., who had always rather admired her, like a racehorse under starter's orders, hardly able to contain herself and her nervous energy. Eliza broke the stillness; she got up suddenly and walked over to the window, turned to face the room from behind Henry's chair, intense interest on her face.

"Do go on," she said. "I imagine there must be more."

"Yes," said Henry, and looked down again at his desk. " 'Finally, I bequeath the remaining two percent of shares in Morell Industries to Miles Wilburn, in the hope and indeed belief that he will use them wisely and well. I also bequeath my Lear jet to Miles Wilburn, as he may find a need for greater mobility in the future, together with the residue of the estate. There remains only for me to bid you all farewell and to say that I hope you will in time see the wisdom of what I have done.' "

The first sound to break the silence was of Eliza laughing; it began as a smothered chuckle and became a gorgeous, joyous peal. "He did have style," she said, to no one in particular, "real style."

Almost simultaneously Phaedria fainted, simply slid out of her chair and on to the floor.

LIVING THE EVENTS of the next hour over and over again in her mind, Roz could remember only nightmarish oddly inconsequential fragments: of C.J. and Henry helping Phaedria into another room; of her own loud and inappropriate demand for a stiff drink; of Letitia suggesting to her that they should go outside together and get some fresh air, and her irritable wretched refusal; of her mother asking inane questions of Peveril, of Letitia, of Susan, of C.J., if any of them had ever met or heard of a Miles Wilburn, and even more inane suggestions that he might be the son, cousin, brother, uncle of various men she had known or that Julian had known; of Camilla, who had become suddenly part of the previously hostile gathering, offering to go through her old address books and diaries (all predictably stored and filed in date order) in search of some kind of clue; of Henry, fussily important, returning to the room and professing as much ignorance of Miles as the rest of them, while volunteering the strangely relevant and unexpected information that he had not drawn up the will, or even set eyes on it until Julian had died and Phaedria had found it in the safe and sent it over to him; of her own savagely swift personal revelation as to the cause of Phaedria's faintness; of Henry's insistence, largely, she felt, for her mother's benefit, that no whisper of the will must reach the outside world, and particularly that part of it centered in Fleet Street; of the departure of the family, in small, disparate groups, oddly subdued (with the exception of Phaedria, glassily pale, but possessed of a strange almost feverish excitement); and lastly the sound of her own voice, the panic and despair she was feeling disguised in a harsh brightness, declaring that she knew that whoever and wherever Mr. Wilburn might be, she would personally hate him unreservedly for the whole of the rest of her life.

"MILES," SAID THE girl from the depths of the bed. "Miles, you just have to get up. It's almost seven, and you have that meeting with your uncle this morning. And you know how important it is. Miles, please wake up."

Miles put out his hand, his eyes still closed, and traced the outline of her breasts, moved down over her abdomen, rested tenderly for a moment on the mound of pubic hair, then moved on, gently, relentlessly, probing her secret places, feeling her soft moistness, parting her. She could feel his penis hardening, rising against her, and her own juices obediently, delightfully, start to flow.

"Miles," she said, in a last desperate effort to divert him. "Miles, please."

"You don't have to ask," he said, smiling into her eyes, deliberately misunderstanding, and for a while everything else was forgotten—the debts, the lawsuit, the trap closing in on him—all lost in a tangle of hair and skin and pleasure and desire.

1

JULIAN MORELL'S ENEMIES OFTEN SAID HE COULD never quite make up his mind whom he loved more, his mother or himself. And certainly anyone observing the two of them dining together at the Ritz one evening in the autumn of 1952 would have been irresistibly reminded of that judgment—watching Julian alternately looking fondly at his mother and almost as fondly at his own reflection in the mirror behind her.

They looked alike to a degree; they were both dark-haired, both tall and slim, but Julian's eyes were brown and his face was long and already threatening to be gaunt. Letitia had deep, almost purple, blue eyes and the kind of bone structure that would look good for another fifty years: high cheekbones and a very slight squarishness to the jaw. She had the sort of mouth possessed by all great beauties of the twenties and thirties—a perfect bow, neither full nor thin—and a nose of classical straightness. But the most remarkable thing about her—and this would not have seemed quite so remarkable to anybody who had not known she was fifty-four years old—was her skin. It was not only much admired, Letitia's skin, it was widely commented upon; it not only inspired admiration, it defied science. It was soft and dewy and extraordinarily unlined, and one of her more florid admirers had once said—rather unfortunately for him—that as he sat looking at her skin, it seemed to him to be more and more like looking into a rose petal.

Julian, on the other hand, could easily have been older than his thirty-two years; he had the kind of looks that settle on a face in their owner's mid-twenties and stay, relatively unchanged, for thirty years or more. He was conventionally good-looking; he had his mother's straight nose, and rather sharply defined mouth, but his eyes were very dark. They were remarkable eyes, curiously expressionless much of the time, but with a capacity to light up and to dance when he was amused or setting out to charm, which was frequently, and to disturb, particularly women; they held an expression that was almost insolent, probing, amused, shrewd; they were hard eyes to meet without feeling threatened in some way or another, pleasurably or otherwise. His hair was a little longer than the current vogue; and his clothes bore the unmistakable mark of much attention and a strong sense of style. His dark gray suit, beautifully and clearly handmade, nevertheless had lapels just fractionally wider, the jacket a touch longer, flaring only a little more at the back, than the classic style his tailor would have offered him; his shirt was not white or cream, but very pale blue; his red silk tie was tied in a Windsor knot; and his shoes, handmade for him by Lobb, were softer, and lighter-looking, than those on most of the feet under most of the tables in the room. His watch was a classic gold Cartier on a black leather strap; on the little finger of his left hand he wore a heavy gold signet ring; and although he did not smoke, he always had with him a slim gold cigarette case, permanently filled with the oval Passing Clouds cigarettes so beloved by the stylish of the fifties, and a gold Dunhill lighter. These lay between them on the table now. Letitia, who had been young in the twenties —and had once most famously danced the Charleston with the Prince of Wales in the Glass Slipper nightclub, an event she was given to reliving in ever greater detail after a glass or two of champagne— and had seen the cigarette as a symbol of emancipation and sophistication, still occasionally smoked before or after a meal through a long black cigarette holder. She was using it now, as she studied the menu, reaching out to cover Julian's hand with her own as he lit it for her, smiling at him through the cloud of smoke; certainly they did not look, the two of them, like mother and son at all, but a wonderful-looking couple amusing and interesting each other intensely.

"Mother," said Julian fondly, "you do look particularly amazing. How long did you talk with Adam Sarsted this evening?"

"Oh, darling, *hours*," said Letitia, smiling at him and stroking his cheek appreciatively. "He takes longer and longer every single time. He's got a marvelous new foundation makeup he wanted to demonstrate, and I do have to say I think it's extremely good. But I had to listen to him extolling its virtues for at least twice as long as it took to put it on."

"Well, he works on his own," said Julian. "He needs to talk about the things he's been doing from time to time. Listening to him is an investment. He was talking to me about that foundation. I'm glad it's good. He's a clever chap. Worth all that money I pay him. Or don't you think so?"

"Mmm," said Letitia thoughtfully. "Just. Yes, I suppose so. But I do keep telling you, darling, the very best cosmetic chemists are in New York. You really should think about finding some people over there. Next time you go I might come with you and talk to a few, if you won't."

"Well, maybe I will—when I go," said Julian, "and I'd love to have you with me. But I honestly don't think you're going to find anyone better than Sarsted. The man's a genius."

"No, he's not a genius," said Letitia. "He's a very good chemist and that's all. He hasn't got any creativity. He isn't inspired. He doesn't have any ideas."

"Mother darling, we have enough ideas between us to keep a dozen cosmetic companies afloat. Stop fussing. What do you want to drink?"

"Gin and tonic. And I'm hungry. Do let's order quickly. Quails' eggs, I think. And the turbot. Lovely. Lots of potatoes and spinach. To give me strength for tomorrow."

"What are you doing tomorrow?"

"Meeting the accountants."

"There's nothing to worry about, is there?" said Julian sharply.

"No, of course not. Don't fuss. You're more of an old woman than I am, Julian, when it comes to money. It's just that I dislike the new man rather, and I know they're going to query the investment budget."

"Are you sure it's the right way to go? Should we talk about it?"

"Absolutely, and no we shouldn't. We've talked about it quite enough already. We need the new factory, and we need a complete new range of filling machinery. Don't worry about it, I'll deal with them. That's my department; you stick to cosmetic concepts."

"Don't patronize me, Mother. I don't like it." The lighthearted look left his face briefly. His eyes grew darker, and he pushed his hair back from his forehead with a rough, impatient gesture. It was an act that his fellow directors and his mistresses came to know swiftly; it meant trouble and got him his way.

"Julian, do calm down," said Letitia. "I'm not criticizing you. I'm simply saying we could do even better with a truly inspired chemist."

"And I'm saying we're quite inspired enough," said Julian. "I don't want any more creativity in the company."

"No," said Letitia tartly, "you wouldn't like the competition. Now get on with your food. Perhaps it's time you did have a new girlfriend. It might improve your temper. Or even," she added, looking at him thoughtfully, "a wife. Thirty-two is far too old to be a bachelor."

LETITIA HAD ALWAYS loved Julian in a curiously unmaternal way, and they had both of them known it; his elder brother James had been the perfect textbook little boy, exactly like his father, serious, quiet, blue-eyed, fair-haired, fascinated by farming as soon as he could walk, tramping around in his Wellington boots after the cowman, up at dawn with his father every day, keeping logbooks of milk yields and stock prices as soon as he could write.

Julian, three years younger, was extraordinarily different, with his dark hair and eyes, his passion for reading, his sociable nature—at five he was already pinning party invitations to the wall in his bedroom and counting the days to each one.

The difference between the two little boys was the subject of much gossip in Wiltshire, and nobody ever understood in any case why a nice straightforward man like Edward Morell had married someone as patently unsuited to the life of farmer's wife as Letitia Farnworth, but there it was. Quite literally blushing with pride, he had brought her down to meet his parents, having met her at a party in London in 1915, and married her a year later.

The reason for that was perfectly simple and straightforward, of course: he had fallen deeply in love with her, and he remained so until the day he died. The real puzzle, and one recognized by the more discerning, was why Letitia had married Edward, beautiful, sparkling, witty as she was, and he so quiet, so shy, so modest. It was on Julian's twenty-first birthday when, given that this was London in 1941, she still managed to orchestrate a very good party for him at the gallant Savoy, that she told him: "You're old enough to know now, my angel, and I don't want anyone giving you a garbled version." She had been engaged to and much in love with a young officer in the Guards, Harry Whigham, who had gone to France and been blown to pieces before her first letter had reached him. Terrified at seventeen by the prospect of spinsterhood, she had seen salvation in Edward Morell. He would not be going to France, because he was farming his Wiltshire property, Maltings; he was good-looking, he was kind, and he was modestly well off. Still in shock from Harry Whigham's death, she accepted Edward's proposal of marriage only three months later. They were married two months after that, this being wartime and the normal conventions having been set aside, and it was only after the birth of James that she fully realized what she had done.

"But, Julian darling," she said, filling her champagne glass and raising it to him for at least the dozenth time that night, "I don't want you to think it was a bad marriage. I made Edward, your father, very happy. He never knew for an instant that he wasn't the great love of my life, and to the day he died I was certainly his."

◆　　◆　　◆

EDWARD MORELL HAD died in 1939. For the duration of the war, James ran the farm while Julian enlisted in the Signals, having rejected the infantry regiments as too predictable, and spent a frustrated two years in England, rising to the rank of captain. Finally by a combination of shameless string-pulling on the part of Letitia's cousin, a colonel in Intelligence, and some sheer bloody-minded persistence on his own, Julian managed to gain an interview with the SOE, the Special Operations Executive, which directed the British leg of the Resistance movement.

Julian had a considerable talent for languages, he was a brilliant radio operator, and he was immensely self-confident; he was recommended for the preliminary selection for F Section and passed with distinction. He then went to Scotland where he learned such assorted skills as living off the land, handling explosives, dropping off a train moving at forty miles an hour, and killing competently in a wide variety of ways.

Finally he was sent to an establishment in the New Forest where he was trained in the more conventional skills of espionage: ciphers, secret inks, and perhaps most crucially, withstanding interrogation.

He was not required, to his disappointment, to set lines of explosives across the Normandy countryside or to scale the walls of German prison camps in order to free his comrades, but what he did have to do required in its own way as much courage, as much ice-cold determination and steadfastness, and it was certainly as essential.

His task was to gather information—perfectly basic, simple information, in the area around Chartres—about such unremarkable things as bus and train routes and timetables, stamp prices, curfew regulations and to relay these facts, so crucial in the planning of covers and escape routes, to SOE in London by radio. His cover was as tutor to the small son of a French comtesse, herself an extraordinarily brave member of the Resistance. Her husband, a colonel in the French artillery, had been killed in the first three months of the war. Julian's code name was Philippe Renard; his age on his forged papers was given as eighteen. The image he set out to project was of someone effete, a little fey, possibly homosexual, certainly timid. It was the first time in his life that he could give rein to his considerable talent as an actor, to display his ability to climb inside another person's skin, however briefly, and he played the part brilliantly. Even Amelie Dessange was half inclined to believe in it, and regarded him with a mixture of tolerance and contempt. Her small son Maurice, on the other hand, adored him and constantly tagged along behind him, a devoted slave.

His radio transmitter, smuggled into the comtesse's house in the gardener's wheelbarrow, was kept in an attic; the door to the tiny room, leading out from one of the servants' bedrooms, was covered by a huge trunk filled with the dead comte's uniforms, medals, and sword. Every night Julian would read to Maurice until he fell asleep, dine alone in the kitchen, and then climb the stairs for his appointment with London.

Julian lived with Amelie Dessange for over a year in a curious mixture of closeness and detachment. She was to him a remote, unsmiling figure who occasionally asked him if he had enough to eat or how Maurice was getting along with his lessons. She was always hurrying about the house, leaving it for brief spells, supposedly to visit her mother in the next village or to take some of her garden produce to the market. He did not like her particularly, but he knew how brave she was and how clever, and he admired her. She was not exactly beautiful; she had rather strange, strong coloring, very dark red hair and immensely freckled white skin. Her eyes, which snapped at him impatiently while she talked, were brown—dark, dark brown, without a fleck of green—and her mouth was narrow and tense. But she had a certain grace and a tension that made him very aware of her sexually. In other circumstances he would have talked to her, made her laugh, flirted with her; as it was, he kept quietly to himself and allowed her to think of him whatever she wished.

One night the Germans came to call, as they put it, a routine visit. Julian was passing along the upper landing on his way to his room, and he heard them come into the hall. They meant no great harm, and there were only two of them. They were simply obeying orders and making sure nothing overtly out of order was taking place at the château, but Amelie was exceptionally rude that night; she shouted at them to leave her house, and when one of them put his hand on her arm, she spat at him. The other grabbed her, shouting at the old man who had opened the door to fetch the boy. Julian, racing down the stairs, watched her, panting, struggling, in the soldier's arms while little Maurice was led down from his bedroom in his nightgown. For a long time they all stood there; nobody spoke, nobody moved. Then the soldier tipped his gun under Maurice's chin, his eyes on Amelie's face. "You should learn some manners, Madame la Comtesse," he said. "Otherwise we may have to teach some to the boy."

He flung her aside, motioned the other soldier to release Maurice, and they left, clanging the door shut behind them. Julian moved toward Amelie as she stood weeping quietly, held out his arms; she moved into them. Maurice joined them, and they stood there, the three of them holding one another in the cold dark hall, for a long time.

The boy was white-faced, sobbing quietly, shaking with fear and cold.

"I'll put him to bed," said Amelie. "Go and take a brandy for yourself and try to sleep."

She started up the stairs. Maurice looked back, holding out his hand to Julian. "Can Philippe come, too, Maman, and read me a story?"

"Of course, and I will come and hear the story, too."

Julian was reading a translation of the *Just So Stories* to Maurice. He found the stories soothing, their humor refreshing and, when he was homesick, comforting. Maurice adored them all. Tonight he read "The Elephant's Child," for a long time, unwilling to relinquish the closeness and tenderness that bound them together. Finally Maurice fell asleep and Amelie led Julian into her bedroom.

It was the first time he had slept with so sexually accomplished a woman. He was not totally inexperienced, but the things Amelie showed him that night, a blend of gentleness and almost brutal passion, stayed with him always. They made love over and over again, until the dawn broke, and they were both exhausted and the world for both of them had narrowed entirely to one room, one bed, to piercing desire, to tender exploration and, again and again, the surging roar of release. In the morning she looked at him as they lay there, unable to feel anything anymore but a sweet weariness, and she kissed him, all of him, first his lips, then his shoulders, his chest, his stomach, buried her face in his pubic hair, tongued his penis gently, and then raised herself on her elbow and smiled at him.

"I haven't done much of this sort of thing," he said, taking her fingers and kissing them tenderly, one by one, "not with anyone who —well, who knew so much. I'm not very practiced."

"You did very beautifully," she said in English. "You are a fine lover. Now"—briskly she got up from the bed and pulled on her robe —"get up. This is not a good idea. It would get out, and the Germans would be suspicious. It must not happen again."

It never did.

IN TIME JULIAN did more challenging and dangerous work. He became, among other things, quite a formidable forger and spent a year in the house of a country postman who produced a large percentage of the documents issued to escaping prisoners en route to the south or to England.

He developed a love of northern France and its lush, curiously English countryside. He was captured and interrogated; he escaped and spent three months of the German occupation in hiding, his cover finally blown, living rough, killing wild animals, catching fish. He made himself extremely ill eating poisonous fungi he mistook for mushrooms and lay for days in a cave, too weak and in too much pain even to crawl away from his own vomit. But he recovered. And he escaped from all of it, returning home in 1945 hugely changed, the charming, flippant boy a complex man, his courage and his brilliance unquestionably established. He had learned to live with solitude and with fear; he had learned to fix his mind absolutely on the end and to disregard the means; he had learned to be ruthless, cruel, devious, and totally pragmatic; he had learned to trust no one but himself, to set aside sentiment, personal loyalty, and, perhaps most crucially, self-doubt.

"I know what I want to do now. With my life, I mean," he told his mother as they sat up late before the fire at Maltings on his first night home.

"What, my darling?" said Letitia, turning the evening determinedly back into a positive occasion. "Tell me. I've thought about it so much. I do hope it's not a career in the Foreign Office or the army."

"God forbid," said Julian. "No, I want to go into the pharmaceutical business. Possibly cosmetics."

"Julian darling," said Letitia, half amused, half astonished, "whatever gave you that idea?"

"Oh," he said, his eyes dancing, enjoying her slight unease with the situation and with this rather unmasculine notion, "this old boy I lodged with near Deauville. You'd have liked him. He was a pharmacist. I worked in his lab with him quite a lot. You know I loved chemistry at school. I'd have read it at Oxford if the war hadn't happened.

"You'd be surprised at what I learned. I can make all kinds of things. A jolly good cough mixture. A sleeping draft. Anti-inflammatory medicine. All sorts. And then I started fiddling around with creams and lotions and that sort of thing."

"Do you mean skin creams?"

"Yes."

"Darling," Letitia said, patting his hand, "I'd sell my soul for something like that. All you can buy now is Pond's cold cream. Too awful. You didn't bring any of your creams back with you, did you?"

" 'Fraid not. But I have got the formulas. And when I've settled down a bit I thought I'd fix up some sort of lab in one of the outhouses and play about a bit. It's fascinating stuff, Mother. I know it's an odd thing to bring back with you from the war, but there it is. I think I could make a business of it. It must be better than an addiction to pornography or a burning desire to write a manual on fifty-five new ways to kill a man. So many of the chaps got bitter and defeated."

"Weren't you afraid of that?" Letitia said.

"No, not at all. I knew I wouldn't; I wouldn't allow it."

It was an extraordinarily revealing remark. Letitia took it in, put it temporarily aside, and then turned back to the future.

"I love the idea, Julian, but how are you going to get started? It's not a world that either of us knows a lot about."

"No," said Julian, accepting her involvement without question, "but we can learn. Would you like to help?"

"Of course I would. I'd love to. But I haven't got any money. Not the amount you'd need, anyway. And James certainly hasn't. It's no use looking here for backing. And I can't imagine there will be any about for quite a long while."

"I didn't mean money. You can always find money if you've got ideas. And I've got lots. And anyway there's going to be a big boom in a year or two. People will be spending money like there's no tomorrow. Or rather, like there was no yesterday. To annihilate. To forget." Another silence. "So I do think it's an excellent time. Both to raise money and to start new ventures. And I really would appreciate your help. I know you'd be very good at it all. Where are you going?"

"To get a bottle of wine. To toast your future."

"Our future," Julian said firmly. "Our company."

HE WAS RIGHT: there was a boom. But it was a little longer coming than he had anticipated. The first two years after the war were almost as austere as the preceding five. Companies were manufacturing as fast as they could, but the Attlee government was obsessed with economic recovery, and everything worth having was being exported. One of the more enraging sights of 1946 was a window full of desirable things bearing the message "for export only." Everything the heart and indeed the stomach could desire was still rationed, and without the patriotic fervor of war to ease the pangs, people were growing immensely irritable.

One night James Morell, who had become increasingly estranged from his brother, came in from the farm, sat down, and ate his supper without a word. Then, after taking a deep breath, he announced that he would like Julian to move out of Maltings. He was planning to be married, he said, and sharing a home with anyone, however agreeable, was not a good beginning to a marriage. The house was his; he ran the farm. Julian had been talking for months about how he was going to start his own business. It was time, James felt, that he got on with it. He had some money, after all; James was tired of supporting him.

Julian, at first amused, became irritable. His outrage increased when Letitia took James's side and said she quite agreed that he should go and that she had no intention of encroaching on James's marital status either.

"We shall go to London together and start a new life," she said, somewhat dramatically, adding that James was perfectly right in his view, that Julian had been talking about his plans for quite long enough and that it was time he put them into practice.

"It's all very well," said Julian, reeling slightly at this double onslaught, "but I don't have any money. I can't get a house in London or start a business. There's no money to be had anywhere."

"Oh, for heaven's sake," Letitia said, "have you not heard of the mortgage? And you have some money your father left you. You said yourself only the other day that it was melting away, as if that fact had nothing to do with you. Very silly. I've thought so for a long time. And anyway, I've got a little money. We'll manage."

James, relieved that the interview with his mother and brother had been less embarrassing and painful than he had feared, said he thought he would go and visit Caroline Reever Smith, the noisily good-natured object of his affections, and hurriedly left. Julian looked at Letitia over the supper table a trifle darkly.

"Thanks for your support," he said. "I hope you realize you've just talked us out of a home."

"Oh, Julian, don't be so ridiculous. You sound like a spoiled child. Of course I haven't. Where is your spirit of adventure? I've talked us into a new one. It'll be the greatest fun. I've been thinking about it for quite a long time, as a matter of fact. Now, I think we should live in Chelsea. In fact I don't want to contemplate living anywhere else. Goodness, I can't even begin to believe it after all these years. Just off Walton Street, I think: Harrods around the corner, Peter Jones down the road, Harvey Nichols, Woolland's."

"You sound as if you're reciting a litany," Julian said, laughing.

"I am. I feel exactly like an excommunicant who's been allowed back into the fold."

"All right. I don't care where we go. Lots of pretty girls in Chelsea anyway."

"Lots. Now, darling, you've also got to think about premises. For your business. Let's forget about starting big and waiting for the banks, and just start. All you need is something very modest, a big garage even would do for now, which you could fit out as a lab. I expect you could contract out any kind of bottling and labeling. The thing to do at this stage is get the biggest mortgage available on the house and keep your capital for the business. You'll find that harder to raise money for, and you'll get a bigger tax concession on a per-sonal mortgage than anything. Anyway, I'll put in any money I can rake up. I've been meaning to sell a few shares anyway; they're just beginning to recover nicely. Only I'll leave it as long as I can."

"Mother, you really are full of surprises," said Julian, looking at her in genuine admiration. "First cash-flow forecasting for the farm, then a capital investment program for Morell Pharmaceuticals, all in one evening. You will be financial director, won't you? And my factory manager as well?"

"Until I get a better offer," said Letitia. "Of course I will, Julian. I've always loved the idea of money and business and making more. It excites me. Only it's something I've never had much of a chance to do in the wilds of Wiltshire. I've often tried to suggest improvements and investment on the farm, but James and your father would never listen to me."

"Well, I'll listen. Gratefully. And as often as I can. And now while we're in such a communicative mood, Mother, and I've sat so politely while you put me just ever so gently in my place, will you tell me something? Something I've always wanted to know?"

"I can't imagine what," said Letitia, just a trifle too lightly.

"Yes, you can. The twins."

"What about the twins?"

"Well, I don't know. I just know there was more to that than you've ever admitted. Some mystery. Something strange."

"Nonsense. Nothing of the sort. They were born prematurely. They died. Nothing more to tell than that." But her eyes shadowed, and her jaw tightened. Julian, watching her, felt the emotion strug-gling in her.

"Mother, please tell me. If it's something that concerns me in some way, I have a right to know what it is. And I can find out anyway. I think James has some idea about it."

"Why?" said Letitia sharply.

"Oh, the odd thing he's said. One night, when we were talking, just after I got home. About how there seemed to be a mystery about it all. How various people still gossiped about it. About all of us. He clammed up after that, wouldn't say any more. But I shall just pester him if you won't tell me."

Letitia looked at him for a long time, then sighed and stood up.

"Where are you going?" he asked.

"To pour myself a stiff drink," she said. "And one for you. I will tell you. If only to stop you worrying James with it. I had no idea that gossip was still going on. Of course James would never ask me; he's much too shy. You do have a right to know, I suppose. And it does concern you. You, but not James. So I would much rather you didn't talk to him about it. Will you promise me that, Julian?"

"Of course." He watched her as she sat down again. "I'm intrigued now, Mother," he said, as lightly as he could, knowing, sensing that what he was to hear was important for both of them. "I can't imagine what you're going to tell me."

"No," she said, "no, you couldn't possibly."

He listened, as she told him, in complete silence. Afterward he sat for a long time, just holding her hand and watching the fire, marveling at her courage and at the human capacity for love and its power to keep silent.

·2·

JULIAN AND LETITIA MORELL SETTLED INTO life in London with a kind of joyous relief, falling hungrily on the city's pleasures and feeling they were both for the first time in their proper habitat. They bought a pretty little terrace house in First Street, just off Walton Street—"I can smell Harrods," said Letitia contentedly—four tiny floors, one above the other. Property prices were just setting off on their dizzy postwar course, and they got it just in time; the house cost two thousand pounds and they were lucky.

It was charmingly shabby, but quite unspoiled; it had belonged to an old lady who had resolutely refused to leave it until the very last all clear sounded, when she had finally agreed to join her family in the depths of Somerset and promptly died. They acquired much of her furniture along with the house, some of it treasures, including some extremely valuable Indian and Persian carpets, but for the most part rather too heavily Victorian for the light sunny little house. Almost everything at Maltings was too big, and although James was generous, urging them to take anything they wanted, neither of them felt they should bring too many remnants of their old life into the new.

They were altogether perfectly happy: it was royal wedding year, and Princess Elizabeth was planning her wedding to the dashing Prince Philip. London was in a party mood, and very busy in every way; bombed theaters, most notably the Old Vic, were being rebuilt, and galleries and museums reopened, holding out their treasures proudly for inspection after years of fearful concealment. The social scene was frantic, as people struggled to re-create a normal pleasurable life. Julian and Letitia lunched, shopped, and gossiped, went to the theater—Letitia daringly bought seats for A Streetcar Named Desire, but actually confessed to preferring Brigadoon—and the cinema —Julian's special favorite being The Secret Life of Walter Mitty, which he saw three times—and listened to concerts. Julian also launched himself on a lifetime passion for cars, and bought himself a prewar Wolseley sedan, scorning the utility-style modern models and feeling, as he settled into its soft deep leather seat and behind its huge steering wheel, that this was for him precisely what First Street and the proximity of Harrods was for Letitia: a wholly desirable place to be.

And they entertained and were entertained tirelessly, a charming if slightly eccentric couple, providing in one deliciously simple package a single man and the perfect excuse to invite him anywhere. No hostess needed to fear she might appear to be pursuing Julian Morell, so charming, so handsome, so delightfully available, but still not quite yet a properly known commodity, or to be hurling him rather precipitately at her single women friends when he could so easily and without any embarrassment be invited to dinner with his mother. And then such were Mrs. Morell's grace, wit, and beauty that no dinner table could be other than adorned by her, no young people could consider her an assault on their fun.

Letitia was having a glorious time. So was Julian. He was now twenty-seven, with that ability to disturb that truly sexually accomplished men possessed, another dimension beyond good looks, attractiveness, or even ordinary sexuality. His entry to a room caused women to fall suddenly into confusion, to lose their place in the conversation, to glance at their reflections, to smooth their hair; and men to feel threatened and aggressive, to look sharply at their wives, to form a closer group, while greeting him at the same time most warmly, shaking his hand, and inquiring after his health and his business.

With good reason: Julian was a most adroit adulterer, seducing quite ruthlessly wherever he chose with a careless skill, and he greatly preferred the company and attentions of married women, not only because of their greater experience in bed but because of the excitement and danger of getting them there. More than one marriage in London in the savage winter and glorious spring of 1948 was ripped apart as a wife found herself propelled by a force she was quite unable to resist into first the arms and then the bed of Julian Morell.

In his early days he found himself in quite extraordinarily delicate situations as poised cool mistresses suddenly metamorphosed into feverish would-be wives, ready to confess, to pack, to leave husband, children, and home and follow him to whichever end of the earth he might choose to lead them. It took all of Julian's skills to handle these situations; gently, patiently, through long fearful afternoons in slowly darkening bedrooms—it was another factor in his success that he was at this point in his life partially unemployed—he would persuade them that they would be losing infinitely more than they would gain, that he was making a sacrifice just as big as their own, and he would leave them feeling just sufficiently warmly toward him to prevent them speaking too harshly of him, and just humiliated enough to be unwilling to reveal the extent of their involvement to any of their friends.

For his first six months or so in London this was the high wire he walked, permanently exhilarated by his success, his only safety net his own deviousness. After that, he grew not only more cautious but busier, involved in the birth of his business and the development of his talents in rather more conventional and fruitful directions. It was a perfect time for him; the boom he had prophesied had finally arrived, and there was a bullish attitude in the country. Investment was available for sound propositions; ideas were the top-selling commodity.

THE MORELL EMPIRE began life as a cough medicine. It was a perfectly ordinary cough mixture—called unimaginatively, if graphically, Morell's Cough Linctus—in three flavors, lemon, cherry, and black currant, but it had two important selling points. The first was that it tasted extraordinarily good and children therefore loved it; the second was that it worked. Given to tired children in the night by tireder parents, it had them asleep again in ten minutes, their coughing silenced, their throats soothed. The reason for both factors was in the formulation, for which the parents and the children had to thank an old man working in the back room of a *pharmacie* in a small town near Deauville, but this was long before a Trades Description Act could prevent anybody from saying anything very much, and Julian had an ingenious and laterally thinking mind. Thus the linctus bore the legend "specially formulated for nighttime coughs."

There was no question of there being any money for advertising, and the labels stuck on the bottles by the hands of the bored housewives of West Ealing, where Morell Pharmaceuticals had its headquarters in an ex-WRVS canteen, were simply printed in white on red, with no embellishments of any kind except a border of medicine spoons twisted together, which was to become the Morell company logo. Nevertheless, the simple message was successfully and powerfully conveyed.

Julian sold the product into the chemists' shops himself, driving huge distances in his Wolseley sedan, its big boot and passenger seats crammed with samples. The pharmacists, used to being fobbed off by crass young salesmen, where charmed by the intelligent, courteous man who could discuss formulas with them and who would always meet orders, even if it meant driving hundreds of miles overnight to do so. Originally reluctant to stock the medicine, those who did so invariably came back for more and, because of the conversations they had had with Julian about formulas, would recommend it with rather more confidence than usual to distracted mothers and worried grandmothers and anxious nannies.

The worried mothers, having witnessed its considerable effectiveness, and coughs being a constantly recurring problem in the pre-antibiotic era, came back for more and still more, recommended it to their friends, and took to keeping a spare bottle permanently in their medicine cupboard, a suggestion added to the original label as a result of one of Julian's overnight delivery drives, the time he always had his best ideas.

They trod a delicate path, he and Letitia; their capital was all gone, and they lived very much from hand to mouth. The pharmacists were slow to pay, and Julian had difficulty getting credit for his raw materials. They fortunately had paid cash for their factory building and had First Street on a mortgage, but for two months they were unable to meet the payment on that. "It's too ridiculous," said Letitia cheerfully, over breakfast one morning, looking up from a pained letter from the building society. "Here we are, dining out every night with the very best people in London—just as well or we'd be quite hungry a lot of the time—and we are threatened with having the roof removed from over our heads."

Julian looked at her warily. "What do you mean?"

"What I say, darling. The building society is threatening to repossess the house."

"Oh, God," he said. "What on earth do we do now?"

"You don't do anything," said Letitia firmly. "Just get on with delivering today's orders and pressing them all for payment. I'm the financial director; I'll go and see the bank."

Which she did. Julian never quite knew what she said to the manager, but he saw her leaving the house, a suddenly much smaller and drabber figure in her oldest clothes, her face devoid of makeup, a plentiful supply of lace-trimmed handkerchiefs in her shabbiest handbag, and returned to his duties as sales manager feeling the future of the company and the home of its directors were in very safe hands.

Before going out to dine with the countess of Lincoln that night, they drank to their modestly generous new overdraft facility in gin and tonic minus the gin, and Letitia assured him they had a breathing space of precisely two months and one week before their cash-flow situation became critical once more.

"And now I am going to go and get ready. I've bought a most lovely new dress with a hundred yards of material in it and a pair of those marvelous platform soles exactly like Princess Margaret's. Just wait till you see them."

"Mother, how can you possibly afford new clothes when we can't buy gin or pay the mortgage?" said Julian, laughing.

"Oh, darling, I have my account at Harrods, and they are dreadfully patient about payment, and we certainly can't afford to look as if we haven't got any money."

"Mother," said Julian, "I don't know what you're doing working for this company. I'm surprised you're not chairman, or whatever a woman would be, of the Bank of England."

"Oh," said Letitia, "I very likely will be one day. I'm just doing my apprenticeship. Now, what you have to do, Julian, is take a very hard look at those customers of yours and which ones aren't paying you quickly enough. We can't afford charity."

JULIAN WAS CERTAINLY not overly charitable with his customers, nor was he yet in a position to refuse delivery to slow payers, although he had learned which of his customers warranted more-time and attention than others, but he was learning pragmatism in places other than the bedroom. One of his very first orders came from an old man called Bill Gibson in a small chemist shop in north London. He had taken two cases of the cough linctus and paid Julian on the spot; moreover he had told his friends in the business to see him and take some of his wares as well. Julian owed him a lot and he knew it. Bill had a struggle to keep his shop going, but it was the only living he had, or knew how to manage, and he had no pension to look forward to; it was literally his lifeblood. Besides, he loved his shop and was proud of it. It gave him a footing of immense respectability and responsibility in the neighborhood, and since the death of his wife it was literally all he had. He lived in permanent dread of his landlord realizing the asset he had and selling his premises over his head.

Six months after launching his company, Julian had still not managed to break into any of the big or even medium-sized chemist chains; he knew that doing so would not only make all the difference to his cash flow and his order books, but would also give him a stature in the industry that so far he lacked.

One night over dinner he met a man called Paul Learmount, who was building up a nice line of business in outer London buying rundown shops at cheap prices and converting them into cut-price chemist shops. He was looking for another in Bill Gibson's area. Did Julian know of any? Julian said he did, that he happened to know a place that exactly fitted Paul's description, and moreover he could put him in touch with the landlord. Four weeks later Bill Gibson was served notice on his premises, a brash young manager arrived to refurbish the shop, and Julian got a huge order from Learmount's central buying office.

He took Bill Gibson out to lunch, commiserated with him over his bad luck, and insisted on giving him a check for fifty pounds to keep him going "until you find your feet again. I'll never forget what I owe you, after all, Bill." To his dying day, Bill Gibson spoke glowingly of Mr. Morell and the way he never forgot to send him a card at Christmastime.

Within another three months demand was exceeding supply to an almost worrying extent. Julian failed to meet a couple of orders, nearly lost a crucial account, and realized he had to double both his manufacturing staff and his sales force.

This meant hiring two people: a salesman to cover the half of the country he couldn't efficiently reach himself, and a second pharmacist. His original pharmacist, a laconic Scotsman called Jim Macdougall, worked tirelessly, twice around the clock if necessary, performing the extremely repetitive task of filling up to five hundred bottles of linctus a day without complaint on the most primitive equipment imaginable, as well as working in his spare time on Morell Pharmaceuticals' second product, an indigestion tablet.

The assistant Julian presented him with was a pretty young war widow called Susan Johns. She was pretty and immensely brave. She was also very bright. When Julian first met her she was deeply depressed, due as much, he thought, to her enforced cohabitation with an appalling mother as to the loss of a husband she had hardly known. Julian would take her out to tea at Lyons' Corner House where she ate hugely and unselfconsciously—"You would, too," she said when he first commented on her enormous appetite, "if you had to live on what my mum produces; a hundred and one ways with dried egg, and they're all the same"—and encouraged her to talk about her life, about her two little girls and the hopelessness of her situation, and what she would have liked to do if things had been different; surprisingly she had not wanted to live in domestic bliss with her husband, or another husband, forevermore, but to get a job as a pharmacist.

"I liked chemistry at school, and I always fancied playing around with all those bottles, and mixing medicines."

"Well, why don't you try to do it now?"

Susan Johns proved to be a moderately good chemist and a brilliant administrator. From the day she arrived at the lab, everything fell into a state of perfect order. Jim Macdougall, who had gone into paroxysms of anxiety at the news that Julian had hired a woman, and a young one at that, was by the end of the first week grudgingly acknowledging that she had her uses, and by the end of the second totally, and by his own admission, dependent on her.

"The lass is a marvel," Jim told Julian as they worked together one evening. "She has a complete inventory of all our stock, she has tabs on what we need to replace, she has a new ordering system, she has every invoice cross-referenced under product and outlet—she worked out that system with your mother, by the way—she seems to understand exactly what our priorities should be, she works unbelievably hard, and doesn't even stop for a lunch break."

"What a paragon," said Julian, laughing.

"Now, Jim," he went on, "I want to talk to you about something else. How's the indigestion tablet coming along?"

"It's fine. Real fine. I have the prototype ready now, and we could start selling it into the pharmacies in a month or two, I reckon."

"How are we on the packaging? Are those boxes really going to be adequate or should we go into bottles?"

"Well, bottles will be safer and will keep the tablets in better condition. But they'll cost twice as much."

"We're up to our necks in debt already," Julian said. "Can't we get away with paying those wretched women a bit less to pack the stuff?"

"No, you bloody well can't." It was Susan's voice; she had come back to collect some order books she had promised Jim to go through that night, and which he'd been unable to give her earlier. She had one child in her arms, and was trailing the other by the hand; all three looked half asleep.

"Susan," said Julian, "what on earth are you doing here with those children at this time of night? It's nearly seven."

"I know, and I was going to do it tomorrow, but the orders were so important, and Mum's out tonight, so I'll have a bit of peace and quiet and I could really make a big impression on them."

"Have you trekked all the way back here from Acton? On the bus?"

"Yeah. Well, it didn't take that long. I saw the bus coming, so I thought what the hell, might as well. Sheila was asleep anyway. And I'm glad I did come back; otherwise I wouldn't have heard you plotting to do those poor bloody cows out of their money."

"Oh, don't be ridiculous, Susan," said Julian in exasperation. "Nobody's planning to do anybody out of anything."

"Planning to try, though."

"Not at all. Simply trying to make the company a little more cost-effective. And, Susan, this is really none of your business. I don't think you should get involved in wage negotiations. You can't begin to understand any of it."

She eyed him contemptuously. "Don't lie to me, Mr. Morell. And don't insult me either. I understand all about it and I think it's disgusting. There you sit, you and your mother, in your charming little house in your posh little street, driving around in your smart cars, complaining that you can't get any decent champagne and that Harrod's won't deliver before nine o'clock in the morning, and you begrudge a few women the chance to get their kids a new pair of shoes before the last ones actually fall to pieces. Some of those wretched women, as you call them, haven't had a decent meal in months. Some of them are doing two jobs, filling your rotten bottles in the day and doing factory cleaning at night, just so they can stay in their homes and not get turned out for not paying the rent. Some of them have got three kids and no husband. The men either got killed or went off with some popsie they met while they were away, while the poor stupid loyal wives stayed at home minding the baby and saving themselves for the hero's return. Just do me a favor, Mr. Morell, and find out what life's really like. Try living on a quarter or an eighth of what you've got, and see how you get on. You wouldn't last a day. Come on, Jenny. We're going home." She turned and walked out.

Julian looked after her, appalled, and then turned to Jim, who had a strange expression of admiration and trepidation on his face. "What the hell do I do with her now? Fire her?"

"I don't think you'll get a chance to fire her," said Jim. "Your problem will be persuading her to stay."

"I don't want her to stay," said Julian, scowling. "That was bloody outrageous, rude, inexcusable behavior. How dare she talk to me like that?"

"She'd dare talk to anybody like that," said Jim. "She's got guts, that girl. And besides, it was true. All of it. Those women do have a dreadful life, some of them. And you don't even begin to know what it's like for them."

"Oh, rubbish," said Julian wearily. "Who created the opportunity for them to work in the first place? Me. Who risked everything to get the company going? Me. Who works all night whenever it's necessary? I do. Who drives the length of the country until I'm practically dead at the wheel? Don't you take up all that pinko claptrap, Jim. Someone should give people like me some credit for a change."

"Why?" said Jim. "Why should they? You enjoy it. Every bloody moment of it. And she's right, that girl. You may work very hard, but you enjoy a standard of living most people can't even begin to imagine. And you have the satisfacton of knowing all the work you put in is building up your own company. You don't need any credit. You have plenty of other things. Now if you've got any sense you'll go after the lass and apologize. Or you'll lose one of the two best people you've got in your company." He grinned suddenly.

Julian scowled at him again. "Oh, all right. But she can't go on talking to me like that. Well, not in public anyway. She's got to learn to draw the line. I won't have it."

"Stop being so pompous, man, and get a move on. She'll be on her bus by now and you'll never see her again."

SUSAN WAS INDEED on the bus, but Julian's car was waiting for her outside the shabby little house in Acton when she struggled wearily along with the children an hour later. He got out and walked toward her.

"Piss off."

"Look," said Julian, "I came to apologize, to say I'm sorry I offended you. There's no need for you to say that."

"There's every need. I don't want to talk to you."

"Why not?"

"Because I don't want to have any more to do with you. I should never have got involved in the first place. I don't like your sort and I never will. So just go away and leave me alone. And pay me for the work I've done this week."

"Susan," said Julian, surprising himself with his own patience, "my sort, as you put it, is giving you the chance of a lifetime. To get out of this miserable dump and make something of yourself."

"Don't you call my home a dump."

"It's not your home, and it is a dump. Working for me, you can have your own home, and lots of other things, too. A career. A life of your own, that you can be proud of. Think of Jenny and Sheila. A good education."

"If you're suggesting I'd want to send them to some bloody neighborhood school, you can forget it. I wouldn't have them associating with those sorts of kids."

"No, of course not," said Julian, encouraged that she had moved outside her outrage and into a more abstract argument. "But you can live in the sort of area where the schools are better. You can buy them books. Send them abroad in due course. Let them choose their own destinies. And," he added with a dash of inspired deviousness, "show them what women can do. On their own. Make them proud of you. Set them an example."

Susan looked at him and smiled grudgingly. "You're a clever bastard. All right. I'll stay. But only if you give the workers a raise."

"Can't afford it."

"Of course you can."

"Susan, I can't. Ask my mother."

"Okay. But as soon as you can, then."

Julian sighed. "All right. It's a deal. But I certainly didn't think I'd find a trade union in my own company at this stage."

"Well, you didn't think you'd be working with someone like me. Do you want to come in and have a cup of tea?"

"No, thanks. I'm—" He had been about to say "going out to dinner" but stopped himself. "Going home. I'm late already, and I've got to get a very early start in the morning. Good night, Susan. See you tomorrow."

"Good night. And—"

"Yes?"

"Well, thanks. Sorry I was rude."

"That's all right. You'd better get those children to bed."

He drove away feeling curiously disturbed. It wasn't until he was getting into bed after an excellent dinner with Letitia and an old school friend that he realized the intense outrage and anger Susan had caused him had been mingled with another sensation altogether. It was sexual desire.

MORELL'S INDIGESTION TREATMENT, as Julian finally called it—the name implying something more medically ethical and ongoing in its benefits than a simple antacid tablet—was a huge success. All the chemists who already stocked the cough linctus took it immediately, recommended it to their customers, and ordered more. Printed on the cardboard pillboxes, under the name, was the message "Keeps the misery of indigestion away," and on the bottom of the box was a helpful little paragraph instructing sufferers to take the tablets before the pain struck, not to wait until afterward, as it doubled the efficiency of the medication that way.

Within weeks orders had doubled, trebled, quadrupled. Julian was physically unable to deal with the deliveries and hired two salesmen-drivers, in whom he invested sufficient time and money to enable them to talk to the chemists with at least a modicum of authority. Jim and Susan were equally unable to cope with the manufacture and to oversee the filling and packaging arrangements. The company acquired a second building in Ealing, twice the size of the first, and invested the whole of the year's profits in paying builders and laboratory outfitters double time to get it operational in a month. Over half the women workers were taken on full-time in the new factory, and Susan Johns became, at the end of her first year, factory manager. It meant she no longer did much of the laboratory work, but Jim had two other assistants working almost full-time on research and manufacture, and Susan's real talent was for administration, not formulation.

She and Letitia were a formidable team. Letitia found Susan not only interesting but challenging to work with. She had a mind like a razor, a great capacity for hard work, and, even more unusually, an ability to exact a similar dedication from other people. Letitia liked her, too. She found her honesty, her courage, and her absolute refusal to accept anything without questioning it interesting and engaging, and she was slightly surprised to find herself amused rather than irritated by the way Susan regarded Julian with just a slight degree of contempt. Susan was constantly delighted by the fresh thinking and innovative approach Letitia brought to the company. Letitia was fascinated by new financial systems. She spent hours reading reports from big companies; she lunched with financial analysts and accountants. Hardly a week went by but she introduced some new piece of sophisticated accountancy, and she drove Julian almost to distraction by constantly updating and changing her methods.

"I really can't see what's wrong with the way you've done things so far, Mother," he said slightly fretfully one evening, as he arrived home exhausted after a long session with the buyer for a chain of chemists in the West Country and found her deep in conversation with Susan over the latest refinement to her system and the effect it was going to have on the next year's wage structure. "I spend my life trying to follow your books and work out fairly crucial basic things like how much money we've got in the bank, and I have to plow through three ledgers before I know if it's okay to buy myself a sandwich."

"Well, I can always tell you that," Susan said briskly. "I understand all the financial systems perfectly well. And buying anything, even sandwiches, is my job, not yours. So there really isn't any problem."

"Absolutely not," said Letitia. "Susan's quite right, Julian. You just stick to your part of the operation and let us worry about ours. If Susan can cope with my systems, then it doesn't matter if you can't."

"Well, thanks a lot," said Julian tetchily, pouring himself a large whiskey. "I had no idea I played such a small part in this organization. You two seem to have something of a conspiracy going. Do let me know when I'm to be allowed to do something more challenging than planning the salesmen's journeys."

"Oh, don't be childish," said Letitia. "You're obviously hungry. It always makes him fractious," she added to Susan. "Why don't you take both of us out to dinner? Then we can try to explain whatever it is you don't understand, and I can put in my request for a new accounts clerk at the same time."

"Dear God," said Julian, "your department will be the biggest in the company soon, Mother. What on earth do you need a clerk for?"

"To do a lot of tedious repetitive work, so that I can get on with something more constructive."

"I think you're just empire building," said Julian, laughing suddenly. "It's a conspiracy between you and Susan to get more and more people employed in the company and keep the wages bill so high that I never make a profit. Isn't that right, Susan?"

"People are the best investment," said Susan, very serious as always when her political beliefs were called into a conversation. "And there's no virtue in profit for its own sake."

"Rubbish," Julian said. "Come out to dinner with Mother and me and I'll show you the virtue of spending a bit of it."

"No, honestly I can't," Susan said. "I must go home. It's getting late."

"Well, at least can I give you a lift?"

"No, it's all right, thanks."

"Let me get you a taxi."

"No. Really. It doesn't take that long from here by bus."

"Susan, it takes hours," said Letitia. "For heaven's sake, let Julian take you home."

"Oh, all right. I would be grateful."

Julian looked at her. She seemed terribly tired. She was basically in far better health than she had been, and was altogether strikingly changed. She had filled out from her painful thinness, had been able to buy herself a few nice clothes, and had had her hair cut properly. The cheap perm was gone and so was the peroxide rinse, and she wore her hair swinging straight and shining, a beautiful nut brown, just clear of her shoulders. Her skin looked clear and creamy instead of pasty and gray. But the biggest change in her was the air of confidence she carried about with her. He could see it in her clear blue eyes, hear it in her voice, watch it as she walked, taller, more purposefully.

"That girl," Letitia said, looking at her across the factory one day, "is turning out to be something of a beauty."

"Yes," said Julian, "I know."

She had looked at him sharply, but his face was blank, his attention totally fixed apparently on some orders. Thank God, she thought. That would never, ever do.

"Tell you what," Julian said to Susan as he pulled the car out into the Brompton Road and headed for Hammersmith Broadway. "How would you like a car to use? You could have one of the vans; we've got a spare, and it would make such a difference to you."

"Oh, I couldn't possibly," Susan said. "Company car? Not my sort of thing, Mr. Morell."

"For heaven's sake, why not?" Julian said irritably. "I'd like it even if you didn't. I'm always worrying or feeling guilty about you, or having to drive you home."

"Good," said Susan, "helps keep you in touch with reality." But she was smiling.

"Look," said Julian, "if you like, if it'll make you feel any better, you can pay me for the use of the car. A bit. Give me what you pay in bus fares. And do the odd delivery, if it fits in. You work such long hours, Susan; you really do deserve it. And it would help with getting the kids to the sitter in the morning. Go on."

"No," said Susan, "honestly I couldn't. I may deserve a car, but I can't afford one. I can't afford to buy a car for myself, I mean. And so I don't think it's right for me to have one I'm not paying for. It would make me feel uncomfortable. And what would the other women think?"

"They'd think you were bloody sensible," said Julian, "and if they could hear this conversation they'd think you were bloody silly."

"I can't help it. It feels wrong."

"Look," said Julian, "how about this? I want you to have a raise. Take the van instead."

"I've just had a raise. Anyway, I can't drive."

"You can learn. I'll teach you myself. Oh, for Christ's sake, you are the most ridiculous woman. Here I am trying to improve your standard of living and you throw my offer back in my face. Don't you want to get on in the world?"

"Not if it means moving out of the bit of it I belong to. Losing touch with my own sort of people. That's the most important thing in the world to me, Mr. Morell. I can't sell out on that."

"But you're already doing a lot for your own sort of people, as you call them, by getting on yourself. Surely you can see that. And I think it's time you started calling me Julian."

"Oh. Okay, but not in the office."

"All right. If you say so. But please think about what I've said."

"I will. And thank you."

She came into his office a few days later, looking slightly awkward. "Mr. Morell, I've thought about everything you said. I agree. I've been very shortsighted. I'd like to take the van, please. On one condition."

"What's that? There can't be many executives who lay down conditions for accepting their own perks."

"You raise the girls' overtime rates just a bit."

"Dear God," said Julian, "so your company car costs me about six times what it would have done. Why on earth should I do that?"

"Because it's fair. Because you can afford it. And because you won't have to waste so much of your time and energy worrying about me on the bus." She was smiling at him now, a confident, almost arrogant smile, but there was, for the first time, real friendship in her eyes.

Julian didn't smile back; he looked at her very seriously and sighed and buzzed through to Letitia, who worked in a small anteroom outside his own. "Could you ask that infernal financial system of yours if we can afford to put the overtime rates up very slightly? Say two bob an hour?"

BY THE BEGINNING of 1950 Morell Pharmaceuticals had expanded sufficiently for Julian to launch into his next phase. He was wearying of patent medicines; he wanted to move into the field that had excited him more from the very beginning: cosmetics. And the cosmetic market was ready for him. There was as much excitement and interest in what women wore on their faces as on their bodies. Fashion had changed in makeup as much as in clothes. During the war the only cosmetics a woman carried in her bag were a powder compact, a lipstick, and possibly some lick-and-spit mascara. Now suddenly makeup had become much more complex. Foundation had become thicker and less naturally colored; rouge was being applied more skillfully and artistically, and was suddenly more respectable; lipsticks were no longer just pink and red, but every shade of coral, lilac, and crimson in between; and eyes had become the focus of the face, with the dramatic, doe-eyed look, a prominent feature of the high-class glamour peddled in the pages of *Vogue* by such high-class peddlers as Barbara Goalen, Zizi Jeanmaire, and Enid Boulting. There was also, in keeping with the new extravagance, a strong movement toward skin care in all its mysticism. Women who for years had been urged, in Miss Arden's immortal words, to cleanse, tone, and nourish their skin, were now feeding it with different creams for night and day, relaxing it with face masks, and guarding its youth with formulas so complex that one required a degree in chemistry to make head or tail of them, but a woman could put them on her face anyway and believe. And belief was what it was really all about.

Julian Morell's talent for understanding women, what they wanted, and above all what they could be made to believe, found itself suddenly most gainfully employed. He knew women wanted above everything else to feel desirable. Not necessarily beautiful or clever, but desirable. To feel, to know, that they could arouse interest, admiration, and above all desire was worth a queen's ransom. And those were qualities he knew could not, should not, be bought cheap. The more rare and luxurious a cream, a look, a perfume was, the more rarity and luxury it would bestow. Anoint your skin with ultra-expensive oils and creams, surround yourself with a rich, expensive fragrance, color your lips, your eyes, with unusual, expensive products and you will feel and look and smell expensive. The other thing about cosmetics, and what distinguished them from clothes, was that every woman personalized them, made them her own. A moisturizer, a fragrance, a color, became, in however small a way, changed, part of a woman's own chemistry and aura and sex appeal. No color, no perfume, was precisely the same on any two women. It was this concept, together with that of desirability, that went into the formulation and personality of the first products in the Juliana line.

Formulating the line was the least of Julian's problems. He knew exactly what he wanted in it—an expensive and complex skin-care line with a strong selling concept, a streamlined color collection, and a fragrance that was not only individual and sophisticated but long-lasting as well. Everyone tried to talk him out of doing a perfume. The only ones with any cachet, everyone said, were French, and he would be wasting his time and money launching an English scent. "It won't be English," said Julian. "It will be French. And the line needs it."

He hired, to help him create all these things, a man called Adam Sarsted, a brilliant lateral thinker and chemist, who had gone into pharmaceuticals from Cambridge and had spent a few months working for Beecham's new toiletries division. He heard Julian was looking for someone, went to see him, fell in love with his entrepreneurial approach, and took a drop in salary to work with him. Together they created Juliana and its first line, Essential Cosmetics. The selling point was that Juliana's new products were invaluable to women, the sort of creams and powders they simply could not manage without.

Julian's biggest problem was selling Juliana into the stores. The rest seemed comparatively easy. He raised the money through a merchant bank impressed by his record over the past two years; he saw Adam's occasionally undisciplined formulation safely into perfectly ordered lines of cleansers and moisturizers, tonics and masks; and he created an advertising campaign with the help of a brilliant team at Colman Prentice and Varley, who took his concept of Essential Cosmetics and turned it into one of the great classics of cosmetic advertising—the Barefaced Truth campaign, a series of photographs of an exquisitely unmade-up face, the skin dewily, tenderly soft, the implication being that with the help of Juliana and its essential-care products, any face could be as lovely. The advertisements appeared on double-page spreads in all the major magazines and on posters over all the major cities and made the elaborate makeup of the models advertising other lines look overdone and tacky. He packaged the range, against the advice of his creative team, in dark gray and white. It looked clinical, they said, not feminine enough; it did not carry any implications of luxury. But set against the pale creams and golds and pinks of the competition on the mock-up beauty counter Julian kept permanently in his office, the Juliana range looked streamlined, expensive, and chic. The creative team admitted it had been wrong.

The perfume, which Julian named simply *Je*, was researched outstandingly. Adam Sarsted went to Grasse and worked for weeks with Rudolph Grozinknski, an exiled Pole, one of the great Noses—an accolade awarded to few—of his generation, and together they created a fragrance that was rich, musky, warm; it exuded sex. "*Je*" ran the copy under a photograph of a woman in a silkily clinging peignoir turning away from her dressing table and looking into the camera with an unmistakable message in her eyes, "for the Frenchwoman in you."

When it was market-researched, over ninety percent of the women questioned wanted to know where they could buy *Je*.

But all this was effortless, set against getting the products into the stores. The most exquisite colors, the most perfectly formulated creams, the most sensational perfume, would never reach the public unless they could buy it easily and see it displayed prominently in the big stores. In London Harrods, Harvey Nichols, and Selfridges were *de rigueur* outlets for any successful line; in Birmingham Rackhams, in Newcastle Fenwick, Kendals in Manchester, and in Edinburgh

Jenners. A newcomer expecting to impress the buyers for these stores and persuade them to give away a considerable amount of their invaluable counter space could only be compared with a ballet student expecting a lead role at Covent Garden, or an unseeded player staking a claim on the center court at Wimbledon.

Nevertheless, Julian knew he had to do it. His first advantage was that, with a very few exceptions, his prey were women. His second was that he had a strong gambling instinct. He took the buyers out to lunch individually, and rather than risk insulting them by attempting to charm them in more conventional ways, he asked their advice on every possible aspect of his line—its formulation, its positioning, its packaging, it advertising—and then paid them the immeasurable compliment of putting some bit of their advice, in however small a way, into practice. It was to the buyer at Harrods that *Je* owed its just slightly stronger formulation in the perfume concentrate, to the buyer from Fenwick in Newcastle that the night cream was colored ivory rather than pink, and to the buyer from Selfridges that the eye shadows were sold in powder as well as in cream form. He then told them that if they would give him counter space in a modestly good position—not demanding the prime places, knowing that would alienate them—he would remove himself and his products if they were not meeting their targets after eight weeks. The buyers agreed. Julian then gave several interviews to the press explaining exactly what he was doing and what a risk he was taking, and the women of Britain, moved by the thought of this handsome civilized man—who talked to them in a way that made them feel he knew and understood them intimately, not only through his advertising campaign and his public relations officer but in his interviews with Mrs. Ernestine Carter in the *Sunday Times* and Miss Anne Scott James of *Vogue*, to name but a couple—placing his fortune on the line in this way, went out in sufficiently large numbers to inspect the line, to try it, and to save him from financial ruin. By the end of its first week in the stores, Juliana had doubled its targets, and by Christmas it had exhausted all its stock.

"WHERE'S SUSAN?" SAID Julian irritably to Letitia one morning the following July. "The cosmetic factory is still running at only eighty percent capacity, and I want to know when she thinks it's going to be at full strength."

"She's just come in," said Letitia, "in something of a tizz, I would say. Very unlike her to be late. Something must be wrong."

Susan was sitting in her office eating a doughnut with savage speed. Julian looked at her anxiously.

"You okay?"

"I'm just furious, that's all. I'm sorry I'm late, Julian, but I had to go and see Mum's landlord. She had a letter this morning saying she had to move out within three months, as he wanted to sell the house."

"Well, that's nonsense. Surely she's protected by law."

"No, she isn't. The house used to belong to the landlord's father. He was a dear old chap, came 'round every week for the rent, nice as pie. But he died, and the son's been looking at all the tenancies, and because his dad never worried about making things official and proper leases, and Mum was just glad to get the place after the war, she just signed something without going into it very thoroughly. All it is is a tenancy agreement with a one-month-notice arrangement. I went and shouted at him, but he said he was doing her a big favor giving her three months, then told me to get the hell out and stop wasting his time."

"Brave chap," said Julian, grinning at her. "Sorry," he added hastily, watching her face freeze. "Look, Susan, let's have a drink after work. I will do anything I can to help."

"Oh, thank you, Julian. I do need someone to discuss this with."

Susan had moved out of her mother's house a year earlier and bought a tiny little terrace house in south Ealing, with the help of a sudden and rather suspiciously timely payment from the War Office. Even Susan couldn't see how Julian could have forged a letter on War Office paper; she underestimated what he had learned in the Resistance movement.

Jenny and Sheila were now ten and eight years old respectively, pretty but rather surly little girls—probably, Julian thought, as a result of spending too much time with their unpleasant grandmother. They went to school within walking distance of the house, and Susan generally found life quite astonishingly easier. It took her just ten minutes to drive her van to the factory in the morning; she was earning, despite her strenuous efforts to keep her salary in line with what she considered equitable, quite a lot of money; she could afford to pay the woman next door to look after the girls after school and during school holidays, and was currently planning a package vacation with them on the Costa del Sol. She was endlessly teased about this, not only by Julian and Letitia but also by Jim and Adam, who never missed an opportunity to point out to her that there were hundreds of people all over the country who couldn't even afford a weekend on the Isle of Wight, never mind jetting off, as they all put it, to the Mediterranean. But, for once, Susan was not contrite. "I've never had a holiday, and we all need one," she kept saying defiantly, poring over her travel brochures.

A week after her disagreeable mother had been served with notice to quit her flat, Susan came flying into Julian's office, flushed and radiant.

"You'll never believe this," she said, "but we've had another letter from the landlord, telling Mum she can stay. He's even sent her a new lease offering her a tenancy for an unlimited period. I just can't believe it. Isn't it marvelous?"

"Marvelous," Julian said, smiling at here just a little complacently.

"Did you—" Susan stood very still, looking at him in awe. "Did you have anything to do with this?"

"A bit."

"What did you actually—"

"Susan darling, I think the less you know about it the better. Otherwise you might say something to your entirely charming mother, or perhaps to someone who might be interested in your knowing anything about it."

Susan looked at him thoughtfully. "It all smacks of corruption a bit, if you ask me."

"I'm not asking you. And I hope nobody else will. Now, if I were you I'd just help your mother sign the lease and get it back to the landlord quickly before he changes his mind."

"Oh, Julian . . ." She stopped and looked at him very seriously. "I do know how good you are to me. And I never seem to thank you properly. How can I?"

"Have dinner with me tonight."

SUSAN ATE HER way through a plate of prosciutto and melon and then some herring before turning her attention to the main course. They shared a chateaubriand, and she ate all of Julian's vegetables as well as her own and worked her way through three rolls and half a dozen bread sticks.

"You really have got the most extraordinary appetite," said Julian, looking at her in admiration. "Have you always eaten so much?"

"Always."

"And never got fat?"

"Never."

"Strange."

"I sometimes wish I could be a bit more—well, round," she said. "Men like it better that way."

"I don't," he said. "I like thin ladies. Preferably with very small bosoms."

"Then I should please you," she said, laughing.

"Yes, you would."

There was a silence.

"And what else do you like in your ladies?"

"Oh, all sorts of things. Long legs. Nice hair. And minds of their own."

"Husbands of their own as well, from what I hear." She meant it lightly, but he scowled. "I'm sorry, Julian. I didn't mean to be rude. I shouldn't have said that."

"Well," he said, pouring himself another glass of wine, "I daresay I deserved it. It certainly used to be true. I don't have time for ladies these days, married or otherwise. Except my mother. And you, of course."

"Tell me why you like married ladies."

"More fun," said Julian lightly. "Less of a threat."

"To what?"

"My bachelor status."

"And what's so great about that?"

"Not a lot," he said with a small sigh. "It gets bloody lonely at times. Don't you find that? Don't you still miss Brian?"

She looked at him very directly. "Actually, no. I know that sounds awful. He was very sweet, but we never had a life together. I don't even know what it might have been like. Living with him, I mean."

"And since then? Anybody?"

"Nobody. No time. No inclination either."

"None at all?"

She looked at him sharply, knowing what he meant. "Not a lot."

"I see."

"I don't think you do. But never mind."

She wondered if he would think she was frigid, devoid of desire, and if it mattered that he did; whether she should try to explain, make him understand that the only way she could cope with her aloneness, the stark emptiness of her most private, personal life and her fear that she would forget altogether how to feel, how to want, how to take and be taken, was simply to ignore it, negate it, deny its existence; and decided it was better left unexplored as a subject between them, that she did not trust either herself or him sufficiently to take the risk.

"What I'd really like now," she said briskly, "is some dessert."

He called the waiter over. "Charlotte russe, please," she said, and upset the waiter visibly by ordering ice cream with it. "And could I have another Bucks Fizz, please? I'm thirsty."

"There is a possible connection," said Julian, laughing, "between the fact you've now had three of them, and your thirst. But never mind." He raised his glass to her. "It's been a lovely evening. Thank you."

"I should be thanking you. As usual. I wish I could do more for you."

"My darling girl, you do a monumental amount for me. That company runs entirely on your efficiency. We would all be absolutely lost without you. I am deeply indebted to you. I mean it."

A very strange feeling was running through Susan. It was partly being called Julian's darling girl and partly the effect of the drinks, but more than anything, she realized, it was simply a sort of tender intimacy that was enfolding both of them, a mixture of friendliness and sexual awareness and a feeling of being properly close to him and knowing him and liking what she knew. The big low-ceilinged room was full now, there was a low hum of conversation and laughter surrounding them, candlelight danced from table to table, an entirely unnecessary fire flickered in the corner, and outside, the sky was only just giving up its blue. She felt important, privileged, and strangely confident and safe, able to be witty, interesting, challenging.

This, she suddenly realized, was much of what having money was about, not just the rich smell of food, your glass constantly refilled, a waiter to bring you everything you wished. It was warmth and relaxation, a shameless, conscienceless pursuit of pleasure, and it was having time to talk, to laugh, to contemplate, to pronounce, and all of it smoothed and eased by self-indulgence and the suspension of any kind of critical faculty for yourself and what you might say or do.

She looked across the table at Julian—graceful, at ease, leaning back in his seat, smiling at her, his dark eyes dancing, moving over her face, utterly relaxed himself, his charm almost a tangible thing that she could reach out for—and she felt an overwhelming urge to kiss him, not in a sexual way, not even flirtatiously, but rather as a happy child might, to express pleasure and gratitude at some particularly nice treat. She smiled at the thought.

"What are you smiling at?"

"I was thinking," she said with perfect truth, "that I'd like to kiss you."

"Oh?" he said, smiling back, "well, do go ahead."

"Oh, Julian, don't spoil a lovely evening." She spoke simply, from her heart. She was suddenly very young again, very vulnerable.

"Well," said Julian, his eyes dancing, "I've had some put-downs in my time, but most of them were a bit more tactfully expressed than that."

"Don't be ridiculous," Susan said irritably, upset at the fracture of her magic mood, "as if you cared what I said to you."

"Susan," said Julian, suddenly taking her hand, "I care very very much what you say to me. Probably more than anything anyone else says to me. Didn't you realize that?"

"No," she said, "no, I didn't," and an extraordinary charge of feeling shot through her, a shock of pleasure and hunger at the same time, confusing and delicious, turning her heart over and leaving her helpless and raw with desire.

She looked at him, and he saw it all in her eyes; and for a moment he wanted her more than he had ever wanted anyone. He looked at her eyes, soft and tender in the candlelight, at the frail, slender, sensuous body, the tough, brave, hungry mouth; he contemplated having her, taking her, loving her, and in one of the very few unselfish acts of his life he put it all aside.

"Come along, Mrs. Johns," he said lightly. "We must get you home. It's late, and we both have a long day tomorrow. I'll get the bill."

Susan stared at him, staggering almost physically from the pain of the rejection and what she saw as the reason for it. Her eyes filled with tears; the golden room blurred.

"Excuse me," she said, standing up. "I must go to the toilet. The lavatory, as you would say. I'd never get it right, would I, Julian?"

"Probably not," he said with a sigh, "and it wouldn't matter in the very least. Not to me. Maybe to you. You've got it all wrong, Susan, but you'd never believe me."

"I'd be a fool if I did," she said. "Let's go."

IT WAS WEEKS before she would talk to him alone, months before their friendship was restored. But finally she came to understand. And she was grateful for what he had not done.

· 3 ·

JULIAN MORELL HAD JUST BANKED HIS FIRST million, having floated his company on the stock exchange a year earlier, when he met Eliza Grahame Black.

He was then thirty-three years old and, besides being extremely rich and successful, was acknowledged one of the most charming and desirable men in London. Eliza was seventeen and acknowledged the most beautiful and witty debutante of her year. Julian needed a wife, and Eliza needed a fortune. It was a case of natural selection.

Julian needed a wife for many reasons. He was beginning to find that having mistresses, whether short or long term, married or single, was time-consuming and demeaning; he wanted to establish himself in a home and a household of his own; he wanted a decorative and agreeable companion; he wanted a hostess; he wanted an heir. What he was not too concerned about was love.

Eliza needed a fortune because everything in life she craved was expensive and she had no money of her own. Being a conventionally raised upper-class girl of the fifties, she anticipated earning it in the only way she knew how: by marrying a rich, and preferably personable, man. She was not too concerned about love either.

Eliza's father, Sir Nigel Grahame Black, was a farmer; he had five hundred acres in Wiltshire and a modest private income. One of his sons was training to be a doctor and the other a lawyer. Eliza came a long way down on the list of demands on his purse, and indeed financing her London season had been largely made possible by her godmother, Lady Ethne Powers, an erstwhile girlfriend of Sir Nigel who, in her garden the previous September, had looked at the potential for investment in her charge—sixteen years old, slender, silvery haired, fine featured, with pretty manners and a huge sense of fun— and handed him a check for a thousand pounds along with a cup of tea and a cucumber sandwich. "Give that child a really good season and she'll be off your hands by this time next year," she said.

She was right. Dressed charmingly in clothes made for her by Ethne's dressmaker, Eliza danced, chattered, and charmed her way through the season, and found her way into every society column, every important party and dance. She adored it all; she felt she had gone straight to heaven. She was a huge success with the young men she met, but that had been something of a foregone conclusion. What surprised everybody, not least Eliza herself, was that she also got on extremely well with the other girls and even succeeded in charming their mothers, something of an achievement, given the fact that she was considerably prettier and more amusing than a great many of their daughters.

This had a lot to do with the fact that she was simply not in the least spoiled. She might have been the youngest in her family, the only girl, and enchantingly pretty, but her mother put a high value on practical accomplishment and a low one on personal appearance; consequently Eliza found herself more sighed than exclaimed over at home as her total lack of ability to cook, sew, pluck pheasants, grade eggs, hand-rear lambs, and indeed perform any of the basic country women's skills became increasingly apparent. She did not even ride particularly well; nobody looked more wonderful hunting, but it was noticeable that she was invariably near the back of the field. Such virtues as she possessed—her beauty, her wit, and a stylishness that became apparent when at the age of twelve she took to wearing her school hat tipped slightly forward on her head and lengthening all her dirndl skirts in deference to Monsieur Dior and his New Look— her family put no value on whatsoever.

Consequently, Eliza grew up with an interestingly low opinion of herself. She did not lack confidence, exactly—she knew she looked nice and that she had a talent to amuse—but she did not expect other people to admire or appreciate her, and when she suddenly found herself that year so much sought after, regarded as an ornament at a party, an asset at a dinner table, it seemed to her entirely surprising and unexpected, a kind of delightful mistake on everybody's part, and it did not go to her head.

SHE STOOD OUT at her party like a star, a jewel. Julian took one look at her, laughing, dancing in the arms of a pale aristocratic boy, and felt his heart, most unaccustomedly but unmistakably, in the way of the best clichés, lurch within him.

"Who is that girl?" he said to his brother who was settling the rest of the party at a table. "The one in cream, with the fair hair."

"That's Eliza, you fool," said James. "This is her party. I thought you'd met her at our place. You've certainly met her parents. Her father's the local MFH, nice chap."

"No," said Julian, "no, I haven't met her. I would remember her if I had."

He sat down and watched Eliza for quite a long time, sipping what he noticed despite his misgivings was excellent champagne, studying her, savoring her, before he made his way over to Lady Powers who was standing on the edge of the dance floor, briefly unoccupied.

He had met her once or twice in London; he smiled at her now and took her hand, bowing over it just slightly.

"Lady Powers. Good evening. Julian Morell. You played an excellent game of bridge against my mother once. Too good. She never forgave you. How are you?"

Ethne Powers looked at Julian and recognized instantly the return on her investment.

"She's pretty, isn't she, my goddaughter?" she said after they had exchanged gossip, news of Letitia, of Julian's company, of the recent flotation, which Julian was charmed to discover she had read much about. "Would you like to meet her?"

"Yes, I would," said Julian, his eyes dancing, knowing precisely what was going through Lady Powers's mind, enjoying the game. "I would very much. And yes, she is extremely pretty. What a lovely dress. Is it Worth?"

"Yes, it is," Lady Powers said. "What a very unusual man you are. How do you know about women's dresses?"

"I make it my business to," said Julian, and then—lest the remark should sound in some way coarse, unsuitable, too alien to this world —went smoothly on, "It suits her very well. Shall we catch her now, in between dances?"

Eliza was flushed and excited. Two of the roses had fallen from her hair and been thrust into her bosom by some overenthusiastic partner. She looked quite extraordinarily desirable, a curious mixture of hoyden and high-class virgin.

Lady Powers moved toward her and raised her not inconsiderable voice. "Darling. Come over here, I want to introduce you to someone."

Eliza looked up at Julian and knew she had quite literally met her match. He stood out, much as she herself did on that evening, as someone of outstanding physical attractiveness and style. He wore his white tie and tails, as he did everything, with a kind of careless grace; his face was tanned, his dark eyes, skimming over her unashamedly, brilliant and alive with pleasure. As he took her small hand in his, she felt his energy, his unmistakable capacity for pleasure, somehow entering her. She met his gaze with frank, undisguised interest.

To her enchantment, after he had bowed briefly over her hand and said "Miss Grahame Black" and smiled at her, he raised her hand to his lips and gave it the lightest, slightest kiss. Something inside Eliza quivered; she felt awed and excited.

"How strange, how sad," he said, "that we have never met before. Could you spare me a dance? Or would that be too much to hope for?"

"Not too much, although not quite straightaway," she said—bravely, for all she wanted was to fall into his arms and stay there for the rest of the night, and was fearful that he might not wait for her if she did not. "I've promised the next one and the one after that, but then it would be lovely."

Julian was completely unlike anyone Eliza had ever met. It was not just that he was so much older than she was; it was his clothes, his cars, his life-style, the things he talked about, the people he knew, and, perhaps most alien to her background and upbringing, the acute importance of money and the making of it in his life. He was obviously immeasurably richer than anyone she had ever met, but that was less significant than the fact that he had made his money himself. Eliza had grown up in a society that did not talk about money and regarded the making of it in large quantities as something rather undesirable; it betrayed an adherence to a code of values and a set of necessities that found no place in upper-class rural life. Nevertheless, he was not what her mother described in a hushed voice as a nouveau. Had he not, after all, lived five miles away from her most of his life and been to Marlborough like so many of the fumbling boys she met, and did he not ride to hounds and dress with impeccable taste? So it was hard to define exactly what made him so exciting, gave him just the faintest aura of unsuitability. She only knew that getting to know him was like discovering some totally new, hitherto unimagined country. And she got to know him, she thought, extremely well and very quickly. He simply never left her alone. At the end of her dance he had said good-bye, very correctly, with the most chaste of kisses on her forehead, much to her disappointment, and driven off to London. She watched the taillights of the Mercedes disappearing into the darkness and fell into a desperate anxiety that she would never see him again. But he phoned her the next morning to thank her for a wonderful evening and ask her to dinner on Monday night.

"I'd love to," she said, her heart soaring and singing above her hangover, "I—I shall probably be back in London with my godmother. At the Albany. Shall I give you the number?"

"I have it," he said. "I made sure of it before I left the ball."

"Oh," she said, smiling foolishly into the phone at this small, important piece of information, "well, then, perhaps you could ring me in the afternoon and arrange when to pick me up."

"I will," he said. "How are you this morning?"

"I feel terrible," she said. "How about you?"

"I feel wonderful," he said. "It was the best evening I can remember for a very long time."

"Oh, good." She could hear herself sounding gauche and uninteresting. "I enjoyed it, too. Well, thank you for ringing. I'll look forward to tomorrow."

Julian took her out to dinner that first evening. The Connaught, he had often thought, and indeed put the thought to the test, had been designed with seduction in mind. It was not just its quite ridiculous extravagance, the way it pampered and spoiled its customers even before they pushed through the swinging doors; nor was it the peculiar blend of deference and friendliness shown by the staff to its favorite customers, or its spectacular elegance, or that of its guests, or even the wonder of its menu, its restrained adventurousness, the treasures of its cellar, the precisely perfect timing of its service. It was the strange quality it had of being something, just a little, like a private house; it had an intimacy, a humanity. He had often tried to pinpoint the exact nature of that quality, and as he got ready for dinner with Eliza, contemplating the undoubted pleasure to come, he realized suddenly what it was.

"Carnal knowledge," he said to his reflection in the mirror, "that's what the old place has." And he smiled at the thought of placing Eliza within it.

They talked, that night, for hours and hours. Or rather Eliza did. She forgot to eat—her sole went back to the kitchen virtually untouched, to the great distress of the chef, despite Julian's repeated reassurances—and she hardly drank anything either. She had no need to; she was excited, relaxed, exhilarated, all at once simply by being where she was, and the enchantment of being with someone who not only seemed to want to hear what she had to say but gave it serious consideration. Eliza was used to being dismissed, to having her views disregarded. Julian's gift for listening, for easing the truth from women about themselves, was never more rapturously received —or so well rewarded.

He sat across the table from her, watching her, enjoying her, and enjoying the fact that he was disturbing her just a little, and he learned all he needed to know about her and more.

He learned that she was intelligent but ill read and worse informed; that she loved clothes, dancing, and the cinema; that she hated the theater and loathed concerts; that she liked women as much as men; that her parents had been strangely unsupportive and detached; that she had been curiously lonely for much of her childhood; that her beauty was a source of pleasure to her but had not made her arrogant; that she was indeed utterly sexually inexperienced and at engaging pains to conceal the matter; and that she was a most intriguing blend of self-confident and self-deprecating, much given to claiming her incompetence and stupidity on a great many counts. It all added up to a most interesting and desirable commodity.

Eliza learned little of him, by contrast. Trained by her godmother to talk to men, to draw them out, she tried hard to make Julian tell her about his childhood, his experiences in the war, his early days with the company. She failed totally; he smiled at her, his most engaging, charming smile, and told her that his childhood had no doubt been much like her own, as they had been such near neighbors, that she would be dreadfully bored by the rather mundane details of how his company had been born, and that to someone as young as she was, the war must seem like history and he had no intention of turning himself into a historic figure.

Eliza found this perfectly acceptable; she was still child enough to be told what she should think and be interested in, and if he was more interested in talking about her than about himself, then that seemed to her to be a charming compliment. It did not occur to her that this aspect of her youth was, for Julian, one of her greatest assets. And she was a great deal older and wiser before she recognized it for the ruthless, deliberate isolation of her from his most personal self that it was.

What he did make her feel that night, and for many nights, was more interesting, more amusing, and more worldly than she had ever imagined she could be, and more aware of herself, in an oddly potent way. She had always known she was pretty, that people liked to be with her, but that night she felt desirable and desired, for the very first time, and it was an exciting and delicious discovery. It wasn't anything especially that Julian said, or even that he did, simply the way he looked at her, smiled at her, studied her, responded to her. And for the first time since she had been a very young child, she found herself thinking of, yearning for, physical contact: to be touched, held, stroked, caressed.

Julian kissed her that night, not chastely on the forehead, but on the mouth; he had had great hopes of that mouth, so full, so soft, so sensual, and he was not disappointed. "You are," he told her gently as he drew back, more disturbed than he had expected to be, wondering precisely how long he would be able to defer her seduction, "most beautiful. Most lovely. I want to see you again and again."

He did see her again and again. Every morning he phoned her, wherever she was, either at home in Wiltshire or at Ethne's flat in the

Albany. If she was in London he insisted on her having lunch with him; he would spend hours over lunch; there was never any hurry, it seemed, or hardly ever. He would meet her at half past twelve, and there was always a bottle of Bollinger or Moët waiting by the table when she arrived, and he would sit listening to her, laughing with her, talking to her until well after three. In the evening he met her for drinks at seven and then took her out to dinner and then to dance at nightclubs; she liked the Blue Angel best in Berkeley Square where Hutch sat at the piano and played whatever he was asked in his quiet, amused and amusing way, the classics of Cole Porter and Rodgers and Hart, and the great songs of that year, "Cry Me a River" and "Secret Love," but Eliza often asked him to play her own favorite, "All the Things You Are," and sat and gazed, drowned, in Julian's brilliant dark eyes and discovered for the first time the great truth of Mr. Coward's pronouncement about the potency of cheap music. They drank endless champagne and talked and talked and laughed and danced until far, far into the night on the small, crowded floor in the peculiarly public privacy created by warmth and darkness and sexy music.

And every night Julian delivered Eliza home to her godmother and her bed, and drove back to Chelsea after doing no more than kissing her and driving her to a torment of frustration and anxiety. He must, she knew, have had vast sexual experience; he could not possibly, she felt, be satisfied with mere kissing for very long, and yet the weeks went by and he demanded nothing more of her. Was she too young to be of sexual interest to him? she wondered. Was she simply not attractive? Was he—most dreadful thought of all—merely spending so much time with her in the absence of anyone more interesting and exciting? She did not realize that these were precisely the things he intended her to think, to wonder, to fear, so that when the time had finally come for him to seduce her, she would be relieved, grateful, overwhelmed, and his task would be easier, more rewarding, and emotionally heightened.

Meanwhile, almost without her realizing it, he aroused her appetite. He did not frighten her or hurry her; he simply brought her to a fever of impatience and hunger, awakening in her feelings and sensations she had never dreamed herself capable of, and then, tenderly, gently, lovingly, left her alone.

THE GRAHAME BLACKS received Julian's request for their daughter's hand with extremely mixed feelings. Clearly it was a brilliant marriage; he could offer her the world and a little more, and moreover he gave every sign of caring very much for her. Nevertheless, Mary Grahame Black had severe misgivings. She felt Eliza was to be led into a life for which she was unprepared and ill suited, and although her perspective of Julian's life was a little hazy, she was surprisingly correct.

Julian's friends were all much older than Eliza. Most of them had been married for years and were embarking on the bored merry-go-round of adultery that occupied the moneyed classes through their middle years. They tended, therefore, to regard her as something of a nuisance, an interloper, who had deprived them of one of the more amusing members of their circle and in whose presence their behavior had to be somewhat modified.

They were not the sort of people Eliza had grown up with; they were not like the friends of her parents or even the more sophisticated friends of her godmother. They were, many of them, pleasure seekers, pursuing their quarry wherever they might find it: killing time, and boredom, skiing for weeks at a time in Klosters or Aspen, Colorado, following the sun to the Caribbean and the Bahamas, racing at Longchamps, shopping in Paris, Milan, and New York, educating their children in the international schools, and spending money with a steady, addictive compulsion. All this Eliza would have to learn— how to speak their language, share their concerns, master their accomplishments—and it would not be easy.

Also, once the first rapture of the relationship was over, Eliza would plainly have to learn to live with Julian's other great love, his company. He was an acutely busy man; he traveled a great deal, and his head and to a degree his heart as well as his physical presence were frequently elsewhere. Eliza was very young and did not have a great many of her own resources; her parents could see much boredom and loneliness in store for her.

There was also that other great hazard of the so-called brilliant marriage, the disagreeable specter of inequality. It was all very well, as Mary Grahame Black pointed out to Lady Powers, catching a man vastly richer than yourself, but for the rest of your life, or at least until you were extremely well settled into it, you would be forced to regard yourself—and certainly others would regard you—as fortunate and, worse than fortunate, inferior. Lady Powers pooh-poohed this, mainly because there was nothing else she could do, but she had to concede that it was an element in the affair and that Eliza might find it difficult.

"But then, every marriage has its problems, many of them worse things than that. Suppose she was going to marry somebody very poor or dishonest or"—she dredged her mind for the worst horrors she could find there—"common. The child is managing to hold her own brilliantly at the moment. She will cope. And she does look perfectly wonderful."

This was true. Eliza did look perfectly wonderful. There was no other way to describe it. She didn't just look beautiful and happy; she had developed a kind of gloss, a sleekness, a careless confidence. The reason was sex.

Eliza took to sex with an enthusiasm and a hunger that surprised even Julian.

"I have something for you," he had said to her early one evening when he came to pick her up from the Albany. "Look. I hope you like it."

He gave her a small box; inside it was a sapphire and diamond Art Deco ring that he had bought at Sotheby's.

"I thought it would suit you."

"Oh, Julian, it's beautiful. I love it. I don't deserve it."

"Yes, you do. But you can only have it on one condition."

"What?"

"That you marry me."

Eliza looked at him, very seriously. She had thought, even expected that he would ask her, even while she had been afraid that he would not, and the moment was too important, too serious to play silly games.

"Of course I will marry you," she said, placing her hand in his in a gesture he found oddly touching. "I would adore to marry you. Thank you for asking me," she added, with the echo of the well-brought-up child she had so recently been, and then, even as he laughed at her, she said, with all the assurance of the sensual woman she had become, "but I want you to make love to me. Please. Soon. I don't think I can wait very much longer."

"Not until we are married?"

"Certainly not until we are married."

"I hope you realize this is what I should be saying to you, rather than you to me."

"Yes, of course I do. But I thought you probably wouldn't."

"I have been trying not to."

"I know."

"But I wanted to. Desperately. As I hope you knew."

"Well, you can. I wish you would."

"Eliza."

"Yes?"

"Will you come to bed with me? Very, very soon?"

"Yes," she said, "yes, yes, I will."

SHE WAS ARDENT, tender, eager to learn, to please, to give, and most important to take. Where he had expected to find diffidence, he found impatience; instead of shyness, there was confidence, instead of reticence a glorious, greedy abandon.

"Are you quite sure you haven't ever done this before?" said Julian, smiling, stroking her tiny breasts, kissing her nipples, smoothing back her silvery hair after she had most triumphantly come not once but three times. "Nicely reared young ladies aren't supposed to be quite so successful straightaway, you know; they need a little coaxing."

"It isn't straightaway," said Eliza, stretching herself with pleasure. "It's the—let me see—the fourth time we've been to bed. And you've been coaxing me, haven't you, for weeks and weeks."

"You noticed."

"Of course. Most of the time," she added truthfully, "I couldn't notice anything else."

He laughed. "You're wonderful. Really, really wonderful. I'm a very lucky man. I mean it. And I adore you."

"Do you really?"

"I really really do."

THEY WERE TO be married at Holy Trinity Brompton at Eliza's own insistence; it nearly broke her mother's heart not to have the wedding in the country, deeply grieved her father, and even Lady Powers was hard pressed to defend her, but Eliza was adamant; she had fallen in love with London and its society and nothing on earth, she said, was going to persuade her to drag her smart new friends down to the wilds of Wiltshire for a hick country wedding.

What was more she wanted a dress from Hartnell for her wedding and that was that; she wasn't going to be married in a dress made by anybody less. Lady Powers told her, first gently, then sharply, that her father could hardly be expected to pay for such a dress, and Eliza had answered that she had no intention of her father paying for it, and that Julian was perfectly happy to do so.

"I imagine your father will be very hurt," said Lady Powers. "I think you should talk to him about it."

"Oh, you do all fuss," cried Eliza irritably. "All right, I'll tell him next weekend. I must go and get dressed now. Julian's taking me to *South Pacific* tonight. We were just so lucky to get tickets."

Sir Nigel *was* very hurt about the dress, and about the location for the wedding; Eliza stormed upstairs after dinner, leaving Julian to salvage the situation as best he could.

"I know you don't like the idea of this London wedding, and I quite understand," he said, smiling at them gently over his brandy. "To be quite honest I'd rather be married in the country myself. But I'm afraid all this London business has gone to Eliza's head, and I suppose we should humor her a little. After all, it is her wedding day, and I very much hope she won't be having another, so maybe we should put our own wishes aside. As for the dress, well, I really would like to help in some way. I know how devilishly expensive everything is now, and the wedding itself is going to cost such a lot and you've been so good to me all this year; let me buy her dress. It would be a way of saying thank you for everything—most of all for Eliza."

The Grahame Blacks were more than a little mollified by this, and accepted reluctantly, but gracefully; but Mary, lying awake that night thinking about Julian's words, tried to analyze precisely what it was about them that had made her feel uneasy. It was nearly dawn before she succeeded, and then she did not feel she could share the knowledge: Julian had been talking about Eliza exactly as if he were her father and not in the least as if he was a man in love.

ANOTHER PERSON WAS deeply affected by the prospective marriage, and that was Letitia. She invited Eliza to lunch at First Street a few weeks after the engagement was announced, ostensibly to discuss wedding plans. Dresses, bridesmaids, music, and flowers occupied them through the first course, but halfway through the compote she put down her spoon, picked up her glass, and said, "Eliza, I wonder if you realize quite what you are marrying?"

Eliza, startled, put down her own spoon, looked nervously at Letitia, and blushed. "I think I do," she said firmly. "I hope I do."

"Well, you see," said Letitia, equally firmly, "I'm afraid you don't. You think you are about to become the wife of a rich man who will be giving some of his time and attention to his company, but most of it to you. I'm afraid it will be rather the other way 'round."

Eliza's chin went up; she was not easily frightened. "I don't know quite what you mean," she said, "but of course I realize that Julian is a very busy man, that he has to work very hard."

"No," said Letitia, "he is not just a very busy man. He is an obsessed man. That company is everything—well, almost everything—to him. How much do you know about it, Eliza? About Morell's? Tell me."

She sounded and felt cross. Anyone who could approach marriage to Julian without a very full grasp of his business seemed to her to be without a very full grasp of him. Realizing that Julian had talked to Eliza even less about it than she had thought, she felt cross with him as well.

"Quite a lot," said Eliza. "I know he's built it up from nothing all by himself and that the cosmetic line is very successful and that he's hoping to start selling it in New York soon."

"I see," said Letitia, not sure whether she was more irritated at hearing that Julian had built up the company all by himself, or that he was planning to go to New York, a piece of information he had not shared with her.

"And do you know about any of the people who work for us?"

"Well, I know there's a wonderful chemist called Adam—Sarsted, is it?"

"Yes," said Letitia. "Some of us are less impressed by his wonderfulness than others. Go on."

"And I met a clever woman called Mrs. Johns. She frightened me a bit," she added, forgetting for a moment she was supposed to be presenting a cool grown-up front.

"She frightens us all," said Letitia cheerfully, "not least your fiancé. Now then, Eliza, there's a bit more about the company that you should understand. First that it is just about the most important thing in the world to Julian. It is mistress, wife, and children, and you must never forget it."

"What about mother?" said Eliza bravely.

"No, not mother. Mother is part of it." Good shot, Eliza, she thought.

"Which part?"

"A very important part. The part that pays the bills."

"So what exactly do you *do* there?"

"I'm the financial director, Eliza. I run the financial side of it. I decide how much we should invest, how much we should pay people, what we can afford to buy, what we can afford to spend. In the very beginning, there was only Julian and me. We've built it up together."

"So it's not Julian's company? It's yours as well."

"Well, it is largely his. I have a share in it, of course, and I know how important my role is. But the ideas, the input, the—what shall we say?—inspiration—oh, dear, that sounds very pretentious, doesn't it?—are his. The company certainly wouldn't have happened without him. But it wouldn't have kept going without me either." She spoke with a certain pride, looked at Eliza a trifle challengingly. "We started it," she said, "on what capital we could rake together, and an overdraft. We worked very hard, terribly long hours. It was all great fun, but it was very, very demanding and at times extremely worrying. Did Julian tell you none of this?"

Eliza shook her head.

"I'm surprised. He usually can't stop talking about it. There were just the three of us then—Julian, who sold all the products, just the patent medicines, no cosmetics in those days, to the chemists, driving all over the country in his car; Jim Macdougall working on formulation; and me managing the money and keeping us from bankruptcy. Just. Susan joined us after the first year or so. She is a remarkable young woman, and Julian is deeply dependent on her."

"What—what do you mean?" said Eliza in a small alien voice.

"Oh, nothing that need trouble you," said Letitia briskly. "I don't mean he's in love with her." She was silent for a moment, remembering the point at which she had feared that very thing. "But she is part of the company, a crucial part, and therefore a crucial part of his life."

"What does she do?" asked Eliza.

"She runs the company. From an administrative point of view. Keeps us all in order. Everything under control. Julian made her a director last year. You didn't know that either?"

Eliza shook her head miserably.

"Well," said Letitia comfortingly, "he's obviously been much too busy discussing your future to talk about his past. But anyway, Susan and I work together a great deal, as you can imagine. The financial side of the company and the administration are intertwined. Obviously. So you see, the company is a huge part of my life as well as Julian's. I just wanted you to understand that before you became part of the family." There, she thought, I wonder what she will make of all that.

"Do you think," said Eliza, a trifle tremulously, "that I could get involved with the company, too? Work there, I mean?"

"Oh, my darling child," said Letitia, unsure whether she was more appalled at the notion or at what Julian's reaction would be, "I shouldn't think so. Julian obviously doesn't want you to have anything to do with it. Otherwise he'd have suggested it by now."

"I suppose," said Eliza, in a rather flat, sad voice, "that's why he hasn't told me anything about it. To keep me well out of it. He probably thinks I'm too stupid."

"Eliza, I can assure you that Julian doesn't consider you in the least stupid," said Letitia firmly. "Quite the reverse. I don't quite know why he hasn't told you more about the company, and I think you should ask him. But you can see how important it was that I should explain. Because when things are back on an even keel and you are settled into a normal life together, you will find that Julian devotes a great deal of his time and attention to the company—a great deal—and I don't want you to think it's because he doesn't love you or doesn't want to be with you."

"No," said Eliza, sounding very subdued. "No, but of course I might have thought that. So thank you for telling me. I'll talk to Julian about it all anyway. I think I should. That was a delicious lunch, Mrs. Morell, thank you very much."

"It was a pleasure. You can call me Letitia," said Letitia graciously. "Come again. I enjoy your company."

"I will. Thank you."

She watched Eliza walk rather slowly up the street, and she wondered just what size hornet's nest she had stirred up.

IT WAS QUITE a big one. Eliza had a row with Julian about what she saw as a conspiracy to keep her from a proper involvement with his company. Julian had a row with Letitia about what he saw as a piece of unwarranted interference. Lady Powers telephoned Letitia and gave her a piece of her mind for sending Eliza away seriously upset. Eliza had a fight with Lady Powers for interfering in her affairs. Out of it all, only Eliza emerged in a thoroughly creditable light. Julian appeared arrogant and dismissive; Letitia, scheming and self-important; and Lady Powers, overbearing and rude.

The worst thing about it all, as Eliza said in the middle of her heated exchange with her godmother, was that they all appeared to regard her as a child, somebody unable to think, act, and worst of all, stand up for herself.

"I am not a child; I am a woman, about to be married," she said. "I would be grateful if you would treat me as such."

But it was one thing to say it and another to confront, in the privacy of herself, the fact that she so patently appeared to everyone—most importantly, the man who was about to be her husband—in such an insignificant light. It hurt her almost beyond endurance. In time she forgave them all, even Julian, but it changed her perception of him, however slightly, and she never quite trusted him again.

SUSAN JOHNS WAS not quite sure how she felt about Julian's marriage; a range of emotions infiltrated her consciousness, none of them entirely pleasing. What she would most have liked to feel, what she knew would be most appropriate, was nothing at all save a mild rather distant interest. The savage jealousy, the desire to impinge on Eliza's consciousness, the scorn and disappointment of Julian's choice of a wife—these were all undignified, unseemly, and uncomfortable. He had told her about his engagement over lunch one day. He had taken her to Simpson's in the Strand, where he assured her she could eat a whole cow if she liked. Over her second helping of trifle, finally unable to postpone the moment any longer, he had told her.

Susan pushed her bowl to one side, fixed him with her large, clear blue eyes and said, "What on earth do you want to do that for?"

Thrown, as always, by a direct question, he struggled visibly to find a route around it. "My dear Susan," he said, "what an inappropriate response to such romantic news. Are you going to tell me what it's all about?" He smiled at her carefully; she met his gaze coldly.

"Don't switch on your famous charm, please. It makes me uncomfortable. And I'm not hostile. Just—well, surprised, I suppose."

"What by? I need a wife."

"Yes," she said, and there was a cold wall of scorn in her eyes. "Of course you do."

"Well?"

"I just don't happen to think that's a very good reason for marrying someone."

"Susan, I'm not just marrying someone. I'm marrying someone who is very important to me. Someone I want to share my life with. Someone—"

"Someone who'll be good at the job?"

He looked at her, and for a moment she thought he was going to lose his temper. He suddenly smiled instead. It was the kind of unpredictability that made her go on, against all the evidence, setting a value on him.

"Yes. If you like."

"Well, I hope you'll be very happy," she said, scooping up what was left of her trifle.

"You don't sound very convinced."

"I'm not."

"Why not?"

"Because," she said, looking at him very directly, searching out what little she could read in his dark eyes, "you haven't said anything at all about love."

◆　　◆　　◆

THE HOUSE JULIAN bought for them was undoubtedly one of the most beautiful in London, one of the Nash terraces on the west side of the Regent's Park, huge and spacious, with a great vaulted hall and staircase and a glorious drawing room filled with light, which ran the entire width of the first floor and overlooked the park. Eliza discovered in herself a certain flair for interior design, albeit a trifle fussy for Julian's taste, and instead of calling David Hicks into her house to style it, like most of their smart friends, she set to work herself, poring over magazines and books, roaming Harvey Nichols and Liberty and antique salesrooms herself, choosing wallpapers and curtain fabrics, innovative color schemes, and clever little quirks of decor—setting a tiny conservatory into one end of the dining room, placing a spiral staircase from the top landing up to the roof—that made the house original and charming without in any way damaging its style. The main bedroom, above the drawing room, was her special love; she shared with Julian a passion for the Deco period, and there was nothing in their room that wasn't a very fine example of the style—a marvelous suite of bed, dressing table, and wardrobe by Ruhlmann, in light rosewood; a pair of Tiffany lamps by the bed; a priceless collection of Chiparus figures on the fireplace; a set of original Erté drawings given to her by Letitia, who had once met and charmed the great man; and a mass of enchanting details, cigarette boxes, ashtrays, jugs, vases, mirrors. The room was entirely white: walls, carpet, curtains, bedspread—"Very virginal, my darling," said Julian, "how inappropriate." It was a stage set, a background for an extraordinarily confident display of style and taste.

On the spacious half landings she created small areas furnished with sofas, small tables, books, pictures, sometimes a desk, all in different periods: thirties for the nursery floor, twenties for the bedroom floor, pure Regency for the one above the drawing room. And on the ground floor, to the left of the huge hall, she created her very own private sitting room, a shrine to Victoriana. She made it dark and almost claustrophobic, with William Morris wallpaper, a brass grate, small button-back chairs, embroidered footstools, sentimental paintings. She put jardinieres in it, filled with ferns and palms, a scrap screen, a brass-inlaid piano. She covered the mantel with bric-a-brac, collected samplers, draped small tables with lace cloths, and in the window she hung a small bird cage in which two lovebirds sang. It was a flash of humor, of eccentricity, and a total contrast to the light and space and clarity of the rest of the house. Julian loathed it and refused to set foot inside it.

"That's all right, my darling," said Eliza lightly. "That room is for me anyway. It's my parlor. Leave me alone in it."

"For what?"

"To entertain my lovers, of course. What else?"

Then she was very busy buying clothes for herself. She not only went to the English designers and shops, but took herself to Paris twice a year to buy from the great names—from Dior, Patou, Fath, Balmain, Balenciaga. She was clever with clothes. She had a very definite, almost stark, taste and a passion for white and beige. She could look wonderful in things from the ready-to-wear boutiques in Paris as well; her beauty was becoming less childlike, but she was slender, delicate, a joy to dress, a favorite customer.

There there was the social life. She and Julian began to give parties that became legendary, and she discovered she had a talent as a hostess, mixing and matching likely and unlikely people brilliantly. Her dinner parties were famous, a heady blend of names, fine wine and food, and scandalous talk. Eliza Morell, like her mother-in-law, had an ear and an eye for gossip and a wit to match it.

She learned very quickly, too, that she was not going to find very much true friendship from within Julian's circle. The women were all at least ten years older than she and, though charming and outwardly friendly, found very little to say to her. They were worlds of experience away from her; they found her lightweight, boring even, and although the Morells were very generously entertained as a couple and people flocked to their house and their parties, Eliza found herself excluded from the gossipy women's lunches, the time-killing activities they all went in for—riding in the park, playing tennis, running various charity committees. She had two or three friends from her debutante days, and she saw them and talked to them, but they had all married much younger men, whom Julian had no time for and did not enjoy seeing at his dinner table, and so she kept the two elements in her life separate, and tried not to notice how lonely she often felt. But her friends were a great comfort to her; she felt they proved to her as well as to Julian that she was not simply an empty-headed foolish child, incapable of coherent thought, and she also found their company a great deal more amusing and stimulating than that of the businessmen and their wives, and the partying, globe-trotting socialites that Julian chose to surround himself with.

BY THE TIME they had been married a year, Eliza was learning disillusionment. In many ways her life was still a fairy tale; she was rich, indulged, admired. But her loneliness, her sense of not belonging, went beyond their social life and even Julian's addiction to his work. She felt excluded from him, from his most intimate self. Looking back over their courtship, she could see that while he had listened to her endlessly, encouraged her to talk, showed a huge interest in everything to do with her, he had rarely talked about himself. In the self-obsession of youth and love she had not noticed it at the time; six months into her marriage, she thought of little else. She would try to talk to him, to persuade him to communicate with her, to share his thoughts, his hopes, his anxieties; but she failed. He would chat to her, gossip even, talk about their friends, the house, the antique cars that were his new hobby, a trip they were planning; but about anything more personal, meaningful, he kept determinedly, almost forbiddingly silent. It first saddened, then enraged her; in time she learned to live with it but never to accept it. She felt he saw her as empty-headed, frivolous, stupid even, quite incapable of sharing his more serious concerns, and it was a hard thing to bear. In theory he was an ideal husband: he gave her everything she wanted, he was affectionate, he frequently told her she was playing her new role wonderfully well, he commented admiringly on her clothes, her decor, her talent for entertaining, her skill at running the household, and he continued to be a superb lover. If only, Eliza thought sadly, the rest of their life were as happy, as close, as complete, as the part that took place in their bedroom. Even that seemed to her to have its imperfections, its shortcomings; the long, charming, amusing conversations they had once had, when they had finished making love, were becoming shorter, less frequent. Julian would say he needed to sleep, that he had an early meeting, a demanding day's hunting, that he was tired from a trip, and gently discourage her from talking.

She had nothing to complain about, she knew; most women would envy her; but she was not really happy. She did not think Julian was having an affair, although she sometimes thought that even if he did she could feel little more excluded, more shut out, than she did already. But she did not feel loved, as she had expected and hoped to feel. She was petted, pampered, spoiled, but not loved, not cared for, and most importantly of all, not considered. It was not a very comfortable or comforting state of affairs.

Eliza was surprisingly busy. In addition to running the London house, she and Julian had bought a house in West Sussex. Lower Marriotts Manor, a medium-size Queen Anne house. It had fifteen bedrooms, a glorious drawing room, and a perfect dining room, exquisitely carved ceilings and cornices that featured prominently in several books on English architecture, forty acres, a garden designed by Capability Brown, and very shortly after they bought it, a stable block designed by Michael McCarthy, an Irish architect who had made a fortune out of the simple notion of designing stables for the rich that looked like just a little more than a set of stables. The stables and yard at Marriotts were a facsimile of Queen Anne stables—lofty, vaulted, and quite lovely. The horses that Julian placed in them were quite lovely, too—five hunters and five thoroughbreds, for he had developed a passion for racing, and was planning to breed as well. Eliza had a horse of her own, an exquisite Arabian mare called Clementine, after the prime minister's wife, whom she flatly refused to take out on the hunting field.

"I want riding to be a pleasure," she said to Julian firmly, "for me and for Clementine, and we are both much happier out on the downs on our own."

"My darling, you can ride her round and round the front lawn, if that will make you happy," he said, "as long as you don't begrudge me my hunting. So many wives get jealous."

"Julian, I have quite enough to keep me jealous without adding hunting to the list," said Eliza lightly. Julian looked at her sharply, but her face was amusedly blank, her eyes unreadable.

Hunting weekends at Marriotts were legendary. Right through the winter the Morells entertained. They gave large house-parties to which came not only the hunting community but Julian's business associates, many of whom had not been any closer to a horse than donkey riding in their childhood. Their socially climbing wives were thrilled to be included in what they felt was a very aristocratic occasion, but they were totally unequipped to participate. Because she did not hunt herself, Eliza found herself forced to entertain these people, and on many a magically beautiful winter afternoon, the red sun burning determinedly through the white misty cold, the trees carving their stark black shapes out of the gray-blue sky, when she longed to be out alone with Clementine she found herself walking the lanes with two or three women, listening to their accounts of purchasing their winter wardrobes or their cruise wear, or playing backgammon indoors with their loud-voiced, red-faced husbands.

She loved Marriotts, rather to her own surprise. She had thought to have become a completely urban person, but she found herself missing the rolling downs of Wiltshire, the huge skies, the soft, clear air, and she looked forward to the weekends more than she would have imagined—especially the rare occasions when she and Julian were alone and could ride together on Sundays, chatting, laughing, absolutely at peace, in a way that was becoming more and more rare.

In the summer of 1955, though, she had to stop riding altogether; she was pregnant.

Eliza had very mixed feelings about her pregnancy. She didn't like babies at all, or small children. She had no desire whatsoever to feel sick or to grow fat, and she resented the curtailment of her freedom for nine months. Nevertheless she had not been brought up the daughter of a minor strand of the British aristocracy without knowing perfectly well that it was the function of a wife, and especially the wife of a rich man, to bear sons. She had a strong sense of the continuity of names and lines, and she was still country girl enough to be totally relaxed and indeed cheerful at the prospect of giving birth and mothering.

As it happened, relaxed and cheerful though she might have been, she was so tiny, so sliver-thin, that Rosamund Morell was born by cesarean section after almost two days of quite excruciating labor, and Julian was told firmly and bluntly by the obstetrician that he was lucky his wife had not died and that another child would undoubtedly kill her. Rosamund was therefore an important baby—the heiress apparent to a fortune and an empire, with no fear of being usurped by a brother at any future date, and the unrivaled focus of her parents' love and attention.

• 4 •

LEE WILBURN HAD JUST COME IN FROM THE beach when the phone rang. It was long distance. "Santa Monica 555-1227? Mrs. Wilburn? Will you take a person-to-person call from London? From Mr. Hugo Dashwood?"

"Yes, yes, I will," said Lee, pushing her hair back from her face, feeling her heart pound, her knees go suddenly limp.

"Lee? Hello. It's Hugo Dashwood. How are you?"

"I'm fine, thank you. How are you?"

"Very, very well. I'm coming to New York next week. Can I come over the following weekend and see you both? Will Dean be there?"

Lee thought very quickly. "Yes, to both. You'll be very welcome. Come on Friday night if you can get away. I'll—we'll look forward to seeing you."

"Yes, I should make it. I have an early meeting Friday morning; then I could leave. I'll take a taxi from the airport. Don't worry about meeting me."

"Okay. Bye, Hugo."

"Good-bye, Lee. And thank you."

She put the phone down; she was shaking all over. That had done it. There was no going back now.

She walked slowly through into the kitchen and poured herself a cold beer. Then she went out into the living room, opened the full-length windows, and looked out at the ocean for a long time. It was the most perfect of Californian evenings, the sky a bright, almost translucent blue, the sun sending a golden dusting on the sea. The beach was still crowded, the white sand covered with people; the surf was gentle, moving almost in slow motion. Lee never got tired of this view, this time; relaxed and at peace from the sun and the sea, she would sit there, enjoying it, drinking it in, and go into an almost trancelike state, wishing she never had to move again. A lot of her friends were taking up yoga and meditation, but she never could see the point in that. Half an hour on the patio with a beer and the ocean, and she felt as relaxed as anybody.

The phone rang again, disturbing her peace. She frowned, went into the kitchen, and picked it up, aiming her beer bottle at the trash can as she passed. It missed, and rolled into the corner.

"Hi," she said into the phone.

"Lee? Hi, honey, it's Dean. You okay? I'll be home in a couple of hours. It's going to be a great weekend. You missed me? I sure have missed you."

"You know I have, Dean," said Lee, smiling into the phone, and it was true; she had. "And I have your favorite dinner for you."

"You're my favorite dinner. Now, honey, you haven't forgotten I'll be away next weekend, have you? I tried to wriggle my way out of it, but I can't. Is that going to be okay?"

"I think I can just about handle it. We've got this weekend, after all. Don't be late, Dean."

"I won't."

She put the phone down, left the beer bottle where it was—she was not a fastidious housewife—and went slowly through the hall and toward the stairs. She caught sight of herself in the long mirror at the end of the room: long, streaky blond hair, blue eyes, freckled face, wearing denim overalls and an old white shirt of her husband's. She looked like a college kid, not a married woman about to commit adultery. She grinned into the mirror and went on upstairs.

She and Dean had met Hugo Dashwood at an advertising conference in New York a couple of months ago. It had been a real treat for her to go—Dean was away such a lot, in his job as representative for a marketing company—and not to have to stay at home and on her own for once, and to see a bit of New York, was just too good to be true. The conference was at the Hyatt, and the delegates were all scattered around the city. Lee and Dean stayed just off Broadway; it was an undeniably tacky hotel, but as Dean kept pointing out to her it was all a freebie, and tackiness was the last thing in the world Lee cared about anyway.

The wives had their own program for a lot of the time, and she had taken the Circle Line tour, gone up to the top of the Empire State Building, and explored the wonders of Bergdorf's and Macy's, ducking out of the more cultural outings on offer, like the Museum of Modern Art and a tour of New York's churches. On the first day there had been a buffet lunch so that they could all get to know one another. Lee hadn't actually taken too much to them—older than she was, most of them, formally and forbiddingly dressed, and very self-consciously good American wives, talking with huge and ostentatious knowledge not only about their husbands' companies but about the advertising industry in general, exchanging telephone numbers and addresses, discussing their husbands' career patterns, comparing company benefits, and constantly interrupting the men's conversations to introduce them to their own newfound acquaintances. Lee decided she preferred her own company; she was standing in the line for the buffet waiting for Dean to finish an interminable conversation with someone about the rival virtues of supermarkets and drugstores as an outlet for cotton balls when a voice that was just like English molasses, as she confided to her friend Amy Meredith later—"If you can imagine such a thing, all dark brown and sweet, but so refined" —asked her if she would be kind enough to hold his place in line while he went and retrieved the book he had been foolish enough to leave in the conference hall. "I don't want to lose it. I am enjoying it immensely, and besides, I'm on my own here—I'm not fortunate enough to have my wife with me to keep me company—and I may need it if I can't find anyone to talk to during lunch."

"Oh, my goodness," said Lee, "we can certainly help you there, my husband and I, but go and get it anyway before they clear it away. I'll hold your place."

She looked at him thoughtfully as he disappeared into the crowd; he was exactly as she would imagine an upper-class Englishman to be —she could tell he was very upper class; he spoke with that David Niven accent everybody had in English films, with the exception of the comic characters, rather clipped and drawly at the same time. He was wearing a gray pin-striped suit, a white shirt, a white and gray tie; he was tall and very slim, with long legs and the most beautiful shoes, in very soft black leather. His hair was dark and slightly longer than she was used to, and he had velvety brown eyes and the most beautiful teeth. She couldn't possibly have asked for a more desirable lunch companion, and felt pleased that she had decided to wear her red sheath dress and pin her hair up in a French twist, so that she looked more sophisticated, instead of leaving it hanging down around her shoulders the way Dean liked it.

He was back in a minute, with a copy of *The Grapes of Wrath* tucked under his arm: "I'm catching up on my American social history," he said with a smile. "Marvelous book. I suppose you've read it?"

"Of course," said Lee earnestly, remembering how she had picked her way painfully through it in high school, and rewarded herself for finishing each chapter with a chapter of *Gone With the Wind*. "I loved it, of course."

"Of course," he said solemnly, "and you do read a lot, Mrs."—he peered at her name tag—"Wilburn?"

"Well," Lee said carefully, "quite a lot. Of course I don't have a great deal of time. But I do enjoy it. When I do." Jesus, she thought, how do I manage to talk such crap?

"And why are you here?" he asked her, moving into safer territory. "Are you one of the delegates?"

"Oh, no," she said, charmed and amused at the same time that he should think her of sufficient status and intelligence to warrant her own place at a conference. "I'm here with my husband."

"And what does your husband do?"

"He's a sales representative for a marketing company. He's very good at his job," she added, mindful of her shortcomings as a professional wife.

"I'm sure," he said. "Can you point him out to me? Where is he?"

"Over there." Lee pointed to Dean, who was furiously distributing his business cards, like leaflets on the subway, to a rather unenthusiastic-looking group. "He'll be over in a minute. He wouldn't miss a lunch." She looked at Dean rather thoughtfully, trying not to compare him unfavorably with the Englishman. She was very fond of him, but nobody could call him a dresser. He had bought a new mohair suit for the conference; it hadn't looked too bad in the shop, but here it seemed too bright a blue, and it had a slightly tacky sheen to it. And then there was his tie. It was a real mistake, that tie, much too wide, with that awful splashy pattern on it. The Englishman's tie, she noted, was discreetly narrow. And she really must, the minute they got home, start doing something about his weight.

"Are you from London?" Lee asked as they reached the buffet table. She helped herself to a modest amount of chicken salad, anxious not to appear greedy and careful to choose something that she could eat easily with a fork. The last thing she wanted to do was drop food on her new red dress in front of this rather intimidatingly suave creature.

"I am."

"And why are you here?"

"To learn a bit about American business methods. I'm opening up in New York, and the more contacts and knowledge I have the better."

"What's your business?"

"Direct mail, I suppose you'd call it," he said. "It's a bit of a new science in England, but it's catching on. And then I thought I'd bring some coals to Newcastle and try it here."

"I see," said Lee, trying desperately not to show that she didn't.

He read her face and smiled, understanding. "Don't worry about it," he said, "old English saying. Let's just leave it at the direct mail. Toiletries mostly."

"Oh," she said as they found a table and sat down, "that's Dean's field, too. He's coming now. Look, he will be interested. I don't know your name; I can't introduce you. Why haven't you got a name tag?"

"Allergic to them," he said. "We don't often use them in England. Silly, I know; they're a very good idea. Anyway, Dashwood is the name. Hugo Dashwood." He held out his hand. "Delighted to meet you."

Lee took his hand and smiled and felt a delicious charge of warm pleasure shoot through her. My goodness, she thought, this guy could be dangerous. The thought was surprisingly interesting. "Lee Wilburn," she said, "and I'm delighted to meet you. Dean," she called to her husband, who was scanning the room anxiously, his overladen plate tipped dangerously to one side, his tie dangling horribly near his potato salad, "Dean, we're here. Come and sit down. We saved you a place."

They became quite friendly after that, the three of them; they had dinner together that evening, and Hugo joined them for breakfast the next day on his way to the conference. They met in the bar of the Hyatt one evening when the last seminar of the day was over, and Dean and Hugo unwound while Lee recounted the events of her day: a tour of the Radio City Music Hall, and a stroll through Tiffany's, which she had found disappointing. "It just isn't as nice as the jewelry shops on Rodeo Drive, not glamorous at all."

She enjoyed talking to Hugo; he had a way of listening that was flattering and that encouraged her to talk, and she enjoyed feeling his eyes on her. She could see he found her attractive, and it made her feel confident and rather grown up; he was so extremely sophisticated and so obviously clever, and she was, after all, a perfectly ordinary American woman. She had majored in psychology, but she knew quite well she wasn't intellectual; she could chat amusingly and even manage an occasional wisecrack when she'd had a beer or two, but that was hardly the sort of thing an urbane upper-class Englishman was going to fall for. Or maybe it was. Anyway, in the meantime it was a wonderful few days. Lee felt more alive, more aware of herself, and a lot more sexy, than she had with Dean in a month of Sundays.

On the fourth and last evening of the conference there was a cocktail party. Lee had dressed for it with great care in a pink shot-silk sheath dress that clung to her body and stopped just below the knee to show off her long, long slender legs. She had bought it at Macy's that morning, and a pair of extra-high-heeled shoes to match; her blond hair was drawn back with pink combs and hung in a straight shining sheet down her back. She was excited and nervous, looking across the room restlessly for Hugo from the moment they arrived.

He wasn't there, and an hour later, as the party began to wind down, he still hadn't appeared. She was disappointed and miserable, and found it depressingly hard to concentrate on what the interminable line of husbands and wives Dean was managing to get a hold of, and hand his cards out to, was saying. She had told one woman how delighted she must be to have left their four children behind, and another how sorry she was to hear she had just installed a new kitchen, when she felt a hand moving gently up and down her arm and a mouth pressed into her ear. "You look wonderful. I'm awfully late. Have I missed anything important?"

She turned, abandoning both wives totally, her face alight. "Hugo! I'm so glad you're here. No, not a thing. It's been terribly boring," Lee said cheerfully and then, realizing what she had said, blushed and tried frantically to salvage the situation. "Er, Hugo this is Mary Ann Whittaker, and this is, er, Joanne Smith. This is our friend from England, Hugo Dashwood."

"Mary Ann White," said the kitchen owner pointedly, holding out her hand. "Which part of England are you from, Mr. Dashwood?"

"London," he said.

"Oh," she said, "we have some very good friends there. They have an upholstery business. You may have met them. Their name is Walker. They live in—now let me see, would it be Willesden?"

"It could be," he said. "There is such a place."

"But you don't know them?"

"I don't think so," he said. "Of course there are a lot of Walkers in London. And it's a big place."

Then suddenly he put his arm around Lee's shoulders and said to Mary Anne White, "You must excuse us now, I'm afraid. We have to meet friends on the other side of the room." And he steered her away. She turned to apologize and saw that he was grinning.

"God in heaven," he said, grasping a glass of wine from a passing tray, "why can't more women be like you?"

"I am really sorry," said Lee, "to have gotten you into that. I would like to say, in defense of my sex, that she was a bad sample, but I don't think I can. Where is Willesden, anyway?"

"A very long way away from the center. Don't apologize. I enjoy such encounters. They amuse me. My only regret is it kept me from talking to you. Here's to you, Mrs. Wilburn, and what I hope will be a lasting association."

Lee looked at him, meeting his dark vivid eyes with her clear blue ones, very steadily. "I hope so, too," she said, composed, in command of the situation suddenly. "If you ever come to California, you must stay with us. We live right on the ocean in Santa Monica. It's a great place to come on weekends."

"I'd love to," he said. "Dean has given me his card. Several, actually," he added, and grinned, but it was a kindly, unmalicious grin. "I don't have any cards at the moment, I've run out, but if you really need to, you can get me at this number. It's my office in New York, but I'm hardly ever there, so it's not very satisfactory, I'm afraid. Anyway, I'll certainly ring you. I've never been to California and I've always wanted to go, so now I shall have a double reason for visiting."

"Good. Do you want to eat dinner with me and Dean tonight? We wondered if you'd like to join us."

"I can't, I'm afraid. I have another engagement. But thank you for asking me."

"That's all right." She felt ridiculously disappointed, her evening suddenly emptied of substance, her pink dress foolishly profitless. He looked at her sharply and then smiled and tipped up her face toward him.

"Don't worry," he said. "We will meet again. I couldn't bear the thought that we wouldn't. I think you are perfectly lovely, and Dean is a very lucky man. And that dress is extremely distracting. It's just as well we're not going to have dinner together; I wouldn't hear a word anybody said. Now I must go; I only popped in to say good-bye. Say good-bye to Dean for me, will you? I don't want to interrupt him."

"I will," she said, "and thank you for coming. It was nice of you to bother."

"No," he said, "not nice at all. I wanted to see you." He paused for a moment, looking at her very seriously. "I find you desirable. Now I must go. Good-bye."

He kissed her lightly on the lips, a gentle, glancing embrace, and then smiled at her and turned away. Lee stood there quite still, a hot, fierce lick of desire stabbing at her, so physically disturbed she hardly knew what she was doing. She went to the ladies' room and shut herself in the cubicle, and sat down quietly and very still on the toilet seat waiting for the throbbing in her body to subside.

Hugo Dashwood spent a weekend with the Wilburns about a month later. Dean and Lee took their duties as hosts seriously and showed him the sights of L.A. in a tireless, enthusiastic forty-eight hours; they took him to Grauman's Chinese Theater and to Griffith Park and the Mount Wilson Observatory; they took him to Beverly Hills and showed him the film stars' mansions; they took him to Muscle Beach where he laughed at the desperate seriousness of the men posing and pumping—"Look," said Lee in awed tones, pointing to one particularly impressive rippling blond mountain, "it's Mickie Hargitay"—and to Malibu, where they sat in a beach bar and he marveled at the compulsive joy and excitement of the surfers and the sea. "I just love it," he said when they finally got back to the Santa Monica house on Sunday afternoon. "I would adore to live here."

"Well, come," said Lee, flinging herself onto the swing seat on the patio and tearing the cap off a bottle of beer. "Bring your wife over. It's not expensive. There's all the opportunities in the world. New people coming in all the time, with the new engineering industries. And they're desperate for young people to come and live here in Santa Monica because everyone wants to be inland, up in the hills. We got free rent for a year and a free television as bait."

"I wish I could," said Hugo, "but I have enough problems coping with living in London and getting a business going in New York. Any more complications would finish me off altogether."

"How's it going?" Dean said lazily. His eyes were closed. He had drunk several beers, and the sun and the alcohol had gotten the better of him.

"Okay. It's tough over there, as you know. But I think it'll work. My main base will always be London, though."

"Why doesn't your wife ever come over?" asked Lee. The last thing she wanted to hear was the minutiae of Hugo's marriage, but she found ignorance more painful than knowledge. The knowledge she had was minimal, not because he did not answer any questions, but because she did not ask many—not wanting to know the answers. Neither did Dean, because he wasn't interested, and Hugo didn't volunteer a great deal of information. Lee was a little disappointed to learn that Hugo wasn't as aristocratic as she had imagined. He was middle class, he told her, and the product of a grammar school rather than Eton, as she had visualized. They knew he had a wife, Alice; that they had been married five years; that she did not get involved with the business, largely through lack of time; that there was a child; and that as families went it was a fairly happy one. More than that Lee could not bear to hear. She pictured Alice as a buttoned-up, frigid English, with an affected accent and a cold stare, and the vision kept her calm and guilt-free. It was based on nothing Hugo had said or even implied.

"She's busy. She has a lot to do. The house is in a dreadful state, and we have a child. She can't keep whipping across the Atlantic for the dubious pleasure of waiting in a hotel room for me to come back from work every day."

"Will you eventually buy a permanent home in New York?"

"Not worth it at the moment. I don't plan to stay on a long-term basis. I want to find someone to run the business for me. If it really takes off, then obviously I would rent or buy a place, but at the moment it's cheaper to stay in hotels when I do come. I'm still doing a suck-it-and-see operation, as we say in Britain."

Dean was now snoring, his mouth hanging open, his empty beer bottle dangling loosely in his hand. Lee took it gently, looking at him in some distaste, and set it on the patio.

"He's always like this after he's been in the sun. He can't take it; not like me. I love it; it makes me feel just—oh, wonderful."

She stretched out on the seat, arching her body. Seeing Hugo looking at her, at the long, slender line from her breasts down to her legs, she stayed still for a moment, holding the pose; then she relaxed and smiled at him.

He smiled back. "You should go and do that at Muscle Beach. You're much prettier than all of them. Tell me how the sun makes you feel."

"Oh, you know, kind of warmed through. Happy, peaceful, good all over."

"Sexy?"

She was surprised by his directness. He was normally rather Englishly reserved. "Yes," she said, "yes, very."

"I thought so." He was silent.

"You look tired," Lee said, jumping up, easing out of the tension. "Let me get you a drink. What time do you have to be at the airport?"

"My plane leaves at nine. Could you ring for a taxi?"

"I'll drive you. Dean has his Sunday homework to do; he's always busy on Sunday night. I get lonely. It'll be a pleasure. Beer?"

"Do you have any whiskey?"

"Bourbon."

"Fine."

She was gone for a while, finding the bourbon, cracking the ice; when she came back, he had drifted off to sleep, too. She sat there, very quiet and still holding his drink. He opened his eyes with a start, looked toward Dean, who was sound asleep, and took her hand, raised it to his lips, kissed it, and smiled at her, then took the drink from her.

"Tell me, Mrs. Wilburn," he said, "why have you not had any children?"

She turned away from him and looked out to sea. "It just hasn't happened, that's all. I'd like them, we both would, but God and Mother Nature don't seem to agree with us." And without warning her eyes filled with tears.

"Oh, darling, I'm sorry, so sorry," Hugo said, using the endearment unselfconsciously, entirely naturally. "I'm an idiot to have asked. I shouldn't have."

"It's all right," she said, smiling at him slightly shakily. "In a funny way I think Dean's quite pleased. It means I can concentrate completely on him."

"Well," he said, "he has a point."

"Do—do you enjoy being a father?"

"Yes. But it has its drawbacks. Children are very demanding."

"And does your wife like being a mother?"

"Yes, I believe so. She finds it difficult at times, of course. All women do, I imagine."

"Yes, I imagine they do," Lee said bitterly.

"I'm sorry," he said. "That was tactless of me. I didn't mean to hurt you. Look, don't worry about driving me to the airport. It's silly. I can get a taxi."

"No, honestly. I like driving, and I love airports. Let me take a shower and fix Dean a steak, and we'll go."

He looked at her and gave her his slow dancing smile. "All right."

THE ROAD TO the airport was busy; the city was growing relentlessly and even the new freeways seemed inadequate. They sat in silence, crawling along, listening to the radio. Pat Boone was throwing his heart and soul into "April Love." It was hot. Lee sighed, pushed the hair off the back of her neck, and threw her head back. "Just think, you'll be cold tomorrow. March in New York. And what about England?"

"Cold."

"Well," she said, "I'd rather be here."

"Lee," he said.

"Yes."

"I do find you very interesting and very, very beautiful. I would like to know you better. Will you remember that?"

She turned and looked at him. "Yes."

"Good."

The traffic had slowed to a complete standstill. The radio was now playing selections from *West Side Story*. Hugo leaned over to Lee, turned her toward him. "Kiss me."

She kissed him. She didn't usually like kissing; it was something rather tedious, and men got so worked up about it, breathing heavily and slavering away. But kissing Hugo Dashwood wasn't like that. He kissed with style, very slowly, very strongly and deliberately, pausing every now and again to stroke her hair, her neck, his hand lingering gently, tenderly, on her breast, and he did not just kiss her mouth; he kissed her eyes and her chin, and her throat. Lee felt as if she were floating, drifting in some delicious, tossing liquid, rising and then sinking, let loose in desire. She sighed, pulled away from him for a moment. He took her face between his hands.

"What do you feel?" he said.

"Everything," she said simply. "Absolutely everything."

"Ah," he said. "Good."

Around them drivers were honking their horns and shouting: "Get a goddam move on," and "Do that off the fucking road." The disc jockey had just started to play "Wake Up, Little Susie."

Hugo sighed, then laughed and drew away from her. "We'd better go or we'll be arrested."

They drove in silence the rest of the way. When they got there, he simply kissed her cheek briefly and got out. "Good night, Lee. I shall hope to see you soon. Thank you for a wonderful weekend."

"Good night, Hugo."

She watched him until he disappeared into the crowd. Then she drove very fast, which was the only other way she knew of relieving sexual tension. When she got home she stayed in the shower for a long time and came out calmer.

She was never able to hear "Wake Up, Little Susie" again without becoming sexually aroused.

SHE WAS ON the patio when he arrived. She was wearing a T-shirt and white slacks. Unusually, for she felt uncomfortable and uneasy without them, she was not wearing either bra or her panties. She had drenched herself in Intimate; her hair was slightly damp from the shower; she looked just about seventeen.

"Lee, you look like an angel," Hugo said, kissing her formally on the cheek. "An all-American angel. It's so nice to see you."

"It's good to see you, too," Lee said, smiling at him. "Can I fix you a drink?"

"That would be nice. A beer, I think. Is Dean not home yet?"

"Not yet," Lee said, going quickly into the house. She reemerged with the beer and a glass, and poured it for him, thinking that she could never remember how amazingly good-looking and sexy he was, and feeling all over again inadequate and crass.

"How was your flight?"

"All right. Long."

"Are you hungry?"

"Not really. I can wait. Why don't you have a drink, too?"

So Lee fetched another beer and sat down beside him on the patio, on the swing seat, and together they looked silently at the ocean. She did think of asking him what he thought might happen over the Suez crisis, just to show she knew there was one, or if he had seen *West Side Story* yet, but it didn't really seem very appropriate, so she just sat there.

Then: "When will Dean be home?"

"Not tonight."

"I see."

That was all he said. No corny response, no come-on, no surprise. Just "I see." Very English.

"Would you like your dinner now?"

"Yes, please, I would."

They sat inside eating steak and salad and drinking red wine, just chatting like any married couple, the way she and Dean did in the evening. It wasn't especially exciting or erotic or anything, just very, very nice.

"I'm tired," he said at last. "Can I go to bed now?"

"Of course," she said. "I'll show you your room."

"Don't worry," he said. "I'll find it. It's the same one, I suppose? You tidy up down here. I'll look after myself. Good night, Lee."

She felt rebuffed, anxious. Was he telling her he didn't want her? she wondered. Was she being foolish and presumptuous? And saying she should tidy up—had he noticed the overflowing trash can, the dishes heaped in the sink, the magazines dumped behind the couch? She was sure Alice would keep the house as neat as a pin all the time. He probably hated her casual ways. She smiled at him nervously.

"I'll fix you some coffee," she said.

"No, don't," he said. "It'll keep me awake, but I'd like some water and a brandy, maybe, to go with it. Perhaps you could bring it up to me in a minute."

And she knew then she wasn't being foolish and presumptuous, that he wanted her as much as she wanted him, that he was simply a courteous, thoughtful man, giving her every chance to let herself off the hook should she change her mind or should he have mis-read it.

She put a pitcher of ice water on a tray with a bottle of brandy and a glass and went quietly up the stairs in her bare feet. Outside his room she listened: silence. She knocked gently and went in. At first she thought he was asleep. She went over to the side of the bed and put down the tray very quietly. As she turned to leave the room, his hand came out and caught hers.

"Don't go," he said, "unless you really want to."

"I don't." She sat down on the bed. He looked at her for a long time, very seriously, and then put out a hand and traced the outline of her face with his finger.

"You're so lovely," he said, "so very very lovely." And then he pushed his hand under her T-shirt and stroked very, very gently her breasts, and then he leaned forward and kissed her on the mouth, gently, repeatedly, as he had in the car.

Lee sat still and silent. She felt her nipples grow erect, a monstrous aching deep within her, but she did not move.

"Lie down," he said. "Lie down beside me."

Her eyes never leaving his face, she slid her T-shirt over her head, took off her slacks, and stood naked before him, smiling.

"No underwear, Mrs. Wilburn? Is this for my benefit, or would that be presumptuous of me?"

"It would," she said untruthfully. "I never wear any. I don't like it."

"I think you're lying," he said, reaching out and stroking her stomach. "I don't believe those wonderful breasts could survive without the help of a bra. Dear God, have you no pubic hair?" he added, sitting up and peering at her with genuine interest.

"I shave it," she said. "Dean doesn't like it. I thought you wouldn't either."

"You were wrong," he said, "but it doesn't matter. Here." And he put his hand on her buttocks and pulled her toward him, burying his face in her stomach, kissing her where the hair should have been, licking her, searching out her clitoris with his tongue.

"It's different," he said, smiling up at her. "I'm not sure if I like it, but it's different. Is that nice? You must tell me."

"Oh, God," said Lee, and it was almost a groan, "it's nice. Don't— don't stop."

"I think I will," he said, "in a minute," and he went on and on, until she cried out with pleasure and an exquisite pain, and fell on him, lying above him, kissing him, licking him, biting him, thrusting herself on to him, and feeling suddenly the immense strong delight of his penis going deep, deep within her, answering her need, gratifying her awful, aching desire. She lay there tearing at him like some hungry animal, rising from him, arching away, and then lunging down again, over and over again, shuddering with pleasure and need; she came once and then again, and still she was hungry, still wanted more. He turned her onto her back, driving into her fast and hard, almost hurting her, stirring places and pleasures she had never known. She felt the waves growing, then breaking, and as she clung to him, calling out in an agony of release, he shuddered into her, with a huge groan of delight and relief.

And afterward they lay together and he took great handfuls of her long blond hair and wound it round his fingers and kissed it and kissed her everywhere, on her eyelids, her nose, her lips, her breasts, saying her name over and over again. And then she felt him growing hard again, and her own need growing, too. Then he took her with him, farther, higher than she would ever have imagined possible; and finally they slept, completely at peace, for a long, long time.

It was midday when they woke; Hugo looked at his watch, groaned, and shook her.

"Lee, it's after twelve. For God's sake wake up. When is Dean getting home?"

And she looked at him through a haze of love and sleepiness, her body sated and yet hungry again, and smiled and kissed him and said, "Next Friday night."

They stayed in bed all weekend, occasionally going downstairs for food and wine and once to swim. They made love until their bodies ached with exhaustion and even Lee could ask for no more.

On Sunday afternoon they finally got up and showered together and dressed and sat quietly in the kitchen, drinking coffee and looking at each other.

"I have to go soon," he said.

"When?"

"My plane leaves Los Angeles for New York at nine."

"Let me come with you."

"No."

"What do you want me to do?"

"I don't know," he said, and she knew it was a lie.

She knew what he wanted. He wanted her to stay with Dean and to be available when he needed her. It was a hard bargain. But she knew she had to settle for it. She had no choice. It was that or absolutely nothing at all.

In time, she could see, she would grow angry, resentful, but now, so filled with him, filled with pleasure and love, she could accept it easily and gracefully.

"I'll come to the airport with you," she said quietly, and was rewarded by seeing the respect in his eyes.

·5·

JULIAN WAS WANDERING THROUGH HARRODS, looking at the cosmetic counters, chatting to the Juliana consultants, and reflecting on their very pleasing sales figures when the idea actually surfaced. He suddenly had a vision of a very different kind of establishment: more than a beauty salon, a little less than a store; something small, intimate, and totally extravagant. It should be, he thought, about the size of a large house, on two or three floors, rather like an infinitely luxurious hotel offering his perfume and cosmetics and all the paraphernalia—treatment rooms, masseurs, steam baths, saunas, beauty therapists, hairstylists—that had become a most necessary accessory to well-heeled life on both sides of the Atlantic. But it would offer other things, too, things to buy, all compatible with a mood of self-indulgence. The atmosphere would be rich and rare, a place that enticed, beguiled, encouraged women into extravagance.

Each department should be small and exclusive, leading from one mood and set of desires to the next, logically extending from cosmetics to lingerie, dresses to furs, hats to shoes. Shopping there would not be a chore or even a business; it would be a series of beautiful experiences, and his establishment would provide a series of different settings for the experiences. It would be a world apart, an excursion into a charmed life. It would not consist of departments and counters and salesgirls and tills; it would be carefully designed into spaces and areas and moods.

Women would come in initially for the cosmetics and the beauty treatments—that would be the lure—but they would stay, and it would be the beautiful things they could acquire that kept them there. It would all be glittering and unashamedly luxurious, outrageously expensive, and totally unique, so that a customer, should she have bought only a silk scarf or a leather belt, would feel she had acquired just a tiny portion of that charmed and charming life.

All these things Julian thought almost without realizing he had thought them. Later, talking to Philip Mainwaring—the marketing manager for Juliana whom he had decided with some misgivings to employ—he found himself describing them in the finest detail. Philip listened politely, as he was paid to do, found himself more impressed than he really wanted to be—he found that Julian's capacity for creativity made his job more complex and difficult than he had envisaged when he took it on—and tried, like the good businessman he was, to talk him out of it.

"What does our financial director have to say about all this?" Philip asked.

"Haven't told her," Julian said shortly. "I think I'll sort out the money first." He returned Philip's look a little coldly. He found the attitude of his younger staff toward Letitia's position in the company —that she must be there only out of some kind of misguided family feeling, that he must have a relationship with her that was odd, to put it mildly—at best irritating and at worst insulting. It seemed to him patently obvious that a company as successful as Morell's was clearly in excellent financial hands and there was no more to the matter than that. Letitia now had a department of five, which she ran with crushing efficiency; she was an innovative and exacting force in the business, and Julian's only anxiety about her was that she was nearly sixty now and surely could not work on into the unforeseeable future. He said as much to Susan Johns one day over lunch at the Caprice. Susan laughed and said she was quite sure that Letitia would outlive them all.

"Including you," said Julian, watching her happily devour a double portion of profiteroles. "You'll have a heart attack any day now. Do you want some more of those?"

"Wouldn't mind. Do you think they know about second helpings here?"

"They should if they don't. Have you ever put on any weight, Susan?"

"Never."

"You're very fortunate," Julian said with a sigh, looking at the dozen or so outrageously expensive grapes he was eating for dessert. "I have to be extremely careful what I eat these days. Middle age coming on, I suppose."

"Don't be ridiculous. Anyway if you're middle aged, so am I."

"How old are you, Susan?"

"Thirty-five."

"You really were a child bride, weren't you?"

"I was. Seventeen years old. Criminal, really."

"Yes," said Julian, looking somber. "It's too young."

Susan, reflecting on the fact that Eliza had been only eighteen when Julian married her, decided they were on slightly dangerous ground and briskly changed the subject. She had gathered from the occasional remark of Letitia's that the Morell marriage was not quite as idyllic as it had promised to be, and it was a subject she preferred to keep not only from talking but also from thinking about.

"I hear you're going to New York."

"Yes. Do you know why?"

"I imagine to sell Juliana into the stores there."

"Yes. And I have another project, too."

"Am I allowed to hear about it?"

"Well," said Julian, signaling to the waiter to bring some more profiteroles, "I suppose as a director of the company you have a right to hear about it. But there is a condition."

"What's that?"

"You don't tell my mother."

Susan looked at him and shook her head in mock disapproval. "My goodness. It must be bad."

"Not bad. A bit risky, perhaps."

"All right, I promise. You need one sensible opinion. Come on, tell me."

He told her of his vision, of how he saw it adding breadth and quality to Juliana's image, of the kind of feel it would have, the sort of women who would be attracted to it, the people he would hope to have working on it and designing for it, where it might be, how it might look. Eliza would have given all she owned to be entrusted with half, a quarter of such a confidence.

"It's a new phase altogether, a new venture. I feel I need one."

"Why?"

"Oh, you know, boredom, restlessness. I always want to be on to the next thing. What do you think of it?"

"I like it. I think it's terrific."

"Good God." He was surprised.

"Didn't you think I would?"

"No, not really."

"Why not? Not my style, I suppose. Too upmarket."

"Now don't start getting touchy, Susan."

"I'm not. I'm just teasing you."

"Good. No, but seriously, I'd have thought it was a bit out of order, from your point of view. Expensive—for the company, I mean. New ground. All that sort of thing."

"New ground is the company's lifeblood. But it will be expensive, won't it? How are you going to finance it?"

"I think I can get the money in New York. If not, I'll raise it here. I'm sure I can."

"What does Eliza—Mrs. Morell think about it?"

"I haven't talked to her about it," said Julian shortly.

"I see."

"I'm going to have a brandy. Do you want anything?"

"Of course not. I never drink at lunchtime."

"Or any other time, I know. Except Bucks Fizz, of course."

"Yes," she said, smiling at him, able at last to remember that evening with pleasure rather than pain. "But not at lunchtime. Anyway, you go ahead. I'll have a cup of tea."

"Now, that really will upset the Caprice. How's the Labour party? Are you going to end up an MP, do you think?"

"I don't know," she said very seriously. "I'd like to, I really would. I do love politics, and I'd enjoy getting something done about some of the things I care about. But I don't know if I'd ever manage it. They're not too keen on women in the Labour party, you know, although they certainly ought to be. It would be such a huge struggle to get elected even, years of fighting and in-fighting, and I'm not sure if I'm ready for that. And it would mean giving up my job, probably, and I certainly don't know if I could face that."

"I certainly couldn't," Julian said.

He spoke very seriously. There was a silence.

"Well, anyway," said Susan lightly, "it's out of the question at the moment. The girls are still at home. Maybe when they're grown up."

"Maybe. I must say I can't quite adjust to the thought of you shirking a fight. You used to thrive on them."

"I know. But I'm older now. Maybe a bit wiser. Anyway, for the next two or three years my work on the South Ealing council will keep me quite busy enough. Then I'll see."

Julian looked at her. She was one of those women who improved with time, who grew into their looks and their style. When she was young, her features had been too angular, too harsh for beauty, prettiness even, and she had had neither the money nor the skill to improve upon the raw material. She was still very thin and not classically beautiful, but she had developed an elegance, and she wore clothes well; her hair hung smoothly on her shoulders, a beautifully cut bright brown. She dressed simply but with distinct style. Today she was in the shirtdress so beloved of the fifties, in soft navy wool, with a full skirt that swirled almost to her ankles, and pulled in tightly at the waist with a wide, soft red leather belt, and plain red pumps. Her skin was pale but clear, her eyes a dazzling light blue; on her mouth, her most remarkable feature, she wore a shiny bright pink lipstick. She looked expensive, glamorous even. What was missing, Julian thought to himself, was jewelry; she never wore any, and her look needed it; it would suit her and her stark style.

"You look terrific," he said with perfect truth. "Is that the new autumn coral lipstick?"

"It is. Mango, it's called. Mum says it's tarty, so I know it must be good and bright."

"It's terrific. Sarsted's doing a good job, don't you think?"

"Very good."

"And how is Mum?"

"Much the same."

"Oh, dear."

"Well, I don't have to live with her anymore."

"Susan," Julian said suddenly. "Why don't you come to New York with me? I could use your opinion, and it would be fun."

Susan looked at him very steadily for a long time. "No, I don't think so," she said at last.

"Why not?"

"You know why not."

He sighed. "Will I ever get the better of you, Susan? Persuade you to do something you don't totally approve of?"

"Certainly not. Are you coming back to the office or are you going to waste even more company time than you have already?"

"You go on," he said. "I'll follow."

When her taxi was out of sight he walked along Piccadilly, up Regent Street, and into Mappin and Webb. He spent a long time there, looking, selecting, and rejecting; finally he chose a two-strand pearl necklace with a diamond clasp and a pair of pearl and gold stud earrings. When he got back to the office he put the box on Susan's desk.

"What's that?"

"Thank-you present."

"What for?"

"For liking my idea. For not coming to New York. And because you deserve it. No strings. But I shall be very offended if you don't take it."

Susan opened the box, looked at the pearls in silence for a long time, and then at him. Her eyes were very bright and big, and suspiciously moist. "You won't have to be offended. Of course I'll take them. And wear them every day. They're simply beautiful. Thank you very much. I—I just don't know what to say."

"Well," said Julian lightly, "you are simply beautiful, too. So you suit each other, you and the pearls. I'll keep you informed about New York. Just in the hope you might change your mind."

But they both knew she wouldn't.

NEW YORK IN the autumn of 1956 was a heady place. It had taken a long time to recover from the depression; in 1939 half a million people in the state were still receiving public assistance. But by the mid-forties the big business giants—IBM, Xerox, General Electric—were all becoming corporations; a new governor, Thomas Dewey, had set schemes for state universities and new highways into motion—six were built in the decade following the war—and Harriman and Rockefeller poured money into the state. In 1955 the New York State Thruway from New York City to Buffalo was opened, and soon after that construction began on the St. Lawrence Seaway.

The new highways meant the real birth of the commuter to New York, and the birth of the suburb; paving a way for ambition, opportunity, and the pursuit of the American dream; they also paved the way for an increasing drift, for the less fortunate, to the ever-growing ghettos. But in the commercial heart of the city there was money, real money, more and more of it, up for grabs. And Julian Morell was in a grabbing mood.

Julian stayed with Philip Mainwaring at the Pierre Hotel, shrine to luxury and a slightly old-fashioned glamour, just across Fifth Avenue from Central Park—and an inspiration for their cause, filled as it was with spoiled, pampered women and extravagant, indulgent men.

They had a huge success with Juliana; Bergdorf's, Bonwit's and Saks all bought it, and promised Julian special displays and promotions when he launched his new young perfume, *Mademoiselle Je*, in the spring. He set up a recruitment drive for consultants selling his range in the stores, interviewing them every morning in his suite; he was looking for women who could not only sell the products but communicate with the customers, sympathize with their anxieties, reassure them, make intelligent suggestions. It was a difficult task; he was looking for a type of woman who would not normally consider selling cosmetics behind a counter. He had managed to find them in London, but it was more difficult to find this particular breed in New York, mecca of the hard sell. At last, after days of intensive interviewing, Julian found a handful and hired them at just over half again the salary all their rivals were getting and said he would pay them no commission. "That way," he said to Philip, "they aren't hammering away, pushing unsuitable stuff at women who don't want any more than advice. It works in London; it'll work here." Then he turned his attention to looking for a building.

They worked their way steadily through midtown New York for

days, marveling at the soaring erratic beauty of the place. Up and down the expensive avenues, Fifth, Madison, and Park; down the side streets; examining new buildings, conversions, buildings in use as offices or as shops. It was exhausting, depressing, and began to feel hopeless.

"Maybe," said Philip as they walked slowly back to the Pierre one evening, "we should think of building."

"No," said Julian, "no, we shouldn't build. I know we need something with a past."

"Julian, we must have looked at everything with a past in New York City and a lot without a future," said Philip. "This place you're seeking doesn't exist. You have to rethink."

"No," Julian said, "I'm not going to rethink. We'll find it. There's no rush. Come on, let's have a martini; it'll cheer you up. Then I'll see if anything's come in for us during the day."

He ordered two martinis and went to the desk to pick up his mail: a huge armful of real-estate agents' envelopes. He carried them over to Philip in the bar, laughing. "Come on, Philip, plenty to do. We needn't be bored."

"I long to be bored," Philip said gloomily, downing his martini in one gulp.

"Oh, nonsense. Where's your spirit of adventure? Have another one of those to stiffen your sinews and bit and— Look, here's something from a residential agent. That's interesting."

He opened the envelope. A photograph fell out of a beautiful house, almost eighty years old, tall and graceful, five stories high, with beautiful windows, classic proportions. It was just off Park Avenue on Fifty-seventh, and it was being offered for sale as a possible small hotel. Julian looked at it for a long time in silence.

"That's it," he said. "That's my building. Jesus, that's it. What do they want for it?"

"Julian, that's a house," said Philip. "You can't convert that into a shop."

"Of course I can," said Julian, smiling at him radiantly. "A house is exactly what I want. I don't know why I didn't realize before. Come on, Philip. Let's go and look at it now."

"But it's dark," said Philip plaintively. "We won't be able to see it."

"Oh, for heaven's sake, man, don't be so negative. Haven't you heard of electric light? It's all the rage. Come on, we can do it easily before dinner."

They walked to the house, a small elegant jewel nestled between two taller buildings. A light hung over the front door, showing off its perfect shape, its delicate fanlight. It was a very lovely house. Julian looked at it in silence; he crossed the street and looked at it still longer. Then he crossed again and knocked at the door.

IT WAS OVER two years before the store opened. An expensive two years.

The first thing Julian had to do was find the money to buy the house and to do the conversion. Most of the larger banks were not helpful. Morell's, and indeed Juliana, did not have the prestige and authority in New York that they enjoyed in London. Julian tried the merchant banks in London, but they were reluctant to put money into an untried venture in New York.

He was just about to try to raise a personal loan when he was put in touch with a young man called Scott Emerson, who headed one of the investment divisions at the Chase Manhattan Bank and who was earning a reputation as having a shrewd eye for a clever investment. Julian went to see him, armed with photographs, cash flow charts, prospectuses, his own company history, and his burning, driving enthusiasm; he came away with a cautious promise—"a definite maybe," Julian told Susan and Letitia on the phone to London—and a life-long friendship. Scott lived with his wife Madeleine and their two children—"Nearly four," he told Julian proudly over lunch that first day, "Madeleine's expecting twins"—on Long Island. He invited Julian to spend the weekend there, and Julian fell promptly in love with American family life. Unlike most Englishmen, he liked the way American children were encouraged to talk, to join in a conversation, to consider themselves as important as adults; he found this charming and interesting. He thought of his small daughter, brought up by Eliza and her nanny in the nurseries at the top of the house, and resolved to change things.

"You must bring Eliza to stay here next time you come," Madeleine said, smiling at him over Saturday breakfast. "We would just love to meet her. She sounds so interesting. It's quite an undertaking, marrying a man with such a huge and demanding business at her age. She's obviously a coper."

"Well, she's very busy," said Julian.

"How old is your daughter?"

"She's nine months old," said Julian.

"That's a lovely age," said Madeleine. "I wish they could stay like that. Our C.J. is just a little older. He'll be down in a minute. His sitter is taking him out for a walk. Maybe when they're older he and your Rosamund can be friends. I'd really like that. Oh, look, here he is now. C.J., come and say hello to Mr. Morell."

The sitter, smiling, carried C.J. over to Julian. The child looked at him solemnly and then buried his head in her shoulder.

"Oh, dear," said Julian, "don't I even get a smile?"

Madeleine held out her arms, took the child; he turned and smiled suddenly at Julian. He had brown hair and large brown eyes; they held a slightly tremulous expression. Madeleine kissed him and then handed him back to the sitter. She went out, talking quietly to the baby under her breath.

"He's sweet," said Julian. "What's his full name?"

"He was christened Christopher John, but the sitter we had then called him C.J. and it kind of stuck. He's very different from his sister; it's funny how you can tell so early. He's quieter, and he doesn't try and push the world around like she did at that age. I don't think he's ever had a temper tantrum. She'll be running for President by the time she's seventeen. But he's such a nice little boy. I suppose he may toughen up."

Julian thought of C.J.'s soft brown eyes, his shy smile, and thought it would be rather a pity if he did.

Julian spent most of those two years in New York working harder than he had ever worked in his life, even during the very early days of the company, in a total commitment to seeing his vision become reality. It was not unusual for him to work right through the night and half of the next one as well. He missed meals, he canceled social engagements, and he expected precisely the same dedication from everyone working with him.

Nathan and Hartman, considered to be the finest architects in New York, had initially been hired to work on the store, and were fired within weeks because their plans didn't meet with Julian's absolute approval; a second firm met the same fate. Then a young French architect, Paul Baud, arrived at the Pierre one evening and asked to see Julian. He had a small portfolio under his arm, and he looked about nineteen. Julian had sighed when he heard he was downstairs; then he said he would give him five minutes and if he hadn't convinced him by then he would have to go away. Baud drew out of his portfolio the plans for a tiny hotel in Paris and a small store in Lyons, the only work he had ever done, and spent the entire night in the bar at the Pierre with Julian, drawing, talking, listening. Then he went away for a week and came back with the plans complete. Julian hardly altered a thing.

He went to Paris for his beauty therapists, knowing that only there would he find the crucial combination of knowledge, mystique, and deep-seated belief in the importance of beauty treatment that would have the women of New York visiting his salons three or four times a week. He installed on the fifth floor an extraordinary range of equipment and treatments—massage machines, passive exercisers, seaweed and mud baths, steam cabinets, infrared sun beds, saunas, and a battery of masseurs, *visagistes*, hairstylists, manicurists, dietitians. There was a small, excessively well-heated swimming pool, a gymnasium, a bar that sold pure fruit and vegetable juices, and a few dimly lit cubicles fitted out with nothing but beds and telephones, where ladies, exhausted from a morning's toil, could sleep for an hour or so before setting forth to buy the clothes, jewelry, perfume, and makeup to adorn their tortured, treated bodies.

Buyers were brought in from all over the world—from Milan, Rome, London, Paris, Nice, San Francisco—men and women who did not just know about fashion but had it in their blood, who could recognize a new line, a dazzling color, a perfect fabric as surely as they could tell their own names, their own desires.

Julian hired a young, greedy advertising agency called Silk diMaggio to promote the store, ignoring the sober advice of Philip Mainwaring to go to Young and Rubicam or Doyle Dane.

Nigel Silk was old money, new style, born of a Boston banking family. He had perfected the art of appearing establishment while questioning every one of its tenets; he was tall, blond—"by Harvard out of Brooks Brothers," Scott Emerson described him—charming and civilized.

Mick diMaggio, on the other hand, was no money at all, the youngest of the eight children of a third-generation Italian immigrant who ran a deli just off Broadway. Mick talked like Italian ice cream spiked with bourbon and wrote the same way. Julian looked at the creative roughs he produced for the poster campaign—a young, beautiful woman lying quite clearly in the aftermath of sexual love under the headline, "The Absolute Experience"—and threw up his hands in pleasure.

"This," he said, "will empty Bergdorf's."

They were a formidable team.

One of its most formidable members was Camilla North.

Camilla North was born ambitious, the daughter of an old-money Philadelphia lawyer and his very, very old-money wife.

So eager had she been to get out into the world and start achieving that she had actually arrived nearly four weeks early; she was walking at seven months old, talking at nine; she was in dancing class at two, riding at three, and reading and writing at four.

By the time she was ten she had become a superb horsewoman and an accomplished dancer and was earning praise for her mastery of both the piano and the violin; by way of recreation she was also learning the classical guitar. She promised to be a brilliant linguist and mathematician and was the only pupil at her exclusive girls' school ever to have gotten a hundred percent on the end-of-year Latin examinations three years running.

The interesting thing about Camilla was that she was not actually especially gifted at most of the things she excelled at. She had minor talents, but because she had a fierce, burning need to do everything better than anybody else, she was prepared to put sufficient, even monumental, effort into it to fill that need. A rare enough quality in an adult, it was an extraordinary thing to find in a child. Her piano teacher, coming to the house to give her a lesson, frequently found her white with exhaustion, on the point of tears, laboring over some difficult piece or set of scales; her mother would often tell people, with a mixture of pride and concern, that ever since she was a tiny child she had risen half an hour early in order to practice her ballet. She was hardly ever to be seen simply fooling around and enjoying her pony, but spent long hours practicing her dressage skills, endlessly crossing and traversing the paddock, changing legs, pacing out figures of eight; she even insisted on learning to ride sidesaddle. And if she was ever found to have fallen asleep over a book, it would have been her Latin grammar and not a storybook.

Camilla went, inevitably to Vassar, a year early. She graduated summa cum laude in languages and also studied fine art. She left in 1956, with a reputation as the most brilliant girl not just of her year but of several years, and also as the most beautiful. She sometimes wondered what she would have done if she had been born plain. Being beautiful was as important to her as being clever; she simply could not bear to be anything but the loveliest and best-dressed woman in a room. Fortunately for her she almost always was. She had a curly tangled mane of red-gold hair, transparently pale skin, and dramatically dark brown eyes. She was very tall and extremely slender; she had in fact a genetic tendency, a legacy from her mother, to put on weight, and from the age of twelve, when she had heard somebody say she was developing baby fat, she had been on a ferocious diet. Nobody had ever seen Camilla North put butter on her bread or sugar in her coffee; she never ate cheese, avocados, cereal, or cookies; she weighed herself twice a day, and if the scales tipped an ounce over 112 pounds, she simply stopped eating altogether until they went back again. She quite often went to bed hungry and dreamed about food.

She always dressed superbly—sharp, stark, slender clothes in brilliant red or emerald or a stinging blue. At college she had been famous for her cashmere, her kilts, her loafers, a supreme example of the preppy look, but as soon as she left, she abandoned them and moved into dresses, suits, grown-up clothes, the severity always relieved by some witty dashing accessory—a scarf, a big necklace, a wide leather belt in some brilliant unexpected color. She loved shoes and had dozens of pairs, mostly classic pumps with very high heels, in which she somehow managed to move gracefully; but she looked best of all in her riding clothes, in her white jodhpurs, black jacket, and long, wonderfully worn and polished boots, her red hair scooped severely back. She occasionally hunted sidesaddle; it was an extraordinary display of horsemanship and she looked more wonderful still, in a navy habit and white stock, a top hat covering her wild hair. So much did she like her habit that she had a version of it made in velvet for the evening; she wore it without a shirt, with a pearl choker at her throat, her hair cascading over her shoulders. It was a sight that took men's breath away, and it was this that she was wearing when she first met Julian Morell.

She was living in New York by then, in a small walk-up apartment in Greenwich Village. It was several months since she had left Vassar, and she had not yet found a job. She had found the debutante and social scene boring, and she had besides considerable hopes and ambitions for herself. She came to New York to seek her fortune, preferably in the arts. She had hopes of working in the theater, as a designer, or perhaps in interior design. She met Paul Baud at a party; he was immediately impressed by her and told her he was looking for designers for a new store. Why didn't she let her talents and imagination loose on a department or two? It was a new challenge for Camilla. She sat at her drawing board virtually without food or rest for almost thirty-six hours before she was even remotely satisfied with what she had done. She delivered the drawings to Paul's office without even asking to see him, so sure was she that she would never hear from him about them again.

She had chosen to live alone, against considerable opposition from her parents, for two reasons. One was that she liked her own company; the other was that she had hardly any friends. Camilla had no idea how to make friends. All her life she had been entirely occupied with struggling, striving, working; she had never had a best friend to talk to, giggle with, confide in, not even as a small girl. She had gone to children's parties; she was pleasant and friendly and nobody disliked her, but nobody liked her particularly either. She was too serious, too earnest, there was too little common ground. Later on, in her teens, she went to fewer parties, because she tended to get left out; she didn't mind, because she was so busy. But at college she became much sought after, because of the way she adorned a room, set a seal on a gathering. She was not exactly popular, but she was a status symbol; she was asked everywhere.

Nevertheless she remained friendless, solitary; and she had no gift for casual encounters. On Sundays for instance, when the other girls went for walks or spent long hours chatting, giggling, talking about men, she would sit alone in her room studying or reading, declining with a polite smile any invitations to join them.

She was perfectly happy; her friendlessness did not worry her. It worried and surprised other people, but it was of no importance to her. What would have surprised other people, also, and was perhaps of a little more importance to her, was that at the age of twenty-one she was not only a virgin, but she had never been in love.

JULIAN WAS IMMEDIATELY impressed by Camilla's drawings, brought to him by Paul Baud late one Friday evening. Feverish with excitement about his project, desperate to make progress on it, he asked to meet her immediately. Paul phoned Camilla in Greenwich Village and got no answer; urged on by Julian's impatience to see her, he called her parents. Yes, they were told by the maid, Miss North would indeed be back that night; she had gone to the opera with her parents and was coming home to Philadelphia for the weekend.

Julian looked at Paul; it was nine o'clock. "Let's go and catch her at the opera," he said. "I can arrange to see her over the weekend."

They waited patiently in the lobby of the Metropolitan Opera House. They heard the final applause, the bravos for Callas's great Carmen, and as the doors of the auditorium finally opened, Julian felt in some strange way this was an important moment, as much for him as for his store. Then the great surge of people began to come out, and he wondered if what he was doing was not rather foolish. How could they expect to find one young woman he had never seen, and Paul had met briefly only once, in this crowd? It was hopeless.

But he had reckoned without Camilla's great beauty and the talent she had for parting crowds; as she walked through the lobby of the opera house in her blue velvet habit, pearls at her throat and in her wild red hair, her brown eyes tender with pleasure at the music she had just heard, people stared and drew aside just a little to look at her. Julian, standing at the main doors, looking in, found himself suddenly confronted by her coming directly toward him. Not knowing who she was, he forgot Camilla North and gazed at her, then smiled, drawn to her, moved by her beauty and her grace. She looked at him, recognizing, acknowledging his appreciation, and then turned and said something briefly to her father who was just behind her.

Paul stepped forward. "Miss North. Good evening. I am so sorry to intrude on your evening, but I liked your drawings so much and Mr. Morell, here, was anxious to meet you as soon as possible to discuss them."

Julian, astonished and amused that this beautiful creature could be his prey, held out his hand to her. "Miss North, I am Julian Morell. Let me add my apologies to Paul's. And extend them to your parents. It is an unforgivable intrusion, but I am in a fearsome hurry with my project. I think we can work together. I wondered only if we could arrange a meeting over the weekend."

Camilla looked at him and recognized immediately a kindred spirit, a fellow fighter, an accomplice in the struggle to do not merely better but best. Where many people would have considered his behavior in haunting the lobby of the opera house a little excessive, ridiculous even, when a phone call on Monday morning would have done nearly as well, to her it seemed entirely reasonable. She smiled at him and took his hand.

CAMILLA AND JULIAN worked closely together for weeks before anything more intimate took place between them than drinking out of the same cup of coffee. Professionally they were completely besotted with each other: each recognized the other's talents, admired the other's style, inspired the other's creativity. Julian, initially overwhelmed by Camilla's capacity for work, by her perfectionism, by her ability to work to the highest standard for countless hours without food or rest, very swiftly came to take it for granted and simply to accept her and her talents as an extension of his own. Camilla accepted this as the highest compliment and regarded his impatient arrogance, his insistence on achieving precisely what he wanted, his disregard for any views but those that concurred with his own, as an essential element in her work for him.

She had initially been hired to design the lingerie and jewelry departments for Circe, as the store was now called. While she worked on those, Julian instructed Paul to search for others to set their mark on the beauty floor and the fur department. But looking at the drawings she produced, the soft, sensuous fantasy world in which she set the lingerie, the ambience of rich, brilliant, hard-edged greed she created for the jewelry, he abandoned his search and told her she was to do the rest. While they worked in the close tension so peculiar to a shared ideal, she grew to know everything there was to know about him as a person; she knew when he was angry, when he was discouraged, when he was afraid of what he had taken on; she could tell in moments whether he was worried, excited, pleased. She could see he was arrogant, demanding, ruthless; she found it absolutely appropriate that he should be so. She was, she realized, for the first time in her life, absolutely happy.

She was a little less happy after she had been to bed with him. Camilla had for quite a long time realized that she had to go to bed with someone before very much time elapsed. It was one thing to maintain your virginity through college; indeed in the fifties that was what a well-brought-up girl was expected to do. But living as a successful career woman in New York City and still maintaining it was something altogether different. She laid her plans with care, but things didn't quite work out the way she had expected. She had managed to present Julian quite late one evening with some drawings that were just sufficiently below her usual standard to require further discussion and work. She had suggested they talk over dinner at a new Italian place in the Village near her apartment; then she had asked him to see her home, as it was Friday night and there were more than the usual number of drunks about. She had made coffee and poured some brandy, which he had drunk rather less enthusiastically than she had, and then sat, edgy and dry-mouthed, hoping rather desperately that some overpowering natural instinct would propel them both into the convertible sofa, made up freshly this morning with some new thick muslin sheets she had bought from Saks, without her having consciously to do any more about it.

Julian, however, did not seem in the least danger of being overpowered by anything. He sat totally relaxed, leafing through *Vogue* and *Bazaar*, pointing out the occasional reference to himself, to Mrs. Lauder's new line, to a forthcoming promotion from Mr. Revson. Finally he leaned back on the couch, looked at her, and said, "What's the matter, Camilla?"

"Nothing," she said, "nothing at all."

"Yes, there is," he said. "First you present me with some damn fool designs and pretend you can't do any better. Then you tell me you're afraid to come home on your own, when you're the most independent woman in New York, and that includes the Lady on Liberty Island. Now you're shaking like a teenager on her first date. What is it?"

She said nothing, nothing at all, simply that she was tired, and he laughed and said she was never tired. Then he took her hand and said, "I may be being presumptuous, but are you out to seduce me?"

And she said, half angry, half ashamed, no, of course she wasn't; it was time he left, it was late; and he said he would certainly leave if she liked, only he would much rather stay if she would like that; and then she started to cry and said please, please go, and he put his arms around her to comfort her, and that was cozy and comforting and reassuring, and she stopped feeling frightened and silly. Then somehow everything changed and he was kissing her, really kissing her, and holding her and stroking her, and at first it was nice, and then as she realized what was happening, she stopped being relaxed and she tautened and shivered violently. He drew back and said, "Camilla, what is it? What's the matter?" And she suddenly took a deep breath and said, "I've never done it before."

She would never forget to her dying day the look of absolute amazement on his face, how he sat back from her, just staring at her, and she was sure he was going to be angry, or amused, and then he said, very gently, reaching out and touching her face, "Then we must take great care that you will want to do it again."

Nevertheless, she did not find it as wonderful as she had hoped, rather more as she had feared, and she felt strangely detached, almost disembodied, as if she were watching from above the bed as he fondled her and kissed her, stroked her breasts and kissed them. He kept asking her if she was happy, if it was all right, and finally, when the moment arrived, as he gently, tenderly entered her, patiently waiting again and again for her to follow him, as he began to move within her, as eventually the movements became urgent, bigger, more demanding, as he kissed her, stroked her, sought out her most secret, tender places, as he shuddered tumultuously into her, murmuring her name again and again, all she could feel, all she could think, as she tried dutifully, earnestly to respond, was a sense of huge relief that it was over at last. Afterward, of course, she lied; she said it was lovely, that no, she hadn't quite come, but she had felt marvelous, that—and this much, at least, was true—it couldn't have been more wonderfully, more gently accomplished and that she was truly truly happy. They fell asleep then; later, waking thirsty and uncomfortable, unaccustomed to the restless invasion of her quietly peaceful bed, she got up and went to the kitchen for a drink of water. When she came back he was awake, waiting for her, his hand outstretched, asking her back to bed; and he did it again, less carefully, more urgently, and it was a little nicer; she almost enjoyed it. And when she awoke in the morning, got up and showered, made him coffee, and sat drinking it with him, she felt quite wonderful, to think that at last, at long last, she was like everyone else, every other woman, no longer set strangely and awkwardly apart.

ELIZA, LEFT ALONE in London, was not only lonely. More miserably, more significantly, she felt isolated, shut out. She tried very hard at first to persuade Julian to tell her about his project in New York, she asked him endless questions, even tried to make suggestions about what the store might look like, what it might sell, what she would like to find in such a place. But Julian would not be drawn in. He answered her questions as briefly as possible, ignored her suggestions, and totally rejected her requests to accompany him on one of his many trips. He phoned her quite often when he was there, asking how she and Roz were. He sent her funny cards, had flowers delivered, and he returned to her with his arms full of presents, impatiently ardent, with a string of funny stories and amusing gossip; but of what he had really been doing, actually achieving, she learned almost nothing. In the end, inevitably, she came to reject the presents, to resent the gossip, and to find the ardor unwelcome.

"Eliza," Julian said in an attempt at lightness when she turned away from him for the third night in a row, "forgive me if I'm wrong, but you seem to find me marginally less attractive than you did a short while ago."

"Yes," she said flatly, "yes, I do. I'm surprised you have taken so long to be aware of it."

"Do I have to look to myself for the reason? Am I growing fat? Boring? Perhaps if you would be kind enough to enlighten me I might be able to do something about it."

"No, Julian," Eliza said, turning over onto her back and looking at him, her green eyes hard and oddly blank, "you're not in the least fat, and I don't suppose you're boring. Although it would be a little hard for me to tell."

"I don't quite know what you mean."

"Oh, for Christ's sake," she said. "Don't be so dense. I see so little of you and talk to you so seldom, how can I possibly know what you're like anymore?"

"That's not fair. You know how busy I am. And I took you out to dinner this evening and devoted myself very thoroughly to your interests, which were, I have to say, a little less than riveting. A nursery school for Rosamund, I seem to recall, and the advisability of refurnishing Marriotts throughout. Oh, and of course your latest purchases from Monsieur Saint Laurent."

"Shut up, shut up!" Eliza cried, sitting up, her eyes stinging with sudden tears. "How can you possibly expect me to have anything to say to you that you might find interesting when I don't have the faintest idea what you're doing from one week's end to the next?"

"Other wives seem to manage. To occupy themselves with something more than trivia."

"Julian," said Eliza, controlling her voice with an effort, "I don't want to have to occupy myself, as you put it, with anything. I want to be busy with you. With our marriage. I want to be involved."

"Eliza, we've been through this before. I have not the slightest desire to have you mixed up with my company. I want a wife, not a business partner."

"And how can I be a wife when I don't even know what kind of areas your business is extending into? I don't want to work for your lousy company, but I would at least like to be able to answer people when they ask me what you're doing in New York and whether the cosmetics are doing as well there as they are in London. I've never even been to New York, I don't know what it looks like, and I'm expected to be able to comment on the comparative merits of Bergdorf's and Saks. How can I begin to understand what might be worrying you, interesting you, exciting you, when you answer me in monosyllables and treat me like a half-witted child? You diminish me, Julian, as a person, and then you expect me to be wholly responsive to you in bed. Well, I can't be. Don't ask me anymore."

There was a silence for a moment. Then Julian got up and walked to the door.

"I think I'll sleep in my dressing room," he said. "I won't say 'if you don't mind,' because clearly you wouldn't."

Eliza, waking in the morning to an empty bedroom, decided this would never, ever happen again. If she could not persuade Julian to share his life with her, then she would have one of her own and make sure she didn't share that one with him. She decided to divorce Julian.

LEE WAS LYING ON THE BEACH DISCUSSING sex with Amy Meredith when she realized her period was late.

She had never been much in the habit of noting down dates; she had long given up serious hope of a baby. Unlike some of her friends she never had any bad cramps, so she didn't have to plan around her period; when it happened it happened, and that was all there was to it. Only this time it hadn't happened.

She looked at Amy, and a huge fist-sized lump grew in her throat; she tried to swallow; her mouth felt dust-dry.

"Lee, for heaven's sake, what is it? You look awful, terrible. Do you feel all right?"

"Yes—no—this is, oh, shit, Amy, what have I done? What have I done? Do you have a wallet calendar? Give it to me quick, quick. Oh, Jesus, Amy, I feel . . ."

Her voice trailed away; she was feverishly counting, checking off weeks. She threw the calendar onto the sand, looked at Amy, her cheeks flushed, her eyes big and scared.

"Amy, I'm late. Really late. Nearly three weeks."

"Well, honey, isn't that good news? Don't look like that. You and Dean have always wanted a baby. What's the panic? Anyway, it probably doesn't mean a thing. Do you have any other symptoms?"

Lee shook her head. "No, I feel perfectly normal."

"Well, then, calm down. When I was trying to have Cary I was late every other month for nearly a year until it actually happened. But I honestly would have thought you'd be pleased. I mean it certainly doesn't matter. It's nothing to panic about. Christ, I thought you were going to die on me."

Lee managed a shaky smile. "So did I. It must have been the sun."

"Lee Wilburn, when did the sun ever give you the vapors?" Amy looked at her friend sharply. "Is something worrying you, Lee? I mean, you know, something that you should tell me?"

Lee looked at her and longed to tell her everything, and knew she never could. If nobody knew, then nothing could happen to her. If she kept quiet, she would be safe. Probably Amy was right and it was just nothing; and if it wasn't, if the unthinkable had happened, if she had to think it, then it was far, far better nobody knew.

In the middle of the following week she began to be sick, not just in the morning but three or four times a day; she seemed to spend her entire life these days in the bathroom. Her breasts were sore; her head ached.

"There's no doubt you're pregnant," said Amy, who had taken to dropping by every morning to check on her and cheer her up. "I know it's hell, but it's such good news, too. And you'll feel great in a little while. Now, listen, you have to start on extra vitamins right away and cut out the booze, of course, just orange juice and lots of fruit, and for goodness' sake you will cut out any medication, won't you? Stop taking all those aspirins you're so fond of. They're toxic. And you should eat bran every morning, too; pregnancy is terribly constipating. And get lots of rest. Have you told Dean yet?"

"No," Lee said listlessly.

"Well, he must have the brains of an ox not to have worked it out for himself. I suppose he's got a lot on his mind. Do tell him, honey; he'll be so pleased, and he can look after you, help some. This place looks terrible, Lee, even by your standards. When did you last clean that sink?"

"I can't remember," Lee said.

"Well, let me do it for you, and then I'm going to take you for a walk on the beach. You look as if you could do with some fresh air."

Lee did as she was told. She didn't have the strength to do anything else. She had just finished a prolonged bout of throwing up when Hugo phoned. She crawled over to the couch and sat there, trying to sound normal as he chatted away about New York and how much he had enjoyed his last trip, and was it still all right for him to visit her and Dean the following weekend?

Torn between a longing to see him and a strong desire to tell him to fuck off, she sat silent. She knew what he was doing, the bastard; he was leaving all his options open, maintaining contact with her while making it perfectly plain he wanted their relationship to remain casual. Next time he wanted to be sure Dean was there as well, lest she think he was taking things too seriously. She suddenly felt violently sick again.

"I have to go now," she said and put the phone down. She rushed to the bathroom, vomited again and again, and then sat on the floor, resting her head tiredly on the toilet, hot tears trickling down her cheeks, hating him, longing for him, wishing she could die.

The phone rang again. It was Hugo.

"Lee, are you all right? You sound awful."

"I'm fine," she said lightly. "Just a bit of a cold, that's all."

"So is next weekend all right?"

"What?"

"Lee, are you sure you're all right?"

"Hugo, I'm all right."

"Good. Then can I come next weekend?"

"Oh, yes, sure. Sorry. That'll be nice."

They arrived together, Hugo and Dean. Lee had made a huge effort, tidied up, made up her face, drunk lots of ginger ale to help control the vomiting.

"You look wonderful, honey," Dean said, hugging her. "Doesn't she, Hugo?"

"Marvelous." But Hugo's eyes went sharply over her, and she was afraid he had guessed.

Later, Dean went to bed early; she tried to make an excuse to follow, but Hugo put out a hand and caught hers.

"What's the matter?"

"Nothing," she said harshly, "nothing at all. Why don't you just leave me completely alone, Hugo, instead of nearly alone? It would be much easier for you."

"Don't be silly," he said gently. "I couldn't imagine not seeing you anymore. It's difficult, that's all. And a little bit dangerous. You must understand."

"I understand all right," she said. "Good night, Hugo. You're in your usual room."

She got just a tiny bit of satisfaction from the expression on his face. He didn't look merely hurt; he looked worried as well.

Lee woke up early the next morning and shot into the bathroom, sicker even than usual. Wandering miserably into the living room a few minutes later, sipping a glass of water, she found Hugo standing by the patio windows.

"You're not well, are you?" he said.

"I'm fine, thank you."

"You don't seem fine." He crossed to the couch, sat down, patted the seat next to him. "Come here. Come on, darling, please. Don't be so hostile. What is it? Aren't we to be friends anymore?"

Lee turned to look at him, and there was all human knowledge and experience in that look: humor, love, scorn, despair. Then she sighed and said simply, "I'm pregnant."

Hugo was silent for a moment; he looked at her intently, searching, exploring her face, her eyes.

He took her hand. "And is it mine? It's mine, isn't it?"

"No," said Lee, "no, no, it isn't. It's not yours; it's Dean's." She pulled her hand away and felt the tears hot behind her eyes. Dear God, she thought, don't let me cry. Not now. Not in front of him.

"Lee," Hugo said, "look at me."

"No, don't. I can't. Leave me alone. The baby is Dean's."

"But you said—"

"It doesn't matter what I said. Obviously I was wrong. This baby is Dean's. I know it is. I know."

"How do you know?"

"Oh, Hugo, stop it. I can count; that's how I know."

"I see."

She watched him trying to analyze what she really wanted, what she really felt. She had so longed to see him again—that was why she had allowed him to come—but she couldn't imagine why. She had thought that perhaps in some miraculous way he would be able to help, make her feel better, but she had been wrong. There was no way he could help her, and he was making her feel worse. They could hardly disappear into the California sunset together. And she had to stick to her plan, of not admitting even to herself that the baby's father might be anybody but Dean. In time, she knew, she could make herself believe it.

She began to feel better soon after that. She couldn't quite figure out why, but she supposed that having confronted Hugo she could only go forward, believing in what simply had to be the truth. Dean was so beside himself with pride and joy when she told him that he didn't even pause to consider that their sex life had been a trifle spasmodic over the past couple of months. He even remarked that it had been worth all the temperature-taking and counting.

He talked nonstop about the baby—what they would do together, he and his boy, for he had no doubt at all about its sex, how they would fish together, play football, camp, ride, hike. Lee listened quietly. She was calm now, serene, happy. She looked beautiful. Pregnancy suited her.

Lee gave birth to her son with the minimum of trouble, albeit three weeks late. They placed him in her arms, and she looked down at the blue eyes, and stroked the downy blond head.

HUGO DASHWOOD, ARRIVING at his New York hotel one day in early January, found a card waiting for him with a California postmark. "Miles Sinclair Wilburn, son of Dean and Lee Wilburn, has arrived," it said. "Born January 2 at 8.30 P.M. at Saint John's Hospital in Santa Monica. Weight 8½ pounds. A big 'un. Mother and baby well. Come and meet him soon."

◆　　◆　　◆

"IF EVER A child looked exactly like his daddy, it's Miles, Mrs. Wilburn. He certainly is a lovely little boy." Father Kennedy at the Catholic church on California Avenue in Santa Monica was chatting to the faithful after midmorning mass; he liked to establish friendships with his flock, make them feel he was an approachable figure they could turn to in trouble. Not that he could imagine Mrs. Wilburn would ever need anyone to turn to; she seemed like such a nice, steady, competent person, not the sort to fool around or leave her little boy to come home to an empty house because she went to work like some of the mothers in the area. With her looks she might even have been tempted to try for work as an extra in the movie studios, but she didn't. She stayed at home and kept house for Miles and her rock-solid husband. Dean didn't attend church often, but he was a nice enough person, he came on Easter and Christmas, and at least one parent attended regularly and was raising the child in the faith.

He suddenly realized that Mrs. Wilburn was looking at him oddly, nervously even, and he wondered what he had said, but then she relaxed and smiled at him, her lovely warm, friendly smile. What a pretty woman she was.

"Thank you, Father. Yes, he certainly is. Of course he's a handful, very very lively, but you would expect that, wouldn't you?"

"You certainly would, Mrs. Wilburn. Boys should be boys. How old is he now? Is he in school?"

"He's going on eight, Father. He's been in Saint Clement's grade school for two years. I can't say he seems to be a genius, but there's plenty of time, I guess. All he thinks about is sports; he just can't wait to join Little League. And Dean, my husband, can't wait either."

"Well, it's nice to see a father taking so much interest in his child."

"It certainly is. I never see them on weekends; they go off fishing together or sit at home and watch football games. Sometimes I feel left out." She smiled gaily, to let him know she wasn't serious.

"Perhaps you'll have another child, Mrs. Wilburn. A girl, maybe. To keep you company." He smiled back, letting her know he wasn't serious either, that he wasn't insinuating that she was doing anything wrong, breaking the laws of the church.

Nevertheless he had wondered. She was young, such an ideal mother. Now, why had there not been another child?

A shadow passed over her face. "I can't tell you how much I'd like that, Father."

He felt guilty for having opened a wound. He patted her hand.

"God works in a mysterious way, Mrs. Wilburn. Who knows what may happen in time?"

"Perhaps. Good-bye, Father. Miles, come along. Your daddy will be waiting to take you fishing."

But Lee knew, as she headed for home that bright October morning; she knew what would happen: nothing, nothing at all. Dean, encouraged by his first success at fathering a child, had never given up hope, but the years had gone by and Miles had remained the only one. She didn't think that Dean actually minded that much. He was so absolutely and utterly wrapped up in Miles; he loved him so much, it frightened her. Another woman in another situation might have been jealous, as she had joked to Father Kennedy, so absolutely second place did she come to the little boy. As it was, she was just thankful, deeply, deeply thankful, that not so much as a shiver of suspicion or mistrust darkened Dean's relationship with his son.

And they were a very happy family. There was no doubt about it. Miles was a very bright, nice little boy. He was naughty, a bit wild, and a bit devious maybe, and very lazy when it came to school. She could see trouble ahead there; it was annoying because he was obviously clever—a bit too clever, she sometimes thought uneasily. He picked things up in a flash if he wanted to, and he had a real flair for numbers; he enjoyed adding them up in his head, which he did terrifically fast. When they went to the supermarket sometimes, and he was waiting for her to check out groceries, he would stand in one of the other lanes and watch the cash register totting up the prices, silently mouthing the figures as they went up and announcing the final sum to the impressed shoppers before the checker did. It became a kind of party trick. People would talk about it and point him out, smiling, and the cashiers would say, "Hey, that's really neat," and tell him what a clever kid he was. Miles liked that; it was one of the things Lee worried about. He loved being the center of attention, being admired, having a fuss made of him, not in the regular way kids did, of enjoying a bit of spoiling, but actually being in the limelight, being stared at, having an audience. She hoped to heaven he wasn't going to grow up wanting to go into the movie business. A lot of mothers encouraged that, of course, but the only thing Miles seemed likely to want to star in at the moment was the baseball team, and that was healthy.

"Mom," said Miles hopefully, pulling on her hand one Sunday morning as they walked down the hill toward their house, "do you think we could have lunch on the pier today?"

"Miles, you know your daddy is planning to take you fishing. Don't you want to go?" Lee said in astonishment. Usually Miles liked nothing better than a day's fishing off Malibu with Dean.

"I'm kind of tired of it. We go so often. And Jamie is going to the pier today with his folks. He says he has something real neat he wants to show me. Please, Mom, could you ask Dad?"

"Well, I don't know," said Lee doubtfully. "He'll have everything ready to go; he was getting the rods out when we left."

Miles scowled. "I don't see why I have to go. That makes two things in one day I didn't want to do."

"Well, Miles, there's nothing anywhere that says you should only do what you want to do. That would be very bad for you. What was the other thing?"

"Going to mass."

"Now, Miles, that's ridiculous. You know you have to go to mass."

"Jamie doesn't have to go to mass."

"Jamie's family isn't Catholic."

"Why do we have to be Catholic?"

"We don't have to be Catholic, Miles; we just are. It's something you're born with and grow up to."

"Dad doesn't go to mass."

"He does sometimes. Now stop this argument, Miles. It's just silly."

Lee always grew uncomfortable when anyone commented on her religion, especially Miles or Dean. It was a bargain she had made with God: if Miles was safely born, she would attend church regularly again. And she hadn't broken her side of it; she had gone not only to mass on Sundays but to confession every fourth Saturday—although there were some things she would never confess to anybody, not even God, never mind Father Kennedy who was a bit of a gossip. Dean had teased her about her suddenly devout Catholicism, but Lee reminded him she had always been a Catholic, just lapsed a bit, and said with some truth that she was so pleased and thankful for Miles's safe delivery that she felt duty-bound to show God her gratitude.

When they got home Dean was indeed ready, all the rods packed up in the hall, beaming delightedly as Miles appeared.

"There you are, son. Ready to go?"

"Yes, he is," Lee said. "Just let him go and change, Dean. He won't be five minutes."

Miles looked back at her defiantly, his eyes so like her own and yet so different; a darker, harder blue, suddenly hostile.

"Do we have to go, Dad?"

Dean looked amazed and hurt. "What do you mean, Miles? Of course we have to go. We want to go. Don't we?"

"No, Dad. Not today."

"Miles, go and change," Lee said quickly. "Go on, run along."

"Do I have to?"

"Yes, you do. Whatever you do, you have to change. I'll talk to your dad."

"What on earth was that about?" said Dean, his plump face bewildered, a little hurt. "When did he ever not want to go fishing?"

"Quite often, possibly," said Lee. "He's never mentioned it before, that's all. He never has to me either. But, Dean, I think maybe he'd like a change sometimes. Do something different. All of us together, maybe. Today he asked me if we could go to the pier. Jamie's going. That would be a nice change for him once in a while. He loves going fishing with you, of course, but maybe every Sunday is a little too much. Don't be upset. Would you mind not going today?"

"Yes, I would," said Dean truculently. "All morning I've been waiting, getting the rods ready. I've been looking forward to it."

"Yes, well, Miles hasn't," said Lee firmly. "It's his Sunday, too. I think you should listen to him once in a while."

"Since when did little boys get listened to?"

"Since there were little boys, maybe. I bet you got listened to."

"I did not."

"Well, you should have." She gave him a kiss. "Come on, Dean. Stay home with me. Just this once."

He softened, grinning at her. "Okay, but you'll have to make it up to me later."

"I will," Lee said.

THE SANTA MONICA pier was a good place to go on a Sunday. "Every day is a holiday here," Miles had once said, and it was true. People always seemed happy, relaxed, in a good mood. Dean, warmed out of his snit, took Miles on the rides and challenged him to a turn at the shooting gallery, and they all leaned over the rail and watched people water-skiing.

"I'd really like to do that," Miles said. "Dad, can I go water-skiing?"

"You certainly cannot," Dean said, instinctively putting out a protective hand and drawing the little boy closer to him. "That's real dangerous, Miles. It's not for little boys."

"I like things that are dangerous," Miles said cheerfully. "When I grow up I'm going to be a stunt pilot for the movies."

"You most certainly are not," Lee said. "I would never allow such a thing."

Miles gave her one of his slow, thoughtful looks. "You won't be allowing me or not allowing me anything, Mom. I'll be doing what I like. I might even be living thousands and thousands of miles away."

Lee shivered suddenly; the day seemed to darken. "If you live thousands of miles away," she said sharply, "you won't be able to be a stunt pilot for the movies."

"I will, too," said Miles, and scowled at her.

"Hey," said Dean, "come on. I thought we were here to please the two of you. Let's go down to Muscle Beach and watch the acrobats."

They went down the steps under the pier and fought their way through the crowds near the Muscle Inn. Massive men, their muscles like skeins of throbbing rope, were posing on the sand, lifting up girls as if they were rag dolls, practicing their strange skills with unsmiling fanaticism. Dean bought beers for himself and Lee and gave Miles an ice cream cone. The beach was packed; it was hot for October, even by California standards. "I should have brought my bathing suit," Lee said. "Maybe I'll go home and get it. Dean, can we have lunch at Sinbad's? I know that's what Miles is hoping for."

"Sure," said Dean, mellowed into total good humor by the holiday atmosphere and the beer. "When is he going to meet his friend?"

"I don't know," Lee said. "Miles, when did you plan on finding Jamie?"

"He said he'd be down after lunch, with his mom and dad. Can we go to Sinbad's, Dad?"

"Sure. If we go now we'll get a table."

They sat in Sinbad's on the pier, eating swordfish steaks. Miles had his favorite, a specialty of the house, au gratin potatoes mixed with slices of bananas. Dean had french fries with his, and coleslaw and pickles and sweet corn. Then he ordered brownies with strawberry sauce and whipped cream; Lee and Miles had sherbet.

"You eat too much, Dean," Lee said, patting his stomach affectionately. "You should cut down a little. It isn't good for you."

"Ah, honey, don't spoil a nice day by nagging."

"I'm not nagging, Dean. Just saying you eat too much." She kissed him quickly on the cheek, not wanting him to think she was seriously criticizing him. "It's only because I care about you. Sorry, Dean. Look, Miles, there's Jamie. There, walking down the pier."

"Hey," Miles said, "hey, look. He has a skateboard. Oh, wow, would I like one of those! Can I go get him, Mom?"

"Sure. Tell him to bring his mom and dad over here to say hello."

When Sue and Gerry Forrest joined them, she said, "Now every kid on the block will have to have a skateboard."

"It was a birthday present from his godfather," Sue said. "I don't think I've ever seen him so excited about anything. He even took it to bed with him last night. He already has about a hundred and fifty bruises."

"Can we go down on the boardwalk and try Jamie's board?" said Miles. "Please, please? He says I can have a go on it. *Please?*"

"Okay," Dean said. "We're coming. But don't blame me if you fall and skin your knees, Miles. I'm sure it isn't very easy."

Miles made it look very easy very quickly. He took two tumbles in swift succession and then suddenly got his balance and took off, swooping down the boardwalk, whooping with excitement.

"Hey," Jamie said, "he's real good. I took a lot longer than that to learn. Miles, come back, come back," he yelled, and started running down the boardwalk; but Miles was far ahead, not stopping, gliding easily away, occasionally wobbling a little, a small, joyous, oddly graceful figure. At last he came back, panting, flushed, his eyes huge and starry.

"Oh, wow," he said, "was that neat! Was that neat! Dad, can I have one? Will you buy me one, please? Please! I'll be so good. I'll do my homework and I'll get good grades and I'll help Mom with the dishes and I'll . . . I'll . . ." He was about to say, "come fishing with you," but he stopped, realizing it was not quite the most tactful thing to say, and anyway, if he had his way, he would never again sit on a boring lake with a boring fishing rod when he could be swooping along with the wind in his hair and the sun on his face, vying with the birds for speed.

"You cannot," Dean said firmly. "Not yet anyway. I don't believe in letting little boys have things whenever they want them."

"Can I have one for Christmas? That isn't so far off."

"Maybe. I'll have a word with Santa nearer Christmastime."

"No, I didn't mean *wait* till Christmas; I meant have it now and not have a Christmas present. Please, Dad, please?"

"No, Miles," Lee said sharply, "you can't."

"But why not? I want one. I want one real bad."

"Lots of us want things real bad," Sue Forrest said, smiling, "but we don't always get them."

Miles looked at her thoughtfully and then turned again to his mother with his sweetest, most appealing smile. "Please, Mom. It would make me real happy."

"Miles," said Lee, "will you shut up? We said no. Now stop it." She was always a little alarmed by the way Miles went for what he wanted. He didn't usually ask for much, but if something mattered to him he pursued it with a mixture of such charm and absolute determination that it was very hard to resist him.

Over dinner Miles tried again.

"I'll pay you interest on the loan for a skateboard," he said suddenly.

"Oh, Miles, don't be silly. What on earth do you know about interest?" Lee said.

"Enough to know it makes lending money worthwhile. You lend me ten dollars for a skateboard and I'll pay you back fifteen in a year. You'll be making a fifty percent profit over twelve months. It's a good deal."

Lee laughed suddenly, ruffling his hair. "Maybe it is. But where would you get the money to repay a loan? And I don't have ten dollars right now. Not to lend, anyway," she added with a sigh. "Now be a good boy, Miles, and help me with the dishes."

"Why should I?"

"Because it would be nice for me," said Lee, hurt.

"Why should I make things nice for you if you don't make them nice for me?" said Miles.

"Miles," Dean said, looking up from the *Times.* "Apologize to your mother this instant. And start helping her."

"I don't see why—" Miles was interrupted by the phone. Dean picked it up, still glaring at him.

"Dean Wilburn. Yes. Oh, Hugo, hi. How are you? Good, good. Great to hear from you. Yeah, I'll hold." He covered the mouthpiece and turned to Lee. "I was wondering when we'd be hearing from him again. . . . Hugo, yes, hi. Sure, sure, we'll be here. We'd love to see you. Lee would be thrilled. Stay for a few days if you can."

"Not too many," said Lee sharply. She dreaded Hugo's visits. They hung over her uncomplicated sunlit life like a dark shadow. They were not very frequent, to be sure, but they were inevitable every two or three months. The very thought of them made her throat dry, her stomach contract, made her want to run and hide, taking Miles with her. What she felt for Hugo these days was a fierce dislike, a deep resentment, mixed with a sharp tug of sexual attraction. The mixture of emotions made her sullen, withdrawn, hostile. She was always amazed that he didn't seem to care and Dean didn't seem to notice. She lived in a state of permanent terror all the time he was in the house that he would say or do something to arouse Dean's suspicions; but she was forced to admire, however grudgingly, his skill at deceit.

Nevertheless, skills faded, watchfulness could slip, memories might falter; every second he was in the house she was sick with fear. He had not visited them for some time, not since May. He had been busy, he said, in England, neglecting his American company. They had had a couple of notes; there had been a card and a five dollar bill for Miles on his birthday, a postcard from Scotland where he and Alice and the children had spent their vacation, but that had been all. She prayed fervently every Sunday, every day almost, that he would not come again; but the God who had given Miles blue eyes and blond hair plainly felt he had done enough for her and had not seen fit to hear or at any rate answer that particular prayer.

"Next Friday, then," Dean was saying. "Great. Lee will meet you, I'm sure. What's that? Okay, I'll tell her to have dinner for you. Bye, Hugo."

He put the phone down, beaming with pleasure; he enjoyed Hugo's persistent friendship, felt it marked him out as a person of some interest and stature.

"He's coming next weekend, honey. On Friday. About dinnertime. Won't that be nice?"

"Very nice," said Lee, walking to the fridge and getting out a bottle of beer, hoping Dean would not notice her shaking hand, her taut voice.

"Miles, I want you to be on your best behavior next weekend," said Dean. "Mr. Dashwood is coming from England, and you know how he always likes to see you and hear about your schoolwork and so on. You come home early for dinner on Friday and stay home Saturday, okay? No going out to play with Jamie or anyone. English kids are very polite. I don't want you letting American ones down."

"I don't like Mr. Dashwood," Miles said, scowling. "I don't want to stay home and talk to him. Always asking me how I'm getting along and what grades I got and what I'm reading, and having to sit and listen while he drones on about his dumb kids in England. He's so— so nosy."

"Miles, don't be ridiculous," Lee said sharply. "Of course Mr. Dashwood is interested in you; he's known you all your life."

"Yeah, well, I wish he hadn't. And I'm going out with Jamie, no matter what you say."

"Miles, I am getting just a little bit tired of your insolence," said Lee. "Just cut it out, will you? Mr. Dashwood is our guest, and he's always very good to you. You have a duty to be courteous to him."

"I don't see why . . ." Miles's voice trailed off into an exquisite, thunderstruck silence. "Gee," he said. "Gee whiz, I'll be nice to him. I'll stay home Saturday. I sure will."

"Good," said Dean. "That's better. That's my boy."

Lee looked at Miles sharply. He caught her eye and gave her his enchantingly sweet smile, his blue eyes wide, guileless.

"I like Mr. Dashwood," he said slowly. "He's kind to me. I forgot for a minute how kind he was."

"Miles," said Lee, "if you say one word to him about wanting a skateboard, I'll tan your hide. I mean it."

"Don't worry," said Miles. "I won't say one word. I swear it. But he'll give me one just the same, I'll bet. He loves giving me things I'm interested in. He's interested in everything I'm interested in. He even said he'd take me on trips if I wanted to go. To England. He told me so." He stood up. "I'll help you with the dishes now, Mom."

Lee stood up, suddenly feeling sick.

"Are you all right, honey?" Dean said. "You look a bit pale."

Lee rushed to the toilet. She vomited violently, then sat on the floor, her head resting on her arm, for a long time.

Dean banged on the door. "Honey, are you okay?"

She came out slowly and sat down heavily on the couch.

"It's nothing, Dean. Must have been the swordfish. I'll be all right. I'll just go lie down for a while."

She lay on the bed twisting and turning, waves of panic and dread going through her, rather like the fierce deepening waves of childbirth. She had been wrong, so wrong, to think that she could get away from Hugo when he was there in this house, growing up, becoming more and more visible every day of her life.

7

ROZ COULD REMEMBER EXACTLY WHEN SHE discovered her father didn't love her. She was six years old at the time, and the incident was fixed in her memory as indelibly and certainly as her own name.

She knew he didn't love her because she had heard him say so. Well, perhaps not in so many words, but he had certainly admitted it. He had been having a row with her mother. They had been shouting at each other in the drawing room of the house in Holland Park where Roz and Nanny and Eliza lived. It was so small you couldn't help overhearing everything. This particular row started when her father returned her to Holland Park after she had spent the weekend with him. She never knew if the happiness of those weekends was worth the misery of their endings. She and Julian had such fun, the two of them. Sometimes he took her shopping and bought her clothes that her mother strongly disapproved of. They often ate in smart restaurants like the Ritz, and he let her stay up late, or they went to the country, to Marriotts, where he was teaching her to ride and had bought her her own pony called Miss Madam, because that was what Nanny Henry always called Roz. He took her for exciting rides in his very special cars, the old ones with lamps sticking out of their fronts and roofs that opened like the hood of a baby carriage—the Lanchester and the Model T Ford and the Mercedes 60; he told her that as soon as she was big enough, about twelve years old, he would let her drive one of them around the grounds of Marriotts, so she could find out what driving a real car felt like.

They had the most wonderful time on those weekends; to have her father to herself seemed to Roz the most perfect happiness. She was very fond of her mother—indeed, she supposed she loved her—but her father had always seemed to Roz the most perfect person; he was so good-looking—much better-looking than most of her friends' fathers—and he wore such lovely clothes, and he was so good at telling her stories and making her laugh and just knowing what she would most like to do. But more important than all those things, he seemed to value her company and her opinions. He never sent her off to the nursery if she didn't want to go; he would explain things to her about his company even when she was a little tiny girl, and he told her it was never too early to learn and that one day the business would be hers; he was never ever going to have any other children, and so Roz was his heir.

"Don't be ridiculous, Julian," her mother had said the first time he told Roz this, when she was only four years old. "How can you expect her to understand such a thing? Anyway, she's an heiress, not an heir."

And her father had looked at her, not her mother, and smiled, and said, "No, she is my heir. Roz will inherit the company, because she is my child and extremely clever, and her sex is quite immaterial."

She hadn't understood all the words, but she certainly understood the meaning—that one day her father's company would be hers, because he thought she was the right person to have it, and no one, no one at all, was going to take it away from her. That promise made everything else worthwhile, even the awfulness of her parents not being married anymore.

And then it was taken away from her.

She and Julian got back from Sussex quite late one Sunday evening. He returned her to the doorstep, and her mother sent her up to Nanny Henry to get ready for bed.

"Do you want a drink, Julian?" she heard her mother say, and her father said yes, that would be very welcome.

"And how are you, Eliza?"

"I'm extremely well. Very happy."

"Good. You don't look it."

"Julian, you have no idea how I look when I'm happy. It was not a state I enjoyed very often during our marriage."

"Well, we won't discuss that now."

Roz, listening on the first-floor landing, heard her mother say casually, "Julian how would you feel about having Roz live with you?"

Roz's heart lifted, leaped; she had to bite her fists to keep quiet. She knew how her father would feel: he would love the idea as much as she did. She had never thought her mother would consider letting her go back home to Hanover Terrace. She waited to hear him say he would take her, to say, "Well, of course, I'd love it," or something like that. But there was a long, an endless silence.

Then: "Eliza, exactly what do you mean?"

"I mean what I say. I just think it might be better."

"For her?"

"Well, yes. Of course for her. I'm not trying to get rid of her."

"You could have fooled me."

"No, Julian, I'm not. But she does so much prefer you. She adores you. You know she does. And I just can't do anything right for her. She's"—and Roz could hear the suppressed laughter in her voice, slightly shaky, but nonetheless there—"she's just like you."

"Really? In what way?"

"Oh, every possible way. Hard to please. Impossible to reason with. Shutting people—me out."

"Poor child. You make her sound very unattractive."

"Well, she isn't very attractive, is she? At the moment? Be honest. She's morose and awkward."

"She seems fine to me. I would agree she isn't physically attractive at the moment. She's going through a very plain phase, and she's so big for her age. It's a shame, poor child. She has enough problems."

"Yes, well, that will pass, I'm sure. So what do you think, Julian? Would you—could you have her for a while?"

Time had stopped for Roz, sitting on the landing in a frozen stillness, her legs cramped underneath her, her fists still crammed into her mouth to stop her making a sound. Surely this was it, the long boring conversation would end, and her father would say yes, of course he would have her, and probably tell her to pack up her things immediately, come back with him now. That was all that mattered, really; it had been very unpleasant hearing him say she was plain— she didn't mind her mother saying she was unattractive—but she had known that already, and if she could only go and live with her father, she would soon become more beautiful. All the people surrounding him were attractive, it was a kind of magic he seemed to work, and she would be happier and she would smile more, so she would look prettier anyway. All he had to say was yes—so why wasn't he saying it?

"No, Eliza, it's absolutely out of the question."

What? What? Roz thought she must be hearing wrongly, that she was imagining his words.

"I couldn't have her even if I wanted to, and frankly I don't. I—"

But Roz heard no more. She got up very quickly and crept to her bedroom and lay down on her bed fully clothed, with the eiderdown pulled over her, waiting for the tears to come. But they didn't. She just lay there, silent, and the feeling returned to her numb legs, which she had been sitting on for so long, in a stabbing agony. The pain was so bad she found it hard not to yell out. But it was nothing, nothing at all, compared to the awful, deathly cold hurt throbbing in her head and her heart.

Roz had learned to live with the hurt, after a while. You could learn to live with anything. Obviously there was a reason for him not loving her, and she spent a lot of time trying to find it. Was it that she was not pretty? It could be. Her mother was beautiful, and so was Granny Letitia, and her father was extremely good-looking; it must be horribly disappointing for them to have someone in the family who was so plain. Of course her father wouldn't want an ugly person living with him; he couldn't be expected to. Then maybe it was because she wasn't clever enough. He was so extremely clever himself, and if he was going to leave her his company—only maybe he wasn't now, maybe he had changed his mind—she needed to be extremely clever, too. Of course he hadn't said that he wasn't going to give her the company, but if he didn't think she was good enough to live with him, then he probably wouldn't think she was good enough to have the company either.

Or maybe it was because she wasn't a boy. He had never said he minded, but Nanny Henry—and quite a few other people, mostly Nanny's friends and some of her mother's luncheon companions, the ladies who arrived at half past twelve and stayed till about four, drinking wine and eating almost nothing and laughing and talking endlessly —had said it would have been much better if she had been a boy and could take over the company. Or—and this was the most frightening thing of all—maybe he was planning to marry someone else and have another baby with her. And maybe that baby would be a boy or a pretty girl or a really, really clever child, and then the company would go to him or her instead.

Nothing that had happened to Roz could compare with this in awfulness, not even the day that her father had taken her on his knee and held her very tight and said he was terribly sorry, but he and her mother were going to be living in separate houses from then on, because they didn't get on very well anymore. And the worst thing of all was not finding out that her father didn't love her; it was finding out that she couldn't love him in the same way either.

She couldn't talk to him about that, of course; she couldn't talk to him about any of it. She simply shut him out and tried not to let him see how bad she felt. She didn't want him to know what power he had to hurt her; she wanted him to think she didn't care what he did. He could buy her as many dresses as he liked and take her to New York and Paris and throw extravagant parties for her on her birthday. One year he took her and her six very best friends to Le Touquet for the day in his own plane, which he piloted himself, and bought them lunch in a very smart restaurant there. Another year he hired the ballroom at the Ritz, and everyone wore long dresses, even though they were only ten, and instead of a conjuror, which most of the girls had, they had a rock group who played all the top hits, and instead of it being in the afternoon, it was from six o'clock till ten o'clock at night. He never stopped trying to please her. He got tickets for shows like *Camelot* and *Beyond the Fringe* and arranged for her to meet the cast afterward, and to premieres of films like *Lawrence of Arabia* and *West Side Story*, and even occasionally to the parties afterward where the stars went. He took her out to expensive restaurants; by the time she was ten Roz had eaten in practically every restaurant recommended by Egon Ronay—and had complained in most of them. He took her to Disneyland; he did, as promised, let her drive some of the cars around the grounds of Marriotts on her twelfth birthday; he bought her not one but two ponies to replace Miss Madam when she was eight, one gray and one chestnut, because she said she couldn't make up her mind between them; he had her stay with him in New York most school holidays; and she had only to mention most casually that she wanted a puppy, a kitten, a new bicycle, a new stereo, and it arrived. And Roz would say thank you politely, formally, but never warmly, never showing her pleasure; and she got great satisfaction from seeing the disappointment, the hurt, in his eyes. She knew he was desperate to please her, that he was frightened of making her unhappy, and she enjoyed the knowledge. It was the only thing that made her feel safe.

Roz hated Camilla North. She had hated her from the very first time she met her, when she went to stay with her father in New York when she was seven. At first she had thought Camilla was just a friend of her father's, one of the many ladies he took out to dinner or the theater and then didn't see again, or not very often. But Camilla didn't go away. She went on being around, first in America and then in London, until Roz couldn't remember a time when she hadn't been there. One of the things she hated most about her was how beautiful she was, with her gold-red hair and her bright red lips and her long red nails; she could see that was why her father liked her, and it seemed so unfair that someone could be liked so much just because she was beautiful.

Camilla came to lunch with them twice in New York that first time, and although she worked very hard being nice to her, asking her endless questions about her friends and her school and her pony, Roz could see perfectly well she was bored; she had that look on her face that grown-ups always had when they weren't listening to what you said, a sort of fixed smile with her eyes wandering around the room a bit. She didn't like the way her father looked at Camilla either, or the way Camilla put her hand over his and kissed his cheek and talked for a long time very seriously about something that had happened in a meeting that morning. Another night she went out to dinner with them; Camilla was looking particularly beautiful, Roz thought, although she didn't like to admit it, wearing a great big shaggy sweater in lovely blues and greens, with a V neck and rows and rows of beads, a pair of very narrow black velvet trousers, and slipperlike shoes. Her father had laughed and told her she looked like a beatnik, and Camilla had said very seriously that he was out of date; beatniks had been around years earlier. He told her not to be so tedious, which had pleased Roz very much. They went to a restaurant called Sardi's, which Roz liked much better than all the other expensive places they had been to; she had a hamburger and a Coca-Cola and felt quite happy, until Camilla said she had a present for her and gave her a little box with a silver dollar in it made into a brooch.

"That's lovely, Camilla," her father said. "Isn't that kind of Camilla, Roz? What do you say? Put it on, darling, and let's see how pretty it looks."

"Thank you, Camilla," Roz said carefully, aware that once again someone was trying to buy her and trying to make her like them, "but I won't wear it now; it doesn't go with this dress."

"Roz, you don't know what does and doesn't go with dresses. Put it on," said Julian. He tried to sound light and amused, but she could see the anger in his eyes and she felt just slightly frightened.

"No," she said, bravely. "I don't want to."

"Roz," Julian said. He had stopped pretending to be amused. "Put it on."

"No," she said. "I won't."

"Oh, Julian," Camilla said quickly, "don't make a big thing of it. If Roz doesn't want to wear it, I don't mind. And she's quite right, aren't you, Roz? It doesn't go with that dress. What a clever little girl you are."

Something snapped in Roz; she could feel a hot rage sweeping over her, could feel Camilla thinking she was getting around her.

"I'm not clever," she said. "I just don't like the brooch. And I don't want to wear it. I feel sick, and I want to go home."

"Don't be ridiculous, Roz," Julian said. "Apologize to Camilla and eat your food. We are not going home."

"I shall be sick."

"No, you won't. Now eat."

Roz ate in total silence. When she had finished the last mouthful she took a deep breath and by sheer effort of will vomited the entire meal onto her plate. It was a trick she would perfect over the years.

Looking at her father across the table, she was rewarded by an expression on his face she had never seen there before. It was defeat.

BUT SHE DID not get rid of Camilla.

Camilla often came to London and stayed at the house in Regent's Park or came down to Marriotts. Roz minded her being at Marriotts even more than in London, because she always thought of it as her father's and her house, and Camilla absolutely ruined it. She was so boring about things and went on and on about whatever Roz said, even if it was a joke or if they were playing checkers, spending hours studying her moves, and if they went riding together, the three of them, Camilla was forever telling her little things she was doing wrong, like not sitting into the canter enough or letting her pony trail his legs over a jump. Camilla was supposed to sleep in one of the guest rooms, but Roz had seen her coming out of her father's bedroom more than once. She knew what happened when a man and a woman were in bed together—intercourse, it was called. Her friend Rosie Howard Johnson had told her, and she had also said it could lead to the woman having a baby. Roz didn't mind too much about the intercourse, but she thought of Camilla having a baby made her feel very sick indeed. Apart from the fact it might be a boy, and that he might get the company, her father might love the baby more than he loved her—if he loved her at all. Sometimes for days at a time Roz managed to make herself forget that she had heard him refusing to have her live with him, but when she thought about him sort of living with Camilla and possibly even having a baby with her, the pain came back so badly it made her breath go away and she felt as if she had fallen and winded herself.

RIGHT FROM THE very beginning of her relationship with Julian, Camilla's main problem had been Roz. She could handle the highly charged matter of working with Julian and sleeping with him as well, and the inevitable speculation and tensions it caused; she could handle the fact that she knew she was not the only woman in his life; she could handle her slightly ambivalent attitude toward sex. And she had no problem at all handling the question of Eliza. Through the divorce, which did not surprise her in the very least, Camilla supported Julian admirably; she allowed him to talk as much as he wished: to question his behavior, to examine his feelings, to express regret, anxiety, remorse—which he did occasionally and rather dutifully, as if he knew it was expected of him. She was careful not to criticize Eliza and was even more careful to avoid hinting that now he might wish to enter into a more serious relationship with her. And she took great care to allow him to spend more time with her than usual between the linen sheets, and to consciously express more affection and tenderness there than perhaps she had done in the past. In brief, she was the perfect mistress. But she was not the perfect stepmother.

Roz quite clearly resented her, feared the impact she might make on her life, and in fact—Camilla had to admit to herself—thoroughly disliked her. She was polite to her—just—but no more; she rejected her overtures of friendship; she cut any conversation with her down to a minimum; and she made it perfectly plain that whenever Camilla was with her and her father she would much prefer it if she was not. Julian had taken an indulgent attitude to this at first, saying easily that Roz would soon get to know Camilla better and feel less threatened by her; later on, weary of the constant hostility between the two of them, unable to ease it in any way, he refused to discuss it or even acknowledge its existence.

The fact that Roz was not a pretty child didn't help; she was not appealing, she did not enlist sympathy, she was big for her age—not fat, but sturdily built—dark-haired and slightly sallow-skinned, with a rather large nose and a solemn expression. The only thing that gave her face any charm at all was her eyes, which were green like her mother's, large, and expressive. But the expression in them was very frequently not in the least charming; she had a capacity to fill them with a kind of brooding intensity, which she would fix on Camilla, or she would make them, like her father's, inscrutably blank.

Later, as Roz got older and Camilla became more involved with Julian, the problem increased. Roz was increasingly difficult to handle; both her parents spoiled her and were afraid of upsetting her, and Camilla could see that she was fast reaching a point where nobody would be able to handle her at all. She was like a badly trained, overexcited thoroughbred, Camilla told Julian. She needed a good long session on the lunge rein at regular intervals. She had been rather pleased with this analogy, but Julian clearly hadn't liked it at all and told her shortly that handling children was extremely easy for people who hadn't got any.

Camilla observed with a mixture of irritation and admiration Roz's manipulative skills. She heard her on the phone one evening, telling her mother that she had been having the most wonderful time with

Daddy and Camilla and didn't want to come home until the next day, when in fact they had all spent a rather depressing afternoon skating at Queen's and then having supper at a dreadful place called the Carvery where you could take as much of everything as you liked and which was supposed to be Roz's favorite place. Roz had sat out most of the skating, saying her ankles hurt, and had refused to eat anything at the Carvery except ice cream and roast potatoes.

Roz was just about nine at the time; Camilla rather bravely volunteered to take her home in the morning by taxi as Julian had several meetings, and on the way she asked Roz to show her Harrods and offered to buy her something. Roz had said she hated Harrods; it was a boring shop and anyway her mother had bought her so much lately she really couldn't think of anything else she wanted; but then, as Camilla delivered her to a rather cool Eliza, Roz had said thank you very, very much and could she please, please go out with her another day and buy her a present for always being so kind to her in New York?

What Camilla felt within her most secret self, the self she crushed ruthlessly into submission most of the time and which only surfaced during the middle of the night—like most obsessive overachievers Camilla was a poor sleeper—was that her own rather irregular situation with Julian made her relationship with Roz worse. Had she been married to him or even his permanent, long-term mistress, sharing his homes as well as his bed, then she felt that Roz would come to accept her, and she could have established a relationship with the child which had some stability. But Julian did not want that; he made it perfectly clear. They had a great many long conversations about it, usually at Camilla's instigation, and agreed over and over again that the success of their relationship was based on their total freedom and the lack of anything in it that smacked of obligation. Camilla was always at even greater pains to assure him and herself that this was precisely what she wanted. She liked him, she told him earnestly, and more than that, she was very fond of him. They had a superb working relationship and an equally superb sex life; they shared many other pleasures and interests—riding, design, fashion—and it would be very foolish, very foolish indeed to introduce any form of long-term commitment into what was a totally pleasurable and undemanding arrangement. But the fact remained that in the middle of the night, when her secret self was asserting itself and having its rather obstreperous say, Camilla knew much of this was quite untrue. She was indeed very fond of Julian, very, very fond, and if she had been caught unawares and asked directly if she loved him she would have said yes. More importantly, there was a lot about him that she didn't actually like very much, particularly in the work situation. She found his ruthlessness with people, the way he used them and discarded them, very hard to accept. He would take an idea from someone and claim the credit for himself if it succeeded and make sure that everyone knew whence it came if it failed. She found his deviousness almost intolerable. He had what amounted to a near compulsion to confuse people, to inform the creative team of some part of his plans and the sales team another, so that only he could bring the whole together. It caused uncertainty, ill feeling, and mistrust among his staff, but it also ensured his continuing indispensability; it kept him totally in control. Camilla saw through this and despised it. She even challenged him on it, but he had a great talent for turning away criticism and disapproval. He would smile at her and tell her she was far too astute for her own good, that if there was one person in the entire company apart from himself whom he could trust to know everything, it was she, and although she knew this to be untrue she was quite unable to prove it.

Then there was their sex life. Camilla continued to try very hard to enjoy sex and to improve her performance constantly for Julian; she never refused him if he wanted to go to bed with her, and she always told him afterward that it had been absolutely wonderful. She hardly ever had an orgasm or even came near it, but she became adept at faking. Her sex therapist told her it was because she would not release her emotions, that she was afraid of her body taking her over. He gave her all sorts of exercises to do, both physical and mental, but they didn't do any good. Fearing that it might be Julian's fault and that they were incompatible, she took another lover from time to time, but it was no better, worse if anything; so then she was left fearing she must be frigid, which was worse still.

She knew what an orgasm felt like because her therapist had taught her to achieve it herself, but even that seemed to her a purely mechanical pleasure, rather like having a drink of water when she was very thirsty, or scratching an itch. It never approached the glorious abandon and heights that she read of and which Julian seemed to experience when they were in bed together.

She had moved in 1963 from her apartment in the Village and had bought a studio in Yorkville, near enough Sutton Place and Julian for convenience, not so near as to make either of them feel stifled. She loved the area, the quiet, sunny streets, the expensive shops, the wealth of museums and galleries, the smart restaurants, the pastry shops, the sidewalk cafés, the entire atmosphere so cosmopolitan and civilized.

Her position in the company was unchallenged, and the most envious, the most malicious person could not but have acknowledged it had been earned, that her success was not dependent on her relationship with the chairman. After Circe's launch, Julian made her design director of the company's stores division; when he opened another Circe in Paris in 1961, he put her on the main board. Two years after that he made her advertising director as well, and creative director of the company worldwide. This meant she had to spend several months of the year in London. She bought a tiny flat in the Boltons and shared her life with Julian exactly as she did in New York, undemandingly, charmingly, and affectionately. But she was very clearly—as even Letitia, who loathed her, acknowledged—in London to work and not as his mistress.

She was brilliant, innovative and, most unusually, had a shrewd commercial sense as well. She never put forward a proposal for a new line, a relaunch, an advertising campaign, without costing it out very carefully, without examining it in all its aspects, and she was equally clever at recognizing the virtue of an idea, a scheme, a suggestion, from someone else. She knew how to delegate and she knew how to lead and inspire. She was an invaluable asset. And Julian needed her very badly.

Circe was a huge, breathtaking success. It stood, a glittering jewel, in the very top echelons of the world's stores. It did not really rank with Bonwit's, Bergdorf's, and Saks in New York, Fortnum and Liberty in London; it had a glamour and style above and beyond all of them, for it had exclusivity, a sense of intimacy that set it closer to the smaller, more specialized establishments—Gucci, Hermès, the Dior boutiques.

The Paris Circe, opened two years after New York, stood on the Faubourg Saint-Honoré and was very similar in feel, a building that had, in living memory, been a house.

But the cosmetic company itself was still at the heart of the Morell empire, and it needed ever more intense attention. Competition in the industry was getting increasingly ferocious in the sixties. Charles Revson was probably at the height of his creative and innovative skills, launching new colors with the brilliance and panache of an impresario. His show was a nonstop extravaganza, with one brilliant promotion after another, six, eight brilliant launches a year, all with dazzling names. The man who gave the world Fire and Ice, Stormy Pink, Cherries in the Snow, was setting a formidable standard. He was also innovative with his products; there were powder blushers, frosted nail enamels, wet-look lipsticks, and above all a mood of constant excitement and innovation. Then there was Mrs. Lauder, rocking the cosmetic world with her high-priced and exclusive line: Re-Nutriv Crème and Extract with its twenty secret ingredients, selling for the awe-inspiring sum of one hundred and fifteen dollars a jar.

The cosmetics industry was discovering science in a big way: Helena Rubinstein had launched a "deep pore" bio facial treatment; Elizabeth Arden had Crème Extraordinaire "protecting and redirecting"; Biotherm had incorporated plankton, "tiny primal organisms," into their creams.

It was a challenging time in the industry, and none of them could afford to rest on their laurels, however exquisitely colored and beautifully perfumed the leaves. Julian responded with a line from Juliana called Epidermelle, which offered a new complex cream containing placental extract for its "cell revival program" and fought back on the color front with a series of promotions based on the concept of the new frenetic fashion of the sixties—his first mini and then micro-mini colors. Pale, pale lipsticks and ultra-pearlized eye shadows sold out in days, and his Eye Wardrobe—the collection of false eyelashes, thick and thin, upper and lower, launched to adorn the little-girl wide-eyed faces of the sixties dolly birds, with their waist-length hair and their waist-high legs—was the sensation of the cosmetic year in 1965.

Nevertheless, Letitia's prophecy that Julian would need to find more and more brilliant chemists had indeed come to pass. He had actually hired not one but three, each overseeing his own branch of a large development team. Two were American, one French, and the rivalry between them was intense—each having deliberately been given the impression that the others were just slightly more brilliant, talented, and experienced—and a great spur to creative activity. He had opened a large new laboratory in New Jersey and greatly expanded the one in England, having moved to new premises in Slough with Sarsted in charge.

However, most of the major cosmetic concepts for Juliana came not from the chemists but from Julian himself. They were the result of several things: his extraordinarily astute understanding of women and what they wanted, his endlessly fertile mind, and his capacity to think laterally about apparently small and unimportant incidents.

He was sitting with Camilla in the New York office over a working lunch one day, discussing the decor of the salons in the Paris store, when Camilla said she would go and get some mineral water to drink. She stood up, looking in the mirror on Julian's wall as she did so.

"Oh, I look awful," she said. "This color has changed on me so badly. The formula just doesn't suit me anymore; the lipstick has gone really dark. I look ten years older."

"I hope it's not one of ours," said Julian absently; then he suddenly froze, staring at Camilla with an expression of intense excitement. "Good God," he said. "Dear Christ. God in heaven. Shelley!" he shouted at his secretary down the intercom, "get me Tom Duchinsky in the lab right away."

"Good God," said Camilla, half amused, half startled. "Do I really look so awful?"

"No, Camilla, you look wonderful. Wonderful. As always. Listen, listen— Oh, Tom, is that you? Tom, listen to me. You know how lipsticks and eye colors—lipsticks particularly—change on the woman due to the acid content of her skin? Do you think you could formulate some quite basic colors that could make a virtue of that fact? Colors that are sufficiently neutral and formulated so that they respond to the woman's chemistry and develop on her? Do you see what I'm getting at? You do? Good. I'd have fired you if you hadn't. What's that? Of course it hasn't been done. Well, it happens all the time, but it's a vice, not a virtue. I want to turn it into a product benefit. And for eye shadows as well. Listen, give it some thought. Camilla and I will be over there in an hour."

"No we won't," Camilla said crossly. "Julian, I have work to do on the new advertising. I can't afford to spend the afternoon in New Jersey."

"Rubbish," Julian said. "If it wasn't for all the new products, you wouldn't have anything to advertise. Come on, I'll drive us. In the Cord. You know you can't resist that."

"Of course I can," Camilla said, crosser still. She found Julian's endless preoccupation with cars intensely irritating and was constantly telling him he would have been far better off with a perfectly ordinary limo and a chauffeur rather than insisting on driving himself around the streets of New York and London in the various exotic vehicles he fell in love with. The white thirties supercharged Cord was his latest folly, as she saw it, with its monster curving mudguards and very long hood set in front of a modestly shaped body. Julian told her as they pulled out of the garage built beneath Circe that he loved it more than anything in the world, with the possible exception of his new brood mare. Camilla was never quite sure whether this kind of remark was a joke or not, but there were times, and today was one of them, when she found it very hard indeed to smile.

LATER THAT YEAR they took a trip to Florida, and stayed in Key West; it was the first time he had suggested they vacation together, and Camilla saw it as important to their relationship. Lying in bed on the third humid night, she was dutifully struggling to arouse the energy to respond to Julian and his protestations of desire when he drew back and looked at her.

"What's the matter?" he said, half amused. "Don't I excite you anymore?"

"Of course you do," she said. "It's just so hot. Let me take a shower and revive myself."

She stood in the tepid water for a long time with her eyes closed, doing some of the mental relaxation exercises her therapist had taught her, breathing deeply and emptying her mind, and some of the physical ones, too, earnestly clenching and unclenching her vaginal muscles, hoping to find in herself some semblance of desire. Suddenly the shower curtains parted, and she saw Julian looking at her with an expression of great amusement.

"What on earth are you doing?" he said. "If I didn't know you better, I would say you were up to all kinds of solitary vices."

"Certainly not," said Camilla, nearly in tears at being caught in such foolishness. "I'm just trying to relax, that's all."

"Well, you had an expression of great concentration on your face. Not relaxed at all. Come on, darling. Let me dry you down and make you feel really good."

He wrapped her in a huge towel, led her to the bed, and massaged her gently through the towel; then he removed it and began to massage body oil into her breasts, her stomach, her thighs.

"Nice?"

"Lovely," Camilla said firmly, closing her eyes, forcing her mind back to her relaxation therapy, saying Pleasure, pleasure, pleasure over and over again silently, like a mantra.

"You feel better. Softer . . . This oil doesn't smell very good," he said suddenly. "Funny how perfumes seem to change in bed"—he bent and kissed her breasts—"in this kind of situation. I wonder—Good God, yes, I wonder . . ."

"What, Julian? What do you wonder?"

"Oh, nothing. Nothing worth talking about now."

"Tell me," said Camilla, who would have thought anything at all worth talking about then.

"No, really, nothing. All I want to do now is just love you until it's light again."

Camilla hastily stifled a yawn, hoping he would think it was a sigh of passion. It all sounded terribly exhausting.

◆ ◆ ◆

SIGNATURE COLORS, THE dazzling new range of lipsticks and eye shadows designed to suit every woman individually, to adjust to her own personal chemistry, and the new Juliana fragrance, Affair, spearhead of an important new element in the Juliana range, were both great successes financially and creatively, launched simultaneously in the spring of 1966 in New York and London. Affair was one of the new all-over fragrance concepts, designed to flatter and adorn the entire body. There was a bath oil, a shower gel, a body lotion, the usual battery of perfume concentrates, and eaux de toilette; and a new product altogether, a body fragrance for the night. "Nighttime Affair," said the packaging copy, "to be stroked and massaged into the skin last thing at night, to surround a woman and her body with the lingering sensuous echoes of Affair until morning." The implications were very clear.

Mick diMaggio produced an advertisement that was so near to soft porn—a woman's body, a man's hand, and a bottle of Nighttime Affair fallen on to the rumpled sheet beside them—that two publications refused to run it, although *Vogue* and *Harpers Bazaar* both adored it. In its first week Nighttime Affair sold out in every store in New York.

Sometimes Camilla North wondered if there was any aspect of her life with Julian Morell that would not become a product.

WHEN ROZ WAS ten years old her parents decided to send her to boarding school. This was partly because they both felt she needed the discipline and stability it could provide and partly because neither of them was prepared to provide it at home. Julian was riding on the crest of wave after wave. Dizzy, exalted with his own success, jetting from London to New York and back again almost weekly, he was considering the possibility of launching Circe in Madrid and Nice. He was exploring hotels, he was investigating a chain of health farms, and he had no time at all to spare for an awkward little girl who was more demanding than all his business interests put together. Had she been more attractive, more appealing, he might have taken her with him sometimes, but she was still a large child, solemn and heavy-featured. Eliza worked hard on her wardrobe and her hair, but she never looked pretty, as so many of her friends did, and her manner was not appealing either; she was truculent and argumentative, and she made no attempt to talk to people if she did not like them.

Eliza was also extremely busy having a great many well-documented affairs both with members of the British aristocracy and the cosmopolitan set, with the twin aims of having a good time and finding a husband. She was achieving the first, although not the second; the English aristocrats, while delighted to enjoy her favors in bed, did not really wish to marry a divorcée, and the cosmopolitan set, while appreciating her beauty and her style, found her in the last resort too English; she lacked their sybaritic indolence, their absolute devotion to the pursuit of pleasure. Nevertheless, her days and her energies were extremely occupied; there was no place in them for a daughter who did her very little credit. Boarding school, it was agreed, was the best place for Roz. It fell to Julian to tell her.

"Mummy and I think," he said to her, over lunch one day at the Ritz, "that you should go to boarding school."

Roz dropped her knife on the floor, panic rising in her throat. "I don't want to go to boarding school," she said firmly, anxious not to allow him to see how frightened she was. "I like being at home."

"Well, darling, you might like it, but we think it would be better for you to go away. You'll like that even better."

"I won't. Why should I?"

"Because you're all on your own. You have no brothers and sisters, and Nanny is getting very old and can't look after you forever, and Mummy and I worry about you being lonely."

"And since when," Roz said rudely, "did you and Mummy decide things together for me? I'd have thought you'd want to do the opposite of what Mummy thought."

"Rosamund, don't be rude," Julian said briskly. He only called her Rosamund when he was very cross with her.

"I don't see," said Roz, determined not to be frightened away from her position, "why I shouldn't be rude. You seem to want to get rid of me. Why should I be polite about it?"

"Darling, we don't want to get rid of you. We think you'd like it."

"No, you don't. You don't know what I'd like. You don't spend enough time with me to find out. And you do want to get rid of me so you can go to New York whenever you want and out to dinner all the time, and Mummy can go rushing off to France with her boyfriends, and have them to stay without having to worry about me being rude to them. You both want to get rid of me. I know you do."

"Darling," said Julian patiently, choosing to ignore her attack rather than defend himself against it, "you're wrong. We love you very much. But going to boarding school is what an awful lot of girls your age do. Isn't Rosie going?"

"I don't know. I don't think so. She wants to go to Saint Paul's. And so do I."

"You don't know anything about it."

She could see he was beginning to lose his temper. She enjoyed that, urging him nearer and nearer the edge. When he pushed his hair back, she knew she was nearly there. She gave a final shove. "Anyway, I'm not going just to please you."

She watched his lips go rather tight and white around the edges. She had done it. But he still didn't say anything really angry. "Well, what you're going to do, Roz, is take your Common Entrance next January, and then we'll go and look at a few schools."

"I'm not going."

"Rosamund," Julian said, "you will do as you're told."

"No," she said. "I won't."

In January Roz sat in the Common Entrance examination and didn't write a word. The headmistress sent for both her parents. Her father came and took her home with him. She had never seen him so angry.

"I hope you don't imagine," he said, "that you are going to get your own way in this. All this sort of behavior does is convince me you are grossly spoiled and you need the discipline of boarding school."

Roz shrugged. "You've spoiled me. It's not my fault."

"No," he said. "No, you're right, it isn't. None of it is. But I am not going to allow you to ruin your life because we have been stupid enough to do it for you so far. You are going to boarding school, Roz, and that is the end of it. Had you behaved more reasonably I might have considered day school. Now it's out of the question."

"No one will take me now that I haven't done the exam."

"Oh, but they will. Your headmistress says you are an extremely clever child, and she is personally writing to the heads of the schools we have chosen for you, with some examples of your work, and you will sit for the individual entrance exams."

"I won't do them either."

"Yes, Rosamund, you will. Otherwise you will go to a school that doesn't require any kind of exam. The sort that exists to help difficult children like you."

"I'll run away."

"Do. You'll be brought back."

Suddenly she stopped being brave, allowed the tears to flow, and once the tears started, the screams followed, the ones she had been silencing for years and years. Her father looked at her in horror for a moment, then stepped forward and slapped her hard across the face. It hurt horribly; she hit him back.

"I hate you. I hate you all. You and Mummy and Camilla. You all hate me. You want to be rid of me. Send me away so I don't interfere in your own precious lives. So you can all do what you like. So Mummy and her boyfriends and you and Camilla can have—" She had been going to say "intercourse," but her courage failed her, and she stood silent, white, her eyes huge, tears streaming down her face, sobs shaking her body.

Her father stepped forward and took her in his arms, and held her close for a long time, soothing her, stroking her, kissing her hair, telling her it was all right, that he loved her, that they all loved her, that they didn't want to send her away, that it was for her own good; they thought she was lonely and unhappy and getting more so.

She didn't believe him. She couldn't remember when she had last believed anyone who told her such things. But she didn't argue anymore or say that she was lonely and unhappy because they had no time for her. She could see she was beaten. Slowly, very slowly she stopped crying.

He held her away from him, looked down at her, wiped her eyes on his hankie.

"Better?"

She nodded.

"Good girl. I'm sorry, I'm so terribly, terribly sorry, Roz, that we've hurt you so much. We didn't mean to."

"Didn't you?" she said.

"No. You have to believe me."

She had learned that when her father said that he was invariably lying. She pulled herself out of his arms and went over to the window. She couldn't ever remember feeling so bad. She wondered how they could possibly go on and on being so cruel to her. It was interesting that her father at least realized it.

She suddenly remembered a request she had been storing up for several weeks. This was clearly a good time.

"Daddy," she said, "can I have a new horse? A hunter?"

"Of course you can," he said. "We'll go to some sales during the holidays."

Once again she had been bought off.

THEY DECIDED ON Cheltenham Ladies' College for her. Roz loathed it; she loathed everything about it from the very first day—the dreary green uniform, the way the students were scattered around the town in houses and marched through it in long lines, the endless games, the misery of communal bathing and dressing, the aching horror of homesickness, the jolly faculty, the way the other girls acted as if they were terribly lucky to be there, the awful food, and most of all the dreadful isolation from the real world. She wasn't popular because she didn't conform; she wasn't friendly and jolly and eager to get on; she was aloof and patently miserable and refused to join any clubs or societies or do any extra lessons. She did what she was required to do; she went there and she stayed there and she worked very hard, because work was the only thing that seemed to make life bearable, and she was always top or nearly top of everything, but beyond that she wouldn't cooperate. She was not going to be happy. That was asking too much.

CAMILLA LOATHED LETITIA. Whenever she allowed herself to consider, however briefly, whether she might, after all, like to be the second Mrs. Julian Morell, she reflected upon the reality of becoming Letitia's daughter-in-law and quite literally shuddered.

She loathed Letitia on two counts: personal and professional. She found it quite extraordinary that this old lady—Letitia was now sixty-nine—should still hold a position of considerable power in the company, and she could not help but feel that Julian was being less than professionally fastidious to allow it. Although Letitia was no longer involved on a day-to-day basis, having retired at the age of sixty-five with a stupendously extravagant party, at which she had danced the Charleston into the small hours at the Savoy, she was still a director of the company, with a most formidable grasp of its workings, a sure and steady instinct for financial complexities, and an equally strong feeling for the cosmetics industry in general. The new financial director, Freddy Branksome, said that the day he was no longer able to consult her on company matters he would take an early pension and go. To an extent he was being diplomatic, but the fact remained that he did give considerable credence to her views and liked to have her at all major financial review meetings. Camilla found this incomprehensible, and was certain that both Julian and Freddy must simply be flattering a vain and difficult old lady. It simply did not make sense, so far as she could see, that a woman with no formal education, no training in business affairs or company management, could possibly be of any value to a multimillion-dollar company. She had tried to say as much to Julian, but he had become extremely angry, told her to keep her business-school nonsense to herself, and said that Letitia had more intelligence and flair in her little finger than did the entire faculty of the Harvard Business School.

On her trip to London in the summer of 1967 she decided once again to try to form an adult working relationship with Letitia. She phoned her and invited her to lunch at the Savoy, which she knew was her favorite place. But Letitia said no, she was on a strict diet and why didn't they meet in the Juliana salon for fruit juice and a salad. Camilla, always grateful to be able to avoid gastronomic temptation and for an opportunity to indulge her body in some therapy or another, agreed and booked herself into the salon for a massage and a sauna for the hour before lunch.

She was now thirty, and against the atmosphere of frenetic pursuit of youth that was taking place in that year, she felt old. London was full of girls who looked seventeen, with silky straight hair tumbling down their backs, Bambi-wide eyes, and skirts that just skimmed their bottoms. Jean Shrimpton's face, photographed by David Bailey, gazed with a sexy tenderness from every magazine cover and every billboard; Marianne Faithful, Sandie Shaw, and Cathy McGowan lookalikes stalked the streets, rangy, self-confident; and through the open window of every car in the capital the Beatles and the Stones sang "Yesterday" and "Ruby Tuesday" and "Penny Lane." It was no time to be over twenty-five.

Camilla sank gratefully onto the massage couch, accepted the beauty therapist's sycophantic exclamations over her slenderness, and then, feeling just pleasantly traumatized from the massage and the attentions of the G5 machine to her buttocks, walked into the sauna, removed her towel, and lay flat on her back with her eyes closed.

She was feeling just slightly sleepy when the door opened. Letitia's voice greeting her made her sit up startled, look frantically around for her towel, and in its absence wrap her arms around her breasts. Quite why she didn't want Letitia to see her naked she wasn't sure, but it seemed in some way an intrusion into her relationship with Julian. She felt Letitia was not looking merely at her body but at what it might offer her son, and that she would find the sight immensely interesting. Camilla didn't like the feeling at all. Letitia was dressed in a terry-cloth robe, with a turban wrapped around her head. She did not remove either, merely sat down on the wooden seat opposite Camilla and smiled at her graciously, her eyes skimming amusedly and slightly contemptuously over her body. Camilla, with a great effort of will, removed her arms and met Letitia's eyes.

"Good morning, Letitia," she said. "How nice to see you. I'm looking forward to our lunch."

"I, too," said Letitia. "And now we shall have even longer together. How well you look, Camilla." And her gaze rested again, lingering interestedly on Camilla's breasts, then traveled down toward her stomach and her pubic hair.

Camilla swallowed hard, closed her eyes, did a relaxation exercise briefly, and said, "Maybe I should go and get dressed, Letitia. I've been here ages already."

"Really?" said Letitia. "They must have been mistaken; they told me you had only just arrived. Don't mind me, dear. I have plenty to think about. Just relax."

"Well," Camilla said, "perhaps I will stay a little longer. Have you been shopping, Letitia?" she added in a desperate attempt to get the conversation onto a comfortingly mundane level.

"No, dear. I don't often shop these days. The shops come to me. No, I've been to see Julian. To discuss next year's budgets and so on. So nice the company is doing so extremely well, don't you think?"

"Marvelous," said Camilla.

"Such a clever man, my son, isn't he?"

"Very clever."

"And you, Camilla, you have done a great deal for the company. I hope he gives you sufficient credit for it."

"Oh, yes," said Camilla, startled by this sudden rush of friendliness and the unexpected tribute, "yes, he does."

"Good. You are unusually fortunate in that case. And in other cases as well, of course."

"Er, yes."

"You seem to enjoy a very special relationship with Julian." Her gaze again traveled down to Camilla's breasts. Camilla made a super-human effort not to cover them again.

"Well, yes. Well, that is to say—I thought . . ."

"Yes, my dear?" Letitia's voice was too sweet.

"That was one of the things I wanted to talk to you about."

"Really? What exactly do you mean?" A wasp was buzzing languidly now near the sugary tones.

"Well, you know, Mrs. Morell, I have always hoped we could be friends. But I imagined you thought I might become deeply involved with Julian personally, and that you might find that difficult to handle."

"What a strange expression," Letitia said sweetly. "No, I don't think so, Camilla dear. I very rarely find things difficult to handle, as you put it. That is one of the advantages of growing older, I suppose. Now, what exactly do you mean—that I would be jealous of you?" And her gaze flicked down again.

"Oh, no, of course not," Camilla said earnestly, "and that's exactly what I want you to understand. There is nothing to be jealous of. My relationship with Julian is more professional than personal. I see him primarily as a colleague, an employer, rather than a man."

Letitia leaned forward, an expression of acute puzzlement on her face. "Camilla, are you trying to tell me that you do not find my son sexually attractive?"

Camilla was so shocked that she did something she had not done for years: she blushed. Furious with herself, desperate to escape the claustrophobic sauna and Letitia's amused, insolent eyes, she stood up and reached for the towel, which had fallen on the floor, bracing herself for the full frontal confrontation.

"How thin you are, dear. Perhaps you should eat a little more. Now, I can assure you," the silvery, flutelike voice went on, "you are very much alone, if that is the case. Most women can't wait to get into bed with him."

Camilla rallied. "I do find him attractive," she said, wrapping herself in her towel, "but I think that some relationships can transcend the physical."

"Balls," said Letitia. She smiled at Camilla sweetly.

"I beg your pardon?"

"I said balls, dear. An old Anglo-Saxon expression. It means rubbish. Balderdash. Poppycock. Oh, dear, you won't know what those words mean either. Your country's vernacular is, if I may say so, extremely limited."

"I do understand you, Mrs. Morell. But I can't agree with you."

"Really? Then what do you do when you are over here staying at my son's house? Talk to him all night long? Hold animated discussions about sales psychology and corporate identity and the design ethic and all those other things you take so seriously over there? I find that very hard to believe."

Camilla struggled not to lose her temper.

"No. Of course we have a—a physical relationship."

"I see. But you don't enjoy it. Is that what you are trying to say?"

Camilla flushed again; she pulled her towel more closely around her.

"No. It's not what I am trying to say."

"Then try harder, my dear. I am only a simple old woman. I can't quite follow your articulate Americanisms."

"What I am trying to say," said Camilla, "is that although I do, since you force me to express it, enjoy my personal—physical—relationship with Julian, what is really important to me is our professional one. I can't imagine my life without that. However much I might admire and enjoy him as a person."

"I see," said Letitia. "How very interesting."

"Why is it so particularly interesting?" Camilla asked boldly.

"Well, dear, forgive me, but it seems to smack of using him. Of using your considerable feminine charms to coerce him into employing you in his company."

"Not at all. I worked for Julian for quite a long time before we—I—he—"

"Had sexual intercourse with you? How charming," Letitia said.

Camilla had had enough. "Mrs. Morell, forgive me, but I am finding this a little embarrassing. Perhaps you would excuse me, I have a lot of work to do."

"Oh, my dear, I am so sorry!" cried Letitia, an expression of great distress on her face. "How thoughtless of me. Of course I have no right to talk to you like this. It is absolutely no business of mine. It's just that Eliza and I were so very close, still are, and I find it hard to be formal when I talk about my son. Now, why don't we both get dressed and move out to the juice bar and you can tell me exactly which aspect of the company you are currently engaged in, to keep you so busy and over here so much."

"Well," said Camilla carefully, determined not to lose her temper, "as you may not know, Julian has put me in charge of the advertising, both here and in New York. Not the creative concept, of course, although he likes me to be heavily involved in that, but I have a major responsibility, reporting only to him, on campaign planning, budgets, media schedules, and of course, overseeing the advertising in all its aspects here. The campaigns don't alter very much, but they need to be carefully anglicized, and we are always ready to consider creative concepts at this end. So I have a lot to do this week. I—we also have to get to know the people at the new agency and see how we are going to work with them."

"I see," Letitia said thoughtfully. "Tell me, is Julian no longer able to afford to employ an advertising manager in New York?"

Camilla looked at her, her eyes wary. "Of course there is an advertising manager, but he reports to me. He is not on the board. I'm surprised you didn't realize that, Mrs. Morell. But I suppose Julian finds it difficult to keep you informed on every detail of the company these days. It must be so different from the old days when he ran it virtually single-handed and you helped him."

Letitia stood up and smiled at Camilla graciously. "He did not run it single-handed, my dear, and I did not help him. We did it together. It could not have survived any other way." She looked at Camilla and then suddenly raised a limp hand to her head. "I am so sorry, but I very much fear I may have to cancel our luncheon after all. I have a very severe migraine coming on. The only thing is simply to get home and lie down in a darkened room. Do forgive me."

"Of course," said Camilla, relief and rage struggling with each other. "Can I have my driver take you home?"

"Oh, no, dear, mine is waiting. He's been with me for years, you know. Ever since the company began. So loyal, all my staff. Goodbye, Camilla, I think I'll get dressed and hurry off. I do hope you will find someone else to join you. I don't suppose you have managed to find many friends in London, as you are so dreadfully overworked."

TALKING TO ELIZA that evening over dinner, regaling her most wickedly with every lurid detail of the encounter, Letitia said, "I do hope for all our sakes, Eliza, he never does marry that dreadful creature. Our lives will become a great deal less agreeable if he does."

• 8 •

LEE LOOKED AT DEAN ACROSS THE BREAK-fast table and wondered for the hundredth, possibly the thousandth, time what she could do to make him eat less. He was, at forty-two, seriously overweight. The last time she had managed to get a look at the scales while he was on them they had lurched up to two hundred forty pounds; that was an awful lot for a man who only stood five feet ten in his socks. It wasn't just the way he looked . . . well, he certainly wasn't the most attractive man she had ever seen, his shirts straining desperately around his huge belly, his trousers slung awkwardly and uncomfortably beneath it. "You'll need them specially made soon," she had said tartly the last time they went shopping together, "or maternity pants, like I used to wear with an elastic panel in the front." She felt his weight was a serious threat to his health and had only last week tried to tell him so. She'd suggested he cut down on the hamburgers, fries, and beer, but he had laughed easily and slapped his gut with his soft, dimpled hand and said he and his belly were old friends and he was damned if any diet was going to come between them.

"If you get any bigger," she said, "you won't have any other friends. You look terrible, Dean."

"Miles," he said to the little boy, who was sitting in the living room reading the comics and munching his way through a bag of potato chips, "do you think I look terrible?"

"No, Dad," Miles said without even looking up.

"There you are," Dean said, "two friends. Miles doesn't mind me being a little overweight, do you, son?"

"No, Dad."

"Honey, you shouldn't worry so much about these things. It's that Amy Meredith with all her crazy nonsense about natural foods and not eating red meat. I never heard of such nonsense. Man was meant to eat meat; he used to live on nothing else. A buffalo steak for breakfast on a good day. Now, you go tell Amy Meredith that."

"I will if you like," Lee said. "She won't want to hear it, but I will. And you're wrong anyway. Man was a hunter-gatherer; he ate nuts and grains as well, and vegetables. And besides, when man was eating buffalo steak for breakfast, he was also going out and killing the buffalo and getting a lot of exercise that way. The only thing you do to hunt your food is walk to the refrigerator and open the door. Please, Dean, at least think about a diet."

"Okay," he said, grinning at her. "I'll think about it. For five minutes every day. Before dinner. Now, why don't you start worrying about something more sensible, like your own figure. You're skin and bone, honey. If anyone looks awful, you do."

"Thanks," Lee said, giving up on the discussion, shooing Miles outside, and turning her attention to sorting the laundry. "At least I won't die of a heart attack."

"No, malnutrition. With all those goddam dance and yoga classes you go to, you could eat twice as much as you do. I'd like it if you were rounder, honey. More of you to get hold of and roll around in the hay with."

Lee thought of his massive weight descending upon her in bed and about the way, these days, she had to climb on top of him if he wanted to make love to her, and looked thoughtfully at him. Maybe this was her chance.

"Dean, if you get to weigh any more you won't be able to roll around in the hay at all. And I certainly won't be rolling underneath you. So think about that."

"Oh, hell, honey, we manage."

"We don't, really," she said shortly, "or rather you don't. Not very often. I miss that, Dean."

"Hey!" he said, beaming at her affectionately, "what about that? Eighteen years we've been married, and my wife still wants to get me into the sack. You always were sexy, weren't you, honey?" He wiped the sweat off his forehead. "Jesus, it's hot. Aren't you hot, Lee?"

"No," she said. "You're hot because you're so overweight. If I was lugging around two hundred pounds all day, I'd get hot, too. Now, Dean, will you please, please think about a diet? Go see Dr. Forsythe if you don't believe me."

"I might."

But he didn't.

That particular morning Lee didn't want to get involved in a discussion with Dean about his weight. She had a lot to do. It was nearly the end of the school year, and she had to get Miles ready for summer camp. She and Amy had their ballet class, and after that they planned to go to the beach. Sometimes Lee wondered if there might not be more to life than ballet classes and the beach. She felt somehow she was missing out on the real world, but she couldn't see what she could do about it now. Nobody was going to give a forty-year-old housewife a job, and besides there was Miles to take care of. He was only ten, and she didn't believe in giving kids latch keys to let themselves into the house with after school; that was where the trouble started and they got in with a bad crowd.

She wondered, as she watched Miles get into the car beside Dean, to be dropped off at school, if the way she felt a lot of the time could be described as happy. Her life was a monotone, without any highs or even promises of highs in the far distance, just a long, level road stretching out ahead. On the other hand, she certainly wasn't unhappy. She had most of what she had always wanted: a family at last, albeit a small one, a nice house, and peace of mind. She valued peace of mind very highly; the only thing that threatened it was the increasingly rare visits of Hugo Dashwood.

Dean was always delighted to see Hugo. He admired him and his English style, and since he had discovered that Hugo had not after all made such a success of his business, had warmed to him still more. Dean had not made too much of a success of his business either. He got by; he had provided for his family and hung on to his job, even made chief district sales rep, but he wasn't exactly Henry Ford. It made him feel comfortable that someone with Hugo Dashwood's obvious advantages had not done so well either. Anyway, Lee thought with some relief, there was no danger of Hugo coming for a while yet. He had said he was spending the rest of the summer in England and would contact them in the fall. She was safe for a while: safe from his probing eyes, his interest in her, his insistent friendliness, his ridiculously pressing attentions to Miles.

Miles at ten could not have been more of an all-American boy, she thought fondly, with his passion for the beach and for baseball. Nobody, nobody at all, could doubt for an instant that he was an all-American boy. Why on earth did she have that thought so often?

Lee had managed by now to persuade herself that the affair with Hugo had never happened. She had done this by every means she knew, from determinedly putting it out of her head, to using the meditation and visualization techniques she had learned in her yoga classes. Most of the time she never even thought about it—it was dead, buried, like a person she might have met long ago—but every now and again, usually when she couldn't sleep, it would rise up inside her, the memories, the knowledge, a suffocating, stifling panic, and she would have to get up and get herself a cup of tea and sit very still, in the lotus position, willing herself into calm. And in the morning, when the sun was shining and Miles was playing in the yard and Dean was tucking into his bacon and eggs, grunting contentedly at her as she set it before him, she would be able to smile at her fears and wonder how had she ever worked herself into such a state, and she would tell herself that nothing could hurt her now.

Only she was wrong; it could.

The phone was ringing when she and Amy got back from the beach that afternoon. "Mrs. Wilburn? This is the hospital. We have your husband here."

DEAN WAS IN the emergency ward when they got there. He looked pale and sweaty; a pretty nurse was taking his blood pressure.

"Hi," said Lee. "I'm Mrs. Wilburn. They said to come in."

"Yes, Mrs. Wilburn," said a nurse. "I'll find the doctor. He wanted to see you."

"How is he?" asked Lee, gently taking Dean's fat, moist hand in hers.

"Not too bad, I think. The doctor will be able to tell you, though."

She disappeared. Lee kissed Dean's forehead. "What happened, hon?"

"I'm not sure. I was just leaving the diner after lunch, and suddenly I felt very sick and dizzy. Sweaty, too. Next thing I knew I was lying on the floor of the diner, and then they brought me here."

"What'd the doctor say to you?"

"Not a lot."

"Does he think it's a heart attack?"

"No. That's what I thought, of course, but he said it wasn't. He said he wanted to talk to you."

"Oh, how do you feel?"

"So-so. Shaky. A little sick."

A doctor walked into the cubicle. "Mrs. Wilburn?"

"Yes."

"I'm Dr. Burgess. May I have a word with you outside, please?"

"Yes, of course," said Lee. Suddenly feeling very sick herself, she joined Amy in the corridor. "Amy, could you go and meet Miles, please? And maybe bring him back here?"

"Sure," said Amy. "Everything okay?"

"I think I'm about to find out." Lee turned as the doctor came out into the hallway.

"First of all, let me reassure you," said the doctor. "He has not had a heart attack. He's had a blackout. His blood pressure is phenomenally high. And it was no doubt increased by the beer he drank for lunch, by the heat, and I imagine by the stress of his job. Now, that in itself is not very serious. He's fine now. But what you have to understand, Mrs. Wilburn, is that if he goes on the way he is he will have a heart attack and very soon. He is grossly overweight, his diet is terrible, and if he has one more incident like this, I wouldn't like to answer for the consequences."

"I see," said Lee. She felt very small. "Doctor, I've tried to make him diet and exercise. But he won't do it."

The doctor smiled at her. "If I had a ten dollar bill for every wife who has said that to me over the past five years I could retire right away up to the Hills. Mrs. Wilburn, you have to *make* him do it. I think he'll be more cooperative now."

"Yes," said Lee, "maybe for a while, but once the fright is past, he'll just relapse into his old bad ways." She felt faint herself suddenly. "Could I sit down?"

"Of course. I'm sorry. Water?"

"No, I'll be okay."

Dr. Burgess looked at her thoughtfully. "You're very slim yourself. Very fit looking. You obviously know about what you should and shouldn't do."

"I do. Of course, I do. And I am careful with my little boy. But Dean—my husband—just lives for his food."

"Well," said Dr. Burgess, "he'll die for it if he isn't careful. Does he suffer from stress?"

"Not too seriously. He takes life pretty much as it comes."

"Well, that's something. Does he drink a lot?"

"Yes. A lot of beer."

"Anything else?"

"Bourbon."

"I see. Does he smoke?"

"Yes. But not too much. After dinner. After lunch."

"How is his health generally?"

"Not too bad. He doesn't get colds and all that stuff."

"Headaches?"

"Yes, a lot of headaches."

"That's the blood pressure. How does he sleep?"

"Very well. Too well."

"How's his libido?"

"I beg your pardon?"

"How often does he want to make love?"

"Oh," said Lee, "not very often." She knew why he had asked that. Amy had told her that very overweight men often lost their sex drive.

"Do you have children?"

"One."

"Was that deliberate?"

"Well, no, not exactly. We—he—well, it never happened again."

"Did you investigate the reasons for that?"

"Yes. A long time ago."

"How long?"

"Before my—our little boy was born."

She began to feel her midnight fears closing in on her, beginning to threaten her. "Is that—relevant?"

"What? Oh, no, not really. Well, it could be. Certainly the loss of libido. Now, look, Mrs. Wilburn, I'm going to keep him in the hospital overnight, and then, providing he's okay in the morning and the blood pressure is down, he can go home tomorrow. But he has to go on a strict diet. He must lose at least seventy pounds, and he must start taking some exercise. Nothing too radical, just some steady walking would be ideal at first. I'm going to talk to him very seriously about his weight, impress upon him how crucial it is. I'll give you some diet information, and I want to see him here in a week. I'll talk to your family physician and explain the situation and ask him to keep an eye on your husband. He should have his blood pressure and his heart rate checked regularly. All right? Are *you* all right now?"

"Yes," Lee said. "Yes, thank you."

But she wasn't. She was seriously frightened.

DEAN EMBARKED ON his new regimen with immense seriousness. He cut out alcohol, gave up smoking, and almost stopped eating red meat and butter and fried foods. Once a week he allowed himself a steak. He said he had to have some pleasure left in his life. He went for a walk every evening after dinner.

Within one month he had lost fourteen pounds, his blood pressure was down, and his headaches were less frequent. After two months he had lost twenty pounds, and his headaches had gone. He looked ten years younger and, he said to Lee one night in bed, he certainly felt it.

"I hate to admit this, hon, but I think the doc's probably right. He said I'd be feeling as lusty as a young man again if I lost weight and got myself back in shape, and I do. Come over here and let me show you how much I love you."

He showed her how much he loved her quite often after that. If some hovering dread hadn't been permanently with her, Lee would have been pleased. As it was, she was fearful, and she didn't know why.

"You never know, honey," said Dean, rolling off her one night and kissing her contentedly, "this whole thing may have been a blessing in disguise. We may manage to provide Miles with a little brother yet."

"Oh, Dean, don't be silly," Lee said quickly. "What difference can losing a little weight make to your fertility?"

"Oh, you don't know, honey, quite a lot. The doctor said obesity and high blood pressure could certainly affect a man's performance, and who knows? It might affect his fertility as well. He thought it was possible."

"Have you been—discussing that with him?" Lee asked.

"I certainly have. Why not? He asked me if there was any aspect of my health that bothered me, and I said, two things: one, I didn't seem to be able to get it up anymore—well, that's cured, isn't it?—and the other, we had always had trouble conceiving children."

"But, Dean," said Lee, feeling sweat cold on her forehead. "You know that was my fault. Not yours. Dr. Forsythe always said—"

"Well, seems he might have been wrong," Dean said. "I don't know, of course, nobody does, but Dr. Burgess says it could be me. Anyway, it doesn't matter. Time will tell."

"But, Dean, I'm forty, too old to have any more children. Even if I could. And besides, Miles is ten. It wouldn't work."

"Nonsense. My mother was forty-seven when I was born. And it would do Miles good. He's spoiled. No, I think we should let nature take its course. I really like the idea of being a dad again."

"I see," Lee said quietly. She didn't sleep until dawn broke.

THREE WEEKS LATER Dean came back from his checkup looking particularly cheerful. "Lee, I've made a decision."

"What's that?"

"I'm going to have some tests done."

"What for, for heaven's sake?" Lee said irritably.

Dean looked at her sharply. "What's the matter, Lee? You don't look too good. Now, listen, we have to take care of you. Because I think we might be able to be parents again."

"Oh, Dean, no, not that again. Please."

"Lee, why on earth not? You've loved having Miles. Why not try to have another baby?"

"Dean, I don't want another baby. I'm forty. There are—risks."

"I know, I know. But if Dr. Burgess says they aren't too serious, then how would you feel?"

"Miserable," said Lee. She spoke without thinking.

"Honey, I don't know what's come over you. I thought you'd be happy about all this."

"About what?"

"There being a possibility that we could have more children."

Lee looked at him wearily. "Dean, it's a very remote possibility."

"Not necessarily. Anyway, Dr. Burgess is arranging for me to have a sperm count. That'll take us to first base. Then we can talk some more. You can't object to that, can you?"

"I suppose not," Lee said listlessly. She felt extremely sick. Dread had settled itself heavily and comfortably on her shoulders. Nothing would shift it now.

A week later Dean came home at lunchtime. Lee heard him shut the front door rather slowly and carefully. She was spraying the leaves of the plants in the living room. He walked in and sat down on the couch. He looked at her, his eyes blank, his face empty of any emotion.

"Dean, what is it? What's the matter?"

"I think you know," he said slowly, "don't you? You know what the matter is."

"Dean, you're talking in riddles. Of course I don't."

"I think you do. I had a sperm count three days ago. You know what the result is, of course?"

"Of course I don't. Don't be ridiculous. How should I know? What was it?"

"Don't play games with me, Lee. You know what it was. It was nix, zero, negative, zilch. I am absolutely sterile."

"Well, probably that's from being so overweight, so unwell, for so long."

"Is that what you think?"

"What else can I think?"

"I'll tell you. You can think that I've always been sterile. That I could never have fathered a child. That's what Dr. Burgess said."

"Well," Lee said, "he doesn't know what he's talking about. What about Miles?"

"Yes, Lee, what about Miles?"

"What do you mean?"

"I mean who did father him?"

"Don't be ridiculous. You know perfectly well you fathered him. He looks just like you."

"No, he doesn't. He looks just like you. Lucky, wasn't it? Supposing he'd had red hair? Brown eyes?"

Lee shivered. "Dean, this is ridiculous. I'm going to call the doctor.

I don't believe any doctor would have said you could never have fathered a child. Is that really what he said?"

Dean suddenly broke down, sobbing like a baby. "No. Yes. Oh, I don't know. He said I was very, very lucky I had managed to father a child, because my sperm count is so low. I asked what the chances were. He said he couldn't say. I asked what the count was. He said I wouldn't understand, but that it was very low. He was clearly embarrassed. Lee, I'm not a fool. I can see when I'm being lied to. Now, will you for Christ's sake tell me who Miles's father is? Who were you fucking then? Who have you been fucking since? Come on, Lee, I need to know. We're not leaving this room until you tell me."

Lee rallied. She took a deep breath, sat down on the couch beside him. "I haven't been fucking anybody. Anybody at all. Not even you very often. Until just recently." She sounded bitter.

"Don't try to change the subject."

"I'm not. It's the truth."

"I don't believe you."

"You don't have to."

Dean's eyes suddenly filled with tears again. He gripped her small, thin hand with his huge one. It hurt. Lee winced.

"I do have to. I do have to believe you."

"Well, for Christ's sake then, Dean, do believe me. Please. I'm telling you the truth. You are Miles's father."

He looked at her for a long time. She did not falter.

Please, please, God, she thought, please let him believe me.

"I can't," Dean said at last. "I can't believe you. I want to, but I can't. Lee, you simply have to tell me. Who was it?"

Lee stood up abruptly. "This is ridiculous. I'm going to fix you some lunch. Maybe you'll feel calmer then."

"I don't want any lunch. Sit down."

"No."

"Lee, will you for fuck's sake sit down? Jesus, I swear to God I'll kill you if you don't tell me the truth."

"Dean, I don't think I can stand this much longer."

"*You* can't stand it!" He laughed shortly, a harsh, cracked sound. "You can't stand it. That's rich. How sad for you. How painful. I am so sorry."

He crossed to the bar and poured himself a huge slug of bourbon. Lee looked at it.

"Dean, you shouldn't drink that. You know you shouldn't."

"Don't you tell me what I should do. You have absolutely no right. No right at all. I'll do what I like."

"Okay." She shrugged. "It's your funeral."

She was to remember saying that for a long time.

THEY SAT IN silence, scarcely moving, for nearly an hour. It was very hot in the living room; Dean wouldn't let her open a window. Most of the time they were silent, just sitting there. Dean drank; Lee watched him.

Every so often he would say, "Who was it, Lee?"

"Nobody," she would say. "Nobody. Let me go."

"No. You're staying here."

Once she tried to walk out, but he stood in front of the door, barring her way. He was very drunk now, red in the face, sweating heavily. He had stopped crying and shouting at her; he was simply waiting, watching her, willing her to crack.

She asked him if she could go to the bathroom. He accompanied her, stood outside the door. Then they went back to the living room. It smelled stale, sweaty, alcoholic. Lee began to feel ill. She sat down on the couch.

"Dean, I feel sick. Could you get me a glass of water?"

"Sure." As he went out, he unplugged the phone, took the handset with him. When he came back, he handed her the glass, tipped up her chin, and looked down into her face.

"You may as well tell me. I'll get it out of you in the end."

She drank the water. "There's nothing to tell."

"You're lying."

"I'm not."

It was exactly like all her nightmares.

At half past three Miles came home from school, banged on the locked door, called out, "Mom, Mom," when she didn't answer.

She looked at Dean. "You'll have to let him in."

"Okay." He suddenly gripped her wrist, twisting it around. "Now, you just keep your goddam mouth shut or I swear to God I'll tell him."

He went out to the door. "Oh, hi, Dad," she heard Miles say. "Where's Mom?"

"She isn't feeling well. She's lying down upstairs. Listen, can you go play with someone for a while?"

"Sure. I'll go to Freddy's. His mom's real nice. She'll understand. Can I take my bike?"

"Sure."

"Bye, Dad."

"Good-bye, Miles." He came back into the living room. "You gonna tell me?"

"No."

Suddenly he raised his fist and struck her across the face. She felt an explosion of searing, aching pain across one eye and tasted the sweet salty flavor of blood trickling from her mouth. For the first time she was seriously frightened.

If only Amy would come, she thought. She would know; she would guess something was wrong. She would get help. But Amy was away staying with her mother.

"It's no use thinking I'm going to get tired," he said. "That I'll let you go. We're staying here till you tell me." He looked at her shrewdly, thoughtfully. "What was it like?" he said. "Fucking some-one else? Was it as good as doing it with me? Did you think about me?"

"Don't be a fool," she said. "Stop asking me these questions. I can't answer them. You know I can't."

"Oh, no," he said, "you're wrong. I know you can. What was it like, Lee? Was his dick bigger than mine? Did you come? How many times? You always were a sexpot." He poured himself another glass of bour-bon, emptying the bottle. He looked down at her, angry, contemp-tuous. "You whore," he said, and all that was in his voice was disgust. "You fucking, fucking whore."

Lee sat quite still on the couch, curled up, her head buried in her hands. Sometime, surely to God, someone would come.

LATER, GOODNESS KNOWS how much later, she heard footsteps on the front steps. The doorbell rang. She stood up.

"Sit down," Dean said, pushing her down. It rang again and again. Then she heard Freddy's mother's voice.

"Mrs. Wilburn! Mr. Wilburn! Are you there?"

"You'll have to answer her," she said to Dean. "She won't go away. She'll call the police if she doesn't get an answer."

Dean went to the door. He didn't open it, just called through it.

"Yes? Who is it?"

"It's Molly Wainwright. Is everything all right?"

Lee heard him open the door a crack. Maybe Molly Wainwright would smell the bourbon on his breath, guess something was wrong.

"It's fine. My wife's just gone to sleep."

"Well, I just stopped by to ask if you would like Miles to stay over. Then Lee can sleep through till morning and she won't have to worry about taking care of him or getting him off to school."

Dean cleared his throat. Lee could hear him making an intense effort to speak normally. "Thank you, Mrs. Wainwright. That'd be fine."

"Could I have his things, please?"

"What things?"

"His pajamas and so on."

"Well, I—that is, I'd rather not disturb my wife right now. Only she would know where they are, you see. Could you lend Miles something, do you think?"

There was a long silence. Surely she'll think that's odd, thought Lee. If she made a dash into the hall, would Mrs. Wainwright hear her? But some strange lethargy gripped her; her legs felt weak, her eyes were half closed. She knew she couldn't make the effort.

"Oh—well, all right." Mrs. Wainwright sounded slightly skeptical. "Is there anything I can do, Mr. Wilburn? Fix Mrs. Wilburn some soup or something?"

"No. No, thank you," said Dean. "Now if you'll excuse me, I must get back to my wife."

"Is she very sick?"

"No, no, she just has a migraine."

"Well, if you need me, you know where I am."

"Sure."

Lee heard the door slam; Dean walked back into the room.

"Okay," he said. "Now we have plenty of time. I'm certainly in no hurry. I'll just open this other bottle of bourbon and then I'll come and sit beside you." He poured two glasses and offered her one.

"Here."

"No, thank you."

"Take it."

"I said no, thank you."

"And I said take it. Now, take it, for Christ's sake. And drink it. I don't like drinking alone."

She took a swig. It was strangely comforting, burning warm in her throat, numbing the pain of her cut mouth.

Dean suddenly put down his glass and touched her face. "You're a pretty woman, Lee," he said. "Very pretty. I still get the hots when I look at you."

Dear God, she thought, how do I handle this one? She smiled at him, trying to lighten his mood. "That's nice," she said. "That's really nice."

She took another gulp of the bourbon. "So is this. I'm beginning to feel better."

It was a mistake. He knocked the glass out of her hand, his face suddenly crumpled unrecognizably in rage. "I don't want you to feel better. Not one bit. I want you to feel worse. You filthy lying bitch. Fucking other men. Having another man's baby. Making me think it was mine. Whose was it, Lee? Whose was it?"

"Dean, I can't go on with this much longer. It was your baby. Miles is your son."

"Make me believe you, then," he said, coming closer to her, grabbing her wrists, searching her face. "Was this how he was conceived? Was it? Like this?"

He kissed her suddenly, hard on the mouth, then threw her back on the couch; he held her down with one hand, ripped her pants off with the other. "Come on, Lee, show me. Show me how you did it. Show me how you did it with him."

He smelled disgusting, of drink and sweat. Lee turned her head away from him, shutting her eyes. "Don't. Please don't."

"Oh, but I want to. I will. Let's see what you can do."

And then it was total horror. He unzipped his fly and fell on top of her, stabbing at her with his penis, clawing at her thighs, her buttocks, with his hands, kissing her again and again, pausing, gasping for breath. He entered her clumsily, impatiently, and began to thrust into her, harshly, heavily. She could hardly breathe, she was crushed beneath his huge weight, she seemed to be drowning in the darkness, the pain, and the foul smell. He pulled out suddenly and drew back from her, looking at her, a hideous smile on his face. "Is this how you like it, Lee? Is this how you did it? Tell me, tell me you like it. Tell me, Lee. I want to know."

She was so afraid she couldn't speak. She lay looking up at him, her eyes huge, desperately trying to say something, anything; no words would come.

"You stupid bitch," he said, "why won't you tell me?" And then he entered her again, brutally, hopelessly, and it seemed to go on forever, and she lay there, hanging on somehow to her sanity, her courage, willing it just to be over. And when finally it was, he lay there, weeping again, and saying, "I'm sorry, I'm sorry," and she stroked his head and said, "It's all right, it's all right," and they stayed there for a long time.

Finally he said he would get her a drink, some tea or something. Yes, she said, tea would be nice, and sat there trembling, not knowing what to do while he went to the kitchen. She drank the tea and persuaded him to have some; he seemed calmer, she was beginning to think she might be able to move from the room.

Then: "I haven't given up," he said softly.

"What do you mean?"

"I won't let you go. Not until you tell me. I have to know."

"Dean, please believe me. There is nothing to tell."

"I don't believe you," he said, perfectly normally, quietly, and then, crossing to the bar, he took a bottle of beer out. "Are you going to tell me?"

"No."

"You are," he said, and suddenly smashed the beer bottle on the edge of the bar, knocking two glasses off at the same time, and came at her with the jagged edge. "Tell me, Lee. You have to tell me."

Lee felt suddenly calm. She saw quite clearly that she was going to have to tell him something; otherwise she would be dead by morning; but she also saw that if she did it right now he would probably kill her anyway. She faced him, steady-eyed.

"Dean, don't. You'll be up for assault, possibly murder. I won't tell you anything until you're behaving rationally. Put that down."

He did put it down, as she had known he would, and sat down suddenly again, looking around him in a slightly puzzled, remorseful way, surveying the mess, the beer over everything, the broken bottle, the smashed glasses.

"Sorry," he said as if he had just knocked a cup of coffee over. "Sorry about that. Now, you were saying?"

"Have some more tea, Dean."

"No, thank you."

"It'll make you feel better."

"All right."

He picked up his cup. "I'm ready. For anything."

Lee took a deep breath.

"Okay, here it is. It was only once. Long, long ago. It wasn't an affair. Honestly. I didn't love him. Just—just a one-night stand."

"I see."

"But—well, yes, I got pregnant. I didn't think I could. I thought I couldn't conceive."

"How unfortunate for you."

"Yes, well. Anyway, that was it. I never ever slept with him again."

"Did you see him again?"

"Hardly."

"Who was it?"

"I can't tell you that."

"You have to."

"I won't."

"Then," he said, "I'll tell Miles."

"Why?"

"Because," he said, looking at her with infinite distaste, "you deserve it. And he has a right to know."

"But you won't if I tell you?"

"Maybe not. It depends on who it was."

"That isn't logical."

"I know. This isn't a logical situation. Do you want me to tell him?"

"Of course not."

"Then you tell me."

Lee looked at him. There was a long silence. Then: "All right. It was Hugo Dashwood."

"Dear God," Dean said, "how bizarre. How incredible. The perfect English gentleman. Fucking my wife. Giving her a bastard baby. And never having the decency to own up."

"He didn't know."

"He didn't?"

"No. I never told him."

"Good God." He turned and looked at her. All the violence, all the anger had suddenly drained out of him. He looked suddenly years older, very frail and vulnerable. "You're quite a woman, aren't you? All these years. Never told him." There was another long silence. "Imagine it being Hugo," he said. "The last person I'd have suspected. It's not British, that sort of thing. Not British at all. I always liked Hugo. Thought he was my friend. Oh, well, at least I know. I feel kind of better now. You should have told me before. Right in the beginning." He sighed. "I feel very tired. I think I'll go up to bed. Good night, Lee. I'll sleep in the guest room."

"All right," she said, disconcerted by his sudden return to normality. "Shall I bring you some more tea?"

"No. No, thank you." He sighed and stood up, zipping up his trousers, straightening his shirt. His eyes were full of tears; he put his hand up and brushed them away. "I still love you," he said. "Very, very much. I always knew you were too good for me. Good night, Lee."

"Good night, Dean," she said, afraid to break the spell. "Good night."

He went upstairs. She heard him going into the bathroom, heard the guest room door open, the bed groan as he fell onto it. Somehow, within her aching, trembling body she found the strength to pick up the empty bottles, to straighten the cushions, to turn off the light. It was only half past ten; it felt as if days had passed.

As she went to her room she could hear his snores; he would not wake now. She would decide what to do in the morning. She went to bed.

IN THE NIGHT the snoring stopped. When Lee went in early in the morning to see if he was all right, she found him absolutely waxen— white and still, scarcely breathing, beyond help. He had taken her bottle of sleeping pills from the bathroom and swallowed all of them, washed them down with the remainder of the bourbon. The verdict at the inquest was suicide while temporarily deranged.

Whichever way you looked at it, she thought, she had killed him.

9

ROZ WAS IN LOVE.

She was not in love, as most of the girls at Cheltenham were, with one of the spotty boys of fifteen or sixteen, one of the band of girls' brothers, who accompanied their parents down to school on Open Day or at the end of term. Brothers were, as far as Roz could see, arrogant, stupid, and tedious, with nothing to say to anyone except "Good term?" or "Er—hello," according to whether they were greeting their sister or their sisters' friends. Nevertheless their prospective arrival caused much giggling, and brushing of hair and excited anticipatory remarks like "I bet he won't remember me" or "Gosh, my brother's not a patch on yours," and the young ladies of Cheltenham went through a formalized mating ritual on their arrival, which consisted in the main of their faces blushing scarlet, their voices rising an octave or so, and their eyes rolling rather strangely as one brother or another was introduced to, or reminded of, them and, if things were going really well, proceeded to suggest that perhaps they might see each other during the holidays at some intimate event like a horse show or a family skiing trip.

Roz did blush at least a little when confronted by her love, but her voice did not rise and her eyes did not roll strangely. She was able to look at him and even answer him when he spoke; but the things that happened to her heart in his presence were much the same as those that happened to the other young ladies: it leapt, it lurched, it rose in her throat and threatened to deafen her with its pounding.

And her love, while not being aware of her feelings, was certainly not indifferent to her. He spoke to her, he inquired after her health and her progress, he remarked on how tall she had grown and quite often on how much he liked what she was wearing. This was not, it has to be said, because he returned her affections; it was because he was employed by her father and was in love with her mother.

David Sassoon was the only son of a modestly successful, fiercely proud Jewish businessman, and having been quite exceptionally good-looking and sexually precocious, he had been expelled from a minor public school, Saint Michael's in Gloucestershire, for being found at the age of fifteen in flagrante with one of the housemaids. This had nearly broken his father's heart, and David had been sent to the local secondary modern in north London to complete his education and learn a few more lessons besides, including, his father hoped, that of humility and the folly of lost opportunity.

David was not, however, so easily defeated. He passed his School Certificate with distinction and became, against all possible odds, the hero of his year. The other boys were impressed by his ability to beat even the most savagely raised bully in a playground fight, and the girls by an equally daunting ability to make three hours in the back row of the cinema, or a sojourn in the park with a couple of bags of chips, an experience of high sensual pleasure.

After school he went to Saint Martin's School of Art where he took every possible prize, graduated with the highest possible honors, and got a job in a large and fashionable design studio in London. Six months after he arrived he was put to work redesigning the packaging for a line of preserves for one of the huge grocery chains. His designs were promptly accepted and put on display. He was then asked to look at the image of the canned goods.

The product manager of canned goods was a beautiful and recklessly sexy girl called Mary, who before long had not only taken David into her bed and her elegant young person but had become pregnant by him. What nobody, least of all Mary, had thought to inform David of was that her father was the chairman of the supermarket chain.

This being the late fifties and abortion being not entirely easy to organize without the passing over of a considerable sum of money, Mary felt obliged to confess all to her father. The consequence was that David was fired not only from the account but from the design company as well and found himself looking for a job without any references.

Fortunately for him, Mick diMaggio, on a trip to London, happened to be in the Juliana offices one day when David was making his somewhat wearisome job-hunting rounds of the studios and offices of London. Mick told Julian he should hire David immediately, Julian said he didn't give a monkey's ass why David didn't have any decent references as long as he had not actually been caught with his hand in the till; and David took the job as assistant design manager in the packaging department with a huge sigh of relief and a resolve never again to be found with his hand in anything, including a till, unless he was one hundred percent certain he could not be fired for it. He had learned something else about himself through this rather salutary experience: that he was savagely, almost ferociously ambitious. He and his work he now knew, had to be very, very successful indeed— so successful that nothing of a personal nature could threaten it.

Some designers worked with their creative instincts alone, some gave more emphasis to commercial demands. A few managed to use both and to throw something else in as well. Mick diMaggio, looking at David's work, put a word to it: guts. David Sassoon took risks on the drawing board. He used colors, shapes, typefaces, that had not been seen in association with cosmetics before. They were not brash or vulgar or in any way shocking, they were beautiful and desirable, but they were also absolutely stunningly new, fresh, rethought. Under David, Juliana took on an entirely new look while retaining its air of exclusivity, extravagance, desirability. A new Sassoon-styled counter display for Juliana making its appearance at Harrods or Harvey Nichols was a major attraction in itself, and the windows he created every Christmas to promote *Je* and *Mademoiselle Je* in all the big stores, including Circe in both New York and Paris, owed more to the cinematic style of Busby Berkeley than to anything taught at art college about window display.

Five years later David was creative director of Juliana, reporting directly to Julian and with a seat on the board. He had a flat on King's Road and a white Mercedes convertible; he spent his nights dancing at the Saddle Room and the Ad Lib, high temples of the shrine immortalized in *Time* magazine as "swinging London," with a string of beautiful girls, each one with longer hair, legs, and eyelashes and shorter skirts than the last. He knew everybody worth knowing in London. He knew the terrible trio of photographers—David Bailey, Terry Donovan, Brian Duffy—and their ever-changing coterie of divinely long-legged, huge-eyed companions; he knew Barbara Hulanicki and her husband Stephen FitzSimon, and indeed had worked with them on some early designs for the first Biba boutique; he knew Cathy McGowan, the star of *Ready Steady Go*; he knew all the most brilliant fashion journalists of the day—Grace Coddington of *Vogue*, Anne Trehearne of *Queen*, Molly Parkin of *Nova*; he knew Mary Quant and Alexander Plunkett Greene; he knew Twiggy and Justin de Villeneuve.

He bought his clothes from Blades; he had his hair cut personally by Vidal Sassoon, who was, they were both at great pains to assure everybody, absolutely no relation; he ate at the Arethusa, and at Nick's Diner, the ultimate gourmet experience in the Fulham Road for young London. His life was a hyped-up fairy story of success and fame, and he was deeply in love with it.

He was also exceedingly good-looking. He had dark curly hair, a slightly swarthy freckled skin, and dark eyes that it was impossible to meet without feeling infected by the naked, unashamed, joyful carnal knowledge that filled them. He was fairly slim, and although he was not very tall, only about five feet ten, he was a curious combination of both grace and power, which emphasized his extraordinary sexuality. David Sassoon did not just look sexy, as one tender young model of seventeen confided to another in the ladies' room at the Ad Lib one night; he felt sexy. "And I don't mean he has hard-ons all the time; he just only has to touch your hand and you start thinking about what it would be like to be in bed with him."

Nevertheless, his reputation was surprisingly blemish-free. He flirted with, he courted, he enjoyed women; but he very rarely took them to bed until he knew them almost as well as they knew themselves.

This was partly because of a deeply held belief of his that women were satisfactory as sexual partners only if they felt at ease, and partly because he was absolutely terrified of finding himself unwittingly in yet another professionally dangerous situation. In David Sassoon's opinion, and indeed his experience, Murphy's Law operated more unfailingly in the bedroom than anywhere else, and he had no desire to see his meteoric career blacked out by the consequences of a night's pleasure, however intense, in the company of a lady who might be the wife, daughter, or mistress of someone who employed him.

ELIZA MORELL, HOWEVER, had seen David across the room at a party Julian had thrown to celebrate the launch of his first health farm— now that he was no longer married to her, Julian perversely greatly enjoyed her company and her attendance at his parties—and had set her sights on him rather firmly. She was talking at the time to Letitia, with whom she was still the very best of friends, and decided she would greatly like to get to know him.

"Letitia," she whispered, "who is that perfectly glorious man with the black curly hair and the divine beige suit? The one who looks a bit like Richard Burton, only with dark hair."

Letitia followed her gaze and then looked back at her amusedly. "That's Julian's latest discovery. His new creative director in London. Awfully clever. A bit abrasive. His name's David Sassoon. Do you want to meet him?"

"Of course."

"He's very dangerous."

"In what way?"

"You know perfectly well what way."

"Then I certainly want to meet him."

David Sassoon in fact proved to be the opposite of dangerous at first. Eliza was disappointed. He bowed over her hand, looked into her eyes with his burning brown ones, and immediately made her feel half undressed. He chatted amusingly with her, danced with her once or twice, told her she was the most beautiful woman in the room, and that he included the ravishing Julie Christie and the divine Penelope Tree in that statement, and then vanished without a trace.

"Rather like a male Cinderella," Eliza said plaintively to Letitia at the end of the party. What David was doing, however, was what he had been doing all his life: safeguarding his own position, or not shitting on his own doorstep, as he described it eloquently if inelegantly to his best friend and colleague over lunch next day.

"I fancy that lady rotten. She's gorgeous, she's sexy, she's been around, and yet right now she needs a jolly good old-fashioned fuck. And I'd like to give it to her. But she's been the boss's wife, and I'm not going to get into that. Or her," he added with a grin.

But he had not reckoned on Eliza's skill at getting what she wanted.

A week later, coming back from a difficult two days in Paris trying to impose his will on the cosmetics buyer for Galleries Lafayette, David found a message on his desk. "Mrs. Morell phoned." He ignored it.

She rang again two days later. "This is Eliza Morell. Do you remember me? Sorry to hound you. I wondered if we could have lunch."

David took a deep breath. "Mrs. Morell, of course I remember you. I'm charmed and flattered, but I think I should say no."

"Why?"

"Your husband might not like it," he said and then, furious with himself, realized what he had said and how unutterably crass it must have sounded.

Her voice was amused. "I don't have a husband, Mr. Sassoon. I've long since divorced Julian, and my second husband as well."

"I'm sorry. You must think I'm quite mad."

"No. A little neurotic perhaps, but not mad. I assure you Julian doesn't mind in the least what I do or with whom I do it. And even if he did I have nothing more incriminating in mind for us than a business discussion. So when shall we meet?"

David knew when he was beaten. "Thursday?"

"Thursday would be lovely. The Walton Street restaurant at one?"

"Fine."

◆　　◆　　◆

SHE WAS WAITING for him when he got there, sitting at a table in the window. The moment he saw her looking at him with the extraordinary combination of innocence and blatant sexuality that she so uniquely conveyed, he knew he was lost, that whatever he might resolve or think to the contrary, if she wanted him she could and would have him.

Eliza wanted him, and she had him.

The business discussion she had managed to create—whisper thin, a request that he should advise her on her new prospective career as an interior designer—was over in half an hour. For two more hours they danced an elaborate sexual quadrille around each other, and finally fell into each other's arms, bodies, and Eliza's bed in the Holland Park house as the October dusk gathered and the clock was striking five.

David stayed for several days; he did not go to work at all on Friday, and right through the weekend they talked and made love with ever increasing delight, drank quite a few bottles of wine, and even ventured out once to walk in Holland Park and to fill the contents of Eliza's fridge, which was extraordinarily bare—"I have to keep thin somehow," she said—and told jokes and played the songs of Stevie Wonder, whose raw, sexy voice seemed totally in accord with the delightful discoveries they were making about each other, and spent quite a lot of time simply looking at each other in silence, happy and almost awed by the perfect pleasure they had found in each other's company.

"I have to tell you," David said quite late on the Sunday night, as they lay in bed and he was smiling at her and dipping his fingers in his glass of wine, wetting her nipples, and kissing them, "I have to tell you you seem to be threatening to be important to me."

"I should think so," Eliza said half indignantly, pushing him away and sitting up. "I don't do this with just anyone, you know."

"No, I can see that. Just with the best. But anyway, there's no need to get upset. I think we have to spend some time together. Do you see any problems there?"

"Not for me. Are there any for you?"

"A few. The main one as I see it is your ex-husband—your *first* ex-husband, that is. Are you quite sure he isn't going to object to this?"

"Of course not," said Eliza, lying down again. "Why should he?"

"I don't know. He's a funny guy. Very possessive within the company. He doesn't like interdepartmental liaisons, for a start."

"He's got a nerve," said Eliza. "Carrying on with Camilla the way he does."

"I know. But he is the boss. I suppose that gives him the right to have a nerve or two. And he has come down very hard on a couple of people having affairs on office territory. He dressed it up, of course, said they were wasting company time. But the real reason is he doesn't like it. He gets kind of jealous, as far as we can make out."

"Well, that's all right," said Eliza. "I don't work for the company."

"I know. But you used to be his wife. It worries me a bit."

"You're really jumpy about him, aren't you?" she said, looking at him interestedly.

"Yes, I am. He's put me where I am today, as they say in the movies. I told you, I've had quite a few chances mucked up by my sexual indiscretions. I can't help being skittish."

"Well," she said, "I don't know if I like coming such a very bad second to your career."

"I'm sorry. I didn't mean it to sound like that. Let's put it this way: there's quite a strong body of opinion in the company that your first husband still cares very much about you and what you do. If I were your ex-husband I would, too." He bent and kissed her breasts again. "I just think we should be careful, that's all. He's a powerful and quixotic fellow. He could hurt both of us."

"I honestly think the body of opinion is quite wrong," said Eliza, "but if you think we should, we'll be discreet for a while. Just for a day or two. Now, put that glass down and concentrate on me for a bit. It's dark outside now, and the shutters are closed. Or would you like me to check there's not a private detective hanging about underneath the lamppost?"

THEY WERE VERY discreet for a while. David kept his flat and only stayed with her one or two nights a week. "It's more exciting and romantic that way anyway," he said. Eliza, deeply in love by now for the first time since her second husband, Peter Thetford, managed to restrain her strong inclination to ring her girlfriends and tell them, and even invented a fictitious new boyfriend for them. She said they couldn't meet him because his wife was madly jealous and had threatened all kinds of dreadful revenge. She rather enjoyed this and elaborated on it so much that in the end she had both herself and the lover threatened by the wife at gunpoint before finally the real story and the gossip broke and William Hickey informed the waiting world, or at least such part of it as read his gossip column in the *Daily Express*, that the beautiful Eliza Morell Thetford had become very friendly with one of her ex-husband's senior executives and had engaged his help in setting herself up as an interior designer.

But Julian showed no signs of jealousy when he phoned her to discuss who should pick Roz up for the Christmas holidays.

"I hear you have enlisted Mr. Sassoon's services as an agent," he said. "Charming fellow. I'm sure he'll be very helpful."

ROZ LOOKED AT her mother as Eliza climbed out of the red E-Type Julian had given her as a Christmas present—he said it was bad for his image to have his ex-wife going around London like a pauper—and thought she had never seen her looking so happy or so beautiful.

"Hello, Mummy."

"Hello, darling. You look—well."

Only Roz, in her acute paranoia about her looks, would have noticed the pause; but she did and she knew what it meant. It meant that her mother couldn't find anything else to say about her appearance—taller, only slightly thinner, shaggy-haired. She looked at Eliza blankly.

"I don't feel very well, actually. I feel sick."

"Oh, darling, I'm sorry. Will you be all right in the car?"

"I expect so, yes, if we can have the windows open." She knew her mother hated that; it blew her hair about.

Eliza sighed. "All right, darling. Where are your things?"

They drove back to London in comparative silence, having exhausted the topic of Roz's term, report, exam results. Eliza was wondering how to broach the news of David, and that she was hoping Julian would have Roz for Christmas.

"Looking forward to Christmas, darling? I've got you a nice present."

"Depends what's happening. Is it Wiltshire, or have you persauded Daddy to take me to the Bahamas?"

"Darling, I haven't persuaded Daddy to do anything. I want you with me, of course. What would be more fun for you?"

"God, I don't care," Roz said. "Wiltshire, I suppose. I can ride there."

"We must get your hair cut tomorrow," Eliza said absently. "I'll book you into Leonard. And then we'll get you some clothes. Would you like that?"

"Not really. You know I hate shopping."

"Yes, but darling, you do need some new things. You've grown a lot."

"No, I haven't."

"Well, anyway, I'm sure you need a couple of things. Now, Roz, I have something to tell you."

"Yes?"

"I have a new—friend."

"Really?"

"Yes. David Sassoon. He works for your father. He's very nice, and I think you'll like him."

"Is he living with you or just sleeping with you?"

"Roz, I wish you wouldn't talk like that. It isn't very attractive."

"Sorry."

"He isn't living with me, but we are very—fond of each other. And he wants to meet you."

"Oh."

"So he's coming around this evening. Just for a meal with us both. I hope you like him."

"I don't really feel well enough to have a meal with anyone, Mummy. I seem to have some kind of a tummy bug. I might just go straight to bed when we get home."

"Now, Roz, that would be a pity. David is coming especially to meet you. Don't you think you could make an effort?"

"Well, I'll try. But I certainly don't feel up to getting all dressed up if that's what you're hoping."

"No," Eliza said, "I wouldn't ever hope for very much from you, Roz. Now I'm sorry, but we really will have to have that window shut."

"All right. I just might be sick, that's all."

ROZ WAS SITTING by the fire in the drawing room, still in her school uniform, when David arrived. She heard her mother open the front door, and settled herself deeper into her chair, picking up the latest *Vogue*, which was lying on the coffee table. She didn't even look up as they came into the room.

"Roz," said her mother, and she could hear the familiar conciliatory note in her voice. "Roz darling, this is David. David Sassoon. David, this is my daughter Roz."

And she looked up and met his eyes, his dark, amused, oddly intimate eyes, and her heart rocketed up and down inside her and she felt slightly dizzy at the same time, and she would have given anything, anything at all, to have been wearing her new long gray crushed velvet skirt and the pink suede boots, and to have brushed her hair properly and to have put some cover-up makeup on the spot on her chin.

David said, "Hello, Roz. It's so nice to have a face to the name. I see you're reading *Vogue*. What do you think of those pictures? Do you like them? They were taken by a great friend of mine."

Overwhelmed by his smile and his voice, which sounded as if he was going to laugh any minute, with its touch of carefully cultivated cockney, and by the fact that anyone at all should ask her opinion about anything other than whether this term had been better than the last, she fell hopelessly and irremediably in love.

Later they all went out to supper to Nick's Diner. She felt better, Roz told her mother; she had probably just been hungry, and she put on her velvet skirt and the boots, did the best she could with her hair, asked her mother if she had arranged her appointment for the next day at Leonard's, and sat between them listening politely, offering her opinion if it was asked for, which it was quite frequently by David, and even from time to time making them both laugh, and she had the best time she could ever remember. She studied David intently all evening, drinking him in, feeling she could never have enough just of looking at him: the riotously curling hair, just short of his collar; his dark, almost swarthy skin; the freckles on his nose, his eyelids, his forehead; his perfect teeth; and his great smile, which was always accompanied by that look of his, his eyes sweeping over your face and settling on your lips, as if he might be thinking about kissing you; and his clothes, oh, she loved his clothes, the printed cream and black silk shirt, and the black flaring trousers that fitted so extremely well over his hips—Roz tried not to look at his hips or to contemplate what else those trousers were concealing—and his black velvet jacket, with the lining that matched his shirt. Roz could hardly swallow, for emotion and excitement, but that was all right. She said she was still feeling a bit funny, but she did at David's instigation have a glass of wine, and that on top of her empty stomach and her excitement conspired to make her a bit giggly and more talkative than usual and then, when they were going home in David's car, to fall into a half sleep. But not so that she could not hear what was said.

"She's had a lovely evening," said Eliza, looking over her shoulder. "She's absolutely out cold. I've never known her to be so talkative. You've obviously made a big hit. Thank you for letting her come."

"I enjoyed it," he said. "Don't thank me. I like her. She's an amusing kid, and I don't know why you keep saying she's plain. She has a great face; I'd like to get her photographed. Terry would love her look."

"Well, he's not going to get a chance to love it," Eliza said briskly. "I know all about your friend Terry Donovan. And I must say you're getting a bit carried away, David. She might look a bit better than she did, but I wouldn't say she's model material."

"Not model, darling, but very interesting-looking, very striking. Anyway, what are we going to do now?"

"I think maybe," Eliza said, with another look at the inert form of her daughter, "you should go home tonight. I want her to get used to the idea slowly. Would you mind terribly?"

"Of course not. I'm an easygoing guy. You should know that by now."

"You're wonderful," said Eliza. "Come on, give me a kiss before our chaperon wakes up."

ROZ FLOATED THROUGH the next day in a dream. David Sassoon—the most attractive, the most sophisticated man she had ever met—had said she was not plain, that she had a great face, and that she was amusing into the bargain. She thought she had never been so happy. She smiled at her mother over breakfast, asked her if they could go shopping after the hairdresser, and then phoned her father and asked him if he would take her out to supper that night. She had never done such a thing before; convinced of her own nuisance value and her own unattractiveness as a companion, she had never had the confidence. She could hear him smiling down the phone.

"Yes, Roz, it would be a pleasure. Now, would you like just me, or shall I ask Camilla? She's here."

"Oh, no," she said quickly. "Let's make it just the two of us. Please."

"Fine. Dress up, then. We'll go to the Ritz."

SHE WALKED INTO the Ritz feeling like a model. Leonard had cut her hair in the new wispy layered look, with little petals of it overlapping one another all over her head and down onto the nape of her neck. Then they had gone, she and her mother, to the Purple Shop and brought her a pair of black velvet breeches, a glorious red silk shirt, some high boots, and a wonderfully flouncy red and purple skirt, like a Gypsy's. Then they had gone on to Biba and bought a long, long black velvet dress, with buttons down the front, which her mother said was much too sophisticated, but which Roz knew showed off her new flatter stomach very well, and a long black coat right to the ground, from next door in Bus Stop, and a huge black hat with a floppy brim. Then she had bought a set of eye pencils and spent the whole afternoon practicing outlining her eyes with them, and then the most marvelous thing had happened: David Sassoon had arrived and found her working on them furiously in the kitchen because the light was better there, and he had said, "Here, let me do that. If there's one thing I can do it's draw." He had held the back of her head very gently with one hand while carefully outlining her eyes with a dark blue pencil, looking at her very intently all the time, until Roz thought she would faint with emotion, and then telling her she looked gorgeous, and when she walked out to her father, sitting in his new black Bentley, with its tinted windows, wearing the skirt and the red shirt and the boots, with her eyes looking all smudgy and big, and her new haircut and she saw him looking at her in genuine astonishment and admiration, she knew that for the very first time since she had heard him say he didn't want her to live with him, she didn't have to feel apologetic about herself.

Later, over dinner, he asked her how she liked David. He seemed quite nice, she said carefully, much nicer than the last one, and he said, good, that he liked David very much and was delighted that her mother seemed happy; but Roz noticed that he pushed his hair back quite a lot during this conversation and that he didn't really seem very delighted, and didn't want to talk about it for long. Testing him, she said casually, "I wonder if they might get married," and he looked very odd indeed, almost angry, and said, "Oh, I shouldn't think so. I don't think that would be a good idea at all," and changed the subject very quickly and asked her if she would like to come for Christmas with him to the house at Turtle Cove on Eleuthera in the Bahamas that he had just bought.

"And Camilla?" Roz asked.

"No," he said, looking almost angry again, "no. Camilla is spending Christmas with her family."

"So it would be just the two of us?"

"Yes. I'd really like you to come, darling. We'd have fun."

And Roz, realizing that for the first time in her life her father really needed her and was depending on her company, looked at him over a forkful of chicken and said, "I'm really sorry, Daddy, but I promised Granny and Grandpa Grahame Black just today that I'd spend Christmas in Wiltshire with them."

"Couldn't you change your mind? Tell them you have to keep your old father company?"

"No," she said, "I'm afraid I couldn't. I don't want to let them down."

The expression of hurt on her father's face added greatly to the pleasure of her evening.

FOR THE FIRST time in her life Roz went back to school feeling quite happy. It wasn't that she wanted to go back to school, but she had had a nice holiday; she had had fun, just like the other girls. She actually found herself joining in their conversations, saying, "Well, we did this" and "I got that," instead of remaining aloof and apart from them. She supposed it was love that made her feel so good. Everyone knew it changed people for the better.

What was more, she was beginning to think that David did return her feelings a bit. He had that way of looking very deep into her eyes when he was talking to her, and smiling very intently at her, and he always noticed what she was wearing and how she looked and re-marked on it, telling her she looked gorgeous. He seemed to like talking to her and hearing her opinion on things. At the New Year's party Granny and Grandpa had given in Wiltshire, he had danced with her several times. Once it had been a real slow dance, and he had held her quite tightly and actually rested his head on her hair and squeezed her hand at one point. Roz had felt so extraordinarily emo-tional and sort of tingly and tense inside that she had gone away and sat in her bedroom afterward, just to think about it and enjoy the memory. When she came downstairs again, he was dancing with her mother and holding her and looking into her eyes, but it hadn't mat-tered because she knew what he felt for her was different and special. When she went back to school he had kissed her good-bye, just lightly on the lips, but she was quite, quite sure he had pressed against them just for a moment, and then he had said he would miss her and he would look forward to seeing her at half term.

"In fact," he said, "I'll come and pick you up, if I can, with your mum. Would you like that?"

She lived for half term, counting the weeks, the days, the hours, and then the most perfect thing happened. When the day finally arrived and she was looking out of the window for the car, it was his car that pulled up in front of the school, and he got out of it all by himself, looking absolutely marvelous in blue jeans and a denim jacket, with his hair even longer. She rushed out to him, and he held out his arms and gave her a huge bear hug and said, "Your mum is terribly busy pleating up somebody's curtains, so I offered to come and get you. I hope that's all right." And Roz looked at him radiantly and said yes of course it was all right, it was marvelous. He said she looked even slimmer and she would soon be too tall for him alto-gether, and she went and got her bag and got in the car beside him and hoped just everyone in the school was looking.

All the way back in the car the radio was playing, the most marvelously appropriate songs like "Let It Be" and "Everything Is Beautiful" and "We've Only Just Begun." Roz sat silent, every so often risking a look at him, and he would grin at her and say "All right?" and she would say "Yes, perfectly," and much too soon they reached London and Holland Park, and her mother came rushing out of the house and said, "Hello, darling. I do hope you didn't mind terribly David coming instead of me."

Roz said, "No, of course not," and thought with great satisfaction how deeply miserable her mother would be when she realized that her lover had grown tired of her and was in love with her daughter instead.

She didn't see all that much of David over half term. He was very busy, but she didn't mind; she had the drive to remember. On the second night her father invited her to supper and to stay the night at Hanover Terrace, with a rather quiet Camilla. He was very polite and charming to Roz and told her she was looking terrific and said he would take her to Marriotts at the weekend for some hunting if she would like that. Roz had said no, she was sorry, but she and her mother and David had all sorts of plans.

Later, when they thought she had gone to bed, she overheard him and Camilla arguing. She crept out into the corridor to listen.

"I'll tell you what I think," Camilla was saying. "I think you're still in love with Eliza."

"Don't be ridiculous," her father said. "Of course I'm not. I probably never was in love with her."

"Then why are you so insanely jealous of David Sassoon?"

"I'm not."

"I think you are."

"I just don't like the way he's taking over my family. My daughter seems as besotted with him as my wife."

"An interesting Freudian slip, Julian. Your ex-wife."

"All right, Camilla. My ex-wife."

There was a short silence. Then Camilla said, "A lot of people in the company are saying they'll get married. How would you feel about that?"

"Oh," she heard her father say, and the lightness of his tone did not fool Roz in the very least, "I'd find a way of putting a stop to it, I expect."

DAVID DID NOT come to collect Roz from school for the Easter holidays; Julian came instead in his latest acquisition, a dark blue Bentley

Continental. Roz tried not to be disappointed and to tell herself how much she would have longed for such a thing only a year ago.

"Hello, Daddy. That's a nice car."

"Isn't it? I knew you'd appreciate it. I've come because Mummy's away for a couple of days."

"With David?"

"No," said her father, pushing his hair back. "David is doing a little work for a change. Mummy's in Paris—working, she tells me. She'll be back the day after tomorrow."

"Oh."

"So you're coming home with me. Only tomorrow I have to go out to a dinner, so you'll be on your own, I'm afraid. I'm sorry. Mrs. Bristow will look after you."

"That's all right." She smiled at him.

A plan was forming in her mind.

"DAVID? HELLO, IT'S Roz."

"Roz, darling, I didn't realize you were home."

She was disappointed. "Well, I am. Daddy's out at a dinner, and I'm all alone tonight."

"That makes two of us."

"Yes, I know. I wondered if—well, if you'd like to take me out to supper."

There was a moment's silence. Then: "Yes, of course I would. What about Parson's? You like that, don't you?"

Parson's was where the *haute monde* ate spaghetti in the Fulham Road.

She smiled into the telephone. "Yes, please."

SHE COULD HARDLY swallow a thing. David was concerned.

"Roz, you're not eating. Aren't you well?"

"I'm fine. Just not hungry. Too much school food."

"Well, you look terrific on it. Very slim."

"Thank you. Could I—could I have some wine?"

"Of course."

He filled her glass and watched her drain it almost at once. He shook his head, looking deep into her eyes with his half smile. "What would your mother say? Taking you out and getting you drunk?"

"I don't suppose she'd care. She doesn't care about anything I do."

"Don't be silly. She loves you very much."

"How do you know?"

"Because she told me."

Roz was silent.

"Roz, look at me."

She looked. She saw his eyes looking at her with great concern and tenderness. Her heart turned over; her tummy felt fluid with excitement and love.

"Roz," he said.

"Yes?"

"Roz, you have this crazy idea that nobody cares about you, don't you?"

"Yes, and it's true."

"It's not, you know. We all care. Your mother. Your father. Me."

"You?"

"Yes. Me." He put his hand over hers on the table. "You're very special, you know. A very special person. I'm extremely fond of you." He smiled into her eyes.

The room blurred. Roz realized her eyes were full of tears. She swallowed.

"Darling," he said, "darling, don't cry." And he reached out and wiped away her tears, very gently.

"Oh, David," said Roz, terrified of breaking the spell, "David, please, will you take me home?"

"Yes," he said, puzzled, "of course I will."

In the car she didn't speak; when they got to Hanover Terrace she turned to him. He was looking almost unbearably handsome and sexy. His eyes moved over her face, lingered on her lips. Roz knew this was the moment, that she had to speak, that he would never have the courage to speak, to take the first move when he had no idea of her feelings, when he thought she simply saw him as an older man, her mother's boyfriend.

"David," she said, and a huge lump of terror rose in her throat; she swallowed hard. "David, I—I—"

"Yes, Roz?"

Words were no good; she had to show him how she felt, give him the opportunity to speak, to show her that he loved her, too. She leaned forward, put out her arms, kissed him on the mouth, wondering even as she did so if real kissing had to mean putting your tongue in the other person's mouth or if there was some way around it; waiting, wondering, every fiber of her alive, excited, tremulous, she felt almost at once that something was wrong. His mouth was dry and still under hers. His arms did not go around her. He drew back in his seat, and when she opened her eyes and looked at him his gaze was fixed on her in horror and alarm.

"Now, my darling, look," he said, in an attempt at lightness, "you don't want to get mixed up with an old man like me. Pick on some lucky fellow your own age."

"But, David," she said, and her voice was almost pleading. "David, I love you, and I thought you loved me. You said—"

"Roz darling, I'm sorry. I do love you. Do care about you. Very much. But not—not in that way. I'm so sorry if you misunderstood. I—I obviously said too much."

"Oh," she said, and a wave of pain went over her, filling every corner of her with hot, shamed shock. "Oh, no." And then desperate, frantic to save herself and her pride, she managed to smile, to laugh even, a tiny forced laugh, and she drew back, groping for the door handle. "Well, of course you didn't. I knew that. I was just joking. I wouldn't dream of coming between you and Mummy."

"No," he said, grasping at this, smiling falsely, foolishly, with relief. "No, I know you wouldn't. We've been such friends, and we always will be. I hope . . . I do hope."

"Of course," she said, "of course we will. I mean—well, I expect you'll be marrying Mummy soon. I hope so, anyway."

Eager to turn the situation around, awkward, crass in his anxiety, he said, "You could be the very first person to know. Apart from me. I haven't even asked her yet. What do you think she'll say?"

And Roz, unable to bear it any longer, jumped out of the car and shouted at him from the sidewalk, "I hope she'll say no. All right? No, no, no!"

And she slammed the door and ran into the house.

THE NEXT NIGHT, a little pale but dry-eyed and composed, she ate dinner alone with her father.

"Are you all right, darling? You don't seem quite yourself."

"I'm fine, Daddy."

"I hear you were out last night. Where did you go?"

"To Rosie's house."

"I see. How is Rosie?"

"She's fine."

"Good."

"Daddy—"

"Yes?"

"Daddy, I don't know if I ought to tell you this, but it's awfully exciting. I think David and Mummy are going to get married. It would be perfectly lovely for me; I would have a proper family again. What do you think about it?"

TWO DAYS LATER, David Sassoon, rushing out of his office at mid-morning to meet Eliza Morell at the airport and to tell her that for the first time in his life he felt ready to commit himself and wanted to marry her, saw a newly delivered letter on his desk marked Private and Confidential. It was from Julian. It offered him the position of design director of the company worldwide at virtually double his present salary, to take effect immediately. The job was based in New York.

The letter finished by saying that David's bachelor status had been a minor but important factor in helping Julian to reach the decision, given that the job would entail a great deal of traveling and, in the first year at least, a crushing work load.

·10·

IT REALLY WAS ONLY A LITTLE LUMP. Lee, feeling it again and again, morning after morning, convincing herself it had grown no bigger, promised herself that next time she had to see the doctor about anything important, she would just mention it and then he could assure her it was nothing, and then she could forget about it. She couldn't spare either the time or the money to go about something that really was absolutely unimportant. Mr. Phillips was a very busy man, and he was so extremely good about her being away when she had to take Miles to the dentist or watch him play baseball or go see his teacher for one of the interminable chats about his outstanding abilities and his equally outstanding laziness. Just thinking about Miles and his laziness made Lee feel tired and limp herself. Not that she would call it laziness, exactly; it was more an absolute refusal to put his mind to anything that did not engage it. He had not been known to write an essay more than one page long; he never read anything more challenging than the sports pages in the newspapers and the *Little League Newsletter*; he regarded history with contempt and science with amusement; he gave the occasional nod in the direction of languages and had a gift for mimicry that made his accent in both Spanish and French virtually flawless; but when it came to math he set himself to his books and his homework with a ferocious determination. He was always top of the class by a very long way and had rarely been known to get a mark lower than ninety percent or a grade lower than A. For some reason he also worked very hard at geography. When pressed by his mother as to the reason he would fix her with his dancing, slightly insolent dark blue eyes and say, "There's a point to it."

"Yes, but Miles, there's also a point to being able to string more than three sentences together on a page," Lee would say.

"Not really," he would say. "What's the telephone for?"

"But, Miles, you have to write letters in business."

"Mom, I don't intend to go into business. Not the kind that needs letter writing anyway."

After a few more protests, Lee would give up, too tired, too busy, too weary of the battle to pursue it any longer.

She was very often—more and more frequently, in fact—very tired. She found looking after Miles, trying to bring him up on her own, earning a living for them both, and keeping the house nice extremely demanding. There simply weren't enough hours in the day.

They had stayed in the house purely on the strength of Hugo's generosity. She had hated taking money from him, but there had been no one else to turn to. Dean's life insurance had been forfeited because he had committed suicide, and she and Miles would have been destitute. Had there been no Miles she would have slept on the beach gladly, along with the other vagrants, rather than ask Hugo for a dime, but there was Miles, and now that Dean had died she had dared to delve into her subconscious and acknowledge that Miles was a burden she could and should lay on Hugo and that the responsibility for Dean's death stood at least in some part at his door as well.

She had hated telling him, hated contacting him, but she had felt, in her unutterable grief and guilt and loneliness, driven to him; it was the first time in ten years she had ever dialed the number in New York, and even then she had hung up three times as the phone was answered before asking for him.

He was in California with her twenty-four hours later, gentle, supportive, comforting. He checked into a hotel, to confound the gossips, and visited her daily. He helped her with the funeral arrangements, sorted through her papers, checked on her financial affairs.

"You're going to need help, Lee," he said on the third day, looking up from a sheaf of papers. "Dean has left virtually nothing. There's a small pension. That's all."

"So what will I do?" she said, fearful, tearstained, shredding Kleenex after Kleenex into her lap, looking at him in a kind of helpless panic.

"Take some money from me."

"No. I can't."

"Why not?"

"I just can't. We're not your responsibility, and besides, you don't have any money."

"You are my responsibility, and I do have money."

"But you told Dean—"

"What?"

"That things weren't going well for you. That you were having a difficult time."

"I was lying."

"But why?"

"Lee, use your common sense. Dean was not exactly a success, was he?"

"He was, too," she said, instinctively indignant, defending the Dean who was far beyond humiliation.

"Well, all right," he said, "maybe he was. But not such a success as I am. I didn't want to rub his nose in that. I was his friend. Friends don't do that sort of thing. Bad form. In England anyway." He was smiling gently.

She looked at him scornfully. "They do other things that are bad form, I gather. Sleep with other men's wives."

"Look, Lee," said Hugo, suddenly angry. "I know I did wrong. But so did you. And you've done precious little to let me help put it right. So just shut up and let me do it now. You need me, Lee. Don't drive me away."

She looked at him through the blur of fresh tears and felt remorseful. It was true. He would have helped. He had done everything he could all those years, everything she had allowed him to—keeping in touch, giving extravagant presents to Miles, making sure she was all right.

"I'm sorry," she said. "You're right. And it was mostly my fault. I shouldn't have blamed you so much."

"Yes, you should," he said, patting the seat beside him on the couch. "But you can stop now. Come here and let me hold you. It's all right," he added as she stiffened in fearful wariness. "I'm not going to seduce you. I think we've both lived well past that. I just think you need some arms around you."

And she had crawled into his arms and lain there, crying for a long time, and he had stroked her hair and kissed the top of her head, and soothed and gentled her, and in the end she did feel a little better.

"Hugo, how will I ever get through this? Forgive myself? Live with knowing what I did to him?"

"Time will do it for you," he said, and there was an odd expression in his eyes. "It is amazing what one does learn to live with. Come to terms with. Forget. No, not forget, but allow to fade. You will never get over it. Not in the way you mean. But a day will come when you will be able to remember Dean with a kind of happiness and to know that you gave him a lot of happiness, too. Don't let yourself forget that, Lee. You made him very happy for eighteen years. That's a long time, and it's a lot to do for someone."

HUGO WAS RIGHT. She did begin to remember Dean more happily and to feel she had done at least a few things right. She did not, as she had feared, go mad with remorse. And life did begin to seem a little more worth living.

She managed to get a job quite easily. She took a quick brushup course in shorthand and typing, paid for by Hugo, and very swiftly found herself working for Irving Phillips, a litigation lawyer who was building himself up a practice in Beverly Hills with impressive speed.

And Hugo had been really good to her. Lee was amazed at how good he had been. He visited them at least every three months, sometimes more often; he had insisted on paying off the mortgage on the house so that she lived there for nothing; he made her an allowance. "For Miles, not you," he said firmly, "so don't go getting proud on me." He called her at least once a week to check that everything was all right. She was intrigued to find that she felt nothing remotely sexual for him anymore, nor he apparently for her. They had become —not without some difficulty, she reflected with a wry amusement— that rarest of rare things, platonic friends. They actually had very little in common. He was far more cultured, educated, sophisticated, than she was, but somehow they always had a great deal to talk about. They would sit and chat for hours, over dinner or walking on the beach, about anything or everything that happened to catch their attention. Hugo told her she made him feel relaxed and easy; he said that when he was with her the stresses and pressures of his other life faded away; he felt like a different person.

"Just as well," she said, teasing him. "Otherwise you might start feeling guilty or confused."

"No," he said, "not with you. I never feel anything bad with you. I just feel peaceful and happy."

And so Lee's life had assumed some kind of order and pleasantness; she felt she could look upon it, if not with happiness, then certainly not with misery, and indeed with less anxiety than had been haunting her for the last twelve years.

Her only source of serious anxiety these days was Miles.

MILES AT TWELVE years old was an interesting child. Too interesting. Lee, analyzing it, as she so often did, in the middle of the night very soon after she had first felt the lump in her breast and totally failed to recapture any semblance of sleep, decided that was why she worried about him. It wasn't that he was particularly bad. He didn't play hooky—or at least did so only once, at Christmas, the year after Dean died, when he had got a job delivering packages to earn some Christmas money, and who could blame a little boy for that? He wasn't insolent; he didn't hang around street corners after school; he was nearly always there when she got home, or with the Forrests or the Wainwrights, with a note pinned on the door saying exactly where; he didn't even tell lies or knock the furniture around like most twelve-year-olds. He simply went his own sweet way and did what he wanted, or rather, being only twelve and a trifle limited in his life-style, firmly refused to do anything he didn't want. And this did not stop at his schoolwork.

Lee had almost given up trying to persuade him to go to church with her. Every once in a while, when he really wanted to please her —and, she suspected, really wanted something to please himself—he would go along to mass on Sunday morning, swallowing Father Kennedy's smiling admonitions about his absence with remarkably good grace, but generally he would simply give Lee his sweet, unanswerable smile and say no, he didn't plan on coming today. Initially she had tried threatening him with the wrath of either God or the church or both, but he had shrugged and smiled and returned to his comics or his TV program without so much as a word of argument. She had even asked Father Kennedy if he would speak to him, and the priest had come to the house once or twice. Miles had listened to his gentle lecture about the mortal sin of not going to church. Then he had looked gravely at Father Kennedy and said, "Thank you for explaining that to me, Father," and absolutely refused to discuss the matter any further. Afterward, when the priest had gone, Lee reproached Miles and said how could he be so rude and unresponsive. Miles said he was sorry, but there was nothing to discuss.. "But why isn't there?" Lee said. "At the very least, God forbid, you could have argued with him."

"Mom, there wouldn't have been any point," said Miles. "He wouldn't have seen it. Waste of breath."

That was his attitude toward most things. If he didn't like something, or the idea of doing something, he just cut it out of his life or did the minimum—like his schoolwork. He didn't argue and make a fuss; he simply didn't do it. As he was now taller than Lee there was very little she could do about it. There was very little anyone could do about it. His teachers could punish him and keep him in after school, but those were punishments for bad behavior and Miles did not behave badly. He was always polite and charming to his elders; he handed his work in on time, such as it was; he never cut class, sat quietly, was not disruptive. But his grades were awful, except in math and geography.

The other reason the teachers found it hard to get too angry with him was that he was such an asset to the school. He played games superbly. He was the best pitcher anyone in the school could ever remember, and although it wasn't his game, he was a fine football player, too. He was the star of all the teams; he could run like the wind and jump in a way that defied gravity. He had beaten every speed and high-jump record in the school's history. In matches against other schools, if Miles Wilburn was on the team, Saint Clement's won.

He was also a talented actor. While other kids giggled and got embarrassed or overacted, Miles simply became the person he was playing. The boy in jeans and T-shirt could become in an instant, with an imperceptible shift of personality, a prince, a king, an old man, even a young woman. Miles's impression of Marilyn Monroe was a joy to behold.

Lee worried about that talent in a way, because she was so afraid Miles would want to go into the motion picture business and start hanging around the studio lots, but he showed no tendency to do anything of the sort. He enjoyed drama at school, but only in a casual way; he did not, as stagestruck kids so often did, form companies and put on productions, or ask to take acting lessons. It was as if he was aware of his talent and waiting to use it when the time came, not on the stage, perhaps, or in front of the cameras, but in life itself. Indeed he used it in this way already. Watching Miles switch from mischievous boy to thoughtful student when his grandmother visited, for instance, to avoid a time- and energy-wasting confrontation with her, or seeing him as a dutiful respectful Young Person in the presence of Hugo Dashwood, was enraging but also amusing. Hugo was not deceived, Lee could see, by the impersonation, mostly because he had heard too much of the other side of Miles from her, but he went along with the charade. He was obviously very fond of the boy and enjoyed his company. She was not quite sure if the enjoyment was two-sided.

Miles was also now exceptionally good-looking. He was very tall for twelve, nearly five feet ten, with golden blond hair, a classically straight nose, a rather sensuously full mouth, and dark, extraordinarily luminous blue eyes fringed by long, curly black lashes—"Like a girl's," said Jamie Forrest in disgust. Jamie, like most of the other boys, liked Miles, hero-worshiped him, almost, for his prowess at sports, but were fiercely jealous of him for his looks, the way he got away with things, and the way that, already, the girls were falling over themselves to get near him.

Miles had a way with girls. He would sit looking at them very intensely, listening to them chattering and giggling, and they would gradually fall silent, discomfited, self-conscious and acutely aware of his attention. Then he would smile his slow, heartbreaking smile at whichever one—or two, or even three—had taken his fancy, and he would wander over and start talking to them.

Jamie and Freddy Wainwright and all the other boys couldn't imagine what Miles could talk to them about. Everybody knew girls had nothing in their heads except clothes and makeup and weren't interested in football or baseball, which didn't leave a lot of room for conversational maneuvers, but Miles managed. In no time at all the girls were laughing and talking with him, and he was laughing and talking back. When they asked him how he did it, he would shrug and say, "Oh, you know," and they didn't like to say no they didn't because it made them sound so hopelessly dense, so it remained a mystery. What they did know was that the prettiest and sexiest girls in the school, like Joanna Albertson who already had thirty-four-inch tits, and Sonia Tullio who had legs as long as a colt's and eyes full of what even the dumbest boy could see was carnal knowledge, made it very plain that the person they wanted to hang out with and meet on the beach on Sundays was Miles Wilburn. It was very irritating.

And so Lee worried. She worried that Miles's grades were never going to get any better and that was really scary, because everyone knew that the war in Vietnam was escalating and any boy whose grades were below a C in college got sent over there. And okay, Miles was only twelve, but six years could go really fast, and at the rate that war was going and the rate young men were getting killed they might even bring the draft age down. She worried that Miles was just too clever for his own good, and too good at manipulating people and getting them to do what he wanted, and she worried that he might suddenly take it into his head to want to be an actor after all; and she worried that he was sexually precocious. Girls were always all running after him, and Lee worried that he would get one of them into trouble. But most of all she worried that he seemed to her in every way to be getting more and more like Hugo.

And that was a worry she couldn't share with anyone.

"I THINK"—AND the doctor's voice was dangerously, threateningly casual—"I think we'd better have a look at this little lump, Mrs. Wilburn. I'm sure it's nothing, nothing at all, just a cyst, but it's good to be on the safe side. We can take it out very easily. You'll only need to be in the hospital for a couple of days. We'll send it off to be analyzed, and then we won't have to worry anymore."

"I see," said Lee. The room spun threateningly, darkened with panic. She felt horribly, sickly afraid. "But if you're sure it's nothing, why do we have to bother? I mean, are you really sure?"

"As sure as I can be without actually looking at it. I mean, it's very small and you say it hasn't got any bigger?"

She shook her head vigorously, pushing back the doubt.

"You breast-fed your baby, didn't you?"

"Yes, I did."

"Yes, well, that's a good thing, a very good thing. How's your health otherwise? Periods regular, all that sort of thing?"

"Yes," said Lee, wondering briefly whether to mention an increase in pain and frequency, and deciding not to. After all, she was forty-two years old, and it was probably the change beginning; doctors were notoriously unwilling to sympathize with women on that.

"Well, let's see, the sooner the better. I'd like to bring you in next week, and then we can get the whole thing over and done with before Thanksgiving. Can you get time off from work?"

"I think so."

"And what about your little boy? Can he stay with friends?"

"Oh, yes. That's no problem."

"Good. Well, I'll have a word with my secretary, and we'll let you know. I expect by this time in a couple of weeks you'll be up and around and feeling just wonderful. Now, I don't want you to worry, Mrs. Wilburn. I'm just taking precautions."

"Oh, I won't worry," said Lee.

THE LUMP PROVED to be absolutely harmless. "Just a tiny cyst," said the doctor, smiling at her in pleasure and self-justification. "You see how right we were to take it out."

Tears of relief and weak joy pouring down her face, Lee said, "Oh, thank you, Dr. Forsythe, thank you very, very much. When can I go home?"

"Tomorrow. Only you must take it easy. You've had a general anesthetic. Promise me you won't go rushing off stocking up for Thanksgiving."

"I promise. I promise." She was laughing and crying at the same time.

FORTY-EIGHT HOURS later she was pushing her cart through the market, getting the weekend groceries when she suddenly felt a huge and terrible weakness and a hot, fierce pain in her belly. She fainted and came to in the manager's office, a wad of towels between her legs. She was hemorrhaging.

That night she had a hysterectomy; a malignant uterine tumor had been discovered.

Lying, weak and tearful, in the bed she had left so happily three days earlier, she asked Dr. Forsythe what might lie ahead. "Is—is that it? Could the cancer be anywhere else?"

"It could," he said, patting her hand gently. "But uterine cancer is the easiest to contain. We may be lucky."

She noticed he did not meet her eye.

"AMY," SHE SAID the next day. "Could you call this number? Just leave a message to say I called."

"Sure." Amy looked at it. "New York, huh? Is this your boyfriend?"

"He's not a boyfriend," said Lee, managing to smile faintly. "Just call him, Amy. No, on second thought, don't. I don't want to worry him. But, Amy, I do think you'd better call my mom. Get her down here soon. I won't be home for a week or so. She's coming anyway, so she can't complain. Miles won't like it, but he'll have to put up with it for a while. And could you tell Mr. Phillips, too, that I won't be back for a week or two?"

"Honey, you won't be back that soon. You have to rest up for a long time after a hysterectomy. Otherwise you just won't get well again."

"Well, never mind," said Lee. "We'll just take it one day at a time. Tell him two weeks for now. Okay?"

"Okay," Amy said.

SHE WAS HOME in two weeks; relieved and happy to be there, she lay obediently on the couch all day, directing operations, running her small household. Her mother, Dorothy Kelly, eccentrically vague but deceptively spry for her sixty-five years, needed directing, but coped physically extremely well. She kept telling Lee she couldn't stay long, that her hens and her goats needed her more than Lee did, but she promised not to go home until things were back under control. It was a promise she had some difficulty keeping.

SIX WEEKS AFTER her operation, when Lee was just beginning to feel stronger, and thinking that very soon she would be able to go back to work and let her mother return home, she developed a stomach virus.

"It's just because I'm run-down," she said shakily to Amy, returning to her couch after a prolonged session in the bathroom. "I'll be better soon."

"I think," Amy said, looking at Lee's ashen, slightly waxy face, "we should call your doctor."

Dr. Forsythe had Lee back in the hospital, ran some tests and scans, and diagnosed cancer of the liver and the bowel. "Inoperable. I'm sorry, Lee. So very sorry."

He held her hand. She clung to it as if she could pull some of his own strong life into her.

"It's not your fault," she said politely, seeking to put him at ease.

"No. Nor yours."

"Of course not." She was surprised.

"Oh, you'd be surprised. A lot of people feel guilty. Feel they could have prevented it. Feel there was something they should, and indeed could, have done."

"Yes," said Lee. "Yes, Amy will say it was the additives in the food I ate."

"Ah," he said. "Yes, a favorite scapegoat right now."

There was a silence. He looked at her tenderly. "You haven't had much luck lately, have you, Lee?"

"No," she said, "I haven't. Will—will it . . ."

"Hurt? No, no more than you can bear. Pain control has become very good. You have only to ask."

"How long?"

He looked at her very steadily. "Not long. Perhaps three months."

She gasped, reeled back as if he had hit her. Then she started to cry, huge, racking, childish sobs, on and on; she hit the pillow, bit her fists, screamed. "It's not fair, it's not fair. I've tried so hard, so hard. Why should it be me, why why why? I hate it, I hate it, I hate everybody, everything. Go away, go away, I hate you. Why couldn't you have seen it, helped me, done something? You told me it was nothing, just a cyst, and now I'm dying and you can only give me three months. You're cruel and you're an idiot. You're a lousy, fucking, useless doctor, and I hate you. Go away, go away."

He didn't go away. He stayed and listened to her, and when she would let him, he held her, held her hand, held her in his arms, like a lover, like a father; gradually she calmed.

"I'm sorry."

"I know. Can I do anything?"

"Yes. Could you ask Father Kennedy to come and see me? And could you call this number and ask this man to come? Explain why. Soon. Please."

Father Kennedy came first. Lee was frightened, as only a sinning Catholic could be frightened.

"Father, I have to confess."

"Very well."

"No, not in church. Here, now. Will you listen?"

"I will."

She told him. She told him everything, about Hugo, about Miles, about Dean. He listened.

"May God forgive you."

"Do you think he will?"

"Christ came to the world to save sinners."

"I know. But sinners like me?"

"Exactly like you. And me. We are all sinners."

She looked at him and smiled. "Father, I don't think you rank as a sinner."

"In the eyes of God I do."

"Well, he must have pretty sharp eyes."

"Merciful eyes, also."

"Father, will you come?"

He understood at once.

"Of course. Whenever you feel it is time."

"Suppose I don't know?"

"You will."

"Will you tell Dr. Forsythe to call you? Just in case?"

"Of course. He always does."

She was comforted.

"Father, what can I do about Miles? I only have my mother, and she's so—well, so unsuitable."

"She is his grandmother, though. And she is willing to take care of him."

"How do you know?"

"She told me."

"Good heavens," said Lee, shocked out of her submissiveness. "When?"

"She came to see me. She said she thought it was her duty. Lee, I wouldn't call her unsuitable. She's a good woman. She's strong, and she loves Miles. She might even be good for him. A little old-fashioned discipline."

Lee frowned. "I know everyone thinks I spoil Miles. But it's almost impossible not to."

"I know." He patted her hand. "He is a beautiful and charming boy."

"But he's so young. Such a baby. So little to be left alone. I can't bear to leave him, Father, I just can't. Never to see him grow up. How will he manage without me?"

He watched her, weeping silently, struggling to control herself.

"He won't be alone, Lee."

"Oh," she said, angry suddenly. "Oh, I forgot. Of course, God will be there. He'll pack his lunch and comfort him when he skins his knees and cheer him on when he plays baseball and make sure he isn't out after dark and listen to him when he's worried and have fun with him on Sundays and invite his friends over and cuddle him and tell him he's a great guy when things go wrong and be on his side when the teachers pick on him and try to make sure he gets to college so he doesn't have to go to Vietnam. Oh, good, I don't need to worry at all."

"God will do some of those things, Lee. Your mother will do others. Some Miles will have to manage on his own. You must have faith, Lee, to save your own happiness during these weeks. They're too precious to waste in misery and doubt."

"I just don't know how you can talk like that. Think like that."

"Talking is easy. Thinking, believing, is more difficult." He smiled at her. "Tell me, is your English friend coming to see you?"

"Yes. Tomorrow. I suppose you think that's very bad." She looked at him, half tearful, half hostile.

"No. I don't think love and comfort are ever bad. Given in the right way at the right time. I'm glad he's coming. Perhaps I shouldn't be, but I am."

"Thank you, Father." She smiled at him, feeling more at ease and happier. "Thank you. Please come again before—before you have to."

"I will. Often. I'll enjoy it. The company of a pretty young woman is always pleasant."

She looked in the mirror at her pallid face, already tinged with yellow, her distended stomach, and grimaced. "Pretty!"

He bent and kissed her cheek. "Very pretty. Now rest. And enjoy your visitor."

HUGO WAS SHOCKED at the sight of her. She could see it in his eyes. He hadn't seen her since she'd had the cyst out—well, it had only been six weeks all together—and he winced as he looked at her. It hurt her.

"Hi, Hugo. Here I am, your golden California girl, a little tarnished. I'm sorry I look so hideous. I can't help it, I'm afraid."

"You don't look hideous. You couldn't. Not exactly glowing, but not hideous."

She was sullen, hostile. "Don't lie to me. I look hideous."

"Okay," he said agreeably, "you look hideous."

"You didn't have to come," she said and started, once again, to cry. Every fresh visitor, fresh intruder into her safe, sick world, made her cry, forcing her as they did to confront her sickness, her imminent death.

"No, I didn't," he said. "But I did come. I wanted to come."

"Good for you."

She was silent. Then: "Did you come from England or New York?"

"England."

"Ah. How's Alice?"

"She's fine."

"How very nice for her," she said bitterly.

"Lee, don't."

"Don't what? Don't care?"

"Don't be angry."

"But I am angry," she cried. "You'd be angry, too, losing half your life, losing your child, being in pain, being afraid. Of course I'm angry. Fuck you. I'm furious."

"I'm sorry."

"Yes, I suppose you are. I'll bet you thought you'd find some peaceful, Madonna-like figure lying back on the pillows, smiling serenely, saying her rosary. Well, death isn't like that, Hugo. It's hard and it's painful and it's elusive and it's ugly. And it makes you angry. Very angry."

She reached out for his hand and gripped it. "I'm so frightened."

"I know. So am I."

"What of?"

"Of losing you."

She was amazed. "Losing me?"

"Yes. Losing you. I can't imagine life without you now. You are the only truly happy thing I have. I love you. I love you so much."

She lay on her pillows, her eyes fixed on his face in genuine, awestruck astonishment. "I never knew."

"I know you didn't. God knows why you didn't. Didn't I behave as if I loved you?"

She thought, looking back over the lost happy years. "Yes. Yes, I suppose you did. I never saw it, but yes you did."

He smoothed her limp hair back from her forehead. "And you don't look hideous. Truly. You look lovely."

She looked at him and smiled, took his hand. "I wish I'd known."

"Why?"

"Well, I would have been nicer to you, for a start."

"You've been very nice to me recently."

"I know, but I was terrible all those years."

"True."

"I was just so afraid— Well, it doesn't matter."

"I know. That I would come and claim Miles."

"Yes."

"As if I would have done that, loving you, loving him."

She looked at him. "Do you love him?"

"Very much. I think he is interesting and clever and charming. Like me."

"No, seriously."

"Seriously I think he's all those things. Seriously I love him. And I'll do everything I can to take care of him."

"But you won't . . ."

"No. I'll never tell him. Don't worry."

"He'll need to be taken care of. My mother is going to move down here. She'll see that he does his schoolwork and doesn't go on the streets, but she won't truly understand him and what he needs. She can't."

"I'm sure Amy will do a lot. And his friends and their families."

"At first. But they have their own families. And they'll slowly stop thinking about Miles in that kind of way."

"Well, I will do my best."

"What will you do? What can you do?"

"Oh, lots of things. I even thought about adopting him. Don't look at me like that. I'm a good liar. I would have thought of something."

"Are you a good liar?"

"Excellent."

"I'm not. Sometimes I wish I was." She sighed and looked at him with a rueful smile. "Miles is a wonderful liar. I can't even tell when he's doing it."

"Well, it can be useful. Anyway, I thought I would make a settlement on Miles, a lump sum, to be held in trust for him. The income will be useful to your mother now. At least they won't have any financial worries."

"Hugo, how can you afford that sort of thing? Are you very rich?"

"No. Not what I would call very rich. But I do have some money and I think I owe it to him."

"And who will look after this settlement? See he gets it?"

"My lawyer in New York."

"Could you give my mother his name?"

"Of course."

"Thank you."

"And then, later, I will see he goes to a good college, that he avoids the draft as long as possible. I know that worries you. And then I will also see he gets a job. A good job. Maybe he could work for me. I don't know. But I won't let him hang around sharing peace and love with the flower children or taking drugs. I promise you that. And I will come and see him very often, talk to him, make sure there aren't any serious problems and that he isn't seriously unhappy, that your mother is meeting all the needs she can, that he isn't too lonely, too lost."

Lee was crying again. "I'm sorry. I can't bear the thought of leaving him. It's the worst, the only thing I really care about."

"I know."

She was silent for a while. Then: "Why do you love me? I mean, what is it about me? I don't really understand. I thought it was just sex."

"It was at first. I thought you were the most beautiful, desirable, sexy woman I had ever seen. You were certainly the sexiest woman I'd ever been to bed with."

"Really?" she said in genuine astonishment.

"Yes, really."

"But how? I mean in what way?"

"It's hard to be specific. I suppose because you didn't think about it. Didn't analyze it. Just wanted it terribly badly and did it."

"Could you tell I wanted it? I mean early on?"

"Oh, yes," he said, kissing her hand, holding her eyes with his own. "From that very first day, that very first lunch. I thought, Now, there is a lady who would be a terrific, gloriously, outrageously wonderful lay. And I was right."

"Okay. So that was the sex. But the love?"

"Oh, the love. That's quite different."

"How?"

"I had to love you without ever getting near you again. So I had to find other things to love. It wasn't hard."

"What were they?"

"Your courage. Your honesty. Your straightforward, sock-it-to-me, let's-get-on-with-life attitude. And then, more recently, still your courage, which has been phenomenal, but also your capacity for happiness. For pleasure. The talent you have for caring for people. I think," he said slowly, stroking her hand very gently, "I am very lucky to have known you. And to have fathered your—our child. I count it as a privilege. And it is the source of great happiness in my life."

"Oh, Hugo," said Lee, a great sob breaking into her voice, lying back on her pillows, closing her eyes, "leave me alone now. Come back tomorrow. I can't bear it."

"All right," he said, standing up. "I'll go. And I will be back to-morrow."

"How—how long can you stay?"

"Awhile. As long as you need me."

"NOW, MOM, ARE you absolutely sure about all this?"

"I'm as sure as I can be," Dorothy Kelly said with a martyred sigh. "The way I look at it, I don't have much choice."

"Well you are sixty-five. That's quite an age to be caring for a little boy."

"And what a little boy. If you'd raised him a little more strictly it might be an easier task. I always told you you spoiled him. Now I have to pick up the pieces."

"Oh, Mom, don't. He's a good boy. Please remember that. Please. And he needs love."

"I know." Her face softened. "It's all right, honey, I will love him. I do love him. You don't have to worry."

"I can't help it."

"Yes, well, it won't help anyone. Least of all you."

"No, I suppose not. Now, Mom, I want to talk to you about money. There really isn't a problem there."

"Why not? Dean never made any money."

"No, but—well, he had a good life insurance policy. Hugo—Mr. Dashwood, you know—helped me invest it, and it's worth quite a lot now. He suggested that we put it in trust for Miles, for when he's twenty-one. The income will be very useful to you in the meantime."

"It must have been a very good policy. How come you got it after Dean killed himself?"

"It was a special one," said Lee quickly. "And also, Mom, if you have any problems, financial or legal, you can call Hugo Dashwood. He lives in England, but he has a small office in New York. They can take messages. You can always call him if it's urgent. Only don't do it all the time."

"I certainly won't," Dorothy said. "I wouldn't want to. I don't like the English. Stiff, unfriendly lot. Living in the Dark Ages most of the time." She looked at Lee sharply. "Mr. Dashwood seems to be a very good friend to you, Lee."

"He is," said Lee firmly, "and he was a good friend to Dean, too. Dean—helped him when he was starting out. He's always said he'd like to repay that."

"I see."

"And you really don't mind coming to live here?"

"I mind like hell," said Mrs. Kelly. "Like hell. How can I say good-bye to my hens? But I know my duty. I always have. I would never forgive myself if I failed in it now. And this is where Miles should be. I can see that. So what must be must be. But it isn't easy."

"No," said Lee. She closed her eyes.

Her mother looked at her. "Are you okay?"

"Just about. It's nearly time for the morphine. That's a bad part of the day."

"Poor kid," said her mother. It was the first and indeed the only time she had ever expressed any sympathy. Lee knew what it meant. She smiled at her mother and took her hand.

"I really am very grateful to you."

"Hmm. Well, I just hope I last the course." There was a pause. "Lee, that affair you were having—before Dean died, the one that caused him to kill himself—is that over? I never asked you, never wanted to know. But now I need to, I guess."

"Oh, yes," said Lee. "Absolutely over."

"AMY, YOU WILL keep an eye on Miles, won't you?"

"Of course I will. You know I will."

"You'll *keep* keeping an eye on him? You won't forget?"

"For God's sake, Lee. We go back a long way. I won't forget."

"He'll need you so much."

"I know."

"Just—just hug him sometimes. And have some fun with him."

"I will. Don't worry about it."

"I can't help it."

"I know."

"Hugo will be down from time to time, keeping an eye on things. He's—he's very fond of Miles."

Amy looked at her deadpan. "I can see that."

"Yes, well."

"He's very fond of you, too, I guess."

"Yes, he is."

"You're not going to tell me, are you, Lee?"

"No," said Lee simply.

"Yeah, well, I have eyes in my head. And a brain. Oh, don't look at me like that, Lee. I won't say anything. I can't. I don't know anything to say."

"No," Lee said. "No, you don't."

"Is—is everything all right with your mom? Money and so on?"

"Yes," said Lee. "No worries about money. There's the insurance and everything. The house is mine. No mortgage."

"Some insurance policy," Amy said.

"Yes."

"How do you feel?" said Amy, looking at her tenderly.

"Lousy."

"You look lousy."

"Thanks."

"Does it hurt a lot?"

"Sometimes. The drugs are very good. Mostly it's just discomfort. And weakness. Weariness. And I can't sleep." She gripped her friend's hand. "Amy, I'm not even scared anymore. I just want it to be over."

"MILES, LOOK AT me. No, on second thought, don't. I'm not a pretty sight."

"You look okay."

"Thanks, hon."

"That's okay."

"Now listen to me, Miles. We have to have a talk."

"Sure."

"You do know, don't you, that I won't be here much longer."

"Yes, I do."

"We have to be grown-up and sensible about this, Miles. No point crying or making a fuss, like I used to tell you about your schoolwork. It has to be done."

"This is different from my schoolwork. I manage to duck out of that. I can't duck out of you dying."

"No," said Lee, thinking she would stifle under the weight of the huge tearing pain in her heart as she looked at him, so much worse than any physical pain she had endured over the past three months. "No, you can't. And I can't duck out of it either."

"Are you scared, Mom?"

"Not really anymore."

"I'm scared."

"What of?"

"Of being without you."

"Oh, Miles." She closed her eyes, swallowed, fought to hold on to herself. "Miles, don't be scared. You're allowed to be sad, but not to be scared. You'll manage. You're so brave. And so tough."

"Like you. You're the bravest person I ever even heard of."

"I try to be," said Lee.

"Was Dad brave? I don't really remember."

"Very brave."

"Why did he die, Mom? I never understood. I think you should tell me. I know he killed himself. Billy Fields told me he heard his mom say that Dad killed himself. And I saw a newspaper clipping that somebody else found in their attic. I just can't think why he would kill himself. All I can remember is us being a really happy family."

"We were," Lee said staunchly. "And don't ever let anyone tell you any different. We were very, very happy. Your dad was happy. Until —until that last day. Then he did something silly. Something foolish. And it went wrong."

"What?"

"Well, you see"—God help me, thought Lee—"your dad was very smart and very good, but he didn't make that much money. He was successful, but not terribly successful. And that bothered him a lot. Then he heard that an old friend had done really, really well, and he got very depressed and felt he was a failure. He also got very drunk. Then he went up to bed and took some sleeping pills. Mixed with the drink and his bad heart, they killed him."

"Oh. That's sad."

"Yes, it was terribly sad. Horrible. But I have learned to think about when we were happy. As you do. Just keep thinking about that, Miles. Don't let anyone take it away from you."

"I won't. Anyway, I feel better now. I wish I'd asked you before. I'm glad you told me." He looked at her, his frightened, loving heart in his dark blue eyes. "Oh, Mom, what am I going to do without you? Who's going to make me feel better?"

Lee couldn't speak. She held out her arms, and Miles, big boy that he was, crawled into them. She smoothed back his hair, kissed his head, stroked his face.

"I'm sorry I don't work at school much, Mom," he said after a while. "Was that what you wanted to talk to me about?"

"Partly," said Lee, grateful to get the conversation on a less emotional level. "Not because I'm cross with you. But because I have such hopes, such high hopes for you. You're so smart, Miles. Smarter than me or Dad"—Oh, God, she thought, I shouldn't have said that —"and you can do so well. Don't throw it away, Miles. You must work harder. Don't let me down."

"You won't be here," he said with simple logic. "You won't know if I've let you down."

"Now, look," said Lee, half laughing, half crying, "is that going to make me feel any better right now, Miles Wilburn? Worrying about you, all day and all night? I want to—to go away feeling proud and confident and happy about you. That's the very last thing you can give me, and it will be such a lot."

"Okay," Miles said. "I promise. I'll work hard. Do you want me to be President? I'll try if you want."

"It might do for starters."

"Okay."

"And I want you to be real nice to Granny Kelly. It won't be easy for her. She won't have her friends or her hens or anything."

"I wouldn't mind her hens. I like hens."

"Yes, well, there's no space for hens in our backyard."

"I don't know," Miles said, brightening up. "There might be."

"Well," said Lee, with the first thankful sigh she had heaved for weeks, "that has nothing to do with me. That's entirely between you and Granny Kelly."

"Okay."

"Now, Mr. Dashwood—"

"Mom, I wish you'd call him Hugo. He calls himself Hugo."

"All right—Hugo. He has very kindly said he will keep an eye on you and Granny Kelly, so if you have any big problems, at school, or about money, or if you think Granny isn't coping, you can talk to him. I'll give you his number in New York. He won't answer the phone; it's not his home number, but a secretary will take a message."

"Okay. Where is his home?"

"In England."

"I know, but where?"

"I'm not sure. In London somewhere."

"He seems real fond of you, Mom." His eyes were probing into hers.

"Yes," said Lee, "well, he's been a good friend for a long time."

"But he's not the friend who was more successful than Dad?"

"What? Oh, good heavens, no."

"I just wondered."

"And with day-to-day problems, you just go to Amy."

"But," he said, and tears filled his eyes and spilled down his cheeks, "it's the day-to-day problems I need you for."

And then Lee started to cry, too, and he climbed right up on the bed beside her and lay clinging to her, sobbing, sounding as if he was three years old.

They stayed there for a long time. And then she said, finally, exhausted, drained of strength and emotion, trying desperately, helplessly, to comfort him, to give him something he could take away with him, "Miles, my darling, stop. Stop crying. This isn't going to do any good at all for either of us."

"Yes, it is," he said, nestling his blond head farther onto her pillow. "I can remember it for always."

SHE DIED EARLY the next morning, the sheets on her bed still crumpled where he had lain.

• 11 •

THINGS WERE DEFINITELY GETTING BETTER. Roz felt life was beginning to go her way.

In the first place she had escaped from Cheltenham, and was spending her two sixth-form years at Bedales: coeducational, progressive, civilized. It suited her well; there was scope for her fiercely individual mind, her rather puritanical approach to her work, her disregard for social conventions. Her self-esteem increased visibly.

"The worst thing about Cheltenham," she said to Letitia, one of the few people she trusted enough to talk to, "was that if you weren't like the others, all giggly and jolly and gossipy and mad on games, it was hopeless; you were just all alone in the world. If you didn't want to be alone, you had to pretend to be like them. Pretending was worse than being alone, though," she added.

"Poor Roz," said Letitia, "five years of that sort of thing is a long time."

"Yes," Roz said shortly. "Well, I daresay it did me some good."

"I hope so, darling. I'm never quite convinced about the therapeutic value of unhappiness. Anyway, I'm glad you like it so much better where you are now. You're looking wonderful," she added.

"Wonderful" was an exaggeration, and Roz knew it, but she also knew she did look better all the time. She was still far from pretty, and probably always would be, but she didn't think anyone anymore could call her exactly plain. She was taller, quite a lot taller, than any other girl in her year. Nobody could quite work out where her height came from—Julian was only six feet, and Eliza was tiny, just about five feet—and half an inch, she always insisted. But there it was, Roz was five feet nine already and still growing, and she was large-framed, too, with wide shoulders and, to her constant misery, size nine feet. "Just you try getting fashionable shoes in that size," she said darkly to anyone who told her it didn't matter. But there was not an ounce of fat on her; she was lean and rangy-looking, apart from most gratifyingly large breasts. Her face was interesting, dramatic, her rather hollow cheekbones and harsh jaw accentuating her large green eyes, her full mouth. Her big nose caused her much anguish, but at least it was straight and not hooked or anything awful, she kept reassuring herself; and her dark hair was thick and shiny, even if it was as straight as the proverbial die, and willful as well. She wore it long now, tied back in a long, swinging ponytail; it wasn't a style that flattered her but at least it kept her hair under control, and stopped it sticking out the wrong way.

She had done very well in her exams and passed eleven of them, nine with A's. she was taking math, economics, and geography, and in her first term at Bedales had beaten all the girls and all but two of the boys in the pre-Christmas exams. She planned on going to Cambridge to read math; her tutor had told Julian that she would probably get in on fifth-term entry rather than doing a third year in the sixth. Nothing pleased Roz more than showing her father how clever she was; it made up for not being pretty, not being a boy, not really being the sort of daughter she knew he would have liked. And loved.

Roz had chosen to forget her own brief foray into love with an older man. What was more, her opinion of the male race, already low, had taken a further dive at David Sassoon's defection to the United States and from her mother's bed the moment success and fame beckoned in even larger quantities than were already in his possession. She had suffered a qualm or two of conscience witnessing Eliza's awful grief over the defection, had tried not to listen, hands over her ears, to the hideous, ferocious scene as David tried to justify leaving—"Darling, I can't afford not to take it. He'll destroy me. Give me a chance to make it over there and I'll set up on my own, and we'll be married." On and on it went, hour after hour, all one night, and in the morning he was gone, leaving Eliza swollen-eyed, ashen, and somehow smaller than ever and very frail. Roz had known she had had at least something to do with that suffering, that frailty, and tell herself as she might that had David really loved her mother he would not have gone, she knew that had she not spoken as she had to her father over those months, David would not have had the opportunity to go. However, she told herself, her mother had caused her a great deal of suffering in her life and certainly didn't seem to have felt guilty about it; moreover, Eliza was tough, she was resilient, and she just didn't need a man who put his worldly success so firmly before his emotional life.

Roz had grown very skillful at such rationalization.

FREDDY BRANKSOME, FINANCIAL director of Morell's, came into Julian's office one morning in early 1972 and shut the door firmly behind him.

"I think we might have a problem," he said.

Julian, who had been studying with some pleasure the latest ad photographs for the autumn advertising campaign, recognized the tone in Freddy's voice that demanded his undivided attention, and set the pictures aside.

"Yes, Freddy?"

"I've been looking at the share register. I don't like it. There's been a lot of buying by someone in Zurich. Big blocks. I smell trouble."

"Can you check it out?"

"I'm trying."

"Takeover?"

"Not yet. But we could be heading for a bid."

"Christ, I wish this company was still mine."

"Yes, well it's a bit late for that. You went public twenty years ago or so. You've still got thirty percent. That's not a bad stake in a company this size."

"Not enough, though, is it? Not when this sort of thing happens."

"Well, it hasn't happened yet. I'll keep working on it."

A WEEK LATER he was back in Julian's office. "More buying. Just in dribs and drabs. Something like twenty percent of all the shares now. I can't make it out."

"But there's nothing tangible?"

"Not yet."

"Maybe it's nothing to worry about."

"Maybe. You okay, Julian? You look rotten."

"Thanks a lot. I feel fine."

"Okay. Sorry I spoke."

"JULIAN," FREDDY BRANKSOME said a week later, "I really don't think you ought to go to New York for a day or two."

"Why not?"

"Because of this situation with the shares. It's still going on. Still worrying me."

"Okay, I'll hang on a bit."

IN THE MAIN bedroom of his château in the champagne-producing area of the Loire, the vicomte du Chene was looking tenderly at the slender, wonderfully sensuous body of his new wife. "My darling darling," he said, punctuating the words with repeated and ever-longer forays with his tongue into her genitals, and postponing in a delicious agony the moment when he could allow himself to enter her with his eager, if somewhat modestly made, member, "you are so lovely, so very very lovely. You have made me the happiest man in France. I cannot believe that you have consented to be"—very long pause—"my wife."

"Oh, Pierre, you're so sweet. It's me that is fortunate. And the happiest woman in France. And thank you for the marvelous wedding present. We can have such fun with it. It was so terribly generous of you."

"My darling, a few shares. It was nothing. In return for your love. And perhaps—"

"Yes?"

"Well, the little matter of course of an heir. To the vineyards. My only unsatisfied ambition now."

"I know. Of course. And I'm sure we can fulfill it. Together. Like this . . ."

"Indeed, my darling. It's just a matter of time. And such pleasantly, wonderfully spent time. If it took all eternity it would be too short."

His bride stretched herself out beneath him, opening her legs, encasing his penis lovingly in her hands, guiding it, urging it into her body. "Yes, my darling," she murmured, raising her hips, pushing herself against him, trying with all the skill she had been born with and learned, to help him to maintain his erection for a few moments at least, to bring him just a little slowly to orgasm. "It would. Now—now—no, my darling, wait, please—aah," and she relaxed suddenly, clenching and unclenching her vagina in a fiercely faked orgasm, as the hapless vicomte's little problem of premature ejaculation once again came between her and her pleasure.

"Ah," he said, "how was it for you?"

"Marvelous. Quite marvelous."

"My darling. My own darling," he said, kissing her repeatedly in a gush of gratitude. "How fortunate I am. How very, very fortunate."

Eliza du Chene, looking up at the ceiling, a yearning void somewhere deep inside her, hoped fervently that the price of revenge and of becoming a major shareholder in her ex-husband's company was not going to become unbearably high.

"THERE'S A VICOMTESSE du Chene on the phone, Mr. Morell." Sarah Brownsmith, Julian's new secretary, spoke nervously. Julian's temper had been extremely uncertain over the past few weeks.

"Who? Never heard of her. Ask her what she wants."

The line went blank for a while. "She says she's one of your share-holders. One of your major shareholders. She wants to ask you some questions about the company."

"Tell her she can't. Tell her it's nothing to do with me."

The line went blank again. "I'm sorry, Mr. Morell, but she's very insistent. She says when you speak to her you'll know what it's about."

"What? Oh, all right. Put her on. But tell her I've only got one minute. Tell her I've got to catch a plane."

"Really, Julian. You can do better than that. Surely everyone knows by now you've got your own plane."

It was Eliza's voice. Julian knocked over his coffee.

"Eliza. What on earth are you doing on the phone? I was expecting some damn fool Frenchwoman."

"No. A damn fool Englishwoman. With a French husband."

"What?"

"The vicomtesse du Chene. *C'est moi.*"

ROZ LOATHED PIERRE du Chene. He was physically disgusting, short and dark, and with an awful smell, a nauseating blend of garlic and strong after-shave, and in spite of that, a kind of lingering body odor as well. And he had those awful sleazy eyes, which were always on her, watching her, half smiling. Often, if she caught him unaware, she found those eyes fixed not on her face but on her breasts or her stomach. He had a little squashed monkey's face with a kind of snub nose and a mustache, and his breath smelled horrible, too, and when he kissed her, which he did at every possible opportunity, she thought she would be sick.

She just hadn't been able to believe her eyes when he came out onto the terrace of the château when she went there for the Easter holidays. Her mother had met her at Nantes in the most beautiful white Rolls Corniche with a chauffeur who was very handsome in-deed; Roz had thought for a wild moment that he was the vicomte, but then they had driven back along the wide straight roads up toward Saumur, Eliza talking endlessly and too brightly about how perfectly wonderful everything was and what fun they were all going to have, and how much Roz would love Pierre, and there was a horse she could ride, and Pierre, a superb horseman, was dying to ride with her, and the château, well—the château was just the most beautiful place Roz could ever imagine, exactly like the Sleeping Beauty's castle, and Pierre was just the best fun in the world, terribly cultured and amus-ing, and she had never been so happy in her life.

Roz, looking at her, thinking she looked rather thin and pale, was a little surprised at this, but she had long since given up trying to understand her mother. Then Eliza said, "There is just one thing, darling. I'd better tell you, in case he mentions it. Well, that is, he *will* mention it. Pierre is fearfully keen for us to have children, or at least an heir. You'll understand when you see the estate. Of course I would love that, too, and I hope it will happen, but—well, just don't be surprised, that's all. You probably think I'm much too old to have babies, but of course I'm not, I'm only thirty-six; that's nothing, really. I just thought I'd better tell you, as I don't suppose you thought it was something your old mother might ever do again. All right?"

"All right," said Roz, extremely confused by this, not sure what she was meant to do or say, but whenever she looked at the awful monkeylike form of du Chene, smelled his breath, saw his awful furtive eyes, she shuddered—and more than that, shuddered for her mother having to go to bed with him, never mind carry his child.

Du Chene didn't actually start in on Roz until the summer. Even then at first, like all comparatively innocent young girls in the hands, literally, of their elders, she thought she must be mistaken. It began with just a pressure on her leg under the table, a squeeze of her hand when she passed him in the corridor. Soon it progressed unmistakably to the patting of her bottom, the massaging of her shoulder as he passed her chair, his hand lingering, straying down toward her breast. Then one evening after supper, her mother pleaded a headache. Du Chene and Roz were sitting alone in the small drawing room, she reading, he studying papers, and he looked up at her and said, "You're looking very lovely, my dear Rosamund."

"Thank you, Pierre. I expect it's the French air."

"Oh, no," he said, "no, it is your own lovely look, your eyes and your skin, and of course your legs; your legs are so tanned. You should wear shorter skirts so that they can be admired."

"Thank you, Pierre, but I don't like short skirts. I'm a little tired now, I think I might go up to bed."

"Very well, my dear, of course you must if you are tired. We cannot have you missing your beauty sleep. Come and kiss me good night."

"No, Pierre, I won't, if you don't mind."

"And why not? I am after all your steppapa. Come, my dear, a little daughterly kiss."

"No, really, Pierre. Good night."

She got up, but she had to walk past him; he shot his little brown hand out and caught hers. "Such a—what do you say?—a tease. It only makes me more excited, my dear."

Roz shook her hand free. "Leave me alone."

She walked swiftly past him, but he still managed, as he released her hand and stroked her bottom. Then he jumped up and, with an unbelievably swift dart, was in the doorway, barring her way. "Just a little kiss. A *petit, petit* kiss."

His breath was foul; Roz turned her face away. But he caught her wrists, pulled her toward him. He was just slightly shorter than she, but he pushed her against the doorway and pressed his wet mouth against hers, forcing her arms above her head and holding them there. Roz acted swiftly; she raised her right knee and thrust it hard into his groin. He groaned softly and let her go; but when she looked back at him as she fled across the hall, his eyes were bright and his cheeks flushed with excitement.

Next morning he did not ride with her, and after she had stabled her horse she came into breakfast nervous about what he might say, but he was, as always, immaculately polite, almost distant, and nodded to her as if nothing had happened between them at all. Eliza appeared at lunch heavy eyed and listless, and hardly spoke.

Roz began to worry about her; she suggested twice that she come back and say with Letitia in London for a while, but Eliza said gaily that it was out of the question, that she wouldn't dream of leaving Pierre even for a short while.

"Well, Mummy, if you don't mind, I think I'll go back a bit earlier. Rosie has asked me to stay with them in Colorado; her new stepfather has a ranch there. I'd love to go. Would you mind?"

"No, of course not," said Eliza, her eyes almost frighteningly bright. "You go, Roz darling, and have fun. When do you want to leave?"

"Maybe on Sunday. Whenever it suits you."

"Fine. Now I think I'll go and have my rest. I seem to be getting old; all I want to do is sleep these days."

"You're not—?" Roz couldn't bring herself to say it, to acknowledge what her mother must be doing, endlessly, horribly, with du Chene.

"Oh, no, darling, not yet. Give me a chance. These things take time, you know."

"Do they?" Roz said.

THE NIGHT BEFORE she was due to leave, the three of them ate outside. Whatever else, Roz thought, this place greatly resembled Paradise. The air was sweet and full of the sound of the poplar trees and the crickets' evening chorus. She looked up at the towers of the château against the darkening sky and across to where they were reflected in the great lake. In the hedges near the terrace there was the light of a thousand glowworms; the new moon, a sliver of silver, was climbing the sky.

"Look," said Roz, "look at that moon. Isn't it perfect?"

" 'Softly she was going up, and a star or two beside,' " said du Chene suddenly. "Is not that a most beautiful English poem?"

Roz looked at him, surprised. "It is. I didn't know you read English literature, Pierre."

"I am full of surprises," he said. "I can quote you the whole of 'Oh to be in England,' by Robert Browning, as well."

"I bet you can't," said Eliza.

"Yes, I can," he said and proceeded to do so, rather beautifully. "You see," he said to Roz, "I am not the ignorant French peasant you thought."

"I didn't think you were anything of the sort," Roz said quickly.

"Good," he said and smiled at her, patting her hand.

Roz pulled it away and felt him turning his attention to her thighs instead. Oh, well, she was going home next day.

She went to bed early; she had just turned out the light and settled into the huge bed when there was a tap at the door.

"Mummy?"

Silence. Another tap, more urgent.

Roz climbed out of bed and went over to the door, which she always kept locked against the threat of du Chene's attentions. "Who is it?"

"Rosamund, it's Pierre. Open the door and come with me quickly. It's your mother; I am worried about her."

She unlocked the door, saw his face, tried to shut it again too late. He was inside the room, pushing her back toward the bed; he was wearing only a robe and it was hanging open. Roz tried not to look at him, just concentrated on fighting him; she was a big girl and strong, but he was stronger. He had her on the bed in no time, pushing her down onto it, pressing his slobbery mouth onto hers, pushing up the hem of her nightdress with his free hand. Then she felt the hand exploring her thigh, and creeping up, up, toward her pubic hair. A hot panic engulfed her; she tried to scream, but his mouth was over hers, attempted to kick him, but she couldn't move.

"Arrogant English bitch," he said suddenly, almost cheerfully, and stood up, shrugging out of his robe. Roz shut her eyes; she didn't want to see. Then in the split second she was free, she raised one long, strong leg and kicked him hard in the chest. He staggered and fell backward and lay splayed on the floor, his hands clutching his penis. He looked more than ever like one of those rather sad-faced small monkeys that hide in the corners of their cages at the zoo.

"Get up," said Roz. "Get up and get out. You're disgusting."

"Oh, Rosamund," he said, "don't be unkind to me. I love you."

"No, you don't," she said. "You're supposed to love my mother."

"No, I love you."

"Rubbish. Now are you going to go, or shall I call her?"

"I'll go." He scrambled up, still covering his parts, and groped for his robe.

"I only wanted to stroke your pussy," he said plaintively. "Your beautiful English pussy."

"Oh, fuck off," said Roz. Then remembering his reaction when she hurt him that night in the drawing room, afraid he would become aroused again if she went on being hostile, she took him by the shoulders and marched him to the door.

"Come along. Time for bed. Good night, Pierre."

He went meekly enough, but at the door he turned once again, with an expression of great sadness. "Forgive me," he said. "I didn't mean to harm you. It's just that you are so beautiful." Roz relaxed her guard, and suddenly his hand was inside her nightdress, feeling for, squeezing, her nipple. "Beautiful," he said, his face millimeters away, "beautiful bitch."

"Fuck off," said Roz again, pushing his hand frantically away.

"That is precisely what I want to do," he said, seizing her breast again, working his hand down toward her stomach this time. "Do you feel nothing for me at all?"

"Yes," said Roz. "Revulsion. Shall I knee you in the groin again, Pierre, or are you going?"

He looked at her, breathing heavily, his face flushed, his eyes still oddly sad.

"I will go," he said, "this time. But I shall not forget you. There will be other holidays."

"There won't. I shan't come. I shall tell my mother in the morning. She'll probably come home with me."

"I'm afraid," he said, "that your mother will not be surprised."

"What?" said Roz, too horrified to be afraid anymore, pushing his hand away from her repeatedly. "You mean she knows?"

"Not about you, of course. But about my very healthy appetite for —well, for young ladies."

"I don't believe you. She wouldn't put up with it. She wouldn't stay."

"My dear child," he said, finally dropping his hand, fastening his robe, "she has no choice. Ask her about her wedding present when you tell her about tonight. Good night, Rosamund. Sleep well."

He raised her hand and kissed it, formally, in a courtly manner. Roz stared after him, then went back into her room, slammed the door, and locked it. She leaned against it, feeling first shaky, then sick. She longed to go to her mother, to be with someone, but Eliza would be with du Chene. It was impossible; she had to cope with this, get through the night on her own. She went through into her bathroom and ran a deep, very hot bath and lay in it a long time, trying to calm herself, to control her panic, her sense of revulsion, of invasion. And what had he meant? What wedding present?

Roz hardly slept. Every time she closed her eyes she saw, felt, du Chene, his horrible clawing hands, his frightful slobbering mouth. She had never thought about sex except in rather abstract terms, or very romantic ones, in the height of her passion for David. Now its worst implications had been literally forced upon her, and she felt damaged, grieved.

Toward morning she finally fell asleep and dreamed, a confused half-nightmare that she was tied down on her bed and he was coming at her, smiling, his robe flapping loose. She felt his hands pushing at her, probing her pubic hair, then moving farther, farther up. She woke up, her head tossing from side to side, her face wet with tears, and her own hands clasped together over her vagina.

She got up, dressed, packed, went downstairs to the kitchens, and made herself some coffee. She was terrified he would appear, but then she saw him walking to the stables and relaxed a little. Now that it was morning, and life was becoming normal again, the nightmare was receding, had become something she could put away, keep under control, like so many of the unpleasant events that had punctuated her life.

What in some ways she wanted, longed to do, was go to her mother, talk to her, tell her, but something stopped her. In the first place she felt it would simply prolong her agony, deepen her own distress.

The other thing was the deeply disturbing fact that her mother was married to this man. She must surely know, or at least suspect, what he was like. Indeed he had said that her mother knew about his behavior.

ROZ TRIED NOT to think about the incident after she went back to school, but then as the term went on she began to have nightmares, to wake up, as she had that first morning, crying, clutching herself, and the nightmares began to grow in intensity. She started sleeping badly. She would put off going to bed until later and later and then, dreading the dreams, slept very shallowly, trying to ward them off. Her housemistress noticed the way she was looking and asked her if she was feeling all right. Roz said yes, perfectly, and worked even harder, acted even tougher. And then one morning, right in the middle of a math tutorial, she started to cry and couldn't stop.

After an hour or so, the matron, alarmed, phoned her father. He was in New York; Eliza was in France; Letitia was on holiday in Florence; and Sarah Brownsmith, completely at a loss as to what to do, consulted Susan Johns, who was, as Sarah said to Susan apologetically, at least a mother herself.

As a result Roz found herself opening the can of worms and releasing them all over Susan that evening in the little house in Fulham where Susan lived and where she had taken Roz, with the school doctor's rather relieved permission, for a few days.

Roz had always liked Susan, but that night she learned to love her. Susan did not do any of the things her father or mother would have done. She did not become hysterical or act particularly appalled or threaten to inform the police or attach the merest suspicion of blame to Roz, and naturally enough, not being Roz's mother, she did not go through the nauseating process of debasing herself, claiming it was all her fault, and offering her the world in order to help her recover.

She merely listened, quietly and calmly, handing Roz tissues, holding her in her arms occasionally when the tears became so overpowering she was unable to speak, asked sensible questions, made her lots of cups of tea, offered her a drink, and even managed to make her laugh by forcing her to repeat, her own lips twitching slightly, the description of du Chene lying naked on the floor, covering his private parts with his little monkey hands.

"Well," she said when Roz had finally finished. She had finally stopped crying, too, and was sitting exhausted but calm in the corner of the sofa. "None of it sounds too bad. Don't misunderstand me; I can see it was perfectly awful, and I think you handled it wonderfully. You've been amazingly mature about it all, but I just don't think you have to go on worrying about it. Your big mistake was not telling your mother that morning, just talking about it straightaway, so it didn't have to fester away for months."

"But I told you," said Roz, tears welling up in her eyes again, "I couldn't tell her. She's having a bad enough time as it is without that sort of thing to worry about, and anyway—"

"I know. You don't want to have to relive it."

"No. I couldn't face it. I'd just got away from him. It."

"Even so, you've been reliving it ever since."

"Yes. Sometimes I can't think of anything else. It's so horrible."

"Of course. Very horrible. Don't get me wrong, I can see exactly how horrible it was."

"Can you? Can you really?" Roz asked, looking at her with suddenly hostile eyes. "I don't think you can. Nobody can, who hasn't gone through it."

"Roz," said Susan briskly, "when I was about twelve, my uncle used to get drunk and wait till my mum and dad were out and touch me up in the front room. I didn't know what to do, whom to tell. I felt somehow I ought to like it because he was grown-up so it must be right. Sometimes even now I can remember how that felt."

Roz looked at her with a kind of desperate hope. "Really? And you —well, you got to—well—"

"Like men? And sex? Yes, of course. Maybe it took me a bit longer than it should have, but once I found someone I could trust, it was fine. You'll find the same."

Roz felt as if a great boulder had been rolled away from her path.

"Look," Susan said, "will you trust me to handle it? I won't make a big deal of it; I'll play it down. But I'll have to tell your father something, because the school is bound to mention it. And I can suggest your mother might need help. Then it'll be out of our hands. All right?"

"All right. Thank you. You're wonderful, Susan."

JULIAN LEFT FOR France forty-eight hours later and returned with the shares back in his possession. A week later Eliza came home, very thin, rather pale, but extremely cheerful, and told Roz she was divorcing du Chene.

"Julian," Susan said, "how on earth did you manage that?"

"It's much better you don't know," he said. "You would be even more disapproving of me than you are already. Which I wouldn't like. Let's just say I gave that little squirt a very nasty hour or so, and he came to see that it was greatly in his interest to do as I asked."

"I suppose you blackmailed him?"

"Mrs. Johns! What an ugly concept." He paused, then smiled at her.

"You did, didn't you?"

"Well, let's say I pointed out to him how very antisocial his behavior was."

"And Eliza?"

"Well, Eliza, of course, was delighted to find herself free."

"Yes, but—"

"But what? You said I should help her. I do a lot because you say so, Susan. I'm always telling you that."

"Did you tell Eliza about Roz?"

"Of course. She was appalled. She really had no idea. If she had, I'm sure she would have left him immediately. But we agreed that she should never discuss it with Roz. On your advice. Again." He was silent for a moment. "We seem to do everything you tell us, my family and I."

A few weeks later Julian Morell asked Susan Johns to marry him.

Not without considerable regret, she turned him down.

·12·

DOROTHY KELLY LOOKED ANXIOUSLY across the table at Hugo Dashwood. She found it hard to talk to him, harder to ask him for help, but Lee had insisted that she could and should, and Hugo himself on his regular visits to Santa Monica had always stressed the same thing.

"It's nothing I can put my finger on, Mr. Dashwood," she said. "But I just don't feel happy about Miles. He isn't working at school, but then lots of boys of fifteen don't. And he seems a mite too interested in girls, but then, at his age I suppose he would be. I think he's a drifter. No sense of purpose. Now, Lee was determined he should go to college. He wants to go to college, he says, but he doesn't seem to understand you have to work to get there. He never does anything. You know what his grades are like. Straight A's in math and geography and Spanish, and D's and E's in everything else."

"Well, look," said Hugo, "it doesn't sound too worrying. Let me talk to Miles. Where is he?"

"Friday afternoon—oh, he'll be playing water polo. He's on the team. He's very good, I believe. And they have a great water polo team at Santa Monica High. I mean not everyone can get on it."

Hugo smiled gently at her pride in the boy who worried her so much, then went for a walk along the Palisades until Miles returned. It was a ravishing May afternoon: hot, clear, brilliant. The surf was up, the sea looked unreal in its blueness. The white beach was modestly littered with people. Cyclists zoomed along the boardwalk, looking like tiny whirling toys from where he stood high above them. He wondered if Miles ever rode the bike he had given him last Christmas. He hadn't seemed very much interested, merely politely grateful.

He decided to drive up to the school and watch for Miles to come out. He wouldn't declare himself, show himself to be meeting him, just observe him. It might be interesting.

He got back in the car and drove along Ocean Avenue and turned into Pico. The school was quiet; most of the kids had gone home already. He parked fifty yards down the street and waited.

Miles came out in a crowd, his arm around the shoulders of one of the prettiest girls he had ever seen. Dark, tall, slender, with big breasts and long long legs, she was quite outstanding. But then, so was Miles. Tall as a man already, with golden blond hair—a pity he chose to wear it hanging down to his shoulders, but that was not an insurmountable problem—and piercing dark blue eyes in his tanned face. He looked wonderful. Hugo felt a stab of pride and another of envy —of his youth, his lack of responsibility, his blatant come-and-get-me sexuality. And he was only fifteen! No wonder Mrs. Kelly was worried.

Miles was dressed all in white—long white shorts, a white sweatshirt, and white loafers. It all emphasized his golden, utterly desirable youth.

The others were going the opposite way; Miles and the girl waved to them and set off toward the ocean and Miles's house. They stopped suddenly, looked into each other's eyes, and Miles bent and kissed her briefly. They were a charming couple. Hugo found it hard to fault them. He let them walk home, waited ten minutes, then turned the car around and drove back to the house.

They were sitting on the patio when he got there. Miles looked wary; he had grown to associate Hugo with trouble. He did not get up or greet him formally.

"Hi, Hugo."

"Good afternoon, Miles."

"Donna, this is an old friend of my mom's, Hugo Dashwood. Hugo, this is Donna Palladini."

"Hi, Mr. Dashwood."

She seemed nice. Hugo smiled at her. "How do you do."

She smiled back. "I love your accent."

"Thank you. Of course we think we don't have one, that it is you who have the accent."

"Is that right? Well, I guess I'd better be getting home."

"Donna, don't go," said Miles, putting out a brown arm. "What's the rush?"

"Mom's expecting me. She'll be worried."

"I'll see you out."

Hugo heard them talking quietly in the hall. "I don't want to intrude," Donna said. "He feels like family."

"He is not family," Miles said. "No way. Don't go, Donna."

"I have to. I'll see you tomorrow."

Miles walked back onto the patio. He didn't look at Hugo, just sat down on the swing seat and picked up a surfing magazine.

"Do you like surfing?"

"Uh-huh."

"Do you do much of it?"

"Some."

"Donna seems like a very nice girl."

"She is."

"Have you been together for long?"

"Hugo, I don't want to be rude, but that really is none of your business."

"Miles, you are being rude. I was only being friendly."

"Sorry."

"So have you?"

"Have I what?"

"Been with Donna long?"

"She's in my class at school. Always has been. So in a way, yes."

"I see. How are your grades?"

"About the same."

"Not so okay."

"Depends which ones you're looking at."

"I suppose so. But, Miles, next year you'll be a sophomore in high school, and after that it's only two years to college. Don't you think you should try to pull up all of your grades? You know you're capable of it."

"Yeah, I know. Don't worry, Hugo, I will. When the time comes, I'll pull out all the stops."

"It may be a little late by then. You'll have missed out on a lot of groundwork."

"No, I can make it up." He yawned. "Hugo, again, I don't want to be rude, but my grades really don't have anything to do with you."

"Well, Miles, they do in a way. I promised your mother I would keep an eye on you, and your grandmother turns to me in a crisis. I do feel responsible for you. If you flunk out now and don't get into college, I shall have to find you something to do. Or I shall be letting your mother down. So don't make me do that, please."

"Okay."

It was an altogether unsatisfactory conversation.

"I think it's his friends," Mrs. Kelly said later when she and Hugo were alone. "They're all like that. No manners. Hang around the beach all the time. Never do anything constructive. I don't think it's healthy."

"I wondered if it mightn't be better for Miles if you moved out of Santa Monica."

"What? Oh, I don't think that's a good idea. He would be really unhappy. He likes school. He loves sports. He'd resent it bitterly."

"Not far away, just out of town a little way. Say, to Malibu. He loves the surf, he told me, and he could stay in the same school. You'd have to drive him back and forth for a year, but you could monitor his friendships a lot more closely, and he couldn't spend a lot of time with some of these undesirable types."

Mrs. Kelly looked at him shrewdly. "That's sensible, Mr. Dashwood. I like that idea. But I certainly don't have time to look for a place to live."

"I'll look. Don't worry about that. You wouldn't mind, though? You wouldn't feel you were losing your friends and social life?"

"Don't have any. Don't like the folks down here. Never have. Affected, I call them. No, I wouldn't mind a bit. And I think it would be good for Miles. I really do."

MILES WAS FURIOUS. Hugo drove him out along the Pacific Coast Highway to show him the house he had chosen, an architect-designed wooden building tucked high into the hillside off one of the small canyons a few miles from Malibu Beach. The view was staggering, a great sweep of ocean taking in both sunrise and sunset. Miles looked at it coldly.

"I don't want to move. I like Santa Monica."

"But, Miles, this is a nicer house, and you have more room and you can surf whenever you want to."

"I can surf in Santa Monica."

"But the surf here is world famous."

"I don't want world-famous surf. I like the surf at home."

"And you will still go to the same school. You can still see your friends."

"Not so easily. I'll have to go to school with Gran in the car and get laughed at. I just won't move. I'll stay with Donna. Her mom is always saying I can stay there."

"Miles, next year you'll be sixteen," said Hugo, desperate at the hostility in Miles's face. "I'll buy you a car." He could immediately see the folly of that one; the whole idea of moving was to make Miles's friends less accessible to him. But it was too late; he had said it now.

Miles looked at him shrewdly. "Can I choose the car?"

"Within reason, yes."

Miles shrugged. "I still don't see why we have to move. And it won't change anything. But I guess I have to say yes."

What nobody realized—not even Mrs. Kelly, who cared for him; not even Donna, who loved him—was that Miles's refusal to work at anything that seemed remotely unimportant and uninteresting was a direct result of his grief for his mother. She had taken with her, when she died, Miles's sense of direction. He had coped with his grief, his loneliness, his need to look after himself, but he had been left a very bewildered little boy. He could get through the days, get himself to school, go out to play, talk to his friends, but anything that required any degree of effort was beyond him. For at least a year he survived on the most superficial level, with only his grandmother to provide all his emotional needs. She did her best, but she was a brusque, impatient woman; Lee had been endlessly affectionate, caring, thoughtful, and fun.

By the end of the first year, he had learned to manage without hugs, treats, a concerned ear, a sense of someone being unequivocally on his side, and he had developed a calm self-sufficiency; but he had no emotional or intellectual energy to spare. Consequently, anything demanding he set aside; and by the time he could have coped with it, the pattern was too deeply established to change. And so he went on, as he had always been inclined, doing the things he liked and that seemed to matter to him, and ignoring the other things. It gave him a very clear and pragmatic set of values, and there was no way he was going to set them aside and start working at literature or history because Hugo Dashwood or anyone else told him to.

TWO YEARS LATER, Miles was not entirely sorry they had moved. It gaver him a certain cachet at school, living in Malibu. And it was a nice house. And he had the car, The car—jeez, it was a good car, a 1965 Mustang, and the old creep had bought it for him just like that. He and Donna had had a high old time in the backseat of that car. Justing thinking about being in the car with Donna gave Miles an erection. He still hadn't exactly done it, not all the way. Donna was so sweet he just couldn't push her, and she was so patient and let him feel her up and kiss her breasts and everything. In any case, however much he complained to her, he knew that in his heart of hearts he wouldn't want a girl who'd let him go all the way. Girls who did that were sluts, and there was no way he was going to go around with a slut. Especially now that he was one of the best young surfers on Malibu Beach. He had a position to consider. Not just any girl would do for him.

And the way Donna had looked at the prom the other night in a kind of Gypsy dress—all red, off the shoulders, with a flounced skirt —well, Miles knew he'd certainly gotten the most beautiful girl in Santa Monica that night. He was the envy of not just his class, but the class ahead of his as well. He'd even wished for a minute he hadn't insisted on wearing tennis shoes with his tux just to make the point that he was a rebel. But there it was; he had worn them, and he certainly couldn't go all the way home to Malibu to change.

The summer stretched before him now; three whole months of surfing, and no schoolwork or grades to worry about. The old creep wouldn't be over; he seemed to appear only at important times, like the new school year or Christmas. He'd wanted to come and watch a swimming match, but Miles had changed the date so many times that the creep had given up and said he'd come another year. Miles supposed he'd have to write and tell him his grades; otherwise he'd be on the phone, and there might be a lecture. But he'd improved a lot lately, and he was still getting A's in math and languages—and C's and D's in the rest. Not bad, for absolutely no work.

So tonight he'd drive into town, pick up Donna, and they'd maybe see a movie with some of the others. Later on, they'd go off and neck for a while, then drive down to the ocean and get some cheesecake and coffee at Zucky's, because necking made you hungry. And then after that park down near the ocean, and neck some more. And after they took the girls home, probably they'd all go over to Tony's No. 5 and have some chili dogs and boast about their conquests and finally get tired of all that and go home to bed. Miles smiled with pleasure and anticipation. Life seemed pretty good.

SHE WAS ON the beach at Malibu when he rode down on his bike later that afternoon. Just stretched out on the sand, with a picnic basket beside her. Miles thought he had never seen anyone so beautiful. She had blond curly hair tied back in a ponytail with a blue ribbon, a tipped-up nose all freckled from the sun, and a curvy smiling mouth. She was a delicious pale brown all over—well, all over that he could see—and she was wearing a sea-green bikini cut so high around the legs that he could just see the palest fluff of pubic hair. Miles swallowed, felt an erection growing inside his surfing shorts, and hurried on.

When he felt better, carrying his surfboard for protection, he walked back past her. She was still alone. He looked down at her and smiled. "Hi."

"Hi."

"Are you alone?"

"Only for a little while. My parents are having a drink at Alice's, and my brother is out there pretending he can surf."

She looked at the surfboard. "Do you pretend or can you really do it?"

"I can do it. And I can surf." He grinned at her; she blushed and looked away, embarrassed at the double entendre.

"I'm sorry. I didn't mean to offend you. I get kind of used to talking to the surfies here. I'll go away if you like."

"No, don't, it's all right. I was awfully bored. Do you live around here?"

"Yeah, up in one of the canyons. Right up there." He pointed.

"It looks wonderful. So romantic. What do your parents do?"

"They're both dead. I live with my grandmother."

He was so used to the fact by now he never thought of it upsetting anyone; he was startled to see her eyes fill with tears.

"How sad. I'm sorry."

"It was sad, but I was small when my dad died and only twelve when my mom went, so I've gotten used to it now. Kind of," he added hastily, not wanting to appear hard-hearted. "What about your folks?"

"They're both in the motion picture business. My dad is a director and my mom is a costume designer."

"Wow. Do you live in L.A.?"

"Yes."

"Whereabouts?"

"In Beverly Glen."

Miles nearly dropped his surfboard. Not in his wildest imaginings had he ever thought of even talking in a friendly way to a girl who lived in Beverly Glen. Some of the richest, most cultured, high-class people in Los Angeles had their homes in Beverly Glen. That was real money, real, real money.

He realized she was looking at him oddly. "Sorry. I guess I looked kinda surprised. I don't meet many folks from Beverly Glen."

"We don't live at the ritzy end. Just a couple of blocks up from Santa Monica Boulevard. I mean it's nice, but it's not Stone Canyon."

"Oh," said Miles.

"What's your name?"

"Miles Wilburn."

"Joanna Tyler."

"It's nice to meet you, Joanna."

"Nice to meet you, too. Are you hurrying off somewhere?"

"No. But your parents might not like you to be talking to a poor orphan from Malibu."

"Don't be silly. My parents believe in democracy. My father is a socialist. That's why they don't send me to boarding school, and that's why we're here on the public beach and not on one of the snotty private ones."

"So where do you go to school?"

"Marymount High."

It was several cuts above Miles's school, but it was still a public school. Miles felt bolder.

"Will you be coming here again?"

"I don't know. Depends how my brother does pretending to surf. Oh, he's coming now. Tigs! Tigs! How'd you do?"

Tigs, thought Miles. What a dumb name. He smiled earnestly at the boy who was approaching them, carrying a brand-new surfboard awkwardly.

"Okay," he said. "It's not as easy as it looks."

"I told you it wouldn't be," she said. "Tigs, this is Miles. Miles, Tigs. Short for Tigger, short for Thomas."

Miles couldn't see how Tigger could possibly be short for Thomas, but didn't want to say so. He shook Tigs's outstretched hand.

"Hi."

"Miles can really surf, Tigs. He could give you a few tips, I'll bet."

Tigs looked at Miles longingly. "Could you really? I'd be extremely grateful."

Miles noticed the boy's accent. He sounded East Coast, different from his sister. Anyway, he didn't seem too bad, and if it was going to make him a friend of Joanna's he would spend all day and all night teaching Tigs to surf.

IF THIS WAS love, Miles thought, it was very uncomfortable. What he had felt for Donna had been much nicer. He had been able to concentrate on other things and had never worried about what he ought to say or wear or do when he was with her. Life with Joanna was initially one big anxiety.

But it was worth it. Every time he looked at her exquisite little golden-brown face, her freckle-spangled nose, her surprised blue eyes, he discovered afresh where his heart was, for it turned right over, not just once but several times.

What was amazing was that she obviously liked him back. Very much. Probably she didn't love him—Miles couldn't in his wildest, most self-confident dreams think that—but liking him was enough for now. He could tell she liked him because she was so friendly. That very first day she had insisted on introducing him to her parents, and they were really nice, too. Her father was a tall, gentle man with golden hair and a shaggy beard, and her mother was small and sparkly like Joanna, but with dark curly hair and a body that certainly didn't look like it had borne two children. They had been nice to Miles and talked to him for a while, and then insisted he come and join them for a drink at Alice's. When Tigs had asked him if he would maybe give him another surfing lesson soon and Miles had said "Yes, sure," Mr. and Mrs. Tyler had said Tigs must bring Miles back afterward for supper or a barbecue or something.

He had been up to their house in Beverly Glen several times now. Joanna had been right; it wasn't one of the mega-mansions, but it was still about five times bigger than any house Miles had ever been inside, a charming Colonial-style white house with God knows how many bedrooms, every one with its own bathroom and Jacuzzi. The house also had a huge living room with a marble floor, antique furniture, a uniformed maid, a kitchen straight out of *House and Garden*, an enormous yard, a massive pool, a tennis court, and three garages. Both Joanna and Tigs had cars: twin VW Rabbit convertibles.

But the Tylers, for all their money, were just the nicest people Miles thought he had ever met—friendly, unsnobby, welcoming, and generous.

His grandmother had been very sniffy about the friendship: "People like that think they're doing you a real favor," she'd said, "letting you into their homes. Don't you get taken in; you'll end up getting hurt."

But Miles didn't see how he could possibly be hurt; the Tylers just seemed to like having him there. The house was always full of people anyway, friends and neighbors. He very quickly learned where Joanna got her friendliness and charm; it came from growing up in a household that was one long party. He found himself there more and more often, and not just after he had given Tigs a surfing lesson. They invited him over every Sunday for a barbecue lunch, and Joanna very often asked him to come and play tennis. He had never learned the game, but he was naturally gifted at all sports and in weeks was playing better than a lot of the other kids who were there.

Not all of the kids were as nice to him as Joanna and Tigs; they clearly regarded him as an upstart, an intruder in their golden world. Miles didn't care. He didn't care about anything at all as long as he could be close to Joanna. And besides, he learned fast. He had a surprisingly acute social sense and charming manners when he put his mind to them; he swiftly absorbed the small differences in behavior between himself and Tigs: the way Tigs stood up when an adult came into the room, called older men sir but did not call older women .

ma'am, let girls go in front of him through doorways, pushed their chairs in for them at the table, used a linen napkin, and ate a little less. He learned to keep quiet about his school and to talk vaguely about Berkeley when people asked him about college. He found that Malibu was a usefully neutral address; a house in Latego Canyon was much better than downtown Santa Monica. Moreover he found, somewhat to his own discomfort, that he felt more and more at home, more comfortable with the Tylers and their friends; he did not feel like an intruder, a cuckoo in the nest, but like a fledgling from Beverly Glen and its environs. He began not so much to look down on his old friends and his grandmother as to regard them with the same kind of detached interest he had originally given the Tylers, as if they were different from him in some way.

It had meant breaking up with Donna, of course, and that had been awful. She had looked at him with infinite scorn in her dark eyes and said, "Okay, Miles, if that's how you want it, go and learn to be a rich girl's pet. Only don't come running back to me when she gets tired of you. And she will." And she had left him then and there, not upset at all as far as he could see, just angry and contemptuous, which had been worse in a way.

He had been with Donna for a long time; everything he knew about girls and their bodies he had learned from her. How soon you could kiss them, how to make them want you to do more, how to stroke their breasts gently, not maul them, what a vagina felt like, how to find the bit that got them excited, when to approach it, how to know when they had their period and to show you knew without actually saying anything, how to reassure them that you weren't going to try to force them to go all the way while actually trying like mad to persuade them. He owed Donna a lot and he knew it, and he felt terrible about leaving her; but love was love, and what he felt for Joanna was utterly different. He had to be free to pursue her—and it.

Miles at seventeen was not only good-looking and attractive; he had a certain confidence about him, a kind of subtlety to his sexuality that persuaded girls he knew his way around better than he did. Girls who didn't know him always imagined that he had been to bed, gone all the way, lots of times. He seemed so much more sophisticated than most of the sweaty, fumbling boys his age. Donna, of course, straightened them out, because she didn't want anyone thinking she was a slut and been to bed with him, but she didn't want people thinking anyone else had been to bed with him either. Nevertheless the initial impression was one of experience.

And this was certainly the impression Joanna got. She was totally inexperienced herself. Apart from a few fumbles in cars after parties or in the garden or maybe occasionally even a bedroom, and a lot of kissing, of course, she had no idea what sex meant. She knew the theory, of course. Her mother was a liberated and civilized woman. She'd had all the right conversations with Joanna and given her all the right books to read as well, but until she met Miles, Joanna had never felt so much as a flicker of sexual desire. That had now, however, radically changed. She could scarcely think of anything else these days. The very first time he had kissed her, slowly, deliciously, confidently, she had felt hot, startled, charged. She had woken in the night with all kinds of strange sensations in her body. Exploring it and them cautiously, she discovered vivid pleasures and sensations; she fell asleep dreaming of Miles and awoke longing to see him again, to be held by him, kissed by him.

Gradually he showed her all the things he had learned with Donna, never pushing her, never worrying her, always reassuring her that he would never, ever do anything she didn't want, or that would be dangerous. Through the summer, Joanna learned a great deal not only about her own body but about Miles's as well—what she could do to excite him, how to get him to excite her, how to prolong the feeling until it was almost unendurable, and then how to relieve it in the delicious explosions of pleasure they could give each other.

In their last year of high school they were both seriously distracted from their studies. They could think of very little but each other and sex. Where the one ended and the other began neither was certain. William and Jennifer Tyler watched them with a fairly benign anxiety. They liked Miles very much, but they were not happy with the fact that Joanna was doing virtually no work and her grades were dropping steadily.

Finally they told her she was not to see Miles except on Sundays until Christmas. If by then her grades had improved, they would review the situation. Joanna stormed and cried and accused them of being snobs and prejudiced—to no avail.

"Darling, we love Miles. We really do. More than almost any of the other boys who come here. But he is a serious distraction. And your work is important." Jennifer looked at her daughter shrewdly. "The last thing we want is to send you away to school now. But if these grades don't improve, that's what we'll have to do."

"You wouldn't be so cruel. You couldn't!" Joanna cried, her eyes big with fright.

"We could. Now, we're not asking a lot. Only that you give him up during the week. Get to work and prove we can trust you."

Joanna wondered how they would feel if they knew they couldn't trust her in other ways, too. In September she had made the trip to Dr. Schlesinger and asked for the Pill. Then she had gone to bed with Miles. After a slightly difficult, painful start, he had proved marvelously clever and skillful, and she sensual and responsive. They spent evening after evening in her little suite, enjoying the most triumphantly pleasing sex, relaxed in the knowledge that her parents, too sensitive and liberated to interfere, would merely walk past the closed doors and never dream of knocking or coming in.

And then they discovered a new pleasure. Accepting the disciplines, the limits set on their meeting, with fairly good grace, they began to experiment with drugs. Miles had been smoking pot for some time; it had been popular with his crowd at school for years, regarded as almost wholesome. "It's organic," Donna had assured him earnestly, passing him his very first joint. And on one or two memorable occasions he and Joanna had tried LSD. Miles had found it at once terrifying and exhilarating. The way it invaded his senses, took him on a journey through colors and shapes and sensations, would have ensnared him very quickly had it not been for a sobering incident that frightened him more than he ever cared to admit.

All the kids at all the Hollywood parties smoked pot; their parents, who smoked it also, for the most part turned a blind eye. But then one night, all the crowd Miles and Joanna went around with were busted at a party just after the New Year. The Tylers and Mrs. Kelly were both woken in the night by the police, along with a lot of other respectable and shaken parents, and told their children would be charged. They had to pay a bail of five hundred dollars for each of them, and also pay a lawyer who made a most luxurious living for himself entirely out of defending Beverly Hills kids against drug charges.

The Tylers forbade Miles ever to see Joanna again; Mrs. Kelly virtually placed Miles under house arrest, contacted Bill Wilburn, a cousin of Dean's who lived in San Francisco, for further legal advice and support, and took the unprecedented step of phoning Hugo Dashwood to enlist his help.

Bill Wilburn didn't like Hugo Dashwood. He had met him at Lee's funeral and found him stiff and overbearing. He couldn't see what his cousin could have liked about him, and he resented the rather proprietary interest he took in the family.

"Good of you to come, Mr. Dashwood, but I think we can handle this ourselves, just keep it in the family."

"I like to think of myself as family, Mr. Wilburn. Mrs. Kelly has asked me to help."

"Whatever you might like to think, Mr. Dashwood, you're not. And I can't see how you can help."

"You may need money."

"We may."

"Let me provide it."

"Why should you do that?"

"I promised Lee I'd keep an eye on Miles. I want to honor that promise."

"I see."

"And I am quite prepared to talk to Miles. To try to help sort things out."

"I don't know if that would be constructive right now," said Wilburn, remembering Miles's nickname for Hugo. "He's very withdrawn."

"I daresay, but he has to realize he can't stay withdrawn. He has to make amends. He has to start rebuilding his life."

"Mr. Dashwood, I'm not making excuses for Miles, and I agree with you in a way, but he's had a terrible shock and he's in a strange state. I would advise against interfering just now."

"Mr. Wilburn," said Hugo, his mouth twitching slightly with suppressed rage, "I think the situation warrants interfering. Anyway, we can come back to that. What is the legal situation?"

"It's not too bad. There are charges against all the kids. There'll be a stiff fine, and a record, I guess. Not good, but not disastrous."

"Will he have to appear in court?"

"Yup."

"When?"

"Next week."

"I'll stay till then."

"You don't have to."

"I want to."

MILES AND HIS friends were fined a thousand dollars each. Any repetition of the offense, they were told, would result in a jail sentence. The judge read them a lecture, and they were driven away from the courtroom by their parents, subdued and silent. Miles was driven away by Hugo.

"Now, Miles, I don't want to pile on the agony and say what the judge did all over again."

"Please don't."

"But I have spoken to you before about your behavior generally, and I simply don't like it. I don't like the direction you are going in."

"I don't care what you like or don't like. It has nothing to do with you."

"That is your opinion."

"It's a fact."

"Only as you see it."

Miles was silent.

"Now then, I have some suggestions to make to you. Miles, look at me."

Miles turned and looked out of the window.

"Miles," Hugo said, "if you are not very careful, I shall have you sent far away, and you will not see any of your friends for a very long time."

"You couldn't."

"I most certainly could. Your grandmother is your legal guardian, and she is most emphatically in favor of the idea. Now will you please do me the courtesy of listening to me properly?"

Miles turned with infinite slowness and presented an insolent face to Hugo. "Okay."

"Right. Now, the first thing I want is for you to promise me never to see this particular crowd again."

Miles looked at him and grinned. "Funny, isn't it? You dragged me away from my high school friends because you thought they were a bad influence. Then I get in with some nicely raised rich kids and look what happens. All kinds of trouble."

"Yes, well, I'm afraid neither a modest nor a rich background is a guarantee against wrongdoing. Anyway, do I have your word on that?"

"I guess you do for now."

"What do you mean?"

"We'll all be kept under lock and key for a while. Most of them are in boarding school, and Joanna's parents have forbidden me to see her." He was silent, his face morose as he remembered his last conversation with Joanna on the phone, her voice shaken with sobs and fear. Not only had her parents been shocked and horrified by the arrest; they had betrayed all their own liberal ideals and thrown the book at Joanna when they found her stash of birth control pills during a search of her room.

"Miles, I don't want a promise with a time limit. These people are not good for you. I forbid you to see them anymore, ever."

"He shrugged. "Okay.""

"Now, I have been thinking. You're an intelligent boy, and I think you could get into a good college. I am prepared to send you to one, a really good one, on the East Coast, maybe. It would be a wonderful opportunity for you. You would have to work very, very hard to get in. You would need a private tutor every night until you went. God knows if you could even get in. But I'm prepared to make the push if you are. Your sporting background might help."

Miles was looking at him thoughtfully. "I don't want to go to some snooty East Coast college. Could I maybe go to Berkeley?"

"Maybe you could. Maybe you couldn't. You don't seem to understand how difficult this is going to be. Are you prepared to make the effort and agree to my other conditions?"

Berkeley! Miles thought. That would be cool. That would impress the world. That would even maybe impress Joanna's parents. Miles sighed. It was probably worth it.

"Okay," he said to Hugo as the car pulled up in front of the house. "I agree. And"—he wrenched the word from himself with an almost physical effort—"thanks."

"That's all right. I want to be proud of you."

Miles thought he might throw up.

"OLD DASHWOOD WANTS to send me to a smart college," he said the next day to Bill Wilburn, who had just read him a lesser lecture and drawn a check from his mother's estate to pay the fine; he had refused Dashwood's offer, saying this was an expense Miles should ultimately shoulder.

"He mentioned some swanky East Coast places," Miles went on. "I said I'd like to go to Berkeley. He said okay."

Bill put down his pen and looked at Miles in genuine astonishment. "That would cost thousands of dollars."

"I know. He seems to have lots of money."

"But why should he spend it on you?"

"Don't know. He seems to feel strongly about what I do."

"Well, you're a very lucky kid."

"Yeah, I guess so."

"What makes you think one of these colleges will take you?"

With the supreme confidence of one who has failed only because he has chosen to, Miles said, "They'll take me."

"Fine." Bill appeared to have dropped the subject, but his mind was seething. What in God's name was this guy about, spending that kind of money on some kid who had nothing to do with him? It didn't make any sense. He decided to do a little investigating before he went back to San Francisco.

"MRS. KELLY, DO you have all the old papers of Lee and Dean's—you know, wills, financial documents, that kind of thing? I'd like to look at them. Just in case this matter gets taken any further."

"They're all in my room. I'll get them for you. Do you think it might?"

"What? Oh, get taken further? No, but it's better to be prepared, just in case. Thanks. Oh, and how much did Lee tell you about this Dashwood character? Just how good a friend was he?"

"Nothing like that," Mrs. Kelly snapped. "Lee never looked at another man after Dean. There was nothing between those two at all. Although I don't mind telling you, as you're family, I wondered about it myself. He's been around ever since I can remember. Before Miles was born. I even asked her about it when she was dying. Dean once did Hugo a good turn, she said, and Hugo always said he'd wanted to repay him. When Dean died he came to see Lee and was a real comfort to her. But not in that way. Not how you might think."

"Okay. I just wondered. He seems to feel pretty possessive about Miles."

"Yes, well, he promised Lee he'd look after him. See he turned out right. I'm an old woman; there's a limit to what I can do. And I've been grateful for his help, so don't you go criticizing him, now. He's been very good to us."

"I won't say another word. Now let me have those papers."

"I want them back."

"You can have them back tomorrow."

THE PAPERS WERE routine: Dean's will, Lee's will, a list of funeral expenses, Miles's birth certificate, doctors' bills for Lee.

Doctors! thought Bill. They always had a lot of information. He wrote down the number of the cardiologist who treated Dean, put the rest of the papers back in the file, and picked up the telephone.

"YES, I REMEMBER Dean Wilburn. A tragedy. He was doing so well; that was the irony. He'd lost a lot of weight. He was getting fitter. And so hopeful."

"About what?"

"Life in general. Of course the one thing he most hoped for wasn't possible. I—" He hesitated.

"What?"

"I shouldn't tell you; it's confidential."

"Dr. Burgess, how can it be confidential now? The man's been dead for seven years. And I'm a relative."

"Even so. Oh, all right. He desperately wanted to have another child. Seemed to think that if he got fit and gave up drinking, all that kind of thing, it might happen."

"So? Could it have happened?"

"Not for him."

"Why not?"

"Because he was absolutely sterile. Totally. A zero sperm count. It puzzled me, because as far as I could see from the tests we ran, he must always have been sterile. I could not imagine how he could ever have fathered a child. I said so to him. I told him he'd been very, very fortunate, that his son was one of nature's miracles."

"Really? Lee never told me any of this."

"Lee? Oh, the wife. Well, why should she? You're only a cousin by marriage. These things are hurtful and difficult in a relationship. Besides . . ."

"What?"

"Oh—forgive me. It's just that some people might—might misinterpret it. Think—"

"Think what?"

"Well, that perhaps your cousin wasn't the boy's father. People are very cynical, you know. Eager to think the worst."

A loud noise like cymbals was beating in Bill Wilburn's ears. He seemed to be seeing the doctor down at the end of a long tunnel. Phrases kept repeating in his mind, tumbling in a wild pattern like a kaleidoscope: "Perhaps your cousin wasn't the boy's father . . . one of nature's miracles . . . a dreadful thing, her husband dying . . . been around ever since I can remember, before Miles was born . . . thousands of dollars . . . he seems to feel strongly about what I do."

He swallowed hard. "Thank you, Doctor."

"My pleasure."

BILL WILBURN WENT for a long walk along the Palisades. The more he thought about it, the more sense it made. Hugo Dashwood was Miles's father. And didn't want him to know. Probably had made some kind of damn fool promise to Lee. Well, it was probably better. There was no point telling the boy now. It would only upset him, make him feel bad about his parents.

Should he do anything, say anything? No, it was all much too delicate. Better to stay quiet. If it was ever really necessary to come forward, he would. If there was any more trouble. Or if anyone ever really needed to know.

· 13 ·

PEOPLE REACTED IN VERY DIFFERENT ways to the fact that Camilla North was at last formally established as Julian's mistress. Letitia was outraged; Susan was hurt almost beyond endurance; Eliza was amused; but the person most deeply affected, and indeed shocked, was Roz.

Roz had thought herself freed from Camilla. She had heard how Camilla, goaded beyond endurance when Julian took up with a much-fêted young model, had resigned from Morell's and set up her own very successful advertising agency in New York. Roz had been amazed—blinded as she was to Camilla's talents by her strong dislike—and she had thought that was the end of a rather long and dreary chapter in her life. Now she had to face not only Camilla's presence again, but the fact that her father clearly wanted it, enjoyed it, and indeed could not manage without it. It changed the part of her life that she spent with her father greatly for the worse; it changed her perception of him in much the same way; and it reinforced her determination not to work for him after she left Cambridge, as everyone insisted on assuming. Camilla was not, to be sure, working in the company anymore. She was spending at least three-quarters of her time in New York, although there was talk of her setting up a London branch of North Creative, her advertising agency, but the fact remained that there she stood, a beautiful, self-satisfied, humorless testimony to Julian's dependence on her, and Roz did not know how to bear the thought of it.

CAMILLA ON THE other hand was perfectly happy. For the first time in her life she had a cause, she was genuinely needed, and she was finding it intensely rewarding.

The cause was Julian's impotence.

God and Julian alone knew what it had cost him to tell her about it. Camilla found the thought quite overwhelming; unemotional as she was, she had felt tears pricking at the back of her eyes as she sat, hands in her lap, listening carefully to him as they sat on the veranda of the house in Turtle Cove, Eleuthera.

He had phoned her at her parents' house in Philadelphia, where she had been staying for a week, and first asked her, then begged her, to come to the Bahamas for a few days.

"I need you, Camilla," he had said, and she could hear the genuine emotion in his voice, so rarely there. "I need you very badly. Please, please come."

And so she had flown to Nassau, and he had met her there in the small plane he kept on Eleuthera, and taken her to Turtle Cove, shown her very formally into the guest bedroom, and said he would be waiting for her on the veranda with some extremely good cold champagne when she was ready. She emerged quite quickly, looking ravishing, in a jade green silk pajama suit from Valentino, her red hair drifting on her shoulders. After she had had half a glass of the champagne, and he had had about three, he began to talk to her about his problem.

It had begun when he was having an affair with Araminta Jones, the new face for Juliana cosmetics, so demanding, so selfish—and so young, Camilla thought to herself sagely—just occasionally, but of course it was a cumulative thing; once the fear was there, the knowledge that it might happen, it did happen again and again. Araminta had not been good about it, not reassuring at all, and then there had been the crisis with the company, the anxiety over the shares and a possible takeover bid; it had grown worse.

"Didn't you take any advice, have any therapy?" asked Camilla. "It's so important, Julian, to get help immediately in these matters, not to try to handle it yourself. You can do untold damage, reinforce the problem . . ."

And yes, he said, interrupting her, yes, he had, as a matter of fact, and only Camilla would know how serious that meant the situation had been, regarding these things as he did with such deep distaste and distrust. He had seen a marvelous woman, and she had been very helpful. He had begun to see an improvement, but then had come the latest series of debacles: the failure of the pharmaceutical launch, Susan's rejection of his proposal—he spared himself nothing in this story, Camilla noticed, not sure whether she was gratified that he was so totally debasing himself or her, or outraged that he should have asked Susan to marry him—Eliza's new and patent happiness with the monumentally rich and powerful Jamil Al-Shehra, Araminta's departure from his life and his bed. And it had all begun again; it was a nightmare of despair and fear. He had become afraid even to try now, and somehow, he felt, indeed he knew, he said, that Camilla, with her great understanding of him and her unique position in his life, and also her very careful and serious approach to sexual matters, was probably the only person in the world who could help.

He sat looking at her in silence then, so unnaturally and strangely anxious and diffident, after what she felt was probably the most, indeed the only, honest conversation he had ever had with her, and Camilla's heart had turned over, and she had felt herself filled with a great warmth of tenderness toward him, and what she supposed was love, and she had smiled and leaned forward and kissed him on the cheek, and said, her brown eyes even more than usually earnest, "Julian, I don't know when I've felt happier or more honored."

She felt something else as well, something that she had rarely felt in her life, with Julian or indeed anyone: a sudden lightning bolt of sexual desire.

CAMILLA KNEW A lot about impotence. She had studied it very carefully as a subject over the years, because everybody knew that powerful women were a threat to men; they emasculated them. While power in a man was an aphrodisiac, in a woman it was the reverse. And being a powerful woman, she had always recognized it as a syndrome and a potential factor in her relationships, and something she should be prepared to face. She had not, however, expected to have to face it in connection with Julian Morell.

She knew a great many possible approaches, both psychological and physical; she knew it was the most difficult problem of all to handle, and quite extraordinarily delicate; and that quite possibly Julian would have to go into therapy whether she could personally help him or not. However, there was obviously no physical reason for it; the root cause was manifestly stress, caused by professional failure and reinforced by an unsympathetic response from his sexual partners; there seemed to be some hope therefore, she felt, that she might be able to help to at least a limited degree.

That night, therefore, after a light dinner, accompanied by only a little alcohol—both at Camilla's instigation—she joined him in the master bedroom and attempted to put some of the theories into practice.

"The most important thing," she told him earnestly, as she drew the sheets over their naked forms and pulled his head gently toward her lovely breasts—"is that you shouldn't even begin to think about having an erection. We should just enjoy the feel of our bodies being together and the sensations of closeness on every level—nothing else."

For three nights she achieved nothing; Julian was increasingly tense and fearful, almost in tears. Camilla, moved by his swift descent from powerful arrogance to helpless humility, tried to remain calm, positive, soothing. They spent their days swimming, sunbathing, sailing; Julian, touched by her devotion and patience, told her repeatedly how much he needed her, wanted her, had missed her. Camilla was perfectly happy. Then on the fourth night he became angry as she lay beside him, trying to soothe his fears, comfort him out of his misery.

"Christ, Camilla," he said suddenly, "just leave me alone, will you? This is a nightmare, I should never have asked you to come. I'm sorry." And he had turned away and shaken her arms off him. A great white anger had come over Camilla, a sense of outrage that he should reject her, even while she understood the reason so well. She also felt a hunger for him, and for sex, so violent she cried out with it.

He had turned again and looked at her with astonishment in his eyes and said, "Camilla, what is it. Whatever is it?"

And she had said, driven out of her usual reserve, her careful, watchful self-restraint, "Christ, Julian, I want you, that's what it is. For the first time in my life I really want you."

"What on earth do you mean?" he said. "We've been having sex for years, marvelous sex," and she had said no, no, they hadn't, it had been marvelous for him, but not for her. She couldn't believe he hadn't realized she had never had an orgasm, with him or with anyone. All her life the whole thing had seemed pointless, futile.

"Do you mean," he said, "that you've been faking all these years?"

"Yes," said Camilla, almost screaming in her sudden rage, "yes, yes, yes. I have been faking, faking orgasms, faking desire. Just to satisfy your monster male ego."

And he sat bolt upright and smiled at her, looking suddenly quite different, younger, more alive. "You bitch," he said. "You clever, devious bitch. I can't believe it of you. I don't believe it. Come here, Camilla, come here. Lie down and bloody well let me help you find out what sex is really all about."

And Camilla, feeling him sinking into her strongly, insistently, reaching her, drawing her into a new wild confusion of liquid pleasure, thought confusedly that this was all wrong, that she should be helping him, healing him, and instead he was helping her, leading her into a new country of hot, soaring peaks and bright exploding waterfalls, and she was lost suddenly. She did not know who she was or what she was doing, but she was moving, following him, climbing him, falling onto him, tearing at him with her hands, her mouth, pulling away from him, feeling him plunging deep, deep into her again, talking to him feverishly, moaning, crying out. She could have gone on, she felt, forever, pursuing this brilliance, this huge, mounting, shuddering delight. She was totally abandoned to him and he to her. And when it was over and they lay quietly apart, still trembling, stroking each other, Camilla wept very gently with pleasure and at long last release, and she looked at Julian, lying there with his eyes closed, an expression of great peace on his face, and saw that his cheeks, too, were wet with tears.

JULIAN CAME UP to Cambridge and took Roz out to lunch to tell her that Camilla would be moving into the house in Hanover Terrace and that from now on she should regard Camilla as at least her unofficial stepmother.

He noticed that Cambridge life seemed to suit Roz. She looked relaxed and somehow younger. She was dressed in the current craze of layers in a dark floral print: a long smock over a full skirt, with a matching turban over her dark hair, and platform-soled blue suede boots.

"You look very nice," Julian added, as a rider to his speech about Camilla. "University life obviously suits you."

"Yes," she said briefly, ignoring the compliment. She looked at him stone-faced and said, "Why not official? Why don't you marry her and be done with it?"

"I would quite like to marry her, as a matter of fact," he said, "but Camilla doesn't want to marry me. Which puts me in my place, I suppose."

"Why doesn't she want to marry you?"

"Camilla values her independence. She is a liberated woman. Like you."

"I don't call it very independent to move into a man's house and let him keep you."

"Roz, I'm not going to keep her. She has her own business. She is a rich woman in her own right."

"Oh. So she isn't going to come back to work for you?"

"Unfortunately not. I wish she would, because she is extremely talented. I miss her input into the company. Her agency will, however, be working on some advertising for us."

"Oh. How old is Camilla?"

"I'm not sure. Let me see, I suppose she must be thirty-six or thirty-seven. Why?"

"Oh, nothing."

"Roz?"

"Yes?"

"Roz, I do hope you and Camilla will learn to be better friends this time round. I'm so extremely fond of you both, it would be nice for me to see you getting on better."

"Daddy," Roz said, "you may be able to fix most things, but you don't seem to understand that you can't order people to like each other. I don't want to be Camilla's friend, and I'm sure she doesn't want to be mine."

"Roz," Julian said, and there was genuine anxiety in his eyes, "why do you dislike Camilla so much?"

"I suppose," she said, watching him carefully, enjoying his insecurity, "because you've always spent a great deal more time and effort fussing over Camilla than you ever have over me."

"Roz, that's not true."

"It's perfectly true."

"Well," he said, in an attempt at lightheartedness, "let's not argue about that. I'm sorry you don't like Camilla and that you're so unhappy about it, but you have your own life now, so maybe I don't have to worry about you and your unhappiness quite so much."

"I don't remember," Roz said, swallowing hard to prevent a rather insistent lump from rising in her throat, looking at him with hard, blank eyes, "you worrying about me and my unhappiness very much when I didn't have my own life."

"Now, Roz, that isn't fair."

"Isn't it?"

"No. I have always put you first."

"Goodness. I didn't realize."

Julian kept his temper with a visible effort. "How's life at Cambridge?"

"It's great, thank you."

"Good. Well, I shall need that brain of yours in the company. I'm glad it's being so well trained."

"Daddy," said Roz, "I've been meaning to tell you for months now. I don't have the slightest desire to work for you. I want to make my own way. Do things on my own terms."

She didn't mean a word of it. She had never wanted the security more, of knowing that he valued her, that the company would one day be hers. But it was worth the risk of losing it just to see the fear and the hurt in his dark eyes.

· 14 ·

ONE COLD, WET MORNING IN NOVEMBER 1979 Julian Morell walked into his office, slammed the door and immediately buzzed for coffee. Sarah Brownsmith looked at the phone and sighed. This was obviously one of the days—increasingly frequent, she noticed—for keeping a low profile.

Julian was running on a fuse so short it ignited almost spontaneously. Everybody had remarked on it, so Sarah did not feel she had to blame herself. Nevertheless, it made life uncomfortable.

She had just switched on the coffee machine and was wondering if she was brave enough to broach the subject of an extra week's leave at Christmas when the phone rang.

"Julian Morell's office."

"Miss Brownsmith. Good morning. How are you?"

The voice was pitched quite low for a woman, at once sexy and brisk. A voice men didn't know quite how to react to. It belonged to Roz, and Sarah's heart sank.

"I'm well, thank you, Mrs. Morell. And you?"

"Very well, thank you, Miss Brownsmith. Is my father there?"

Sarah felt Julian needed Roz on such a day like a dose of strychnine; nevertheless she was the only person in the world, apart from his mother and Camilla North, who she could not refuse to put through.

"He is, Miss Morell, but he's—"

"Tied up at the moment. Of course. What else? Is he free for lunch?"

"No, I'm afraid not."

"Put me through to him, would you, Miss Brownsmith?"

Sarah did so. Two minutes later Julian pressed the intercom.

"Sarah, cancel my lunch with Jack Bottingley, would you? And book a table at the Meridiana. I'm meeting Roz there at one."

ROZ PUT DOWN the phone. She was actually feeling a little nervous. It was one thing persuading her father to see her at the snap of her fingers, to give her whatever she desired as soon as she asked for it, but what she wanted from him today was something rather more

· 236 ·

considerable than a yacht, a horse, or a new wardrobe from Paris or New York. Moreover, it meant going in for some considerable diplomacy on her part, some nibbling at least of humble pie, neither of which she had any talent for or practice in. Nevertheless it had to be done.

Roz had decided that the time had come to claim her birthright. She had wearied of pretending she didn't want it; of working hard but a trifle halfheartedly for other people, for Jamil Al-Shehra, her mother's latest lover, for Marks and Spencer, even for Camilla North, who she had to admit had taught her a great deal. What she wanted to do now was work for her father, to serve her apprenticeship, and to start scaling the real heights. And she knew she would scale them fast.

In addition to her two years' work experience, as her father rather contemptuously described it, Roz had just spent a year at the Harvard Business School. It had been the happiest of her life and the most fascinating. Cambridge had seemed like prep school by comparison. Money, deals, politicking, power—it all fascinated her, made her heart beat faster, gave her a sexual thrill. That was what she wanted, great slices of it; she was prepared to work and sweat and suffer for it. She didn't want men falling at her feet or into her bed; she had sampled some of both, and it had left her for the most part bored and unimpressed. She wanted men where she decided to put them, preferably several seats beneath her on the board.

She knew, she felt in her bones, that she would be able not just to deal with any business situation but to win in it. When she looked at some of the hypothetical problems she had been set to crack at college, when she read the financial pages of the papers, which she devoured daily, it seemed to her she was almost clairvoyant; she could see not just to the end of a problem, a development, a takeover bid, but beyond it. She considered not merely every angle that seemed relevant but a dozen more that did not. She took not just facts and figures into her equations but people, situations, geography, history, even the seasons of the year and the time of day. She knew as surely as she knew her own name that she had a brilliant company brain. All she needed now was something to practice on. She needed her father's help to get it, and she didn't relish asking for it.

JULIAN REACHED THE chic whiteness of the Meridiana five minutes before Roz did. He ordered a bottle of Bollinger, greeted a few of the disparate people he knew there—Grace Coddington, fashion editor of *Vogue*, looking divinely severe in a Jean Muir dress; Terence Conran, charmingly jovial, a fresh cigar in one hand, a glass of Sancerre in the other; Paul Hamlyn—and watched his daughter swing in through the door. He hadn't seen her in months. After Harvard she had stayed with friends in New York and had only been back in London for a week. She'd lost weight and let her hair grow, and as she bent to kiss him, he noticed she had acquired a very expensive-looking necklace, thick gold inset with diamonds and emeralds, which he certainly hadn't bought her, her mother was unlikely to have given her, and she would not have bought herself. Interesting. Who was she seeing with that sort of money?

"Roz," he said. "How nice! How are you? Let me take your coat. I've ordered champagne. I thought this should be a celebration."

Roz sat down, took a glass of champagne, ordered some prosciutto and plain grilled sole, and looked at her father with genuine, if slight, concern.

"You look tired, Daddy. Have you been overworking?"

"I expect so. I enjoy it, you know. It makes a distraction from my social life."

"Aren't you enjoying your social life?"

"Not much. How about you?"

"Not much either. How's Camilla?"

"Camilla is very well," Julian said carefully, wondering if she read the gossip columns. "We had dinner with the father of a friend of yours the other night. Tom Robbinson. Weren't you at school with Sarah, or was it Cambridge? I know she was at your twenty-first birthday party."

"School. Haven't seen her for ages. She was the despair of Cheltenham. She's getting married, isn't she?"

"Yes, after Christmas."

He sighed. The thought of weddings always depressed him. "Nice necklace, Roz."

"Yes," said Roz, "it was a present."

Her tone closed the subject. Julian opened it again.

"From anyone I know?"

"No."

"I see."

"Someone I met at Harvard," Roz said quickly, seeing her father was fast growing irritated by her lack of communicativeness. "Someone called Michael Browning. He came to give a lecture. He lives in New York. He's divorced. I just see him sometimes. May I have some more champagne?"

"Of course," said Julian. He looked at Roz thoughtfully. He knew Michael Browning well. He had made a fortune out of soft drinks in

California, moved to New York and into supermarkets, and ran his business by instinct and the seat of his pants. Not the kind of man he'd really want sleeping with his daughter, which seemed likely if he was buying her that sort of present. But maybe it was a hopeful gesture on his part. At any rate, clearly Roz wasn't going to give any more away just now. He changed the subject.

"How's Mummy?"

"Fine." Roz sounded wary.

"And the charming Mr. Al-Shehra?"

"Oh, charming as ever. He's a darling. So kind to me. He keeps a horse for me at the house they've bought in Berkshire, him and Mummy."

"How nice of him," Julian said shortly.

She put down her fork. "I want to talk to you about something, Daddy."

Julian looked at her, his eyes the familiar blank. "And what is that, Rosamund?"

Things weren't going too well, Roz realized; he never called her Rosamund unless he was displeased with her. She wished fervently she had been less awkward the last couple of times she had seen him.

"It's advice I really need, Daddy." She had rehearsed this bit of her script carefully.

"About?"

"About a job."

"A job? I see."

He was looking at her with an odd, rather shrewd amusement. Roz squirmed, but met his gaze steadily.

"Could you elucidate?"

"I've been offered a job. It is marketing, but they've said I can move around. Really get to know the company."

"Have you? By whom?"

"Unilever. That's what I need advice about. It's such a huge company. Michael—lots of people have said it might swallow me up. What do you think?"

"I don't think the job's good enough for you. You've got a Cambridge degree, you've got some valuable experience, and you're an honors graduate of Harvard. You don't want to start working for some sweaty brand manager from East Anglia."

"How do you know he'll be from East Anglia?"

"They always are."

"That's"—Roz had been about to say "ridiculous," but she managed to stop herself—"really interesting."

"What is?"

"That you don't think I should do it."

"Why?"

"Because I don't think so either."

"And what do you think you should do?"

Roz looked him very straight in the eyes. "Work for you."

He hadn't expected that, and he was impressed by it. It took a kind of courage for her to lay herself so totally open. He had it in his power to reject her absolutely, and she knew it, and knew, moreover, that he was quite likely to do so. Clearly she had even more guts than he'd thought. He put her to the test. "I don't think it's possible."

"Why not? Is it because I've—"

"Rejected me?" He looked at her again with amused eyes.

"Yes. Oh, Daddy, I was just being silly. Young and silly. I'm sorry if it hurt you. It must have seemed very ridiculous. Ungrateful. But you must have known I didn't mean it."

"You seemed to at the time. And you weren't all that young. The last conversation I remember was only about six months ago. How old are you now?"

"Twenty-three."

"Well, anyway—" There was a long pause. Roz braced herself to look at him. He was smiling. "That's not the reason."

"What do you mean?"

"I mean the reason I can't offer you a job is that we don't take Harvard people. Company policy."

Roz went limp with relief. "Daddy, that is just ridiculous. You're joking."

"Not at all. I'm perfectly serious. I warned you before you went there. Only you were busy telling me it didn't matter." He smiled at her again.

"Well it's mad."

"Why?"

"Because Harvard people are the best. Brilliantly trained."

"That's only your opinion."

"No, it's not. It's a very valid, widely held opinion."

"By whom? Other Harvard people? Your friends? Michael Browning?"

"No, people I've talked to. Companies I've applied to. They all want Harvard people. They say their power to analyze and apply theory to practice is outstanding. You're losing some of the best business brains in the country with a policy like that. Whose cockeyed prejudice is it?"

"Mine."

"You should change it."

"Convince me."

"How?"

"From inside the company."

"All right, I will."

She had become so absorbed in the argument that she hadn't noticed where he was leading her. She stopped abruptly, looked at him furiously for a moment, and noticed that his eyes were looking more benign than she had seen them for a very long time.

"Oh, God," she said, "I wish you'd stop playing games with me."

LETITIA MORELL HAD a visitor that afternoon. There was nothing she liked better than entertaining, and at the age of eighty-one she still gave excellent dinner parties. She was wickedly amusing; she broke all the rules, thinking nothing of seating a beautiful nineteen-year-old next to an elderly relic of the British Raj fifty years her senior, or a confirmed homosexual next to a highly desirable, and desirous, divorcée and watching them all having the evening of their lives. People would go to some lengths to get a dinner invitation from Letitia Morell—drop hints, ask her to dinner repeatedly themselves, phone her casually on some weak pretext—but it was none of it any good. To qualify you had to be good-looking or amusing, preferably both. You could be poor, socially modest in exceptional cases, not always entirely well mannered. But you could not be dull.

She still dressed beautifully. She found shopping a little tiring, but many of the designers were charmed and delighted to visit her in First Street with toiles and drawings and take her order; and she was still very slim and trim, her latest passion, introduced to her by the Vicomtesse du Chene, being yoga. It was not at all unusual to arrive and find her dressed in leotard and tights, sitting in the lotus position in her drawing room.

It was thus that her visitor, the vicomtesse herself, found her that November afternoon.

"Darling! How lovely. Nancy, make us some tea, will you? You do want tea, don't you, Eliza? And I think I'll go and change. I get cold in this ridiculous outfit after a bit."

"Of course." Eliza's smile was a trifle too bright. Letitia thought she had probably been crying.

"What is it, darling?" she said, returning in a navy cashmere two-piece outfit and beige calf-length boots, looking just about fifty-five years old. "You're upset."

"No," Eliza said brightly. "No, not at all. I'm getting married."

"My darling! How marvelous. But how on earth have you managed that? I thought Arabian marriages were sacred. Should we be drinking champagne rather than tea?"

"No. Not yet. Well, it might help. Yes, please. Yes, they are sacred. But I'm not marrying Jamil."

"My goodness. What an entertaining child you are. Nancy, will you please bring us a bottle of Bollinger from the fridge and two glasses? Have some yourself if you want it. Now then." She raised her glass to Eliza. "Who is it and why? And why have you been crying?"

"It's Peveril Garrylaig."

"Good heavens. A proper title in the family at last. And a good one, too. A countess. Oh, my grandmother would have been relieved."

"Do you know him?"

"Of course I do. I think he's charming," said Letitia firmly, wondering what, apart from a title, the bluff, born-middle-aged, widowed earl of Garrylaig could possibly offer Eliza that Jamil Al-Shehra could not.

"Well, then, you know what a charmer he is. I adore him. And he adores me. Of course it'll be a big change, living in Scotland, but I always did have a sneaking liking for the country, and the castle is just beautiful, Letitia, quite the most ravishing place. You will come and stay, won't you?"

"Darling, of course I will. All the time. Now then." She looked sharply at Eliza. "What does Mr. Al-Shehra have to say about all this?"

"He's quite happy about it," said Eliza briskly. "Clearly we couldn't go on forever how we were and, well—oh, Letitia, I can't bear it, I simply can't bear it. Please, please tell me I'm doing the right thing."

Tears were streaming down her face. Her green eyes searched Letitia's blue ones wildly, frantically, looking for relief from her pain and her grief.

"Tell me more, darling, when you're ready. I can't tell you anything until I know what it's all about."

Eliza told her. She told her that there was no real future for her with Al-Shehra; that the most passionate love affair could not last forever; that she was forty-three years old and most assuredly not getting any younger; that she was afraid of being alone and lonely; that she wanted to be safe, with a status of her own again; that she was truly, truly fond of Peveril or she wouldn't be doing it; and that she was so unhappy she thought her heart was not just broken but exploded into a million tiny fragments.

She did not tell her that Al-Shehra had wept in her arms the night before, that he had made love to her that morning so sadly, so tenderly, so exquisitely, that she still felt faint remembering the sensations, and that it had taken every fragment of her courage not to change her mind.

"But you do see, Letitia, don't you? It was all right at first, the mistress of a wildly rich Arab potentate, or tycoon or whatever he is; it's all right when you're young, but think of being fifty, sixty, and still in that position, always terrified of new young women coming along, having no status, no standing. I couldn't face it, Letitia; I just couldn't. I need to be married. I have to do this."

"And when did the affair with Peveril begin?"

"It isn't an affair, Letitia," Eliza said with the shimmer of a smile. "Peveril is a gentleman. We shall go to bed on our wedding night and not before."

"How charming. How refreshing. Well, all right, when did you meet him?"

"Last month. At Longchamps. Jamil wanted to take me to the Arc de Triomphe, but then he got gambling and I got cross. Peveril was there with his sisters. One of them knew Julian; he'd been at her coming-out dance. Well, we started talking, and he asked me if he could take me out to lunch one day in London, and it all went on from there."

"It's not very long," said Letitia, frowning.

"I know, and everyone's going to say that, but I have to get it settled quickly, and Peveril wants to; he's lonely and why should we wait?"

"To make sure you're doing the right thing?"

"No, I don't want to do that. Because I might not be. But if I'm not I'll make it work just the same. Just you watch me. He's a good man, and a kind one, and I won't let him down."

·15·

MILES HAD GRADUATED FROM BERKE-
ley, to his own surprise as much as
everyone else's, summa cum laude in
mathematics.

Smiling happily, he walked across
the campus toward Hugo and Mrs.
Kelly, who had attended his graduation along with Father Kennedy—an
ill-assorted trio, he thought, but what
the hell. He looked superb, a beautiful, successful golden boy. He had had
four glorious years; it showed.

"Hi."

"Hello, Miles. Well done."

"Thanks, Hugo."

Mrs. Kelly's eyes were full of tears. She was angry about them and
sniffed fiercely. "Congratulations, Miles. I wish your ma was here."

"So do I." But he didn't look sad. He didn't feel sad. Not really. It
was too long ago. It was the future that mattered now.

Miles looked assured, successful, easy, and he felt deeply pleased
with himself.

LATER THAT NIGHT, when they were home and Father Kennedy had
gone back to the parish house, the three of them sat in the house in
Latego Canyon and watched the sunset.

"What next, Miles?" said Hugo.

"You tell me," Miles said cheerfully.

"What do you mean?"

"I kind of thought you would be helping."

"In what way?"

"Getting me a job."

"Oh, no, Miles, you've misunderstood me, I'm afraid. I've no intention of finding you a job."

"God, Hugo, why not? You're a rich man. You have a company.
Can't you find a space for me?"

"No. I can't."

Miles was genuinely astounded; he looked physically winded, betrayed.

"But why not?"

"Because I simply don't believe in that sort of thing."

Miles shook his head, smiling. "I'm just not hearing all this."

"What do you mean?"

"I mean, all these years I've been slaving away—"

"At my expense."

"Okay, but you offered. Slaving away, thinking it was all with a clear end in view. That you'd help me get a good job."

"I will help you, Miles. But I'm not giving you one."

Miles stood up. He looked at Hugo with deep contempt. "I can't believe anyone can be so mean."

"Miles!" said Mrs. Kelly. "How dare you? After all that Mr. Dashwood has done."

"What's he done?" Miles said. "Signed a few checks. Is he going to put himself on the line, present me to his company, his fancy friends and associates? He is not. I'm on my own now, Hugo, is that it?"

"Possibly. With a damn good college education behind you. I don't call that alone."

"You've built me up, given me fancy ideas and a sound education, encouraged me to think I was worth something, taken me away from my friends, and now you're dropping me right back where I started. Thanks a lot."

"This really is the most extraordinary way to look at things, Miles."

"Is it? I'd have thought it was your way that was extraordinary. To have the power to help and refuse it."

"I'm prepared to do what I can. To speak to some associates, perhaps. To give you good references."

"Spare me. I don't want any lousy job anyway. Good-bye, Hugo."

MILES TOOK TO the beach. He joined the other surf bums who made it their life; he spent every day waiting for the wave, or riding it. Occasionally he earned a little money. He would pump gas, deliver the odd grocery order, wait on tables at Alice's, maybe push a little grass. He smoked a lot of grass, but nothing more harmful than that; they all did. It was a strong brotherhood they had, the surfers. They had total loyalty to one another, none at all for the geeks, the incompetent newcomers who got in the way. Their only concern was waiting for the bitchin', the real quality surf, and enjoying it.

Hugo came from time to time, and he and Miles had terrible arguments. Once Mrs. Kelly asked if he could maybe do what Miles wanted, give him a job. Hugo said he couldn't. He really couldn't. Especially not now. Not after all Miles had said. But he would stay in touch. And he begged Mrs. Kelly not to give up. He felt Miles needed her, needed them both.

But Miles didn't need anybody. All he needed in the world was the surf and the sun, and his board, and the sweet dizzy feeling that was like sex, of elation and release when he caught a good wave and rode it in to the shore.

And nobody was going to take it away from him.

· 16 ·

ANNICK VALERY, WHO HAD EXPECTED to dislike Roz heartily and to find working with her an unpleasant experience, found very little in her work to criticize and, even more to her surprise, liked her very much.

The Paris office of Juliana was the least active, from a marketing point of view. Most of the creative work on the cosmetics was done in London with considerable input from New York.

Roz found herself working as a junior brand manager on the color ranges, as opposed to skin care and perfume, which meant to a large degree simply watching sales figures, overseeing the translation on packaging, checking distribution, watching and adjusting price levels, and rubber-stamping media schedules. It was not inspiring, it allowed little if any scope for creative flair, and it involved an enormous amount of tedious routine work. She could have sulked; she could have traded on her position and slacked; she could have thrown her weight around. She did none of those things; she worked very hard and efficiently, made modest suggestions about prices and packaging, always had her paperwork up to date, and made a point of spending at least one day a week behind the counter in one or another of Juliana's outlets.

Annick reported very favorably on her to Julian after the first six months and passed on a couple of suggestions Roz had made, which were clearly based on extremely sound judgment.

"She is a clever girl, and she works very hard. She suggested to me that we price up all the lipsticks, make the eye shadows a slightly more budget line, and sell them together. Just as a promotion. I think it will work."

"Why?" said Julian. "Sounds a bit cockeyed to me."

"Because she says women use up their lipsticks and want more. The eye shadow is never finished. So they will spend more replacing a lipstick they like and will buy more eye shadows, simply to get the new colors."

"I don't follow."

"But it is so simple," said Annick, surprised at his denseness. "If a woman likes a lipstick, it is because of not just the color but the texture, the perfume, even. So she will pay much more for it. It is a personal thing. Eye shadow is different. It is just the fashion, the colors. If you sell the two as a pair, you will persuade her to buy an eye shadow she is not perhaps ready for, especially if it is cheaper. And she will also pay more for the lipstick, because it comes as part of a package."

"Yes, I see," said Julian. "It might work. Test-market it in the next promotion."

It did work. Sales increased by about ten percent in all the stores offering the new seesaw prices, as Roz had privately named them.

"It's very good," Annick said happily to Roz as they went over the sales figures at the end of the first two months. "You are clever. Your father will be pleased with you, I think."

"I hope so," Roz said. "He's the boss. Come on, Annick, I'll buy you lunch."

ROZ WAS ENJOYING Paris. She had a tiny flat just off the Tuileries, and with Annick's help she was learning to dress well. She had discovered the joy of French clothes and the way French women, whether rich or poor, could put together and accessorize an outfit so that the end result was not just stylish, but witty as well.

She began to look very chic; eighties fashion in any case became her well: the pantsuit which suited her rangy walk; the short skirts, which showed off her superb legs; the strong, bold colors; the dashingly patterned knitwear, which flattered her dark coloring; and the infiltration of the fitness craze into the fashion industry via the "sweats collection" of Norma Kamali, with her rah-rah skirts, leggings, and sweatshirting tops with huge shoulder pads all perfectly suited Roz's dynamic, athletic style.

She had her dark hair cropped short, which emphasized her large green eyes and her wide mouth, making no concessions to prettiness but everything to drama. She learned to make up superbly, to wear strong colors on her lips and dramatic shapes on her eyes. She had her father's natural physical grace; she moved, sat, and stood well. And she dieted and exercised ruthlessly, running in the Paris streets early every morning, working out in the Juliana salon most evenings, pushing herself harder and harder, until there was not an ounce of fat to be seen on her lean, long body. She looked sleek, elegant, expensive. And the look pleased her.

She managed to enjoy her work, dull as it was. She felt she was learning things that really mattered, and she also had a very close and good friend. She liked Annick more than she had ever liked any other female, apart from Susan. Annick was very young, only two years older than Roz herself, fiercely ambitious and hardworking—both qualities Roz recognized and respected. But work was very far from everything to her. She was amusing, irreverent, warm, and supportive, and perhaps most important, she put no value whatsoever on Roz's background or position. She made it perfectly plain that she liked her for what she was, no more or less, and never referred to her father or asked why Roz was working with her.

And then there was Michael Browning.

He was in love with her. Seriously in love with her. Roz could tell this quite clearly, and the novelty of being loved wholeheartedly made her very happy indeed. It improved her temper, shrank the chip on her shoulder to manageable limits, increased her self-confidence, even in her appearance, and enabled her to regard the rest of the world with a little more tolerance.

"You're a bitch, Rosamund," he had said to her frequently, from the very beginning of their relationship. "A hard, bad-tempered bitch. And it turns me on. Don't change. I adore you."

Being adored by Michael was a dizzying experience. He was thirty-five years old, a rough, tough Brooklyn diamond. His father had run an all-night deli, and Michael had worked in it from the age of fourteen. At sixteen he had observed the ever-soaring sales of soft drinks and wondered if there mightn't be room for a new one. He talked about it with an acquaintance who owned a factory, and together they came up with Fizzin' Flavors, a line of new imaginative mixtures in drinks: orange with lemon, blackcurrant with apple, pineapple with grapefruit. Michael's father shook his head, put the soft drinks on a back shelf, and they stayed there. Undeterred, Michael took six crates with him on vacation to California and set up a stall near the boardwalk in Venice. They sold in a day, which he had known they would. Next day people came back for more, which he hadn't been so confident about, and were disappointed at having to settle for 7-Up and Pepsi.

Michael flew home and went to the bank. The loan officer lent him five hundred dollars against his father's surety. It wasn't much, but it filled a lot more crates; he shipped them to Venice and sold them for half again as much as he had last time.

Then he went looking for another small soft drinks factory.

IN FIVE YEARS Michael Browning was a millionaire with a chain of supermarkets. He was married to a nice Jewish girl from Brooklyn called Anita, whom he had impregnated on their second meeting in his newly acquired penthouse just off Madison.

Both families were very happy, and given the size of the penthouse and Michael Browning's fortune, Anita's parents were easily able to ignore the fact that she looked just a little plump on her wedding day and that Michael Browning the Third was born a couple of months early.

Five years later Michael was a multimillionaire, heavily involved in oil as well as food chains and married to another, rather less nice Gentile girl from Washington, whom he had seduced on their second meeting, in the Waldorf-Astoria where he was chairing a conference.

Anita Browning took one look at the ravishing, ice cool blonde on her husband's arm in the society column next day and knew when she was beaten. She took him to the cleaners for two million dollars and refused him access to little Michael and baby Sharon except at Thanksgiving, Hanukkah, and an occasional weekend at her own specification if she particularly wanted to go off on her own. Michael minded this very much, but there was precious little he could do about it.

Carol Walsh left Michael Browning in 1975, wooed away from him by some older, more socially acceptable money. Michael was left with a profound mistrust of marriage and a strong need for the company of women, the more beautiful the better. He did not have too much trouble finding them.

He was not very tall, just a little over five feet ten, and neither was he conventionally good-looking. But just looking at him, as Carol Walsh had remarked to her best friend the day after the seduction, made you think about sex. Michael Browning exuded sex, of a strangely emotional kind. He made women think not merely about their physical needs but about their emotional ones as well. He made them aware not only of their bodies but of their minds. As a result, he was extraordinarily successful not only in bed but in persuading women to join him there at the earliest possible opportunity.

He was dark-haired, with a slightly floppy preppy haircut, "Designed to bring out the mother of the bastard in us all," Anita had been heard to pronounce in tones of absolute contempt more than once. He had brown eyes that looked as if they had seen and profited by every possible variety of carnal knowledge; a nose that only just betrayed his Jewish origins; and a slightly lugubrious expression that relaxed into good humor rather slowly, a little reluctantly, even. This expression, an entirely natural asset, was nevertheless of great value to Michael Browning in his relationships with women; they felt he must be sad, that he had some problem, some sorrow, and they went to some trouble to ascertain what it might be and whether they could help him with it. By the time they had discovered there was no problem, he could, should he so wish, persuade them to do almost anything.

And then there was his voice. Michael Browning's voice was unique. "It sounds," Roz had said to Annick, uncharacteristically poetic in her attempt to describe it, "like a voice that started out perfectly ordinary and then had a fight with a dozen men and then got soothed again with honey and hot lemon, with a slug of bourbon thrown in for good measure."

"*Mon Dieu*," said Annick. "And what does it say, this voice?"

"Oh," said Roz vaguely, "not an awful lot, really."

This was quite true. Michael Browning was not a raconteur, not a dazzler at dinner tables. He spoke with that particular form of Brooklyn succinctness that is so charming when a novelty and so wonderfully reassuring to those who have grown up around it. If he was asked a question, he would answer very fully—he was not a man who spoke in monosyllables—and he could be thoughtful and amusing in conversation. But women in love with him waited in vain to be told that they were beautiful or charming or all that he had ever wanted. He told them instead the simple truth—that they were a great piece of ass, that they were terrific company, that he wanted to go to bed with them as soon as possible, that this or that dress looked good on them—all in that gravelly-silken voice, while at the same time looking at them mournfully and interestedly with those dark brown eyes, "as if he'd never met anyone quite like you before," Roz said on another occasion.

He did not dress particularly well. Roz joined a long line of women who tried to improve his wardrobe with a total lack of success. He was quite simply uninterested. He bought his clothes in all the right places. His shirts and ties came from Brooks Brothers; he had his suits tailored at J. Press; his shoes were from Paul Stuart; and he acquired all the perpetually crumpled Burberrys, which he lost relentlessly, in London at Harrods. But he never looked stylish. He always looked as if he had borrowed someone else's clothes, which didn't quite suit him but managed to fit him fairly well.

He lived in a penthouse duplex on Fifth Avenue, right across from the park, one block up from the Pierre. It was much too big for him, but it was useful when Michael and Sharon, and the ferocious English nanny who Anita insisted should accompany them, came to stay for the weekend. The duplex was a shrine to new money. It had marble floors throughout; a pond and a waterfall in the lobby; a living area with a sunken floor and so many mirrored walls you hadn't the least idea where you really were; a master bedroom with not only a Jacuzzi, a sauna, and a sun room, but a small swimming pool as well; a large number of very expensive paintings by fashionable New York artists; a fully equipped gym; a music room complete with a computer-drive piano and a synthesizer so that Michael could indulge in his hobby of composing variations on the works of Bach, Mozart, and even Wagner when he was feeling particularly creative; a playroom for Michael and Sharon, which made the toy department at Macy's look rather poorly stocked; and a roof garden bearing trees and shrubs so big they had to be hoisted by crane from Fifth Avenue fifty floors up the face of the building.

Perhaps the most surprising thing about Michael Browning was that, despite his considerable wealth, his success, and the constant parade of women in and out of his life, he remained a comparatively nice unspoiled man. He had, of course, forgotten some of life's minor hazards; he did not have to worry about letters from his bank manager, or do his own cleaning; he could go on vacation when he wished either alone or in the company of any number of beautiful women; he could acquire for himself anything at all that he wished for, which was a great deal, one of his greatest faults being an insatiable greed; and he could rid himself of anything he had ceased to like, be it a set of Louis Quinze chairs, a jet-propelled surfboard from Hammacher Schlemmer or a complete gold-plated dinner service, to name the three most recent, without giving a thought to how much money he might be losing in the process; but the fact remained, that despite a rather strong streak of self-interest and a complete inability to deny himself whatever or whoever he wanted, he was kind and honest.

He had an extraordinary and genuine interest in everybody; he could become as deeply engrossed in conversation with the teller at the bank about his vacation or with the cleaning lady in his office about her grandchildren as he could in his own multimillion-dollar deals. It was not in the least unknown for a new secretary to go in for dictation and spend the next thirty-five minutes showing him photographs of her parents' silver wedding anniversary celebration and being encouraged to describe painstakingly exactly what the cake had been like and the precise age and state of health of her father's great-aunt, who had somehow managed to take up a prominent position in nearly every shot. He did not do this sort of thing to charm people, as a means to an end; he simply had a great capacity for wanting to know about people, for finding out what they were really like, and for very much enjoying himself in the process.

Which was precisely why he had fallen in love with Roz.

ROZ HAD BEEN responsible for his invitation to Harvard. She had suggested to one of her professors that he would be an interesting guest lecturer, having heard her father and Freddy Branksome mention him, and had consequently been assigned the task of meeting him in the shabby splendor of the Boston railway station, escorting him back to the college, and attending a luncheon, along with several other carefully selected students, in his honor. She had dressed for the occasion with great care in a white gabardine jacket and jodhpurs from Montana, with very pale beige flat-heeled suede boots; her hair was tied back with a silk scarf; she carried a large beige canvas bag from Ralph Lauren. She looked expensive, classy, stylish. Michael Browning's first words made her feel less so: "Are you the chauffeur from Harvard?" He had gotten off the train and stood looking around him in his rather hopeless way. At first she couldn't believe anyone so rumpled, so unimpressive, could possibly be the undisputed king of the cut-price food market, self-made and self-hyped, whom she had heard and read so much about. However, there was nobody else leaving the New York train looking any more impressive, or rather nobody who was clearly looking for someone and waiting to be looked after, so she stepped forward and said, "Yes, I'm the chauffeur. Mr. Browning?" and he had looked at her very solemnly and said, "Miss Morell?" and she had felt a strange lurch somewhere in the depths of herself and had led him to her car and driven him back to the college.

She knew precisely when she had fallen in love with Michael Browning, and it had not been the first time he kissed her, or when he had told her he wanted to go to bed with her more than he could ever remember wanting to go to bed with anyone; not even when he told her she had a better and quicker mind than the men he most respected, or that if she should ever need a job, he would give her one at ten grand a year more than anyone else could offer. It wasn't even when he said that he hoped his small daughter would grow up into just such a woman as she was. It was when he said, "Hey, are you Julian Morell's daughter?" and she had said, "Yes, I am as a matter of fact," and he looked at her consideringly and very seriously, and said, "That has to be quite an obstacle race."

Roz had felt at that moment that after spending much of her life trying to explain things to people who spoke another language she had found herself in a country that spoke her own, where people understood not just what she was saying but why she was saying it; and she had actually stopped the car and looked at Michael Browning very seriously in a kind of pleased disbelief.

"Hey," he said, "did we run out of gas or something?"

"No," she said, "no. I'm sorry. It was just what you said."

"About your father?" he said, and smiled at her again. "Did I hit the button?"

"Very hard," Roz said briefly, starting the car again.

"You're a terrible driver," he said after they had gone a few more miles in silence. "You drive like a New York cab driver."

"Thank you."

"Sorry. I didn't mean to be rude."

"Well, you were."

"I know. It happens all the time."

"Can't you control it?" Roz asked, smiling in spite of her irritation.

"It seems not. I've been in analysis and had deep hypnosis and electric shock treatment and it just goes right on."

"How unfortunate for you."

"I get by."

"So I understand."

"I find the English accent really sexy," he said suddenly. "It's kind of lazy."

"And do you find laziness sexy as well?"

"Oh, absolutely. One hundred and one percent sexy. I have to tell you, you could make me feel very lazy," he added as an afterthought.

Roz felt confused, disoriented. The conversation seemed to be meandering down a series of wrong turns, not at all the dynamic businesslike route she had imagined.

"Do you like giving lectures?" she asked in an attempt to haul him back onto the main highway.

"I don't know. I never gave one before."

"Oh."

"It could be interesting. I'll tell you afterward. Do I get to see you afterward?"

"I don't know. I suppose so. Briefly."

"Well," he said, "briefly's better than nothing."

THE LECTURE, UNREHEARSED, unstructured, often funny, told the students more about food retailing than they had ever imagined they might need to know. Afterward he sought Roz out at the buffet lunch, gave her his card, and told her to phone him next time she was in New York. Roz said she never went to New York.

Three days later she got a call from him.

"This is Michael Browning. I thought if you were never going to come to New York, I would have to come to Harvard."

"Why?" said Roz foolishly.

"Just to take another look at you. Make sure I got it right."

"Got what right?"

"Well," he said, and there was a heavy sigh down the phone, "it's those legs of yours. They're coming between me and my sleep. Were you born with them that long, like a racehorse, or did they just go on growing, like Topsy?"

"I think," Roz said carefully, feeling oddly dizzy and happier than she could ever remember, "they were quite short when I was born."

"I'd really like to take another look at them. And the rest of you as well. Do you ever eat dinner?"

"Just occasionally," she said.

WHEN HE WAS first getting to know her, Michael Browning was unable to believe how spoiled, truculent, and outrageously self-obsessed Roz was.

He looked at her, and he wanted her, but he was not quite sure that he could take her on. Then he got to know her a little better, learned of her wretched childhood, her totally unsatisfactory parents, the painstaking indulgence of her every whim that had gone on through fifteen years of recompense, and he had known that he could.

He treated her rough at first. He told her she had no right, no one had any right to be so angry, so hostile, so aggressive, so self-pitying. He told her of girls he had grown up with, who had been raped by their mothers' boyfriends or their own fathers before they reached puberty, who had had to go on the streets to fill their bellies, who had had their first unanesthetized abortions at twelve, their fifth or sixth at fifteen, and then he dared her to go on being sorry for herself.

Then, having broken down some of her defenses, he set to work on the rest. Roz was sexually, as well as emotionally, a mess. Quite apart from the fearsome attentions of the vicomte du Chene, her history was unhappy.

By the time Michael Browning came into her life and her bed, she had a great need for skill and kindness as well as passion. He provided them; he coaxed her and cosseted her, teased her and tormented her, took her and fulfilled her, night after glorious night. He taught her to know what she wanted and ask for it; he taught her to please him and to please herself; he taught her to think about sex and to give it her attention, just as she did to food and clothes and work. He turned her into a sexual being aware of her own sensuality and what she could do with it, possessed of great pleasures and new powers. Despite strong desires and instincts of her own, she was, she felt, his creation in bed. She sometimes wondered uneasily if he wished her to become his creation in other things as well.

He flew to Paris at least once a month for the weekend, amused and charmed, for the time being at least, by her bid for independence. They seldom left her apartment those weekends. Occasionally he would, in one of the grand gestures he so excelled in, take her off to the south of France or to London or Venice. "So that I can know you in the biblical sense—in another place," he would say. "It might make a difference."

Roz supposed she was in love. She had very little knowledge of love, although she had seen the worst excesses committed in its name; but if being filled with thoughts and concern and desire and joy by someone was love, then she felt she was experiencing it now.

She consulted another of her visitors, her mother, an expert she could only suppose, on the subject, but Eliza was charmingly vague.

"I can only tell you, darling, that you'll know if it is love. Not if it's not. Not the first time, anyway."

"Oh, Mummy, surely you can be more precise."

"No, Roz, I can't. There's nothing precise about love. That's what's so dangerous."

ELIZA WAS IN Paris shopping. They were lunching in the Hotel Meurice. Eliza was picking her way painstakingly through a tiny grilled sole; Roz was eating steak tartare with rather more enjoyment. Eliza looked at her; she had never seen her so happy. Her skin, her eyes, even her hair glowed; she was wearing a smudgy pink cotton sweater with full linen trousers from Ralph Lauren, a long rope of pearls around her neck. Eliza, more formally dressed in a short black linen dress from Valentino, looked equally relaxed. Newly married to Peveril in that summer of 1980, she was surprisingly happy. Letitia had been right; the pain had eased.

It had been a quiet wedding in the private chapel at Garrylaig. Letitia had been there, and Roz, and Peveril's sisters, and Eliza's parents, and that had been all. Eliza had worn a ravishing ivory silk dress by Yves Saint Laurent, and had managed not to look ridiculous with wild roses in her silvery hair, and Peveril had worn his kilt and a look of such love that Letitia had felt her eyes fill with tears. Perhaps this time the child had done the right thing. Roz was also looking softer, tender, moved. Whoever this man Michael Browning was, he was undoubtedly doing her good.

Eliza was now intent on doing up the castle, which had had no mistress for ten years. Quite what the earl of Garrylaig thought of the new furnishings and pictures that were finding their way on to his austere walls was doubtful. He had already learned not to criticize his new wife, and as prettying up the place, as he put it, seemed to keep her happy, he held his tongue as century-old brocades were packed away and replaced with silks and chintzes, and cavernous halls were filled with seventeenth- and eighteenth-century sofas, chaise longues, and escritoires. He spent more time than ever in pursuit of the grouse and the deer. What did it matter, after all, he thought, as long as his bride was content and out of mischief? She looked after him beautifully, catering to his every whim, and seemed to find him agreeable and attractive. Peveril was well content and found himself looking forward to bedtime more and more.

"You're a fine filly, my dear," he would say, slapping her fondly on her tiny backside, "very fine. I'm a lucky chap."

Which indeed he was, and Eliza felt perfectly entitled to regular trips to London and Paris to spend his money and see her daughter, with whom she was suddenly finding it easier to communicate. She was rigidly faithful to Peveril, besides being truly fond of him, and she was enjoying being a countess and her new situation in life. She had fun shocking her Scottish neighbors and importing her London friends into the castle, and she was perfectly happy inflicting her slightly excessive taste on its decor.

"It sounds dreadful, Mummy," Roz said after listening to her for most of lunch, describing the color scheme for the main guest room. "More suitable for Surrey than Scotland. Pink chintz in a castle? It's like poodle-clipping a deer. Whatever does Peveril think?"

"Oh, don't be so superior," said Eliza, more than slightly miffed, for she greatly admired her own taste. "Peveril likes everything I do for him. And he's thrilled with the way the castle's turning out. It was so horribly uncomfortable and bleak before. Well, you saw it. Don't you honestly think so?"

"No, I liked it," Roz said. "I like austerity. And I thought it had great dignity. You'll take all that away if you're not careful. Anyway, it doesn't really matter. How is my new stepfather?"

"It does matter," said Eliza. "It matters very much to me. I'm putting a great deal of time and effort into that place, Rosamund. I don't want aspersions cast upon it by my own daughter. Anyway, I don't see much evidence of any interior design skills in your own home, my dear."

This was true. Roz, who was at last demonstrating some taste, albeit modest, for clothes, cared nothing for her surroundings and would have agreed to spend the rest of her life in a twelve-foot-square attic, provided it was warm and clean, had she been asked.

"Oh, don't be so touchy, Mummy," she said. "I'm sure it's quite all right, really, and I know Peveril thinks you're wonderful. Have another glass of wine and let's talk about something interesting."

"Like what?" said Eliza, a trifle sulky.

"Me."

"And what is so interesting about you?"

"Well, I need a bit of advice."

"What about?"

"A man."

"Ah. This Browning person."

"Yes."

"I don't really like what I hear about him, darling. He has an appalling reputation with women. What exactly do you want advice about?"

"Michael has asked me to marry him."

"Oh, good God, don't," said Eliza. "Whatever you do, never marry his sort. It's quite wrong."

"Mummy," said Roz, half amused, half intrigued, "what advice to be dishing out to your only daughter! Do I just continue as his mistress, then?"

"If you want to, if you enjoy it. You're so lucky these days, Roz, not having to have at least one ring on your wedding finger before you can go to bed with anyone. When I was a girl, virginity was still almost obligatory for a bride. Have fun, darling. But don't marry Michael Browning."

"Why not?"

"Because you'll be divorced in two years. Six months into the marriage he'll have a new mistress. Believe me."

Roz sighed. "He says he loves me."

"I'm sure he thinks he does."

"He says I'm different."

"We're all different. Take no notice."

"He says he wants to settle down."

"No man of thirty-five wants to settle down."

"He says he wants more children. I'd like that."

"Oh, for heaven's sake, Rosamund, I can't believe you can be so naive and stupid! Why on earth do you want to go having babies at the age of twenty-four? It's absolutely ridiculous."

"You were twenty when you had me."

"I know, and it was a terrible mistake. The marriage was a terrible mistake. I was much too young. I hadn't lived at all. Nor have you. Just enjoy the man, Roz. Besides, I thought you were intent on building a proper career."

"Well, I am. But Michael says he won't interfere. He says I can carry on with it."

"Rosamund," said Eliza darkly, signaling at the waiter, "Michael Browning would not be interfering for about forty-eight hours. If that. I have learned a few things in my misspent life. Now, have some more wine," she added, "and, darling, you'd better have some black coffee. You've got to go back to work. Please, please believe me, Roz. A career is far more important and worthwhile at your age—probably at any age—than a man."

"But I can have both."

"Darling, you can't. Perhaps if you should find some milksop of a man who'll do exactly what you tell him and who thinks you should be allowed to do what you like. But not a man like Browning."

"I don't see how you can be so sure," Roz said sulkily. "We've talked about it for hours and hours. Michael is very proud of me. He wants me to do well."

"Rosamund, he won't want you to do well. Doing well will mean you not being there when he wants you. Men don't like that."

"Don't they? I really think he might. Oh, I don't know," Roz said with a sigh, draining her glass. "I do absolutely adore him. And he is such fun."

"Well, that's all right," Eliza said. "Just go on having fun with him."

"MICHAEL, I'VE TOLD you, I just want more time to think about it," Roz said earnestly. "I'm not saying no. I'm not even saying probably no. I just need to think it through."

"Oh, God," Browning said wearily. "Don't use your Harvard jargon on me."

They were sitting in a café on the Champs Elysées having a breakfast of croissants, orange juice, and champagne. It was Saturday midmorning, and the sun was shining; Michael had spent the night on a plane and was tired and irritable and blind to the pleasures in front of him. He had dropped a box into Roz's lap as the waiter filled their glasses.

"That's for you, Roz. Part of a deal."

"What kind of a deal?"

"You get that and I get you."

Roz opened the box. Inside was a diamond ring of monstrous proportions, a huge solitaire set in a rough-cut chunk of gold spangled with tiny sapphires. She looked at it thoughtfully.

"It's gorgeous. Simply gorgeous. I love it."

"Put it on."

"I can't. Not if it's what I think it is."

"Rosamund, if you don't know what that is, you've got even less sense than I thought. It's a diamond. You've heard of diamonds, haven't you? This is a big one. The goods. It's to show you what I think of you."

"You know what I mean."

"Yes, I know what you mean. And yes, it's an engagement ring, Roz. I really want to marry you."

"Why?"

"Because I love you. God knows why, but I do."

"I love you, too. But things are fine as they are."

"I don't agree with that. I want them settled. I'm sick of flying in here every other day. I want you with me."

"Where do you mean?"

"New York."

"I've just been offered a new job. In London."

"London! Why didn't you tell me?"

"I didn't know. I was only offered it yesterday."

"Well, turn it down. Or say you want to go to New York instead."

"No, I can't."

"What do you mean, you can't? Your father's got offices there."

"Michael, my father isn't slotting me in somewhere just to suit me. He's given me a proper job to do. It's important. It's a promotion."

"Oh, for Christ's sake, Rosamund, how important is it to get a promotion in your father's company?"

"It's terribly important, Michael. Terribly. I can't believe you don't understand. I really have earned it. I'm going to be marketing manager of all the Juliana color products in the U.K. It's a terrific job."

"And I suppose the competition was really stiff for this terrific job?"

"Oh, don't," said Roz angrily. "You don't know my father. He wouldn't give me any job he didn't think I could do."

"I do know your father, and I think he would."

"Well, thanks a lot." Roz drained her coffee cup and called the waiter. *"L'addition, s'il vous plaît!"*

"Oh, for Christ's sake get off your high horse and have some more champagne."

"No, thank you. I want to keep my head clear."

She was finding the conversation difficult and terrifying. She kept hearing her mother's voice saying "You can't have both" and pushing it resolutely to the back of her head. It wouldn't stay there.

"Rosamund, I really want you to have a career. It's one of the things I value in you. I love it that you want to do well. But I want you to do well with me."

"But, Michael, I can't come to New York now. I can't give up my job and be a proper good wife to you. Not yet."

Michael picked up her left hand and slid the ring onto it. "Please wear it."

"I can't."

"You can wear it. That doesn't commit you to a life sentence of picking out shirts for me at Brooks Brothers and arranging the flowers for our dinner parties, which is what you seem to think I want."

"No, I don't think that, of course I don't. But if I did marry you, if I was your wife, I'd want to be a proper one. I've seen too many wrecked marriages. And this way I'd be cheating. Well, I feel I would."

"Look, wear the ring. And say you'll marry me soon. I'm not insisting on next week. You can do this important job for a while if you really want to. I'll wait. Please, darling."

"Michael, I'm not going to promise anything."

"Why not? What harm can it do?"

"You have to keep promises."

"Oh, for God's sake, stop playing games."

"I'm not playing games. I just—"

"What?"

Roz looked at him suddenly. He was white-faced with exhaustion; he had a night's growth of beard; his voice was shaking with rage and some other emotion, she wasn't sure what. In a rare moment of unselfishness, she realized she should stop hitting him when he was down.

"I just want time to think. Come on."

She stood up and held out her hand. "Let's go back to my flat and you can go to bed for a couple of hours."

Michael's eyes flicked over her. "You going to join me?"

"If you like."

"I do like. I sure do."

AT ONE O'CLOCK he was still asleep. Roz rolled out of bed cautiously and crept out of the room. She felt exhilarated, recharged, absolutely alive. Sex with Michael Browning did that to her. Not just her body, but her emotions and her intellect had all been absolutely engaged, focused on the taking and giving of pleasure. She was left with a surge of adrenaline coursing through her; she felt she could literally have flown in the air.

She made herself a pot of strong coffee and wandered into the bathroom, looked at her face, flushed, worked over with love, and smiled at it. Perhaps, perhaps, after all, Michael could be, would be, enough. She wished for that, at that moment, more than she had ever wished for anything in her life.

Then she looked at the great ring on her finger, where he had put it, and she thought about her father, about London, about her new job and the passion of excitement she had felt when he had phoned her about it, telling her she had earned it, that he was impressed with her work, that he knew she could do it and do it well, and she knew that she could not, would not, give it up. Not for all the rings, all the money, all the sex, all the love in the world. It was difficult, because she wanted love, and she needed it; but the choice had to be made.

A milksop of a man, she thought sadly, hearing yet again her mother's voice. That's what I shall have to find.

In the event it wasn't really very difficult.

C. J. EMERSON arrived at Harvard just as Roz was leaving, a charming, gentle young man whose only real ambition in life had been to study archaeology. His father, however, had rather different ideas for him. He was only moderately successful himself, lacking the necessary drive and ruthlessness to head up empires and make fortunes; but he had had moments of inspired vision and had backed some brilliant investments. Scott Emerson's reputation on Wall Street was front rank.

None had been more brilliant than the one he had pushed through in 1957 when Julian Morell had come to him with his proposals for Circe. The friendship forged then had endured through the years. They lunched, dined, talked, and at times still worked together. They had visited each other's houses, became involved in each other's children.

Scott was impressed by Julian's immense success and fortune; he admired it, but he did not envy it. He had watched his personal unhappiness grow, seen his uncertainties and his agonies, observed his straightforward optimism become something darker and more complex, and he found himself, somewhat to his own surprise, increasingly content with his own more mediocre achievements and his extraordinarily happy family life.

Scott Emerson in 1980, then, found himself viewing the thirty years to come in the same sanguine spirit as he had viewed the thirty that had so pleasantly passed. His daughters were all doing well; only his son was causing Scott the odd moment's anxiety. More than a moment, as he confided to his friend Julian Morell over lunch at the Oyster Bar in Grand Central Station one spring day. The two of them sat and looked, each from his own standpoint, at the pretty girls around them, shedding like so many fluttering butterflies their coats, their boots, their scarves, their gloves, and emerging in the delicious, slightly self-conscious sexiness of light, clingy dresses of neatly cut, figure-hugging skirts and jackets, of higher heels and silky stockings. Scott looked and regretted, just perhaps for a fleeting moment, that such pleasures were purely visual; Julian enjoyed, for perhaps just a little longer, the reflection that the pleasures might be extended.

Settled into their martinis, their oysters ordered, the room surveyed, they turned their minds to more important matters: to the present and the future of their families.

"C.J.'s a dreamer," said Scott, gazing a trifle morosely into his martini. "He's gone to Harvard, but his heart's not in it. Not really. He wants to be an archaeologist. I ask you, Julian, what kind of a job is that?"

"A fascinating pursuit," Julian said, "but I don't think I'd actually call it a job. More like recreation. I didn't know you had such things in your country anyway, Scott. I didn't think there was anything to dig up."

"Well, hell, of course there isn't, that's why it's such a crazy idea. He wants to travel, spend years on sites here, there, and everywhere, do a graduate course at Oxford. That's no life for a young man; I told him so. Where's your ambition? I asked him. Where are you aiming for in the world? I said he could have a job at any time at the bank, but he wouldn't hear of it. It worries me, Julian, because I think he'll drift his life away if he's given the chance. And I won't have that."

"No, you shouldn't," Julian said. "Young men should have proper jobs. I quite agree with you. Make their way in the world. Take life on. Plenty of time for dreaming when they're older. Nothing makes me angrier than this modern tendency to put the pursuit of happiness and self-fulfillment and some bloody silly ideals before the real stuff of life. I wouldn't have it if it was my son."

He spoke with surprising passion. Scott looked at him sharply. He wouldn't have expected a man with no son and no experience of such matters to feel so strongly, to have given the subject so much thought.

"What about Roz?" he asked tentatively, wondering if she was failing her father in this matter, as she had in so many others. "Is she frittering her life away, buying clothes and so on? How's she doing?"

"Very well," said Julian, more warmly than he had spoken of Roz since she was a little girl. "She's working for me and she's working very hard. She's got brains and she's got push. She's very, very ambitious."

"What a waste," said Scott, half humorously, half enviously. "How ironic that you should have one daughter with all the traditional male virtues, and I should have one son with apparently none of them."

"Well, work on him," said Julian briskly. "Don't let him throw his life away. Tell him there's plenty of time for archaeology when he's retired and during his vacations. Ideal sort of occupation then."

"I have. I've tried that one. And he does try to see it my way. He's a good boy, and he's working quite hard at Harvard. But I worry about him over the long term."

"Harvard might well sort him out. Roz loved it. Did her the world of good. I shouldn't worry too soon, Scott. Have another martini. Ah, here are the oysters."

BUT SIX MONTHS later Scott was still worrying. C.J. had scraped his way through Harvard and was now sitting at home in Oyster Bay writing endless applications for jobs he didn't want. He was a tall, slender young man, with a pale softly freckled face and large dreamy brown eyes. He wore his clothes casual, his hair long, and he never seemed to be entirely present at any occasion.

He could be witty and entertaining when he felt relaxed and appreciated, but his charm was low-key and diffident. At twenty-five he felt as confused about life and his future as he had at eighteen, and he could work up no feelings at all for money and business, profits and power. The prospect of having to find a job and work among such things, his father's assumption that he would change his mind and grow to like the idea, depressed him utterly. He loved his parents deeply and wanted to please them, but it seemed to him this was too much for them to ask and for him to give.

He knew, deep in his gentle bones, that there was no real question of him actually being permitted to spend his life on the great digs of the ancient world, but he kept hoping against increasingly forlorn hope that a more pleasing occupation than wheeling and dealing on Wall Street might come his way. Publishing, perhaps, he thought, or antiques, but he had made little headway with applications in that direction. You needed contacts in that world as much as any other, he had discovered.

Nevertheless, he did finally get an offer of a job as an assistant editor with Doubleday at a modest salary. He looked up from the letter at the breakfast table, his brown eyes shining.

"I've been offered a job, Dad."

"Have you, son?" said Scott, putting down his coffee and beaming benevolently at him. "What is it? Did that opening at Citicorp I gave you lead to anything?"

"Er—no, not exactly," said C.J., who had kept that particular letter of rejection to himself for several days, bracing himself to tell his parents. He had had several rejections, and each one had upset them more than the last.

"No, it's not banking; it's publishing."

"Publishing?" said Scott. "I didn't know you knew anything about publishing."

"Well, I don't know much," said C.J., "but I don't know anything about banking either. And I think I'd like publishing better. This is a wonderful offer. I'm going to be an assistant editor at Doubleday. It's a terrific opportunity. I'd really like to take it, Dad."

Scott looked at him and bit back the words of discouragement and disappointment that were struggling to get out. The boy had shown some initiative, after all, and Doubleday was a good firm. He smiled at him.

"That's great, C.J. Well done. When do you you start?"

"In a month, Dad. So you don't mind?"

"No, son, not at all. I'm proud of you. You got there on your own initiative, and that's a hell of a good thing to do. Write and accept it. Now, here's a letter from Julian. What's he got to say, I wonder?"

He started to read and then drew in his breath sharply.

"C.J., listen to this. Julian Morell says he has an opening for you in his London office. He wants you to join the management team of the hotels division. He's hell-bent on opening more of them, God knows why, and he's got guys working on it night and day. He needs people to do feasibility studies of various sites worldwide. You'd be working on that side. It's a hell of an opportunity, C.J. You'd do well. He says you could stay with him in London for a few weeks while you're finding somewhere to live. He'll pay you handsomely, too. It says here, 'Tell C.J. he can have five grand and a BMW for starters.' Now that really is great, C.J., isn't it? Listen, it would make me so happy to think that Julian and I could really put our friendship to work."

"But, Dad, I already have a job. I don't want handouts. It's very kind of Mr. Morell, but I'd rather not take it. You just said it was very good that I landed the job at Doubleday on my own initiative. And I don't want to go to London."

"Why on earth not?" Scott said. "I'd have thought it would be just the greatest. All those old buildings, and you could go do your digging on weekends. I don't understand you, C.J., I really don't."

"Dad, I know you don't and I'm sorry. But my life is here, and my work is here, and I want to stay. I don't want to work for Julian Morell."

He was quite pale. By nature he was so conciliatory that every word pitted against his father felt like a self-inflicted wound.

"Well, think about it at least," said Scott, disappointment echoing in his voice. "Don't write to Doubleday for a day or two, and I won't write to Julian."

"Okay," C.J. said with a sigh.

"There's my boy. Now I have to go. I have a medical checkup this morning; this damned ulcer is getting worse. Say good-bye to your mother for me when she comes down. See you later, C.J."

"Yes, Dad," C.J. said absently. He sat reading and rereading the letter from Doubleday for a long time. He was determined not to go to work for Julian Morell. But he trembled at the thought of the battles that lay ahead.

In the event there were no battles. Scott's ulcer proved to be cancer and C.J. could not deprive him of the pleasure in the last year of his life of seeing his son go to work for his oldest and dearest friend.

He did not actually hate the job quite as much as he had expected. C.J. was a carer, and hotels were in the caring business. Having overcome his initial distaste, he found he could actually get quite interested and involved in how best to ensure the maximum comfort, visual delight, and pleasure of one person for twenty-four hours a day.

Julian Morell was swift to realize that where C.J. worked, people tended to think more visually, more imaginatively, and he encouraged and nurtured him. He was a brilliant employer. As with his own daughter, he gave C.J. no special privileges, attention, or opportunities, until they were earned. And as in the case of his own daughter, they were earned quickly. In eight months C.J. was promoted to deputy marketing manager, Morell Hotels Europe, at a hugely increased salary, every penny of which he earned.

Julian had taken a considerable gamble in giving him a job at all, but it had paid off. And it was making Scott very happy as he lay failing in his huge bed in the house in Oyster Bay.

ROZ WAS VERY unhappy. More so than she would have believed possible. She missed Michael Browning with every fiber of her being; she hated every beginning of every day.

When they had finally parted, at her instigation and against appalling opposition from him, she spent forty-eight totally wakeful hours, wondering if she could stand the pain and the knowledge of what she had given up. She, who had been looking for love ever since she was a tiny girl sitting on the stairs and hearing her father's voice rejecting her, had thrown it wantonly away. And not just love, but appreciation, acceptance, admiration, physical pleasure, simply so that she could be seen to be a worldly success and to be taking up her position as her father's rightful heir. And it might well be worth it—indeed she had to believe it was—but the price was horrifically high. She had expected to feel bad; what she hadn't expected was to feel bad for so long. As the days became weeks, and the weeks a month, two, and her pain continued, she became angry and resentful.

It was very hard, even after this time, to stick to her decision; not to lift the phone, not to write, not to get on a plane. By one simple action, she knew, she could feel well, healed, happy again; but somehow she resisted. She had to.

At first she had expected Michael to make approaches to her, to try to make her change her mind. But such behavior was not his style. He was a proud man. If Roz told him she couldn't give him her life, he was not about to crawl around her trying to change her mind. They had one last night together, when he made love to her again and again, angrily, despairingly. "This is what you are losing," his body said to her through the long, endless hours, "this pleasure, this hunger, this love," and in the morning he got out of bed and left without saying another word to her, not even good-bye.

She had wept for hours. That was in itself a rare event; she surprised herself by her capacity to feel. Physical pain, this was; her skin was sore, her head felt bruised, her joints ached. She couldn't think clearly or concentrate or remember anything at all for more than sixty seconds. That went on for weeks. It was only when she botched up an important presentation that she remembered sharply and with a kind of thankfulness why she had subjected herself to this: precisely so that she could work and impress and succeed and excel.

She went home that night and took a sleeping pill, set her alarm for five-thirty. By six-thirty she had run three miles, showered, and dressed; by seven she was in the office dictating memos. That day she instigated a complete reevaluation of all Juliana's outlets, made a review of the advertising, arranged presentations from five new agencies, called the studio in for a major briefing on repackaging three of the lines, and tried to persuade her father of the wisdom of putting small, Circe-style boutiques in his hotels.

"I think it would work, Daddy. Let me give you some of my ideas."

Julian looked at her white, drawn face and her dark eyes raw with pain and saw how he could help her. "Actually," he said, "I've been thinking about that for a while. I'm not convinced it's right, though. I'd like a report soon, Roz. I can't wait months. Can you let me have it in three weeks?"

She looked at him with weary gratitude. "Yes, I think so. Yes. I can."

He looked after her with great respect as she went out of the room. He was deeply thankful that the affair with Browning was over, but it wasn't entirely pleasant to see her so patently wretched.

Roz was too unhappy to think very rationally at the time, but later on it was to occur to her quite forcibly that she could perfectly well have done her new job in New York under the aegis of Miss Bentinck, overall marketing director of Juliana, rather than in London under her father, and continued to see Michael at the same time. It was yet another example of her father's power over her and his insistence that she recognize and accept it.

THE REPORT SHE delivered was excellent: clear-sighted, financially well based, persuasive. Julian, who had not had the slightest intention of putting any boutiques in his hotels, agreed to do a test at the one in Nice and at the London Morell. As this came under C.J.'s domain, he called him in.

"Have lunch with Roz, C.J., and talk to her about her ideas. They're interesting. She thinks these boutiques should not be just expensive little shops but should have properly planned merchandise and fashion consultants to coordinate accessories. It's a good idea. Let me have your views on it."

C.J., who was pushing himself equally hard to try and numb himself against the pain of his father's death, hurled himself into the project with fervor. He didn't particularly like Roz, but he admired her and her ideas, and he enjoyed working with her. Personally she terrified him, but on a business level she was a delight. Her brain was much more incisive than his; she could see her way through a problem or situation with extraordinary clarity. She was a brilliant analyst and a very clever negotiator. But she definitely lacked flair and fashion instinct, her own appearance apart, and C.J. possessed both; they made an unbeatable team. It was a source of great sadness as well as huge pride to Madeleine Emerson that Scott missed seeing his son's promotion to junior vice president of Morell Hotels by just three months. Roz was given the same title at the same time. It was an interesting period in the Morell empire.

"C.J.," ROZ said one night just after Christmas, "why don't we go through these designers' names over dinner? I'm really hungry."

C.J. looked at her warily. He was less frightened of her than he had been, but she was still far from the kind of dinner companion he would have chosen.

Nevertheless, it was a pleasant evening. They got through the list of designers, and a bottle of champagne, in half an hour and by the time the first course arrived they were sitting isolated from the buzzing and shrieking of San Frediano's restaurant in the Fulham Road in a kind of euphoric relaxation. Roz was enjoying herself for the first time in months.

"Oh, it's the best feeling in the world, this," she said happily. "Don't you think so, C.J.?"

"Being round half a bottle of champagne?"

"No, you fool, you know perfectly well what I mean. Finishing a difficult job and knowing you've done it well. And knowing you've earned being round half a bottle of champage. What a ghastly expression, C.J. Is that an Americanism?"

"My father told me it was a Briticism," said C.J., smiling at her. She looked very good; she was wearing a white silk shirt and tan leather jodhpurs with high boots; slung casually over her shoulders was one of Edina Ronay's Fair Isle sweaters. She was leaning back in her chair, her long legs thrust out into the aisle between the tables, threatening to trip up the waiters as they hurtled past. Almost for the first time he realized she was a very attractive woman in her strong, slightly forbidding way.

"How are you feeling about your father now?" Roz asked. "Awful still?"

"Pretty awful."

"I'm sorry."

"Yeah, well, it's not so bad for me, I guess. It's my mother who's really doing the suffering. She's been so brave. She loved him so much. They were the whole world to each other. I guess not many people grow up looking at a happy marriage. It's a great privilege."

"One I wouldn't know about," said Roz, sad rather than angry for once about her parents' spectacular inability to form satisfactory relationships with anyone, let alone each other. "Is she all right? How does she cope?"

"Not too badly. The girls are all in New York, and they see her a lot, and I go over quite often and call her all the time. But it doesn't really do much good. It's Dad she wants. I'm just glad I was doing what he wanted me to do when he died."

"That's a very unselfish sentiment. What a nice person you are, C.J."

"You sound surprised."

"Not about you. I'm always surprised by niceness."

"Why's that?"

"I haven't met an awful lot of it."

"Are you feeling better?" C.J. asked, anxious to change the direction of the conversation.

"What do you mean?" She looked suddenly defensive.

"Oh, I'm sorry." C.J. grew confused and nervous again. "I guess I shouldn't have asked. Here's our food. Can we have some more champagne?" he said suddenly to the waiter.

"C.J.!" said Roz. "What decadent behavior."

"My father always said champagne was cheaper than psychiatry," said C.J., smiling at her, "and it worked a darn sight better. I think he was right."

"Do you need psychiatry? Do I?"

"I do," said C.J., looking suddenly serious. "Or something like it. I'd be in analysis if I was in America."

"C.J., what is it? No, you don't have to tell me. I'm prying. I'm sorry."

"No, I'd like to," he said, and to his total embarrassment and misery his eyes filled with tears. He blew his nose. "It would be a relief, in a way. Although you're the last person I expected to tell."

"Why?"

"Because you scare the shit out of me."

"So I see," said Roz, "and it's deeply flattering. Now, come on, C.J. Just forget I'm so terrifying and you don't like me and all that and just spill the beans."

C.J. looked wretchedly down at the table. "I—well, I think—that is, since Dad died, I—well, I don't have any sexual feelings at all. It scares me, Roz, it really does. I'm not attracted to anyone. I don't even want to be. I'm not suggesting I'm impotent or anything drastic like that. I just feel—dead."

"You mean sexually dead?"

"Yes."

"What about emotionally?"

"What do you mean?"

"I mean, don't you think about girls and falling in love with them and all that sort of thing?"

C.J. looked at her, surprised. He had not expected Roz to look at his problem with such sensitivity and imagination. "Well, I worry about it. About not being in love. Not being able to be. But I haven't met anyone in ages who made me even think positively about it."

"You mean you haven't met anyone you like enough or fancy enough?"

"Both."

"How awful."

"It is."

"No dreams even?"

"No dreams even," said C.J. sadly, and then suddenly he smiled. "What a strange girl you are, Roz."

"What do you mean?"

"You're so tough and clever and ambitious—"

"And terrifying."

"And terrifying. And yet you seem to understand the most surprising things."

"Like what?"

"Well, loneliness. Isolation, dreams. That really is strange. For you to talk about dreams."

"Oh, I'm a mass of contradictions," Roz said, somewhat bitterly. "I've just been through the mill myself, C.J. That's how I know what you're talking about. I dream a lot. In fact, I get all my sex in my sleep at the moment."

"Well," said C.J., "at least you're getting some." And totally unaware of the comedy of the situation, he heaved a shuddering sigh.

Roz sat there, and a whole range of emotions filled her. She felt sadness for C.J. and pity; she felt remote and sad for herself; she felt a strong urge to giggle; and strongest of all and quite unbidden, she felt a great lick of desire. And she knew precisely what she would have to do.

"C.J.," she said almost briskly, "drink your coffee and take me home. I'm very, very tired. Could you call a taxi, do you think, while you're paying the bill? I'm going to the loo."

C.J. looked after her miserably as she disappeared. He had made a fool of himself, but at least she was clearly not going to attempt to comfort him or offer any advice. He should be grateful for that. And frightening as she was, he knew she wasn't a gossip. His misery was in safe hands. He paid the enormous bill, collected their coats, and was standing in the doorway when Roz appeared, looking briskly cheerful, in a cloud of perfume. "Got a taxi?"

"Yes."

"Good."

INSIDE ROZ'S FLAT, which surprised him by its lack of style, its blanket decor of beige and white, its dull born-again Conran furniture, its dearth of pictures and books, Roz kicked off her shoes, threw her coat on the sofa, put on a record—*Forty-Second Street*—and disappeared into the kitchen.

"Make yourself comfortable, C.J. That's what they say, isn't it? I won't be long."

C.J. paced up and down the living room. "Evening shadows fall!" cried the record player provocatively. He felt sick. He felt like a rabbit in a trap. He would have bolted if he'd had the courage, but he didn't. He wondered how he could have been such a fool, and had just decided to put in for a transfer to Sydney in the morning when Roz appeared with two mugs of coffee.

"Okay. I want to go over that list of designers just once more. I think we may have rushed it."

C.J. felt a surge of gratitude. She was a clever girl. She knew exactly how to defuse the situation after all. He relaxed suddenly.

"I felt that," Roz said.

"What?"

"You relaxing."

"Ah."

"Now, don't go all tense again, C.J. Get the list."

"Okay." He went out to the hall where he had left his briefcase. When he came back she patted the sofa beside her. "Let's see. Are you quite sure about Jean Muir?"

"Quite."

"I'm not."

"Why?"

"Too subtle. Zandra certainly. Belinda Belville almost certainly. But I'm doubtful about Jean. Give me your hand, C.J."

He was so relaxed, he gave her his hand without thinking. Roz raised it to her lips and he looked at her, startled. "Roz, don't."

"Why not?"

"I don't like pity."

"You're not going to get any."

"Ah."

The record had mercifully stopped; all he could hear, thundering somewhere inside him, was his heart.

"Kiss me."

"Roz, I can't."

"Why not?"

"You know why not."

"I don't. Kiss me."

"No."

"Then," she said, taking his face in her hands, "I shall kiss you." And she leaned forward very, very slowly and kissed him gently. "Was that so dreadful?" she said, drawing back.

"Not dreadful at all."

"I liked it, too. I shall do it again."

And she did.

"How was that?"

"It was great," said C.J., and then suddenly drew back from her and collapsed into the corner of the sofa, roaring with laughter.

"C.J., what is the matter with you?"

"This is too ridiculous. It's like *Some Like It Hot.* You know, when Tony Curtis has told Monroe he's impotent and she's really trying to get him going, and he keeps saying 'Nothing' every time she asks him how he feels. It's just ridiculous!"

"Well, thanks," Roz said, slightly nettled, but then she started to laugh, too, and fell against him, and then she turned her face up to him and pulled him down against her. And he kissed her again and then again, and "Still nothing?" she said, aping Marilyn Monroe's baby voice.

"Yes, something," C.J. said in a flat midwestern accent, and then, his eyes still full of laughter, he pushed her upright and unbuttoned her shirt and began to slide it off her shoulders, and as he looked at her breasts naked under the silk shirt he felt at the same time a dreadful stab of terror and panic and a great lunge of desire, and he stopped smiling altogether and froze quite, quite still.

"Oh, C.J., don't be afraid," she said in a voice so soft he would not have believed it of her, and she pressed his head very tenderly against her breasts, stroking his hair, and as he took one of her nipples in his mouth, played with it, teased it, she began to moan very, very quietly. And then suddenly he felt everything was totally out of control, and a white-hot need came into him that was blind, driving, deadly. He was tearing at her clothes and his own, and kissing her everywhere, her face, her shoulders, her breasts, her hands, and drawing her down on top of him. He felt her thin back, her tight, hard buttocks, and then her soft moistness, so tender, so yielding at first, and then so hungry and so strong, and he turned her and entered her with a great surge of triumph. He had only been in her for the briefest of times, it seemed, settling, searching, and feeling her juices flowing to meet him, when it was over in a shuddering agony of relief, and the months of misery and loneliness were wiped out, and he lay weeping on her breast. And Roz lay too, hardly begun to be satisfied, aching with hunger, weeping for the loss of Michael for the first time in months, but smiling nevertheless; and in her ears she could hear, as if she was in the chair on the other side of the room, her mother saying, "Find some milksop of a man who'll do exactly what you tell him."

She looked up into his slightly anxious brown eyes and smiled, and reached out a hungry hand, cupping his balls, caressing them with light, feathery strokes. "C.J.," she said, "do it again. Now. Before I scream."

C.J. did it again.

HE DID NOT always do quite what she told him. At first. After a heady two months, when they saw each other three times a week, in secrecy, and went to bed together whenever they could—and during which time she managed to improve his performance considerably—Roz asked him to go to Paris with her one weekend, ostensibly on business. She booked them into the anonymity of the Paris Hilton and, on Saturday morning after some particularly satisfactory sex, proposed to him. C.J. refused.

"You know as well as I do, Roz, it wouldn't work."

"Why wouldn't it work?"

"Because you're the boss's daughter, for a start. And you'd try to boss me around. And we're too unalike to make a go of it."

"You once said," said Roz, bending down to kiss his flat stomach, "that you wouldn't mind my being your boss."

"Well, I wouldn't, in a business context. But I don't want to be bossed in my marriage."

"Maybe I could learn not to."

"No, I don't think you could."

"C.J., I really think we could be very happy."

"I don't."

"But why not? I fancy you rotten. I enjoy your company. I"—and there was a fraction of a second's hesitation—"love you."

"No, Roz, you don't. And I don't love you."

"I see."

"Rosamund, I adore you. I think you're a terrific lay. I admire you. But I don't love you. You can't have thought I did."

"God in heaven!" Roz said. "How I hate being called Rosamund. It always heralds disaster. And I did think you loved me."

"Roz, I never said—"

"Oh, go to hell," she said angrily, climbing out of bed. She went into the bathroom, reappeared dressed and made up, and walked over to the door.

"Where are you going?"

"To see Annick. To discuss sales figures. That's all I'm really fit for, isn't it? Work. Let's keep things in order. Good-bye, C.J."

"Roz, please!"

She was gone, slamming the door behind her. She took a taxi to Annick's flat and stormed up the stairs.

"My goodness, Roz, what is it? What is the matter?"

"Nothing! Everything!"

"Have a drink. Tell me."

"Thank you. I'll have a brandy."

"Before lunch! This must be bad."

"Oh, it isn't really, I suppose," Roz said, sinking into Annick's deep leather armchair with a huge sigh. "It's the old story. I want to marry someone and he doesn't want to marry me."

"Not—not Michael Browning?"

"Oh, no," said Roz, with a wry grin. "He did want to marry me. It's ironic, isn't it, Annick? He would have married me and it would have been disastrous for me. This one would work, and he won't. And I don't know what to do."

"Forget him," said Annick. "There is no point in marrying someone who is not right for you."

"I think he is, though, that's the point."

"Well, *chérie*, even if he is you can't force him. And besides, Roz, why are you in such a hurry to get married? It is not so very long since

you finished with Michael. You have your career. I don't understand."

"I don't quite myself," Roz said slowly. "I only know I really, really
want to be married. I want to be wanted, and I want everyone to
know I'm wanted. A lot of people thought Michael ended our relationship. I don't like that. And I'm afraid of being alone. Ever since
Michael I've been afraid of being alone."

"And your career?"

"That's no problem. Of course I want my career. But I want to be
married, too. I want it all, Annick. We all do, our generation. Don't
you?"

"Perhaps."

"Oh, Annick, what am I going to do? How am I going to persuade
him?"

"I don't know, *chérie*. Truly. After all, the good old days when
women trapped the men are gone, are they not?"

"How do you mean?"

"By becoming pregnant. *Mon Dieu*, how many men got caught
like that. But not anymore. And what a disastrous beginning for the
marriage anyway. Have another glass of brandy, Roz, and tell
yourself there are other pebbles in the river, or whatever it is you
say."

"Fish in the sea," Roz said slowly. "Thank you, Annick. Good
advice. You're right, of course."

SHE WENT BACK to the hotel that night and found that C.J. had
checked out. She was not bothered. She had a little time. Back in
London she sought him out after a few days, apologized for making a
fool of herself, and said they might as well be friends. Loving friends.
C.J., relieved to see a peaceful end to the conflict, agreed. Within ten
days she had seduced him again. After a month, they were back
where they had been—passionate lovers—with one difference: Roz
told her father about the relationship.

"You won't believe this, Daddy. But we really really get on."

"Darling, I'm delighted. Surprised. But delighted. My oldest friend's
son. It's charming. I suppose I shouldn't encourage my daughter in
an irregular relationship, but I'm so fond of C.J. and I know he'll take
care of you."

"Don't say anything to him, will you? He's so shy."

"Of course not. But it is very nice news indeed. What delightful
hands I am finding my company in."

Roz had correctly anticipated her father's pleasure, but she had not quite thought through how deeply her future in the company might be affected by a marriage to C.J. The two of them—or rather the one of them, she thought wryly—could make an uncontested takeover for the whole thing in the fullness of time. Her father was sixty-two. He couldn't go on forever. Any fear that somebody might emerge—the specter of a son being born to Camilla, or indeed to anybody, was receding steadily these days, thank God—would be greatly diminished if Julian's only child—she wondered idly, occasionally, why he always referred to her as his only daughter—was married to the son of his oldest friend and that son already a proven asset to the company. Roz smiled to herself over the glass of champagne her father had poured her. How very nicely everything would work out.

THREE WEEKS LATER they were having a lazy Sunday breakfast in C.J.'s flat in Primrose Hill when Roz put down the *Sunday Times* and looked at him just slightly nervously.

"C.J.," she said, "I have a tiny problem."

"What's that?" said C.J. He was learning to be wary of her. "Can I help?"

"I don't know. Probably not." She paused and took a sip of coffee. "My period's rather late."

C.J. looked at her intently and rather oddly and put down his newspaper.

"What do you mean?"

"What I say. My period's rather late. Ten days, actually. What do you think?"

"I don't know," said C.J. "I don't know what I think. Or I hope I don't. Is it often late?"

"Well, sometimes. Not often. Bit worrying, isn't it?"

"I thought you were on the pill."

"I am. But it's a low-dosage one and you do have to be terribly careful about not forgetting and even about taking it at the same time each day. Maybe I slipped up. I don't think I did, but I might have."

"How do you feel?"

"Fine. Perfectly fine. Although—"

"Yes?"

"Well, the only thing is, I'm terribly hungry all the time. But I certainly don't feel sick or anything like that. Oh, don't look so worried, C.J. I'm sure it's nothing. If it hasn't arrived by Friday I'll have a test done. Now let's get dressed and go for a walk or something. Don't you want to go and explore Spitalfields, or somewhere equally exotic?"

"What? Oh, no, it doesn't matter," said C.J. absently.

"Well, anyway, you choose. I don't mind where we go."

COMING OUT OF the shower, she looked at C.J. He was staring out of the window, his face blank and white, his eyes somehow sunk into his face, darker than ever and full of fear.

· 17 ·

"I JUST CAN'T STAND THIS ANY LONGER, Miles," said Dorothy Kelly. "Either you get yourself a job or I'll tell the police about all that dope you're smoking."

Miles looked at her across the table and smiled his enchanting, irresistible smile.

"You wouldn't, Granny Kelly. I know you wouldn't. You couldn't."

"I would and I could."

"But you'd have to prove it. How would you do that? You'd have to bring them down to the beach or up to my room and watch them catch me in the act."

"I'm prepared to do that. For your good."

Miles smiled again. "I don't believe it. I just don't believe you'd come marching down to the beach with the law in tow and say, 'Look, Officer, there he is. That's my grandson, and he's smoking a joint right now.'"

"I would."

"Then I'll have to keep an eye open for you." He got up, kissed her fondly, and walked toward the door.

"Where are you going?"

"To the beach. Where else? With a mountain of grass."

"Miles, please come back. Let's talk about it. It's not just the dope. I'm scared you're going to get onto stronger stuff. You're throwing your life away, and I just can't bear to see it."

"Granny, I swear to you I never touch anything else. Ever. I don't need it."

"That's what they all say."

"I know. And okay, maybe a couple of the guys take a snort now and then, but not a lot of it. And certainly not me. I can't afford it. Now stop worrying."

She looked at him as he stood there, leaning gracefully against the door frame. Whatever he was doing, he managed to look as if he was posing for a photograph in some glossy magazine, and yet he was entirely unselfconscious. His great beauty was like a present that he didn't really want, something he was mildly pleased to have been given, and then put carelessly aside, unused. And yet it was not wasted, was not really unused at all. It opened doors for Miles, that beauty, made him welcome, sought after, everywhere he went. Women fell in love with it, and because of its singular nature, it did not repel men either; it lent Miles desirability. On a man with ambition it would have been dangerous; on Miles with his complete lack of concern for any kind of a future, it was in safekeeping. He was now twenty-three and a little over six feet two. His golden hair hung over his shoulders and halfway down his back. He was slim, but not thin, not gangly, and quite fine boned, with a long graceful neck and a beautifully shaped head. He had a high forehead and a perfectly straight nose with very slightly flaring nostrils. His eyes were exceptional—dark, dark blue, flecked with brown—and his lashes were so extravagantly long that women became irritated just contemplating them. But it was his smile that made his looks exceptional and that saved them from the cliché: it was sweet and all-embracing, but it also contained much humor and just a touch of self-mockery. You felt when you saw it that you were part of a conspiracy, that you'd been taken inside a charmed world, that you knew its owner and you liked him, and that he was anxious that you should not think he cared in the very least about how he looked or whether you might care either. He was constantly being approached by the photographers who came to Malibu to shoot fashion spreads or advertisements or commercials, to model for them; he had been asked not once but three times by movie people who had, in the way of all the best Hollywood fairy tales, watched him as he filled their gas tanks, delivered their groceries, or simply walked along Sunset with his swinging rangy grace, to come and test; several had suggested he go to casting calls for this or that film; but to them all he threw his most brilliant regretful smile and said that was really nice of them and he was really really flattered, but he had no wish to be a model, the film business did not interest him, and he was actually much happier doing what he did.

Which was almost nothing.

It was eighteen months now since he had graduated from Berkeley. After his first angry outburst he had relaxed into a lazy contentment. As far as Mrs. Kelly could make out he didn't see any girls at all. Or certainly not committedly. There were girls at the beach parties in the evening, but they were hangers-on who came and went; none of them were part of the surfing community, and Miles brought none of them home. She felt sometimes that even if he could get committed to sex that would be better than nothing, and then she hastily stifled the thought and told herself that at least he was doing no harm the way he was.

Apart from the dope smoking, he seemed to be leading a blameless life. He never asked her for money; he wouldn't take money from anybody. When he neded some, which wasn't very often, he earned it. He was strangely easy to live with; when she wasn't irritated by his idleness, the waste of his life, she couldn't help enjoying his relaxed, good-natured company. He spent many evenings just sitting in the swing out on the lawn high above the ocean, talking to her about anything that happened to engage him at the time, asking her opinion on things, listening carefully and consideringly to her answers. He didn't exactly challenge her views—that would have been too exacting for his philosophy of minimum intellectual effort—but he would gaze at her from the depths of his blue eyes and say, "Do you really, really think that's right?" and she would say, nettled, "Yes, yes, I really do," and he would raise his eyebrows mildly and smile at her, and shrug and resume his survey of the evening sky, and she would find herself against her will questioning her own views. He was kind to her and thoughtful; he never stayed out late without telling her, he almost always came home to dinner, he brought her occasional presents, he took her for drives into Santa Monica. He did the marketing and took care of the garden. He stopped short of the housework and the cooking, but he would fix things for her if she asked him. And he often told her she was the only person who had never let him down.

"Now, Miles, that is ridiculous," she had said, the first time he voiced this opinion. "How can you say that, when all these years Mr. Dashwood has taken so much interest in you, visited you, encouraged you to make something of your life?"

"All he did," Miles said, his eyes distant, "was turn me into some kind of hobby. When it began to be hard work, he was gone."

"Well, I don't see it like that."

"Don't you, Granny? Oh, well."

And the subject, like so many, many others, was closed.

"Miles, I think we should move," she said to him one day.

"Granny Kelly, what for? Where to? You know I like it here. You know you like it here."

"I don't like it that much. I've never made friends. I've never felt at home. Not really."

"You have me. I'm your friend."

"I know that, but you'd be mighty big-headed if you thought that was enough."

He sighed and smiled at her regretfully. "I guess you're right. I'm sorry. But I really don't want to move."

"I do. And maybe it's my turn."

"Well, you could go and I could stay."

"No, Miles, I want you to come with me."

"Granny, I'm twenty-three. I can go—or stay—where I like." He was smiling, but there was an edge to his voice.

"I know that, but I think you owe me something. Some loyalty. Some return."

He was silent for a while. Then: "Well, maybe. Where are you thinking of going?"

"The Bahamas."

"The Bahamas! Why?"

"I have an old friend there. In Nassau. I got a letter from her six months ago. She has a big house. It's beautiful, Miles; you'd like it. She lives alone, and she's lonely. She suggested I go and stay with her for a while. I didn't because I didn't want to leave you. But I think I will. For a week or so, at least, just to see if I like it. I asked her how she'd feel about us moving there, and she said she thought it would work out real fine."

"For you and her maybe. Not me."

"Why not?"

"Granny Kelly, you know why not. I like it here. There's no surf in the Bahamas. I wouldn't know what to do."

"You could get a job."

"I could not get a job. I don't want to get a job."

"Miles, have you never wondered what we live on?"

"Well, you have some money from my mom's insurance—my dad's, really. And the house. And I bring in enough for food."

"Yes, that's true. But if I chose to withdraw my support from you, I could. And you'd get pretty hungry and uncomfortable pretty fast."

He went over to her and kissed her. "You wouldn't do that to me. You wouldn't want me to be hungry and uncomfortable."

"I just might. I'm pretty tired of being uncomfortable myself. I don't like this climate that much. And I'm lonely, as I said."

Miles sighed. "I'm sorry you're lonely. It was terrible of me not to realize that. I'll try to stay home more."

"Miles, I don't want you to stay home more. I want friends of my own. I think we could have a good life in Nassau. It's a great city. I've been reading about it. There would be opportunities for you."

"I don't want opportunities."

"I know that, but I want them for you. Think about it. Please."

"All right, Granny. I'll think."

Thinking was cheap.

Partly out of a sense of guilt about his grandmother's loneliness, partly out of a wish to make her think he was indeed giving consideration to her plan, Miles stayed home the next day and worked in the garden. The surf was virtually flat anyway. Toward evening he drove the truck down to the beach to tell his friends he'd join them the next day. The beach, when he got there, was swarming with police. He drove home again thoughtfully.

That night two officers from the Los Angeles narcotics squad called at the house. Miles went to the door.

"Evening, sir," said a thickset, bullnecked cop with shifty black eyes. "Are you alone here?"

"Good evening, Sergeant. No, I'm not. My grandmother's here. She lives with me."

"Could we come in?"

"Why?"

"We have reason to believe you may have drugs on the premises."

"Now, what leads you to that line of reasoning, Officer?"

"Those guys on the beach. Your friends."

"Some friends," said Miles lightly. "Do you have a search warrant?"

"We certainly do."

"Okay. You'd better come in."

Mrs. Kelly appeared from the kitchen wiping her hands on her apron.

"Miles, what is it?"

"These gentlemen feel we may have drugs in the house, Granny. Do you have a stash anywhere? I certainly don't."

"This is not a laughing matter," said the sergeant with a look of such menace that even Miles felt a heaving shudder somewhere in the region of his bowels. "You have a police record, Wilburn. You were convicted and fined for a drug offense, as I am sure you will remember, and your friends did lead us to believe, quite strongly, that you have drugs in your house."

"Okay," Miles said. "Go ahead and search. You won't find anything."

They started in his room, and they wrecked it. They ripped open pillows, quilts, curtains; they tore out drawers, tipped out cupboards, threw books, clothes, tapes, and records on the floor. They moved into the bathroom, emptied the linen closet, the laundry hamper, tipped the entire contents of the medicine cupboard into a plastic bag.

They went through Mrs. Kelly's room, too, tore her mattress up, ripped her curtains down, rummaged through her underwear drawers, tipped her jewelry box out on the bed. They searched the kitchen, too, every drawer, every cupboard. Then they turned their attention to the living room, taking up every cushion on every chair and turning out her beloved china collection from the corner cupboard onto the floor with reckless, deliberate carelessness. When they had finished, and gone through every box and case and old jar in the garage, too, taken the seats out of the car, the saddle off Miles's bike, they looked at the two of them with an expression of odd suppressed anger.

"There doesn't seem to be anything. We might come back. Would you like us to clear up for you a bit now?"

"No," Mrs. Kelly said. "Just go."

She was stiff-backed and tight-lipped until the car had vanished down the hill. Then she suddenly collapsed in one of the cushionless chairs, her eyes frightened and full of tears.

"Granny Kelly, don't," Miles said, taking her in his arms. "I'm sorry. So sorry."

"Miles, did you have any drugs? Where did you put them?"

"Yeah, I had some hash. I flushed it down the toilet. That was all, though. They were looking for coke, but they'd have been really pleased to find the grass. It would have satisfied them for now."

"When did you flush it? Why?"

"This afternoon. I saw them on the beach. I thought they might come."

"Oh, Miles."

"The bastards," he said, in a sick quiet anger, "the bastards."

"They are, Miles, the police. They are pigs."

"I don't mean the cops. I mean my friends. My friends, squealing on me. How could they do that to me after all we've been to one another? How could they?"

"I don't know, Miles."

"You see. Everyone lets you down in the end. Lets me down, anyway."

He looked at her and kissed her wrinkled, sunburned forehead. "Except you. What a performance, Granny. You were great. You made it almost worth it."

"Not quite, though."

"No." He was silent for a while, looking at the mess. Thinking.

"Maybe," he said slowly, "maybe we should think seriously about going to Nassau."

NASSAU DIDN'T SUIT Miles. He felt lonely, bored, hemmed in. He couldn't believe he had been stupid enough to agree to come. He spent most of his days wandering through the back streets and the markets, wondering how he could escape back to California. On the face of it, it didn't look easy.

They had left quickly and very quietly. Only Father Kennedy had been informed of their destination, and that in the vaguest possible terms. Mrs. Kelly had not sold the house or even put it on the market; she simply put everything under covers and locked it up. She said she didn't feel it was really hers to sell, and one day maybe she might want to go back. Miles had said that now that he was over twenty-one wasn't it his? But she said no, Mr. Dashwood had bought it for her, it was in her name, and there was no way she was letting Miles get his idle hands on it.

"And besides," she said tartly, "I didn't think you'd want to taint yourself by accepting anything from Mr. Dashwood, Miles Wilburn."

Miles shrugged. "Maybe not."

He had never gone back to the beach; he couldn't. The betrayal went deeper than that of friend by friend; it was brother by brother, the brutal violation of a whole lovely life-style. He could not believe that the fellowship, and what seemed to him the inherent goodness of life on the beach, could have been hacked to death in five minutes by a team of cops, and that a dozen or so close brothers under the sunburned skin had sold him down the river for nothing more than the insincere promise of a more lenient sentence or a lower fine. He felt more than hurt; he was sickened. He had lost faith, trust. He didn't know where to go or what to do. And Nassau suddenly had seemed as good as anywhere—from a distance.

Flying in late one November afternoon, stepping out of the plane into the warm windy air, looking at the black faces everywhere, hearing the musical accent, discovering immediately a way of life that made California seem desperate and aggressive, he had been briefly intrigued and charmed. Mrs. Kelly's friend, Marcia Galbraith, had sent her car for them, driven by Little Ed, her chauffeur. Little Ed was six feet five inches tall and almost as wide; the name had been bestowed upon him by his father, Big Ed, who had driven for Marcia's father until he died at the age of eighty-three. Little Ed was now sixty-seven. He took them on a brief tour of Old Nassau before delivering them to Mrs. Galbraith's mansion. Miles and Mrs. Kelly, looking out at the grand Colonial-style white and pink houses, the policemen in their banana-republic white uniforms with their pith helmets and gold braid, the tourists driven about in the open carriages, felt they had come to a new and romantic country and smiled happily at each other.

Inside the Galbraith mansion, hidden behind high walls near

the center of the town, Mrs. Galbraith waited for them with after-noon tea.

It was served in a silver tea set and brought in by Little Ed's wife, Larissa. They sat in the shabbily grand drawing room filled with or-nate furniture, painted cabinets and gilt chairs overlooking a cool, shady garden, all palm leaves and extravagantly flowering shrubs, fluttering with small brilliant birds, and drank tea and nibbled wafer-thin cucumber sandwiches. Later Marcia Galbraith showed them their rooms, equally shabby, equally grand, both with verandas set with rocking chairs, looking over the garden. They had big high four-poster beds draped with brocade; they were lumpy and piled with worn chintz quilts. The walls were hung with portraits of Galbraith ancestors, and above their heads whirring fans with whirling arms shot the hot air around and around the room. The whole place had a strange, dreamlike quality. Miles felt as if he were watching a film or reading a book. He half expected it all to vanish and to find him-self safely back in the house in Latego Canyon. Dinner would be at seven, said Marcia. No need to dress tonight, as they were tired. Miles went out for a walk and found himself near the water, look-ing at the high bridge over to Paradise Island and the modern sky-crapers, and wondered what he would find to do here to pass his days.

Dinner, served by Larissa, four courses, each separated from the last by a ritual with finger bowls and glasses of ice water to clear the palate, was tedious and endless. Marcia, who proved to be a little more than slightly senile, reminisced about her days in the last war when the Windsors had been resident at Government House, and she and her husband St. George Galbraith had been frequent guests, and she had helped the duchess—"So charming, so very very kind"—with her Red Cross work. Miles and Mrs. Kelly went early to bed.

Over the days that followed, Mrs. Kelly settled down, settled in, began with astonishing speed to pick up her old friend's affectations, lethargic accent, ladylike ways. She bossed Larissa about, took up petit point, went out shopping, and exchanged her rather sexless, shapeless clothes for some girlishly flowing skirts and lacy blouses. She also managed to persuade Little Ed that some hens would be a useful addition to the household and could be kept at the bottom of the exotic garden.

"I feel," she said happily to Miles, rocking a little too vigorously for a true lady, on her veranda after lunch one day, "that I have come home."

Miles kissed her hand, which seemed appropriate under the cir-cumstances, and smiled down at her. "Good," he said.

AFTER A FEW days, wretched with inactivity, he crossed the bridge and spent the day on Paradise Island. He sat on the silvery white beach and looked at the sea, so much greener than its California counterpart, so still, so dull, it seemed to him. He looked at the hotels, stacked one upon the other with no breathing space between. He studied the people, the tourists, who looked mostly rich and old, and thought he had never been so lonely, or so unhappy. Later, he found there was more to like; but that day he was in despair.

And then he met Billy.

Billy de Launay was the son of Nassau gentry; his father was in the civil service, and his mother had grown up in the Windsors' court. Billy had been sent to Hampden Sydney, where he had graduated with great difficulty. Now he was home "resting," as he put it to Miles, before he decided on a career worthy of his education and intelligence. It wasn't easy to find. Billy was not unlike Miles to look at, being blond and blue-eyed. He did not have Miles's outstanding good looks, but he was very prepossessing nonetheless, with the old-fashioned, slightly fey charm of his background and upbringing.

He and Miles met at a lunch party given by the de Launays, to which Marcia Galbraith had been invited and to which she insisted on bringing her old friend and her old friend's son. The ladies were both dressed in outlandish creations of flouncing lace, and carrying parasols. Miles was good-naturedly out of character in white flannels and a navy blazer.

Billy de Launay came up to him, smiling broadly, and held out his hand. "Hi. I'm Billy de Launay. You must be Miles Wilburn. I've been hoping you'd come. I'm just about starved to death for company here. Can I get you a drink?"

"Sure," Miles said, smiling back at him.

"Bloody?"

"Sure," said Miles, smiling. "Love one. Thanks."

"How are you enjoying Nassau?" asked Billy, detaching two Bloody Marys from the tray of a passing waiter and handing one to Miles. "Having fun?"

"Not a lot," said Miles, and then realizing this must sound rude, hastily added, "I mean, in Nassau generally. This is a great party."

"I don't think I'd go that far," said Billy, laughing. "We're a trifle short of young blood in Nassau. What do you do, or what are you going to do?"

"Don't know," said Miles cautiously. "I'm—waiting and seeing a bit." He smiled his glorious smile at Billy. "I have plenty of time."

"You do," Billy said, responding to this philosophy with gratitude and pleasure. "We both do. Plenty. I keep telling Daddy there is absolutely no rush, that it's crazy to go into something I'm not sure about just for the sake of getting into order, but he doesn't see it that way."

"None of them do," said Miles, recovering swiftly from the cultural shock of hearing a six-foot-tall twenty-three-year-old refer to his father as Daddy. Ivy League talk, he supposed. "They all feel we should follow them onto the conveyor belt the minute we're out of college and stay on it till we drop off. I think there has to be more to life than that."

"Me, too," said Billy, beaming delightedly at him. "Here, have another Bloody."

"Thanks."

"Where did you go to college?"

"Berkeley."

"Uh-huh. What did you major in?"

"Math."

"God!" Billy's gaze was respectful. "And how did you graduate?"

"Summa cum laude," Miles said with a shrug.

"Jesus. Why hasn't some bank snapped you up?"

"I didn't want it to."

"Did you even try?"

"Nope."

"Good man! Your parents are dead, aren't they?"

"Yeah."

"I'm sorry. That must be, well, hard."

"Not really. It was a long time ago. My grandmother brought me up."

"Is she your guardian?"

"Yeah. And some old guy put me through college. He was a friend of my parents."

"He sounds like a good guy."

"Kind of," Miles said briefly. "I didn't really like him."

"He must be kind of sick you're not using your education."

"Yes," Miles said with relish. "I think he is."

Billy, realizing there was more to this story than he was going to hear just now, dropped the subject. "Met any girls here?"

"Haven't met anyone under eighty till today."

"Well, there are a few. Pretty damn dull, though. Not many game ones."

"That's bad."

"Yeah, it is. The talent is over on Paradise Island. The older ladies, you know."

"I have seen a few."

"Well, hell," Billy said, "you don't have to stop at looking. They're really hot, half of them. Married to rich old guys who can't get it up half the time."

"Uh-huh."

"Honestly, Miles, you can get most of them just with a smile. With your smile," he added, without even a touch of envy, "you could get all of them."

Miles decided he liked Billy more and more. "But how do you meet them?"

"Oh, it's easy. Just hang around the pool at some of the hotels or at the Mirage Club. That's a good place."

"Yeah, but how do you get into those places?"

"Oh, it's easy. You just walk in, settle down, look as if you're staying there. Dress the part. Club tie, battered old tennis hat, that sort of thing. I'll show you. The club's harder. I've actually had to pull out of there. There's a funny old French guy who runs it. He wears a morning suit every day, he's really spaced, and he's gotten to know me. Once you're there, the women just come flocking. It's so easy. After that it's parallel parking all the way."

"Sorry?"

"Parallel parking. Fired up. Sex. All the way. You know?"

"Oh, sure," Miles said, laughing. "I know."

Billy laughed, too. Miles might be just a bit of a dork. He obviously hadn't been anywhere too smart to school, and he seemed to be a bit slow on the uptake a lot of the time, but he was a really nice guy, and living almost next door. There was nothing socially that Billy felt he could not fix. Miles was clearly good-natured and a quick study; he could teach him all the right things to say and how to behave. It was all too good to be true. Life was obviously going to look up a lot.

IT DID. BILLY and Miles had a marvelous time. Billy had been absolutely right. Just as Miles had suspected, many of the rich, bored ladies were indeed all too ready to spill their sexual largess over the bodies of two charming and totally available young men. What was more, Miles discovered, his innocence was considerably in his favor. Women of thirty-five, forty, forty-five, painstakingly tutored in every possible variation, legitimate or deviant, of sexual behavior were delighted to find themselves in bed with near virginal material.

The main trouble, from Miles's point of view, was that there was still no financial advantage in this pastime. There was absolutely no way either he or Billy could actually take money from their activities. They saw the whole thing as a lark, as fun, as something to do, and there was no way the ladies would give them any. Having an entertaining time with some charming boy who was clearly from a good family was one thing; paying for the entertainment would have put a very different complexion on it.

The young men were constantly being given presents—ties, silk shirts, belts, wallets—all very nice accessories, particularly when they were moving on from one liaison to the next, but that was all. Nevertheless Miles did occasionally wish some of the presents could be turned into cash. The occasional belt or wallet provided him with a few dollars, but the market value for such things was poor. One particularly rich and—it had to be said—plain, lady had given him a Cartier watch, but Miles could not bear to part with it. He had, he was discovering, a serious liking for beautiful and prestigious things. He wanted more and more of them, and he would rather go without spending money for a month, as he frequently did, than part with anything of lasting value. Nevertheless it was frustrating. Because their work, as they called it, left their evenings free, they both liked to gamble. Billy had a little money, which he was generous with, but it never seemed to last for more than an hour, even on a good evening, and besides, Miles had his pride. He had tried to persuade Mrs. Kelly to give him a bit more, but she was increasingly withdrawn into her new persona of genteel widow, along with her friend. She had aged a lot in the year they had been in Nassau. Relieved of the strain of caring single-handedly for Miles and worrying about his future, she had suddenly descended into confusion and delusion. She was, after all, nearly eighty, and she had had a lot to cope with. Miles, who genuinely loved her and was truly grateful to her, did not want to intrude on her new happiness. He could wait. It was not, after all, her problem. He was a young man of rare integrity, as Billy and he often agreed.

The solution to their monetary problems came from a rather unexpected source: the doorman at the Bahamian Palace, who had grown fond of them and saw them in a rather benevolent light.

"You boys play tennis?" he asked them one day as they wandered out, blinking slightly, into the sunshine after a long afternoon's work in the shaded air conditioning of two of the hotel's finer suites.

"I do," said Billy. "Played for Hampden. How about you, Miles?"

"Some," said Miles. "I could brush up on my game. Why?"

"They need a new tennis pro here. I'd apply if I were you. They might take on the two of you. It wouldn't interfere with your other occupation, I wouldn't imagine. Might even help it along a little bit." He grinned and winked at them. "Go and see the manager now. He's by the pool."

MILES AND BILLY played a test game, charmed the manager, who was pleased with the notion of what was clearly old money on his staff, and Billy got taken on immediately. Miles was told to polish up his game and then he might be allowed to work with his friend on busy days. Given his facility for sports, he was on the courts at the Bahamian Palace in three weeks.

They benefited in two ways: they had a cash income, albeit a modest one, and they were able, as the doorman prophesied, to pursue their prey with greater and more graceful ease.

Billy's parents were initially unhappy with the arrangement, but swiftly came around to the view that any employment was better than none, and at least were relieved of continuing to give Billy his modest allowance, which in their straitened circumstances was a relief. Mrs. Kelly was almost speechless with delight at the news, as presented by Miles, that he was working as sports and social manager of one of the island's most prestigious hotels.

Miles, in possession of his own money for the first time in his life, felt strangely exhilarated. He had never really made the connection between work and money, had not thought of getting a job as the route to worldly delights. In any case, worldly delights had never interested him before; the surf had come cheap. But sitting in the gilded air of the Palace, taking in heady whiffs of the rich aroma of real money, studying the women he was making love to, who somehow managed to look rich even naked, looking at their jewels, their clothes, feeling against his skin the sensation of silk sheets, savoring the almost sensual pleasure of good champagne, he felt a swiftly growing desire for more and more of it.

He changed his outward appearance. Basing much of his style on Billy's, he cut off his long hair; he bought himself suits, shirts, and ribbon belts, knotted silk cuff links, loafers, and one of L. L. Bean's Norwegian sweaters, a whole wardrobe of Lacoste shirts, and even, in a fit of sartorial madness, sent for some madras Bermudas from Trimingham's. He looked supurb, an outstanding example of money of the very oldest kind.

He had proved, as Billy had suspected, a talented student of the social school Billy put him through. He learned all the right preppy phrases and words and attitudes; he changed his accent slightly from his Californian drawl to something based more on Tigs Tyler's than Billy's. He learned to display the peculiar WASP brand of ennui rather than his own more ingenuous Californian laid-backness.

And yet he remained true to himself and his roots. He never lied about his background, never disowned Granny Kelly, never set aside his happiness and his loyalty to Santa Monica High School and his days on the beach. He became something interesting and unique: a carefully stylish, rich blend of old-money behavior and modest philosophies put together with his looks, his charm, and a genuine sweetness of disposition. As a result, he found hardly a door anywhere that would not open for him. For the first time in his life he felt a sense of anticipation. He wondered where he might find himself next.

·18·

ON THE DAY THEY WERE TO MEET, both Phaedria Blenheim and Julian Morell woke up feeling exceptionally irritable.

Phaedria switched off her alarm, sank back deep under her comforter, and reviewed the events of the day ahead for possible reasons. There was only one, and it came to her very quickly. It was to have been her day off, and she had lost it; a day out hunting with the Avon Vale had been replaced with an as yet unconfirmed interview with some boring old fart of an industrialist.

"Why me?" she said furiously to her editor the night before, shaking her head at the can of beer he was offering her. "You know it's my day off. I'm going hunting. Jane'll be here, and she can do it every bit as well as I, probably better because she'll care. I won't. Please, Barry, please don't make me do it."

"I'm sorry, Phaedria, but Jane can't do it every bit as well as you. I need you there tomorrow. It's important. And you might like to remember I pay you to care," he added a trifle heavily.

"But why? What's so special? Some boring plastics company. What's in that for the Women's Page?"

"Its chairman."

"Its chairman? Oh, Barry, come off it. Since when did the chairman of a plastics company have anything interesting to say to women?"

"Not just plastics, Phaedria. Pharmaceuticals. And cosmetics. And department stores and hotels. Don't you ever read press releases?"

"Of course not."

"Well, you should. Read this one and stop looking so bloody constipated and have a drink. Sit down. Go on."

Phaedria glared at him, slung her coat down on his spare chair, took the can of beer from him, and leaned against the wall, skimming the release:

MORELL PHARMACEUTICALS TO OPEN BRISTOL
PLANT. FOR IMMEDIATE RELEASE.

The multimillion-dollar worldwide Morell Pharmaceutical Chain will open its new plant, the most technologically advanced in Europe, in Bristol in two weeks' time. The plant, which is situated on the Fishponds Estate, incorporates a factory, a marketing and sales division, a research laboratory, and a conference center. It has been designed to entirely new specifications incorporating the very latest technology.

The chairman of Morell Pharmaceuticals, Sir Julian Morell, knighted for his services to industry in 1981, will be coming in person to officially open the plant and will hold a conference for selected members of the press at the same time. An invitation is attached.

There was much more about Sir Julian's other business interests, his pharmaceutical work and its vast benefits to mankind in general, and those in the Third World in particular, the drugs he had launched, most notably one of the first low-dosage oral contraceptives ten years earlier, and his various extraordinarily well deserved awards for services to industry. Phaedria read the release stone-faced and looked at Barry.

"Still can't see it. It sounds totally boring. I'm going hunting."

"Phaedria, you are not going hunting. You're going to get an interview with Julian Morell."

"Barry, for Christ's sake, it's a press conference. Every half-assed reporter for miles around will be there asking him the same half-assed questions."

"I know that, darling, but you're going to get an exclusive."

"And what will be so big about that?"

"Phaedria, you ought to read the papers a bit more as well as the press releases. Julian Morell is a great character. And a great womanizer," he added, "and he hasn't given an interview for ten years. He's developed a phobia about the press."

For the first time Phaedria's expression sharpened. She slithered down against the wall and sat on the floor, taking another can of beer from Barry.

"Okay. Tell me about him."

"More or less self-made. Impoverished second son of the upper classes. Well upper middle. Started with a tiny line of medicines just after the war. Went into cosmetics. Then plastics, pharmaceuticals, paper. Department stores. That's probably the big one. Never heard of Circe?"

"Never."

"Well, there isn't one in London—yet. But there's one in Paris and

Milan and New York. And Beverly Hills, I expect. Very, very expensive. Makes Harrods look like Marks and Spencer, that sort of thing. Oh, and there's a chain of hotels."

"Called?"

"Called just Morell. Like—well, like—just Hilton. Anyway, he's made a billion or two."

"And what about the women?"

"Well, he's only been married once. Can't remember who to. But there've been a lot of mistresses, all beautiful, and a lot of scandal. He's always in the gossip columns."

"Barry, I didn't think you read the gossip columns," Phaedria said, laughing.

"A good journalist reads everything in the other papers," Barry said slightly pompously. "You have to. You need to know what's going on. I'm always telling you that, Phaedria."

"I know," Phaedria said, "I know I'm bad. I just can't be bothered half the time. I'm not really a journalist at all, I'm afraid. Not like you," she added, getting up and patting his hand fondly. "All right, you've intrigued me. I'll go. I shall continue to complain, but I'll go. Now, have you fixed the interview?"

"No. They turned me down. That's precisely why I want you to go. I reckon you'll get one."

"Why?"

"You know damned well why. Don't play games with me. Now go home and get some beauty sleep. You're going to need it."

"Thanks," said Phaedria. "All right, I'll try. But I want another day off instead. And you can send Jane to the mayor's banquet, okay?"

"Okay."

"Don't forget."

"All right, Phaedria," Barry said wearily. "I won't forget."

"You probably will. But I'm not going to do it anyway. 'Night, Barry."

"Good night, Phaedria. See you tomorrow."

"Perhaps. I might elope with Sir Julian and never come back."

"That's fine by me. Elope with him if you like, but get the copy in first. Bye, darling."

"Bye, Barry."

Barry looked after her thoughtfully as she walked out through the newsroom. She had been with him two and a half years now on the *Bristol Echo*, and she drove him to distraction. She was everything he disapproved of in a woman and in a reporter, and yet he lived in dread of her leaving. She was a talented writer and a clever interviewer; she could entice new thoughts and pronouncements out of anybody. The most overdone, rent-a-quote actor, the most cliché-ridden, party-line politician suddenly, under the scrutiny and influence of Phaedria Blenheim, found an original line, an unpredictable view, which they read themselves with surprise and pleasure, and they refreshed and invigorated their own tired battery of quotes with it for months to come.

She was also extremely beautiful, which was clearly another asset; she could persuade any man to talk to her and pour his heart out, and she had little compunction about publishing intimate little confidences and details that had been made to her "strictly off the record, darling," taking the view that any public figure who was fool enough to trust a journalist deserved absolutely anything he got.

On the other hand, she was quite right when she said she wasn't really a journalist. Her knowledge of the world was extremely scanty; she scarcely knew who the Home Secretary was, and certainly not who ran the Soviet Union or China, or even Ireland and, more unusually in a woman, who Prince Andrew's latest girlfriend was, or whether Elizabeth Taylor was marrying for the fifth or sixth time. She was actually far more interested in horses and hunting than in seeing her name in ever-bigger by-lines. Her job financed her horse and her riding—just. Barry knew, and was alternately irritated and amused by the knowledge, that she also capitalized on his rather indulgent attitude toward her to get days off when she wanted to hunt or attend a race meeting.

But she filled her pages—he had made her women's editor a year ago—with original and charming ideas, and she delivered the goods every week, even if it came in dangerously close to deadline, and he knew it would be a hundred years before anyone as talented came the way of his paper again.

She had started working for the *Echo* as a typist and gofer, but had soon become a full-time reporter. She worked very hard, she enjoyed what she did, and she was nice to have around. She was a touch abrasive, and she knew her value, but it did not make her arrogant, she mixed in with the others, learned to drink and swear and swap filthy jokes, and became, in short, one of the blokes. And she was extremely happy.

Barry grew very fond of her. Often, when everyone else had gone home, they would go to the pub and talk. She was a good listener; almost without realizing it, he had told her everything about his marriage, his career, his love for the *Echo*, and his one great terror in life —retirement.

It was a long time before he found out much about her. It came out gradually in bits and pieces, tiny pieces of confidences spilled over just one too many beers or in the intimacy born of working closely together long and late. She was an only child and she had looked after her father ever since she was ten years old, when her mother had run away to South America with his best friend and had never properly communicated with either her husband or her child again.

Augustus Blenheim was an academic, and earned his living lecturing in literature and writing biographies of virtually unknown writers; it was her father that Phaedria had to thank for her name. "No, it isn't Phaedra," she would say patiently, a hundred, a thousand times over the years, "it's Phaedria. Different lady."

And then she would explain—or perhaps not explain, depending on her audience—that Phaedria was one of the characters in Spenser's *Faerie Queene*, and the personification of Wantonness. Why any father, most people would wonder, while keeping their wonderings to themselves, should inflict upon his daughter so strong an association with such a quality was a considerable mystery. But Phaedria did not seem to have held it against him. It was a pretty name, and she liked it, and besides she loved him so much she would have forgiven him far more and much worse.

They had lived together, father and daughter, in the same house in Chelsea all their lives, and Phaedria had come home from school every day with a mountain of homework and had shopped and cooked for him before settling down to it. At the weekends they did the housework together, went to the cinema, visited friends, mostly academic or literary colleagues of Augustus's, experimented with recipes, played chess, and talked interminably. They were all the world to each other; it was a perfect marriage. Phaedria had few friends her own age; she was perfectly happy with her father's. Occasionally one of the less reticent women in their circle would tax Augustus with Phaedria's rather unconventional social life or suggest to her that she go to more parties and perhaps even on holiday with her contemporaries, but they would both politely say things were perfectly satisfactory as they were, and ignore any attempts to change anything. Nobody ever managed, or even tried, to come between them.

The effect of all this on Phaedria was complex. It made her fairly incapable of relating to any male very much under the age of her father; it matured her in some ways emotionally and retarded her in others. It made her self-reliant; it meant she was not daunted by any person, however brilliant or famous, or any situation, however difficult or challenging; it also ensured that she remained a virgin.

Even at Oxford, when she finally began to make friends with men who were her contemporaries, she found herself completely incapable of entering into a sexual relationship with any of them. Having missed out to a large degree on any kind of emotional education, having had no mother, sisters, or even friends to talk to about sex and love or about how she felt about anything, she grew up self-contained and innocent. She learned the facts about sex from school and books; she had to handle her first period, her early sensations of desire, and the transformation of her own body from child to woman, entirely alone.

She entered her third year at Oxford intact, with a reputation for being fun, funny, intelligent, beautiful, and absolutely not worth even trying to get into bed. Men initially saw her as a challenge but, confronted by her patent lack of interest in the matter, gave up. Nevertheless, she was popular; she had a capacity to listen and a lack of self-interest that made both sexes pleased to have her friendship. But she remained, unknown even to herself, very lonely.

And then she had met Charles Fraser-Smith, the darling of the gossip columns, blond, tall, heavily built, a superb rugger and polo player and a brilliant classics scholar. What nobody except Phaedria ever knew was that he was homosexual. Phaedria not only knew, she became his best friend and even, for one night, his lover. Although she knew it was futile, she found herself falling in love with him. But when he was unable to return her affection, Phaedria was devastated and painfully cut him out of her life.

After Oxford she settled in Bristol because the parents of an Oxford friend lived there in a big house in Clifton, and let out bed-sits to students. What she had seen of Bristol she liked; it was architecturally nice, very lively, and near enough to the country to be able to ride. She moved down with no clear idea of what she was going to do, but she had her typing and her shorthand skills, and she knew she could support herself. She did a series of temporary secretarial jobs, found some good stables, began to ride regularly and bought her own horse, slowly formed a new circle of friends and, without being fully aware of the process, began to forget about Fraser-Smith. She also began to think about a proper job. She had not got a useful degree and, despite her expensive education, had to be content with typing and filing for a series of people who had less than half her brains.

Two things really interested her: fashion and journalism. "And you know the rest," she said to Barry one night, over the hundredth or so half of bitter, "and here I am."

"And I'm delighted you are," he said fondly, patting her hand. He had a great deal of time for her; she wasted no time whatsoever on self-pity.

PHAEDRIA GAVE QUITE a lot of thought to what she would wear to persuade Sir Julian to talk to her exclusively. She was clever with clothes; she had never had any money to spend on them, but she had that eye for shape and length, a flash of color, an unexpected accessory, that ability to haul together three or four disparate items of clothing into something coherent and original that is called style and that is as ingrained and inborn as the ability to carry a tune or to spell correctly.

It was no use today, she thought, trying to dress up. Multimillion-aires would not be impressed by Wallis copies of Jean Muir or even Jaeger. Better dress down and chic, she decided, spraying herself in Guerlain's Jicky, the perfume she always wore, and pulling on a cream silk shirt and a pair of straight-legged Levi's. She added soft brown leather calf-length boots, a wide brown belt, and a soft leather jacket she had bought secondhand at the flea market in Paris; and after a moment's hesitation she put on an antique gold chain and locket. She hauled back her cloud of wild dark hair and tied it with a brown and cream Hermes scarf her father had given her for her birthday, and after a moment's consideration set it free again. She put a little shadow around her dark brown eyes and applied a slither of lip gloss, then slung a notebook, a pen, and three pencils into the canvas and leather fishing bag she used as both handbag and brief-case.

"Right," she said, smiling at herself in the mirror. "Sir Julian, here I come."

JULIAN ALWAYS GAVE a good performance on these occasions. His charm and his capacity for lateral thought tended to cut neatly through the tedious razzmatazz of a mass conference. By the time he had unveiled the plaque—less pretentious than cutting a tape, he thought to himself as he did it, but still bloody silly—made his short speech, and answered five of the six journalists' questions he had promised himself, he felt himself on a downhill run. He had actually picked up the sheaf of papers in front of him on the table and smiled charmingly at the assembled company and the mayor and other local dignitaries when a female voice rang out through the hall.

"Sir Julian, may I ask you about women?"

The assembled company laughed; it was a neat line. He could not afford to be unreceptive. He put the papers down again, shaded his eyes against the glare of the lights, and smiled charmingly.

"I'll try to answer. Which particular aspect of the female race were you interested in, Miss—er?"

"Blenheim. Phaedria Blenheim. *Bristol Echo.*"

Ah, that one. The one who'd requested an exclusive interview. Clever stuff. She would need putting in her place. "What is your question?"

"How many women will you be employing? In your management team here, that is, rather than on the factory floor."

Julian smiled again. He couldn't see her clearly, but the voice, indisputably Oxbridge, told him exactly what she was like: confident, assertive, and too clever for her own good, as his mother would probably have said.

"As many as earn their place in it, Miss Blenheim. I have a good record in equal opportunity. I have several women on the boards of several of my companies, both here and in the United States. Including the major parent company. You really should do your homework a little more carefully."

"Oh, but I have," said Phaedria. "I've learned that the board of Juliana and Circe is largely female. In the case of the hotels and the pharmaceutical company, however, your record is less good. With the exception of Mrs. Emerson, of course."

A slight buzz went around the hall. Julian pushed his hair back. Brian Branscombe, recently appointed head of Morell Pharmaceuticals, half stood up, but Julian shook his head at him and smiled again into the lights. "Do go on, Miss Blenheim. I had clearly underrated your capacity for research."

"Thank you," said Phaedria. "I think I have made my point. The record in other companies, particularly in Europe, is better. I thought perhaps as this was a new plant, you might feel you could be a little bolder."

"How interesting," Julian said. "Well, Miss Blenheim, as you are clearly something of an expert on management matters, perhaps you would care to submit a proposal to me. In writing, of course. I would be most interested to read it. In the meantime I can only say that there will be several women on the management team here in Bristol, and in due course they will be available for interviews to you and your colleagues."

"And you, Sir Julian. When will you be available for an interview?"

"Miss Blenheim, I am under the impression that that is precisely what is happening now."

"No," Phaedria said, "this isn't an interview. This is a floor show."

She was walking down to the front of the hall now. Julian suddenly saw her emerging from the blurred darkness; she took form, became more than a voice, a purveyor of silly questions, aggressive observations, posturing clichés. He looked at her and his breath caught. A great cloud of wildly tangled curly dark hair, pale oval face, luminous dark eyes; young, so young she looked, younger than his own daughter, younger than any woman he had looked at sexually for years. And that was how, he realized suddenly, he was looking at her: as a man appreciating, admiring, desiring, a woman. It happened with a speed, a force, that physically startled him; he felt suddenly confused, unable to remember what she had asked.

And Phaedria, sensing in some instinctive way the stab of emotion, the surge of interest, paused, looked at him more sharply, and was moved by what she saw. Style he had, this man, and humor and a strange grace; but what hit her hardest was a sense of sexual energy, directed exclusively at her. It was a cataclysmic moment that both of them would remember for the rest of their lives.

Brian Branscombe, finally deciding to arrest the tedious Miss Blenheim in her nicely shod tracks before she could do any more harm to his carefully orchestrated conference, stood up on the platform. "Miss Blenheim, thank you for your question. I trust Sir Julian has answered it to your satisfaction. Ladies and gentlemen, a buffet lunch is now being served in the hospitality suite. Unfortunately, Sir Julian has to leave for an urgent meeting in London very shortly after lunch, but he will be joining us briefly. You can put any further questions to me or to our press officer. Thank you for your interest and time. Do please adjourn next door."

The guests and the press moved as one hungry man toward the next room; only Phaedria remained, standing quite still, her eyes fixed on Julian's face.

"Miss Blenheim," said Branscombe, a trifle impatiently, "do please go next door and help yourself to lunch."

"Well, I did wonder," said Phaedria, motionless still, "if I could have a few words—"

"No, Miss Blenheim, you cannot. I'm sorry. Sir Julian has to leave very shortly. Sir Julian, let me take your papers. If you will just follow me . . ."

"Just a moment, Brian. Miss Blenheim, was there anything else?"

"A lot," said Phaedria briskly, seeming to wake, coming to herself again. "I'd like to ask you about so many things, Sir Julian."

"Miss Blenheim," Branscombe said again, "please. Sir Julian is on an extremely tight schedule. Do excuse us."

"Miss Blenheim," said Julian, ignoring him totally, "I do have to go. It's quite true. But I would be happy to give you an interview. What are your plans for the rest of the day? If you have time, you could fly back to London with me now and I could give you an hour or so. Then I'll send you back here."

"There's no need."

"I pay the helicopter pilot," he said, and smiled at her.

"Right," said Phaedria, smiling back. "I do have the time. I'll just call my editor. Thank you, Sir Julian. I do appreciate it very, very much."

"It will be my pleasure," he said, and she thought she had never heard that word so blatantly caressed.

Branscombe, clearly irritated, showed her to his office, and she phoned Barry.

"Barry? It's Phaedria. Listen, I've got it. The exclusive. I'm flying back to London with Julian Morell now in his chopper. Stylish, huh? Expect me when you see me."

PHAEDRIA HAD NOT expected to like Julian Morell. She had thought he would be interesting and charming but arrogant and shallow. She found him interesting and charming, and unpretentious and thoughtful.

She also found him sexually attractive; her senses had not recovered from the shock they had received. She felt disturbed and irritated with herself at the same time. Sitting looking at him across his desk, her stomach still unsettled from the helicopter flight, she found it impossible to relax, to set herself aside, to concentrate on him and what she could extract from him. She knew he was sixty-two, but she found it hard to believe; he looked easily ten years younger. His hair was only slightly flecked with gray, his skin was lightly tanned, he was very slim. He was superbly, if predictably, dressed: classic gray three-piece suit, gray and white striped shirt, with a button-down collar, she noticed. "Are you the man in the Brooks Brothers shirt, Sir Julian?" she asked. Yes, he said, yes he was. His son-in-law brought him half a dozen of the things every time he visited New York, which was fairly frequently. "I wear them all once, and then file them away." His tie was red, with a black line in it, very discreet, his watch a wafer-thin Cartier, his cuff links plain gold. There was no suggestion of vulgarity, of showmanship; he was simply a beautifully dressed conservative Englishman.

He was good to listen to as well, she thought. His voice was light and level, neither aggressively public school nor flattened out Middle

Atlantic. It had great charm, that voice, an ability to take certain words and phrases and warm them, lend emotion to them, or to toss humor into a remark, self-mockery even, without a fleck of emotion crossing the bland face, the dark, dark eyes.

He sat and looked at her with such pleasure, such patent interest, that Phaedria felt exposed, vulnerable. Short of leaving the room, there was nothing she could do to escape his examination. He had said little in the helicopter. He had studied papers and signed letters, having asked her to excuse him. "When we get to my office, I shall be entirely at your disposal. Which I trust will please you."

They had landed at Battersea Heliport and been met by a pale blue Rolls Corniche convertible. Phaedria was surprised by this, the first hint of ostentation she had seen. "Goodness," she had said, "what a nice car!"

Yes, he had said, he liked cars, always had; they were one of his hobbies, as no doubt she knew, being such a careful researcher. "And do you like cars, Miss Blenheim?"

No, she said, not really. They were just a means of transport to her, but his other passion, horses—now, that was something she did love, and his eyes had danced over her face, and he had talked to her about horses, thinking to discover she knew nothing about them at all, pleased and surprised to find he was wrong, that she could converse about bloodstock and flat racing and hunting with confidence and knowledge.

"Do you have a horse, Miss Blenheim?"

"Yes, I do. A hunter. A six-year-old gray mare."

"And what is her name, this young gray mare?"

"Grettisaga."

"That is a very unusual name."

"Yes. It's nice, though, don't you think? I expect you know the tale well?"

"I fear not. Which tale?"

"*The Grettisaga*. It's a fourteenth-century Icelandic story. It bears a strong resemblance to *Beowulf*. William Morris has done a translation."

"I see. You are clearly a very literary person."

"Oh, not really. My father thinks I am woefully ill-read."

"And who is your very well read father?"

"His name is Augustus Blenheim. He's an academic. He writes books and gives lectures on literary figures only about two other people have ever heard of. His current obsession is Charles Maturin, an Irish Gothic novelist. His dream is to be asked to make a television program about someone, but I think it would draw such a small audience that the channel showing it would go right off the air."

"And I suppose you owe your very unusual name to your father?"

"Oh, yes," Phaedria said with a cheerful sigh, "of course. Do you know who Phaedria was?"

"Let me see. Did she not marry Theseus?"

"'Fraid not. You've failed the test. No relation to her whatsoever. That was Phaedra. Phaedria was a character in—"

"I know," said Julian suddenly, "don't tell me. In—not Chaucer, no, Spenser, wasn't she? *The Faerie Queene.*" He smiled at her triumphantly. "Do I pass?"

"Do you know what quality she represented?"

"No, I don't think I can go that far."

"Well, then you do pass. Not very well, but better than most. She was Wantonness."

"I see. And how well does your name become you, Miss Blenheim?" He spoke lightly, he smiled charmingly, but Phaedria could feel him reaching out to her, taking a small but irrevocable step toward intimacy, and she felt at the same time warmed and confused.

"That is a question I never answer," she said. "Whoever asks it."

"Ah," he said, "an unoriginal one, clearly. Forgive me."

"Very unoriginal. But yes, I do. Forgive you, I mean. Where are we going?"

"My office is in Dover Street. I'm surprised you didn't know that. Your research was so extremely thorough."

"Yes. I'm sorry if I was rude. About your daughter and everything. I didn't exactly mean to be."

"I forgive you. But why did you have to be at all? Exactly or otherwise?"

"I had to get you to notice me."

He turned slightly in the car and looked at her for quite a long time, his eyes moving slowly from her hair to her face, pausing there, exploring her own eyes so tenderly, so questingly, that she looked away briefly, confused, lingering on her mouth, and then, quite briefly, but with an unmistakable confidence, on her neck, her breasts. And then he smiled and said, "I don't think you had to be even inexactly rude to do that."

"Not true," she said, pulling herself together after what she felt to be an endless silence. "Would I ever have made so much as another question if I hadn't been so—so bothersome?"

"Possibly not. And I would have regretted it greatly." He looked away from her then, out of the window for a long moment. They were traveling slowly along the Embankment; the river looked beautiful, goldenly gray in the winter sunshine. "Do you like London?"

"Only quite. I prefer the country."

"That's nice. I think I do, too. Because you can ride?"

"Yes. And because I like space to myself."

"That doesn't sound like a journalist."

"I'm not really a journalist," said Phaedria. "My editor is always telling me that."

"Really?" he smiled, genuinely amused. "In what way are you not really a journalist?"

"I'm not interested in the world at large and not really interested in newspapers. Only my bit of them."

"Then why do you do it?"

"Because I'm good at it, and I like writing."

"And interviewing famous people?"

"Everyone says that. No, not interviewing famous people. Most famous people are extremely boring."

"On behalf of us all I apologize," he said, and smiled his dancing smile. "Or perhaps I am being presumptuous. Perhaps I don't qualify as famous in your book."

"No," she said, "honestly, you don't. Famous is—well, you know, really famous. Instantly recognized. Peter Cook. Olivier. Maggie Smith."

"I feel very humbled. But you're right."

"I'm sorry. I didn't mean to be rude again."

"You weren't. I was being arrogant. Have you interviewed all those people?"

"Yes."

"And were they really boring?"

"Actually, those three weren't. Not at all. But they were exceptions." She looked at him and smiled. "I think you are probably another."

"But I thought I wasn't famous."

"Well, maybe you are a bit. But you aren't boring. So far."

"Good."

The car was swinging up Whitehall; the traffic, as it so often and inexplicably did in London, had cleared. Peter Praeger, Julian's chauffeur and bodyguard, and probably the most discreet man in London, half turned his head. "Straight to the office, Sir Julian? You don't want to stop anywhere for lunch?"

"No, thank you, Pete. Sarah has something waiting for me in the office. Sarah is my secretary," he said to Phaedria. "Terrifyingly efficient. We are all frightened of her. Aren't we, Pete? We do what she says."

"We certainly do, sir. Will you need me any more today? You don't want me to bring you anything from the house?"

"No, I don't think so. But I have a dinner engagement. Can you come at seven to the office?"

"Yes, Sir Julian. Would the engagement be in London or out of town?"

"The Meridiana, Pete. And I won't be late."

"Fine. Right. Here we are, sir."

Phaedria, climbing out of the car, looked up at the offices with interest. She had expected some modern block; she found one of the original gray eighteenth-century buildings, with large white admittedly fake Palladian doors, and the original windows.

Julian pushed one of the doors open himself, then stood aside to let her pass, taking his briefcase from Pete. "In you go, Miss Blenheim. The lift's over there. Just a moment."

He went and spoke briefly to the girl at the reception desk and then came over to her. They got in the lift. "Top floor. My office is in what is known as a penthouse suite."

"It sounds rather debauched."

"I'm afraid it isn't. A great deal of very hard work goes on there, and that's all."

"I see."

Nevertheless, she was not surprised to find the suite, his personal offices, so stylish, so unbusinesslike: the lobby, with its sofas, its plants, its Tiffany-style lamps on low tables; the small rather more impersonal office beyond that where sat the terrifying Miss Brownsmith, who nodded briefly as they went through, skimming a thoughtful eye over Phaedria; and beyond that again, Julian's own office. Phaedria looked around in delight, drinking in the white and chrome, the Symonds and Lutyens desk, the curving bookshelves, the lacquered floor lamps. "What a beautiful room."

"I'm glad you like it. Many people don't."

"I'm amazed."

"It's a little subtle, I find, for general consumption. People expect either very grand eighteenth-century style, a sort of cross between a boardroom and a brothel, or pure Conran. They can't cope with this at all."

"Well, I think it's marvelous."

"I'm glad you like it. I am very fond of the Art Deco era. Probably because I was born in it. Although I fear it's beginning to be more historic than nostalgic." He buzzed for Sarah Brownsmith. "Ah, Sarah, could we have that lunch I hope you have been keeping for me? We're very hungry. Is there enough for two?"

"I think so, Sir Julian. Would you like wine or Perrier?"

"This is an occasion. We would like wine. No, more than that—champagne. Bring in a bottle of the Cristal, will you, Sarah? And some Perrier as well, we have work to do. Miss Blenheim, I presume you would like a drink? Sarah, this is Phaedria Blenheim, a journalist from the *Bristol Echo*. She has come up to interview me. Now is there anything I need to know urgently? If so, I'll deal with it now, and then I want to be left alone for an hour or so. No calls or anything. This is an important interview."

Phaedria met Sarah Brownsmith's politely amused gaze, resisted an almost overpowering urge to wink at her, and moved over to look out of the window at Dover Street.

"Do you want lunch first, Sir Julian, or the messages?"

"Obviously lunch, Sarah; it's nearly half past three, and I have a guest. Just have it brought in, please, and then give me the messages quickly."

Sarah Brownsmith's revenge for this small piece of arrogance was swift and heady. "I'll give you all the messages," she said, as Julian poured two glasses of champagne and held one out to Phaedria. "Then you can decide for yourself which are important. Miss North wants to know why you haven't rung her about tonight. She said to impress upon you that you were to be at the restaurant by seven sharp. Susan Johns says if you don't call her this afternoon about the marketing plans for next year she will resign immediately from—now what was it?"—she consulted her notebook—"ah, yes, your bloody ego trip of a company. She said it was very important I give you that message verbatim."

"Thank you, Sarah. Anything else?"

"Freddy Branksome says it's crucial you sign the audited accounts today; otherwise we shall all be in jail by Christmas."

"Yes?"

"Richard Brookes wants to know if you actually want to ensure a lawsuit from Mrs. Lauder or if you would consider renaming your new line. He must have a definite answer today."

"Fine."

"And your mother says if she doesn't hear from you by four she will be extremely displeased with you."

"Thank you, Sarah. I hope you haven't forgotten anything."

"I don't think so."

"Good. Get my mother on the phone, will you?"

"Yes. And Miss North?"

"I will ring Miss North later," Julian said lightly. He pushed his hair back. "Thank you. Now then, I don't want to be disturbed."

"What about the accounts?"

"The accounts will have to wait. I believe the jails are very full toward Christmas. I doubt if they will have room for us."

"Yes, Sir Julian."

She closed the door behind her. Julian smiled at Phaedria. "She is an excellent nanny. She likes to remind me I am imperfect and in need of discipline."

"So I see."

"And you also see what an extremely important person and how high-powered I am, and how my staff trembles at the sound of my name."

"Yes. I do."

The phone rang. "Mother! Hallo. What? Yes, I know I didn't ring you last night, and I'm truly sorry. I was working with Freddy on the accounts. What? Well, we had a little supper later. No, Camilla was not with us. Well, your spies are lying. Now, darling, I promise to come and see you tonight. Without fail. How are you? Good. I may have a friend with me. What? No, it won't be Camilla. I know she's bad for your health. Poor girl, I never can see what harm she does you."

Phaedria, watching him closely, saw his face darken suddenly. "Mother, I can't get into that now. I've got somebody with me. Yes, I have sent Roz some flowers. I know it's dreadful waiting for a late baby, but she'll survive. Other women do. She was a fortnight late herself. Serves her right. Bye, darling, I must go now. See you later. What? Oh, about seven." He put down the phone, walked over to Phaedria, and refilled her glass.

"Now then, Miss Phaedria Blenheim. What do you want to know about me?"

SHE HAD JUST finished telephoning her story through to the *Echo* from Sarah's desk when Julian appeared in the doorway.

"Was that all right? Was he pleased?"

"Very."

"Good. My extremely valuable, moderately famous time has not been wasted, then?"

"Of course not," she said, pushing the certain knowledge that she had done a lousy job to the bottom of her consciousness. She looked at Julian, about whom she knew so little more, and she did not wonder for a moment why she had not pushed him in the very least for information about himself beyond his companies, his money, his houses, his tastes. There was much she wanted to know about Julian Morell, much that she needed to know—about his first and only wife and why he had not remarried; about his daughter and how, if at all, he rationalized having both her and his son-in-law holding significant positions in the company; about his very long association with Susan Johns and the closeness with him that gave her the right to insult him considerably and publicly through his secretary; about the demanding Camilla North, who was clearly not going to be met at seven o'clock sharp or indeed at any time during the evening; about his mother, who had worked in the company from its founding and was still, by all accounts, an active constituent—but it was not to be shared, any of it, either with her editor or her readers.

As for herself, she had time on her side; she could wait.

"I would like to buy you a drink," he said, "preferably several. But I have a slight problem."

"You've already given me several drinks."

"Maybe. But that was work. I would like to move you into the pleasure category now."

There it was again, that gentle, insistent pressure into intimacy. Phaedria started putting papers into her fishing bag, her head bent, glad to have a reason not to look at him, wondering confusedly at the warmth stirring somewhere in the depths of her body. "I see."

"Are you busy this evening? Do you want me to send you back to Bristol? Because I will. You have only to say so."

"No," she said, as he had known, as they had both known she would, looking up suddenly and meeting his eyes. "No, I don't. I can stay in London."

"Good. Now then, I wonder how you'd feel about coming to see my mother before we go on for—what? Dinner perhaps?"

Sarah Brownsmith, working on the small computer on the other side of her office, wondered if Phaedria had any idea at all how much that invitation meant.

"YOU'LL LIKE MY mother," said Julian as the car made its slow, painful journey along Saint James's.

"Good. Will she like me?"

"I think so. I think definitely yes."

"Then I shall like her."

"And then, after that, I thought we would go out to dinner. If you have time. Where would you like to go?"

"I have time. Why not the Meridiana?"

"Why the Meridiana?"

"I imagine you have a table booked. You said you were going there this evening."

"Oh, now, here we have the journalist at work, do we not?" He sounded faintly irritated. "Not missing a single thing. No, I don't have a table booked. I canceled it."

"Pity," said Phaedria, undismayed by his change of mood.

"Why?"

"Because I like it."

"Well, that is a pity, but anyway, we can't go there, because several people I know are going, and I don't want to see any of them. Where else do you like?"

"I love Chez Solange. I like Bentley's Oyster Bar. And I love Inigo Jones in Covent Garden. Do you know it?"

"I do. How is it that you are so *au fait* with London restaurants? I thought you were a provincial girl."

"Absolutely not," said Phaedria firmly. "I grew up in London, and my father is a great gourmet."

"Are you a great gourmet, too?"

"A small one."

"Good. Then let us go to Inigo Jones. It's certainly an imaginative menu. I'll book a table from my mother's house. Tell me more about your father. Tell me about your mother. What does she do, if anything?"

"I haven't the faintest idea," Phaedria said, and there was no bitterness, no emotion of any kind in her voice, just a blank indifference. "She left us when I was ten. She wrote at Christmas for a few years. I think I last heard from her on my twenty-first birthday. She sent me a card."

He looked at her with great interest. "How appalling."

"Not really. I had my father. We were perfectly happy."

"You don't seem at all damaged by the experience."

"Who knows? It's hard to assess, isn't it, that kind of thing? I might have been greatly damaged. But I don't think so."

"I find that encouraging," he said.

"Why?"

"My own daughter has had—well, a difficult life. My wife and I divorced when she was very small. I have always worried about the effect on her. But perhaps she will prove as undamaged as you."

"Perhaps."

"She's about to have a baby," he added.

"Yes, I know."

"Dear God," he said, half amused, half irritated. "Is there anything about me you don't know?"

She met his gaze steadily, the warmth inside her stirring again. "I think there's a lot."

He smiled. "Good." Then he looked at her more seriously. "This is very odd, what we are doing, you know. It has only just dawned on me how odd it is."

"What?"

"Well, that you should be coming to meet my mother and then agree to have dinner with me when you should be safely back home in Bristol, typing your articles, or whatever you do in the evening. Is there nobody to worry about you?"

"Nobody."

"Don't you have any friends?"

"Of course I do. But they don't monitor my every movement. Some evenings I see them, some I don't."

"I see. So you live alone?"

"Yes."

"Do you have a boyfriend?"

"No."

"Don't you think it might be a little rash, spending the evening with me? I might prove to be a lecher, or a miser or a bore."

"You might. In each case, I could just go home."

"To Bristol?"

"Of course not. To my father's house in Chelsea."

"Then," he said, smiling, his eyes dancing, "I shall relax."

"MOTHER, THIS IS Phaedria. Phaedria Blenheim. She is writing a series of articles on captains of industry. She's started with me."

"Really. How interesting. Which of the other captains are you interviewing, Miss Blenheim?"

"Clive Sinclair, Richard Branson, Alan Sugar, John Bentley."

"And for which publication?"

"The *Bristol Echo*."

"How nice. And has my son given you some good copy?"

"Not yet," Phaedria said. "I'm hoping it will improve."

Letitia sparkled at her. "It probably won't. He can be very dull when he wants to be. And he lies a lot. Look out for that. What would you like to drink?"

"Goodness, I'm not sure."

"Well, if you're not sure, you'd better have champagne. Such a catholic drink, I always think. Julian, go and get a bottle, will you?"

She looked at Phaedria. "How pretty you are. And such a lovely name."

"It's from *The Faerie Queene*," Julian said.

"Well, of course it is, I know that," said Letitia briskly. "Wantonness, wasn't she, Phaedria? You must get so tired of being asked if it suits you."

"I do," said Phaedria. She wasn't quite sure about the form her relationship with Julian Morell was going to take, but she was certainly in love with his mother.

BROUGHT STRANGELY CLOSER by the interlude with Letitia, they sat in the restaurant, yet another bottle of champagne in the ice bucket beside them. Phaedria, half drunk, totally relaxed, sat with her elbows on the table, her chin resting on her hands, smiling at Julian.

"What a lovely lady," she said.

"She is. Although not always."

"Isn't she? I can't believe that."

"Come, now," he said, "nobody is lovely all the time. Or are you?"

"Me? I'm hardly ever lovely. Horrid most of the time."

"I don't think," he said, "that I can believe that. You seem a consistently nice person to me."

"Not at all. Look how belligerent and rude I was this morning."

"You were just doing your job."

"Doesn't that count?"

He seemed surprised. "Of course not."

"So you can be thoroughly unpleasant in the course of duty, and it doesn't really matter?"

"I don't think it does."

She looked at him thoughtfully. "I don't think I'd like to work for you."

"Working is not what I have in mind for you."

The warmth again; she looked down, confused, flushed.

"I was very impressed," he said, "by the way you summoned up all those names for my mother."

"What names?"

"The captains of industry you are supposed to be interviewing."

"I'm a good liar," she said, smiling, "when I have to be. Are you?"

"Not very."

"Why did you have to tell her that story anyway?"

"I thought it best for her to think our relationship was purely professional," he said lightly.

"Why?"

"She doesn't trust me with young ladies. With any ladies. I didn't want a lecture in the morning."

"Why not? I mean, why doesn't she trust you?"

"With good reason, I'm afraid. I have a bad reputation with women. Your research must have told you that."

"A little."

"Does it bother you?"

She looked at him very directly. "Not really."

"Good. How old are you, Phaedria?"

"Twenty-four." She shook back her mane of hair and looked at him very directly. "How old are you?"

"Sixty-two."

"Older than my father." It was an oddly intimate statement.

"Does it matter?"

"What do you mean?"

"You know what I mean."

"Yes," said Phaedria. "Yes, I do."

He took her hand suddenly. "I find you very beautiful. I find the way I am feeling very surprising. Please tell me about yourself."

"All right. But you must talk as well."

"Very well. We shall swap story for story and see how we get along."

He put out his hand and stroked her cheek, very gently; she turned her head and rested it in his hand. She smiled. "I think I shall run out of stories first."

"We shall see."

They talked for hours. Warmed, relaxed by the wine, the strangely delicious sensations invading her body, his beguiling interest in everything she had to say. She talked of her childhood, her love for her father, their strangely intense relationship, her fear that her mother might return and invade it; of her days at Oxford, of her unwillingness to become involved with anybody. She talked of her work, of the people she had interviewed. "Everybody must ask you this," he said. "Did you ever fall in love with any of them, have an affair?" No, she said, never. She did not regard them as people at all; they were objects, part of the job, her ambition, the delight she took in her work. She also spoke of occasional anxiety for the future and where her rather singular approach to life might lead her.

"It seems to me," he said, "that you have led a most blameless life."

"Fairly. And you? You haven't done much swapping yet. Come along, tell me about you."

"Well, not blameless," he said, "not blameless at all," and he began to talk, as he had not talked for years, freely, easily, about Eliza, about Roz, about the years in New York, about Camilla, about—very briefly —Susan. But, as for Phaedria, there were boundaries to the confidences; he was not prepared to go beyond the ones he had set.

He told her of his years in France during the war, of the early days in the company. He talked about his mother and the fun and the pleasure they had had in London in the early days, and how in fact it had never stopped.

And Phaedria listened, as she so skillfully did in her work, silently for the most part, attentively, occasionally asking a quiet, thoughtful question, and she learned more in two hours than most people did in two months, two years.

Suddenly he stopped, looked at her slightly warily, and smiled. "You are a very dangerous person to talk to," he said. "You tempt one to say too much."

"Can one say too much?"

"One certainly can."

He was silent; then he reached out again and touched her face. "What do you think?"

She knew what he meant. "I'm not sure."

"Ah."

"Perhaps I should go."

"Where?"

"Home."

"Don't go," he said. "Not yet." He took her hand again, looked at her intensely with his dark, questing eyes, searching, half smiling, disturbing her.

Phaedria closed her eyes briefly and swallowed; she felt faint.

"Now I have to ask you something," Julian said. "Something important. Something I have to know."

"What?"

"Have you been to bed with many men?"

"No."

"Ah. Any men?"

"Yes and no."

"Are you a virgin?"

"Yes and no."

"My God," Julian said, dropping her hand and laughing, signaling to the waiter, "you're hard work. Are you always so mysterious?"

"I try to be. I don't like giving too much away."

"You certainly succeed. Let me take you back to my place. I have some very interesting etchings."

"No thank you," said Phaedria. "I really don't want to go back to your place. I hate men's places."

"That's a very sweeping statement. My place is very nice."

"I'm sure, but I don't want to go there."

"There's the office."

"Any etchings there?"

"Kind of. You've seen most of them."

"I suppose so." She looked at him with sudden interest. "Do you have any pictures of the stores? And the hotels? I'd really like to see those."

"Dear God in heaven, I hadn't anticipated having to compete with my own company for your attention. Come along, let's forget the brandy. Plenty in the office anyway."

HE UNLOCKED THE big white door to the Dover Street office, let them in, followed her into the lift. It was a small, intimate space; he pulled her hard against him, turned her face up, and kissed her suddenly, fiercely. At the top the doors opened abruptly, the lights came on automatically; he looked down and saw her face, startled, raw with surprise and desire.

"You look very different from this morning."

"I feel different."

"Do you really want to look at photographs of my stores?" he asked, smiling gently, teasing her.

"No, not now."

"You disappoint me."

"Don't joke."

She walked away from him with an effort, suddenly nervous, unsure of what she should do. He followed her, turned her around, looked at her and smiled. "Don't be frightened."

"I'm not frightened," she said, "but you will have to take care of me. I am half a virgin."

"I promise I will." He smiled down at her. "I don't know exactly what you mean, but you can tell me later."

He took off their coats, first his, then hers, and then, his eyes never leaving her face, he unbuttoned her shirt, slid it off her shoulders. Her breasts were small, firm, almost pubescent; he looked at them for a long time, then bent his head and kissed them tenderly at first, then harder, working at the nipples with his tongue. Phaedria, her head thrown back, limp, shaken, forgot everything except her need to have him, to know him utterly, to give to him, to take, take, take. She moaned; he straightened up.

"Let's get undressed. We aren't giving our bodies much help."

She lay on the carpet, shivering, watching him; she had been a little afraid that he would look less good, less youthful, without his clothes, but he didn't. He was tanned all over; his stomach was flat, his buttocks taut and firm. His penis stood out starkly; she looked at it with frank interest.

"Now, you must have seen one of these before."

"Yes, but it wasn't so big."

"Ah," he said, "I expect you say that to all the boys."

And he smiled, defusing her fear, and began to stroke her gently, insistently, first her breasts, playing with the nipples, smoothing the skin; then her stomach, stronger, harder. Then he moved his hand into the mound of her pubic hair, gentle again, unthreatening, and then, as she began to move, involuntarily responding to him, he sought her clitoris with his finger, probing, questing, and smiled as he felt the swelling and the wetness.

He was kneeling above her now, bending now and again to kiss her; again and again she thrust herself up toward him, her arms stretched out, her hair spread about her, looking like some strange, Pre-Raphaelite painting, an embodiment of desire.

He made her wait a long time, until she was quite ready for him. Then very, very slowly and gently, he began to enter her, pushing, urging, withdrawing every time he felt her tense. She was tight and tender, despite her desire, and still afraid, deep within herself. He waited for her again and again, following her pattern, understanding her ebbing and flowing, and gradually, very gradually, she abandoned herself absolutely to him, relaxed beneath him, softened, opened deeper and deeper, and then suddenly she gathered herself and it was a different movement altogether, it was hungry and grasping and greedy, and then she cried out and trembled and clung to him, and he knew she was there, and that it was safe for him to join her. And afterward she lay and cried, sobbed endlessly in his arms, and couldn't tell him why.

"I'm happy," she kept saying. "I'm happy. I can't bear it. Please, please don't go away."

"I'm not going away," he said. "Never. I shall be here with you always. Don't cry, my dearest, dearest darling love. I'm not going away. Shush, shush, Phaedria, don't cry."

And in the end she stopped and turned toward him, her face all blotched and smudged with tears and exhaustion and sex, and smiled and said, "How wonderful you are."

"No," he said, "not wonderful. Not wonderful at all. I loved it. I love you."

He had not said that for years; it frightened him even as he spoke.

And Phaedria, who had said it only once before and had been rejected and was frightened also, looked at him very seriously and said, "I love you too."

SHE MOVED INTO the house in Regent's Park the next day.

· 19 ·

FATHER KENNEDY WAS HAVING SERIOUS problems with his conscience. Mrs. Kelly had made it perfectly plain to him that she didn't want anyone to know where she and Miles were going; indeed had entrusted him with the information under pain of great secrecy. It was essential for several reasons, she had said, that nobody knew: the police might come inquiring for Miles; those no-good friends of his from the beach might want to find him; and kind as Mr. Dashwood was, she didn't really want him knowing either. If she and Miles were to make a fresh start, she didn't want him turning up, upsetting Miles, interfering. She felt bad about it in a way, but Hugo could have done more to help and he was being just plain stubborn now, digging his heels in as hard and as awkwardly as Miles, only Miles was little more than a child, and Mr. Dashwood was old enough to know better. It could have made all the difference in the world to Miles and his future if he had given the boy a job in his company, and it wouldn't have hurt him any. Sometimes, she had said, she wondered if Miles wasn't right when he said that Mr. Dashwood was ashamed of him, and of her, as well.

Father Kennedy had the advantage—or maybe the disadvantage—of knowing rather more about Hugo Dashwood and his relationship to Miles than Mrs. Kelly or indeed anyone else in the world did, and he found it very hard to understand why the man wouldn't help his own son. He had often thought about the puzzle over the years, ever since Miles had graduated so well and then wasted himself. Obviously it would be very damaging for the boy, even when he was grown up, to learn that his mother had had a sexual relationship with another man and that the father he had been so fond of had not been his father at all. It would inevitably lead to the painful realization that the reason for his father's suicide had been his mother's adultery. The whole story was obviously best left untold, especially since Miles disliked Hugo Dashwood so much. That was a sad thing, under the circumstances.

But on the other hand, that should not keep the man from giving Miles a job. He was clearly fond of him, proud of him, and besides, a man did not put a boy through college if he was ashamed of him and didn't like him. He was as good as the boy's guardian. Why should he persist in this strange, stubborn attitude?

Father Kennedy could see all too clearly why some truly poor people behaved badly, refused to help themselves, let alone others, but he could not see why a man who clearly had more than his fair share of the world's bounty should not pass a little of it on to his own flesh and blood. It wasn't as if Miles was an unattractive young man; quite the reverse, he would be a credit to anyone.

Well, as Father Kennedy had learned as a very young priest, there was no accounting for human nature, and it was not for him to try. His duty as God's extremely humble servant was merely to accept people as they were and do for them what he could.

And now here he was, confronted by Hugo Dashwood, just flown in from New York, clearly agitated, and demanding to know where Miles and Mrs. Kelly had gone. And he really did not know what to do. This was always the difficult one: when knowledge came into your possession not through the confessional—when it was sacred, and not, even under threat of death, to be revealed—but from conversation, confidences, when it could be argued it was yours to make a judgment on, to do with what you thought best.

And what would be best now? Did he respect the confidence of an old friend and do what she had asked, or did he use his knowledge of her whereabouts to rescue her grandson from a life of shocking idleness at best and, at worst, from the very serious danger of mortal sin?

"I need to find them," Hugo Dashwood had said, sitting down earnestly in front of him and looking the very picture of remorse and anxiety. "I have been terribly wrong, and I want to make amends. I want to offer Miles a job before it's too late."

"Well, I'm sure that is very heartening news," said Father Kennedy, playing for time while his old mind roamed around his dilemma, "and Mrs. Kelly would be pleased to hear it. I am not altogether certain how Miles himself would take to the idea now, though. It's been a while now since he graduated, and I suppose he has gotten used to a life of idleness. If you will forgive me saying so, Mr. Dashwood, I'm afraid your change of heart may be a little late."

"You may be right, Father, but we shall never know unless I can find Miles and put it to him. If I don't, there is certainly no chance at all that my change of heart, as you put it, will benefit him."

"Would it be too inquisitive of me to ask where this job would be? Would you be taking him to England with you, or to New York? Or would it be somewhere here in California?"

"I wouldn't take him to England. I think that would be too much of a culture shock for him. No, I have a small wholesale business in New York, supplying toiletries to drugstores—soaps, toothpaste, that sort of thing—and I could fit him in there quite easily. I need some younger salesmen. I think he would do well."

"And do you think he would settle in there? Do you think he would be happy?"

Hugo sounded impatient. "It would be a marvelous opportunity. I think he would settle down quite quickly. It's what he has wanted, after all."

"It's what he wanted once. He was hurt not to get it at the time."

"Father Kennedy, he is not a child. He has to learn the ways of the world. Things do not necessarily drop into our laps at precisely the moment we want them. They did not for me, and I am sure they have not always done so for you."

Father Kennedy reflected, not for the first time, that the English had an unfortunate way of sounding pompous and distant when they probably didn't mean to. "Indeed they have not," he said. "Most of the people I've worked with all my life would say the same thing of themselves. And it does people very little good when things do drop into their laps. Struggle is spiritually enhancing. Would you not agree, Mr. Dashwood?"

"I would, Father."

"You are not a Catholic?"

"I am not."

The old man was silent for a while, looking at him shrewdly. "And what would become of Mrs. Kelly if Miles were to go to New York?"

"I don't quite know. I would certainly try to look after her. She has been very good to Miles."

"She has indeed. And she is anxious to protect him."

"Father, I hope you are not implying Miles needs protection from me."

"Not from you, Mr. Dashwood. From unhappiness. From idleness, from falling into unfortunate ways."

"Which I fear he has despite her efforts."

"Indeed."

Hugo leaned forward earnestly. "Father, I cannot tell you how very much I want to reestablish contact with Miles. I want to make amends. I want to help him, to give him a chance, to make something of his life. I think it is time I managed to be more to him."

Father Kennedy looked at him. "I hope, Mr. Dashwood—and forgive me if this sounds impertinent—I hope you would not be of a mind to change his perspective on life."

Dashwood met his eyes steadily. "I don't know exactly what you mean. But I give you my word I would do nothing, nothing at all, that would make Miles unhappy, that would make him think differently about his background or change his mind about anyone who had cared for him."

"I'm glad to hear that, Mr. Dashwood. It puts my mind at rest. Miles is a loyal and a very well adjusted young man. It would be a terrible shame if that was to change."

"I agree with you."

Father Kennedy stood up, his gentle old face calm and suddenly decisive. "I don't think I can tell you where they are, Mr. Dashwood. I think it would be a grievous betrayal of confidence. But I will write to Mrs. Kelly and tell her what you have told me. And then it will be for her to decide."

"Do you not think, Father, that Miles should have a say in the decision?"

"I think he will. Mrs. Kelly wants to see him settled and doing well. I'm sure she will consult him in the matter. I'll write to her tonight."

"Thank you."

·20·

"SHIT," ROZ SCREAMED OUT. "Shit. C.J., C.J., I can't stand it. Stop it, stop it, oh, Christ, it hurts. It hurts."

She had been in labor for twelve hours, ever since, as Letitia was to remark later, she had heard about the arrival of Phaedria in her father's life.

It was Eliza who had brought her the news, as she sat sulkily and vastly pregnant in the house she and C.J. had bought in Cheyne Walk. The drawing room was on the first floor; she had a chaise longue in the window overlooking the river, and for days she had lain there trying, as her yoga teacher and her natural childbirth instructor had told her, to relax and think positive thoughts, to visualize her body opening gently and letting out the huge child it was nurturing. All she could visualize was her office, ever more disorganized, she felt sure, the many strands of her business life tangled, her staff taking matters into their own hands, making the wrong decisions, wrecking the painstakingly constructed edifice of her own particular empire.

She had continued to go into the office every single day until her gynecologist had expressly forbidden it, telling her that her membranes were going to rupture any moment. Roz did not care whether they ruptured or not, as long as she went into labor, but she could see that it would not be very impressive or professional to sit or stand in a large pool of water in the boardroom, so she had reluctantly given in. She stayed at home after that and made everybody's life a misery, insisting that papers, letters, marketing plans, and budgets be sent to her daily, countermanding other people's decisions, altering her own, dictating endless memos to her hapless secretary, and circulating them to the entire company, putting forward proposals for new hotels, stores, cosmetics, even hospitals. "Well, why not, Daddy?" she had said when Julian phoned her to point out the folly of one particular plan. "You have an excellent reputation in the pharmaceuticals industry now. Why not capitalize on it? Hospitals are big business in the States." She demanded to see every note, the minutes of every meeting, every letter, and came close to demanding a transcript of every phone call that C.J. wrote, attended, or made.

C.J. was wretched. While Roz had been active and in control of her life, she had paid lip service to making the marriage work. She had been polite to him, pretended to listen to his views, both professional and personal, and had hired Robin and Tricia Guild to decorate their house in the way he wanted, she having absolutely no interest in the matter. She had even gone with him with a fairly good grace to stay with his mother in Oyster Bay for a week in lieu of a honeymoon—"Well, after all, C.J., we certainly don't need one, too ridiculous"—and had continued to see that sex was as satisfying and as frequent as it had been before their marriage. But now she had stopped trying; she was angry and miserable. She felt too ugly and sick and bored and uncomfortable to do anything but let her true feelings for him show. And her true feelings were a mixture of contemptuous fondness and an almost permanent irritation.

She managed to keep this hidden, with considerable effort, from her father, whose approval seemed—somewhat ironically, she felt—more and more crucial to her, and from her mother and grandmother, who had both told her in very clear terms that she was making a serious and a very destructive mistake in marrying C.J. in the first place. She had had no answer for Letitia, but she had looked at her mother in rage and despair and said, "Mummy, I'm doing what you told me to. How dare you not support me now?" Eliza, horrified by all the threads of all the lives she seemed to have so disastrously tangled together, had begged her to reconsider and said over and over again that she had been wrong, that she should never have advised any such action, that she would be no party to it. But Roz had gone ahead. Whether Eliza agreed with her or not, marrying C.J., so far as she could see, was going to ensure her most of what she wanted from life: her father's approval, her future assured, and a husband and home of her own.

Unfortunately she had not been able to see very far.

C.J., who had been able to see quite far enough from the very beginning, was in a state of rising panic. He was in an untenable position, with no hope of escape. Julian had sent for him the morning after Roz broke the news of her accidental pregnancy. C.J., braced for a bawling-out and in the slightly forlorn hope of dismissal from the company, had been confronted by a magnum of champagne, an outstretched hand, and a promotion.

"I couldn't be more delighted. Roz tells me you want to get married straightaway. I think it's an excellent idea. I'm going to put you in as president of the hotels division, reporting direct to me. You'll need more money, as a family man. God, I wish your father were alive to see this."

C.J., reflecting that none of this would have happened if that had been the case, agreed fervently, and then asked, slightly nervously, whether Roz was to be given a new job as well. "I don't see her wanting to report to me."

Julian laughed. "Neither do I. Yes, I'm giving her a go at the stores. She's always wanted them. Starting her off as vice president Europe. Then, when she's had the baby and is ready, she can move on. She won't want to do too much just yet."

He was wrong, of course. Roz did want to do much too much. She was wild with joy and triumph at getting her hands on the stores at last. She worked fourteen, fifteen hours a day and demanded the presidency as her baby's birthday present. She got it.

Rather to her surprise, to everybody's surprise, pregnancy suited her well. She was never sick; she did not feel tired; she enjoyed the new sensations within her body, her comparative serenity, the feel of the baby kicking, even her new statuesque shape; being so tall, she carried the baby well. Even more to everybody's surprise, she decided on natural childbirth and went to classes, earnestly practicing relaxation and breathing every day, attending yoga classes, seeking out a doctor who would allow her to deliver the baby in the way she had chosen, who would not insist on giving her drugs or using any unnecessary medical procedures.

"This is a natural process," she told everybody firmly. "I plan to experience it naturally and handle it myself."

Eliza, who still had rather uncomfortably vivid memories of Roz's own birth, was skeptical. "Of course it might all work wonderfully, darling, but I do think you'll be glad of some kind of pain relief at least in the later stages."

"I don't see why," Roz said. "Cordelia has seen countless babies delivered by her method and none of the women needed any drugs at all. You can be your own pain relief, Mummy. You didn't understand in your day."

"Maybe not," said Eliza. "Who is Cordelia? A doctor?"

"No, she's my natural childbirth teacher."

"Is she qualified to teach such things?"

"Of course. She works with midwives and doctors. She's the one who recommended me to Dr. Partridge. He is a very advanced obstetrician, totally opposed to medical interference."

"I would have thought that was a contradiction in terms," Eliza said. "And anyway, what is Cordelia's method? Does it all take place in darkness with water beds all over the place? I was reading about something like that last week."

"Well, you read the wrong magazines. Not water beds—that's just silly—but some women do have their babies in warm water. Cordelia's method is a bit more straightforward. Basically, you learn to listen to your own body and follow what it wants. I mean, you might want to deliver your baby on all fours, or standing up. It's all much more natural than lying down, anyway."

"It sounds rather tiring to me," said Eliza. "And this is what Dr. Partridge thinks as well, is it?"

"Of course. And he has booked me into a private hospital with a modern birthing room, C.J. can be there, and Cordelia as well, to encourage me. I'm looking forward to it."

"Good," Eliza said. "I'm delighted."

"Honestly," she said to Letitia later, "I think pregnancy has affected her brain. Roz, of all people. I'd have thought she'd have favored a Cesarean. I didn't argue with her. You can try, but I think we're actually lucky she isn't insisting on having this baby in the middle of a field. Or Hyde Park," she added. "Oh, dear, C.J.'s so unhappy about it, too."

Letitia, who felt that C.J. must be unhappy about a great deal more than the method by which his baby was going to enter the world, tried very hard to change Roz's mind as well, without success. Roz was convinced that her mother and grandmother had suffered in childbirth simply because of archaic conditioning, and she was deaf to any advice they had to give her.

She would have her baby as she did everything else these days: the way she wanted.

"HOW ARE YOU, darling?" Eliza said, entering the drawing room at Cheyne Walk, her arms full of white roses.

"Lousy," Roz said. "Can't sleep. So uncomfortable. The baby's so big now it can't move at all. I feel as if I'm going to burst."

"Well, never mind, darling, it's only twenty-four hours now at the most, and then Dr. Partridge will take you in."

"I know, but Cordelia is most unhappy about it. She says induction ruins the natural pattern of labor. I really think I might not let him."

"Roz," Eliza said firmly, "with great respect to Cordelia—whom I do hope I never have to meet, incidentally—she is not a doctor, and nothing will ruin the natural pattern of labor more swiftly for you than a dead baby. Do stop being ridiculous."

Roz looked at her mother, startled; she was not usually so firm. "All right," she said crossly, "there's no need to start lecturing me."

"Sorry, darling. Now, listen, I have the most divine bit of gossip for you. You just aren't going to believe this."

"What?"

"Your father has a new girlfriend."

"Since when?" said Roz sharply.

"Since the day before yesterday."

"Oh, Mummy, he's always in bed with someone or other. That's not gossip."

"Well, I think it might be. She's living at Regent's Park already."

"Good God. What on earth will Camilla have to say?"

"A great deal, I hear. Apparently she's flying back to New York this afternoon."

"Well, who is this woman?"

"Hardly a woman, darling. Younger than you."

"What?"

Eliza was so busy arranging the roses that she did not see Roz's face go white, her eyes blaze.

"Yes, really, that's what's so intriguing. She's twenty-four years old. Extremely beautiful, apparently. Sarah Brownsmith has met her; she came to the office. She's a journalist. She interviewed your father and never went home again."

"Who told you all this?" Roz sounded strained.

"Well, lots of people. Letitia met her; he took her there for a drink. Well, that's pretty significant, wouldn't you say? She said she was charming, and very beautiful."

"Yes, yes, so you keep saying. And?"

"Well, I rang Sarah and managed to get a bit out of her, but you know how irritatingly discreet she is. So then I rang the housekeeper at Regent's Park and asked if your father had any guests at the moment, and she said yes, a young lady. She has the most unusual name, she's called Phaedria, Phaedria Blenheim. And—and this is the most ridiculous thing of all—I'm sure it can't be true—but Angie Masterson was having a drink in the Ritz early yesterday evening, and Camilla was there with a friend. Angie said she looked absolutely dreadful, white as a sheet—not that Camilla would ever look really awful—and Angie heard her say—well, she *says* she heard her say, "And he's talking about marrying her." Well, it's obviously nonsense, but I don't see why Camilla should make things sound worse for herself than they really are. Can you imagine anything more absurd? He's sixty-two, marrying a child of twenty-four. Oh, it can't be true. Now, darling, what can I get you?"

"Nothing," said Roz, who had turned very pale and was gripping the chaise longue. "I don't want anything. I feel sick." Tears had formed in her green eyes, and she was looking at her mother with a mixture of panic and misery.

"Roz, darling, what is it? Is it the baby? Shall I call Dr. Partridge?"

"No," Roz said, breathing heavily, the tears falling. "It isn't the baby. Damn the baby. You wouldn't understand. Oh, shit, I can't stand it. Just go away, Mummy, and leave me alone. Actually I do want something. I want a drink. A big one."

She was in labor by lunchtime.

MIRANDA EMERSON WAS born that night, a noisy, healthy ten-pound baby. During the delivery, Roz had screamed, kicked the midwife as well as Dr. Partridge, sent Cordelia packing, bitten her husband's hand so hard she drew blood, and then suddenly at the end of it delivered her baby with extraordinary ease and swiftness and a beatific smile on her face.

"Isn't she lovely, C.J.? Isn't she absolutely lovely?" she said, sitting up in bed half an hour after the delivery, the picture of rosy health, Miranda in her arms. "What on earth have you done to your hand? Why is it all bandaged up?"

"You bit me," C.J. said, not a note of reproach in his voice. "Hard. It bled."

"Oh, God, I'm sorry. I really didn't know what I was doing. Did I bite that silly bitch Cordelia as well?"

"No."

"Pity. I will if ever I see her again. What a load of balls. Pain management indeed. Never mind; it's over now. Don't you think she's beautiful?"

"She's lovely," said C.J., looking somewhat nervously at the small wrinkled face, the mop of black hair, the tiny waving hands. "Lovely."

"Did you ring Mummy?"

"Yes. She's very excited. She's coming over later."

"Tonight? How lovely. I want everyone to see this baby. What about Daddy?"

"Yes, I spoke to him."

"Where was he? At home?"

"Not at first. Some girl answered the phone. Said he would be back soon. She seemed to know about the baby. I don't know who she was. Then he called here and said he's coming over in the morning. Sent lots of love."

Roz scowled. In her euphoria she had temporarily forgotten the new mistress. A girl of twenty-four. She found it almost impossible to believe. A cloud of fear and rage was cast briefly over her happiness. She remembered with a rush how passionately she had needed the baby to be a boy. For a second she looked at her daughter with regret; then she shook herself. Who needed boys? Women could fight as well as men. Miranda was hers, her own creation; she would train her from this moment.

CAMILLA, SITTING ON the plane drinking distilled water and nibbling raw vegetables, the only food she ever allowed herself on flights, found the whole thing hard to believe. She was hurt, she was angry, she was humiliated, but most of all she was, she discovered, slightly amused. It really was a trifle pathetic that a man of sixty-two should be swept off his feet by a girl young enough to be his daughter. Or his granddaughter.

Camilla knew exactly what had happened to Julian; she had spent a great deal of time discussing the syndrome with her analyst over the past eighteen months. It was a mid-life crisis. Male menopause. He was perhaps a little old for it, but its manifestations—a panicky rush into a new relationship, a desperate grab at youth—were classic and unmistakable. It usually coincided with the waning of the sexual powers, and the new relationship was seen as a remedy, a revitalization. As Camilla allowed herself a short and pleasant contemplation on Julian's sexual powers and their vulnerability and her own singular position with regard to them, she wondered how he would manage without her in the future. Once or twice over the years, when things had been rather less than one hundred percent for him, he had turned to her again for help, and she had given it generously, grateful, she had to admit to herself, for his unique need of her. There then would follow a period of great affection, and many promises of faithfulness. The promises were always broken, and Camilla always managed to persuade herself that his other relationships were trivial, short-term, and that she should not allow herself to overreact, should not throw away so much that was good about her life with Julian Morell along with the little that was bad.

And usually she was right; the affairs did not last, particularly those with younger women, who swiftly tired of being forced into a middle-aged life-style, however glamorous, and moved on. And there was absolutely no doubt in Camilla's mind that this would happen now. Phaedria Blenheim—very young indeed, even by Julian's standards —was clearly not going to spend the rest of her youth tied to someone so much older than she, however rich he might be. No doubt she had found his wealth irresistible—she was by all accounts very hard up—but wealth was a commodity that very soon palled. In a year's time, her wardrobe full of couture clothes, her wrists and neck hung with jewels, her body expensively exercised and massaged and tanned, already bored with her old husband's old friends. Miss Blenheim would be looking, idly desperate, for a young lover, a friend, a soul mate, someone who spoke her language, shared her tastes, saw the world from her own viewpoint. And she would no doubt find him. Well, good for her.

She bit savagely into a stick of celery, remembering with fierce misery the session with Julian yesterday morning. He had been very frank, totally out of character; he had called her quite early, about eight o'clock, apologized for not taking her to dinner the night before, and asked her to join him for breakfast at the Connaught. She had gone along, mildly revengeful but serene and in control nonetheless. He had stood up as she entered the dining room and looked at her very seriously. He was clearly tired; his eyes had the shadows of a sleepless night in them, and his mouth was tense, unsmiling.

"Camilla, good morning. Come and sit down. Breakfast?"

"Honey in yogurt, please, and decaffeinated coffee."

He repeated her order to the waiter.

"Is the yogurt live?" she said.

The waiter looked at her with exquisitely polite disdain. "I will inquire, madam. What shall I do if it is dead?"

"Cancel my order," Camilla said coolly. "And bring me some freshly squeezed orange juice and strawberries instead."

"Certainly, madam."

"You're not eating," she said to Julian in surprise. He usually ate well at breakfast time, the only meal in the day when he indulged himself.

"No, I'm not hungry."

"Are you feeling unwell?"

"No."

"Julian, I wish you'd consider a macrobiotic diet, for a short time at least. It would do your system so much good. So cleansing. So detoxifying. I found an excellent dietician in Covent Garden. He draws up individual diet sheets according to life-style and metabolic requirement and—"

"Camilla, I really don't want to discuss my diet. I have something very serious to tell you. Something that may—that will distress you. I'm sorry."

She sat and looked at him, quite still, her face composed, devoid of emotion. She did, as she always did in stressful situations, one of her relaxation exercises—letting go slowly and completely from the belly inward, breathing in very slowly through the nose and gently out through the mouth. It always worked; it kept her utterly in control.

"What is it?"

"I have to end our relationship. At once."

"I see."

His face was working, anxious, almost afraid. She had never seen him look so vulnerable.

"I have found—met someone else."

"When?"

"I beg your pardon?"

"When did you meet her?"

"Yesterday."

"I see. Love at first sight."

"Perhaps."

"Well, this is not really very unusual, is it? I am totally familiar with this scenario. Now, who is this person? Do I know her?"

"No, you don't. She's a journalist."

"Would I have heard of her?"

"I very much doubt it. She is not at all well known, although she's very talented."

"Of course."

"Camilla, I can see this must sound quite absurd. But I can only tell you that I feel I can't go on seeing you. Not now. It would be—dishonest."

"Good heavens, Julian, what an interesting word to find on your lips. I didn't know you were familiar with it. She must be a very exceptional person, to lead you to think in such terms."

"Yes," he said, "yes, I think she is."

Camilla was having a little trouble with her relaxation therapy. She felt tense, shaky, rather faint. She took a deeper breath, closed her eyes for a moment, tried to wipe her mind blank.

The waiter returned, with her breakfast "The yogurt is live, madam."

"What? Oh, I don't want it. Take it away."

"Do you want the strawberries instead, madam?"

"No," Camilla said, teeth clenched, voice low. "I don't want anything. Just some coffee."

"Certainly, madam. Decaffeinated?"

"No." She was almost shouting at him, in an agony of misery. "I want real coffee. Full of caffeine. Strong. Black. With sugar. All right?"

"All right. Certainly, madam. I'll bring it at once."

She looked at Julian and thought how much she had loved him, how much, at that moment, she hated him. "How old is this person?"

He looked at her, then looked away. "Twenty-four."

"Twenty-four!" Camilla began to laugh—wild, hysterical laughter. "Twenty-four years old. How pathetic. Even by your standards. What a stupid, hopeless gesture. Julian, it's a classic. I suppose you realize that. A classic grab at youth. A negation of yourself, a rejection of where you really are, who you really are. I feel sorry for you, deeply sorry. And for her. How long do you think it will last?"

"A long time, I hope. I intend to marry her."

Camilla sat staring at him, quite, quite still, her face ashen, her eyes wide with horror. Her stomach heaved; she thought she might be sick. Then she leaned forward and, in perhaps the first, the only truly spontaneous, unpremeditated action of her entire life, slapped him very hard twice across the face.

"You poor deluded bastard," she said very clearly, so clearly everyone in the dining room could hear. Then she picked up her bag and walked quite slowly and deliberately out.

It was only when she was safely in a taxi that she began to cry.

THE FIRST PERSON Roz had talked to, bared her soul to about Phaedria, was Susan. She found her very receptive.

Susan found herself reacting strongly and rather painfully to Julian's prospective marriage. She had imagined herself to be entirely free of any emotional involvement with him. She was, in fact, happily involved with Richard Brookes, an executive with the company, and was seriously considering marrying him—"Although at our age it does seem a little ridiculous," she said, "and I'm certainly not having anything but the smallest most badly publicized wedding." She had watched Julian leading Camilla through the elaborate and disagreeable dance she had visualized for herself over the years, and she had thanked God, and her own common sense and judgment, that she had escaped it. Then he had sat her down in his office one morning —the same day as he had had the confrontation with Camilla at the Connaught—and told her that he was very much in love and planning to marry again. She had felt sick, and savagely jealous.

She had managed to smile, to tease him mildly, to tell him he was too old for such nonsense and that he should wait maybe another twenty-four hours before finally committing himself, but the words came out with difficulty, and the smile was frozen onto her mouth.

"I know it sounds absurd," he said, kissing her fondly on the cheek, accepting her good wishes. "I know I am old enough to know better and that I am acting rather rashly, to put it mildly. I can only tell you that what I feel for Phaedria I have never felt for any other woman, so I can only presume it must be love. It has come to me rather late, but I have to be grateful that it is here at all. And you with your clear-sightedness and great knowledge of me should surely understand."

"I do, Julian," said Susan, a twist of pain in her heart as he admitted finally—and somewhat brutally—that whatever he had felt for her, it was not love. "I do understand. Does—that is, have you told Camilla?"

"I have," he said with a heavy sigh. "This morning. Over breakfast. At the Connaught," he added, a trifle unnecessarily.

"I don't suppose it mattered much where you told her," said Susan briskly. "In fact, it might have been better to do it somewhere just slightly less public."

"Yes, I think you're probably right," he said. "I'm afraid she was very upset. More than I thought she would be."

"Julian," said Susan, standing up, unable to bear it any longer. "Sometimes I find it very hard to believe you think at all. Especially about people and how they might feel. I must go; we have a great deal of work to do, you never did phone me yesterday about the marketing plans."

"Oh, I'm sorry," he said. "I'll go through it all with you later."

"If you have the time," she said.

As she looked back, she saw an expression on his face that was very seldom there: it was uncertainty.

ROZ SAID FOR many years how appropriate it had been for her and Phaedria to have met in the bathroom.

Two and a half weeks had passed since Miranda's birth and the arrival of Phaedria in her father's life. She knew she was being ridiculous in avoiding her, but every day she told herself that tomorrow she would be able to face meeting her, or at least face arranging to do so, and every day she felt an even darker horror at the thought. Roz was not a coward; she flinched from very little; but the prospect of having not only to meet Phaedria but to smile at her, to be nice to her, to express pleasure at having her in the family, seemed quite beyond her endurance. And so she continued to hide, to make excuses. Letitia and Susan had pleaded with her, her father was on the brink of losing his temper, Eliza had given her a very sharp piece of her mind, and still she said no, she couldn't; she still felt unwell, weak, not up to such a confrontation—while looking radiantly healthy, attending her yoga classes, visiting the office for ever longer periods each day, and calling meetings at the house.

It was C.J. who finally persuaded her. He put down the phone at breakfast one morning and said, "That was your father. He wants us to have dinner at his house tonight. I said I thought we could and you'd call him back."

"I won't go," Roz said, panic rising. "I can't. I don't feel at all strong today. What about Miranda? How could you, C.J.? Call him back, please, and say no. Maybe at the weekend."

"Rosamund, you look extremely well to me, you have a meeting in the office, remember, which I'm sure you won't want to cancel, and I haven't noticed Miranda preventing you from doing a great deal over the past two weeks. Now, for God's sake pull yourself together. You're making yourself look like a complete fool."

Roz looked at him startled, impressed as always when he stood up to her. She managed to force a smile. "All right, C.J. I certainly don't want to look a fool. I'll come."

"Good. Call your dad back, will you? I have to go now."

He walked out of the room without looking at her. Roz looked after him thoughtfully and then picked up the phone and dialed Hanover Terrace. Her father answered.

"Daddy? It's Roz."

"Hello, Roz." He sounded brusque, impatient.

"Daddy, we'd really like to come tonight. I'm feeling much better, thank you. I might have to bring Miranda, though. She's a bit colicky, and I don't want to leave her with Nanny."

She could hear the warmth, the relief in his voice. "Roz, I'm delighted. I'll tell Phaedria, she'll be so pleased. And of course bring Miranda. That will be lovely."

"She might yell."

"We won't mind a bit. Good-bye, darling. See you about eight."

"Yes. Bye, Daddy."

Roz put down the phone and went up to have a bath. She suddenly felt quite genuinely weak and shaky. On the way she looked in on Miranda, who was being bathed.

"You'd better yell good and loud tonight, baby," she said.

The nanny, a young Norland-trained embodiment of efficiency, looked at her in surprise. Roz didn't bother to explain.

She went to her meeting in the office, a financial review of the stores' various performances in various cities of the world—New York still led the field, Paris was down, Milan up—and spent an hour with her secretary dictating letters and arranging a trip to Paris so that she could study Circe's performance and see Annick at the same time. She decided to go home and rest up for the ordeal of the evening, and took the lift up to the penthouse to use the ladies' room there while her car was brought around to the front of the building. As she stood in front of the mirror, brushing her hair, wondering if the half stone she had still retained was settled entirely onto her chin, the door opened behind her and a girl walked in. Roz glanced at her, half smiled, and then looked at her more carefully, taking in properly what she saw: long, curling dark hair falling past her shoulders, a pale, rather serious face, and a slender red crepe dress with a gently swirling skirt that Roz recognized instantly as being from Jasper Conran's latest collection. The impact hit her gradually, like a slowed-down film. The girl's walk seemed almost to stop, her head to turn toward her inch by inch, the hair floating, drifting up in the air; a smile began, tenuously, cautiously to appear on her lips. Roz felt as if she was falling. The room swam; she closed her eyes, leaned on the dressing table.

As if from a great distance she heard the girl say, "Are you all right? Here, sit down. Let me get you a glass of water."

Roz straightened, hauled herself back to normality with a huge effort. "I'm fine," she said, meeting the brown eyes, the concerned face with a hard, distant stare. "Absolutely fine. Thank you," she added with ill-disguised reluctance.

"Are you—you must be Roz? I'm Phaedria." She was holding out her hand.

Roz, with enormous self-control, took it. "How formal! How do you do?"

"It feels a bit formal. How are you? Are you sure you're all right? How is the baby? I'm so looking forward to tonight."

"I'm perfectly all right, thank you. So is the baby."

There was a silence. Phaedria was looking at her uncertainly, searching for something else to say. "I'm just going to have lunch with—with—"

"My father? How nice. Do give him my love."

"Why don't you join us? It would be fun."

"Oh, I don't think so," Roz said, managing to smile graciously, sensing Phaedria's discomfiture. "Thank you," she added. There was a long silence.

"Well," Phaedria said, "I'd better go. He doesn't like to be kept waiting, does he?" She was floundering now.

"Perhaps not," said Roz. "He's never seemed particularly to mind waiting for me." She smiled again. "We'll see you tonight."

"Yes. I hear you're bringing the baby. That will be lovely, I shall look forward to meeting her."

"No, I'm not bringing her," said Roz. "I think after all it would be better if I didn't."

She managed to imply it would be seriously bad for Miranda's health if Phaedria met her.

"Oh," Phaedria said, "oh, all right. Well, good-bye Roz. Nice meeting you."

"Good-bye," said Roz.

She watched Phaedria walk out of the ladies' room rather quickly, and smiled at herself in the mirror. It might be a long war, but she had certainly won the first skirmish.

THE DINNER WAS dreadful. Roz had dressed to kill, fearing to look disadvantaged beside this paragon. She wore a black silk jersey dress from Chloe with the newly fashionable wide shoulders, and an above-the-knee skirt that showed off her endlessly long, slender legs to their very best advantage. It did her very little good. Nothing, nothing at all, could have prepared her for or helped her through the agony of watching her father looking at Phaedria in adoration, asking her opinion on everything, encouraging her to talk, praising the way she had adjusted to her new life, organized the dinner that evening, charmed the housekeeper, done the flowers herself. Dear God, thought Roz, any moment now he'll start saying how exquisitely she goes to the lavatory.

Roz knew her own performance was superb. She talked as charmingly as she knew how, questioned Phaedria graciously about her life as a journalist, admired the food and Phaedria's dress—another Conran, black crepe this time—teased her father, but only very gently, about his wicked past, and asked Phaedria most politely if she would forgive her if she and Julian talked shop very briefly after dinner. "Literally shops. You know, I expect, that I'm president of Circe," she said, smiling across the candlelight.

"Of course," said Phaedria, "I do know. Yes, you withdraw, and I'll stay here. C.J. and I can tell dirty stories over the port."

It was the first sign of retaliation. Roz looked at her sharply, startled, then smiled again.

"Do be careful," she said. "C.J. has a terribly weak stomach."

She was quite unable, however, to say anything at all about the marriage, or even to congratulate them. She tried several times, but the words literally stuck in her throat, a hard, dry lump, and each time she had to take a huge draft of the superb claret her father had brought out for the occasion, swallow it desperately as if it were beer or water, and change the subject. Nonetheless, she felt, as she kissed him lovingly and proffered her cheek to Phaedria, she had got through it all extremely well.

Later that night, however, C.J., lying awake in the bedroom next to hers, which he now occupied permanently, thinking about her and the performance she had put on, heard her weeping for a long time and wished there was something he could do to help.

"PHAEDRIA, WE HAVE to think about the wedding."

"Oh, good."

"No, I'm serious."

"So am I. I like weddings."

"Now, we can play it two ways. We can sneak off and go to a registry office and not really tell anybody. Or we can do it in style. Ask everybody—and it would have to be everybody. What do you think?"

"What do you want to do?"

"I don't care. I want you to do what you want. I suppose I have a marginal preference for the sneaking off."

"Let's do it in style."

He was surprised. "All right. If that's what you want."

"When shall we do it?"

"Too late before Christmas now, if we're to do it in style. January? Here or in the country?"

"Oh, let's do it in the country. That would be much nicer. Then we can involve the horses."

He laughed. "They'll like that."

THE FOLLOWING WEEKEND Julian took Phaedria to Marriotts for the first time. She fell in love with it. She wandered through its beautiful rooms, looking for a long time out of each window, so as to imprint each individual view on her mind. She insisted they eat lunch sitting at either end of the huge table in the dining room. She explored the attics, investigated the cellars, walked around the gardens, exclaimed with delight at the stables, and rode with him across the downs in the falling dusk, laughing, exultant.

"We must bring Grettisaga here. She would love it. Can I go and fetch her myself?"

"If you want to. Take Tony with you."

"Who's Tony?"

"My groom. You can't manage on your own."

"Yes, I can," she said, and for the very first time he heard a tinge of irritation in her voice. "Of course I can. I can drive a horse trailer. I've done it hundreds of times."

"Phaedria, it really isn't very wise. It's a long way. Suppose you had a breakdown or a puncture?"

"I'd fix it."

He sighed. "Wait till next weekend, and I'll come with you."

"No. I want her here sooner than that. Stop fussing."

Later that night, as they lay in the big bed upstairs, with the shutters open, ghostly moonlight falling across the pillow, she said, "Julian?"

"Yes, darling?"

"What am I going to do about Roz?"

"What do you mean?"

"She hates me."

"Phaedria! It's not like you to be hysterical."

"Julian, I am not being hysterical."

"Forgive me, darling, but I think you are. Those are very strong words. You've only met Roz twice. How can you possibly claim she hates you? It's nonsense."

"Julian, I am capable of making a judgment. I can tell when people don't like me. And Roz doesn't. Well, she more than doesn't like me. As I said, she hates me. She won't speak to me unless she has to. She won't even look at me. I've suggested lunch; I've asked if I can come to see her in the office. I've really tried. She won't meet me even a quarter of the way. And I find it very difficult."

"She came to dinner with C.J."

"That was to please you."

He picked up her hand and kissed her fingertips. "I think you're merely not having quite the success with Roz you've had with most other people. Which is natural, in a way. She has a rather—intense attitude toward me, and she's bound to be a little wary. Now, look, my mother adores you, Richard and Freddy are both dying of love for you, all the staff in Hanover Terrace dote on you, even Eliza wants to be your best friend. I haven't been on such good terms with Eliza for years. Can't you be content with that, and let Roz come round in her own time? She will. She likes you very much, she told me so."

"Did she?" Phaedria said. "How nice. Julian, please stop patronizing me. I am not a child, even if I seem like one to you."

"Phaedria," Julian said, dropping her hand and drawing slightly away from her. "I think this is a little absurd."

"Really? You call my objecting to Roz's total animosity absurd? I'm disappointed in you, Julian."

"I think," he said, and she could hear the ice in his voice, "we have enough real problems to confront without you manufacturing a nonexistent hostility from my daughter."

"It is not nonexistent."

"I happen to believe it is."

"Then you should open your eyes a little wider. And perhaps you would like to tell me what real problems we have?"

"A great many. I'm amazed you have to have them spelled out. We have an age difference of nearly forty years. However much we may both deny it, there are awkwardnesses in that. I have a very large company to run—which, if I may say so, you have not made much of an attempt to acquaint yourself with. I also have several households to maintain, and there are serious practical problems in that. You need to understand each one and its own particular system; you need to know each staff and to win their trust. You've made very little effort in that direction. You haven't bothered to buy yourself many decent clothes. You haven't suggested we do any entertaining. Your main concerns seem to be whether or not you can get a job on *Vogue*, and being reunited with your horse."

Phaedria was silent for a while; then she got out of the bed.

"You bastard," she said, "you lousy bastard. I've known you just over three weeks and you throw that pile of garbage at me. How dare you?"

She walked over to the door, pulling her robe on.

"Where are you going?"

"Back to London."

"Don't be absurd."

She slammed the door.

She had no clothes to put on; she wasn't going to go back into the bedroom. She went into one of the spare rooms and found some jodhpurs—probably Roz's, she thought, pulling them on with vicious rage, or one of Julian's other unfortunate mistresses'. Downstairs she took one of the jackets hanging on the utility room door and a pair of Wellington boots. She let herself out of the door. She was too excited now, too amused by her own adventure to feel upset.

They had driven down in the Corniche; the keys to that were on the table next to Julian. She walked over to the garage where he kept the cars; it was unlocked. There were five cars inside, including three very early models: an open 1903 Fiat; a first edition Chevrolet, its name written elegantly right along its bonnet; and a Cunard-bodied Napier. Even in her rage, she did not quite dare to take one of them. But nearest the door was the Bugatti; ravishingly elegant and low-slung, with its sloping running board and majestically curved mud-guards. That would do. Unbelievably, the keys were in it; Julian had been playing with it that morning.

Phaedria got in and, trembling slightly, tried to start it; it roared obligingly at the second attempt.

She smiled triumphantly, and eased it forward; it was deliciously easy to drive. Safely out of the garage, she let in the throttle and cautiously put her foot down. Clear of the house and halfway along the drive, she increased her speed. This was fun. . . .

She could remember the way—just. The night was clear, which made things easier. Down the lane for two miles, then right at the turn to Steyning and then it was signposted to the A24. She had a bit of trouble making the lights work, and she had to stop twice and wipe the windshield with her hand, but otherwise it was easy. She hoped the petrol would last; she wasn't going to find a garage open here in the middle of the night. Her mind was blank now, except for rage; pain, she supposed, would come later. She found it almost impossible to believe that a man as charming, as gentle, as civilized, as loving as Julian had been to her, could convert so swiftly into an arrogant, manipulative monster. All at a breath of criticism of his daughter. She shuddered; she felt outraged, blindly, furiously angry. She put her foot down harder.

Suddenly in the rearview mirror she saw headlights. It might be someone else, anyone, but it was certainly very likely to be Julian. The lights flashed; she drove on. It was Julian, in the Corniche; the lane was so narrow he couldn't overtake her. He was driving quite hard behind her now, honking and flashing his lights. Phaedria sud-denly started to laugh. This was revenge, however brief, and it was extremely sweet. There was nothing he could do, just for a short heady while. He was impotent; he couldn't touch her. She hoped the sensation was painful. It would almost certainly be novel.

At the end of the lane, her triumph swiftly ended. The road wid-ened; she tried to go faster, but the Bugatti suddenly began to slow down, its petrol exhausted. The Corniche swung wide of her, then pulled in tight in front of her; she had to stop. Julian leaped out, dragged her out of the driver's seat and slapped her hard across the face.

"How dare you! How dare you take that car? Have you any idea how valuable it is?"

"Yes," said Phaedria coolly. "C.J. was telling me about it at dinner. Well, Julian, you seem to want me to become more familiar with all the precious and important things in your life. I thought I'd start with the cars. Now, if you could just give me a lift to the nearest garage, I can get a can of petrol and carry on."

She was breathing heavily, her eyes huge and brilliant with anger. As she stood there, confronting him, contemptuous, unafraid, the jacket fell slowly open and revealed her bare breasts. Julian looked at her, and slowly his expression totally altered. Rage became hunger, hostility turned to tenderness, and he reached out and tried to take her in his arms.

"Don't touch me," said Phaedria, pulling the jacket angrily around her. "Just don't. I want nothing more to do with you. Ever. Leave me alone."

"No," he said, "I can't do that," and he half pushed her, half dragged her into the backseat of the Corniche, slamming the door behind them.

"I'm sorry," he said, pushing the coat down off her shoulders, kissing her frantically on her lips, her neck, her breasts. "I'm sorry, I'm sorry, I'm sorry, and I love you so much. Please, Phaedria, please forgive me."

And she, stunned by the swift conversion from anger to desire, which she felt in her own body as well, kissed him back, fiercely, greedily, reaching for him, tearing at his clothes, ripping open his trousers, pushing down her jodhpurs, and flung herself back onto the seat, pulling him on to her, thrusting herself desperately against him, frantic for the feel of him inside her, filling her, moving her, leading her into her sweet, hot explosion of pleasure. It was over in minutes; they lay, breathing heavily, silent, looking at each other warily. Then Phaedria suddenly smiled. "You bastard," she said, and kissed him very tenderly on the mouth.

Three days later Julian gave her the Bugatti.

THE WEDDING DATE had been set for the first of June. On the night of Phaedria's flight in the Bugatti, after they had reached home—towing the Bugatti, to the accompaniment of much swearing from Julian, who refused to leave it in the lane—after they had gone back to bed and made love again, after Julian had begged her to forgive him again and again, after she had said, without believing it for a moment, that perhaps she had been mistaken about Roz, after they had slept briefly and Phaedria had woken first to a still, cold day, she had told Julian that January was perhaps a little soon for the wedding. That maybe they should know each other a little better first. That it would do no harm to wait. And besides, the weather would be nicer, they could have a marquee, the gardens would look beautiful.

And Julian had been quite unable to change her mind.

TOWARD THE BEGINNING of March Julian went to see his dentist. Sitting in the waiting room in Weymouth Street, leafing idly through copies of *Country Life,* he saw an advertisement for a house and his heart was as startlingly stopped as it had been when he had first seen Phaedria Blenheim four months earlier.

The house was on the corner of Picadilly and one of the small streets tipping down the hill toward Saint James's, just east of Fortnum's. It was tall and gray and beautifully proportioned, and it had been in use for the past few years, said the advertisement, as a hotel. It was for sale for three million pounds and could easily—so the advertisement said persuasively—be converted into offices or flats. Julian had other ideas for it.

He canceled his appointment, tore out of the building, and took a taxi down to Piccadilly. He got out and walked to the building, half afraid to confront it, to look at it, lest it was not as the advertisement said, lest once again he should be disappointed, robbed of his prize. But he wasn't. It stood graceful and unspoiled, so far as he could see, five stories tall, not at all unlike the house on Fifty-seventh Street in New York, with a fine arched doorway and beautiful stonework. Inside it was a nightmare; the staircase had been ripped out, lifts installed, most of the paneling stripped out, the ceilings lowered. The perfectly proportioned big rooms upstairs had been halved or quartered, the doors lined, the walls covered with built-in cupboards. What the hotel chose to call bathrooms had been crammed into corners; the decor was fifties kitsch, with a heavy slug of baroque glitz.

Julian didn't care. It could be restored, made beautiful again, brought back to life. And it was exactly what he had been looking for, waiting for, for nearly twenty-five years. He felt as if he had come home.

◆　◆　◆

"I HAVE A present for you," he said to Phaedria that night. She was sitting at her desk in the room she had chosen for herself in Regent's Park, the one that had been Eliza's parlor. It looked a little different now. The walls were white, the ceilings were white, the floor was white; there were black blinds at the window and a big black desk in the middle of the room. There were books on floor-to-ceiling shelves on one of the walls, and a stereo system with a huge mass of tapes and records on another. On a low table by the window was a mass of magazines, not just English, but French, American, Italian, German. And the room was full of flowers, a huge extravagant mass of color, on the desk, the table, the shelves, even in a giant vase on the floor.

Here for several hours a day Phaedria sat working. She had not yet managed to get a fashion job, although she wrote the occasional free-lance article. She had been commissioned by the Society of British Fashion Designers to write their history from year one, and she was deeply engrossed in it. She was also surprisingly, and rather charmingly, busy with plans for her wedding.

"What's that, Julian?" she said slightly absently.

"Here you are." He handed her a key.

"Julian! Not another car?"

"No. Something bigger."

"What?"

"Come with me, and I'll show you."

He refused to say a word as they drove down Baker Street and Park Lane and turned into Piccadilly. As they reached Fortnum's he slowed down and pulled over to the curb.

"There you are."

"What?"

"That. There. That building."

"I can see. It's very nice. But what about it?"

"It's yours."

"Mine! But I don't need a building."

"Yes, you do. It's going to be the London Circe. It's your wedding present."

"Oh, my God," said Phaedria. "Oh, for heaven's sake . . . Oh, Julian."

·21·

ROZ WAS SO ANGRY WHEN SHE HEARD about the store she actually threw up. Julian told her about it over lunch at the Ritz, presenting the event as something to be celebrated. He explained that he was giving it to Phaedria as a wedding present and that he was sure she and Roz would be able to work together on it amicably if they put their minds to it. He had said much the same thing to Phaedria the night before. For the first and last time in their lives Phaedria and Roz were in total agreement: this, they could both see, was the beginning of a very long war. They also both had great difficulty in believing that Julian could actually think they would be able to work together. There was an expression in his unfathomable brown eyes, which Roz had grown up with, and Phaedria had begun to recognize. It meant danger, meant games were being played, meant checkmate. It was there now.

"Excuse me," Roz said and half walked, half ran to the bathroom.

Kneeling on the floor, trying to recover herself, tears streaming down her face, she wondered where this fearsome situation was going to end. The specter that had haunted Roz all her life, ever since she could remember, that of a small sibling, seemed suddenly terrifyingly close.

She stood up slowly and wearily and washed her face. She studied it as she put on her makeup and brushed her short dark hair. It might not have beauty, but it had a great facility that face, something inherited from her father—a capacity not to show the emotion behind it. She was going to need that capacity a great deal, she realized, in the months ahead.

"SORRY, DADDY. I suddenly felt awfully sick."

"Are you all right, darling? You do too much."

"Rubbish. You can't do too much. You've taught me that all my life."

"Maybe, but I didn't really intend that philosophy to be applied to a period just after having a baby. Miranda is only—what?—four months old? You don't realize it, but you're still recovering."

"Oh, Daddy, you sound like Dr. Partridge. Silly old fart," she added.

"You're referring to Partridge, I trust, and not to me."

"Of course."

"From what I hear, he is a silly old fart. But if he's been telling you to take life a bit easier, I would echo him."

"Well, I'm not going to, so you can both stop. Now tell me exactly what this business with Circe and Phaedria means."

"In what way?"

"I am the president of Circe Europe, am I not?"

"You are."

"Circe London, therefore, will come under my control."

"Well, yes. But only officially. I want this store to be Phaedria's. She has a considerable feel for fashion and for decor. I think she'll make a good job of it. She has some interesting ideas."

"Oh, good," said Roz.

"Obviously I can't ask her to report to you."

"Obviously."

"But she'll need help, particularly on the administrative side, budgeting and so on."

"Temporarily, I presume."

"I beg your pardon?"

"If the store is to be hers, surely she will want to handle the whole thing. She won't want anyone interfering with her budgets or her staff or her long-term planning. Not after the early stages. It would be an untenable situation for her."

"Possibly."

"Not possibly, Daddy, obviously."

Expressionless face met expressionless face.

"So," Roz went on, "in the long term, Circe London will be an oddball, under different control, out of the system. Is that going to work?"

"I don't see why not. Providing you are kept informed of what is going on. Clearly Phaedria will be working to guidelines. She's not going to turn it into a downmarket chain store."

"Hopefully."

"Roz, don't be negative."

"Sorry." She threw him her most charming smile. "No, I'm sure she won't. She's a clever girl. And she has great taste."

"Doesn't she? She's beginning to do some extremely nice things to the house. And to Marriotts. Why don't you come down this weekend? Bring Miranda. I don't see enough of her."

"Are you hunting?"

"Yes, we're going out on Saturday with the Crawley and Horsham. Do come."

"I might. Yes, thank you. It would be nice. I'll talk to C.J."

"Good. Now I'll think over what you said, about Circe. I can see there might be the odd anomaly. Nothing that can't be sorted, but it could need some thought."

Round one to me, Roz said to herself. She gave her father her most brilliant smile. "Thank you for lunch, it's been lovely. I'll see you on Saturday."

"Why not come on Friday night? Phaedria cooks dinner herself then, and it's always delicious."

"No, thank you," Roz said hastily, feeling sick again at the thought of Phaedria's culinary skills. "It would be difficult. C.J.'s working late. No, we'll come early on Saturday."

"It'll have to be very early if you're going to come out hunting with us."

"It will be. Miranda gets me up at half past five. Bye, Daddy. Give my love to Phaedria."

"I will. You'll enjoy riding with her; she's very good."

"I look forward to it."

She would defeat that paragon if it was the last thing she did.

"ROZ, DO YOU have five minutes?"

Roz looked up. Phaedria stood in the doorway of her office. She was wearing her wolf coat and long black boots; she looked as if she'd stepped straight out of the pages of *Cosmopolitan*.

"Not quite five," said Roz, her distaste written very plainly on her face. "I'm late for a meeting already. I thought perhaps you might have been invited. We're discussing the architecture of the Beverly Hills Circe. You know we're opening one, of course?"

"Of course. I didn't know you were involved in it, though."

"Oh, didn't you?" said Roz. "How odd. I imagined my father told you everything about his business. Yes, the president of Circe in the States, Harold Fowler, is retiring next year. I think it's a fairly foregone conclusion that I shall take over the whole lot then."

"I see."

"Anyway, I imagined you'd want to take quite a close look at all the stores before getting to work on your own. Just to make sure it's in line."

"Possibly."

"Well, I would have thought it would be essential. Still, you have your own ideas, I imagine."

"Yes," Phaedria said. "Yes, I do. Plenty. Which is precisely what I wanted to talk to you about. We need to get together."

"Well, let's pencil in a meeting," said Roz, "but it will have to be a few weeks from now, I'm afraid. Do you mind if I set the date? I imagine my diary is a little fuller than yours, just at the moment."

"I doubt that," Phaedria said sweetly. "I am extremely busy myself, you know, with the arrangements for my marriage to your father. If it can't be within the next ten days, I'll just have to proceed on my own and hope we can iron out any problems later."

Roz wasn't sure if it was the first or the second half of this brief speech that made her feel sick again.

"JULIAN, WHY DIDN'T you ask me to the meeting about the Beverly Hills Circe? It would have been so helpful to me, hearing how that was going to be started from scratch."

"Darling, I did suggest it to Roz and she was all for it, but then she told me you and she had a very comprehensive meeting of your own planned and she'd be able to fill you in on the details then. It seemed more sensible, when you've got so much on your plate at the moment."

Phaedria had learned not to discuss Roz with Julian.

"I see. Well, in future, could I be put on the circulation list for store meetings anyway? I'll find the time."

"Of course. I'll let Roz know. I'm sure she'll be delighted."

"I'm sure."

"PHAEDRIA, ROZ AND I are going to L.A. next week to look at the Circe site, meet the architect, all that sort of thing. I think it might be a good idea if you came, too. What do you think?"

"Oh, Julian, I'd love it. I've never been to L.A. Never been to the States, as a matter of fact. Have you—discussed it with Roz?"

"Of course. She's delighted."

"PHAEDRIA, IT'S ROZ. Look, I don't want to interfere, but I really would suggest you get Paul Baud to help you with the plans for Circe. He's done most of them, including the first, and he is brilliant. Quite the best in the business. He'll help you keep to the house style, so to speak, and yet he'll listen to your own ideas. Just a thought."

"Thank you. I'll think about it."

"PAUL? IT'S ROZ. I'm absolutely fine, thank you. I still miss Paris, though. I can't think why you don't live there all the time. How's New York? Good. Listen, I need your help. Now, I do want you to be very discreet about this, because it's a bit delicate. You know my father's getting married again? Yes, isn't it delicious, and she is just so nice, none of us can believe our luck. You'll love her. Well, anyway, and this is the difficult bit, for me, you may have heard my father's giving her a building as a wedding present, to turn into the London Circe. You did? Yes, well, look, she's going to need a lot of help. No experience at all, and frankly, *entre nous*, she's going to make a complete hash of it if we're not very careful. Only of course I can't say anything to Daddy. Anyway, I've suggested she consult you, and I think she will. Look as if you're holding her hand and guiding her, and just quietly take over. She has some extremely dull ideas, as far as I can make out, and she really needs to be talked out of them. And both my father and I basically want the London Circe to be a little different. Just slightly more—well, quite a bit more avant-garde. You know. We've discussed it, and I know he's a little worried by some of Phaedria's ideas. Or rather the lack of them. He won't say anything to her, of course, nor can I. It would be terribly unkind, and we do want to encourage her. So we—well, I—thought you were the person to help us all through it. What? Well, the stores are my baby now, you know, I don't want this one going wrong. But obviously I can't interfere. You can see my difficulty. Yes, I do have a real baby as well now; she's adorable. You must come and meet her. So if she rings you, Paul— No, not the baby, you fool, Phaedria, will you be helpful? And terribly discreet? Marvelous. Thank you so much. We've never needed you more."

"RIGHT," ROZ SAID, settling a large pile of files on the boardroom table, "Let's get to work, Phaedria. Have you spoken to Paul Baud, by the way?"

"Not yet. But I do agree he's the best person. Thank you for suggesting it."

"Perfectly all right. I do want to help. We have to make this thing work, after all."

"Quite."

Brown eyes met green in total mistrust.

"Let's start with basics," Roz said. "How do you see the store? I mean, what image?"

"I thought very much the same as all the others. There's nothing that would be more disastrous than to have a kind of rogue Circe in London of all places."

"Well, obviously that really is up to you. I am totally unvisual, as my father is always telling me. I wonder whether perhaps you should consider a slightly different look."

"And would you be happy with that?"

"I was under the impression," said Roz, "that my happiness was of no relevance in this whatsoever. But possibly yes."

"Oh, all right," Phaedria said with a sigh. "Let's get down to budgets." She felt instinctively that any suggestion from Roz should be treated with deep suspicion.

"DADDY, IT'S ROZ. Look, you'll be pleased to hear Phaedria and I had our meeting today, and it went quite well. I think we can work together all right."

"Good."

"She has some quite nice ideas. The only thing is, I really don't think you should get involved at all."

"Why not?"

"Because she's feeling inhibited enough by me being involved, and she plans to consult Paul, which seems a good idea. I think if she feels your hand on things as well, she'll lose all confidence."

"Well, as long as you and Paul keep a firm eye on it and make sure nothing radical happens, I'll stand back."

"I think you should. It'll work better that way."

"JULIAN, COULD I talk to you about Circe, please?"

"Darling, I'd rather not. I'm terribly busy. It's your project. You have perfect taste, and I trust you. All right?"

"All right."

APART FROM HAVING to endure Roz's company—made more unendurable by the pleasant front she put on for her father's benefit—in Los Angeles, Phaedria greatly enjoyed her trip to the States, brief as it was. She had expected to find New York exhilarating, but she had not been prepared for its beauty. She spent a whole day as a tourist, just walking up and down the streets, in and out of the stores. She went to the top of the Empire State Building, she did the backstage tour of Radio City Music Hall, she skated in Rockefeller Center, and that evening she insisted Julian take her through Central Park in a horse-drawn carriage.

"We'll die of cold."

"I won't. You can keep me warm."

"Come on, then."

"I love it here," she said happily as they huddled under the rug Julian had brought from the Sutton Place apartment—"The ones they give you are threadbare," he said. "Can we spend lots of time here?"

"We could. I tend not to these days. Less involved than I was with this side of the world."

"Well, let's get more involved. Can you keep a horse in New York?"

"It's difficult. There is one place, on the upper West Side, the Claremont Stables. It's like a multi-story garage; you ride up a ramp. Not very satisfactory."

"Oh, well, maybe it's not a very good idea, then. What happens tomorrow?"

"We have a Juliana board meeting in the morning, and then I thought we'd spend the afternoon at Circe."

"Is Paul Baud here?"

"No, Roz asked him to go to Paris to have a look at the store there. It needs refurbishing, apparently. She's in a panic to get it at least partly sorted for Easter."

"What a pity. I did want to meet him."

"Well, isn't he coming to London to talk to you?"

"I haven't decided."

"Oh? I thought you had."

"No, not yet."

"Ah. I must have got it wrong."

SHE WAS MORE enchanted still by Los Angeles. Everyone had told her she'd hate it, but she loved it. She loved everything about it—the sunshine, the buildings, the traffic, the freeways lacing their way across the city, the glitz of Beverly Hills, the tackiness of the Sunset Strip, the palm trees waving above their heads, the ocean beating its way remorselessly onto the white beaches. She longed to explore further, to go along the coast, but Julian was reluctant to leave the city.

"We have a lot to do," he said rather shortly when she protested, "and not a lot of time."

"I'll go off on my own, then."

He looked at her rather coolly. "I thought you came here to work."

"I did."

"Oh, Daddy, don't be such a slave driver," Roz said. "She came to observe. I don't see why she shouldn't go off if she wants to, just for half a day. She's never been here before. We can brief her afterward."

Phaedria met her eyes with a grudging admiration. "No," she said, "thank you, Roz, for your concern, but Julian's right. I should be here."

The site they had acquired for Circe was right on Rodeo Drive, almost next to the Rodeo Center, precisely opposite Elizabeth Arden.

"Brilliant," Roz said happily. "Just brilliant. Worth waiting for."

The architect brought in to design the store had ideas never before even whispered of in connection with Circe. He saw it white, airy, stark; Phaedria watched Julian thoughtfully as he briskly demolished ninety percent of his ideas and then slowly moved into a qualified acceptance of the remaining ten percent. Perhaps the faint indication she had picked up from Roz that she might do something similar in London should be given more attention. Perhaps she had been wrong.

"ROZ, IT'S PAUL."

"Paul! Hello. How are you?"

"Very well. How was the Los Angeles site?"

"Perfect."

"And the new designer?"

"Very interesting. Totally revolutionary."

"And how did these revolutionary ideas go down with your father?"

"Surprisingly well. As I said, he does seem to be very much looking for a change."

"Good. Well, perhaps it is time. Now, I have talked to Phaedria."

"And?"

"You are right. She is most beautiful. And charming and intelligent. I liked her very much."

"I'm so glad."

"But I do not agree with you about her abilities. I found her full of ideas."

"Oh, good."

"She seemed interested in a more modern look. I told her I thought it was possibly a good idea. So we are proceeding cautiously along those lines."

"Excellent. I wouldn't be too cautious if I were you."

"JULIAN, I VERY much want to have a formal meeting to present my plans for Circe to you and Roz."

"All right, darling. I'm sure that's the way to do it. I'm very, very busy, though. Couldn't you manage just with Roz?"

"Of course not."

"Why of course?"

Her eyes met his with just a touch of amusement.

"You're the boss."

"RIGHT," SAID PHAEDRIA. "Let's get down to business right away, shall we? I thought I'd start with the cost estimates."

Roz looked startled. "I didn't realize you'd done any."

"Of course," Phaedria said coolly. "I don't see how we can possibly discuss architecture and design if we don't know what the financial implications are."

"Quite right," Freddy Branksome said briskly.

For the first time Roz felt a stab of fear.

Phaedria presented her budget clearly and succinctly. She had estimates from contractors covering external and internal work; she had a budget for architecture, another for design, and a preliminary one for fittings and fixtures. Freddy, the financial director, sat beaming at her, clearly enchanted; he was not used to seeing financial considerations given such high priority.

"So, at a very rough estimate, we're talking about something like ten million pounds, assuming we can get the work done within the year."

"Well, you can't," Roz said. "It's absolutely impossible."

Phaedria looked at her. "I don't agree. I've talked to several contractors. They all say twelve months is not unreasonable."

"They always say that."

"Possibly. But with heavy penalty clauses, it should be perfectly feasible."

"Maybe. But I doubt it."

"Well, let's move on," Julian said, slightly impatiently. "What about the designs, Phaedria? The budget sounds reasonable to me."

"Right. Now then, as you know I have worked with Paul Baud quite closely on this project. We spent a lot of time looking at the existing Circes, discussing them in the light of some of the work other stores have been doing, notably Harvey Nichols, and also the shops like Joseph and Rive Gauche. While Circe is clearly unique, it equally clearly cannot be studied in isolation. Markets change, consumers change, fashions change. Money, quite a lot of money, is in new hands. People who a few years ago would not have considered going into Circe will now be shopping there."

"What kind of people?" asked Roz. "Typists?"

"No, not typists. Obviously primarily our market will still be women in their thirties and above. But there is a great deal of money in younger hands. Real money. What I think of as designer money. Stylish money. There's a new breed of professional woman who wants and needs clothes that are very expensive, very stylish. She probably has much more fashion sense than her mother or her older sisters. And a lot less time. I think we have to consider her. Clearly much of that area is down to merchandising; I would like, for instance, to institute a department where a woman can get an entire wardrobe put together for her consideration as a result of a preliminary consultation on her taste, life-style, and needs. But I don't want to get too deeply into that now. The point I'm making is that we should consider these women when we look at the style, the design, of Circe."

She paused. "I talked to Paul Baud along these lines, and we discussed, among other things, the look of the Los Angeles Circe in relation to the New York one. Very different. Paul was very enthusiastic, surprisingly so I thought, about change. About a contemporary look. I liked his ideas. Here they are."

She pulled out the screen, walked over to the carousel cassette of slides, and flashed the first image onto the screen. It showed a detailed color drawing of the foyer of Circe: all white, with Deco-style lights and a low, curving reception desk. "That would be for a store guide, to welcome people personally, tell them where everything is. Then we go through sliding glass doors into the body of the store."

Another image came on the screen. "Paul based his ideas for the ground floor rather on Saks in New York, or even Tiffany's, where you get a panoramic view of the store, less claustrophobic, less fragmented."

Julian's face was expressionless, taut.

"The predominant color throughout the store would be white, the predominant sensation one of space. The beauty floor would also be more open, more spacy, than we have grown to expect from Circe." She clicked the button again. "Clients would, for some treatments, be in a large, open salon. Then"—another slide—"we looked at fashion. We conceived a very large space with departments opening from it at regular angles—one at two o'clock, if you follow me, one at four, and so on. They would not be shut off from one another as they are now, but an impression of seclusion would be given by screens and plants. I—"

Julian held up his hand. "Excuse me, Phaedria. Forgive me for interrupting you. I have to say I feel we are all wasting our time. This —concept of yours bears absolutely no relation to anything that Circe stands for. It offers no intimacy, no luxury, no exclusivity. I am particularly concerned by the plans for the beauty floor. The whole principle behind Circe is a sense of privacy, so that a woman can be as relaxed as if she were in her own home. I fear you have grossly distorted the Circe concept. I think the only thing to do at this stage is go back to basics and begin again."

"But—"

"No, really, I don't think there is anything to be gained by further discussion. I would urge you very strongly to do a little more research into the needs and desires of our past customer before you sacrifice her on the rather dubious altar of what you conceive as the present. Now, if you will excuse me, I think I will forgo lunch. I have a great deal of work to do. But, please, the rest of you stay."

He was white, clearly shaken, and oddly angry. Roz felt a stab of pleasure shoot through her, strangely akin to sexual desire. Freddy Branksome looked uncomfortable. There was a silence as Julian stood up and picked up his files.

"Please sit down." It was Phaedria's voice, very calm, with just a tinge of amusement in it. Roz looked at her sharply.

"I would rather not."

"I would rather you did. And do me the courtesy of allowing me to finish my presentation."

He gave her a look that was very close to dislike. Then he sighed and sat down. "Very well. But I have only ten minutes."

"Fine. Now then"—she looked at them and picked up the control button again—"as you can see we did a lot of work along these lines. I enjoyed working with Paul Baud, and I think he has vast and valuable experience. However, returning to the new customer, and yet still looking very carefully at the old, I think there is much more work to be done. I have begun doing it."

She clicked the button. "I decided in the end to take a rather revolutionary step and talk to a designer with no direct experience in retailing but a great deal in company style."

"Indeed?" Julian said dryly, still angry, still distressed. "And are we allowed to ask this person's name?"

"Of course," said Phaedria. "You know it well. It's David Sassoon."

Freddy, looking at her as she stood there fighting the first great political battle of her life, wondered just how aware she might be of the sexual dynamite delivered in that simple statement and decided it was most unlikely that she was not totally aware. He looked at Julian swiftly, nervously, for a reaction, but his face was smooth, expressionless.

"I see," he said. "Do go on."

"Right. This is our view of the reception, the foyer, call it what you like."

They looked. It was like looking into what Freddy described afterward, in a most uncharacteristic fit of lyricism, as a grown-up fairytale book. It was as if William Morris had had a love affair with Kate Greenaway and they had run away together to the twentieth century. David Sassoon had used an airbrush to create the effect of actual photographs rather than designers' sketches; the effect was very powerful. His Circe, and Phaedria's, was light, airy, lovely, awash with sea greens and blues; huge tangly ferns stood in the corners; embroidered tapestries hung on the walls. The floor was white marble, the ceiling white and high. Big lamps with blue glass shades hung tantalizingly here and there, their light falling tenderly on low counters set with jewelry, perfume, hats, gloves; one felt a compulsion to walk forward, to examine, to explore.

"None of this merchandise would be for sale," explained Phaedria briskly, breaking the spell. "It is there simply to draw the customer on into the store. Now here we have the main ground floor."

In the same color scheme, imbued with the same spirit of romance, it was broken into segments purely by pools of light. Between the lights, the small, jewellike departments, it was dimmer; in here the floor was no longer white, but the same soft greenish blue.

"I am investigating coloring the marble; it might be cold. Carpeting could be a possibility, but I don't like the idea. Let's move up to the beauty floor."

The beauty floor saw William Morris on a tropical island: huge, exotic flowers grew in white urns, a waterfall splashed brilliantly against the marble walls, a pool of brilliant blue water lay in the middle of the room, white water lilies lying languorously on its surface.

"Then all around it are the small treatment rooms, totally private, but each one with its coordinating theme of water and flowers. There will be a Jacuzzi in every room, and winter jasmine, clematis, anything that will grow indoors, climbing up at least one of the walls. The horticulturalists' bill will probably rival the beauty therapists'. Each room will also have a dressing table, a proper one, as you see, stocked with the entire Juliana line, but not remotely clinical. Vases of flowers, big powder puffs, hairbrushes, and white wicker chairs will give something of the feel of a conservatory. But as you can also see, out in the reception area, by the pool, more big chairs and lounges, so that people can sit and talk and drink fruit juices or whatever. It will have to be very, very warm, so they can wear just robes or—as they do in the Sanctuary in Covent Garden, just towels round their waists. Women are exhibitionists, when they know they've got good bodies; they should have a chance to be that as well as to be totally private."

She clicked again. "On the floor below, in the lingerie department, we thought a change of color scheme, to pink, so that it looks as much like a boudoir as possible."

The boudoir was dressed with brocaded wallpaper, brass wall lights with pink glass shades, charming eighteenth-century prints, small groups of chairs, dressing tables, beds with draped heads, lace spreads, and cushion covers, and scattered everywhere, as if waiting to be put on, was the merchandise—nightgowns, robes, undergarments, camisoles.

"Of course this may not be practicable. There would be security problems, but a few things dotted about would be worth losing, I would imagine."

Another click: "The fashion floor. More conventional, but again as you will see, a series of suites, an office perhaps, a drawing room, a salon, a conservatory, with the appropriate clothes in each one. Again, there could be a problem with security, but I think as a device, it could be made to work. And here we have all the color schemes brought together, the greenish blue, the pink, the white, so that the customer is aware of a coherent feel throughout the store."

She paused. "That is as far as David Sassoon and I have gone for now. We wanted to get your reaction. Perhaps we could discuss it over lunch."

Phaedria walked over to the window, let the blind up. She saw first Julian's face, surprised, almost awed, but soft with pleasure; then Freddy's, smiling at her fondly; and finally Roz's face, quite, quite blank, green eyes looking at her with a disturbing mixture of hatred and respect. And there was something else in those eyes, something that gave Phaedria more pleasure even than the respect. It was fear.

·22·

GAMBLING, MILES REFLECTED, WAS like surfing and sex. It completely wiped out everything else. That was its charm.

He and Billy had become more and more besotted with gambling lately. They had had a few lucky nights, left the Paradise Beach Hotel riding high with several hundred dollars in their pockets, and felt they couldn't go wrong.

They could.

Within the space of a week they owed, between them, nearly a thousand dollars. Desperate, they had begged the manager for time to pay.

"You boys have been coming here long enough to know better. I want you to pay back that marker in forty-eight hours."

"We will."

"Will your dad give you any money?" Miles asked as he and Billy walked disconsolately over the bridge toward the Old Town.

"Nope. I wouldn't dare ask him in any case. I'm in enough trouble as it is. What about your grandma?"

"Not a chance. She doesn't have any."

"So what do we do?"

"I don't know."

"You could sell your watch," Billy suggested.

"I could. But I'm not going to."

"You might have to."

"Billy, I'm not going to. I told you."

"Miles, you don't seem to understand. We're up against it. This is real life, not a rehearsal. We could be in dead trouble. And I mean dead."

"Don't be melodramatic."

"I'm not."

"You are."

"Oh, for fuck's sake, Miles, grow up."

Miles looked at his friend sharply. His face was drawn and pale in the harsh light of the street lamps.

"You're really worried, aren't you?"

"Well, of course I damn well am. You should be, too."

"Sorry. I didn't realize how serious this was."

Miles sold his watch. It brought in just enough to pay off their debt and leave them a hundred dollars to take to the roulette table.

They put fifty dollars on the twenty-one black. Just for the hell of it. The wheel spun. Twenty-two.

"Nearly," said Billy. "Let's try again. Twenty-five dollars."

The wheel spun again. Endlessly. Twenty-two again.

"Okay," said Miles. "Third time lucky. Twenty-five dollars on twenty-two black."

The wheel spun. Time froze. Miles stood motionless, concentrating totally. He could not have told anyone even his own name. Go on, you fucker, stop. Twenty-two. Twenty-two. Twenty-two.

The wheel stopped. Twenty-two black.

"Jesus," said Billy. "We did it. What's that?"

"Odds are twenty to one. That's five hundred dollars."

"Great," Billy said. "You got half your watch back. Let's go."

"No, not yet. Let's stay a while."

"Miles, don't. You can't go on winning."

"Why not? We went on losing. I'll be careful."

A blonde in a black dress, all hair and eyes and breasts, heard him and laughed. "I'll pace you. What are you betting?" she said.

"A hundred dollars."

"Wow. On what?"

"Twenty-two black."

"You just got that."

"I know."

"All right." She pushed a pile of chips onto the twenty-two black. The wheel spun. Billy looked away.

"Hey," he heard the girl's voice, gritty, delighted. "You did it. Twenty-two black. I won two thousand dollars."

"Yeah," said Miles. "We both did."

He felt tense, high, heady. Just like sex.

"Again?" She was laughing.

"Yeah. Again."

Hauling the will together. Could you? Again? Pushing yourself. You could. Feeling the power, the thudding heart, the pounding, soaring blood. Just like sex.

"What number this time?"

"The same."

"Can't be."

"It will."

It wasn't. Miles lost five hundred dollars. Billy pulled at his arm. "Come on. Let's go."

The girl looked at him, winked at Miles. "Him or me?"

Miles looked at her and smiled his wonderful, radiant, self-mocking smile. "Him. Come on, Billy. I'm with you."

She looked amused. "Okay, he wins. Will you be here tomorrow?"

"I guess so."

The next night Miles won five hundred dollars and the next five thousand. The girl was there. She was sexually aroused by the game. So was Miles. Billy stood back from the tables, afraid. Afterward he went home alone and Miles took the girl down to the beach and made love to her three, four times, reliving the tension, the fear, the spins on the wheel, the absolute will to win, the heady power of the numbers.

The next night he lost three thousand dollars. The girl left him sitting at the table. The next night he won ten thousand. The girl took him back to her hotel. He still didn't even know her name.

And the next night he lost five thousand dollars, and the next five thousand, and finally he was left with a marker for four thousand to pay back in a week.

He walked home alone, shakily sobered. He woke Billy up. Billy gave him coffee, counsel, comfort. But he didn't have four thousand dollars.

"Jesus," Billy said. "What will you do?"

"I don't know."

"What about the girl? She had money."

"She was a shill—a gambling whore. She had no money. It came from her pimp. He's in at the casino."

"Ah. Didn't you realize that?"

"I'm not sure."

"Miles, you're crazy."

"I know."

"They'll get very mean."

"I know."

"Is there anyone with that kind of money? Who'd give it to you?"

"I don't think so. No. Oh, I don't know."

"What about the old guy who put you through college?"

"I couldn't ask him. I'd rather get beaten up."

"You'll get worse than beaten up," Billy said with conviction.

"Oh. Well, anyway, I still would. I could ask my uncle, but I don't think there's anything left. Or—yeah, that's it. The house."

"What house?"

"The one in Malibu."

"It's your grandmother's."

"I know. But it ought to be mine. I could borrow against it."

"Do you have the deed?"

"No, but it must be in the house somewhere."

"Miles, you really are something," Billy said in tones of great admiration.

The next day, when Mrs. Kelly was taking her afternoon nap on the veranda, Miles let himself silently into her room. She slept soundly these days; she was old and weary, and she had had several glasses of Madeira with her lunch.

In a box under her bed, he found what he wanted: the deeds to the house. Wrinkled documents in a tatty envelope. He took them out and looked at them and smiled; then he went straight to the bank.

"THESE ARE NOT in your name, Mr. Wilburn."

"I know. They're my grandmother's."

"I can't let you have any money on these without her signature. Also, we need a transfer deed, making the property over to you. Signed by you both, with witnesses. And even then I have to draw up a legal charge."

"What's that?"

"It's a document saying you've borrowed the money; we hold the document until the loan is repaid. I have to put a time limit on that, of course. Perfectly simple, no problem in any of this. But, as I say, first we need your grandmother's signature on the transfer deed—witnessed."

"But she's—well, she's very old. She's almost senile."

"Doesn't alter matters."

"What would?"

"Nothing."

"Uh-huh. Well, thanks anyway. I'll be back."

"GRANNY KELLY, WOULD you sign this for me?"

"What's that, Miles?"

"Just a form saying I'm over twenty-one. I've applied for a job at the casino."

"The casino! What kind of a job is that?"

"Better than no job. You've been trying to get me to work for years. You've finally succeeded. You should be pleased. Please sign it. Oh, and we have to get Little Ed and Larissa to witness it."

"Miles, this is just ridiculous. Just for a job? Are you sure this is right?"

"Granny, the world's changed a bit lately. You don't realize."

"Maybe not. Oh, all right. Providing you go check on those hens and collect the eggs. I don't trust Little Ed one bit. I know he's taking them."

"You can't trust anyone these days, Granny."

"RIGHT, YOUNG MAN, here you are. A draft for four thousand dollars. To be repaid in three years." The bank manager was avuncular, smiling. "That's a lot of money. Don't you go off with that to the casino, now."

"Oh, I wouldn't do that."

"Glad to hear it."

He paid the gambling debt, stayed away from the casino, stayed away from the women in the hotels. He concentrated on his job on the tennis courts. But he was unhappy, lonely. Billy's father had finally put his foot down and was sending him off to work in a bank in Washington.

Billy seemed quite happy about it. "I could use a little respectability. Don't you ever want it?"

"Want what?"

"Well, you know, normality. A job. Salary. A regular life."

"Billy! Do you?"

"Yeah." He grinned sheepishly. "Yeah, suddenly I do. I really don't mind being shipped off to Washington. I'm looking forward to it. Except I'll miss you."

"Billy," Miles said, smiling at his friend, "you're out to lunch."

But when Billy had gone, he did wonder if a regular life might not have its charms.

IN MARCIA GALBRAITH'S desk was a small bundle of letters, all of them addressed to her friend, Dorothy Kelly. She took care that Dorothy never saw her letters. You never knew; someone might try to tempt her back to California and away from Nassau and Marcia. And besides, Dorothy needed looking after, now that her mind was going, and Marcia and Little Ed and Larissa were all so devoted to her, protecting her from reality. She didn't want to be bothered with things like letters.

Among the letters in the bundle were two from Father Kennedy in Los Angeles and one, forwarded via Los Angeles from Hugo Dashwood in New York.

·23·

JULIAN TOOK PHAEDRIA TO THE house on Eleuthera in the Bahamas for their honeymoon. It was a low white mansion set just above a small curving bay, palm trees hanging gently over the silvery white beach; she fell instantly in love with it.

Julian flew them in himself to the village airfield at Marsh Harbour in the small plane he kept at Nassau. She sat gazing spellbound for the entire flight at the fairy-tale sea beneath her, the strange variations in the color of the water, the mystical, uninhabited, almost swamplike green islands, the dark, dark blue swaths of the deep waters, the pink etching around the small white patches of land set in the blue-green sea.

"That's the coral," he said. "Tomorrow we'll go snorkeling on the reef near the house. Then you can meet the fish."

That evening they wandered along the beach, picking up coconuts and conch shells, looking at the slick of moonlight on the sea. Phaedria sank down suddenly, laughing, on the warm white sand and said, "This is a cliché of a honeymoon, Julian Morrell."

"I'm sorry."

"Don't be. I love clichés. I'm a journalist, remember?"

He lay down beside her. "I do. Could we add to the clichés, do you think, and make love in the moonlight?"

She looked at him thoughtfully. "Bit corny. But I like that, too."

"Come on, then," he said, reaching for her, kissing her forehead, her nose, her neck.

"Oh, Julian," she said, "I will, I will."

EARLY NEXT MORNING the houseboy took them out in the small motorboat and anchored on the reef while they swam, and Phaedria marveled at the peaceful, enchanted world she found beneath the sea, the filigree coral, the clear, clear water, and the rainbow-colored, friendly, quaintly smiling fish.

"Oh, I love it, I love it," she said as they sat later on the veranda of the house drinking fresh iced lemonade, sinking her teeth into a papaya. "Why didn't you bring me here before?"

"You were too busy wanting to go to L.A. and New York and opening your own store and organizing a wedding. If you remember. We shouldn't really be here now; it's much too hot. I usually come only in the winter. But I wanted you to see it, I thought you just might like it."

"Oh, I do, and I don't mind the heat. I love the sun."

"Yes, but you must be careful. This is real sun. Very dangerous. Not to be sat in."

She ignored him, as she so often did, and got badly burned. For three days she lay, feverish and in pain, in the cool bedroom with the whirring fans, and he sat with her and bathed her skin and read to her from *Anna Karenina*, which he pronounced as suitably romantic and sad for the occasion.

"You're a stupid girl," he said to her when she finally felt better and sat up, weak but cheerful, demanding breakfast. "You should do what I tell you. You've wasted three days of our week here, and I haven't even been able to make love to you. What a honeymoon."

"I'm sorry. Can't we stay longer?"

"No," he said, mildly irritated. "We both have to get back. You know we do."

"Sorry. All right. But we have three days left, don't we?"

"We do."

"Well, let me start making amends straightaway. Come into bed beside me, take those silly shorts off, and show me that you've forgiven me."

"I'm afraid of hurting you."

"It'll be worth it. Please."

"All right. I'll be very careful."

"Not too careful."

"All right."

"AND DID YOU enjoy your wedding?" he asked her suddenly as they sat eating breakfast some considerable time later. "Was it worth all that worry and work?"

"I really enjoyed it. Every minute. Did you?"

"Surprisingly, I did. I spent the whole day thinking how special you were and that I didn't deserve you at all."

She looked at him, tender in the aftermath of love, distressed at the thought that she had nearly not been there at all.

"I do like Susan," she said suddenly. "She's very brisk and I'm not sure she likes me very much, but I can see why you're so fond of her."

"She is a very special person," he said. "And I'm very glad she's married Richard Brookes. He'll make her a much better husband than I ever would have."

There was a silence. Phaedria smiled at him, took his hand, kissed it. "I love you when you're humble. And honest."

"Then you can't love me very often," he said and laughed.

"No. I don't. Didn't your mother look wonderful?"

"Absolutely wonderful."

"How old is she?"

"Eighty-five."

"She's amazing. That was some Charleston she did with David. Imagine him being able to do that."

"Imagine." He sounded short, tetchy. Phaedria looked at him, amused.

"Don't you like David?"

"Well enough."

"Enough for what?"

"To work with him."

"Is that all?"

"I think so, yes."

"Pity. I wanted to ask him down to Marriotts for the weekend when we get back."

"What on earth for?"

"To work on Circe. He doesn't have much time to spare during the week. Would you really rather I didn't?"

"Yes, I would. Tell him to make time."

She sighed. "Pity. I thought it would have been a fun weekend as well."

He was silent. The subject was clearly closed. As it was their honeymoon, she did not try to reopen it.

BACK IN LONDON, relieved of the pressures of planning her wedding, she began to work in earnest. David's drawings were completed, specifications were drawn up, the work put out for bids.

Phaedria put her mind to merchandise, to her scheme for a wardrobe consultancy, to hiring buyers, to finding new designers as well as established ones, to selecting, and mostly rejecting, jewelry, fabrics, shoes, furs. She wanted, was determined at this stage, to be as painstakingly and personally involved as possible, to put herself in the position of her customer and see, feel, try, everything for herself. She bought collections from Sonia Rykiel, Missoni, Krizia, Valentino ready-to-wear; from the States she imported Anne Klein, Ungaro, Cerutti; from France Dorothée Bis, and Emanuelle Khanh. There were shoes from Maud Frizon, Ferragamo, and Charles Jordan, hats by Freddy Fox and Patricia Underwood, and a dazzling costume jewelry department bedecked with designs from Butler and Wilson, Chanel, Dior. She learned to haggle not just about money but about exclusivity and time as well. She discovered the great retailing nightmares—holdups in production, in customs; a delivery of hats that failed to reach her on time because the straw had not arrived from China, a set of silk dresses because a factory in Hong Kong had been closed for a fortnight by an epidemic of flu. She poached staff shamelessly from other stores: from Brown's, Harvey Nichols, Fortnum's. She considered new departments—gifts, pictures, interior decor—and rejected most of them as too impersonal, out of line with the Circe concept. The only one she was totally confident about was a flower room, as a part of the foyer, a small bower styled like a conservatory, set with wicker chairs and tables, stacked with every conceivable flower, with rose trees and jasmine and daisy bushes in pots, urns filled with lilies and orchids, and roses, and myriads of dried flowers hanging from the ceiling, stacked in baskets around the walls.

"Women will buy them, of course, but men will come in and buy them, too. It will be the most beautiful, caring, exclusive flower shop in London. Made for people in love."

Favorite and well-known customers would receive a spray of white lilies on their birthdays and wedding anniversaries from Circe; little girls would get nosegays of sweetheart roses and forget-me-nots.

It was a charming concept; it brought the front of the shop alive.

She began to think about sales staff: "I want them to be young— Don't look at me like that, Julian."

She looked at advertising agencies, PR companies, talked to the press herself as well, began to plan a launch party that rivaled her own wedding in splendor and complexity. Things were proceeding fast; she was determined to achieve the impossible and open by the spring. And the more people told her she couldn't, the more she knew she could.

ROZ HAD BEEN carefully avoiding any involvement with Phaedria. She knew this was a mistake, that it was at best unbusinesslike and at worst childish, but she was angrily aware of the ever-extending ripples of Phaedria's power; she could feel them lapping onto the shores of her own empire, and for the time being, until she could find some way of defeating her, she was merely hoping that Phaedria would hang herself sooner rather than later on the huge lengths of rope Julian was clearly prepared to hand over to her.

She was also oddly and miserably jealous of Phaedria's relationship with David. She had not thought about David sexually for years. He had become a much loved avuncular figure, and she was relieved and happy that he and her mother had managed to become friends once more, but he was a person for whom she had a very special fondness, and it riled her dreadfully that he was clearly so close to Phaedria.

In addition to riling her, it interested her. Even Roz could not believe—knowing David, knowing his singular attitude toward her father—that they were likely to be lovers; nevertheless there did exist the clear possibility that her father might think that they were. That seemed to Roz a very large case of dynamite indeed.

JULIAN CAME INTO the first liaison meeting looking particularly bland.

"Right," he said. "Now, hopefully, these meetings can be kept short and not take up too much of our time. It may be that in due course the two of you can handle them yourselves and not need to involve me."

Roz and Phaedria looked at him in a hostile silence.

"My concern, as you both know, is that your work is, to an extent, overlapping and there is a certain lack of communication. It is vital that there be two-way traffic of information between you. Clearly you, Roz, as president of the stores, need to be well informed on Phaedria's plans—"

"In theory, yes," Roz said, interrupting him. "In practice, surely, as the London store is so exclusively Phaedria's, there is very little input I can make. She seems perfectly confident and is moving very fast, aren't you, Phaedria?"

"Roz, that is not the point, as you must realize," said Julian, his irritation beginning to surface. "Phaedria's confidence and competence are not in question—"

"I'm so glad," Roz put in sweetly.

"Roz, I would be grateful if you will let me finish the occasional sentence—"

"Sorry."

"What matters is that you should be aware of what she is doing, so that you can build it into your overall picture of the store development worldwide. London is crucial to that picture."

"I agree," said Roz. "It just seems rather dangerous that it should be potentially a separate entity."

"Roz, that is the whole point of these meetings," Julian said, his eyes growing very hard. "To make sure it does not become a separate entity."

"Are you saying that if I disagree with any of Phaedria's plans, I have the authority to block them?" said Roz. "Surely not."

"Not block them, no, of course not. But discuss them, talk your objections through, yes, certainly."

"I see," said Roz. She looked suddenly rather sleek.

"How—detailed might these objections be?" Phaedria asked mildly.

"Oh, for God's sake, I have no idea," said Julian. "That is clearly the sort of thing that will emerge over the weeks ahead."

"I think we should discuss them now," Phaedria said. "Obviously on large matters—budgets, designers, color schemes, for example— it would be not unreasonable for Roz to have a view—"

"Not entirely," said Roz, looking amusedly arrogant, a perfect toying with a very new recruit to the first form.

"But if," Phaedria went on steadily, apparently unmoved by this, "I am to talk to Roz about every hat, bracelet, salesgirl, before making a decision, progress is going to be rather seriously halted. Just in case she disagrees with a great deal of what I am doing," she added sweetly.

"Phaedria," said Julian, "if you cannot establish in your own mind the proper limits of your own influence, then I would have serious doubts about your ability to handle this project at all. I expect you and Roz to be able to work out a modus operandi and stick to it. That is all. Initially I will be available for consultation on it, if absolutely necessary. Please get to work implementing it straight away. Now then, I do feel that you need a really first-class assistant, Phaedria. Someone with a background in marketing and experience in design and retailing as well. Instinct alone is hardly sufficient under the very serious commercial circumstances you are operating in. Roz, I'm sure Phaedria would appreciate some help in finding someone. You have so many contacts. Give it a bit of time, would you?"

"I'm very busy indeed at the moment," Roz said. "I don't really have that sort of time to spare. Couldn't Susan handle it? It's her area."

"I don't think so, no," said Julian. "Susan's area, as you describe it, is overall company management, which may incorporate personnel, but certainly doesn't include it as a day-to-day concern. Besides, you are in the retail field every day. You must constantly meet people who would be suitable for the job."

"Not at the assistant level, no," Roz said.

"Then be kind enough to descend to it for a while," said Julian. "Now, Phaedria, while I think of it, you'll have to find someone to work with you on the design aspect of the store for a few weeks. C.J. needs Sassoon on some vital refurbishing of the hotels. He's taking him off to the States next week."

It was hard to say which of them was more angry with him.

"HELLO, ROZ. IT'S nice to see you."

Roz looked up. She had been sitting at her table at the Caprice for half an hour after her lunch guest had gone, trying to concentrate on the spring promotions for Circe New York and the merchandising plans for Circe Beverly Hills. Roughly twenty-five of the thirty minutes had been occupied with a savage contemplation of Phaedria. The only consolation was that there seemed little chance of her having a baby while she was apparently so committed to her work.

She looked up. Michael Browning stood in front of her, his expression as wryly solemn as always, his dark eyes exploring her face with a tentative tenderness.

Roz actually felt her heart lurch three distinct times, moving within her. She closed her eyes briefly, trying to compose herself, and then, surprising herself with her calm, smiled back at him. "Michael! What on earth are you doing here?"

"Looking for my raincoat."

Roz relaxed, started to laugh. "Why should your raincoat be here?"

"It was here last night. Now it's gone."

"I expect you left it in a taxi, not here at all. Never mind your raincoat, what about you? Why are you in London?"

"I'm buying a few little supermarket sites."

"How nice." She was silent, just looking at him, drinking him in.

"Aren't you going to ask a raincoatless man to sit down?"

"Sorry. Do sit down. Have a coffee."

"That would be nice."

He looked at her, quietly studying her face, her hair, her clothes. She was wearing—and thanked God for it—a particularly flattering outfit: a short peplumed jacket in navy suede by Sonia Rykiel, with a long bias-cut swirling skirt; it made her look taller, more graceful, more slender even than she actually was. Michael smiled at her.

"You haven't changed much."

"Why should I have?"

"Quite a lot has happened to you."

"I suppose so."

Her heart was taking off again. Keep calm, she said desperately to herself. Keep calm. Don't think, don't feel, don't do anything. Help-lessly, horrified, she heard herself say, "It's so nice to see you. I've missed you such a lot."

"I miss you too, darling."

Her eyes met his. She smiled. "How long are you here for?"

"That's a leading question. About five days. Could you fit lunch into your high-powered schedule?"

"No, honestly, Michael, I don't think that's a very good idea."

"Dinner, then?"

"No. Absolutely not."

"Okay," he said calmly. "Lunch will do. Where would you like to go?"

"I wouldn't."

"The Connaught tomorrow?"

"I have a meeting."

"Thursday?"

"I don't know. I'll see."

"Fine. See you there at one. I'm staying there," he added.

IT WAS A foregone conclusion, really. They lunched; Roz talked; Michael listened. She talked to him about all the things she had sworn she wouldn't: about C.J., about Phaedria, about her terror of losing everything.

He looked at her sorrowfully, and shook his head. "You should have married me."

"I know."

"I still have the ring."

"I don't believe you."

"I do. I take it with me everywhere. Can't think how I haven't lost it. Look. Here it is."

He got it out and handed it to her. She opened the box, looked at the ring, remembering everything about the day he had given it to her—Paris, the sunshine, the breakfast, the sex. Her eyes blurred.

"Put it on."

"I can't."

"Put it on."

She put it on.

"Great. Now let's go upstairs and get married."

◆　　◆　　◆

ROZ DIDN'T LEAVE the Connaught until six o'clock the following morning. She had forgotten, or rather her body had, how sex could really be—the questing hunger, the frantic concentration, the way her body felt slowly and sweetly filled and then the wild, glorious progression, deeper and deeper, bigger and bigger, as she rose, rode, swung, soared into orgasm.

She lay, after she had come the first time that afternoon, half laughing, half crying, her body still throbbing, still shuddering gently, and wondered how she had endured the stillborn dull despair of the sex she and C.J. had known lately.

"That wasn't too bad," said Michael mildly, reaching out to her, stroking her face, moving down to her neck, her breasts. "I didn't mind that so much. Did you?"

"It was okay," said Roz, smiling as she had not smiled for months, warmly, peacefully, joyfully. "Okay for starters."

"Jesus, I've missed you. All of you. Every last inch of you."

"Well," she said, "you certainly know all those inches."

"I do, I'm glad to say. Did you miss me?"

"Oh, not much."

"You're lying."

"Yes, I am."

"Has it been worth it?"

"I don't know. I don't think so. No, of course it hasn't."

"Good. Have you been happy?"

"Not really. No."

"Excellent."

"You bastard."

"No, I'm not a bastard, Roz. Actually, I'm a regular nice guy. I've played by the rules. I've let you do things your way. I wasn't even going to look you up. It was an accident I saw you there, in that restaurant. You're the bastard. I imagine in your liberated world women can be bastards."

"I suppose so. Yes, you're right. I know it. It's all my fault."

"And are you truly sorry?"

"I think so."

"Truly, truly sorry?"

"Yes, truly, truly."

"Good." He turned toward her, his hand moving steadily, purposefully, down over her flat, smooth stomach, into the hidden warmth he had just reclaimed. "Now, this may take a while, but I plan to make a little more of you my own again. After that we can order tea and have a talk."

"I don't want to talk," Roz said, her voice low, desperate. She knelt up, pushed him over on his back, straddled him, drew his penis into her wet, hungry body, threw her head back, and rode him, almost detachedly, plunging, thrusting, exhorting, demanding from him her long, fierce eruption of pleasure.

And Michael Browning, detached also, looked at her face in all its ferocious abandonment, and wondered if there could be another woman anywhere with the same power to take hold of his heart.

CIRCE, LONDON, OPENED on May 1, 1984, in a blaze of publicity, with a party that lasted for eighteen hours, beginning with a charity lunch and fashion show—entailing a panic of nightmare proportions, with half the clothes from New York held in customs until the actual morning of the day, culminating in a drive down the M4 by Lady Morell herself and a ticket for speeding, but at least a fully clothed set of models—and ending with a champagne breakfast the following dawn. Circe was widely acknowledged by the press, the trade, and the customers to be the most exciting, original, and beautiful environment for shopping that London had seen for decades.

Nigel Dempster gave it his lead story under the headline "All in the Family":

> The beautiful new young Lady Morell, wife of billionaire Sir Julian, has proved her worth with a dazzling coup. She has taken the distinctly ropy Windsor Hotel, Piccadilly, and turned it into a pleasure dome, a store called Circe, which will undoubtedly prove to be the happiest of stamping grounds for London's rich and style-obsessed. Although there are other Circes, in Europe and the United States, Phaedria Morell assures me that hers is unique. Phaedria—her name is that of a character in Spenser's *Faerie Queene*, the personification of wantonness—has been working very closely with David Sassoon, head of corporate design in Sir Julian's company; a rare empathy is reported between the two. Mr. Sassoon has strong connections with the Morrell family; he was once romantically involved with Sir Julian's first wife, Eliza, now countess of Garrylaig. With Mr. Sassoon, the countess was at the opening of Circe, looking very

much younger than her forty-eight years, and apparently the best of friends with her ex-husband's new wife.

Lady Morell, who was once a journalist and met her husband when she went to interview him, says she is now hoping to turn her attention to some of the other Circe stores.

This could cause fireworks in the family; Rosamund Emerson, Sir Julian's daughter, who is president of Circe Stores worldwide, guards her empire jealously. Roz, who is married to C. J. Emerson, and has a baby daughter, Miranda, has been seen several times in recent months dining with New Yorker Michael (ByNow Supermarkets) Browning. "He is an old friend of the family," she told me.

ROZ WASN'T IN a terribly good mood. She was having a late breakfast at home and trying to summon the necessary courage to go to the office. What was worse about all this, apart from the stuff in Dempster's column about her and Michael, was that she knew the thinly disguised brickbats were actually not deserved. Phaedria had had some new ideas and the store looked beautiful, but the implication that all the other Circes were old hat, somehow burned out, was monstrous. Oh well, the storm would undoubtedly pass. The good news were the innuendos in the story about Phaedria and David. If there was one man her father was ferociously jealous of, it was David Sassoon. Any suggestion, however unfounded, that Phaedria might be involved with him should affect him very satisfactorily. She still presumed it was unfounded; maybe it wasn't. The rows reverberating across Regent's Park and the Sussex Downs these days, and indeed by telephone across several continents, were reportedly growing in noise and frequency. Interesting.

She had just poured herself another coffee when the phone rang.

"Roz? Hi, it's Michael. I love you. Will you marry me?"

He made this call most mornings at about seven, quite undeterred by the twin facts that it was two A.M. in New York and that C.J. might well be sitting beside her.

"Hello, Michael. I just might today. Life is bad here."

"Is hubby there?"

"No, he's gone to the office."

"Can I come around?"

"Where are you?"

"At Heathrow."

"You're not."

"I am."

"How long will you be here?"

"Couple of days."

"Why are you here this time?"

"To twist your arm."

"Oh, God. I have enough problems. Look at the *Daily Mail*. Nigel Dempster's column."

"I've already seen it. I was pleased."

"Why?"

"That arm's been twisted halfway around already. Can I come?"

"No. I'm going to the office. I'll meet you tonight. Will you be at the Connaught?"

"Yup."

"Oh, I'm glad you're here. Problems notwithstanding. Bye."

"Bye, darling."

WHEN SHE GOT into her office her father was at her desk. He had the *Daily Mail* in his hand. "Have you seen this?"

"Of course."

"Don't you care?"

She shrugged. "Not terribly."

"Why not? For God's sake, Roz, why not?"

"I'm not sure. Maybe because it doesn't seem to make much difference. Michael and I are having an affair. Everybody knows anyway."

"Roz, this can't go on."

"What do you mean?"

"This affair. You're married; you have a child."

She looked at him, amused. "Forgive me for saying so, Daddy, but such old-fashioned morality does not become you."

He looked at her, his eyes dark with anger. "What are you intending to do?"

"I don't know."

"Are you thinking of divorcing C.J.?"

"I told you, I don't know."

"I won't allow it, Roz. You both have important positions in this company. It wouldn't work."

"Daddy," Roz said, walking around her desk, reaching across him for some files, looking at him very directly, "you can't not allow me to do anything. I'm an adult. Stop playing games with me. With all of us."

"You're not behaving like an adult," he said, "and I am not playing games."

He got up, pushed past her, and walked out of the office. She suddenly felt as she had when she was a little girl and told him she wouldn't go to boarding school. She had done everything she could to defeat him, but she had ended up at Cheltenham just the same.

PHAEDRIA WAS WORKING on her follow-up advertising campaign for the summer for Circe when Julian walked into her office. She looked at him warily. He had been charm personified during the endless party at the launch, smiling at her indulgently, telling everyone how clever she was, how proud of her he was, how marvelous he thought the store was. Then they had got home and he had been distant, withdrawn.

She had taken a bottle of champagne from the fridge and gone up to him, put her arms around his neck, tried to kiss him. "Shall we celebrate? Aren't you pleased?"

"Oh, yes, delighted," he said almost coldly. "But I'm very tired. I think I'll go straight up, if you don't mind. You do what you like."

"Julian, I can hardly celebrate by myself."

He looked at her, his eyes hard. "I would have thought you'd have done enough celebrating for now, Phaedria. With a great many people. Good night. I'm going to bed."

She had stared after him, shocked, hurt. For the first time since their marriage, they had slept separately, and she had lain tossing and turning for what was left of the night, trying to understand, trying to remember Letitia's words, to see him as threatened and in need of support and understanding, and only succeeded in perceiving a small-minded, jealous man in serious need of a brisk kick in the ass.

So far she had had no opportunity to administer it; he had left before her for the office, without a word.

He looked at her now with hostility in his eyes and threw the *Daily Mail* down on her desk. She smiled, determinedly bright. "Aren't you pleased with it all?"

"Not all of it, no."

"What do you mean? It's a huge success."

"Yes, it is. And I fully acknowledge it. What I am not pleased with is this report in Dempster today. About you and Sassoon."

"Oh, Julian, don't be ridiculous. It's only a bit of nonsense."

"I happen not to like nonsense. Especially when it makes me look foolish and denigrates my wife."

She stared at him. "That's a very interesting viewpoint."

"What do you mean?"

"Interestingly feudal. It's me that's denigrated, Julian, if anyone is, me, the person, not your wife."

"Don't be absurd."

"I'm not being absurd. Anyway, I don't feel in the least denigrated. I see this for what it is, a way of filling a column inch."

"Yes, well, I suppose you would regard it in that way. You are still a reporter at heart."

"Sometimes," she said, "I wish it wasn't only at heart."

"Well—unfortunately, perhaps—things have changed. Now can I make it quite clear that I do not want you working with Sassoon on anything, ever again, and I don't want to read this kind of thing ever again. All right?"

Phaedria's eyes met his, amused, slightly contemptuous.

"I'm awfully busy," she said. "I really don't have time for this. There's a journalist from the *Sunday Times* waiting to see me. Sorry, Julian. Please excuse me." She pressed her buzzer. "Janet, could you ask Catherine Bennett to come in now."

·24·

THE PARADOX OF THE VIRGIN bride is that she is potentially more promiscuous than her experienced sisters. If her bridegroom proves a disappointment, she will inevitably seek the long-awaited, much vaunted pleasure elsewhere, and if he proves a delight she will almost equally inevitably wonder if other bodies in other beds might not be more delightful still.

Phaedria Morell had, to all intents and purposes, been a virgin bride, and her bridegroom had shown her considerable delights. Nevertheless, over a year having passed since he had led her to her somewhat unconventional marriage bed on his office floor, she found herself restless, excited, disturbed. Her earlier anxieties about her own sexual capacity had been shifted, if not entirely removed, by a new and even rather dangerous self-confidence; she had begun to change more than she realized.

Her success, her newfound power, and her pleasure in it, the gloss and sleekness Julian's money had bestowed upon her, had all conspired to make her greatly sought after. She had none of the problems experienced by Eliza thirty years earlier, of having to fit in with Julian's circle, of having no status, no life of her own. She found herself at the center of a fashionable world, of designers, photographers, journalists; she could pick her friends, her social circle, from a group of people with whom she felt entirely at ease, who pleased and amused her, and whom she seemed to please and amuse. Wherever she went and whatever she did, she found attention. She was photographed, interviewed, sought after; scarcely a day passed for a while when her picture or her pronouncements, and very frequently both, did not appear in the press. She was a frequent guest on talk shows. Labeled by *Tatler* "Leader of the Chat Pack: Cafe Society 1980 Style," she was recognized everywhere she went. She was stared at, remarked upon, exclaimed over. And she became increasingly pleased by it. She would scarcely have been human had she not; from the near obscurity of a two-bit job on a provincial paper, she had become seriously famous, sought after by stylish society in New York as well as London, flattered and praised everywhere she went. And when the flattery and praise fell from the eyes and lips of attractive men, and attractive young men in particular, she found it and them quite irresistible.

A year after her wedding, her name had been linked with at least three highly, and visibly, eligible young men: Bruce Greene, racehorse owner and polo player; Danny Carter, a truculent young working-class photographer who had made love to her, if not literally, constantly and disturbingly with his voice and his camera lens through several heady afternoons behind his locked studio door; and Dominic Kennedy, a twice divorced self-made millionaire, who phoned her every morning as soon as she got into the office and invited her to dinner before finalizing his arrangements for the evening with anybody else.

With all of them she flirted, lunched, and occasionally—when Julian was away—dined. She let nothing more carnal come to pass between herself and them than an occasional mildly sensuous kiss. She had no real intention of having an affair with anybody; nevertheless she enjoyed and was reassured by the attention of other men; she toyed with the ultimate conclusions, she meditated upon the possible pleasures, and she was careless of her husband's reaction.

That summer Phaedria gave a costume ball on midsummer night at Marriotts. Three hundred guests came for dinner, and another three hundred arrived at ten as the dancing began. The drive to Marriotts and all the lanes leading to it for five miles around were lit with torches, and the grounds were spangled with five thousand fairy lights. The dancing took place in two sea-blue marquees, the bands performing against great theatrical sets of fairyland designed by Damon Austen, a brilliant new recruit to the Royal Shakespeare Company who was rumored to be one of Lady Morell's admirers. Even the grounds had been adorned with great drifting garlands of green gauze hanging from the trees. Boats drifted on the lake, each one lit by hundreds of candles, bearing a champagne breakfast, which was served as dawn broke, and as the sun rose, exactly on cue, a pair of white peacocks, Phaedria's Christmas present to Julian, appeared and strutted about the lawns, giving out their strange pagan cries. The costumes were dazzling: fairies danced with hobgoblins, mermaids with centaurs, princes with beggarmaids; the grounds appeared, in the dusky flickering light, to be filled with creatures of another world, some with ornate masks. Phaedria—dressed as Titania, in a green silk chiffon dress designed by Zandra Rhodes, her face made up theatrically strange in blues and greens, her hair drawn back from her face with a rope of pearls, her feet bare—looked quite extraordinary. Even those who knew her well stared at her, newly impressed by her beauty. Only the host, wandering apparently benignly about his guests, smiling, talking, dancing with all the most beautiful women, with the notable exception of his own wife, refused to participate in the fantasy and wore white tie and tails. The ball was featured in every popular newspaper and in *Tatler* and *Harpers Queen*, claimed three entire pages in *Ritz* magazine, and even made the sign-off story on the news at ten. Lady Morell was clearly now established, or so said the media, as one of the great partygivers of her generation.

Julian was initially amused and then patently irritated by the way she had become a minor celebrity and her reaction to it; Phaedria enjoyed his irritation. She saw her success as a way of redressing the balance a little in their marriage; she was no longer a nobody, a mere recipient of his favors. She had power of her own, albeit limited. She could give as well as take, hold her own in his life, and after eighteen months of being made to feel excessively fortunate, she was enjoying the sensation.

Julian seemed more jealous of her fame, of the column inches she was consuming day by day, than of the young men. She wasn't sure if he was really unmoved by her lunch companions and by the insinuations in the gossip columns, but he certainly seemed to be. It annoyed her a little. She would have liked him to exhibit at least a touch of possessiveness, but he did not; he looked at her with his cool, blank gaze, when they were out together and she was surrounded with her circle, when the stories reached him or he read them in the paper, and said he hoped she was enjoying herself, managing to imply that it was both unlikely and unattractive if she was.

Except in one case. One name on her lips, she knew, could cloud a morning, wreck a dinner, destroy a weekend. One man threatened her peace of mind and her marriage—the one with whom she had every reason to be innocently occupied: David Sassoon.

JULIAN MORELL WAS working on a new cosmetics line. It was the first he had given his total attention to, put aside other work for, for years; he was totally engrossed in it, spending much time with the chemists in New York. The concept was an absolute secret. Nobody—not even Annick Valery, who was now *directrice de beauté* for Juliana worldwide; not even David Sassoon, who was working on the packaging; not even Phaedria Morell, who was supposedly privy to all the workings of her husband's mind—knew absolutely what it was. It was a complete line; that much everybody knew; it was to be high-priced and very original; it was to be launched for Christmas; there was an all-time-high advertising budget, using posters, cinema, and television; and a new model had been signed up exclusively to represent it, a brown-eyed ash blonde, called Regency, who was seventeen years old and who was reportedly consoling Mr. Morell in his great unhappiness over the famously bad behavior of his new young wife. Both the reports and the unhappiness were only a little exaggerated.

Phaedria tried to talk to Julian about the range, to show her interest, to offer her opinions, but he brushed her aside almost contemptuously. "You know nothing about cosmetics, and besides you're far too busy with your own life these days."

"Julian, that's not true. I can make the time easily, you know I can, and I'd like to talk to you about it. It's obviously terribly important to you."

"Well," he said, looking at her oddly, "that's very good of you, but frankly I don't have the time to go through it all with you, when really I feel you could contribute very little. But thank you for your interest."

Phaedria turned away, afraid he would see the tears behind her eyes; he still had the power to hurt her.

"Incidentally," he said, "I'll be away for a few days. We're shooting some commercials in Paris."

"Could I— Would you like me to come with you?"

"Oh, I don't think so. A waste of your time. You must be extremely busy with Christmas planning for the store. I hope you can improve upon those designs for the window displays. They're very poor, in my opinion."

"Yes, well, if I could work with the right person—I mean people— they might not be so poor."

"If you mean Sassoon, I really cannot believe that you regard him as a suitable person to work on window displays. Phaedria, David Sassoon is head of corporate design in this company. He cannot be expected to concern himself with trivia. If I may say so, you are showing a severe lack of understanding of the areas of control and how to use them."

"You may say so," she said with a sigh, "and I expect you're right. But the fact remains there's nobody decent in the display department."

"That," Julian said, "is patent nonsense. There is considerable talent in the display department. It is entirely your responsibility to motivate it properly. Talk to Roz about it. I'm sure she'll be able to help."

"Yes," she said, "I will."

He left for Paris in the morning in his private jet, with Regency, David Sassoon, and several people from the advertising agency. Phaedria, looking at the photograph the publicity people had organized and brought to her desk for approval, felt oddly bereft.

When Julian came back three days later he was curt and short-tempered. She had been looking forward to his return, had organized dinner at home for the two of them, and had a bottle of champagne on ice.

"I'm sorry, Phaedria, I have to go out for dinner."

"Who with?"

"What's that? Oh, Freddy Branksome. And I'm looking in on Roz and C.J. later. I have to talk to C.J. about the new Morell in Acapulco. Don't wait up for me. I shall probably be very late."

"Julian—"

"Yes?"

"Julian, I don't mind waiting up for you."

"Darling," he said, and he managed to turn the endearment into something cold and distant, "I'd really rather you didn't. I can't concentrate on things if I've got half a mind on getting back."

"Oh," she said, "all right."

"Get those displays sorted out?"

"What? Oh, yes, I think so."

"Roz any help?"

"No. She's—been away."

"Where, for God's sake? The Beverly Hills Circe opening is only weeks away. She can't afford to be away."

"Julian, I don't know where she's been. She's probably been in L.A."

"Oh, all right. I'll find out from C.J. See you in the morning."

"Good night, Julian."

ROZ HAD NOT been in Los Angeles. She had taken advantage of her father's absence to go to New York for three days, ostensibly to check on Circe's Christmas plans, but actually scarcely leaving Michael Browning's penthouse and his bed. A couple of phone calls and a late-night conversation with C.J. made this abundantly clear to Julian; he was furious.

He sent for her in the morning; she came in looking wary.

"Good morning, Rosamund. How are you?"

"Very well. How was Paris?"

"Excellent. And New York?"

"Very good."

"How are the cosmetic promotions going in Circe? Particularly the gift with purchase?"

"Very well indeed."

"Good. How clever you are, Rosamund."

"What makes you say that?"

"Oh, a conversation I had with Iris Bentinck. She said you hadn't been anywhere near Circe, and yet you seem to have managed to garner a considerable amount of information."

"I see."

"If you're going to lie, Roz," he said, "do it properly. Do some background work first."

"Yes, well," she said, "you should know."

He looked at her and half smiled. He was always impressed when she stood up to him.

"Fortunately the promotions are going well," he said. "Now then, has Phaedria talked to you about the window displays here?"

"No."

"I'll get her in. She needs some help."

"Ah."

Phaedria walked in; she looked tired. She had been dancing at Tramp half the night with a group of friends. Julian had arrived home before her and gone to bed, merely asking her over breakfast if she had enjoyed herself. He looked at her now with something close to distaste.

"Phaedria, if you talk to Roz after this meeting about the windows, she may be able to help before it's too late. It's almost the end of August, you seem to be sailing very close to the wind to me. Is everything else under control for Christmas?"

"Yes," Phaedria said, meeting his eyes with equal distaste. "Absolutely."

"Good. Because I want you to go to Los Angeles for a few days next week."

"Why?"

"I want you to look at the store. I want your opinion on what's going on there."

"I see. Both of us? Roz and me?"

There was a long silence.

"No," said Julian. "Only you."

Roz walked out of the office.

◆　◆　◆

THAT NIGHT, ALMOST incoherent with misery and rage, Roz talked to Michael Browning for over an hour on the phone. "I hate her, I hate her. It's so unjust. Why should I have to endure it?"

"Roz, it's not Phaedria's fault. Surely you can see that. Your old man has the two of you out there on that chessboard he calls his company, and I would say it's probably check. If not checkmate."

"All right, then, I hate him. I hate them both."

"Leave them both and come with me. I won't play games with you."

"No, I know you won't."

"Please, darling. Don't be so dumb. Just walk out on the lot of them."

She sighed. "Right now I feel I just might. I feel so—used."

"Yeah, well, you're in the clutches of a real champion at that game."

"Maybe. I can't help feeling it's about time I got a break."

A WEEK LATER she did. She was trying to call C.J. in Washington; he had been there working with David Sassoon on the new corporate image for the hotels.

"Your husband went to New York this morning, Mrs. Emerson. You should get him at the Morell there at lunchtime."

C.J. was distant, cool. "I may stay here a few days. We're finished in Washington."

"How was it?"

"Okay."

"Is David staying there with you? Or is he on his way back?"

"No. I thought you knew."

"Knew what?"

"He's flown out to L.A. Phaedria called him. She's there, and she wants him to look at Circe. I thought you'd be going."

"No," Roz said. Time seemed to have frozen around her. It was extremely quiet. "No, I'm not going. Well, enjoy New York, C.J. Give my love to your mother."

"Sure. Bye, Roz."

"Good-bye."

SHE AND HER father had their weekly progress meeting three days later. He was unsmiling, his eyes at their most blank.

"Everything under control?"

"Yes."

"Good. I thought we might look at Sydney as a site for Circe. Why don't you go over for a week or two and see what you think."

"You've always said Sydney was wrong for Circe."

"I've changed my mind. I was wrong about Beverly Hills."

"Yes."

"Take C.J. and Miranda with you. Make a holiday of it."

"Don't try to charm me back into submission, please. I'm finding all these games with Phaedria very hard to take. And I certainly don't want to go to Australia with C.J. I'm probably going to divorce him." She was only testing her father's reaction; she had given a divorce almost no serious thought at all.

"Roz, you can't do that. Absolutely not."

"I can."

"No, you can't."

"How will you stop me?"

"If you do," he said, his face smooth, "if you even suggest such a thing, I shall give the stores to Phaedria. All of them."

Roz felt as if she had just fallen from a great height. She felt light-headed, dizzy, distant; he seemed a long way away.

"You couldn't."

"I would. She has great talent. She's original."

"And I'm not?"

"Not especially."

"God," she said, "you really are a bastard. A manipulative, evil bastard. Well, do that. Give them to her. I don't care. I shall go to work for Michael. That's just fine."

"Oh, excellent," he said. "You can redesign the ByNow supermarkets for him. That would be a good project for you. You'd like that, wouldn't you, Rosamund?"

"I could do anything for Michael. He has enough money. I could start a new line of stores myself."

"You could. You wouldn't have much expertise behind you, though. Not in him, would you? Not much flair. It would be very difficult. I have all the best people in retailing tied up. And if you found any brilliant new people, I should probably find I needed them more. And what do you think people would say? They would compare what you were doing very unfavorably, I would imagine. Poor Roz, they'd say, you see, she didn't have it in her, really; it was all just handed her on a plate. She's nothing without her father. You wouldn't like that, would you? You need success and admiration and power. I think you would be making a huge mistake."

Roz suddenly hit him, sharply across the face. Then she stood back, frozen into stillness, stunned by her own courage.

Julian stood looking at her, equally motionless. He was breathing heavily. There was an odd expression on his face, almost one of puzzlement.

"Why are you doing this?" Roz cried, almost in anguish. "Why? Why can't you leave me alone?" Tears had filled her eyes; she was very white.

"Roz, Roz, don't. Please don't be so hostile. I'm trying to help you. Trying to save your marriage."

"I feel hostile. I hate you. I hate you more than I would have believed possible. And on the subject of marriage, maybe you should take a look at your own."

"What do you mean?"

"Where is that original, beautiful wife of yours right now?"

"She's in Los Angeles. I told her to go."

"She is indeed. And do you know who's there with her?"

"What do you mean? Nobody's with her."

"At this very minute David Sassoon is there. You didn't know that, did you?"

"I don't believe you."

"You don't have to. You can ring the Beverly Hills Hotel yourself and check, as I just did. They're both there, for another two days. Together."

PHAEDRIA WAS LYING by the pool at the Beverly Hills Hotel when she was paged. "Call for Lady Morell. Call for Lady Morell."

She sighed. She was half asleep, sun-soaked, happy. She had been working for almost twenty hours, and she wanted to stay where she was, not moving, for a little longer.

She had enjoyed the last few days. She had been well aware of the personal risk she was running, calling in David; but when she had arrived in L.A. and seen the way the designer there had been slightly too extravagant with the open space and, just minimally too cautious with color, how the windows were just a fraction too close in feel to all the other windows up and down Rodeo Drive, she had, without any thought for anything at all except Circe, put in a call to Washington, where she knew he and C.J. were. She had expected only to talk to him, to describe the problems, maybe to put him in touch with the other designer. When he had said he was free and would come over, her spirit lifted at the thought of defying Julian, of showing him, if necessary, that she was not to be told what to do.

Whatever the sexual and marital considerations involved, David's arrival had solved her professional problems. He had stayed forty-eight hours, at least forty of which they had been awake and working, or eating and talking shop. They had both, oddly but tacitly conscious of their slightly compromising situation, avoided lengthy dinners and any but the briefest sojourns by the pool, and the one time he had attempted to probe her feelings on her situation and her marriage she had closed the slightly forbidding shell of reserve she wore around herself and made it very clear that he was not to try to open it again. It had been tempting, though, for she longed for a confidant, yearned to talk not only about Julian but about Roz as well, but David was the least likely candidate for such a role, and certainly not in the dangerous situation they were in, and she knew it.

So now he was gone; she had driven him to the airport in a rented car, he had kissed her good-bye in a brotherly—or would it be fatherly?—fashion, and she had returned to the Beverly Hills and its pool and its pampering power, to recover for a day or two.

She needed to recover; she was tired from the strain not only of the last forty-eight hours but of the previous few months. She was beginning to find Julian seriously dispiriting. His jealousy, his constant criticism, and his arrogance were very destructive. She had tried to be tolerant, but she was too busy fighting for her own survival most of the time to have any emotional energy left for him. What she would not do was give in, when she was quite convinced he was wrong. She was prepared to listen carefully to his point of view, to consider his criticisms, to take note of his experience, but after that she would, if it seemed necessary, come out fighting.

But it was difficult—difficult to hang on to her self-respect, difficult to work effectively and efficiently, difficult above all to nurture and enjoy what was after all a very young and delicate marriage.

So for all those reasons, she was tired, she had been enjoying her brief rest, and she didn't want it to end. She remained motionless, merely raising a slender sun-browned arm. One of the small swarm of waiters who hovered, permanently watchful, near the pool appeared instantly in front of her.

"There's a call for me," she said. "Would you bring me a phone, please?"

"Certainly, Lady Morell."

"Hello?' she said, picking it up on his return. "Yes?"

"Phaedria?"

"Yes? Hello, Julian. Where on earth are you?"

"In reception."

"In reception where?"

"In reception here."

"Good God. Well, you certainly are full of surprises."

"I try to be."

"I'll be right out."

SHE WALKED INTO the foyer of the hotel, carelessly graceful, dressed only in a minute blue bikini, a white terry-cloth robe swinging loosely around her shoulders, her feet bare, her hair loose and slightly damp from swimming. In a place well used to beautiful women, she still attracted attention.

She kissed him lightly. He looked at her.

"You look tired."

"Yes, I was working most of the night."

"Indeed? On what?"

"The merchandise. I've found a marvelous new designer."

"A new one? How nice."

She looked at him, puzzled. "Julian, why are you here?"

"I wanted to see you."

"Why didn't you ring first?"

"Then I wouldn't have surprised you."

"No. Well, shall we go up to the suite? I expect you'd like to change."

"You have a suite, not a bungalow?"

"Yes."

"Why? I keep a bungalow here."

"I know, but I don't like them particularly. I feel—oh, I don't know, vulnerable."

"I see."

"Well, let's go up. Would you like a drink?"

"No, thank you."

"All right."

She followed him into the lift and into the suite, wary, baffled. The bellhop brought in Julian's suitcase. When the door was closed he took her by the shoulders and turned her to him.

"Where is he?"

"Where is who?"

"Sassoon?"

"Oh, don't be ridiculous."

"Phaedria, I know he's here."

"He is not here."

"I don't believe you."

"Would you like to search the hotel?"

He looked at her closely, then released her and sat down heavily on the bed. Phaedria walked over to the window, looked out at the brilliant sunshine, the blue carefree sky, so poignantly contrasting to the dark mood in the room; then she turned.

"He was here, though, until this morning."

"I see. In this room, or did you share another suite?"

"Julian, I really feel desperately sorry for you. You just can't go on in this ridiculous, melodramatic fashion. I am not having an affair with David Sassoon. Neither of us has the slightest inclination to do anything of the sort. If he is in love with anyone, it's Eliza, still. I like him very much. I think he's fun, I love working with him, and I think he's very attractive. But I am not in the business of having affairs, unlike you."

"Phaedria, be careful!"

She looked at him unafraid. "I am married to you, I care about you, and I am much too busy and too sensible to risk losing you."

"Me and all that goes with me."

"That was vile."

"The truth often is."

"I don't think you are very well acquainted with the truth, Julian. Anyway, who told you David was here? Roz, I suppose."

"Can we leave the ridiculous vendetta between you and Roz out of this?"

"It's very difficult, when most of the unhappinesses between us can be laid directly at her door."

"Phaedria, grow up, for God's sake."

She looked at him, her eyes full of a strange pain.

"I'm trying to, Julian, believe me. I'm not getting a great deal of help from you. Are you going to accept what I said about David or not?"

"Phaedria, even if I accepted, even I believed you—and I don't know that I do—how could you ask Sassoon to come here, to stay in the same hotel, after I expressly forbade you to have any more to do with him?"

"That was precisely the reason. Or one of them. That you forbade me. If you'd asked me, sensitively, I might have felt different, might have tried to understand. The other was, of course, that he was the only person who could do what I wanted."

"Indeed. Where? In bed?"

She crossed to the closet, pulled her suitcase out. "This is ridiculous. I'm going."

"Don't."

"Why not?"

"Because I am going," Julian said. "Immediately. That will save you the trouble of packing."

"You're mad."

"I think not. If anyone is mad, I think it is you."

He left immediately without another word. While he was waiting for his plane at the Los Angeles airport, he phoned his lawyer.

PHAEDRIA ARRIVED HOME at Regent's Park forty-eight hours later. It was very late; the house was in darkness, utterly quiet. She put down her bags, and went silently upstairs. She was not sure what she might find—that Julian was not there at all, that he was in bed with someone else, that he was alone and hostile, refusing to speak to her. She pushed open the bedroom door. He was in bed alone, asleep, completely still; he did not stir. For a horrific moment she thought he was dead, had taken an overdose and it would be her fault. Then he suddenly moved, turned over, still asleep. She looked at him; for the very first time, she noticed, remorseful, almost afraid, he looked older. His hair was grayer; his face, relaxed in sleep, was suddenly more lined, looser. He appeared very vulnerable.

She sat down on the bed beside him and looked at him for a long time. Then she rested her hand gently on his shoulder and bent and kissed his forehead. He woke, quite easily then, not startled, just slowly moved into consciousness, opened his eyes and looked at her in silence.

"I'm sorry," she said. "I was quite, quite wrong. Cruel and arrogant and wrong. Please forgive me."

"Oh, Phaedria," he said. "I'm glad you're back. I thought I might not see you again."

"You don't know me very well, do you?" she said, pulling off her clothes, climbing into bed thankfully beside him.

"Not very. But I'm beginning to learn."

ROZ WAS SLIGHTLY regretting her action. It seemed to have achieved nothing; her father and Phaedria appeared to be closer than they had been for some months. David Sassoon, of whom Roz was very fond, was cold and distant toward her, and Michael Browning had been very outspoken in his criticism.

They had met in Paris for the weekend and were lying in bed in a suite at the Crillon. Whenever Roz was really down, Michael took her there and spent the weekend in bed with her, making love to her, feeding her, pouring the finest champagne down her throat, showering her with presents and flowers, and conducting his apparently tireless campaign to entice her away from her husband, her father, and the company. So far, as he frequently observed, he was not having a great deal of success.

"You're nuts, Rosamund. Crazy. All that kind of thing can accomplish is damage to yourself. You won't win any battles that way. You have to box cleverly, darling. This is not kindergarten. Remember Machiavelli."

"I didn't think you knew anything about Machiavelli," Roz said sulkily. "You're always saying you had no education."

"As usual, you weren't listening. What I am always saying is that I didn't have a *conventional* education. Machiavelli is compulsory study for any ambitious young man."

"Well, what do I have to remember about him anyway?"

"Machiavelli said you must either promote or execute. In other words take totally decisive action. No half measures."

"I don't see what you mean. I'd love to execute Phaedria, of course. But I can't. And it isn't up to me to promote her."

"I don't agree. Well, obviously your old man has to do the actual promoting. But you should encourage him. Make him think you're coming around. Get him to give her more than she can handle. That way you'll get rid of her far faster. An execution, masquerading as a promotion. Best of both worlds. And your hands will be clean."

THE PRESENTATION TO the sales force of the new line, at the annual sales conference, took place in Nice. Julian liked to make the sales force feel important, pampered. He installed them all in good hotels, gave them two days off to enjoy the place, and then put on an impressive show with the maximum of razzmatazz.

Everybody who mattered was there, whether directly involved with the cosmetics or not, Julian's rationale being that this was still, however large and successful, a private company, a family affair. David was there, Roz was there, Letitia was there, Susan was there, Regency was there as the face of the campaign, and this year, of course, Phaedria was there.

The conference always followed the same theatrical form: Act One was a big general presentation by Freddy and Richard on the company and its success; Act Two was a more detailed one by Annick

Valery on the brands and their success; then there was an intermission, which took the form of a superb lunch and the announcement of the award winners for highest retail sales, highest trade sales, saleswoman of the year, and so on; and then in the afternoon the curtain went up on Act Three as the new products took the floor.

This was the moment when Julian himself first spoke, and this year more than ever it was the high spot of the conference.

"What we have for you today," he said, "is the first complete line of Juliana cosmetics since Naturally. I felt it was time for a completely new look, a new feel; we have moved away from softness into something much more positive, more exciting, in a way. And so we have created a line, something quite different, a departure for Juliana, designed for the new woman.

"It is called Life-Style, and it is deliberately simple—a set of colors, of skin care, of fragrance, which this new woman, the working woman, the powerful, busy woman, will instantly recognize as the straightforward, swift route to beauty that she needs, and that nobody else is providing. We have cut out much of the complexity of cosmetics, particularly in the skin care products; we're offering just two very simple sets of products—morning and evening. Even the fragrance line will follow this concept; we are taking the mystique out of perfume and simply offering one strength, one presentation—halfway between a perfume concentrate and an eau de toilette—plus a bath and body range."

Roz, watching the consultants, was suddenly sharply and instinctively aware of a hostility. It was only several years of attending these conferences that enabled her to pick it up. A novice—Phaedria, for instance—would not have noticed the slightly wall-eyed expression behind the false eyelashes, the fixed hardness of the heavily glossed lips.

Annick Valery took over next, presenting the products in detail. Again the reaction was muted, slightly flat. Julian moved on to the advertising: six-foot-high photographs of the model Regency's face were unveiled, and the TV commercial was shown: Regency waking, showering, making up, driving, chairing meetings, lunching, and then dining with a man, presumably her inferior, face unseen, and going home to her lonely, presumably powerful, bed. The commercial was a series of endless stills, intercut very fast to give the impression of movement. The background music was fast, modern, obscure. At the end of the presentation Regency herself walked to the front of the stage dressed in a simple black wool dress by Chanel, worn with pearl and gilt earrings and a long pearl rope, her ash-blond hair tied back with a black ribbon.

"I feel honored to have been chosen to represent the new Juliana woman," she said carefully, giving them her—literally—million dollar smile. "I hope you will like her as much as I do."

This long speech closed the presentation. Applause followed—mild, polite applause. Again Roz read the mood of the consultants, the sales force, and the message was clear: *This girl, this near child, is not the Juliana woman.*

THE NEW LINE sold into the stores fast. The cosmetics buyers had great faith in Julian Morell and in Juliana. Neither had failed yet. The advertising campaign broke: Regency's face—glossy, confident, just slightly contemptuous—looked down from billboards and out of every glossy magazine and television screen.

The Christmas rush in the stores began. The cosmetics houses were engaged on their annual bonanza. Revlon, Lauder, Chanel, Mary Quant, were propelled off a thousand counters and into a million shopping bags in a great wave of perfume, promotion, and hype.

And on the same counters, in the same stores, Life-Style by Juliana remained: uninvited, unwanted, a wallflower at the ball, and Regency's fixed smile seemed to grow a little more desperate every day.

Julian dismissed the failure completely. It was a hiccup; it meant nothing. Maybe the line had not been absolutely right for Christmas, it would start selling hard in the new year. No, Regency was not too young. Her face was perfect; she had the look of today, if not tomorrow. It was a look that public opinion would warm to. Yes, the packaging was absolutely right, clean and chic, like the message of the line. Of course it should not be softened; the new woman was not soft.

The consultants had had it too easy for too long; this was a new concept and they had to work harder on it. When it started to sell, when the public recognized it, accepted it as what they wanted, which they assuredly would, then the sales force would relax and feel more comfortable with it.

Phaedria had never admired him more. She half expected him to let down his guard to her, to admit something was wrong, but he did not; he continued to behave as if everything were wonderful, as if Life-Style were breaking all records. Even when he came into Circe for the Christmas party and saw the new products piled high on the counters, he managed to smile with complete assurance and convey the impression that he was delighted with their progress.

He criticized much that Phaedria had done: he still didn't like the windows, he was unhappy with many of the clothes on the fashion floor, he complained that the flower shop looked messy, he said the lingerie department was hopelessly understocked. But of his own mistake looking him so painfully in the eye he said nothing, nothing at all.

The only sign she could detect that anything might be seriously troubling him was that he had not made love to her for weeks.

CHRISTMAS WAS COMING, and to Roz's utter astonishment and horror, C.J. had asked Phaedria if he and Roz and Miranda could spend it at Marriotts. Phaedria and Julian were both delighted, C.J. told her. "Especially your father. So you can't back out."

"How could you, C.J.? How could you make me spend Christmas, of all times, with her?"

"Roz, I don't see where else is going to be any better for you. And I would certainly like to go. I don't see that the three of us would have a happy time on our own. At least it will be more fun for Miranda. And besides, you need to strike some sort of truce with your father. This will help. You should be grateful to me."

"Couldn't we spend Christmas with your mother?" Roz asked, casting desperately around for an escape from the trap that was closing in on her.

"She's got a huge house party planned—Francesca is getting engaged—and frankly I just can't face it."

"Well, I can't face this."

"Roz"—he turned to her, his gentle face totally transformed by anger and misery—"I have to face a great deal that I don't like. Every day of my life. Just do me the rare kindness of letting me have my way for once. Just for a day or two."

Roz looked at him and felt a wave of misery, not for herself but for him. She had ruined his life, willfully and thoughtlessly; she had made him very unhappy, and he did not deserve it. She put out her hand. "I'm sorry, C.J. Really I am. Yes, we'll go to Marriotts. Perhaps you and I should talk."

He shook her hand off, looking at her with a cold distaste. "I don't think so. There's nothing to say. I am trying to work out what to do, and it's very difficult. But meanwhile I see no point in a painful dialogue."

Roz walked up to her room, feeling the madness closing in on her. What was she doing? Michael had begged her to spend Christmas with him in the Caribbean. Why wasn't she going with him? She had told him she couldn't possibly leave the baby, not feeling able to explain that spending Christmas with him would be an open declaration of war between herself and her father, and he had rather surprisingly accepted this without argument. He was having Michael and Sharon for the New Year in any case and was rather pathetically having the duplex decorated accordingly, with a Christmas tree in every room—two in the children's bedroom—and a great pile of presents under every one. Roz, who had never met Michael and Sharon, feared for their character, but Michael assured her they were great kids: "Just like their mother, no Browning in them at all."

And so, with a heavy heart, she packed for Christmas at Marriotts, wondering how she was going to endure it. But at the last minute the party was greatly improved by the arrival of Letitia and a car literally filled with presents. Garrylaig Castle was too cold for her these days, she said, and she wanted to spend Christmas with her great-granddaughter.

Phaedria, who wanted to be busy and to have as little time as possible to spend sitting with her guests, gave the entire staff Christmas Day off and did all the cooking herself. Christmas morning passed fairly smoothly; they went to church, exchanged presents, and had a late lunch, during which Letitia kept them entertained with stories of Christmases past. Afterward she said that she and Miranda should go and have a nap and everyone else could clear up.

"One of the great joys of being very old and very young," she said, scooping the child up, "is that we don't have to be helpful."

"Lunch was great, Phaedria," C.J. said, pouring himself a third glass of port and waving the bottle hospitably about the table. "You're a great girl." He was fairly drunk.

"She is," Julian said, smiling benignly at her across the candlelit table. "Let's drink a toast to her. To Phaedria."

"To Phaedria," said C.J.

"Phaedria," Roz said through clenched teeth. She thought no one would ever know what that moment had cost her.

"You look absolutely beautiful, Phaedria," C.J. said. "Beautiful. Doesn't she, Julian?"

"She does. Not a day over twenty-six."

"I don't know how you do it," C.J. went on. "All that cooking and organizing and running the company and—"

"Not quite running the company," Roz said, her voice sickeningly sweet. "Not all of it."

"Oh, give her time," said C.J. "Just a little bit of time."

Phaedria shot him a warning look; it was too late.

"I'll bet she could run the whole outfit. Easily," he said, draining his glass. "I suppose she will one day, right, Julian?"

"Possibly," Julian said blandly. "But not for a very long time, I hope."

Roz was white, clutching her glass very tightly.

"Well, I think that would be a wonderful thing," C.J. said. "What a successor for you."

There was a strange cracking sound: the delicate stem of Roz's wineglass had snapped. Phaedria looked at it—the jagged edge, the red wine spilled on the white tablecloth, Roz's blazing eyes—and shivered.

"Come on, C.J.," she said. "Let's get a bit of fresh air before it's dark. Julian? Would you like to come for a walk?"

Julian was looking at Roz thoughtfully. "What's that? Oh, no, I don't think so. I might even join the other babies upstairs for a rest. You go on. I'll just help you clear that up, Roz."

He went to the kitchen in search of a cloth. Roz, still sitting at the table, still holding the broken glass, looked at Phaedria. She tried, she wanted, to remain silent, but she couldn't. Her self-control, which seemed to her these days to be an increasingly fragile thing, suddenly splintered like the glass.

"You aren't going to win, you know," she said savagely. "Whatever you do, however much you try, I won't let you win."

"Oh, Roz, I don't want to win," Phaedria said wearily. "Whatever that might mean."

"You're a liar," Roz said. "I don't believe you." She knew she was making a fool of herself, losing her dignity, but she couldn't stop. "Of course you want to win. You want to take my place in this company, you want it for yourself when my father dies, along with his money. That's all you want; it's all you ever wanted, but nobody, nobody else at all, seems to be able to see it."

"Perhaps because it's not true," Phaedria said quietly. Her eyes were fixed on the jagged glass. She seemed frightened. Her fear gave Roz pleasure, made her feel better.

"It's true," Roz said almost cheerfully. "I know it's true and you know it's true, and it seems to be our little secret." She stood up suddenly; she was taller than Phaedria. She began to walk slowly toward her, holding the glass. Phaedria, backing away clumsily, suddenly found herself against the wall.

"Roz, please," she said, and there was a tremor in her voice. "Please."

Roz slowly raised the glass. She had no intention of hurting Phaedria with it, but this moment was revenge for all the months, all the misery, all the humiliation, almost for the loss of her father.

"Roz!" It was C.J.'s voice from the doorway. "Roz, what the hell are you doing? For God's sake, put that down."

He sounded calm, authoritative. Roz turned and looked at him, then put the glass down quite gently.

"It's all right," she said. "I wouldn't dream of hurting her. Then everyone would feel sorry for her as well as being in love with her. Do enjoy your walk with my husband, Phaedria. You're welcome to him."

She walked quickly out of the room, up the stairs, and into her room; Letitia, who was coming down from settling Miranda for her nap, heard her crying and knew there was nothing, nothing at all, that she could do to help her.

ROZ WENT INTO her father's office one morning in January; she looked tired and drawn. Julian and Phaedria had been away for a fortnight on Eleuthera, and this was his first day back in the office. He was skimming through some magazines and newspapers; he looked at her with concern.

"Roz, you don't look well. Are you all right?"

"Yes, thank you. I just wanted to talk to you."

"You know I'm always happy to talk to you."

"You may not be too happy about this."

"Try me."

"I've spent a bit of time at Circe while you've been away. The sales figures are disastrous."

"Oh, Roz, don't be absurd. How can they be disastrous after—what, nine, ten months? It's still in its earliest stages. Still in a heavy investment situation. Circe New York took three years to break even, never mind show a profit."

"Of course. But it was steady growth, however small and slow. London did quite well in the first three weeks and it's been falling steadily ever since. And certain departments are a disaster."

"Like?"

"The fashion consultancy—only one client since Christmas. The lingerie—too tacky looking. There's a feeling those suites of rooms don't work."

"How do you know?"

"I've talked to the staff. They're very demoralized. And they feel out on a limb. They got a great deal of attention in the beginning, but they say they hardly see Phaedria these days. They feel abandoned."

"Well, let's get her in," said Julian, slightly wearily. "I can see it's a problem. Have you told her all this?"

"Of course not. She's—you've been away."

"Sarah, get my wife in here, would you?"

"Yes, Sir Julian."

Phaedria came into the office ten minutes later. She looked pale. "Sorry. I was on the phone to L.A."

"Phaedria, we seem to have a problem on Circe."

"Really? In L.A.?"

"No, here. In London."

"In London? Who told you?"

"I did," Roz said.

"Ah."

"Apparently certain departments are doing extremely badly," Julian said.

"Really? Which?"

"The clothes consultancy—no clients. The lingerie—no sales. What do you think about that?"

"Not a lot," Phaedria said. "It's early days. In any case, I knew about it. We have time."

"Apparently the saleswomen feel abandoned," Julian said. "They say they haven't seen you, can't talk to you about their problems."

"For heaven's sake," Phaedria said quietly, "how could they have? I've been away with you."

"And before that in L.A."

"Jesus, Julian, what are you trying to do to me? The two of you? Of course I've been in L.A. I've been terribly busy. At your behest."

"Originally at yours. You wanted to be involved."

"Yes," said Phaedria, keeping her temper with an effort, "I suppose I did. I suppose I did take on too much. It hasn't been easy, Julian. You seem to forget I'm a novice at this game."

"You seem to find plenty of time," he said, icily smooth, "for your other activities."

Phaedria followed his eyes to his desk. A copy of *Vogue* lay there opened at a spread of photographs of her by Danny Carter; the *Daily Mail* carried a story about her involvement in a charity fashion show, under the aegis of Dominic Kennedy.

She looked at him steadily. "All right. I have been doing—some other things. But I have been working hard on the store as well. None of what Roz says is true. Well, it's strictly true, the figures aren't good.

I knew that. But they're very far from disastrous. That's absolute nonsense. It's a bad time. The lingerie department had a marvelous Christmas. Now it's obviously down. I talked to all the departments at length just before Christmas. I had formed some ideas, which I was going to discuss with you. But luckily I've had some help. You really have been working hard on this, Roz. How kind, how extremely kind of you to keep such a close eye on Circe in my absence. Snooping around, putting words into my staff's mouths, thoughts into their heads. That's what it amounts to. How dare you? And you, Julian. With all your experience, all your years and years of staff relations and company management, how extraordinary that you didn't think for one moment that I might need advice, guidance, support. I could say I wasn't going to take this any longer, but I'm not prepared to give in to either of you. I will not be beaten. I'm going to my office now; I have several people waiting to see me. Perhaps we could reconvene this meeting later, when we have a few more facts at our disposal. Oh, and Julian," she added, turning and confronting him, her eyes steady, "did Roz happen to mention the figures for Life-Style at the same time? I thought not. They make even the lingerie department look healthy."

Roz watched her thoughtfully as she walked through Sarah Brown-smith's office and into the lift. She was learning to fight dirty. That was interesting. Roz felt a pang of something quite close to admiration. Then she turned to her father. There was an expression on his face she had not often seen there. It was panic.

MORE AND MORE these days Phaedria wondered exactly why she was so determined not to give in. It would be so comfortable, so easy, to walk out, say good-bye to them all, embark on her own life, which would, after all, be easy now. She had made a name for herself; she had friends, contacts. She did not think she was happy anymore. She found that hard to admit, but searching through the painful days, the increasingly lonely nights, she could find little pleasure. Julian didn't seem to love her in the least. Occasionally he was tender, kind, appreciative, even more occasionally loverlike. More and more often he slept alone. He had made love to her once or twice in the house at Turtle Cove, but it had been with a kind of frantic fervor, as if he had been trying to prove something. There was none of the confident, joyful pleasure she had fallen in love with.

And then there was Roz. Some days she felt, in a near-feverish anxiety, that it was Roz who was married to Julian, so close, so alike did they seem, and she was the interloper, the intruder on the relationship. Julian never acknowledged that there was any kind of problem with Roz. He ignored Roz's rudeness and hostility and continued to treat her with patience and courtesy; Phaedria compared it with the impatience and intolerance with which he talked to her and wondered how she was expected to endure it.

LOVE SUFFERETH LONG and is kind, Michael Browning thought to himself as he waited for Roz's plane at Kennedy Airport one evening in late February. He felt he had suffered for longer and had been kinder than most men would have been, and right now he was finding it hard to think why. He was tired, he was hungry, and he was wearying of the game of piggy in the middle he seemed to have been playing with Roz and Julian almost as long as he could remember. Who was in the middle he wasn't sure, but he sure as hell wasn't winning. On the other hand, he wasn't losing either; Roz was still there, in his life, in his bed, and in his heart for that matter. It had to be love, he thought. There could be no other explanation for a relationship that continued to thrive, to give pleasure, against such odds as almost continuous separation, Roz's refusal to commit herself to any kind of permanence, which cast him as supporting player to a leading lady. Well, he had finally had enough. He was about to step into center stage. No matter what it cost him, what it cost Roz, the situation had to be resolved. It was unendurable.

She was walking toward him now, smiling, looking pale and tired but happy, in a long fur coat and high brown leather boots. He felt at the same time a surge of love and pleasure and a stab of irritation that she should be so remorselessly confident of him.

"Hello, Michael."

"Hi, darling." Despite the surge of love, he held back, kissed her formally, distantly. Roz didn't notice. She was immune to subtleties of behavior unless they took place in the boardroom.

"Ghastly flight."

"I'm sorry. What went wrong? Did they take a wrong turn?"

"I think they must have. I seem to have been up there forever. And I'd seen the film. And the woman sitting next to me talked about her grandchildren all the way. Oh, God, Michael, let's go home."

"Okay." He was used to her litanies of discontent; he had learned to ignore them. The thing about Roz, he thought—and it always amazed him that nobody realized it but him—was that beneath the bad temper, the bitching, the chips on both elegantly sloping shoulders, was a funny, sexy, nice woman. You just had to dig a bit. Michael had dug.

"What do you want to do this evening? Eat out? Stay in? I have Rosa standing by just in case."

"I want to stay in, with you, without Rosa. Let's get some food delivered. I want to have you in every room in the place."

Michael looked at her and struggled to maintain his equilibrium. He had more serious, more important intentions for the evening than making love on a lot of different floors, beds, and couches.

"That's nice to hear. But I want to talk to you."

Roz's heart sank. She knew what that meant. Another attempt at exacting a promise from her, another demand for commitment. He was growing weary at last, and it frightened her.

"Michael, don't, please. Not this weekend."

"Weekend? I thought it was five days."

"Well, long weekend. I have to go back on Monday. I'm sorry. I was going to tell you."

"For Christ's sake, Rosamund, why?"

"Well, my father's called a full board meeting to discuss the new company. I have to be there. Surely you can see that."

"Yes," he said, "I can see it."

She misread his mood. "Good. I knew you would. I'm sorry. Let's go and find the car."

"I'll go find the car. I don't see a lot of point in your coming with me. Why don't you just stay here and get the next plane home? You can prepare for the board meeting better, really put on a good show, impress your father, give one in the eye to your rival. Go on, Roz. Go and get yourself a flight."

"Oh, Michael, don't be ridiculous."

"I am not being ridiculous. I love you and I need you, and if you felt half as much for me you wouldn't even think of rushing back for some two-bit board meeting. Which no doubt he's called because he knows you're here. Well, does he know you're here?"

"Yes," she said, very quietly.

"Will you stay?"

"I can't, I can't, not yet, not now. You're asking too much."

"Go fuck yourself."

He gave her a look of despair, of hostility mingled with such love that tears filled her eyes. She put out a hand, put it on his arm.

"Please, Michael, don't."

"Don't what? Don't get sick of you making it clear that I come a very poor third to that father of yours and his shitty company? That you'll find a place for me in your busy schedule in between board meetings and takeovers and, of course, sticking yet another knife into the back of that poor goddam stepmother of yours. Jesus, Rosamund, I don't know where you learned to fight so dirty, to cheat so thoroughly, but it sure was a fine training school. Well, I'm through, with it and with you. Just get the hell out of my life. I won't be messing up yours any longer."

Panic tore through Roz; she felt shaken, weak; there was a roaring in her ears.

"Michael, don't, don't. Please stay. I have to talk to you."

"Really? Suddenly you have to talk. All the times I've wanted to talk and you've ducked, dodged, dragged me into bed, anything to avoid the confrontation. Well, I don't want to talk right now, Roz, or ever again."

He walked away, fast, pushing through the crowds. Roz looked at his disappearing back, sobs tearing at her throat, her heart wrenched into terrified fragments. She couldn't bear it, not again, not that pain, that loneliness, that aching, racking misery. Nothing, nothing was worth that.

She ran after him, stumbling, frantically calling his name, but he wouldn't turn or look back. He went through the glass doors. His car was waiting; she stood, tears streaming down her face, watched him get in, lean back, close his eyes, and then the traffic and the darkness swallowed him up.

ROZ WENT TO see her father, pale and drawn, but dry-eyed on Monday morning, a look of ferocious determination on her face.

"I've done what you want."

"What do you mean?"

"I've finished with Michael. Again."

"Roz! I'm sorry. I know what this must have cost you."

"Yes, well, I'm planning that it should cost you."

"What do you mean?"

"I've kept my share of the bargain, Daddy. Let's have yours."

"Roz, you're talking in riddles."

"No, I'm not. You said if I divorced C.J. you'd give the stores to Phaedria."

"Yes. And I meant it."

"Okay. Well, I'm staying with him. So you can give them to me."

"You have them. You know you do."

"No, I don't. Not all of them. I want London, too."

"Roz, you know that's impossible."

"I don't see why."

"Circe London is Phaedria's own. It was a wedding present. She created it."

"Yes, and she's done well. Now I want it."

"Rosamund, you can't have it. Now can we forget this nonsense? I'm delighted you've come to your senses, and I'm sure I can find a new section of the company for you to run if that's what you want."

"I don't want a new section. I've told you what I want. I want the stores. All of them."

"And I've told you you can't have them. We have a board meeting to get to. We're already late."

Roz looked at him. "You're a cheat, you know. A liar and a cheat. You cheat on us all. Even your beautiful new wife." Then she smiled. It was a dangerous smile. "How was Paris, Daddy?" she said. "And how is Camilla these days?"

·25·

MARCIA GALBRAITH TUCKED HER old friend into bed for her nap and drew the curtains tenderly. Dorothy had certainly gone downhill faster than she had expected. When she had come to Nassau three years before she seemed the stronger of the two of them. Marcia had looked to Dorothy for help and support, thinking she would take care of her in her frail old age. Well, life did funny things to you, and here she was, feeling stronger suddenly and in command of everything, and here was Dotty, confused, fragile, in need of care. She had looked for a mainstay and had found a burden.

She wondered what was going to happen to the house in Malibu. It was all very well, Dotty living here, and she was pleased to have her, but it seemed awfully silly just leaving that place empty and rotting, when it could be converted to money in the bank.

She wondered where the deed was. Presumably in Dotty's box under her bed with all her other stuff, the pictures of Lee and her will and everything. She felt for the box; it was there. Cautiously Marcia pulled it out and tiptoed out of the room.

"DOTTY," SHE SAID that night, casually, over supper. "Have you thought of selling your house in California?"

"No, no," Mrs. Kelly said firmly. "That's mine. I wouldn't sell it."

"It isn't a lot of use to you, Dotty. Not sitting there. You should convert it into money."

"I don't want Miles to have the money. It won't do him any good."

"Nobody's saying Miles should have the money, Dotty," said Marcia patiently. "You should have it. In the bank. Earning interest."

"Me? What for?"

"Well, Dotty dear, I've never said anything before, but I'm not getting any richer. Times are costly. It would be a real help if you could put a bit in now and again."

Mrs. Kelly was stricken. Emotion cleared her brain. "Marcia! You should have said something before. Oh, my! I certainly have been thoughtless and selfish. You're right. I'll put the house on the market right away."

"I'll do it for you, Dotty. You don't have to worry about any of the details. Just give me the deed. I'll go down to my lawyer in the morning and set the wheels in motion."

"All right, Marcia. That's very kind of you. I'm sorry, really sorry. I never intended to take your charity. I've been paying a little something into your account each week, and I thought it was enough."

"Well, Dotty, not quite, not anymore. Give me the deed, dear, and I'll see to it."

"It's in my box under my bed. I'll get it after dinner."

"All right, dear."

Marcia thought it best for Dorothy to discover for herself that the deed wasn't there.

"MILES, DO YOU have any idea where the deed to the Malibu house might have disappeared to?" Marcia said the next day. "Your grandmother can't find it, and she's upset."

It was true; Dorothy was wandering around the house, searching endlessly in the same places, becoming increasingly distressed.

"The deed? No idea at all. Why?"

"Well, I've been talking to Dotty, and we have decided that the house should be sold."

"Really? Why?"

"We need the money, Miles. This house isn't cheap to keep up. That's a lot of money, I'm told, sitting there in California, and I could use it. Or some of it. It might not have entered your idle head that you've been living here rent-free for three years. I think I have a right to some money."

He looked at her. Then he smiled, his most disarming smile. "Of course. You're right. I couldn't agree more. Don't worry, Mrs. Galbraith, I'll find the deed."

THE BANK MANAGER was nice, but firm. He couldn't let Miles have the deed back until he paid off the loan. There was the original four thousand dollars and then there was that other thousand he'd borrowed last year. Of course it wasn't much set against the value of the house, but nonetheless, the deed must stay with the bank.

"But we want to sell the house."

"Well, that's all right. Put it in the hands of a realtor. Nothing to stop you doing that."

"Okay. Thanks."

"IT'S OKAY, MRS. Galbraith," Miles said that afternoon as his grandmother slept. "I'll see to selling the house. I guess it's mine in a way and my responsibility."

"It is not," said Marcia, indignant on her friend's behalf. "That house is your grandmother's. She's always said so. No, I'll see to it, Miles. Just give me the deed when you find it."

"I have found it, Mrs. Galbraith. It's at the bank."

"The bank! How did it get there?"

"I guess Granny must have taken it there and forgotten. You know what she's like these days."

"I'll ask her."

"No, don't."

"Why not?"

"You know it upsets her when she realizes how vague she's become. Let's just leave the deed there, and I'll go ahead and organize the sale. Okay?"

She looked at him doubtfully. "Okay. Which bank?"

"Her bank, of course." He met her suspicious eyes with his wide, candid blue ones. "Does it matter?"

MARCIA GALBRAITH'S LAWYER and Miles's bank manager were members of the same golf club. Over just one too many bacardis one afternoon, the bank manager, knowing the lawyer's connection with Marcia, remarked on what nice manners young Wilburn had and what a rare pleasure it was to find such a phenomenon these days. The lawyer agreed and cited several examples of young men who had no manners at all, whereupon the bank manager went on, with extreme indiscretion, over yet another bacardi, that it had been a pleasure to be able to help young Mr. Wilburn with a loan the year before, and asked his friend the lawyer what he thought, purely as a matter of interest, a house in Malibu, California, might be worth these days, as Miles was in the process of selling one. The lawyer said he had no idea and that he also had no idea that young Wilburn was a man of such substance.

On Mrs. Galbraith's next visit to his office, he made the same observation. Marcia looked at him, her eyes deceptively innocent. "I always thought the house belonged to his grandmother," she said. "She's a very frail, confused old lady. I know I shouldn't be asking you this, but could you possibly find out if the house really is in Miles' name?"

The lawyer hesitated. He didn't like using a friendship. But two old ladies in distress surely needed help. "I'll see what I can do," he said. "Try not to worry."

He asked her to come to his office three days later. "No, Mrs. Galbraith," he said, "you're wrong. Mrs. Kelly definitely signed a transfer deed, turning the house over to Miles. Nothing to worry about, I'm sure. Can I help in any other way?"

"Not for now. But thank you very much. You've been really kind."

Marcia's blood was up; she was enjoying herself.

Later that day she asked Dorothy if she had ever thought of putting the house in Miles's name.

"Of course not, Marcia," Mrs. Kelly said, irritated out of her vagueness. "How many times have I told you I would never let Miles get his hands on that house? He'd just squander the money. If he's ever going to get a decent job, he certainly can't be handed thousands of dollars on a plate."

"No, Dotty," Marcia said. "He certainly can't."

She went back to her lawyer. "Could you find out a little more?" she said. "Discreetly. I don't want Miles suspecting anything."

The lawyer did.

"I have to tell you, Mrs. Galbraith," he said, "that boy seems to have been borrowing on that house. Five thousand dollars all together. Are you sure your friend doesn't know anything about it?"

"Quite sure."

"Well, the money's been borrowed. Not much, of course, in view of what the house is worth, but if that signature was obtained unlawfully, the boy could be in trouble."

"Yes," said Mrs. Galbraith. "Thank you. I'll let you know if there's any more to be done."

MILES WAS IN love. He had met her at the hotel, and she was just seventeen years old, with long, silvery blond hair, huge blue eyes, and freckles dusted prettily on her tip-tilted little nose. Her breasts were tip-tilted, too, just a little, and her legs were as long as a colt's. She had a disposition as sunny as her hair, and her name was Candy McCall. She should have been in high school, but her father had taken her out for a while. He thought it would be good for her to see some of the world. So far the world had consisted of Acapulco and Nassau. Candy wasn't too impressed, but it was better than school.

Candy's father, Mason, a candy manufacturer who currently was married to Candy's fourth stepmother, Dolly; Candy hated her. They were staying in Nassau for a few weeks while Dolly played the roulette table and got a tan, and Mason did some property deals.

Until Candy met Miles she had been frantic with boredom. Despite her virginal appearance she'd had several boyfriends, most of whom had been granted the pleasure of her small, neat body; Miles, who had a sure instinct for anything to do with sex, recognized her experience, and her capacity for pleasure, instantly and easily.

"Don't give me that," Miles said good-naturedly when Candy squirmed under his exploring hands, pushing them gently, modestly away. "You know you want it as much as I do."

"I know nothing of the sort," she said, smiling up at him, her small freckled nose wrinkling, "I am not that kind of girl."

"Show me what kind you are, then," Miles said. They were lying on a rug on Candy's balcony, on the penthouse floor of the Bahamian, out of view of anyone except the most determined cat burglar. He stood up and pulled off his shorts. Candy looked up at him, his tall, golden body, his glorious face, his magical smile; then she knelt in front of him.

"This sort," she said, and took his penis in her mouth with a gentle hunger.

After that they were seldom apart.

"MILES," MARCIA SAID after breakfast one morning, "I want to talk to you."

"Sure," said Miles, sitting back in his chair and smiling at her. "Here I am."

"Not now. When your grandmother is asleep this afternoon."

He looked at her slightly warily. "I'll be working."

"I know how important your work is, Miles, but maybe just this once you could arrive a little late."

"Not too late. I have a game at three."

"Fine. We'll talk at two."

An odd unease gripped Miles; a shadow came over the sun.

THAT EVENING, AFTER his afternoon games, Candy found Miles drinking a beer and looking miserable.

"Miles, what's bothering you? Tell me. I won't split on you or let you down. I might even be able to help."

He looked at her. "I don't see how. Unless you can give me five thousand dollars, and I don't think even that would make much difference."

"Well, tell me anyway. Come on."

So he told her—that Mrs. Galbraith had guessed what he had done; that she had threatened to go to the police; that her lawyer knew, too; that unless Miles repaid the money within a month, she would tell his grandmother and the bank. "I kept telling her I didn't have the money, that I couldn't pay it back. She just said I'd spent it and it was my duty to put it back."

"She sounds crazy."

"She is."

"What about your grandmother?"

"If she knew what I did, it would really send her right over the top. Poor old lady."

"You're real fond of her, aren't you?"

"Yeah. She's been very very good to me."

"Don't you have anyone else in the world who could help?"

"Nope. Not really."

"No relatives?"

"Only an uncle. He doesn't have any money."

"Could he get some?"

"I don't think so."

"Well, who put you through college?"

"Oh, some guy."

Candy looked at him and laughed. "Miles, what do you mean? What sort of guy?"

"A creepy old guy. Friend of my parents."

"He sounds pretty nice to me. Creepy or not."

"Well, maybe. But I fought with him. Pretty badly."

"I can't image you fighting with anyone."

He looked at her almost with surprise. "I never have before. Or since. Only with him."

"What did you argue about?"

"He wanted me to get a job, and I thought I could work in his company. He said I couldn't. He was lousy to me. I wouldn't have any more to do with him."

"So you said you'd never speak to him again, just because he wouldn't give you a job." She looked amused. "You're a spoiled baby."

"You don't understand." Miles never got angry or defensive. "Anyway, I haven't been in touch with him for years."

"Maybe you should now. Maybe he could let you have the money."

"No," Miles said. "No, I couldn't go begging to him. I'd rather go to jail."

Candy shrugged. "Suit yourself. I hear the Nassau jails are pretty unpleasant. Come on, let's go upstairs. Dolly will be coming back from the beach soon. I don't want her to see you."

"Why not? I like older women."

"Ugh!"

THAT NIGHT MILES sat in his room in Marcia's house, thinking. No matter which way he turned, there was no escape. He thought of running away, back to the beach, but they would know exactly where to look for him. He wondered if he should go somewhere else. Miami, maybe. He could work there in the hotels; but they would find him there, too. Mrs. Galbraith wouldn't give up.

Anyway, he didn't want to leave his grandmother alone with her. At least not until he had this thing settled. He felt she needed him.

"GRANNY, I WANT to talk to you."

It was afternoon, and her mind was at its clearest. "Yes, Miles."

"Granny, I want to write to Hugo."

"Oh, Miles. That is real good news. What brought that on? Though why he should want to hear from you I can't imagine."

"I'm going to do what he says. I want to tell him I'm going to get a real job. He'll be pleased. I guess I owe it to him, after what he did for me, putting me through college and everything."

Mrs. Kelly shot him a shrewd glance. "This is awfully sudden, Miles."

His face was totally open. "I know. But I guess I finally realized I can't go on playing tennis forever."

"Playing tennis? I thought you were working at the casino."

"Yeah, well, a little of both."

She sighed. "I surely would like to see you settled. And so would Mr. Dashwood. What are you thinking of doing?"

"Banking, I guess. I thought I'd go to Miami. That way I could come down and see you regularly. It isn't far."

"Well," she said, "I certainly will miss you. But it will make me very happy."

"Good. So could I have Mr. Dashwood's address?"

"I only have the one in New York. We never had the one in England. I'll get it for you. Wait there." She paused. "You're not going to him for a job again, are you, Miles?"

"No, Granny, I swear I'm not."

"Good. Because you'll just open up old wounds, that's all."

"I know."

"It's funny," she said, "we never heard from him. He promised to write, you know."

"Yeah, well," said Miles. "He was a pretty strange guy."

MILES WROTE THE letter. It was scary. He waited. He didn't have long. Mrs. Galbraith was mercifully a little vague about time. But her lawyer wouldn't be. April came. He began to feel frightened. He had written to several banks in Miami. Most of them wrote regretfully polite letters back, telling him he was a little old for a job as a trainee. Two asked him to come for an interview. He couldn't afford to go, so he wrote polite letters, stalling. One bank wrote back and told him to forget it.

Candy was leaving soon. Dolly was bored, and Mason's deals were nearly done.

Mrs. Galbraith stopped him one day and told him she hadn't forgotten their conversation. Miles didn't dare antagonize her further. He smiled his most charming smile. "Don't worry, Mrs. Galbraith, I'll get the money very soon. Please have faith in me."

"Even if I did, Miles, I'm afraid my lawyer doesn't."

Finally a letter came.

> Dear Miles,
> I was absolutely delighted to get your letter. It seems a very long time since we met, and I do assure you I have missed you. You were an important element in my life for a long time, and it was a considerable loss.
> I am very pleased to hear that you are going to get a job. I always felt you had such potential and a great future. I have several connections in banking in Miami, and I would of course be delighted to put your name forward. I think New York or Washington might be better for you than Miami, although of course if you want to stay near your grandmother, I quite understand.
> How is she? Please give her my regards.

*With reference to your request for a loan for $5,000, I am of
course happy to consider it, but I would like to know a little
more about your reason for requesting it. I know this may
annoy you, but I cannot help worrying about your past record
with drugs, and I want to be assured that you have completely cut yourself off from all that sort of thing. I have given
a lot of thought to your situation, and it seems to me that
you are very much alone in the world. I realize you are twenty-
six, but that is not a great age, and I feel you need some
support and help, on perhaps a more formal basis.*

*I would very much like to see you. I feel we have a great
deal to talk about on both a business and a personal basis,
and there is something that I have decided it is important
you should know. I shall be coming to Nassau toward the
middle of next month, and we can perhaps have a long talk
then. Providing I am satisfied that the $5,000 is to be put to
good use, I will give you a check then and have my lawyers
draw up the papers in connection with your allowance.*

Thank you again for writing.

Yours ever,
Hugo Dashwood

"Miles," said Mrs. Galbraith, "it's been just about four weeks now.
I wonder if you've made that arrangement yet?"

"Nearly, Mrs. Galbraith. The check is on its way."

"It had better be. My lawyer has already drafted a letter to your
bank."

"WHAT DO I do?" he said to Candy. "What do I do now?"

She was still on vacation in Nassau. Her stepmother had found a
new toy boy on the beach, and her father was discovering the joy of
shooting craps in the casino.

"Didn't the old guy deliver?"

"Sort of."

She read the letter. "He sounds pretty generous, considering."

"Oh, sure."

"Well, would you shell out five thousand dollars just like that?"

"I guess not."

"And he's going to give you an allowance."

"Big deal."

"Well, it is."

"Maybe. But, Candy, I need the money now. I got a letter from the bank this morning asking me to go and see them. I'm in real trouble."

"You'll just have to tell your grandmother the truth."

"I can't. It's hard to explain, but I just can't do that to her. I think it might really break her. Send her over the edge. She's half nuts already. She needs to think well of me."

"She won't think well of you if you get arrested for fraud."

"I know. But I'm going to hang on as long as I possibly can."

"Couldn't you tell this Dashwood guy it's urgent?"

"I'd have to tell him why, and I don't think that would be a good beginning."

"What *are* you going to tell him?"

"I think ordinary debts would be a safer excuse. Cost of living, you know? Overdraft. More respectable, somehow. Only that could obviously wait three weeks."

She looked at him. "Listen, we're going to New York next week. Why don't I look this old guy up?"

"What good would that do?"

"It might help. I could explain that you're in trouble. Old men like me."

"I'll bet they do," he said, smiling in spite of himself.

"Come on, Miles. Let me. Give me his address."

"All right," he said. "I guess it can't do any harm. Meanwhile I'll just have to stall. You can't lend me a hundred dollars, can you? Just so I can go for this interview in Miami?"

"I'll ask Dolly. I'll say I want a dress. She'll do anything to try to make me like her."

"You're an angel, Candy."

"Yeah, well, let's have a bit of earthly pleasure. Just for now."

CANDY CALLED HIM from New York a few days later.

"Miles, it was really weird. I went to Mr. Dashwood's address. It's a really funny place on the Lower East Side. But it isn't a place at all. Not really."

"What do you mean?"

"Well, it's just a scruffy room, in an awful building, with a lot of pigeonholes for letters and a weird woman, who said she was in charge. I said where could I find Mr. Dashwood, and she said she wasn't allowed to give his address, and that it was just a forwarding house."

"That is weird."

"I said it was really urgent, and she said that didn't make any difference; she could only pass messages on. I tell you what, Miles; I really don't think he can be as rich as you say. I mean, I was expecting a real impressive place."

"Me, too. Well, thanks for trying."

"That's okay. Sorry. Did you get the job?"

"Haven't heard. Even if I do, they won't give me five thousand dollars on my first day, will they?"

"I guess not. Well, in two weeks the old guy will be down to see you. So you should be all right."

"Yeah. Well, I hope so. When are you coming back?"

"Next week. Love you."

"Love you, too."

IN DESPAIR, WITH very little hope, Miles wrote to Bill Wilburn, asking him for a loan. All he could do now was wait. And hope the bank and the lawyers would drag their feet.

·26·

CAMILLA NORTH KNEW PERFECTLY well what had brought Julian back to her. It was not love or desire. It did not necessarily mean that his marriage had been the disaster that she had prophesied, or that it had simply signified male menopause at its most acute. It was fear, and Camilla could offer the unique gift of sexual reassurance that Julian needed.

She found that was enough.

In offering her gift and having it received, she received much herself: gratitude, tenderness, and trust. Through the long nights, between her linen sheets, Camilla learned of Julian's marriage, of his disappointment, disillusionment, and despair. He was, she found, extremely fond of Phaedria, but he had found himself in the position of a man who had imagined he was buying a toy pistol when actually he had obtained a deadly high-caliber revolver. He hadn't acquired a wife; he had acquired a clever business partner and a highly visible personality, and he didn't like it. Camilla wondered at the girl's foolishness. She was by all reports intelligent, surely intelligent enough to realize that the male ego was a fragile thing and that the ego of the middle-aged male was poised to splinter into a thousand pieces at the first threat of rivalry—in whatever field.

Camilla smiled to herself as she sat in her executive office on Madison Avenue just opposite Brooks Brothers, remembering with fierce vividness the pleasure of her reunion with Julian in bed. He might have been uncertain and fearful with Phaedria, and in his abortive attempt to seduce Regency, but with Camilla he was as powerful, as skillful as she could ever remember. And since she had grown, greatly to her own surprise, more sensual in her middle age, was less inhibited, more imaginative, greedier—largely, she was sure, as a result of some very intensive and lengthy sessions with a new, highly aggressive female therapist—their lovemaking was very satisfactory indeed.

"And just who exactly have you been doing this sort of thing with for the past two years?" he had asked with surprise and pleasure, and a gratifying tinge of jealousy.

No one, she had assured him, with her usual, painstaking honesty, no one at all. "I have learned to communicate with myself, be in touch with myself, that's all."

"Well," he said, settling his head gratefully on her magnificent breasts, "that must be extremely nice for you. Oh, Camilla, what is it about you that I cannot live for very long without?"

"I'm not sure," she said. "I feel the same, you know. My analyst says it's probably because our ego instincts and our sex instincts are deeply compatible, both in ourselves and with each other."

"Balls," he said, lifting his head, smiling at her, lazily moving his hands over her flat stomach, her beautiful slender thighs. Then, seeing the outraged expression she wore whenever he questioned her psycho fixation, as he called it, he added hastily, "I mean, balls are part of it. And bosoms. And this. And this. And this . . ."

CAMILLA WAS NOW highly successful. She had her own advertising agency, North Creative. Her clients were among the richest and glossiest in town, in fashion, beauty, drinks, and interiors. She had a small penthouse on the newly fashionable Upper West Side and a house in Connecticut, where she kept a fine string of horses, rode with the Fairfield Hunt Club, and gave brilliantly orchestrated house parties to which she invited a careful blend of clients and friends.

She was happier, more relaxed, than she had ever been in her life. She had long ago given up any idea of marriage. Her new analyst had taught her to respect herself, what she had, and what she wanted. "I have learned to give myself permission to experience pleasure for its own sake," she explained to Julian, "rather than desperately seek to justify it or to claim new territory." If she wanted to have an affair, she knew she should have it and enjoy it. As a result she was perfectly content to continue as mistress to Julian Morell for as long as they both wished without making any further demands on him. It seemed a very amicable and satisfactory arrangement.

JULIAN RETURNED TO London from Paris via New York early in March, looking fit and happy. Phaedria looked at him warily. She had learned to trust none of his moods; the good ones could change swiftly, and the bad ones stayed stubbornly the same. But he seemed genuinely pleased to see her. He avoided sleeping with her on his first night at home, saying he was tired, that his jet lag would wake him at two. She accepted it resignedly, prepared for more to come, but in the morning she woke to find him sitting on the bed, looking at her, his eyes warm and tender.

"I think we should begin again," he said, sliding into bed beside her. "I have missed you very much."

And Phaedria, feeling she should be cool, controlled, distant, but finding herself hungry, eager for him for the first time in months, turned to him and smiled, and said, "I've missed you, too."

Later he said he would stay at home and would like her to do the same. They lunched together and then went back to bed. He gave her some presents: a Hockney swimming pool painting, which he said would remind her of the Los Angeles she had fallen in love with, a Deco Diamond clip, an edition of the *New York Times* from the day she was born.

"Oh, Julian," she said, "what have I done to deserve this?"

"A lot," he said, "but I want to ask you for more."

"What?" she said, smiling still, but cautious, wary. "What do you want?"

"I want you to give up Circe," he said. "It's taking up too much of your time, of your attention; it's causing many of our troubles. I think you—we would be better without it."

"Give up Circe? Julian, I can't. Two years of my life have gone into that. I love it; it's too important to me. Don't ask for that."

"Two years of my life have gone into you. I love you, too; you're too important to me. I have to ask. Please, Phaedria, please. For me. Because I love you."

"I can't. If you loved me you wouldn't ask. Besides, the me that you love is not a passive nobody of a wife."

"You don't have to be a nobody to be a wife. Most women see it as quite a rigorous job."

"Well, I don't." She sat up and looked at him, flushed, angry. "I couldn't."

"No," he said, sitting up himself, drawing away from her in the bed, "you couldn't. That ego of yours wouldn't let you. It's yourself you're in love with, Phaedria, not me, and that great heap of hype you've built around yourself. That's what you can't give up, not Circe, not the job. Being a star, being featured in magazines, being sought after, interviewed on talk shows—that's what you really want, not the work, not the store at all."

"It's not true!" she said. "You're lying." But she spoke without conviction.

"And even if it wasn't true, if it was just the work, if you were doing the most important job in the world, would you really sacrifice our marriage, our happiness, to it? Don't you think that is something worth subjugating yourself to, Phaedria? Probably not. I'm afraid the person I fell in love with doesn't exist anymore. And it makes me very sad."

"The person I fell in love with never existed," Phaedria said bitterly.

"Oh, Phaedria," he said, and his eyes were full of pain, "do you really believe that?"

"Sometimes," she said, tenderness for him rising up in spite of herself.

"And other times?"

"Other times, I suppose, he's still there."

"So will you not do this for that person? Give up your work. You need not do nothing. We can find you something else to do."

"And who—who would care for Circe? Take it on?" she asked in a sudden reckless act of surrender.

"I don't know," he said easily. "It would move back under the umbrella of the stores division, I suppose. Does it matter?"

"Yes, Julian. Yes, it does."

"Oh, well." He sighed, reached for his watch and looked at it. It was the first sign that he was returning to real life. In a flash of temper she snatched it from him, threw it across the room. He looked at her, startled, and then he smiled. "I like making you angry. It does wonderful things to you. Remember the flight in the Bugatti?"

"Of course I remember," Phaedria said. "I learned a lot about you that night."

"I suppose you did. The darker side. Well, you lost a hero and gained a car."

"I'd have preferred to keep the hero."

"Phaedria, we have to live in the real world. That's why I want you to give up the store. We have problems; Circe doesn't help them."

"But—" she began and then stopped. There was no point in arguing with him. He was too skillful, too devious for her. She always ended confused, half won over.

"I suspect I have no choice. If I want to stay with you."

He looked at her, startled. "Is there any doubt about that?"

"It doesn't seem there is, no."

He kissed her hand, her hair, her face; he looked into her eyes and smiled gently, tenderly, with no hint of triumph. "I know you won't regret it."

He fell asleep then, and Phaedria lay beside him watching the early spring sunshine playing on the walls; she felt unutterably weary, bereft, bereaved, as if she had lost someone dear to her.

A MEMO FROM Phaedria went around the company a week later. She had decided, so it said, that the work of continuing to run the store was too demanding for her to reconcile with the increasing demands of her life as Lady Morell. Launching it had been challenging and rewarding, but now she was anxious to pass on the day-to-day running to Rosamund Emerson, in her capacity as president of the stores division. She was confident that Mrs. Emerson would preserve the store in the mold she had so carefully created; discussion between them had revealed that Mrs. Emerson had no desire to change any of her concepts substantially. A memo sent out concurrently from Mrs. Emerson said that she had enormous respect and admiration for Lady Morell's work and hoped that she would continue to work with her on the store in a consultant capacity.

If Phaedria had not been so heartbroken and Roz had not been so triumphant, they would both have argued a great deal with the actual author of the memos. As it was, neither of them had the stomach for it.

"YOU DON'T LOOK very well, Phaedria darling." Julian sounded concerned, anxious. "Why not go away for a few days?"

"I don't want to go away."

"Why not? You have the time now. Do you feel all right?"

"Yes. No. Oh, I don't know. I suppose it might help. Where would you suggest?"

"Why not L.A.? You like it there. Get a bit of sunshine."

"All right. It does sound lovely. I have nothing else to do."

She flew to Los Angeles ten days later, spent three days lying by the pool, another one shopping and, unable to help herself, checking on Circe L.A., and felt at least physically better. She was still wounded, still uncertain about how she should conduct this strange marriage of hers, but she felt she had at least the strength to go on trying.

Roz had been quieter, easier, lately; Phaedria had scarcely seen her. It wasn't just the triumph over the store: that seemed to have done her very little good. She looked dreadful; her misery over the breakup with Michael Browning was very obvious. Phaedria was curious as to what he might be like. She wondered if she would ever meet him. He had to be a man of formidable character to love Roz, but he obviously did—or had. And she had clearly loved him, too. It was strange to think of the Roz she knew experiencing an emotion as tender, as positive, as love. It didn't seem possible that her ferocious heart could contain it. But it had, and now that heart had been broken. Sitting there in the sunshine, thousands of safe miles away from her, Phaedria could almost feel a pang of pity for her.

She felt a great deal more pity for C.J. He was having a very hard time; Roz was taking out all her misery, all her frustration, on him. He could do no right: if he was away, even for a day, she demanded he come back again; if he was anywhere near her at all, she could patently not wait to get rid of him; if he agreed with her, she was contemptuous; if he disagreed, she set about him like a harpy. Phaedria, who had talked to him only once on the subject, had decided that whether he realized it or not, he was merely biding his time, waiting for fate to deliver him into a happier situation, more loving arms—after which he would be gone, she devoutly hoped, without even a pause for further thought. She would miss him, but she planned personally to help him pack.

Sitting by the pool eating her lunch the day before she was due to leave Los Angeles, Phaedria wondered what was to become of her. Was she to become one of the ladies who lunch? A bored born-again shopper? No. Most assuredly not. She didn't really want to work for Julian in any other capacity. She felt the whole circus would start again, and she couldn't face it. Could she return to her writing? Get a job on a magazine? She couldn't see it working. It would have to be a token, a charade of a job, given to her because of who she was, something to be dropped whenever Julian snapped his fingers and demanded her attention, to be with him, entertain him, stand at his side. That was not what she understood of work. Was there some other job she could do? Run an art gallery? Start a stud farm? Become some designer's patron? None of it seemed satisfying, or even real.

"God," she said to the glass of champagne she was drinking, "what on earth is to become of me? What have I done?"

Well, it was too late now; she had done it. She had to live with it. And with Julian. For better or worse. For the hundredth, probably the thousandth, time she asked herself if she was still in love with him and for the hundredth, the thousandth, time she had to say she didn't know. She found it hard to imagine being in love with anyone at all at the moment; she lacked the emotional energy. Maybe when she had adjusted to her new life, she would start to feel again.

She had been sobered by Julian's attack on her when he had asked her to give up the store. Even while she recognized much of it had been unjust, there was no doubt at all that she had become much in love with her own image, her own hype, her dizzy, glossy life-style.

And it wasn't a very pretty thought. It was the ugliness of the thought, and realizing how far she had come from the direct, self-respecting person she had been, that had really persuaded her to give up the store, not Julian's declaration of love for her. If she was about to turn into the sort of person she herself would have despised, she needed to do something about it. It had taken great courage, but she had begun.

She was due home on the Thursday midday; Julian had told her he was flying up to Scotland for forty-eight hours to talk to some forestry people, but that he would be back on Saturday. He sounded loving, conciliatory, on the phone; she found herself at least looking forward to getting home to him. Maybe it would all be worth it, if they could restore their relationship to some semblance of its original pleasure and delight.

She got to the L.A. airport at midafternoon and was about to check in on her flight when she saw a flight to New York posted, leaving in an hour. Now, that would be fun. She loved New York. She could go to the apartment on Sutton Place tonight—she had the key—and then do a day's shopping and visit the Frick, which she had never yet managed. Nobody was expecting her home; feeling like a truant schoolgirl she booked a seat on the flight.

It was late when she got to New York—midnight, with the time change. She got a cab easily; she sat back, tired, happy, excited. She could sleep late, then have a day of self-indulgent pleasure all by herself. She still loved her own company.

The apartment building on Sutton Place was in darkness, the doorman half asleep. She let herself in quietly, humming "Uptown Girl," which had been playing on the in-flight stereo, throwing off her coat, walking through to the kitchen, fixing herself a cup of coffee. She felt suddenly alive again, a free spirit; she should do this more often.

What she really wanted now was to sit in bed and watch a movie on TV. That would end a perfect day. She wandered back through the hallway and down the long corridor to the big master bedroom, still humming. Suddenly she heard a noise, quiet voices; then, as she moved again, a responding silence. She waited, desperate with fear, and then, in the slowest of slow motion, she watched as the double doors of the bedroom opened. Julian stood there, wearing nothing but a robe, his face pale and appalled; all she could see, beyond him, was a white face and a mass of red-gold hair spread across the pillows.

◆　◆　◆

THE ONLY REAL decision was exactly where to go. She could have gone home to her father, but the complexities of trying to explain to him what had happened were so daunting that in her weak, sickened state she could not face them. She could have gone back to her friends in Bristol, but somehow that offended her sense of rightness. She had moved beyond and away from them; they would not be able to help her now. And her current circle was too new, her position in it too ephemeral to be close enough.

Letitia had been supportive and very kind, but when all was said and done, Julian was her son, she was in her late eighties, and there was a limit to the amount of hostility and conflicting emotion she could be expected to be asked to bear.

David Sassoon soon offered to take her in, to put her up, but that seemed unfair; she would only jeopardize his position in the company. He swore he didn't mind, but it would clearly be an impossible situation for all of them. Eliza phoned, assuring her of support, sympathy, and a home for as long as she wanted it, but that, too, although it appealed to her sense of humor, seemed to verge on the ridiculous, and poor Peveril would have found it very difficult to cope with. Regretfully she turned the invitation down.

For want of anywhere else to go, she booked into Brown's Hotel while she recovered her equilibrium and wondered exactly what to do.

Clearly she couldn't stay with Julian; she had no intention of doing so. Public humiliation was obviously a permanent possibility, and she wasn't going to expose herself to it. She wouldn't starve; simply selling some of her jewelry would keep a family of fourteen in considerable luxury for many months. But what was she going to do with herself? She had been robbed, in that brief shocking moment, not only of her husband and her love—for she did love him, very much, she discovered, in the sickening physical blow of her jealousy—but of her home and her life-style as well. And in the midst of her rage and jealousy she felt guilt and remorse as well: would Camilla ever have reclaimed Julian if Phaedria had been the devoted wife that Julian had clearly wanted? And now her days were not only empty of Julian, they were empty of purpose and interest as well, with not even the doubtful new pleasure of playing the devoted wife. She knew she must, in time, try to get a job of some sort, but at the moment she had no stomach for it. She felt ill as well as wretched; she could only struggle through the days.

Everyone tried to help her, each in a different way: Letitia implored her to reconsider; Eliza told her to take Julian to hell and back; C.J.

wrote her a charming letter assuring her of his love, support, and friendship and promising to do everything he could to help; Susan phoned her, oddly concerned, saying how sorry she was. Even Roz sent a brief note that said she was sorry to hear what had happened. It was a considerable gesture; Phaedria wondered what on earth could have inspired it. Guilt, she supposed.

She was right.

But of course nobody could help. She felt lonely, wretched, and worst of all, she felt a fool. How could she, naive and unsophisticated, have possibly imagined she could accomplish a successful marriage with a man forty years her senior, a man of almost unimaginable wealth, power, and influence? It was simply arrogance, as she now perceived it, and she felt deeply ashamed; of all her wounds this would surely take longest to heal.

The other thing she had to endure was physical illness. As April turned to May she became more and more listless, lethargic, increasingly nauseated. Her back ached, she felt dizzy, she had no appetite, she was losing weight. Eventually she went to her doctor.

Victoria Jones was young and perceptive. She saw at once what was the matter with Phaedria, wondered at her blindness, and decided to lead her to the reason herself rather than shocking her with it in all its complexity.

"Well, obviously you aren't going to be feeling well," she said briskly. "You've had a terrible time. How are you sleeping?"

"I'm not."

"Appetite?"

"Haven't got one."

"Getting any work done?"

"I haven't got any to do," Phaedria said and burst into tears. "And that's another thing," she said, sniffing into the tissue Victoria had handed her. "I keep crying. I never cry normally. I feel just—oh, unlike myself."

"Well, you've got plenty to cry about. Periods regular?"

"Yes. I think so."

"When was the last one?"

"Oh, I—oh, God, I don't know. Does it matter?"

"It might be useful to know. Here's a calendar."

Phaedria looked at it, absently at first, then more intently, going back over the weeks, thinking. Then she suddenly looked up at Victoria, her cheeks very flushed, her eyes bright with tears. "February sixteenth," she said quietly.

"Nearly three months."

"Yes. I suppose it could be all the trauma."

"It could."

"But you don't think so?"

"Honestly, no. Not put together with the nausea and the lassitude," said Victoria.

"Oh, God," Phaedria said. "Oh, my God."

SHE WAS SITTING in the upstairs drawing room when he came in; she heard the car draw up, the door slam, his steps in the hall, then heavily, slowly, coming upstairs. She tensed, then stood up and walked to the doorway.

"Hello, Julian."

"Phaedria!" He looked first startled, then nervously pleased. "What on earth are you doing here?"

"I came to get some things. And I—I wanted to see you."

"I see." He sighed, looked at her searchingly. "You don't look well. What is it?"

"Would you expect me to look well?" she said, suddenly angry.

"I suppose not. I'm sorry."

"It's—it's nothing, really."

"Would you like a drink?"

"Yes, please. A glass of white wine."

"I'll get it."

He came back with her wine and a glass of brandy for himself. "Are you managing all right?"

"Oh, yes, thank you. You'd be surprised how well I'm managing."

"I wouldn't," he said. "I wouldn't at all. I have the utmost respect for your capacity to manage. I miss you," he added, his voice very low. "I miss you terribly."

A silence. Then: "Does there have to be a divorce?"

"Oh, yes," she said, "I think there does."

"Is there no future in my telling you how sorry I am? That I love you? That I would give anything, anything, to have you back?"

"I don't think so. I do believe that you're sorry and you want me back, but I know it would happen again. If not with Camilla, then someone else."

"And if I made a promise?"

"I don't think you could keep it."

"Oh. Oh, well." His voice was oddly flat, unemotional.

"I think it really is hopeless."

He sighed. "Maybe."

"And it isn't all your fault either."

"No," he said, "you're right. Nearly, but not all."

"You were right about me. I did neglect you—well, our marriage. I cared too much about the store, my own life, everything. I am terribly, terribly ambitious. I didn't know I was, but you set it free, made me that way."

"I know. I blame myself."

"Well, I don't think you should. Not really. And then there's Roz. That could never, ever have worked."

"No. Of all the pain I feel, that is worst. That the two of you couldn't somehow have lived together, worked together."

"You didn't help, you know."

"I tried."

"Julian," Phaedria said, looking at him, suddenly so angry that her lassitude and sadness left her, "that is a lie. You did not try. You made things a hundred, a thousand, times worse. Why do you have to deceive yourself about it? About everything?"

"I don't think I am deceiving myself," he said. "I think I really tried."

"Well, in that case, either you don't know what you are saying or, as usual, you're lying. You just cannot tell the truth, can you? You just can't. Truth is a total stranger to you."

"You're right, I don't find it easy. But for you, because I love you, I'd like to try. Will you let me?"

"What do you mean?" she said, puzzled. "What do you want me to do?"

"I want you to listen to me. Let me tell you about myself."

"Well," she said, intrigued by the notion, momentarily removed from her misery and her anger. "I think you should answer some questions rather than just talk. That way you're less likely to get carried away. Why did you marry me?"

"Because I fell in love with you. And I found you very arousing sexually."

"Was that all?"

"No."

"What else?"

"It flattered my vanity, I suppose, that someone so young, so beautiful, should want to marry me."

"Anything else?"

"I was lonely."

"It's getting less pretty, isn't it? Is that all?"

"No," he said, and she could see the struggle he was having, to fight through to the truth. "I rather liked the idea of the to-do it would cause."

Phaedria looked at him, her eyes first cool, then suddenly filled with amusement. She smiled at him for the first time. "I like this game."

"I'm not sure if I do. Can I sit down beside you?"

"No. Stay over there. I need to see your face."

"This really is an inquisition, isn't it?"

"It was your idea. Okay. Now then, did you really not think there would be a problem with Roz?" Phaedria asked.

"I really didn't."

"Are you sure?"

"Yes. I'm quite sure," he said after a moment's thought. "I had no idea she felt so strongly about me. Or rather about the company and her place in it."

"We'll come back to that one. Did you find being married to me as you'd expected?"

"No."

"How?"

"You were much more difficult."

"Good." She drained her glass; she felt pleasantly dizzy and strangely powerful. She had forgotten about the baby, about why she was here; this was the most fascinating conversation of her entire life.

"Did you—did you sleep with anyone besides Camilla?"

"No."

"Really no?"

"Really no."

"What about Regency?"

"No. I didn't sleep with her. She—she didn't want to," he added painfully, dragging the words out.

"Julian," she said, and she had to pour another glass of wine and drink half of it before she could face her own question, even, quite apart from the answer, "what is it about Camilla? Why do you go back to her again and again? Do you love her? Or is it just sex?"

He was silent for a long time, not evading the question, just thinking. Then he sighed and said, "I suppose, in an odd way, I do love her."

"Oh," she said, and it was like a cry of pain, of fright, in the big room.

"No," he said, moving toward her, holding out his arms. "No, you don't understand. Don't look like that, darling, please don't. Come here."

"No," she said, her eyes hard behind her tears. "Don't touch me. Don't come near me."

"All right. But may I go on?"

"I suppose you have to."

"At various stages in my life," Julian said, "when I have been under very heavy pressure of one kind or another, I—I have become impotent. When I feel threatened. Textbook stuff, I suppose. Camilla," he added, his lips twitching, "is very strong on textbook stuff."

"You mean she cures you? Helps you get it up? My God."

"Phaedria, don't be crude."

"I still can't understand you going to her. When you're supposed to love me."

"I do love you."

"You can't. You simply can't."

"I do. Do you love me?"

She was taken aback by the suddenness of the change of direction. "Yes. Yes, I think I do."

"Did you sleep with Sassoon?"

"No, I didn't."

"Did you want to?" The questions were coming faster, harder. He was flushed now, breathing heavily.

"No. Not at all. Why were you so jealous of him?"

"I don't know."

"That's not the truth."

"Because Eliza loved him."

"Do you still love Eliza?"

"Yes," he said suddenly, looking at her in astonishment. "Yes, I think I do. I didn't love her when I was married to her, but I have loved her greatly since. And I always will. She has a hold on my heart," he added, "as you do."

"I seem to be sharing your heart with quite a few people. Anyone else while we're on the subject?"

"No," he said quietly. "Not now."

There was a silence. Then: "Why did you marry me, Phaedria?"

"I wanted to."

"Is that all?"

"Yes."

"Why, though?"

"I thought you were clever. Interesting. I—loved you. You made me feel safe." She finished her wine. "That's ironic, isn't it?"

"I'm afraid so." He looked at her piercingly, suddenly. "Phaedria, why have you come here? Tonight? So late. There is a reason, isn't there? It's not just a desire to talk, to discuss the formalities of a divorce. The lawyers can do that. There's something else. Please tell me."

She was thrown off her guard by the switch from past to present. She stood up. "No. There was something, but I've changed my mind, I don't want to tell you. Not now. I'm going. I'm sorry, Julian. I really did love you, and maybe I still do, in a way, but I can't live with you. You're better on your own, and so am I."

"Well," he said with a sigh, "perhaps you're right. I love you, too. Very much. How ridiculous this is."

"Yes," she said, suddenly, for some inexplicable reason, light-hearted, "it is quite ridiculous. I shall miss you dreadfully, horribly." And she smiled at him suddenly, a warm, friendly, loving smile. "Perhaps we can be friends. Loving friends."

"Ah," he said, catching her mood. "That would be nice. But how loving, I wonder? And what kind of love?" And he looked at her, his eyes dancing, and as he looked, Phaedria suddenly felt herself physically assaulted by a bolt of desire. It filled her, it consumed her, it was like a great, fierce fever, and she looked back at him, startled, helpless with it.

"Come here," he said lightly, "let me kiss you good night. But not, please, not good-bye."

And she moved toward him, her eyes still fixed on his, wondering that he could not see, feel, how she felt. Perhaps, perhaps, if she could only get out of the house quickly, she would be safe, and he would never need to know. She raised her face to his, thinking that in one moment, one moment, it would be all right, it would be over, but he touched her and it was like a charge. She shuddered, looked up at him, into his eyes, and she saw at once that he had known, had felt it, too. She moved into his arms, drew his head down toward her.

"You bastard," she said. "You make me so angry." And very gently, very slowly, she began to kiss him.

"I love you," he said. "I love you so much. Please say that you love me, too."

"I do," she said. "You know I do."

"Come along," he said. "Come along to bed." And unprotesting, childlike, she took his hand and followed him, and all the way upstairs he talked to her, endlessly, telling her he loved her, he wanted her, he had missed her, and she listened, enchanted, caught once more, helplessly, in the spell of sensuality with which he had first ensnared her. She lay on their bed and looked at him, her eyes never leaving his as he undressed her, stroking, kissing, sucking each of the places he knew most aroused her—her neck, the hollow of her throat, her shoulders, her breasts—lingering there, feeling the leaping, quivering response. Then, urgent suddenly, he was tearing off his own clothes, telling her over and over again how much he wanted her, how much he loved her, and then, swiftly, unable to wait any longer, he was in her, and she felt him grow, seek, yearn for release, and it came so suddenly, so fiercely, they cried out together, and then he was lying, looking at her, with tears in his eyes, and for the first time since she had known him, she felt he was vulnerable and that she was safe.

"I love you," he said. "Don't ever leave me. Tomorrow we will begin again."

"I don't know," she said. "Perhaps we can. I love you, too. But I still don't quite know."

"You will," he said. "You will. Promise me you will."

"I can't promise you," she said. "Not yet." But she fell asleep, sweetly contented and untroubled.

IN THE MORNING she felt extremely ill. She slithered out of bed and into the bathroom, and was sick over and over again. It must have been the wine, she thought; she had not felt so bad before. She should not have drunk it; she would give it up at once. She stood up and looked at herself in the full-length mirror, so slender, so small-breasted, and reflected upon the secret within her and how it would change her body, how her breasts would become veined and heavy, and the flat stomach swollen and ripe. She remembered with a gentle shock that she had not told Julian, that he had no idea what they had accomplished, and she smiled at the pleasure it would give him and the promise it brought to their life. She washed her face, brushed her hair, and walked back into the bedroom, into the sunlight, where he lay still asleep, to wake him and tell him.

"Julian," she said, bending over, kissing his cheek, his hair, "Julian, wake up. I have something lovely to tell you."

He turned, still half asleep, and looked at her, and she was to remember that look for the rest of her life: first love, then pain, then panic; and then he cried out, hideously loud, and she said, "What? What is it?" but he couldn't speak; he was beyond it. He tried, but it was quite quite impossible.

JULIAN FOUGHT DEATH for days. He lay in intensive care after not one but three massive coronaries, battling against it, pushing it away.

Phaedria sat with him, watching him drowning in it, sinking, gasping, surfacing, seeing him afraid and more than afraid, frantic, trying to speak to her, impotent, helpless.

"He's trying to tell me something," she kept saying to the doctors. "He's trying to talk to me. He's desperate. Can't you see? How can I help him? Can't you do something?"

No, they said. There was nothing. He was beyond speech. This often happened; people did appear to be desperate to talk, but usually it was nothing important. They had nothing to say, really. There was nothing to worry about; she was doing all that could be done, just being there, calming him. But she knew she was doing nothing of the sort.

She felt afraid herself, contaminated by his fear. She talked to him endlessly. She told him she loved him, she tried to calm him, to give him courage, hope, faith. And all the time his eyes looked at her in a deep despair.

He died, looking at her still, his hand in hers, her gaze locked in his. And afterward, as she gazed down at the still, sterile shell that he had suddenly become, all the charm, the grace, the tenderness shockingly gone, she realized with a piercing sense of grief and shock that she had hardly known him at all.

· 27 ·

WOMEN ARE NOT ASKED TO BEAR any pain greater than that of losing a child. Letitia lay in her brass bed in First Street and felt she would never sleep again. She could not cry; she would not cry. She was afraid of tears, of the sweeping wave of pain that they released. She was fighting to hold back that wave, to control it; she knew if it came she would sink and drown in it. In a few days, perhaps, she would be able to manage it; for now, dry-eyed, breathing a little heavily with what felt like a physical effort, she lay and held it at bay.

She was helped in her struggle by her thoughts of the rest of the family and of Phaedria, widowed before she had begun properly to know what marriage was, and with the added pain of a pregnancy to endure alone. Letitia had no doubt that she would come through; she was tough, and she was brave, but that did not diminish her grief and her misery. And there was grief; Letitia was almost relieved to see that grief. She had always felt that Phaedria had loved Julian, that she had married him for that reason, not for the money, the power, the fairy-tale transformation he could work upon her life, but she had been alone in her judgment at the beginning and had sometimes over the past two years begun to doubt it. Whether the marriage had been a success she had no real idea; the last few weeks of it had been very sad. Phaedria had, at least, been with him when he died, when he had been taken ill; there must have been a reconciliation of some kind, but it had clearly been brief. When Letitia, summoning a strength from she knew not where, had gone to visit Phaedria at the house the night after Julian died, all she had said over and over again, her voice cracked with pain was, "I didn't tell him, Letitia. He didn't know. I didn't tell him; he didn't know."

She had thought at first that Phaedria had meant she hadn't told Julian she loved him, but later when she had tried to give her a brandy, a sleeping pill, anything to calm her, she had said no, no, the least, the very least she could do was take care of her baby, of Julian's baby, and Letitia had looked at her, shocked and still with pity, and wept with her for a long time.

And then there was Roz. Roz had reacted strangely—angrily, fiercely—when she was told the news that Julian was in intensive care and not expected to live. C.J. had broken it to her and then phoned Letitia in despair, saying Roz was raging, screaming, blaming Phaedria, saying it would never have happened had she not married Julian, saying she should be there with him, not Phaedria, and then, when Phaedria had said of course she should come, should see him, should say good-bye to him, Roz had said, her voice icy cold, "I do not intend to share him with her now."

Roz had stood stone-faced throughout the funeral at the small Sussex church. She had not wept until she tossed a small bunch of white roses onto the coffin as it went into the ground. Then she turned swiftly and ran, sobbing as she went, into the trees at the back of the graveyard. She would not come out, would not speak to anyone, until the last car had left, insisting that everyone—her mother, her husband, her grandmother—go and leave her alone. Then she walked, slowly, heavily, an almost ghostly figure, toward her own car.

Phaedria had kept the service very simple; the only dramatic gesture she made was when she placed some keys in the grave, on top of the coffin, nestling in her own flowers, white lilies, with a card that said simply "From Phaedria, with my special love."

"The keys of the Bugatti," she explained to Letitia with a half smile at the house later. "It was a very special present to me and I wanted to return it to him. No one will ever drive it now."

Roz had not returned to Marriotts but had driven back to London and locked herself in her bedroom in the house on Cheyne Walk. She had emerged the following morning, dry-eyed, perfectly dressed, and had thrown a tantrum because her driver was not available to take her to the office, being rather fully occupied ferrying funeral guests to the airport. From then on, she had seemed normal. Someone, she said, had to keep the company going, and it looked as if the task had fallen to her. If anyone proffered sympathy, she gave them a terse nod. Otherwise she did not mention her father's death at all.

Until the reading of the will, two weeks after the funeral. That occasion drew the family together in a white heat of emotion and tension and then tossed them apart again as if they were so many rag dolls.

Remembering the events of that day—of Camilla arriving so bravely to confront them, summoned by Julian from wherever he might now be; of Roz, so powerfully, fearsomely angry and hurt; of Phaedria, so freshly wounded, so suddenly frail—Letitia wondered with a mixture of horror and fascination at the cruelty of her son. In a way she was almost glad; it eased her grief, gave her something else to focus on. And besides, being angry with him, being ashamed of him, was oddly healing.

·28·

PHAEDRIA MORELL WAS NOT BE-
having quite as a widow should.
Well, not as a grieving widow,
at any rate, as Henry Winterbourne, amused and slightly
shocked, remarked to his wife
Caroline the day after the will
had been read.

Henry—all of them—had ex-
pected a long period of mourn-
ing, of grief, a tacit withdrawal
from the battleground that Julian
had so unequivocally created. Especially in the light of her pregnancy, which she had confirmed to Henry with a cool, even amused
look when he inquired after her health: "I am indeed, as some of you
may have guessed, going to have a baby."

But at ten o'clock the next morning, there she was in Henry's office,
a little pale, to be sure, but beautifully dressed in a shocking pink wool
crepe dress, her hair caught back with the seed pearl and coral combs
Julian had had made for her as a souvenir of their honeymoon, and a
pair of very high-heeled pink suede shoes that Henry could only cat-
egorize to himself as flighty.

She had her briefcase with her, and she had sat down in the big
chair opposite Henry's desk, looked at him with an expression that
was cheerful and determined in equal measures, and told him that
there was a great deal of talking to be got through and work to be
done.

"I want to find this person, Henry, this Miles Wilburn, and I want
to find him quickly. The situation until we do will clearly be intolerable. In fact I would go so far as to say," she added, with the hint of a
smile and of conspiracy in her eyes, "I am anxious to find him before
—well, shall we say before anyone else does?"

He returned her look steadily. "I do understand exactly what you
are saying, Phaedria. Unfortunately, much as I would like to help
you, I don't think I can enter into any kind of an exclusive search on
your behalf. I am the Morell family's solicitor and have been for many
years. It would be extremely difficult, unethical even, for me to report
solely to you."

"Oh, of course," said Phaedria, "I understand that, Henry. I assume that you could instigate some searches, or perhaps hire a detec-

tive agency to do so, and report to us all on whatever you are able to find out. I know how busy you are, and I wouldn't dream of making too many demands on your time. But it is a pressing matter, as you must agree. The need to find this Miles Wilburn is immediate and crucial. There is a large and complex company to run, and trying to do so will be virtually impossible while Roz and I have absolutely equal shares in it. We don't always see eye to eye, as you may have heard."

"Well, yes, I had heard some reports to that effect," Henry said, smiling his charmingly benign smile at her, "and I can see there would be considerable difficulties. But—well, forgive me, Phaedria, for being so frank—are you actually planning to become involved in the company and its day-to-day administration straightaway?"

"I am," she said coolly, opening her briefcase. "Absolutely straightaway. I have a meeting with Freddy Branksome and Richard Brookes this afternoon. There is clearly a great deal I need to learn and know, and the sooner I begin the better."

"Oh, I think so, yes," said Henry. "Phaedria, the more I look at this whole thing, the more I think we do need a private detective agency working for us. A really good one. I'll find an agency at once and get things rolling straightaway."

"That would be very helpful. Thank you. Although I have a nasty feeling that at least one of the really good agencies may already be in the employ of Mrs. Emerson."

"I WANT THIS person found," said Roz, fixing Andrew Blackworth with a steely gaze, "and I want him found quickly."

Andrew Blackworth was not what she had imagined; he was not sleek and sharp-looking; he was about forty-five years old, short, rotund, and rather learned-seeming. She liked everything about him.

"We have a long way to travel," he said, "perhaps literally."

"Yes," she said, abandoning reluctantly her vision of finding and coercing Miles Wilburn onto her side within the space of seven days, "yes, I suppose so. But then again, given some luck, we might do better."

"We might indeed. And of course, in us you have considerable skills working for you as well as luck. Skills and contacts. Are you prepared to put your trust in those?"

"Yes," said Roz, "yes, I am."

"Good. Now, in order to utilize those skills, I need all the information you can possibly give me."

"You're welcome to it. But there really isn't any. None at all."

"Could I talk to the widow?"

"No," Roz said. It was a flat, final sound; it brooked no further discussion.

PHAEDRIA WAS SITTING at the huge desk that had been Julian's, a neat pile of papers and files at her left elbow, a legal pad in front of her, which she was covering rapidly with notes. Richard Brookes and Freddy Branksome, who had both been expecting to spend most of the afternoon humoring her and dispensing sympathy, were slightly disconcerted by the turn events were taking.

"What I'd like," she said, looking at them composedly, "is a complete breakdown of the structure of the company, the relative value of its different components, its assets, its liabilities, and perhaps, from both of you, an assessment of its strengths and weaknesses. Nothing too technical"—she smiled briefly—"but a kind of gut reaction, with facts and figures to support it, where necessary. For instance, I have a hunch, just a hunch, that the hotels are not making us a great deal of money and are costing us dearly in terms of personnel, hassle, and investment. On the other hand, they obviously provide a high-profile visible asset. I'm also not really very sure about this new communications company. I imagine that's an investment in the future— satellite TV and so on. Could you clarify that a little for me, please?" She looked at them both and smiled. "I must seem very ignorant, foolish, even. But I am desperately anxious to familiarize myself with this company and assess what my future role might be. I want to keep it running successfully. For Julian's sake."

"Of course," Richard said, "and we will do everything in our power to assist you. Won't we, Freddy?"

"Absolutely everything," said Freddy. "But, Lady Morell, there is one thing. It's a little delicate, but it has to be broached."

"I know what you mean," she said. "Roz Emerson. She has at the moment an equal share in the company, equal say in its future, equal power. I understand and appreciate that. Clearly she and I will have to establish a modus operandi. But she has the advantage at the moment of knowing rather more about it than I do. Its structure and so on. She's worked in it for years. I've been involved for only a very short time."

"Right," said Freddy uncertainly. "Er—right. But will you—that is—" His round red face was perspiring, his bright blue eyes were anxious.

Richard looked at him and smiled, then turned to Phaedria, stretching his long legs out in front of him, looking at her with frank appreciation and a certain degree of wariness at the same time. She was going to take some dealing with, this lady. Lucky old sod, Julian had been. How had he done it? And how could he have perpetrated an act of such wanton cruelty on her as he had done with that will? And on his daughter, for that matter. Roz might be a tough nut—although Susan was extremely fond of her and always claiming that she was not as tough as she seemed—but he suspected in any case that Phaedria Morell could and would match her, blow for blow. God in heaven, what a bloody mess.

"What my learned friend is trying to say, Lady Morell," Richard said, with his careful, lazy smile, "is that we will need to know just how you intend to work here. How involved you plan to be. How often you will be in the office. Where. That kind of thing. We have to work with both of you, you see, and we have to be—well, tactful, to put it mildly. Indeed we are statutorily obliged, I would say, to deal with both of you on all matters of policy, finance, the whole damn thing."

"Of course," said Phaedria, "I understand. I am not trying to coerce either of you into anything. I give you my word that after today there will be no meetings at board level that will not involve Mrs. Emerson as well as myself. I will keep her abreast of everything, as I would expect her to do me. As to your question about how often I intend to be here, the answer is all the time, every day. Possibly including the weekends. After all," she said, flicking a brief glance down her own body, meeting their eyes with frank amusement, "I will not be able to ride or hunt for the next few months, so I may as well work. And I shall base myself here, in this office. Someone has to use it."

"Really?" It was Roz's voice; she was standing in the open doorway. "I don't quite see that, Phaedria. Nobody *has* to use it. It can be locked up. It was my father's office, and you have no more claim on it than I do. We are absolutely equal partners in this company at present, and I fail to see why you should make assumptions, and indeed implications, by taking your place at his desk."

Phaedria looked at Roz; she was white, her green eyes blazing. She was dressed in black and looked fierce, dramatic, almost frightening. Richard and Freddy shifted awkwardly in their chairs. There was a long silence; then Phaedria spoke.

"Freddy, Richard, perhaps you would leave us for now. We have matters of policy to sort out, as you were saying earlier. We can continue this meeting tomorrow morning if you're free. Any time—to suit you."

"Fine," Freddy said, gathering up his files. "We'll sort out something between us."

"Absolutely," Richard said, rising to his full, gangling height, "and as you were saying, Lady Morell, it is essential that both you and Mrs. Emerson should be present at all major meetings in future."

It was a graceful, diplomatic remark. Phaedria gave him a grateful look. "Indeed. Shall we fix a time now?"

"I'm afraid," Roz said, tapping lightly on the desk, where she had sat down, in a clear piece of territorial reclamation, "I shall be out of the office tomorrow. All day. This meeting, whatever it's about, will have to wait."

"As you wish," said Richard, bowing to her ever so slightly. "We are at your service, Mr. Branksome and I. Are we not, Freddy?"

"We are indeed," Freddy said, hastily leading the way to the door. "Good afternoon, Lady Morell, Mrs. Emerson."

The door closed behind them. Phaedria faced Roz, her eyes contemptuous. "Roz, whatever you may feel about me—and I can hazard a very clear guess—we do have to work together, and I see no future whatsoever in holding public brawls. Please can't we confine any emotional discussions to occasions when we are alone together?"

"My God," said Roz, "my God, Phaedria, you have a lot of gall. You knew my father just over two years, and yet you inveigled your way into his company, and now within days of his death you're trying to step into his shoes. You have no right to sit at this desk, in this office, no right at all, nor to hold meetings with the executives of his company; the only rights you have here are mine as well, and I intend to see I don't lose any of them."

Phaedria looked at her in silence for a while. Then she stood and picked up her files, her notes, her briefcase. "You're absolutely right, Roz," she said finally, "and I'm sorry. I was making assumptions that were quite wrong. Either we should share this office, which frankly I don't see working, or I should have one of my own. This one, as you say, can be locked up. For the time being. One of us can move into it in the fullness of time."

Roz stared at her. "I'm sorry, I don't quite follow you."

"Don't you?" Phaedria met her glance with clear disbelief. "I'm surprised. One of us is going to win this war, Roz, sooner or later, and at that time, the victor can move in and claim the throne. Meanwhile, I will speak to Sarah about an office for myself. I'm going home now. I'll see this room is locked before I go." She buzzed on the intercom. "Sarah," she said, "could you please speak to whoever is in charge of such things, and organize me an office. As near to Mrs. Emerson's as possible. Oh, and Sarah"—she looked very straight at Roz for a moment—"make sure it's no smaller than Mrs. Emerson's office, will you? I don't want to be working under unfavorable conditions."

ROZ FELT AS if there were a great raw hole at the heart of her that was bleeding endlessly. She thought she had known what misery was until now. Had she not been propelled into this bitter battle with Phaedria, she would have given in, lain down, and let the world take care of itself. She felt weary, sickened, by her father's treachery, and totally wretched at her loss. He had enraged her, fought her, and manipulated her ever since she could remember, and most of the misery she had ever felt could be lain at his door; nevertheless she had loved him deeply, helplessly. She received little of the comfort afforded to Phaedria, the tide of sympathy, love, concern, that was flowing her way from every direction. Roz had not been with him at the end; there had been no reconciliation. He had died thinking she hated him. He had never known, would never know, how much she had loved him, admired him, longed for his approval, how he had always, since she was a tiny child, occupied the prime, the most important, the most tender place in her tough, hurt little heart.

During the long sleepless nights now, she relived the happy times with him, the weeks she had spent at Marriotts, riding beside him on Miss Madam, looking up at him, trying to do as well as he, braving wide ditches, long, fast gallops, anxious to earn his look of approval, his praise; walking the downs, talking endlessly, her small hand in his, dining with him alone in the huge dining room while he solemnly had her glass refilled with wine and water and consulted her on whether he should buy this horse, that car; sitting beside him, driving some of those wonderful machines, long before she was legally old enough, up and down the drive and tracks of Marriotts, seeing his surprise and pleasure at her skill with them; the visits to New York, dizzier and more exciting all the time as she grew older; the intense pleasure and joy she had felt at his acceptance of her into the company, at his recognition of her skills, his delight at her success. She even relived her wedding day, most of it a panicky blur, the happiest, the best moment being his face looking up at her as she came down the stairs at Marriotts in her dress, Julian's face, naked of everything but love, and his voice saying, "Rosamund, you are the joy of my life." And all through the years, the fear, the terror, the nightmare, that someone would come along, some woman young enough to give him another child, a child he would love as much as, more than, he loved her.

And now he was gone, and he had never known any of it; he had thought she hated him, despised him, that she wanted to see him hurt and wounded, when all she had really longed for was his unequivocal love.

In her anguish, all pride gone, lonely, fearful, she had phoned Michael in New York. He was polite, kind, sympathetic over Julian's death, but distant, declining her invitation to come to England. He had said very little, but she knew what the refusal meant. It meant "I was not good enough while your father was alive, and I am not going to come running to you now that he's dead."

She even turned to C.J., but he was remote, withdrawn. He, too, had loved Julian, who had been a second father to him, and he was saddened by his death. He could not pretend feelings that did not even exist for a woman who had shown him nothing but coldness and distaste for so long.

She reflected, too, in these long sleepless nights, on Phaedria and her hatred for her, on how she was going to win the battle that lay ahead, and on what was to become of them all. And now there was the child, the child she had feared and dreaded for so long. Well, at least her father had not known about it. That seemed to Roz something to be grateful for. She genuinely doubted very much if the child was Julian's; it seemed so unlikely on every possible basis, and her outburst at the reading of the will had been genuine. She had seen it as the possible explanation of her father's behavior, the answer to the riddle. That had not of course explained his equal cruelty—for cruelty it had to be seen to be—to her. On the other hand, she deserved cruelty. Tossing and turning on the huge banks of pillows with which she tried to tempt sleep, Roz heard again and again her voice as she taunted her father into giving her the store: "You're a liar, a liar and a cheat. . . . How is Camilla? . . . I want the store, I want it. . . . I want . . ." She seemed to have ended up with very little.

NEXT MORNING AT breakfast she dispatched Miranda upstairs with Nanny, then turned to C.J., who was reading the *Financial Times*.

"C.J., I want to talk to you."

"Really?" His face was blank, his voice pleasantly polite. "About what?"

"I think we should get divorced."

He looked at her, grave, detached. "You're probably right. All right." He turned back to his paper.

"C.J.?"

"Yes?"

"C.J., is that all you have to say?"

"Yes," he said with a calm smile. "What else could there be? My usefulness to you is over now. Your father is not here to punish you for divorcing me. Why keep me hanging around?"

"Oh, C.J., don't be ridiculous. It's not like that."

"Isn't it? I think it is." He slammed the paper down and looked at her, his face white, his eyes blazing with fury. "For years, Roz, you've used me, simply to get what you wanted—a home, status, your father's approval, sex, I think, originally. I forget. Now you can't quite think what I can do for you. I irritate you, so you are going to send me packing. Well, that's fine. I'll go. But I'm not in a hurry. I like this house. I love London. I have been commissioned to write a book. I would find it easier to do that from this house. I have my study, and I don't want to spend a lot of time looking for another place to live."

"You didn't tell me about the book. What's it about?"

"There was no point in telling you about it," he said. "I knew you wouldn't give a fuck." C.J. never used bad language; it was a measure of his despair about her. "It's about the shifting location of fashionable London."

"I see."

"So I think I'll stay for a while, if you don't mind. Or even if you do. Besides, I don't want to leave Miranda. I'm surprised at you, Roz, after all your endless horror stories about your own childhood, exposing your daughter to divorce."

"I think," she said, wincing with pain, "we can handle it à bit better than that."

"Do you? So far I haven't seen much proof of it, from your side. Anyway, I'll be leaving the company. You'd better have a board meeting about it. The hotels will need a new president. I'm going upstairs now to get Miranda. We go for walks every morning and look at the boats. You didn't know that, did you?"

"No," she said, "I didn't."

As he walked out of the door, she felt suddenly utterly alone.

"C.J. IS LEAVING the company," she said, walking into Phaedria's office without knocking later that morning. "We had better discuss the consequences."

"I'm sorry," said Phaedria, "really sorry. Glad for him, because I always felt he hated it, but sorry for us. He was so good at it."

"I don't really think you have much idea what being good at running hotels implies," said Roz, "but you do happen to be right. He was. Quite good, anyway."

Phaedria looked at her. "Roz," she said, "we have to work together. Given that, don't you think we should at least attempt to observe the formalities and be polite to each other? Apart from anything else, it's counterproductive if we squabble all the time."

Roz walked over to the window and looked out. She was silent for quite a long time. Then she turned and looked at Phaedria oddly. "All right," she said, "let's attempt it. As long as you appreciate that it is only a formality."

"I do," Phaedria said, "I certainly do." She was dressed in brilliant red today, her hair piled high on her head in a tumbled waterfall of curls; she was carefully made up, she wore the Cartier necklace that matched her rings, and dazzling diamond and emerald earrings.

Roz stood for a moment, her eyes skimming contemptuously over her. "You dress rather strangely," she said, "for a pregnant widow."

"LADY MORELL, I have Mrs. Morell on the phone. Can I put her through?"

"Please do."

"Phaedria?"

"Yes, hello, Letitia. Are you all right?"

"I'm fine. Feeling much better. How are you?"

"Perfectly wretched, thank you. Were you sick when you were pregnant?"

"No, I was very good at being pregnant. Just bad at giving birth."

"God, it's awful," Phaedria said. "I don't know whether it's better to eat and then be sick or not eat and feel even worse."

"Oh, I'd eat," said Letitia emphatically. "Do you feel hungry?"

"Not really. Well, a bit. I do want certain things. Spicy things. Steak sauce. Did you ever hear of anything so unchic?"

"Not really, darling, no. Well, I wondered if you'd like to have dinner with me tonight? I'll have a big bottle of steak sauce on the table for you; I'll send Nancy out to Harrods for it now. I presume they'll have it?"

"I expect so," said Phaedria, laughing. "It sounds lovely. Thank you, Letitia. I'd love to come."

"All right then, darling. About eight. There's something I want to talk to you about. Apart from just wanting to see you."

"I hope I won't be late. Roz will be out of the office all day and can only begin an absolutely crucial meeting at five."

"Oh, dear," said Letitia. "She obviously isn't making things easy for either of you."

"LADY MORELL, I have Mr. Emerson on the line. Can I put him through?"

"You certainly can. C.J., hello. This is sad news about your resignation."

"Not for me."

"No, I suppose not."

"Phaedria, I wondered if you could possibly have lunch with me?"

"Well, I'd love to, but I don't know if it would be wise. I don't think Roz would be pleased."

"I don't care."

"No, but I do."

"You really don't have to. She's just taken the helicopter up to Manchester. Says she has to see the guy at the communications company. We don't have to go anywhere; I'll come to the office."

"How very cloak and dagger. All right, yes, I'll get Sarah to organize something. I have a new office, by the way. Immediately beneath Roz's. I thought tactically beneath was better than above. See you here at one."

"Fine."

He arrived with a bunch of white freesias and a bottle of white burgundy.

"C.J., you are naughty. You can't give me flowers."

"I can do what I like. Roz wants a divorce."

"Yes," Phaedria said, looking at him sadly. "I thought she might."

"Don't look like that. I don't mind. I feel sort of—well, discarded, but otherwise, it's a relief."

"Will you go back to New York?"

"No, I don't think so. I don't want to leave Miranda, and I have a book to write about London."

"C.J., how marvelous. I'm so pleased. Tell me about it." She pressed the buzzer. "Sarah, could we have those sandwiches? And also could you bring a vase in?"

She started arranging the flowers while he talked. He looked at her and thought what a remarkable person she was, and wondered how Julian could possibly have treated her so badly. There had to be an explanation; if only to provide it to the world, he was determined to help her find it.

"Phaedria, I'd like to help."

She looked at him over her glass. "What do you mean?"

"I'd like to help you find Miles Wilburn."

"C.J., that's sweet, but why?"

"Because—" He paused, trying to find exactly the right words. "Because I think you deserve it."

PHAEDRIA ARRIVED AT First Street that night well after nine.

"Letitia, I'm so sorry. The meeting went on and on, and then I had letters to sign. Please forgive me."

"Of course I do. It couldn't matter less. Drink?"

Phaedria shuddered. "No, thank you. Could I have some Perrier?"

"Of course. What does your doctor say about all this?"

"I haven't seen her since—" Her face clouded, drained of color; she sat down and looked at Letitia, suddenly very white and shaken.

"Darling, what is it? Are you all right?"

Phaedria tried to smile, and failed; she shook her head, unable to speak. Letitia crossed over to her and took her hand.

"Tell me. What is it?"

"Oh—I don't know. I'm sorry. It's stupid, really. It's just that—well, I haven't seen my doctor since the day before Julian died. I haven't even thought about it. You asking made time telescope suddenly, if you know what I mean. I felt I was back in her room. It was a sort of ghostly feeling."

Letitia looked at her keenly. "It isn't easy, is it?"

"What do you mean?"

"Being alone in a pregnancy."

"No, no, it isn't. How do you know, though, Letitia? I didn't think you ever were."

"Well, I was in a way, my darling. In a way. Let me tell you about it. It might make you able to feel you can talk to me, turn to me. That I'll understand."

"I do anyway. But yes, please do. I'm intrigued."

"Well," said Letitia, "it's a long story. I'll try not to make it too long. When I was only seventeen years old, I was engaged to someone called Harry Whigham. He was a captain in the Guards. He was terribly handsome and charming, and I loved him very much. Very much. He went away to France and was killed in the war. I was distraught. Of course. And lonely and lost and terrified that I would never find anyone else. All the boys I knew were going to France, and most of them were not coming back. I had a horror of being a spinster, like most young girls then. Then I met Edward Morell, Julian's father. He was kind and good, and he adored me, and I thought—well, I suppose I managed to think I loved him. And he wasn't going to go away to France because he was a farmer. So I married him. That was in 1915. James, Julian's brother, was born a year later. And we were perfectly happy. Well, perfectly content, anyway.

"In 1919, after the war, I went to stay in London for a few days with my grandmother. She had always been opposed to the marriage with Edward. She thought he was"—her lips twitched—"very middle class. I suppose I inherit my dreadful snobbery from her. Anyway, we went out to the theater one night, and after the play, we were waiting for a cab when someone tapped me on the shoulder. I turned, and there was Harry Whigham. Only of course it wasn't; it was his younger brother, Christian, but he was just terribly, terribly like him. It was the most dreadful appalling shock, I felt absolutely ill. Fainted, in fact. I came to lying on the sidewalk, with everybody fussing and Christian fanning my face. He was looking at me very, very intently, and I was in his arms, his coat over me. I remember it all so clearly; he had on a black evening coat over his dinner jacket; he looked so handsome, so unbelievably handsome and—well, that was it, really."

Phaedria sat absolutely motionless, her eyes fixed on Letitia's face. She hardly dared to breathe for fear of interrupting her.

"My grandmother, who had always liked Harry, asked Christian to join us for supper. It all seemed like a dream; all I could think of was that I was with Harry again. Or nearly. Before he left he asked if he could come to call the next day. My grandmother not only encouraged him, she arranged to be out and for half the staff to be out as well. She was very wicked, I'm afraid. And so was I."

"So—so what happened?"

"Well, darling, I'm afraid a great deal. It was all very disgraceful. Of course everybody nowadays thinks affairs and adultery are the invention of the late twentieth century, but I do assure you, they have always gone on. Christian and I had a wild affair. Aided and abetted by my grandmother. Oh, it was wonderful. I stayed in London for another week and was with him every day, very often alone. He begged me to leave Edward and run away with him, but of course I couldn't. I said it was impossible, that we must never meet again, that Edward was a good, kind man, that I did love him, and that Christian must go away and never, ever see me again. I remember my words still. I said, 'There is nothing for us, absolutely nothing at all.' Only I was wrong, of course." She was silent for a moment, just looking at Phaedria. "There was Julian."

Phaedria said nothing for a while; then she put her arms around Letitia. "How did you bear it?" she asked.

"Oh, you bear what you have to," Letitia said. "There was nothing else to be done, nothing at all. When I found I was pregnant, I did think of trying to tell Edward that it was not his child, but what would have been the point? It would only have made trouble, caused pain. So I kept silent. Edward had no cause to suspect. He was delighted at the thought of another baby. I found my comfort and happiness in Julian. But then—well, he did look very different from James and Edward, and nobody in Wiltshire, in Edward's circle of friends, liked me very much. I didn't fit in. Someone had seen me with Christian in London; there was talk. Of course I tried to laugh it off when people made remarks about Julian having brown eyes while Edward and I were both fair and had blue eyes. But it was—difficult. Then when Julian was nine or ten weeks old and I was still frail, Edward came in, sat down at the table, and burst into tears. It was dreadful. He said someone had been drunk and blurted out that Julian was not his son. He clung to me and begged me to tell him that he was, that it was a lie. He was sobbing; he was drunk himself. So of course I said that it was a filthy lie, that people were jealous of him, of both of us, that Julian was his son, that there was no truth in any of it."

She was silent for a long time, her eyes filled with tears.

Phaedria sat utterly still, her eyes fixed on Letitia's face. "How awful for you, how sad, and how brave you had to be. How did you do it? How did you get through?"

"Oh, very much as you are," Letitia said briskly. "By just getting on with life. It's the only thing to do."

"I suppose so." Phaedria was pale, almost awed. "So Julian was actually illegitimate. Did he know?"

"Yes, he was, and yes, he did, although not until he was grown up and Edward was long dead. When Julian came back from France, I told him. I'm not sure I should have, in a way."

"Why?"

"Oh, I don't know that it served any useful purpose. And I think in a way it encouraged his extraordinary instinct for intrigue. And for deceit. I don't know." She sighed. "One makes a lot of mistakes in one's life. And they become clearer as you get older. There's an old Irish saying, you know, which my father used to quote: 'Old sins cast long shadows.' It's true. You think something is far, far away, buried in the past, and it isn't at all. It travels with you always, ahead of you even, into the future. I feel that sin of mine certainly did that. And now, you see, some sin of Julian's is casting its own very long, dark shadow."

"But, Letitia, why does it have to be a sin? Perhaps this Miles person is someone Julian wanted to help, to benefit."

"Well, darling, if he is, why didn't we all know about him? Why all this mystery and cloak-and-dagger nonsense? It really is quite extraordinary. So unnecessary. Oh, I could shake him." She smiled suddenly. "It helps me to get cross with him. I don't hurt so much."

"You must hurt terribly," Phaedria said, reaching out to take Letitia's hand.

"Yes, I do. Terribly. There is nothing, no pain, like losing a child. Take care of that baby, Phaedria. No other love has the strength, the power, of the love a woman feels for her child."

"I will," Phaedria said, looking at the sad, suddenly old face before her. "I will. For your sake I will. And thank you for telling me. It helps; I don't know quite why."

"I hoped it might, and I thought you ought to know now. Tell me, darling, how do you feel? Apart from physically? Any better at all?"

"No. Not really. But I feel so rejected, somehow. As if Julian has just—oh, I don't know, thrown everything in my face. And I can never, ever have the comfort of thinking he trusted me, loved me at all. And nobody else could think that either. It's awful. Letitia, I don't know what to do. I simply don't know how to bear it."

Letitia looked at her. "I don't know either," she said. "I just wish I could help you. What I do know, though, which might comfort you, is that Julian did love you. Very much. I know it's very hard to believe, but it is true."

Phaedria was silent. Then she said, "You know, Letitia, all the time, all those three days before he died, I kept feeling he was trying, struggling, to tell me something. But he couldn't. He couldn't speak, couldn't write, couldn't do anything. They kept saying I shouldn't worry, that it was normal, but I did feel he was desperate. Perhaps that was about the will, about what he had done."

"Poor Julian," Letitia said quietly. "If that is what it was, how dreadful. Now than, let's have something to eat. It's terribly late, you must be starving. Nancy's made something I think you'll like. It's chicken marengo, and you can drown it in steak sauce if you want to."

"Sounds wonderful."

"Good. Come on, then."

"Incidentally," she said carefully, a few minutes later, as she watched Phaedria pick halfheartedly at her food, "a private detective has been hovering around me. Hired by Roz. Did you know about this?"

"No, but I'm not surprised."

"Well, that's something. I didn't want to commit myself to talking to him until I'd seen you. Of course I shall help him in any way I can to find this Miles Wilburn. But I just wanted you to know."

Phaedria looked at her and smiled. "Thank you. What is he like? Awful?"

"No, he seems rather nice. Quite civilized and gentle. Not like the ones on television at all. A bit like an English Hercule Poirot."

"Goodness. And what sort of thing does he want to know?"

"I'm not too sure. I don't think he knows himself. I imagine he just wants to hear everything I can tell him about Julian. To see if he can pick up any clues."

"And do you think he will?"

"No, I don't, I really have never heard Julian mention anyone called Miles, or Wilburn. But he may unearth something from the depths of my mind. I hope so. The only thing I do feel—it's partly hunch, but there is some basis for it—is that this person, whoever he is, is more likely to be in America than here. I really think it would have been rather difficult for Julian to establish a strong link with him or his family here in England without one of us picking up some hint of it. And he did spend such a lot of time over there, especially in the sixties and seventies. I do think, also, darling, you should talk to Eliza. She says she doesn't know anything, but she's so scatty. Careful prompting might help."

"Yes, but I don't know what to prompt. And I don't feel well enough to go haring up to Scotland. But I suppose she'll come down here, if I ask her."

"Of course she will. Any excuse to come to London. And just let her run on. That's all you need to do in the way of prompting."

"All right. Oh, by the way, Letitia, this may sound like a funny question, but do you happen to know if Julian could type?"

"Oh yes," said Letitia. "He typed rather well. He learned during his Resistance training during the war. Why?"

"Oh, just a query over the will. Whether he could have drawn it up himself. It seems he could have. Incidentally, I have a detective working for me, too," said Phaedria with a smile.

"You don't! How intriguing, darling. What's his name?"

"He's an amateur. His name is C. J. Emerson."

"Phaedria, that sounds very unwise to me."

"Not really. Roz wants a divorce. C.J. is moving out. He offered his help. I was doubtful at first, but actually I think he might do rather well. He has an investigative mind. He likes little odd facts and things, and he remembers them, stores them away. He really wanted to be an archaeologist, you know."

"How sad that he wasn't. That he had to get mixed up with Roz, I mean. Two unhappy people."

"Yes."

Letitia looked at her. "I hope he's not falling in love with you," she said. "I've always thought he had a soft spot for you. Do you think he is?"

"Absolutely not," Phaedria said firmly. "But even if he was, it wouldn't matter too terribly, I daresay. Roz doesn't give a toss about what C.J. does. My God—" She stopped eating and shuddered, looked at Letitia, stricken at her own thoughts. "Can you imagine anything more dreadful, though, than if someone Roz did give a toss about was in love with me? That really would see me in the morgue."

MICHAEL BROWNING ARRIVED at Heathrow three days later.

He had been feeling remorseful ever since Roz's cry for help, and his refusal to respond to it. Near psychotic fixation apart, Roz had genuinely loved her father. Michael reckoned she must be feeling pretty wretched. He owed her his support. He had absolutely no intention of resuming their affair. Some old-times'-sake friendship was about the most he could offer. Even with her father gone, he had no illusions as to where he would come in her list of priorities, especially if all these rumors about the will and the company were true. That was all very intriguing. He wondered what on earth the old bastard had been playing at. He wasn't too sure of the facts of the case. The *New York Times* and the *Wall Street Journal* had both carried the news of "certain complexities" in Julian Morell's will. But *People* magazine had also jumped on the story. They had clearly had trouble getting enough details, and had run only a paragraph, but it was fascinating reading. "Wills and Wonts," it was headed:

> Billionaire tycoon Julian Morell, who died three weeks ago, reportedly left a bizarre will, bequeathing two equal forty-nine percent shares in his company to wife Phaedria and daughter Roz, and the remaining two percent to a so far unnamed party. The famously feuding women now find themselves put in a neat corner by Big Daddy, neither able to claim control and forced to work together

in close disharmony. Neither of them was available for comment, but the countess of Garrylaig, Eliza, first wife of Sir Julian, mother to Roz, and guardian angel to Phaedria—who is rumored to be pregnant, although estranged from her husband for the weeks prior to his sudden death—predicts a speedy discovery and recovery of the missing heir.

"Holy shit," Michael Browning had said under his breath as he read the article on the London-bound plane. He signaled to the hostess. "Could you get me a whiskey, please? I suddenly have an awful thirst."

"EXCUSE ME."

Michael stood in the reception area at Dover Street, dripping wet. He had, as always, lost his raincoat. Just as well he was in London. Although of course nowhere else would it be pouring rain in the middle of June.

"Can you tell me where to find Mrs. Emerson?"

"Certainly. Second floor, turn right at the lift, and it's the big office on the left. Can I have your name, please? I'll tell her you're here."

"No, thanks. I want to surprise her."

"Mrs. Emerson doesn't like unannounced visitors."

"She'll like me."

"No, I really can't."

Michael looked at the receptionist with his mournful face, his spaniellike brown eyes. "I really want to surprise her. Can you deprive a drowning man of his last wish?"

"Well . . ."

"Thank you. If she fires you I'll give you a job."

He decided to walk up the stairs; he hated elevators and it was only one flight. Being an American, the second floor to Michael Browning was actually the first. He ran up the stairs, pushed through the swinging doors, waited momentarily outside the office, and then opened the door.

"Hi, darling."

But the face at the desk, looking at him, was not what he had been looking for, seeking, even, he realized with some surprise, longing for. It was not Roz's face. It was nevertheless a rather beautiful face, very, very pale, with large dark eyes, and a cloud of dark hair. Michael Browning did not take a great interest in clothes, but he could see that the brilliant red dress with the wide shoulders added greatly to its owner's striking appearance.

"Yes?" she said, somewhat shortly.

"Oh, I'm sorry," he said. "I was looking for someone else."

"So I gathered."

"I'd like to say you'll do," he said, sounding rather morose, "only that would be corny, and I'm afraid it wouldn't be absolutely true. Although as substitutes go, you set a pretty high standard."

The substitute stood up, whiter than ever, and rushed toward him. "Excuse me," she said. "I'm going to be sick."

When she came back, shaky and a little dizzy, he was still there.

"Hey," he said, "you look terrible. Here, come on and sit down." He took her hand, led her gently to a chair. "I don't usually have that bad an effect on people. I obviously have a problem. Can I get you a drink of water?"

"Oh, yes, please. There's a fridge in that cupboard there. Thank you. I'm really sorry. Horrid for you. Nothing personal. It's just that I'm going to have a baby. And it doesn't seem to like me."

"Now, that's really bad," he said, looking at her with concern. "Are you sick a lot?"

"An awful lot."

"All day? Or just in the morning?"

"All day."

"You really shouldn't let that go on, you know. It's bad for you and not good for the unfriendly baby. What have you tried?"

"Nothing, really."

"Okay, well, here's an idea. My first wife had terrible sickness, and in the end she licked it. Now, you take a lemon, and you just lop the top off it. Think of it as an egg. Get a little sugar—do you have that here?"

"I believe we do," Phaedria said, her lips twitching.

"Right, you sprinkle just a little onto the egg."

"You mean the lemon?"

"Yeah, the lemon. And then when you feel sick, or every ten minutes or so, you suck it. Try it. It can't do any harm."

"Thank you, I will. It sounds awful, but I will."

"And when is this ungrateful monster due?"

"Not for an eternity. November."

"You should have passed beyond being sick by now. What does your doctor say?"

"I haven't asked her. I'm seeing her tomorrow."

"Well, you should have seen her a long time before tomorrow. This certainly is a rather primitive society. In the States you'd be having your twenty-fifth checkup by now. Do you plan to give birth to this child in a ditch or something?"

"No. Well, hopefully not." She looked at him and smiled. He smiled back.

Phaedria felt a very odd sensation—a small, meek, but very determined lurch somewhere deep within her. A slight shifting of her solar plexus. An illusion that the room was warmer, brighter. She stifled the sensation and looked at him again, taking in the solemn face, the lugubrious dark eyes, the thick floppy hair—and the indisputably damp suit.

"You're very wet."

"I certainly am. Are you surprised? This is London, right? And it is June."

"Yes, but most people wear a raincoat."

"I lost mine."

"Ah."

"In fact I plan to buy a new one this afternoon. In Harrods."

"You could get one nearer than that. Simpson's. Austin Reed."

"I know. But they know me in Harrods."

"Do you buy raincoats there very often?"

"Oh, all the time. I only have to show my face in the department and hordes of women rush at me bearing Burberrys."

She laughed. "All right. Now then, who is this darling you're looking for?"

"I beg your pardon? Oh—sorry." He smiled again. "I'd forgotten. Too interested in you and your baby." The shift again; the brightening. "Yeah, well, you probably know her. It's Roz. Roz Emerson."

"Yes," Phaedria said, "yes, I do. Slightly. I'd ask my secretary to take you up, only she's not very near at the moment. It's the next floor. Directly above this room. Shall I let her know you're here?"

"No," he said, "I want to surprise her."

"I hope she likes your sort of surprises," Phaedria said briskly.

"I think she will. Thank you, Miss—er, Mrs.—"

"Morell. Phaedria."

"You! You're Phaedria! My God, I didn't expect you to be quite so good-looking." He studied her in silence, drinking her in; then he smiled again. "Well, you really are a nice surprise."

"Thank you." Another slightly bigger shift.

For God's sake, she reminded herself, you're a grieving widow, four months pregnant.

"And you are?"

"Browning. Michael Browning."

"Oh, my God, I'm going to be sick again."

"I'll bring you some lemons," he called to her departing back.

"MICHAEL, MICHAEL, I love you. I love you so, so much. It's so good to see you." Roz was more than slightly drunk; they were lunching in the Caprice. Michael, most of his lofty resolutions gone, was sitting back looking at her thoughtfully.

"Do I get to spend the rest of the day with you? Since you love me so much?"

"Michael, I can't. I just can't."

"Ah."

"Michael, do be fair. I had no idea you were coming. I have three major meetings this afternoon. I have half the company resting on my shoulders these days you know. It's serious work."

"Not half, darling. Forty-nine percent."

"You've been reading the papers."

"I certainly have."

"Well, what do you make of it?"

"Very odd. I told you he was a devious old buzzard."

"Yes, well, so you always said." Her face darkened. "Do you know the whole story? Or at least the half of it that we know?"

"Not really."

"Well, he left forty-nine percent to me and forty-nine percent to the wife—the widow."

"And who holds the key?"

"I don't know. Nobody knows."

"You're kidding."

"I wish I was. Some man called Miles Wilburn. None of us have ever heard of him."

"None of you? Not even the old lady? Or that frosty lady with the red hair?"

"No. None of us."

He was silent for a while. "Weird."

"It is."

"So what are you going to do?"

"Find him," Roz said. There was an expression of absolute determination on her face.

"And then?"

"Get him on my side."

"Exactly how?"

"I'll find a way."

"Poor fucker."

"I beg your pardon."

"You heard. I don't like his chances. How are you going to find him?"

"The lawyers are on to it. I have a detective agency working on it, too."

"Is Lady Morell also trying to find him?"

"No doubt she is."

"Some contest."

"I intend to win."

"I'll bet you do."

"Michael, you're not being terribly nice to me."

"You haven't been terribly nice to me."

She looked at him, held his gaze, and took his hand; and in that moment all her toughness, her selfishness and greed left her eyes, and they were filled quite simply with longing and love. "I know. And I'm truly, truly sorry."

"Well," he said, fighting to retain some semblance of judgment, "I think I'll wait and see. Are you sure you can't come back to the hotel with me now?"

"I'm sure," she said, and he could see the immensity of what that cost her. "I'm sorry, but I can't."

"Ah." He was silent for a moment; she looked down, fearing she might crack, weaken, even cry. Then he smiled, kissed her cheek.

"It's all right, Roz. That was unfair of me. I shouldn't have asked. I wouldn't cancel three vital meetings either, just on the off chance of a glorious afternoon in the sack. Can I see you tonight?"

"Yes, most certainly tonight. This evening. I'll be there at seven."

"What about hubby?"

"I'm divorcing hubby."

"Just like that?"

"Just like that. Well, I suppose he'll be divorcing me. He has enough grounds."

"Well, that's sad."

"Is it?"

"Of course it is. Jesus, Roz, you're a tough cookie. It's always sad when a marriage ends. You have to think that."

"Well," she said, "maybe. But we never really had a marriage, C.J. and I. Just an arrangement."

"Of your making. Rosamund, much as I love you, dearly as I like to be with you, desperately as I long to have you in my bed again, I want to make it very plain that I will not play some minor part in any convenient arrangement of yours. Is that clear?"

"Yes, Michael. Quite clear. I promise."

He looked at her warily. He had learned not to trust her promises.

PHAEDRIA AND C.J. began their detective work that night. Phaedria unlocked the huge desk in Julian's study, and they sifted patiently hour after hour through papers, letters, documents. Everything was meticulously filed, perfectly ordered; most of it was administrative stuff, deeds to houses, details of staff, invoices for work done, letters from lawyers in America, France, the Bahamas, about property, cars, horses, planes. Some of it was personal: there were letters from Roz at boarding school, brief, harsh, dutiful; and earlier ones, which she had written to him when he was in New York, when she was a little girl, loving, sad, brave little notes asking him to come home, to take Mummy back to Regent's Park, telling him of her successes at dancing, at riding, at school; there were snapshots of her on her pony, in her ballet dress, in her first school uniform, and several of her with Julian, holding his hand, sitting on his knee, sitting on her pony beside him. Phaedria studied them in silence; her eyes filled with tears.

"This is awful, C.J. It makes me feel so sad. He really really loved her. And she must have loved him so much. I don't think I can take much more of this. I shall end up giving her my share and just retiring to the country."

"Yes, I know," said C.J. "I used to feel sorry for her, too. But I don't anymore. Other people have tough childhoods. You did. But they survive. They don't turn out to be psychopaths."

Phaedria laughed shakily. "She's not exactly a psychopath. But I suppose you're right. Oh, look, here are the wedding pictures, with Eliza. Goodness, she was beautiful. And, oh, C.J., look at Letitia. What a marvelous-looking woman she was. Is."

"She is such a very old lady suddenly," said C.J.

"Yes, I'm afraid she is. But she's amazingly brave. She's an example to us all. Well, there's nothing here, C.J., is there? We may as well call it a day."

"I guess so. You look tired. Why don't I fix you a drink before I go?"

"That would be lovely. I am tired. It's not exactly easy, what I'm doing at the moment."

"Roz giving you a hard time?"

"Very. The thing is, I could easily give in and just let her carry on for a bit. I still hold forty-nine percent, so she can't do anything much without me. But I just know she'd start politicking in earnest if my back was turned. I have to show my mettle."

"She certainly seems much happier," C.J. said with a sigh. "Browning's been over."

"Yes. I know. I met him."

"Really? How did that happen?"

"He came to my office by mistake."

"I hear he's quite charming."

"Yes," Phaedria said briefly. "He seemed quite nice."

"I guess she'll marry him now. In the fullness of time."

"I guess she will." She looked at him, but his face was blank.

"How's the flat-hunting?"

"It's good. I have a nice place, I think, just off Sloane Street. I've made an offer. Now what would you like to drink?"

"Hot milk with honey in it. A real nursery bedtime drink. Can you manage that?"

"Sure. Now I think the next thing we have to do is repeat this same operation in New York. In Sutton Place."

"God," said Phaedria, "I don't think I could possibly find the strength to fly over there just now. And my memories of Sutton Place are not the happiest."

"You really have had a tough time, Phaedria. I suppose you've considered not doing all this? Just letting things go. You could settle down happily with your baby, probably marry again, spare yourself all this pain."

"No," Phaedria said firmly. "I haven't considered it for a moment. Not one. The company matters desperately to me. It's the most important thing I have left of Julian, apart from the baby, and I intend to keep it alive, in my own way. And I feel that, in doing what he did he made it clear he wanted me to remain involved in it, caring for it. Otherwise he would have left it all to Roz. No, C.J., I have to carry on."

"Well, I just thought I'd mention it. Phaedria, would you like me to go to Sutton Place? And to the offices in New York? I wouldn't mind. I know where everything is. I have the time. And"—he smiled at her suddenly—"I'm not pregnant."

"Well, that's true. Oh, C.J., I'd love it. But are you sure it won't upset your book schedule?"

"It will," he said cheerfully. "But I don't mind. Now I'm going to get your drink. You just wait there."

When he came back with it she was asleep, her face peaceful, childlike, her hair tumbled on the cushions.

ELIZA PROVED NO more able than anyone else to help in the hunt for Miles Wilburn. Phaedria asked C.J. to phone Camilla while he was in New York—unable to bear to talk to her herself. The only other person worth talking to, Phaedria decided, was Sarah Brownsmith. Sarah, she felt, probably knew more about Julian, both his public and his private life, than anyone in the world. And she was clearly anxious to help. She had even moved her office down from the penthouse in order to act as Phaedria's private secretary and to prevent Roz from claiming any kind of injustice. Phaedria asked her to organize lunch for them both one day, and said she wanted to ask her some questions.

"I really need all the help I can get," she said as they sat down together. "Anything at all you can think of. However unimportant."

"Well," Sarah said, "I have no notes, no addresses, no names, that are going to do you any good. I have been through everything, and this Mr. Blackworth of Mrs. Emerson's has already been to see me, as you know."

"Hmm. Let's go at it a different way. Sarah, you knew him a very long time. Can you think of any time he might have behaved differently?"

"Not really. He was, considering how spoiled he was, very balanced, I always thought. Although—" She looked at Phaedria quizzically. "There was something."

"Yes?"

"Well, it was quite soon after I came to work for him. Right at the beginning of the seventies. In 1971 to be precise. He became very depressed. Very depressed indeed. In fact, one morning I did actually find him in tears. I've never told anyone this, of course—there was no reason for me to—but I suppose it might be relevant now: He did at that time see a doctor quite regularly."

"Goodness," Phaedria said, "this is intriguing. What sort of doctor?"

"Well—a psychiatrist."

"My God. How regularly?"

"Twice a week for nearly a year. I had the impression he was very troubled."

"This is truly extraordinary. Nobody, nobody at all, has ever mentioned anything about this. That he was so unhappy or anything. Do you by any chance remember this doctor's name?"

"I can find it. Just a minute."

She came back with her address file. "Dr. Friedman. Margaret Friedman. She practiced in the Marylebone Road. I have her number. Would you like it?"

"I certainly would. Sarah, you're an angel. Thank you."

"It's a pleasure, Lady Morell. Would you like your nap now?"

"No, I'm much too excited to sleep. Try this number straightaway, will you? I can't wait to talk to her."

But Dr. Friedman, the receptionist said, was away for a fortnight. She would be happy to make an appointment for Lady Morell on her return. Would an early morning be convenient? Yes, quite convenient, said Lady Morell, just as early as Dr. Friedman liked.

"Very well," said the brisk voice on the other end of the line. "Eight-thirty on Monday, August first."

With which Lady Morell had to force herself to be content.

·29·

MILES THOUGHT MIAMI WAS JUST about the most awful place he had ever been to in his life. It made the early days in Nassau look like paradise. Even the relief of getting old Marcia off his back, with Bill Wilburn's totally unexpected help—God, why hadn't he asked him before?—didn't make life seem much better.

At first sight, the beach had looked all right, and there was at least the suspicion of surf rolling in; but he discovered very quickly that it was nothing but a huge man-made people park, covered with a lot of very old people and an endless procession of film crews. It had no soul, unlike the beaches of California, no shape to it, and no land behind it, just mile after mile of high-rise buildings. He liked the south end better, Old Miami as it was called, with its little colony of Deco hotels and buildings, but it was still basically part of what seemed to him the same nightmare, just concrete and more concrete, straight lines and endless streets. What he couldn't understand was how proud and pleased everybody seemed to be with the place. The number of tourists, they kept telling him, was rising every year, every month—at least five million last year. An incredible number of new roads were being built, and all kinds of new developments, like Bayside, the waterfront development, and then there were all the wonderful things like the Seaquarium and the Metrozoo, and had he been to the Everglades and the Tropical Garden and . . .

Miles smiled his lovely smile and said, no, not yet, but he was certainly looking forward to it. Then he got his head down at the bank, took the cheapest room he could find, and immediately set about saving his fare back to Nassau.

IT WAS MRS. de Launay, Billy's mother, who saw the advertisement.

"Look at this," she said to her husband excitedly. "Someone wants to contact Miles. At least I suppose it's him."

"Must be," he said. "There can't be many Miles Wilburns around. I wonder if Marcia has seen this."

"Probably not. Should I show it to her, do you think?"

"Well, of course you should, Alicia. It could be important."

Alicia was shy. "But she might think I'm interfering. She might already have seen it. I don't like to."

"All right." He shrugged. "Have it your own way."

"Oh, well—maybe I should."

She went to Marcia's house later that day. Marcia was doing her needlepoint; Dorothy was asleep upstairs.

"Forgive me for interfering in your business, Marcia, but I wondered if you'd seen this."

"What's that, Alicia?"

"It's an ad in the paper. For Miles to get in touch with some lawyers in England."

"Well, for heavens' sake," Marcia said. "Let me see. Good heavens. I wonder what that can be about."

"Usually they're about money, Marcia. Legacies. You know. Someone might have left him a lot of money."

"I doubt it. No one in that family has a penny to their name."

"Well, you never know. Don't you think you should at least tell Dorothy—Mrs. Kelly?"

"Yes, I expect you're right, Alicia. Thank you for letting me know. Now, would you like some tea?"

Marcia thought hard about the advertisement after Alicia had gone. It might well be that the boy had come into some money. But so what? It was very nice without him, and if he didn't have to work in the bank in Miami, he would probably come back and hang around the house all day. And if it was a lot of money, he would probably move away and take Dotty with him. He was genuinely very fond of her and had often said that one day he would make a new home for them both. Marcia didn't want Dotty to go away. Not now. She felt proprietary toward her. She felt that Dorothy was hers to look after; she couldn't imagine life without her. And there was certainly no way Miles would put any of his money in her direction. She would end up lonely, and poorer than she was now. Once the house in Malibu was sold, she and Dotty would be very well off.

No, there was absolutely nothing to be gained by letting Miles see this advertisement. She put it with all the letters under her bed.

BILLY DE LAUNAY saw the advertisement too, in the *Washington Post*. Now, this was really interesting. This might explain why Miles hadn't heard from the old guy: he'd died. This was an English lawyer, after all, and it looked like Miles might actually be going to get some money. That was what these kinds of ads usually meant. Lucky Miles.

He sighed. It was a shame Miles was such a lousy correspondent. He never heard from him these days, although Miles continued to send him a note whenever something interesting or exciting happened to him. Oh, well, they could catch up on everything when he went home for his summer vacation.

Billy hoped Miles would see the ad. It would be awful if he missed it. He never read the papers, except maybe the headlines. He tore it out and wrote to Miles that night, enclosing it and demanding an invitation to the blowout he hoped Miles would be hosting if it meant what he thought it did.

He mailed it to the house in Nassau, not knowing Miles's address in Miami. Marcia filed it carefully with the others.

FATHER KENNEDY READ the advertisement in the *Los Angeles Times*. He always studied those columns closely in the extremely forlorn hope that one of his flock might have come into some kind of legacy, however small. They never did. But God moved in very mysterious ways indeed, in his experience, and it was worth keeping an eye open. He wondered what had happened. It looked as if Mr. Dashwood might have died and left Miles some money. Maybe there'd been a reconciliation. Well, that was nice; but Father Kennedy had always felt it very sad that after all his efforts on the boy's behalf, poor Dashwood had received very nearly no thanks at all.

He imagined Miles was sure to see it. Mrs. Kelly certainly would; she was a great one for reading the papers. Strange, she had never answered his letters. She had promised to write, even suggested he take a vacation in Nassau one day. Oh, well, promises were cheap. Father Kennedy was used to the vagaries of human nature. He thought it would do no harm to forward a copy of the paper to Miles. He just might miss it, and that would be a dreadful thing. He sat down that night and wrote a long letter to Mrs. Kelly, enclosing the clipping. He really hoped she would reply; he would like to see her again.

Marcia looked at the envelope with the Los Angeles postmark, guessed its contents, and put it with the others. She was beginning to wonder if she was doing the right thing. Whoever was looking for Miles seemed to want to find him pretty badly.

IN HER HOUSE in East Hampton, Long Island, Mrs. Holden Taylor, Jr., was reading the *New York Times* over breakfast, as she always did before embarking on a hectic day of tennis, lunching, shopping, and menu planning. She skimmed through the law reports—Holden liked her to know what was going on in his world—and was looking idly at the Public Notice column when a name sprang out at her. A name that caught her sharply somewhere in the region of her heart, a name that spelled sunshine and beaches and old cars and smoking grass and glorious, wonderful sex, the kind that Holden simply never quite managed, however hard they both tried to pretend that he did. Miles! Miles Wilburn. Just reading the name, she saw him as suddenly and clearly as if he were standing there, those amazing dark blue eyes, the heart-catching smile, the long blond hair—well, that was probably cut short now—heard his voice, soft and lazy and slow. Miles. She would never forget him, ever. They said you never did forget your first love. They seemed to be right. So what had happened? Had someone died and left Miles some money, and as it was an English solicitor's address in the paper, would it be Hugo Dashwood? It seemed very likely. That was very good of him, when Miles had been so hostile and rude to him.

Oh, God, what would she give to see Miles just once more. Joanna shook herself. She hadn't even thought about him for years—well, not seriously—and now here she was like a bitch in heat just because she'd read his name in the paper. Pull yourself together, Joanna, she said to herself, and get to planning that menu. She was giving an important dinner party on Saturday; she had invited some incredibly high-powered advertising woman that Holden had met somewhere. Just thinking about her made Joanna nervous. Apparently she was brilliant and clever and had her own agency, and she was amazingly beautiful, too. Camilla North, she was called; she was in her mid-forties and looked just about thirty. And she rode to hounds sidesaddle. Oh, God, what on earth could she serve up on the plate of such a paragon?

Joanna covered the table with recipe books and temporarily forgot all about Miles Wilburn.

·30·

DR. MARGARET FRIEDMAN looked at Phaedria across her desk.

"Good morning," she said, her eyes taking in an enormous amount without appearing even to have left her appointment book: the beauty, the pregnancy, the money. Margaret Friedman did not know a Ralph Lauren shirt from a Marks and Spencer one, nor a Cartier ring from a junk job from Fenwick's, but she could nonetheless tell you in an instant where her clients stood on the socioeconomic scale, what kind of school they had been to, which kind of car they drove, whether they lived in town or the country, whether they had children. It was one of the things that made her so good at her job.

"Good morning," said Phaedria. "It's very good of you to see me at such short notice. Thank you."

"Joan said you sounded—well, not entirely happy. I do like to help when I can."

"I'm—well, I'm all right. It's just that—well, I do have a problem."

Margaret drew a notepad toward her. "Let's start with a few details, shall we? Now your full name is—"

"Phaedria Morell."

"And you're—forgive me, but I do read the papers—Julian Morell's widow?" The dark eyes looked at Phaedria, politely noncommittal.

"Yes."

"I'm so sorry. This must be a very difficult time for you."

"Well," said Phaedria, with a rather tight little smile, "it certainly isn't easy."

"And you're pregnant."

"Yes."

"How do you feel?"

"Awful."

"I'm not surprised. Would you like some tea?"

"No, thank you. Do you have any lemons?"

"I do. In hot water?"

"Yes, please."

She ordered Joan rather briskly to bring in some hot water and lemon and then sat back in her chair. "Now then. Where should we begin?"

"About fifteen years ago," said Phaedria.

"I'm sorry?"

Phaedria smiled. "It's all right. I'm sorry. I must be a terrible shock to you. There's nothing wrong with me. At least I don't think so. Not psychiatrically. It's just that—oh, it's such a bizarre story, I don't know where to begin. You may not be able to help at all."

"Let me try."

"About fifteen years ago my husband came to see you."

"Yes, he did. Did he tell you that himself?"

"No. His secretary told me. You see, my husband has left a very complicated will. This is confidential?"

"Yes. Yes, of course."

"Well, we are trying to trace someone. Someone he left an important legacy to. We thought you might be able to help."

"I can't imagine how."

"My husband was rather a complex man. He was not at all straight-forward."

"Perhaps."

"Anyway, his secretary knew he had been seeing you in, I think 1971. We thought—that is, I thought—if you could tell me what he came about, it might throw a bit of light on his life."

"Possibly," Margaret Friedman said carefully.

"I feel so silly," Phaedria said suddenly. "You must think I'm mad."

"On the contrary, I think you're very sane. You should see some of the others, as they say. And I do assure you that no story comes as a surprise to me."

"Let's get down to basics," said Phaedria. "Do you remember why my husband came to see you?"

"I'm not sure. I'd have to look in my notes."

"Could you do that?"

"I could certainly pull his file, but before I commit myself to talking to you very much more, I'll have to know a bit more about you."

"Why?" said Phaedria, her eyes wide with disappointment.

"Well, you seem very stable, and I'm sure you are. But you must realize I might—I'm not saying I necessarily would be—I might be promising to tell you something that would make you very unstable indeed."

"Oh, I'm sure it wasn't anything really ghastly. It couldn't have been. Someone would have known."

"You'd be surprised, Lady Morell, how people don't know about ghastly things. Close their minds to them. Tell themselves they can't be true. Of course I'm not suggesting your husband was a murderer or anything. But I can't give you a blanket promise to tell you whatever it was he came to see me about without knowing you a little better." She smiled. "When's the baby due?"

"November."

"Then we must take care of you. Where are you having it?"

"Saint Mary's, Paddington. The Lindo Wing."

"Very sensible. Now, what I'd like to do is have a chat with you now, learn a little more about you, and then if you can come back in a day or two, I'll have looked at your husband's file, and I can talk to you with a bit more confidence."

"Oh, God," Phaedria said, her voice suddenly shaky. "Look, I can see that you have to be careful, but honestly I am very stable. I don't need counseling; I just want to unravel this mystery. I can't stand it much longer. I don't see why you won't help."

She suddenly burst into tears; Margaret Friedman handed her tissues and watched her sympathetically for a few minutes. Then she said, "You may not need counseling, but you do need help. Why don't you begin at the beginning? I honestly think it'll make you feel better."

When Phaedria had left, an hour later, Dr. Friedman got out the file on Julian Morell. She felt she owed it to herself to check through it. But as she had known, there was no need. She could remember absolutely everything that was in it.

PHAEDRIA WAS FAST asleep when the phone rang.

"Phaedria? It's C.J."

"C.J., it's two in the morning."

"I know. I'm sorry to wake you. But I have some news."

He heard her snap into wakefulness. "What? C.J., what? Where are you?"

"In New York, at the Sutton Place apartment."

"Oh, God, of course you are. I'm sorry. I'd forgotten for a moment. Well, go on, what have you found?"

"Something quite strange. In Julian's desk."

"What? For God's sake, C.J., what?"

"I thought I'd wasted my time at first. Nothing in it remotely interesting. Then I was fiddling with one of the small top drawers—it seemed to be too shallow somehow—and, well, it had a spring back, and there inside it, right at the very back, was a box. A locked document box."

"And?"

"I forced it open and found some pretty odd things inside."

"What sort of odd?"

"A few snapshots of a little boy. No name or anything."

"What does he look like?"

"Fairly standard. Blond hair. Snub nose. Nice smile."

"What else?"

"A card announcing a birth. It's him—Miles. Miles Wilburn. Born 1958. In Santa Monica."

"Oh, God. C.J., who is he? What is all this? Who was this card from?"

"Someone called Dean Wilburn. Saying 'Come and meet him soon.' "

"Does it give an address?"

"No. You know those cards, Phaedria, they're just name, weight, date, time, that sort of thing. Nothing helpful like an address, for us detectives to discover."

"You're a great detective, C.J. You really are. You should take it up for a living. I can't believe all this. But what on earth does it mean? Does it say where he was born, this child?"

"Yeah, Saint John's Hospital, Santa Monica."

"Well, maybe we could track him down through there."

"Maybe."

"Anything else?"

"Yeah, a clipping from a newspaper, an obituary of someone called Lee Wilburn. The usual thing, you know, after an extended illness. Beloved mother of Miles. The service was conducted by a Father Kennedy of Santa Monica."

Phaedria was silent for a minute. "Poor Lee, whoever she was. Poor Miles. What year was that?"

"Um, let's see, 1971."

"So Miles would only have been, what, twelve or thirteen. How sad. What about his father?"

"No mention of him. Not even in the obit."

"Oh, C.J., I don't understand any of this."

"Neither do I. And there's one more thing, a list of graduations from the University of California at Berkeley in 1980 listing Miles Wilburn. He graduated summa cum laude in math. He's obviously not dumb. Whoever he is."

"No more photographs?"

"None. Julian obviously believed in keeping his memorabilia to a minimum. Look, I have to go and see my mother tomorrow, but I'll fly straight back to London the next day. We can talk then and decide what to do next—go to L.A. or whatever. I just had to let you know."

"Of course. Oh, C.J., what on earth do all these people have to do with Julian? It's so mysterious. Oh, God, I don't know whether to be pleased or worried."

"I think you should be pleased. Otherwise I'm wasting an awful lot of time and effort."

She smiled, and he could hear her mood briefly lightening. "All right, I'll be pleased."

"Good night, Phaedria."

"Good night, C.J. Sleep well. And thank you."

Phaedria couldn't go back to sleep. She lay tossing, uncomfortable, agitated, with visions of a small boy with blond hair dancing before her eyes, and the words "beloved mother of Miles" flickering fretfully inside her head.

ROZ LOOKED AROUND the boardroom. Phaedria was at one end of the table, Richard Brookes at the other. Susan, Freddy Branksome, and George Hanover, sales director of the entire group, were sitting side by side with their backs to the window. They all, even Phaedria, had their eyes fixed on her face. She was, in that moment, Susan thought, extraordinarily like her father—determined, utterly in control, fixing their attention on her.

"I want to discuss the pharmaceutical division," she said. "I think we could be missing some valuable opportunities for expansion."

This was Roz's latest game, and it was tactically important in her war against Phaedria. She would fix on some aspect of the company, study it fiercely for days, acquaint herself with every possible detail of its strengths and weaknesses, and then pounce, call a meeting to discuss it, with the least possible warning.

Phaedria was clearly losing confidence now. She would make a statement; Roz would contest it, express a view, demolish it. Richard and Freddy and even Susan, with her determined fondness for Roz, her support for her cause, watched this slaughter with distaste. Roz had the big guns on her side; Phaedria was confronting her with an elegant pistol loaded with blanks.

PHAEDRIA MADE HER way wearily up to the penthouse and let herself in. She drank the iced Perrier Sarah had left for her, ignored the prawn salad, and lay down on the bed in the small room off the main office. She wondered how much longer she could go on, how much more public humiliation she could take, how many more blows at her self-esteem she would have to endure.

And what was she doing it for? C.J. had been right: she could easily give in, let Roz have the company, just go away somewhere and enjoy herself, have her baby in peace, bring it up somewhere far removed from this nightmare of intrigue and politicking and self-doubt.

It was a monstrous legacy and one that had very little to offer her. And just where was that bloody Miles Wilburn? Was she ever going to find out what his part was in the nightmare? And if she did, then what? What good did she think he could do her? How was she to get hold of his two percent anyway? Would she have to marry him? Buy him? How could you have done this to me, Julian Morell? she thought. Why did you expose me to this pain, this humiliation?

How Julian must have despised her. He certainly couldn't have loved her. Bastard! She found herself thinking in these terms more and more often these days. If he walked in here now, she thought, I'd kill him! Then the irony of that struck her, and she smiled suddenly; she relaxed on the bed. Deep within her the child stirred, the strange sweet fluttering she waited to feel day by day, entranced by its increasing strength and urgency; it made the whole thing somehow bearable, worthwhile, important.

"We'll do it," she said aloud, looking down at the considerable hump now situated where her flat stomach had been, stroking it tenderly, smiling at it. "We'll do it. For your daddy's sake. No, not for your daddy's sake—forget I said that. For your mother's. I'm the one who counts around here. Don't you forget it." She closed her eyes; she felt her head slowly skimming into the lack of coherent thought that meant sleep was imminent. She allowed her mind to wander; she thought about the little boy with blond hair, the woman, the beloved mother. Poor Lee, she thought drowsily, poor Lee. Dying so young. In 1971. The words formed a refrain in her head: Dying so young in '71, dying so young in '71.

And then she sat up suddenly alert, her heart thudding, her hands damp. In 1971. Lee had died in 1971. The year Sarah had said Julian was so depressed. When he had begun to go to Dr. Friedman.

She turned on the bed, reached for the phone, dialed Dr. Friedman's number feverishly, her mind a tumult.

"Could I speak to Dr. Friedman, please? This is Lady Morell. Yes, it's very, very urgent. Very urgent indeed."

·31·

"NASSAU?" SAID ROZ. "NASSAU? ARE YOU sure?"

Andrew Blackworth was used to being patient. "Yes," he said. "I'm quite sure, Nassau is where Bill Wilburn last saw his nephew."

"Well, go to Nassau, of course," Roz said impatiently. "I don't care in the least how expensive it is. You seem to be doing quite well. Do you have anything further in the way of information?"

"Nothing at all," he said. "But I don't see that as an insurmountable obstacle."

"No, I would hope not. Yes, do go on down there, Mr. Blackworth. At least for a few days. Keep in touch, though, won't you? I don't want you to disappear utterly."

C.J. WAS JUST beginning to think about making his excuses for leaving Oyster Bay and his mother earlier than he had promised when he remembered that Phaedria had asked him to talk to Camilla before he left New York. He sighed. He didn't particularly relish the thought, but he could see that he was probably the best person to talk to her. There were no violent emotions raging in his breast against her, or in hers against him; they had had a civilized working relationship. She had been perfectly courteous and composed with him at the reading of the will; he viewed her a great deal more benignly than did a lot of other people in the family.

He walked through into the hall and dialed the number of her agency. Miss North was out, they said, taking a late lunch. Could she call him back in a half hour?

Certainly, C.J. said. He would be in all afternoon. The secretary sounded shocked at any suggestion that Camilla would fail to call within the half hour, and took his number. Almost exactly thirty minutes later the phone rang.

"C.J.? Hello. This is Camilla North. You called me."

"I did. How are you, Camilla?"

"Extremely well, thank you. C.J., I'm glad you called. I can imagine what it's about, or I think I can, and I do actually have some news for you. I didn't know quite what to do with it. That is, I didn't know who to call. Could we meet for a drink? Perhaps the Palm Court at the Plaza?"

"Sure," he said, intrigued.

CAMILLA WAS WAITING for him when he got there. She really was a lovely woman, he thought, studying her before she had seen him; nobody would ever think she was forty-eight. No wonder old Julian had been so besotted with her. She was dressed in a loose white silk dress with wide shoulders and sleeves cut off sharply at the elbows. She was tanned, and her long legs were bare. Her red-gold hair was clipped back from her face, and she wore a heavy gold chain and matching bracelet from Chanel. She looked classically, sleekly beautiful. C.J. went up to her and held out his hand.

"C.J. How formal!" She kissed his cheek. "It's nice to see you. I was sorry to hear about you and Roz."

"Yes, well, thank you," he said. "It's never easy, is it?"

"Well, of course," she said, very cool, very composed. "I have never been married, and therefore never divorced, but I have been through a breakup or two."

She smiled at him, and he noticed for the first time the lines of strain by her mouth and a shadow in her eyes. It must have been very hard on her, Julian's death, indeed the whole ghastly business. No sympathy, and plenty of pain.

"Yes," he said, gently commiserating, "I know. What would you like to drink?"

"A Bloody Mary, I think. To go with my day."

"How is the agency? And what are you doing in this godawful place in August?"

"Working. I have a lot going on. And you?"

"Oh, same kind of thing."

"I heard you'd left the company."

"I have. I'm researching a book."

"C.J.! How nice. What on?"

"London," he said, and then seeing her puzzled eyes: "I'm here visiting my mother."

"Ah," she said, "I see."

"So what news do you have for me, Camilla?"

"I think I have a lead for you." She told him she had been to a dinner party with her new lawyer, Holden Taylor, and his wife, Joanna. The talk had turned to college days, and Joanna was reminiscing about her first boyfriend, whose name was Miles Wilburn.

What had reminded her of him had been seeing an advertisement in the *New York Times*.

"Hmm, that is very intriguing. Where does your friend Joanna live?"

"On Long Island."

"Camilla, you're great. This news could be a real breakthrough."

He looked at her and smiled, and she thought how extraordinarily nice he was, quite the nicest person in that whole ghastly clan; maybe it had something to do with his nationality. She was also struck for the first time by how attractive he was. He did not have exactly striking looks, but they were the kind she liked and understood: gentle, well bred, understated. He was always so well dressed, too, and his manners were perfect; Camilla settled deeper into her chair and prepared herself to enjoy the evening ahead more than she had expected.

"You see, I came to New York for another reason as well," he explained. "I find the whole business of Julian's will so intriguing that I decided to do a little investigating."

"Ah," she said. "Tell me what you've found so far."

"Well, I found some stuff in Julian's desk that points to L.A. Camilla, did he go to California a lot when you first knew him?"

There was humor in her eyes. "Who could ever guess where Julian was? But no, not so far as I can remember. He always resisted the idea of having a store there, or a hotel. He said he didn't like the place."

"Intriguing."

"Yes. Well, he was an intriguing man, whatever his faults."

"Camilla, do you remember Julian getting any calls from someone called Lee Wilburn?"

"No. No, I don't. But then he got an awful lot of calls." She looked at him and smiled suddenly. "He was very clever at covering his tracks. I doubt if he'd have had anyone call him at home."

"No, but maybe in an emergency?"

"Maybe. But it's all so long ago, isn't it? I mean it's hopeless trying to pick up trails at this distance."

"I guess so. Although we don't seem to be doing too badly."

"No, you don't. What will you do now?"

"I think, if you don't mind, I might talk to this Joanna Taylor on Long Island. Can you give me her number?"

"Of course."

"This is very nice of you, Camilla. I don't really see why you should help any of us."

She shrugged. "I felt very bad about my being in the Sutton Place apartment when Phaedria walked in. I didn't behave very well. I'd like to make amends."

"Well, you're very generous. Can I show the family's appreciation by buying you dinner?"

She looked at him consideringly. "That is a very attractive idea, C.J. Thank you."

They had a pleasant and relaxed dinner and, both being lonely, frustrated, and in need of some harmless diversion, ended the evening, to their mutual surprise and immense pleasure, between Camilla's muslin sheets.

C.J. WENT TO see Joanna the next morning. He liked her immediately. She was pretty and sharp and funny, and she was delighted to talk about Miles.

She had obviously been seriously in love with him; she still talked of him with a kind of wistful intimacy. He had been her best friend, she said, as well as her boyfriend. She had met him on the beach at Malibu in 1975. "Ten years ago, goodness, aren't we all getting old."

He had been living with his grandmother, a nice old lady named Mrs. Dorothy Kelly, and he had been at Santa Monica High School. "Then Mr. Dashwood came along and sent him off to Berkeley. Miles was very smart; he did really well."

"Who was Mr. Dashwood?"

"I don't really know," Joanna said. "He was a hazy figure. I only met him very briefly once. He hardly ever came to see Miles. But he was a friend of the family, and he was rich, I guess. Anyway, he did a lot for Miles. Miles never really liked him, though, I don't know why."

"He should have," said C.J., "if Dashwood put him through college. That isn't cheap."

"I know. Anyway, Miles was hurt because Mr. Dashwood wouldn't give him a job in his company. That was when he went off and became a beach bum. Miles, I mean, not Mr. Dashwood. And Miles said he'd never see him or speak to him again."

C.J. was beginning to dislike Miles.

"When did you last see him?"

"Oh," she said, her face shadowy, "I guess it was about 1981. Yes, that would have been it. I tried—we all did—to change Miles's mind, to make him get a job, do something with his degree, do something useful. He was intelligent and very attractive—presentable, you know —but he just wouldn't. He was so angry and kind of strange suddenly. He just went off and more or less dropped out of our lives. I used to go and see him and his grandmother sometimes in the evening, but somehow I felt he didn't want me anymore either. So I gave up, too."

"Do you have a picture of him?" asked C.J., his heart beating suddenly fast.

"Well," she said, looking suddenly guilty. "Yes, I do. I'll go and get it."

She came back with a faded color snapshot. "It's old. I don't suppose he looks like this now. But anyway, there you are. I got rid of all the others."

A face smiled at C.J. It was an indisputably nice face. A very good-looking face, probably, he thought, if you could see it properly. The boy had long blond hair, blue eyes, and a ravishing smile. He was wearing a white T-shirt; he looked happy, relaxed, very California, and he had signed the picture, "Jo, from Miles, all my love."

"I can't—"

"No," she said, "I'm sorry. I would rather you didn't take it. It's kind of personal."

"Of course."

"What are you going to do?" she said.

"What would you suggest?" he asked. "Do you have any idea where he might be?"

"None. But you could look in L.A. He might still be there. On the beach. Try his grandmother. I can give you her address. Oh, and I'll tell you who else you could talk to. Father Kennedy in Santa Monica. He and Mrs. Kelly were great buddies. Miles used to say she was his temptress." She laughed. "If only you could have seen her. But she was so good to Miles. And he did love her. He really really did."

"And you have no idea where we could find this Mr. Dashwood?"

"Honestly, no. I mean, he could be anywhere. England. New York. Anywhere."

"Why England? Why do you say that?"

"Because he was English," she said. "I thought I'd told you that."

"ALL RIGHT," MARGARET Friedman said. "Ask me some questions."

Phaedria leaned forward eagerly. "When my husband came to see you, was he very unhappy?"

"Fairly. Certainly not happy."

"No, well, silly question I suppose. Was he—well, had he lost someone he was very fond of? Had someone died?"

"Yes."

"A woman?"

"Yes."

Phaedria was silent for a while. "Was she his mistress, do you think?"

"I think she could have been."

"Was he still in love with her when she died?"

"In a way, perhaps. But, he was more sad than heartbroken. I think she was much more of a dear friend. I got the impression your husband was not rich in close friends."

"No," Phaedria said. "I'm afraid that's right." She looked at Margaret Friedman. "Did he talk much about a little boy?"

"Not a great deal. This lady did have a little boy. And your husband was concerned about him."

"What about her husband? Do you know anything about him?"

"Yes, he had also died. Earlier. A year or two, I think."

"I suppose that would explain why Julian was so concerned about the little boy. He was an orphan."

"Indeed."

Phaedria looked at her and sighed. "I feel you're keeping an awful lot from me."

"Why should I do that?"

"You've told me why. You said you had to know more about me before you could tell me anything much."

"I think I've told you a lot. I'm keeping my side of the bargain quite well. Let's talk a bit more about you now. How are you feeling?"

"All right. Very tired. But less sick."

"I meant emotionally."

"Pretty bad. I miss Julian terribly, of course."

"Of course. Do you feel anything besides sadness?"

"Yes," Phaedria said, suddenly meeting Margaret Friedman's detachedly interested eyes. "I feel angry. Absolutely furious. I don't see how he could possibly have done this to me. Half the time I'm grieving because I loved him, and the other half I'm raging because I hated him. It's awful."

"It's healthy."

"Is it?"

"Well, don't you think so? If he were still alive, you'd be furious. Why should his being dead make a difference?"

"I hadn't thought of it like that," Phaedria said. "But it does, because it's so much worse. I can't talk to him, find out why he did it, why he hated me so much."

"I'm sure he didn't hate you. Quite sure. But if you really thought, hard and constructively, you might find a few clues as to why he decided to do it."

"I have thought. I've thought and thought. I can't come up with anything except that he wanted to make me miserable."

"Let me help you think. We may come up with something better than that. All right?"

"All right."

PHAEDRIA'S DRIVER WAS waiting outside with the car when she came out, drained, exhausted, but strangely more peaceful.

"Dover Street, Lady Morell?"

"I suppose so," she said and sighed, and then on an impulse: "No, Pete, take me to First Street. I'd like to see Mrs. Morell. It's only twelve o'clock, she's sure to be there."

"Certainly."

"And Pete, let's stop off at Harrods and get her some flowers."

"Very good, Lady Morell."

She sank back in the car, her mind blank, vaguely anxious that she should be in the office, but equally sure that she would be unable to cope with its demands for an hour or two. It would be nice to see Letitia; she was always so comforting, so affectionate, such fun. It would be nice to talk over the past twenty-four hours with her, but she couldn't; it would be unfair, too much for her to cope with. She had survived Julian's death surprisingly well, but she had aged a lot just the same, and the ongoing stress of the mystery was taking its toll. She really was the pivot of the family, Phaedria thought; what would they all do without her? Even Roz talked to Letitia from time to time, and loved her. She managed to transcend all the rivalries, all the passions, all the jealousies and in-fighting and yet without ever being pious or sanctimonious, indeed she managed to defuse it all, make it seem rather amusing and silly. It would be nice to see her now, nice just to talk to her. She wondered if she should have warned her she was coming, but no, she always encouraged people to just drop in, and it was a good time, just before lunch, she wasn't resting or anything, and she wouldn't have gone out.

Pete pulled up outside the house. "Shall I wait, Lady Morell?"

"Yes, please, Pete. I'll only be a short while, and we may be able to give Mrs. Morell a lift somewhere as well."

She scooped the white lilies she had bought into her arms, walked up the steps to the front door, and knocked three times very briskly. The door opened at once and Phaedria found herself looking up into the mournful face of Michael Browning.

Her first instinct was to bolt. Nobody, except perhaps Dr. Friedman, could have told her why, but it was extremely strong. It was also ridiculous. She stood there looking at him; he looked back at her in silence.

She was wearing a brilliant sea-blue silk dress that slithered gracefully over her burgeoning stomach and stopped at the knees; her long legs were bare, and she wore low-heeled blue pumps that matched her dress. Her wild hair was tied back in a blue silk bow. With the lilies in her arms and the distress in her eyes, she looked exactly like a painting by Burne-Jones.

Michael Browning reached out and in an instinctive desire to comfort, to calm her, touched her cheek. Phaedria drew back as if she had been stung.

"Hey," he said, "don't look so frightened. I won't bite you. Come in. How's the unfriendly baby? Grown, I see."

"Yes. Sorry—that is, well, I won't stay, not if you're here. Just give Letitia these. I'll be back another time."

"Now, look," he said, his eyes exploring her face amusedly, "I don't know what I've done to frighten you so much, but I promise I'll stop now. Don't be silly, of course you'll stay. I'm here for a drink, and then I'm taking Letitia out to lunch. Why don't you join us?"

"Oh, no," said Phaedria, sufficiently recovered from her shock to smile, almost to laugh. "Thank you, but no. Not in public, not with you."

"Well, thank you for the compliment. Maybe in private, then," he said, returning the smile. "I don't mind."

Letitia suddenly appeared in the hall.

"Phaedria, how lovely. Come on in, darling, and sit down. Are those for me? Thank you. I have a new maid, you know—Nancy finally decided to retire—and she's hopeless with flowers. I'll do them myself. Now then, what will you have? A drink?"

"No, thank you," Phaedria said, "and I won't stay. You're busy."

"Nonsense. We have all the time in the world, don't we, Michael? He's taking me to lunch at Langan's, so we can get to know each other better. Roz brought him over and introduced him to me last night, and I felt it couldn't be left at that. After all, he's almost part of the family and he doesn't know anything about me at all. Now, don't be ridiculous, Phaedria. Come along in and sit down. You look exhausted."

"I'm all right. Yes, could I have a cup of hot water with some lemon in it? And some sugar."

"Ah," Michael said, beaming at her delightedly. "I knew the lemon would help. How much longer is it to term now?"

"Just over two and a half months."

"You look thin," he said critically. "Are you eating all the right things? Taking vitamins? Getting enough fresh air?"

"I certainly am," Phaedria said, determinedly cheerful. "Never has a pregnant lady been so carefully looked after."

"I somehow doubt that," he said gently, suddenly serious.

Phaedria, meeting the dark eyes, felt all at once confused, disturbed. "Well, you're wrong," she said. "I go to classes—"

"Not those dreadful relaxation classes!" said Letitia. "Not natural childbirth again, Phaedria, please!"

"Again?" Michael said. "This is not your first baby?"

"Oh, this is," said Letitia briskly. "But surely Roz must have told you about her experiences in childbirth? No? My God, that poor child, she got in the grips of an extremely expensive lunatic who didn't seem to believe in anything more powerful in the way of pain relief than a little light massage. I'm pleased to say she gave as good as she got. Even in childbirth, it seems, Roz is a formidable woman."

"I have to tell you I believe it," said Michael. "I haven't heard any of this, though. What did she do?"

"Kicked him very hard a few times. Swore so loudly and violently that the other women complained. Bit poor C.J. It was a very—what shall we say?—active birth."

"Yeah, well, I don't know about all that," Michael said. "In New York they still more or less knock you out."

"Much better," Letitia said.

"Yeah, but I think it's a good idea if the father can be there. If he possibly can. It's kind of good for him, I guess, even if it doesn't do the mother any good."

There was a strange sound from Phaedria, halfway between a sigh and a sob; she was looking out of the window, fighting back the tears. Michael and Letitia looked at her, stricken.

"Oh, my God, what a stupid goddam thing to say!" Michael jumped up, sat beside her, and put his arms around her. "Phaedria, I'm sorry. Please forgive me. Here, look, have a good cry. Go on, don't fight it. Take my handkerchief, take two. I always have plenty to spare so I can lose them. Go on, just cry."

And she did, she sobbed for five minutes or so, on and on, like a child, all the stress of work, the anxiety of her pregnancy, the trauma of her morning with Dr. Friedman, breaking in her heart in a waterfall of grief. Michael sat holding her, mopping what he could see of her face with his handkerchief. When she had finally stopped, she looked up at him with half a crumpled, wounded smile and said, "I'm so sorry. Look at your shirt."

"You don't have to worry about this shirt," he said. "It's amazingly absorbent. I always wear it just on the off chance that some lady may burst into tears on it. There, now, you see? It's drying off already. Now take this handkerchief and blow your nose. That's better."

She blew her nose, and then as unselfconsciously as he, sat there for a while with her head on his shoulder, resting herself and her emotions.

"I'm so sorry," she said after a while. "Now I've spoiled your fun lunch."

"Nonsense," said Letitia, "but I really don't think we can leave you now. I suggest, Michael, that you go down the road to Harrods and buy us a picnic. I'll cancel the table at Langan's. We can make sure Phaedria is getting her proper diet and then send her home in the car with Pete."

"Fine. I'll go right away. Phaedria, is there anything you don't like?"

"Everything."

"I'll find something you do like. It'll be a challenge."

When he had gone Phaedria looked at Letitia and smiled shakily. "He's so nice," she said. "Much too nice for Roz."

"Indeed." Letitia looked at her ravaged face and decided this was no time to give her even the mildest hint of what she had foreseen, with hideous clarity, as she watched Michael holding Phaedria in his arms on the sofa.

TWO WEEKS LATER Phaedria flew to L.A. in search of Father Kennedy. C.J. was almost hysterical with anxiety at the thought of her going on her own. He said he would go with her, but Phaedria pointed out with perfect truth that Roz would be so angry if she found out that she would probably come after them, and she would also guess the reason for their trip. "I can concoct a story about checking out the store or doing some buying or just taking a vacation. I deserve one, for God's sake. She'll never know."

"But, Phaedria, you're seven months pregnant. You're mad; you'll make yourself ill. You'll have a miscarriage."

C.J. had watched her go through passport control with a sense of deep foreboding.

SHE ASKED THE Bel Air Hotel for a car; she wanted some freedom to explore. They provided her with a Mercedes SE convertible, and she set off after breakfast with the top down and a set of very good maps.

She had found Father Kennedy working in a small office with just space for a shaky desk and chair. He had a host of papers spread in front of him, and he was shaking an extremely old and cumbersome-looking adding machine.

"That machine doesn't look too terribly healthy," Phaedria said as she came in.

"It's not. Like me, it has seen far better days. What can I do for you?"

"I hope you'll be able to help me find someone."

"And who might that be?"

Phaedria suddenly felt rather frightened and a little faint. "May I sit down?"

"Oh, now, what am I thinking of? Of course you must sit down. Come along with me, and we'll find you a chair."

She followed him as he took a decrepit chair outside and set it in the shade. A pair of cats sat looking at Phaedria interestedly as she sank down into it. Father Kennedy settled himself beside her on a three-legged stool.

She looked at him—a plump, white-haired old man with all the patience and candor on his face that only a long life given to the ungrateful and undeserving could provide—and felt she was in safe hands.

He looked at her for a while in silence, and then said, easing her into the conversation, "I expect it's Miles you've come about?"

Yes, she said, yes, it was. She needed to know about him, not just where he was, but who he was, how well Father Kennedy had known him, and whether she was wise to pursue him across half the world. She explained who she was and why she wanted to find him; she felt it was the only fair basis from which to ask him what she needed to know.

Father Kennedy talked to her with great tenderness and care. He answered only her questions; he gave her no more information than she asked for, and even then he tempered his words with great thoughtfulness, rewriting history just a little in the telling to make the story easier for her to hear.

Yes, he had known Miles since he was a tiny little boy, and his parents too. Nice people they had been, good and loving parents, a happy family.

Dean had died of an overdose of sleeping pills when Miles was only about ten or eleven. The verdict had been suicide, but he had been such a calm and a cheerful man that it seemed unlikely. There was certainly a reasonable possibility that he had been drinking and had taken too many pills in his confusion.

And Lee—now, that had been a terrible thing. Cancer she had died of, and only a young woman, in her early forties, but her death had been very peaceful; he had been there with her when she died. His only sorrow had been that Miles had not been there. People said children should have no part of dying or death, but he thought it was important for them to see that there was nothing to be frightened of and to know it as the part of life that it was.

The boy had been all right at first, very sad of course, but he had been doing well at school, and he had been a wonderful athlete. Later on, though, he had stopped working, wasted his talent, and fooled around a bit. That was when his grandmother had moved out to Malibu with him.

And that had been when he met the girl, a sweet little thing, Joanna, and such a nice family, very well off and so on, but with no silly ideas. They had been so good to Miles. And of course it had been a wonderful thing when he had been able to go to Berkeley and do so well there.

Yes, indeed, that had been when Mr. Hugo Dashwood stepped in and paid the boy's tuition. Now, wasn't that a fine gesture for a man to make? He had been a gentleman, Mr. Dashwood had, and it was the greatest pity that Miles had fallen out with him.

No, he had no idea where Mr. Dashwood was now. He had never seen very much of him. Indeed he had seldom visited Miles in those later years, and the few meetings that took place were not happy. He had had an idea that Mr. Dashwood lived in New York, although he was English, and certainly the address that Mrs. Kelly had had was not in England. Indeed he had not heard of him for some time.

He believed Miles had been very angry that Mr. Dashwood had not offered him a job in his company. He had felt in some way that it was his due. Of course it was not, and it was very foolish of Miles to think that way, but the fact remained that if it had been possible, it would have made the greatest difference to Miles and his life. But then, on the other hand, Mr. Dashwood had been so good to Miles, so generous, it was hardly fair to expect any more.

What had Mr. Dashwood been like? Oh, a very typical Englishman, Father Kennedy would have said, a fine-looking man, very tall and slim, and what he would always have imagined an upper-class Englishman would be like, but Lee had told him that Hugo had gone to neighborhood schools and made his way in the world himself. No, he was afraid he didn't have any photographs of Hugo. He had had a wife, Lee had told him, with an old-fashioned name. Alice, that was it, and two or three children, boys if he remembered rightly. He had been a good friend to Lee as well as to Miles and done a lot for her after her husband had died.

The house in Malibu was still empty, Father Kennedy said, although it was up for sale; if she wanted to go and have a look there, it would do no harm; it was only half an hour's drive away.

And where was Miles now? Well, he supposed there was no harm in telling her the address, although he had written there himself and not had an answer, so it was possible that they had moved on. He had been sad to lose them, Miles and Mrs. Kelly. He hoped they were well. If she went out to Malibu one of the neighbors might have a more recent address.

"Now, I wouldn't go rushing off to Nassau if I were you," he said, looking at her with concern in his faded blue eyes. "I really don't know that they are still there, and it would do you no good in your condition. Write to this address, child, and see what comes of it. Mrs. Kelly's friend is called Marcia Galbraith. That is the lady they were staying with. You may have more luck than I."

"I probably will," said Phaedria, standing up and smiling down at him. "Thank you, Father. You have been so very kind. I can't tell you how grateful I am. How can I thank you?"

"Oh, it was nothing," he said, smiling back at her. "A small donation to the refuge would be wonderful, though."

Phaedria thrust a hundred dollars into his hand. "Take this for now. When I get home to England, I will see that a trust fund is set up for you, supplying you with a regular income."

Father Kennedy believed her. She was a sweet, pretty child, and he wished her nothing but well. But he watched her drive away with a certain foreboding. He hoped she wasn't going to learn anything about Miles that would cause her distress.

LATEGO CANYON, FATHER Kennedy had said. Make a right just after Pepperdine University. Here it was. Phaedria swung in, drove cautiously up the winding dusty road. She had to stop twice just to drink in the view: the interweaving hills, the sea, the endless range of headlands. It caught hold of her heart; she wanted to stay forever.

She drove on, about three or four miles. "Then the road will fork," the priest had said. "Take the left fork. Two miles on, there is a white house. That's the one."

And there it was, the white house, built cleverly on three levels into the hill. There was a parking space in front of a garage. She pulled in and parked. Then she got out and looked at the house. It was definitely empty.

Phaedria wandered around it, up and down the steps, peering in through the windows. It was desolate, dusty, still. The furniture was covered in sheets, but she could tell that it was modern furniture, neat, soulless. No clues.

Everything was locked. Every door, every window. She tried the garage. That was locked, too. She had just sat down on the grass to rest for a while and try to think what she wanted to do next when she heard a voice.

"Can I help you?"

Phaedria jumped. A man stood on the grass, smiling at her; friendly, helpful.

"Sorry, I didn't mean to startle you. We live next door. These folks moved years ago. Never sold the house, though. Are you looking for them or looking to buy the house?"

"I'm looking for Miles and Mrs. Kelly," she said. "Do you know where they've gone?"

"Can't rightly say," the man said. "Mrs. Kelly kept pretty much to herself, and Miles was no good. We didn't have much to do with them."

"I see." Phaedria was silent. "Well, thank you anyway. I thought I might find a clue or something, but everything's locked."

"Did you try the shed down there?" The man pointed to a hut on the lower lawn. "That might be worth a try. They left in a mighty big hurry. They didn't take hardly anything with them at all."

"I'll try," said Phaedria. "Thank you."

She clambered down to the lower lawn and pushed cautiously at the shed door. At first she thought that was locked, too, but she gave a second, harder push and it yielded.

Her heart thumping violently, she went in.

It had obviously been Miles's shed; in it was his skateboard, an old surfboard, a bike, some roller skates. She looked at them, mildly charmed by the personality that was emerging. But there were no clues to his whereabouts.

Then she saw the satchel, an old bookbag, really, stuffed into a corner. Phaedria looked at it for a long time, then cautiously, as if she might be burned, reached out and picked it up. It was dusty, covered with insects. She shook it, took it outside, and sat down again on the grass.

The bag was full of letters. Letters from girls at school, all with patently big crushes on Miles, letters from Granny Kelly written on his birthdays, all urging him to work hard and do better at school right in the same breath as wishing him happy birthday; heartbreaking letters from Lee, written when she was in the hospital, telling him how much she loved him, how she trusted him, how she wanted him to be good.

And then a last few, stuffed right to the bottom of the satchel—typewritten letters from Hugo Dashwood. One was very old and faded, dated 1971, thanking Father Kennedy for his kindness to Lee before her death; another dated two years later, saying how pleased he was to hear Miles had made the swimming team, but he hoped he would still go on working hard at school as well; and finally three more recent, undated, all rather admonitory in tone, telling him that he should stop fooling around on the beach and get himself a job, that he was fortunate to have such a good education, that he owed it to his parents' memory as well as to his grandmother and indeed to Hugo himself to show what he could do.

Phaedria read them in silence, wondering at them, at the heat of emotion so obviously contained in them, at the proprietary tone. Whoever Hugo Dashwood was, he had felt very strongly about Miles. And moreover he could type. Odd, that. Not many men typed letters. Well, if the signature was anything to go by, it was just as well. It was virtually illegible, just a scrawled "Hugo"—if she hadn't known the name, been looking out for it, she would not have been able to make it out at all.

Phaedria sat looking at the letters for a long time, aware that they were engaging her attention on some quite different level. And then she became aware that her brain was focusing very strongly on that signature and that her heart was suddenly thundering and that the sun seemed suddenly almost unbearably bright. A darkness came over her briefly, a frightening, rushing, hot darkness. She closed her eyes, swallowed, put out a hand to steady herself. The entire earth seemed to heave beneath her.

Then she opened her eyes, took a deep breath. "Don't be absurd," she said aloud. "It isn't. It couldn't be."

She stood up. She felt shaky, weak. She took the satchel and climbed very slowly back up to the car and sat in it for a while. The baby, still all day, suddenly woke up and started moving energetically inside her; it had less room now, the movements were different, stronger, but more forceful somehow, more controlled.

The normality of it made her feel better, hauled her back into the present.

"Let's go home," she said to her baby, to Julian's child. "Let's go home and have a rest."

She started the car and drove very, very slowly down the hill. It took her a long time to summon sufficient courage to drive onto the teeming highway, but she finally managed it. Then she headed back into Los Angeles.

Tomorrow she would go and see Father Kennedy again. Ask him

some more about Hugo Dashwood, but now she just had to get back and lie down. A strange taut pain was ebbing and flowing at the base of her back, and her head throbbed. She was terribly frightened.

AFTERWARD ALL PHAEDRIA could remember of that night was bright lights. Bright lights coming toward her from other cars: the bright welcome lights of the hotel, there at last to receive her after the nightmare drive of fear and pain; the bright brilliant light as the doctor summoned by the anxious hotel manager looked into her eyes and then, as gently, as carefully as he could, said he had to move her to the hospital, that her baby was being born; the fearfully bright lights in the hospital corridors as she was rushed through on a gurney, silent, stoical through her terror; the piercing white light of the delivery room as she was taken in, moved onto the bed, her legs put in stirrups, her pulse, the baby's heartbeat, taken feverishly, anxiously, her own pain set aside, taken no account of, not through disregard or callousness but out of urgency, necessity. The light came and went then. Sometimes it was dark, almost peaceful, but then again and again she kept surfacing into the room, the pain, the brightness. You're doing well, they kept saying. Not long now, hang on, hang on. Now rest, relax, breathe deeply, and she would start to sink, and then, there it was again, the awful wrenching tearing in the center of herself, so fierce, so violent she could not see how her body could survive it.

And then at last, quite quickly they told her afterward, not more than an hour after she had arrived, the great primeval urge to push, to go into the pain, to let it carry her forward, onward, to endure it somehow, anyhow, because through it, at the end of it—there, now, Yes, she heard it—was the cry, the triumph, the new life, the love. Love such as she had never imagined, never even begun to know, a great invasion of her every sense, love at first sight and sound and touch and smell. And they placed her daughter in her arms, a tiny—too tiny—scrap of life, a great mass of dark hair and surprisingly wide dark eyes, just for a moment, just so that she would know that this was what for the rest of her life she would fight for and give to and be concerned about, over and above everything else she ever knew.

Then they took her away again. She was two months early, they said; she must go quickly to the special care unit, to an incubator, to be cared for, to be stabilized. Phaedria wept, sobbed, tried to climb off her bed and follow them, but the doctor said no, she could not go, that the child would very probably be all right, that caring for preemies these days was a most advanced science, that seven months was considered almost full term, that she must not worry, but should try to rest. And then at last they moved her away from the brightness into a quiet, dim, peaceful room, and Phaedria, soothed by the assurances, exhausted, triumphant, fell asleep.

IN THE MORNING the news was good. The baby was lively, hungry, breathing well. Phaedria said she was to be called Julia, and ate an enormous breakfast. Later they took her down in a wheelchair to the preemie unit, and she sat and gazed enraptured at the tiny wonder she had created, she and Julian, as she moved and stretched and curled up into her prenatal shape again; sneezed, clenched and unclenched her hands, kicked her tiny legs. They let Phaedria put her hand into the incubator and touch her, feel her soft, silky skin. She put her finger in the tiny fist; Julia took it, gripped it, hung on. Phaedria smiled triumphantly: the baby was strong.

Two days later she was not doing so well; she had developed a respiratory infection. "Nearly all premature babies do this," said the doctor, trying to soothe her out of her wide-eyed terror. "She's strong. Try not to worry; she should pull through."

Twenty-four hours later she was still holding her own, but plainly was distressed; she was restless, feverish, she wouldn't take the breast milk Phaedria was expressing for her and the nurses were trying to give her.

Phaedria sat and watched her for almost thirty-six hours, scarcely moving, hardly sleeping; she was afraid to close her eyes lest she should open them and see the baby still, dead, gone. While she looked at her, she felt she could keep her safe. In the end, the doctor led her away, saying she would collapse if she stayed any longer, that she could do nothing for Julia, that she must rest. He put her to bed and sat with her, trying to reassure her; as soon as he had gone she climbed out of the bed again and dragged her poor, sore, weary body down the corridor, back to Julia's side.

"Don't leave me," she kept whispering urgently, fearfully, to the fragile, brave little piece of humanity. "Stay with me. I need you. I can't lose you, too."

Toward the end of that night she fell asleep and awoke suddenly to see the tiny body still, lifeless. She opened her mouth and screamed endlessly.

A nurse came running to her, took hold of her, and shook her. "Stop it, stop it," she said, frightened herself. "You must be quiet."

"I can't, I can't," she said, tears of fright rolling down her face. "My baby's dead."

But no, they said, no, she is not dead; she's better. Look, she's peaceful, sleeping. She's going to be all right.

And even then she would not leave. She stayed, exhausted, just watching and looking and loving the baby until another day had passed, and then finally, seeing her pink, kicking, healthy, however tiny, she trusted them and agreed to leave her for a while and go to bed.

PHAEDRIA DID NOT recover as quickly as she should have. She stayed in the hospital for another week, and then, because they said Julia could not leave for two weeks more, maybe three, she moved back into her bungalow at the Bel Air, driving in every morning to sit with the baby, feed her, hold her when she was allowed, and coming home in the evening to rest and recover.

It was a strangely happy, almost surreal time. She loved best—guiltily, because she was not with her baby—the evenings, when she would sit on her patio, utterly at peace, drinking in the scents of the flowers, watching the swans, hearing the conversation, the laughter, the music drifting quietly from the main body of the hotel, concerned briefly only for herself, and rediscovering the sensation of happiness.

There had been endless excitement, of course, when they had heard in England what had happened. Phone calls and letters and great banks and baskets and bowls of flowers arrived, and boxes extravagantly gift-wrapped in Beverly Hills, containing presents for Julia, tiny dresses, shawls, bonnets, coats, and enormous, ridiculous soft toys, golden teddy bears and great pink bunnies, three, four, five times larger than their small owner. Eliza flew over to see her, bringing a minute white silk dress and matching coat from the White House, a cobweb-fine hand-crocheted shawl from Letitia, and a tiny gold locket set with sapphires that Letitia's grandmother, the Dowager Lady Farnsworth, had worn in her own cradle and bequeathed to Letitia in her will. David Sassoon came to visit and gave her a Hockney print of Los Angeles: "Clever girl. What better place could you possibly have chosen to have a baby?"

Susan came, greatly to Phaedria's surprise and pleasure, a little reserved but friendly just the same, bringing boxes of cookies and chocolates and strawberries. "I do remember how marvelous it is to be hungry again, and you must need little doggy bags to take to the hospital."

Phaedria's father, Augustus Blenheim, came, jerked into reality by concern and love.

C.J. came, with an exquisite engraving by Frith of a baby. C.J. looked anxious and concerned, but with a hint of "I told you so" in his eyes and his voice. "And I'm sure it could all have waited, there was no point tearing out here. Roz has made no progress at all, as far as I know."

Phaedria, still nursing her quiet fear, unable to confront it, to recognize it as real, had allowed the night of pain and the days of terror that had followed in its wake to blank it out. She did not even tell C.J. she had seen Father Kennedy, merely sat and nodded and said how right he had been.

And then one day, toward the end of the time, when Julia was nearly strong enough to leave and she was sitting, peaceful and happy, in the evening sun, reading *The Water Babies*, which someone had sent to Julia and which Phaedria had rediscovered with immense pleasure, she heard footsteps and looked up and there in front of her was Michael Browning.

"Now, you're not going to faint and you are not going to be sick," he said, placing a bottle of Cristal champagne on the table and producing two glasses from his pockets, "and you are certainly not going to run away. And before you ask, Roz has no idea I'm here."

He looked at her as she sat, frozen with shock, silent, her eyes huge brilliant smudges in her pale, still face. "Aren't you going to greet me?" he said. "I've traveled three thousand miles to bring you this. I hope you like it."

And he produced from yet another pocket a book, a tiny leatherbound volume, a first edition of Christina Rossetti's poems. "I bought this because of the birthday poem. I thought it was appropriate. I guess your heart must feel pretty much like a singing bird just now."

"Michael!" Phaedria said, kissing him gently on the cheek. "I didn't know you were a literary person. What a lovely present. Thank you."

"This is a man," he said, taking off his jacket and sinking into the chair beside her, "who won the English Lit runner-up prize at Sethlow Junior High two years running. Champagne?"

"Do you know I haven't had any yet? Eliza offered me some, but I refused. I wasn't ready for it. But today, yes, I really would like some."

"Well, it's time you did, and it's just as well," he said. "Otherwise I would have drunk it all."

She looked at him, smiling with the absolute pleasure of his company, untroubled for the moment by thoughts of what might lie before or behind them. He looked, as always, slightly rumpled; it was not just his clothes, it was his hair, which looked perpetually in need of a comb, his rather shaggy eyebrows, his disturbed—and disturbing—brown eyes. She thought, not for the first time, how extraordinary it was that a man so devoid of most of the obligatory qualities of conventional male desirability—height, looks, stylishness—could have such an ability to project sexuality with so acute a force. She wrenched her mind away from her deliberations with an effort and smiled at him. "It's so nice to see you. But why are you here?"

"I'm here," he said simply, "because I wanted to see you. I was in Los Angeles anyway; I have two companies here. I knew where you were, and I suddenly decided to come rather than go racing back to New York for a lonely weekend. I am family—or nearly. I felt I should greet the new member."

"I'm glad you did."

"Well, now," he said, leaning forward, "tell me all about this baby. I hear she is beautiful. Are you all right? Are they taking good care of you?"

"The baby is beautiful. She has dark hair and the most wonderful dark eyes. She's tiny, but growing very, very fast. She eats and eats and eats."

"From you, I see," he said, his eyes lingering briefly, pleasurably, on her changed, swelling breasts.

Phaedria saw the look and felt a strange stabbing somewhere in her heart; she looked down, away from him, flushed.

"Yes," she said in an attempt at lightness. "I have proved to be a fine dairy cow."

"Good. And how much does she weigh now, this little calf?"

"Oh, nearly five pounds. She was only three and a half when she was born. So thin, so tiny; now she's getting quite fat."

"I'd like to see her," he said. "Could I, do you think? Would it be possible?"

"You could," she said, touched, moved by his genuine interest, "but not tonight. Tomorrow. I will take you to the hospital and introduce you to her. Where are you staying?"

"I don't know. Would they keep me here, do you think?"

"We could ask."

"Good. I'll try now." He went through the French doors, into her sitting room and picked up the phone. "You pour me some more champagne. This is a very nice little pad you have here. I'm surprised you don't stay."

She laughed. "I would if I could. I feel it's half home. I've been terribly happy here. But we have to get back, Julia and I. We have to wake up, get on with reality."

"What a pity," he said. "Dreaming suits you. Ah, Reception? Do you have a room for tonight and maybe tomorrow as well? You do? No, I don't mind. That's fine. Browning. I'll come and check in right now."

"Excuse me," he said, putting down his glass. "They want to inspect me. They only have a small room. I guess that means only big enough for three. I'll be back. Have you had dinner?"

"No."

"You need feeding up. Why don't you ask me to join you for a nice big juicy T-bone?"

"I don't like nice big juicy T-bones."

"I'm easy. I'll eat anything."

"All right," she said, laughing, "then please stay and have dinner with me."

ROZ WAS FRIGHTENED and she didn't know quite why. On the face of it she was doing well. With immense ease she had gathered a good many reins into her exquisitely manicured hands during the few weeks Phaedria had been away. People no longer felt inhibited, by loyalty to or sympathy for Phaedria, and allowed Roz to take visible control. The management staff, heading the various companies, impatient for decisions on this and that, for go-aheads, for direction on expansion moves, hamstrung earlier by the ridiculous charade Julian had orchestrated, found her quick, shrewd, brilliantly decisive. Predictably hostile to the notion of being ultimately answerable to two young women, experienced businessmen found themselves grudgingly more receptive to acceding to one. The wholesale exodus of management talent, which had threatened the company after Julian's death, was slowing; people were waiting, seeing what might happen, what Roz—increasingly Roz—might do.

Roz, exhilarated, excited by what she was accomplishing, but exhausted nonetheless, had fears that haunted her frequently sleepless bed. She knew she was still fighting a crisis of confidence, that she needed a personal team behind her that could lend respectability and status to her accession. She knew that, however brilliant her own mind and training, the one crucial quality she could not possibly lay claim to was experience.

She looked into the distance and could see no end, no turning, even, that might indicate a byway, a respite. She faced a long, relentless straight highway.

She traveled it all day—she was in the office by seven-thirty most mornings—and she traveled it much of the night as well, leaving the building often at ten and taking work home with her. She hardly ever saw Miranda, she briefed her domestic staff in notes, and in the months since her father had died she had not once eaten a meal with anyone other than a business contact or Michael Browning. And that was the other reason for her fear. She knew she was pushing their relationship, straining his tolerance to the furthest possible parameters. She occasionally spent the weekend with him in England, still more occasionally flew to New York. She paid lip service to listening to his problems, his demands, but in fact her contact with him on any genuine level was restricted to sex and a demand that he listen to her. And she did not know how much longer he was going to put up with it.

C.J.'s departure from the household, and indeed the company, was a great relief. She was able, as soon as he had moved into his new flat near Sloane Street, to feel quite fond of him again. He was the perfect ex-husband—undemanding, good-natured, polite. He took over Miranda almost every weekend. He had agreed to go ahead with the divorce as fast as possible, and he had remained loyal; he did not go bad-mouthing her all over London, as she was uncomfortably aware he would have been justified in doing.

She had a feeling he was helping Phaedria with the hunt for Miles, but she really did not care. Such was her contempt for C.J.'s intellectual capacities, his lack of shrewdness, that she could not imagine they were going to be very successful, certainly not as successful as she was, with the loyally dogged Andrew Blackworth working on her behalf. The latest news had been that Miles was working for a bank somewhere; the crazy old woman who had finally revealed herself in Nassau hadn't had a clear idea where. It probably wasn't the right Miles, she thought wearily. In the very few moments when she had time to think at all, she wondered at the fact that Miles Wilburn had so completely failed to materialize. The lawyers had advertised so painstakingly, and if the flood of fakes, from half the major countries in the world, who had presented themselves to the offices of Henry Winterbourne either in person or by letter or phone call, had seen the advertisements, why had not Miles himself? And who was this Hugo Dashwood, for God's sake, that Henry Winterbourne had discovered through Bill Wilburn in California? None of it made sense.

She woke up late that Saturday morning and decided she had to speak to Michael. What was the time? Ten o'clock. Damn, only five in New York. Oh, well, he should be pleased to hear from her just the same. He had always told her to ring him any time. Michael could wake up and go back to sleep with the ease with which most people took a drink of water. Maybe she would give him another hour.

She got up, lay in the bath for a long time, thinking about Michael and how much she would like to be with him, wondering even if she might fly over for twenty-four hours, then dressed slowly, fetched herself a coffee from the kitchen and dialed his number.

It was answered by his butler, Franco, a good-natured, efficient, and loyal man, who shared with his master a distaste for untruth and an irritating ability to answer the most intensive questioning without giving anything away at all.

No, Mr. Browning was not here. No, he had gone away, he believed, on a short business trip. Yes, he had gone by air; Franco had ordered the car to take him to Kennedy himself early yesterday. An internal flight. No, he had no number.

Where could he be, where could he be? Who could he be with? Roz looked out of the window at the golden October sunlight dancing on the Thames and shivered. It seemed to grow darker. That fear that followed her everywhere had suddenly grown very big.

THEY LOOKED AT the baby and admired the baby, and then Phaedria had fed the baby. Michael asked most charmingly if he could stay while she did so, and she, surprised at her own unselfconsciousness, said of course he might, if he wished. Michael cuddled the baby and remarked on her great beauty, and he talked to the nurses and extracted news of an imminent engagement from one and a suspected pregnancy of her own from another. Phaedria talked to the pediatrician and extracted a promise that Julia could fly home in another week, and when the baby had been finally laid in her crib and, after a brief protest, gone to sleep, Michael suggested a picnic. "Or do we just stay here with her? I don't mind at all, if that's what you would like."

"I do usually," she said doubtfully, "but the nurses are always telling me to go out more. They have masses of my milk in the fridge, so I suppose we could."

"Right," he said. "It will do you good. Let's go to the beach."

So they drove out of Los Angeles and along the coast road, past Malibu, and on to Paradise Cove. Michael produced from the trunk of the Mercedes a picnic basket, an armful of towels, two blankets, and a beach umbrella. Phaedria watched entranced.

"This is like an act at the circus. When did you get all that?"

"The hotel did it, early this morning. Come on."

He set the umbrella in the sand, spread out the blankets, and opened the hamper. It contained a bottle of exquisite California Chardonnay, another of Perrier, a modest heap of smoked salmon sandwiches, and a large bag of peaches, cherries, strawberries, raspberries. "And I even have bathing suits for us both. You're right about the hotel filling every human need. If I had asked for a trio of naked ladies to come in juggling flaming torches on unicycles, they would have said, 'Certainly, Mr. Browning,' and had them there before I could say 'room service.' Do you feel like swimming?"

"I'm not sure. Sunning anyway. You are wonderful."

"I know. There are some pretty amazing sights over there," he said, pointing to the far side of the beach.

"What?"

"That's the nude beach. Never been there?"

"No. And I don't think I want to now," she said, laughing.

"Don't you like the naked form, Lady Morell?"

"Very much," she said, "but not on a lot of strangers."

"Then I look forward to being your friend," he said. "Now, don't start looking frightened," he added, seeing her eyes fill with confusion and alarm. "I was only joking. Eat your food, like a good nursing mother. You need nourishing."

"All right," she said, and he watched her relax again.

They ate slowly, drank the wine, watched the surfers, soaked up the sun. Phaedria thought of Miles, spending his days here, in this very stretch of ocean. He began to materialize for her, a lean brown body, sun-streaked hair, swooping interminably in on the waves, pursuing nothing but pleasure. She longed to know more of him, to meet him and talk to him, to find out what sort of a man he could possibly be.

"Hey," said Michael, who had been watching her, "where are you? Back in that hospital?"

"No," she said, smiling, hauling herself back to the present, "more or less here. I was looking at the surfers and envying them rather. I love the sea and I love the sun. It makes me feel good right down in my bones."

"Me, too. It's hot, though. That delicate English skin of yours will burn. Do you want some sunscreen?"

"It's not delicate, not really, but it might be a good idea. Did the hotel send that, too?"

"Of course."

"Yes, please. Could you put some on my back?"

He opened the bottle and began to spread the lotion over her shoulders and her back, smoothing it in slowly, rhythmically, gently massaging the tender nape of her neck, down her spine, over her shoulders, his fingers stopping just short of her breasts. Suddenly, shockingly strongly, she wanted his hands on them, more than she could ever remember wanting anything; she closed her eyes, pulling herself tautly together, lest he should feel her tipping over into desire. "Thank you," she said quickly. "That's fine. Shall I do yours?"

"No," he said, "no need. I have skin that resembles a tortoise's shell more closely than anything else." He looked at her closely, saw the raw flicker of sex in her eyes, and smiled.

"You worry too much," was all he said.

A little later on, Michael went over to the water and Phaedria lay down under the umbrella. When he came back, not having quite entrusted himself to the surf, which was running high, she was asleep. He sat and looked at her for a while, his face an interesting blank.

She woke up quite suddenly, looking startled, and sat up. "We must get back," she said, "quickly. We've been gone too long."

"Calm down," he said, smiling. "It's only three o'clock, and I don't suppose they'll let that baby starve. We'll go back if you like. But don't panic."

She relaxed again and lay back on the bed. "I'm sorry. I just worry about her all the time."

"Of course. I would, too. And we'll go in a minute. Are you sure you don't want to swim?"

She shook her head. "No, it's so lovely just lying here."

"Why wake up at all?"

"I have to, Michael. I can't give up now. I can't."

"I don't see why not. You have all the money you need. You have a gorgeous baby. You're beautiful. Talented. Why not just enjoy yourself?"

"I wasn't born," she said, "to just enjoy myself."

"Okay," he said, "do something else. Sell out to Roz. Take the money and run. Start your own newspaper or something."

She smiled. "Do you know, I've thought of doing that. I just might in the fullness of time. But first I have to resolve this mess. Somehow."

"Okay. Are you any nearer?"

She looked at him. "Yes," she said. "Quite a bit. I haven't found him, but I know who he was. Is."

"Really? And who is he?"

"Do you really want to know?"

He lay down on the sand beside her, turned his head toward her. "Okay, I'm in a listening mode. You should know by now I find people kind of interesting."

She told him. About the collection of things in Julian's desk, about Father Kennedy and her conversation with him, about Miles, who he was, his small rather sad history, even about Hugo Dashwood and his role in it. All except the letters and the signature. That she was not even acknowledging to herself.

THEY DINED ON the patio of her bungalow, reluctant to break the spell of privacy, of solitude. After dinner they went into the sitting room and closed the French windows; the nights were getting cold. Michael poured them both a brandy. They sat and looked at each other.

"Right," Phaedria said, "let's talk about you."

"How long have you got?"

"As long as it takes."

So he told her: about his childhood in Brooklyn, about selling soft drinks on the streets of California, about Anita, about Carol, about Little Michael and Baby Sharon, about making a fortune, about his constant willingness to risk everything and lose it all again.

She listened, attentively, silent, drinking him in, enjoying his roughly rich voice, his humor, the attention to and pleasure in unexpected detail that was so much a part of his charm, his ability to haul his listener into intimacy; when he had finished she said, "And— Roz?"

"Oh, no," he said, smiling to her, "I think that's a subject we should not discuss. Not now. Not yet."

"What do you mean?"

"You know what I mean."

"I suppose I do."

She was silent.

"So now we know all about each other," she said.

"I wouldn't say that."

There was tension in the room so strong that Phaedria felt she had to get up, move about. "Would you like another drink?"

"I guess so," he said slowly, as if he had come back from a long way away. "Then I'll go to bed. And tomorrow I have to fly back to New York."

"It's been a lovely day."

"Yes, it has."

"You are," she said suddenly, smiling at him, quite relaxed, "the nicest man I have ever met. Ever."

He looked at her thoughtfully. "I don't know how much of a compliment that is. You've met some real stinkers, that's for sure. Been married to one of the best."

"Julian wasn't a stinker," she said, indignant, defensive. "I can't let you say that."

"Jesus!" he said. "I seem to spend my life listening to women defend that monster. Just exactly what did he do to you all? Phaedria, honeybunch, just think what he did to you. He cheated on you, he manipulated you, he lied to you, and he left you with this goddam corporate ballet to orchestrate. Of course he was a stinker."

"Well, maybe, in a way. But I—" She was silent.

"You loved him?"

"Yes. I did. I really did. God knows why."

"God has to be the only one who does. Funny thing, love. It has no respect for persons. Look at me: I've loved a greedy Jewish mama, an ice-cold, nicely bred ice maiden, and probably the biggest bitch in Christendom. Really loved 'em all. And now . . ." He was silent. Then he looked up at her, and his eyes moved over her face, lingering on her mouth. She felt herself tremble.

"Phaedria, I—"

"No," she said quickly, with panic in her voice, "don't. Don't even think it."

He laughed, the tension gone briefly. "You can't do that. You can't tell a man what to think and not think. You're taking away one of our most inalienable rights. Besides, you don't know what I was thinking."

"No," she said, her voice small, a little sad. "No, I suppose I don't."

"Oh, God," he said, "I hate it when you're sad. Don't be sad. Of course you knew what I was thinking, what I was feeling, what I was going to say. And if I had said it, you'd probably have thrown up or something. I find myself in a no-win situation here."

"Yes," she said, trying to sound lighthearted, too, in spite of the awesome conflict in her, the yearning and the panic. "Yes you are." But her voice came out sounding dull and bleak.

Michael looked at her; she was sitting in the chair opposite him, tension in every particle of her; looking down at her hands, the glass she was holding, the great waterfall of dark hair obscuring her face.

"Phaedria," he said, "come and sit down here. Next to me."

She looked up at him, her eyes meeting his, full of longing and fear; and in a great rush of tenderness and concern he held out his hands.

"Come on."

"Why?"

"God, you make things complicated. Because I want you near me, that's why."

She hesitated, looking at him, considering; then in a visible rush of courage, moved over to him.

"That's better. It's all right; I'm not going to crush you in my arms or anything. Although I have to say I find it a little insulting that you seem to find the prospect so alarming."

"You know why I do."

"Yes," he said, smiling at her again. "Of course I do. I find it quite alarming myself for the same reason. You know," he added, leaning back, looking thoughtfully into the soft darkness outside the window, "Roz isn't really so terrible. Nobody realizes it but me, but she isn't. Underneath all that toughness and bitchiness and anger is really quite a nice, funny woman. You'd be surprised."

"Perhaps I would," Phaedria said carefully.

"I now she's been vile to you. I know she's been vile to a lot of people. But there are always reasons. And one of the main reasons was that charming, dangerous father of hers, whom you loved so much."

She nodded. Suddenly, surprisingly, tears formed in her eyes, spilled over; he reached out and wiped them tenderly away. "Poor baby. I'm sorry. I shouldn't have criticized him and I shouldn't have threatened you. It's much too soon. You did love him, and you've had a bad time. You must miss him like hell."

"Yes," she said, "I do. I really do miss him. I'm sorry. I'm always crying all over you."

"Well, it beats throwing up." He looked at her for a long time, his eyes exploring her face. "We seem to have a penchant, both of us, for loving difficult people. What a shame. When we could probably have been so much happier loving nice easy ones. Like each other. Well, maybe we'll never know."

"Maybe," she said.

"I'M NOT GOING TO LIE TO YOU," said Michael. He stood looking at Roz across the vast width of the living room of his New York duplex.

"Okay, then," she said. "Where were you?"

"In California."

"Why?"

"Business. And a bit of pleasure."

"Without me?"

"I get precious little pleasure with you, Rosamund."

"I presume by pleasure you mean sex?"

"Wrong in one. No sex."

"I don't believe you."

"Roz, when have I ever lied to you?"

She hesitated.

"I never have, have I?"

"No. You never have."

"Okay, then. No sex."

"What were you doing?"

"I was," he said, choosing his words very carefully, "meeting a new friend."

"God, Michael, you are being irritating. What kind of friend?"

"A young friend."

"Female?"

"Female."

"I see. And what did you do with this new young female friend?"

"Not a lot. Fed her. Talked to her. Looked at her. Gave her a present."

"What sort of present?"

"A book."

"And what did you do the rest of the time?"

"Lay on the beach. Swam a bit. Talked. Ate. Drank."

"And then you came home again?"

"I did."

"Do I," she asked in a most uncharacteristic piece of self-exposure, "do I have to worry about this girl?"

"No," he said, "not for a moment. Come here."

She moved toward him; he took her in his arms. "Now can we drop the subject, please? I really don't want to talk about it anymore, and I have a hell of a day ahead of me. You're taking today off, but I have to work. You can stay here or go out shopping, whatever you like, and then come and meet me at six at the Algonquin. Okay?"

"Okay," Roz said, and sighed. She was still very unhappy.

ROZ SPENT THE day shopping and getting her hair done. Then she went back to the duplex and sat for a long time, as the room darkened, feeling alternately angry and wretched. She also felt very alone and, in some strange way, duped, cheated of territory that was rightfully hers.

She decided she needed a drink. Franco was out and wouldn't be back for an hour or so before dinner. She wandered into the gleaming stage set of a kitchen and found a glass, went to the fridge and took out a tray of ice cubes. While she was dropping some cubes in her glass, she noticed the basket of book matches Michael kept on the top of the fridge; he had been collecting them for years. They told better than anything where he had been, eaten, stayed.

She glanced idly into it as she poured some scotch into her glass. Suddenly she froze, rigid with shock and fear. Right on the top, the very latest addition, was one of the small cream boxes with silver lettering in which the Bel Air Hotel packed its matches.

The Bel Air! Phaedria was at the Bel Air. Had Michael been there? Had he seen her? Was it possible? Surely not. Surely, surely not. It wasn't— It couldn't be. He wouldn't even look at that bitch, wouldn't betray Roz. It would be the utmost, infinite treachery. No, it must be a mistake. Anyway, maybe Phaedria was gone by now. No, she wasn't. She was leaving next week. Well, maybe Michael had had the matches for some time. Maybe he had been rummaging through them, and it had just come out on top. There had to be a reasonable explanation. There had to be. He couldn't betray her like this, not with Phaedria. Roz drank a very large glass of scotch and poured herself another. Then she crossed over to the phone and, holding the matches, dialed a number.

"Bel Air Hotel," said a smoothly purring voice. "May I help you?"

"Yes," Roz said, carefully turning her voice into something slick and efficient, not remotely like the high-pitched hysterical wail she felt struggling to escape from her. "This is Mr. Browning's secretary. Mr. Michael Browning. Mr. Browning stayed there over the weekend. He has lost his raincoat. I wonder if he left it at the hotel?"

"One moment, ma'am. Let me check with the housekeeper."

There was an endless, endless pause while the phone was silent, occasionally crackling gently. Roz had to bite her fist to stop herself from screaming. "Ma'am? No, Mr. Browning didn't leave a raincoat behind. We don't have much call for raincoats here, of course." The voice was politely amused, obviously hoping Roz would share the joke.

"I see. But he was there? I haven't made a mistake and confused hotels?"

"No, ma'am. He was here. Friday and Saturday night. But no raincoat. I'm sorry."

The voice was filled with the slightly hyped-up charm that was essentially Californian. Roz just heard that and then no more. She had a rushing in her ears; she closed her eyes and put down the phone.

She sat drinking her second scotch and then her third, wondering how she could possibly survive the agony she was enduring.

PHAEDRIA HAD BEEN living at the Bel Air for so long she couldn't imagine having to return to reality. To organizing her own household, to being in the offices every day, above all, to looking after the baby all by herself. It felt very frightening.

While Julia had been at the hospital, cared for by the nurses, although she had longed to have her with her all the time, she had felt safe. No harm could come to her. If the baby got a cold or colic, or if she wouldn't nurse, someone would take care of her. If there was a real crisis, the pediatrician was on hand. Now the safety net was about to be removed from underneath her, and Phaedria was extremely nervous. It was all very well for everyone to reassure her that the baby was now at her normal weight, that she was, if anything, more robust than a full-term baby leaving the hospital, that she knew as well as anybody how to care for her; Phaedria still didn't feel ready to take on the responsibility.

Besides, she was taking Julia away from the warmth and sunshine of California into the raw dank hazards of an English November. How would she possibly be able to adapt to that?

Just fine, said the pediatrician. "I presume you're not going to be living out-of-doors. That your house has some form of central heating? That your child will have a crib of some kind to sleep in?" His lips twitched slightly.

In the end Phaedria had to accept everybody's judgment and prepare to take Julia home.

She had spent most of the week thinking about Michael Browning.

She found it rather alarming how much she had focused on him. He filled her head and her heart, and she had hardly a thought that had not contained him. What was that Quaker expression that had always charmed her? Thee pleasures me. Yes, that was what Michael did to her; he pleasured her, made her feel joyful and warmed and safe and almost physically cared for. He introduced a kind of charm and delight into everything; life was heightened and lightened when he was there, and bleaker and darker when he was not. She liked, too, the fact that she clearly amused and delighted him, that he made her feel interesting and important and—and oh, God, yes, and something else, too: he made her think with quite appalling relentlessness and vividness of sex. She was not sure quite how he did that. It was partly the way he looked at her, the way his eyes flickered over her body sometimes, the way he smiled, not just into her eyes, her face, but suddenly disarmingly as his eyes were resting on her breasts, her legs, her stomach as though these places inspired such thoughts of joy and delight that he could not contain himself, could not remain solemn. It was also partly the blatant sensuality in his eyes, the way he moved, even the way he spoke, certainly the way he laughed, and partly the sudden amused comment, the half serious observation that revealed a strong sexual focus; but if she had tried to explain it to anyone who had never met Michael Browning she would have failed utterly. Other women had tried in the past and failed also.

Well, it was not to be. Her sadness, her regret, the physical ache he had induced in her for him paled into insignificance at the thought of Roz and what she would do if she discovered that Phaedria and Michael were lovers. Had even thought of being lovers.

She had been afraid of Roz even when she was married to Julian. Now she was, quite literally, physically terrified, and she set the thought of Michael aside as determinedly, as irrevocably, as if it had been some food, some substance that would injure her, damage her fatally.

She was also terrified at the thought of returning to the mine field that was the company. She dreaded to think what Roz might have engineered in her absence, whose confidence she had gained, whom she had persuaded to regard Phaedria as a half-witted usurper into the company's power structure. The temptation to sell out, to let her have it all, to go, was fierce, and yet she never allowed herself seriously to consider it. Julian had left her half the company, and he had left her Julia, although he had not known it, and she had to safeguard the one for the other. She could not betray what limited trust he had had in her. She owed him that at least.

At least now she felt well, strong, ready for battle. On the other hand, she knew she would never again be able to fight with the same total commitment. She would have Julia to worry about, to get home to, to be with; she wasn't going to have her growing up wondering who she was. However good the nanny, however/efficient the staff, Julia needed her; and she was going to have her. Delegation was the key; she must find it and put it in the lock.

She had done a lot of thinking in the long, often tedious days in the hospital and in the quiet evenings in her bungalow. If this nonsense was ever to be resolved, simply trying to divide everything in two pieces was not the answer. There had to be some lateral input of thought. The trouble was that, on this subject at least, Roz thought only vertically.

It seemed hopeless, unless one or the other of them managed to find Miles and manipulate him into cooperating. And that seemed increasingly unlikely.

TOWARD SIX O'CLOCK, Roz suddenly remembered, through the haze of misery and rage, and several extremely large whiskeys, that she was supposed to meet Michael at the Algonquin. Well, that was all right. She could talk to him there as well as anywhere. It might enliven things a little for the other people there. It was a pretty dull place a lot of the time. She called out to Franco who had come in and was working in the kitchen, and told him to get her a cab.

"You won't get one now, Mrs. Emerson. It's rush hour."

"Well, I have to get to the Algonquin. And I'm not going to walk."

"Would you like me to drive you? I can have the car out in front in five minutes."

Roz looked at him, thinking. Walking might not be a bad idea. It was only ten blocks, and she needed a clear head. The traffic would be appalling, and she would have to sit and listen to Franco's running commentary on the deteriorating condition of New York all the way.

"No, it's all right, Franco, I think I'll walk after all. The traffic will be terrible."

"All right, Mrs. Emerson. Will you and Mr. Browning be coming back here for dinner?"

"I'm afraid I don't have the faintest idea," she said, making it plain that the decision was hers, rather than Michael's, where they dined. "I haven't yet decided what I want to do this evening."

She liked putting Franco down; he was so bloody devoted to Michael, so eager to impress upon her the democratic nature of their relationship. Roz thought there was only one place for servants and that they should know precisely where it was.

MICHAEL WAS SITTING at a table in the Blue Bar and drinking bourbon when she arrived. He saw her standing in the doorway, and his heart lurched. She was difficult, she was overbearing and monstrously self-ish and unreasonable, but she was very, very sexy. And she was plainly in a feisty mood. Her eyes were brilliant and snapping, her face was alive, her entire body spelled out energy, power, resolution. He smiled to himself.

"Hi, darling! Come and sit down. What would you like to drink?"

"Scotch on the rocks," Roz said to the waiter. "A double."

Michael looked at her quickly. She didn't usually drink liquor, and certainly not in large quantities. He noticed suddenly that she was flushed and that her voice was slightly odd.

"Are you okay?"

"Oh, yes," she said, and her voice was just a little too loud and harsh. "I'm absolutely fine. Never better. But then, I always did enjoy good health. As you know, I'm not someone to cave under at the least strain. Would you say, Michael?"

"No," he said, and there was puzzlement in his voice. "No, I wouldn't. It's that good British stock you come from, I guess."

"Not necessarily," she said. "Not at all. I could name a few examples of British stock who are pretty damn feeble. Who take almost two bloody months recovering from having a baby. Who sit about whining and expecting the world to come running to them, from thousands of miles away if need be." She drained her glass, leaned back in her chair, and called to the waiter. "Bring me another of these, will you?" Then she turned back to Michael. "So how was my dear stepmother last weekend, Michael? Sitting up and taking notice yet? Or still lying back on her pillows like some pathetic Victorian heroine, trawling sympathy from anyone in sight?"

"Ah," he said quietly. "So that's it."

"Yes," said Roz. "That is it. And how was it, Michael? How did you find her? Pretty damn ready for you, I would say. I bet she's like a bitch in heat underneath that fey, little-girl charm of hers. She pulled my father into her bed fairly fast. Well, there's no fool like an old fool, they say. You, I would have thought, might have been expected to be a little more sensible. I was obviously woefully wrong."

"Roz, don't be absurd."

"Absurd! In what way am I being absurd? Perhaps you expect me to be delighted that you went sick-visiting? And saw fit not to tell me. I would say that tells its own story, Michael. Or am I to believe that you simply gave her some grapes and admired the baby? Now, that really would be absurd. Deeply absurd. I mean, I don't admire her style myself, but I am told she is considered not exactly ill to look upon. And you are, by your own admission, frustrated at the moment. And I daresay she is—or rather was—too, by Christ, although God knows how many lovers she might have had before or after my father died. I still don't believe that child is his."

"Roz, you are making several serious mistakes," Michael said quietly. He was still sitting quite easily in his chair, watching her, listening to her. The fact that the entire room was doing the same bothered him not in the least.

"Really? What mistakes am I making? I hope you're not going to try to tell me I'm mistaken in thinking you have been in her bed—and in her so elegant personage. She must be a hell of an easy lay, and so conveniently far from home and from anyone who might have known or disturbed either of you. How was it, Michael? Is she good in bed? Does she have any clever tricks you hadn't met before?"

"I wouldn't know," he said. "Shall we continue this discussion at home?"

"Oh, I like it here," she said. "Where is my second drink? Waiter! I asked you for another scotch. Bring it over here, would you?"

"Rosamund, he isn't going to. Leave him out of this. It isn't his fault, poor guy."

"No, but it's yours," she cried, quite loudly, her face by now contorted with fury. "It's absolutely yours. How dare you go out there to California, to her, seeing her, screwing her, while I was safely thousands of miles away in London? How dare you?"

"I did not screw her," he said quietly. "I didn't touch her."

"Oh, yes, and I'm the President of the United States. Don't give me that, Michael. Don't insult me any more than you have already."

"I'm trying not to," he said, and there was an edge of searing anger suddenly in his voice that quieted even her. "I did go to see Phaedria, yes, and the baby. I went because I was out there on business, and it seemed like a nice idea. I like Phaedria; she's charming and agreeable, which is more than I can say for you most of the time. And she's had a tough time, to which you have contributed greatly. I did not, however, go to bed with her. I might well have been tempted to, not having had a great deal of carnal pleasure lately, thanks to your good self and your insane obsession with that company of yours. But I did not, and it was much to my credit and to hers that the only physical contact I experienced over the whole weekend was with her very charming baby—who, incidentally, greatly resembles your father. I only hope she grows up to be more agreeable than his other daughter. I'm going home now. Perhaps you'd like to settle the check."

He walked out, leaving the room entirely silent and Roz frozen to her chair, her face ashen, her eyes huge and brilliant, and an icy fear taking grip on her heart.

LATER THAT EVENING Michael called the Bel Air Hotel.

"Phaedria, hi. How are you?"

"I'm fine. What's the matter?"

"Well, I thought I should call you. Tell you to double-lock your door. Batten down the hatches." He tried to sound amused, light-hearted, but he failed.

She knew immediately what he meant. "Roz found out?"

"Yup."

"But there was nothing to find out."

"She found that kind of hard to grasp."

"Oh, God. Oh, Michael, what shall we do? Where is she?"

"Christ knows. I imagine on her way back to London. She just left. She flew in this morning. I don't think she'll be coming out to L.A., but she just might. I'm very, very sorry."

"How did she find out?"

"I don't know. I really don't."

"Oh, it's so ridiculous," said Phaedria. "There's nothing to know, nothing at all. But I can see she wouldn't have believed that."

"No. I'd have a little trouble with it myself, though, wouldn't you?"

"I suppose so. Yes."

"Serves us right," he said. "I knew it was a mistake."

"What? Coming to see me?"

"No," he said, and his voice warmed her, stroked her over the telephone. "Not seeing more of you. The rest of you."

"Well," she said, "I shall just have to go back to London and face her. I can't stay here."

"You wouldn't like to come and hide with a lonely, frightened man for a day or two?"

"No," she said firmly. "You've got me into enough trouble. I'm going home."

"Lady Morell," he said, and there was a wealth of admiration in his voice, "you are a dame with balls."

◆　　◆　　◆

BACK IN LONDON, the weekend wound wearily on for Roz. The nanny had taken Miranda up to Scotland for a day or two to stay with her grandmother; the house was empty, silent. She roamed about it, restless, miserable. She felt she had been asked to bear too much; she didn't see quite how she was going to stand it. She was alone, she was frightened, she was wretchedly unhappy, she was humiliated. She thought of going to see Letitia to talk to her, but rejected the idea, shrinking from the pain of explaining, of exposing herself to Letitia's particular brand of rather pragmatic sympathy. And Susan, dear Susan, her refuge in times of trouble, was away with Richard in France, inspecting their new property.

She hurt physically: her back throbbed, her head ached, her legs felt heavy and weak. She tried to eat, in the knowledge that on Monday she was going to have to make an appearance, to make some decisions, put on her endlessly impressive performance. Phaedria would be back at the end of the week; Roz couldn't afford to let them see her weaken now. But the food tasted disgusting; she couldn't swallow it.

She decided to go out, to get some air; she walked for miles along the embankment, from Cheyne Walk all the way to Westminster and then on to Blackfriars and still farther, to Tower Bridge. As she walked she thought about C.J. and the London he loved so much, about how she had refused over and over again to go with him as he explored it, about how little he had complained, merely gone off with his maps and his reference books, in search of happiness, interest, discovery, and she had been grateful, relieved, to see him go. Well, he was gone now, permanently. She had lost him—odd how it suddenly seemed to be a loss—and it seemed she had lost Michael, too. How horribly wrong her life was turning out, when only two years ago she had seemed to hold everything she wanted in her hands. A nightmarish panic took hold of her; she felt as if everything was out of rhythm, distorted, slightly mad. She grew oddly frightened; she felt she must get back to her own territory, not be in strange places and alone. She hailed a cab and went home to Cheyne Walk, sobered, miserable.

In the end she turned to work. It proved, as usual, to be the panacea. It never failed her. She always found serenity and calm, sheer pleasure in work.

She settled at her desk in the study next to her bedroom and with sheer force of will set her mind to the company and its demands. Initially she went through her pending files, catching up on detail, answering memos, checking minutes, cross-referencing appointments in her diaries. But on Sunday evening she got out some files and looked at the performance of the various companies over the past year. The stores were doing fine, including London now, which was a bittersweet pill to swallow; the cosmetic company was flourishing, only she yearned to do things with that, expand into the body business, open some more health spas; the hotels were a bit iffy; the pharmaceutical company was expanding faster than the rest; plastics and paper were both doing fine. Only the new communications company looked as if it might be in serious difficulty. Roz would sell that if she had her way. But Phaedria would never agree. Oh, God, if only, if only she had a bit more power. She could see the way ahead so clearly, and knew exactly how to steer the company through it.

She was in the office at seven-thirty the following morning. She felt excited, exhilarated, her misery briefly forgotten.

She settled at her desk, pulled out her dictating machine, began to construct a careful, discreet document. She was totally engrossed in it when she heard footsteps in the corridor. Now, who could that be, and why hadn't she had the sense to lock the front door? It was far too early for any of the regular staff to come in, and the cleaners came at night. Maybe it was the doorman, come in early. She heard a knock on her own door; she frowned. "Yes? Come in!" She heard the door open; still half engrossed in her work, she paused before she looked up. When she did, she thought she must be hallucinating.

A ludicrously beautiful young man stood in front of her, leaning with an almost mannered grace against the door. He had sun-streaked, untidy, rather long blond hair and very dark blue eyes; there was a night's growth of stubble on his tanned face; he was tall and slender and was dressed in jeans and a very crumpled white shirt, a denim jacket slung over one shoulder.

His eyes traveled over Roz appreciatively, slowly, carefully, taking her in. Then he slowly smiled, a glorious, joyous, pleasure-giving smile that she could not resist, could not, despite her weariness, her anxiety, help but return.

"Hi," he said. "I'm Miles."

·33·

MILES WILBURN AND BILLY DE LAU-
nay often remarked that the most
amazing thing about the whole
story of Miles's inheritance was
not so much that Marcia Galbraith should have tried to do
what she did but that she should
have succeeded for so long.

"For months and months half
the civilized world was looking
for you," said Billy, "and you had
no idea. It sure beats fiction."

"Yeah," said Miles. They had been sitting in the Nassau airport at
the time, waiting for Miles's flight to be called.

"God knows what else she's been keeping from you," said Billy.
"Did you ask her?"

"No," Miles said. "No point. But I did ask her if she'd kept anything
from Granny Kelly. I made her turn over all of her letters."

"And?"

"Well, there were several from old Father Kennedy. Granny would
have loved to get them. That did make me mad. And in one of them,
he said that old Hugo wanted to contact me. So it was kind of important."

"And you still don't know how he fits into this?"

"Nope. But maybe soon I'll find out."

Billy had been having a marvelous time in Washington. He was
doing well at the bank, he had grown increasingly charming and
good-looking with the years, and he was much in demand by debutante mothers at parties everywhere. Instead of going home to Nassau
for August, he was invited by the mother of one Marilyn Greaves,
who fondly imagined him to be a great deal richer than he really was,
to summer with them at Mount Desert Island in Maine. Being beset
with the twin problems of deflowering Marilyn and keeping from Mrs.
Greaves his family's true financial status, Billy let almost two months
go by before he returned to the matter of Miles and where he might
be. It wasn't until he wrote to his parents—a rare event—and asked
them to tell Miles to get in touch next time they saw him that he
heard about what was going on. His father told him Miles had gone
to Miami to work in a bank; he had no address, but he would ask
Marcia for one. Shamed into honesty, Marcia gave Mr. de Launay
the address, but Billy's letter was returned.

Marilyn Greaves was still absorbing a lot of Billy's attention, and he was a slow correspondent; it was the end of October before he actually wrote to Miles in care of the bank and two more weeks before Miles replied.

Miles's letter made interesting reading. He had tired of life at the counter and had walked out of the bank one day at the end of August. He had taken a bus down to Coconut Grove, found it much more to his liking, and had been working at Monty Trainer's down on Dinner Key for the past couple of months. He occasionally went down to the bank to pick up letters, which made life simpler, as he kept moving around in the Grove; they had been real nice about him leaving so precipitately.

He was planning to marry Candy McCall, but wasn't saving much money. He'd love to see Billy. When was he coming down south?

Billy, on his way home for Thanksgiving, stopped off in Miami and sought Miles out. While they were getting gloriously drunk together, Billy asked him what had happened when he phoned the number in the advertisement.

HENRY WINTERBOURNE HAD just come into the office when Miles called. He and Caroline had celebrated their fourteenth wedding anniversary the previous evening. The effect of the combination of a bottle of champagne each, a bottle of Beaune over dinner, several large brandies, and Caroline's refusal to mark the occasion in what seemed to him a more appropriate manner later in bed had left him bad-tempered as well as severely hung over.

He snatched up the phone when it rang and, nursing his head with the other hand, spoke tetchily into it. "Yes?"

"Er, Mr. Winterbourne," said the easily frightened temporary secretary who was filling in until Jane came back from holiday on Monday, "there's a long-distance call for you. The name is Wilburn, Mr. Winterbourne. Miles Wilburn."

Henry forgot his hangover. "Good Christ. Put him on."

The voice that came three thousand miles over the wires to him was a charming, slightly husky California drawl.

"Hi," it said.

"Er, good morning," said Henry.

"This is Miles Wilburn. I believe you wanted me to contact you."

"I did. Where are you calling from?"

"Coconut Grove, Miami."

"Would you—shall I call you back? Give me your number."

"I'm in a phone booth."

"Then ring off and call me back, reversing the charges."

"Okay. That's really nice of you."

Whoever he was, Henry thought, he had nice manners.

"Right," he said, slightly more himself by the time the international operator had put Miles through the second time. "Tell me why you're calling now. We've been trying to reach you for months."

"It's a long story. I just heard you were looking for me. My grandmother's friend had been keeping letters and stuff from me. She's a little confused."

"I see. Do you have any idea why we're looking for you?"

"None at all," Miles said.

"Did you ever meet Sir Julian Morell?"

"I beg your pardon?"

"Sir Julian Morell—did you know him?"

"No, I didn't. I never even heard of him. I kind of thought this must have something to do with Mr. Dashwood."

"Ah." Henry thought quickly. The mysterious Mr. Dashwood surfacing again. Who the hell was he? Why did all these Americans know him? "Was—is Mr. Dashwood related to you?"

"He certainly isn't." Miles sounded just mildly put out. "He's just—well, what you might call a family friend, I suppose."

"I see," Henry said again. His headache was returning. "Well, Mr. Wilburn, we obviously have a lot to talk about. Can you give us evidence that you are indeed Miles Wilburn?"

"I have a birth certificate. Would that do?"

"Very probably," Henry said carefully. "I think you should come to London. My secretary will book you a flight immediately. Do you have a passport?"

"Yes."

"Excellent. Then I suggest you come straight here on Monday. Providing we can get you on a flight on Sunday. From Miami?"

"No," Miles said. "I'll be in Nassau."

"Fine. I will have a car meet you at London Heathrow."

"Okay," Miles said. "That's really nice of you. Good-bye, Mr. Winterbourne."

Henry thought he had never, in twenty-five years of practice, come across anybody quite so unemotional. What was the expression they used in California? Laid back. Yes, that was it.

Well, how extraordinary. After all these months. Good God, he must let Roz know. He rang the Morell offices to discover that she was in New York. What about Phaedria? She would like to know. But it was the middle of the night in California; he would ring her later. Meanwhile he wanted his coffee extremely badly.

Later, Phaedria was out; she had taken a car and not said when she would be back. She was usually back by evening, though. Should they have her call him?

He and Caroline were leaving for Paris for the weekend to further celebrate their anniversary. No, he would surprise everybody on Monday morning.

"No," he said, "it's all right. No message."

"STAY THERE," ROZ said, jumping up, holding up her hand as if to prohibit him from suddenly vanishing again. "Don't go away."

"I just flew three thousand miles to come to this place. I'm not going away until I find out what I'm doing here," Miles said with a second, yet more dazzling smile.

"Would you like a coffee?"

"I certainly would. Black, no sugar."

"I'll go and get it. Just wait here."

Miles looked after her as she disappeared down the corridor, puzzled by her agitation, and then shrugged. He had heard the English were a little tense. Old Hugo had always seemed stiff and awkward. If they were all as uptight as this girl, he wasn't going to enjoy them much. She was interesting-looking, though. Not good-looking, exactly, but she had a lot of style. She reminded him of someone. He couldn't think who.

Roz came back into the office, a coffee cup in either hand. "There," she said. "I hope it's okay."

"It will be. Pan Am's coffee taste like gnat's piss. Not," he added, smiling at her, "that I've ever actually tasted gnat's piss."

Roz sat down again at her desk and gazed at him in total silence. She couldn't stop. Partly because of his remarkable looks, and partly because she couldn't believe he was really there. Miles met her gaze steadily, a sliver of amusement in his dark blue eyes. Then finally he smiled. "Will I do?"

"I beg your pardon?"

"Do I pass? Have you examined me enough yet?"

"Oh, I'm sorry," Roz said, smiling back. "Do forgive me. It's just that—well, we've been looking for you for so long, it seems odd that you should just—well, materialize. Like a ghost or something."

"Nothing ghostly about me," Miles said cheerfully. "Feel." He held out a brown hand. Roz took it, shook it, laughing.

"How do you do. I'm Rosamund Emerson."

"Pleased to meet you. You know who I am. So you're not one of the Morells?"

"Oh, yes," Roz said quickly. "Yes, I am. I'm Julian Morell's daughter."

"Ah. So who is this guy?"

"You really don't know?" Roz said, astonished, not believing, even after all the accumulated evidence, that the link between Miles Wilburn and Julian Morell was still so absolutely inexplicable.

"No. Why should I?"

"Well, because—" Roz stopped, suddenly aware of the need for a degree of caution. "It's terribly complicated. The lawyers should really tell you."

"Oh, God!" He put his hand to his forehead in horror. "I forgot. I was supposed to be met by your lawyer's car this morning at Heathrow. But I got an earlier flight out of Nassau. He'll be sitting there wetting himself. Can we do anything about that?"

"Oh, so Henry knew you were coming?" said Roz. "Why the hell didn't he tell us?"

"I don't know. Now, what about this poor guy in the car?"

"Oh, don't worry about him," Roz said briskly. "He's paid to sit and wait for people."

"Some job," said Miles. "I don't envy him. Well, maybe we should tell your lawyers anyway."

"Yes, we should. But Henry won't be up yet even. He keeps academic hours. Don't worry, we'll call later. Are you hungry?"

"I sure am."

"I am, too. Let's go and get some breakfast. Now, let's see"—she looked at him doubtfully—"they won't let you into the Connaught in those clothes. Or the Ritz. Oh, God, where can we go?"

"Mrs. Emerson, I only want a coffee and some bacon. Do you have to wear a tux for that in England?"

Roz laughed. "Sorry. Practically, yes, if it's high-class coffee and bacon."

"Then let's go find some of the lower-class kind."

"All right. We'll go to Shepherd's Market. And I don't really answer to Mrs. Emerson. Call me Roz."

"Okay."

"WHAT I WANT to know," she said as he swooped hungrily into a plate of bacon, mushrooms, tomatoes, and fried bread at one of the early morning sandwich bars in Shepherd's Market, "is how you found us in Dover Street."

"Oh, well, your stuffed shirt of a lawyer kept mentioning Morell. I got into Heathrow early, didn't know what to do, checked through the phone book, and there it was. The Morell Corporation, Julian Morell Industrials, God knows what else. I decided it was worth a try. That somebody might be here. And I was right. Which was nice," he added, smiling, "very nice."

Roz was suddenly aware of a warmth in her, comforting her, cheering her. "Nice for me, too," she said. He held her gaze for a moment with his lazy blue eyes. Just slightly discomfited, she looked away.

"So where is Mr. Emerson?" Miles asked, pushing his empty plate back, looking hopefully into his empty coffee cup. "Don't they give you refills here?"

"Mr. Emerson is in New York," Roz said in tones that totally discouraged further questioning on the subject, "and no, I'm afraid England has not discovered the secret of eternal coffee. Not yet. Some of us are working on it. Let me get you another cup."

She picked up his cup and walked over to the counter with it. Miles watched her. She certainly had a great pair of legs.

"There. Good and strong. How are you feeling?"

"Fine." He seemed surprised by the question. "Shouldn't I be?"

Roz smiled. "Most people complain about feeling tired after a transatlantic flight."

"Yeah, well, I'm young and strong." He grinned at her. "Could I have some toast or something?"

"Yes, of course." She called over to the girl behind the counter. "Three rounds of toast, please. With butter."

She turned back to Miles. "Just exactly how old are you anyway?"

"Twenty-seven."

"You look younger."

"How old are you?"

"Twenty-nine."

"You look older."

"Thanks."

"I didn't mean to be rude," he said hastily. "I'm sorry. But you do look kind of—well, stressed out. Tired. You look like you could do with some California sunshine."

"Oh, God," Roz said, "I would just adore some California sunshine."

"You should go there. Seriously. It would do you good."

"That's where you come from, isn't it?"

"How do you know that?"

"You'd be surprised what a lot we know about you."

"Jeez," he said. "Why do I matter so much?"

"We'll tell you very soon."

"So how did you find out where I came from?"

"A roundabout route. From your uncle is the short answer."

"Who, Bill, up in San Francisco? How did you track him down?"

"He answered our advertisement in—let's see, July, I suppose it must have been."

"Bastard," Miles said. "He didn't tell me. Or maybe he did, and the letter got holed up with all the others by old Marcia."

"Who is Marcia?"

"A crazy old woman my grandmother lives with. She had a whole stack of letters addressed to me and my grandmother, all the newspaper clippings people had sent from all over."

"And you and your dad and mother lived in L.A.?"

"Santa Monica."

"But they're both dead?"

"Yup." He looked at her and grinned. "It's all right. I don't really feel like the tragic orphan. It was a long time ago. I can hardly remember my dad dying. My mom—well, that was a long time, too, but I remember it—her more clearly."

"Tell me about her," said Roz.

"She was really pretty. She had blond hair and very blue eyes, and she was fun. She was always laughing. She gave me a real nice childhood. She loved the beach; we were there a lot. We lived near the ocean."

"And she died of—what?"

"Cancer." He was silent for a moment, the memory suddenly brought sharply into focus. "She was young. Only forty-three."

"And you were—what?"

"Thirteen. Just a little bitty boy." He sighed, then smiled at her. "It was very sad. I remember wanting to die, too, so I could be with her again. I missed her so much."

"After your mother died, you and your grandmother stayed in Santa Monica?"

"For a few years. Then we moved out to Malibu. This old guy, Hugo Dashwood, thought I was getting into bad company in Santa Monica. He bought a house in Malibu for us."

"He sounds like a very generous person," Roz said thoughtfully. "Who was he?"

"A friend of my parents."

"He must have been rich."

"Yeah, I guess so. He sent me through college, too."

"This man—this Hugo Dashwood. What was he like?"

"He was English," Miles said. "Very English."

"Where did he live?"

"I don't know."

"You don't know! He bought you a house and sent you to college and you don't know where he lived? When did you last see him?"

"A long time ago. But I did write to him recently. I'm not very proud of it, but I did."

"How recently?"

"Last summer."

"Why?"

"I needed some money really badly. I'd done something stupid."

"What? Not drugs?"

"No, no, not drugs. But I'd—borrowed some money on the house in Malibu, and I had to pay it back. I didn't know where to turn. I wrote to him. He wrote me a letter back and said he was coming to Nassau to see me in June. But he never did. I never heard from him again. My uncle lent me the money, though."

"Well," she said briskly, "I think we should ring Henry and tell him you're with me. He must be terribly anxious about you."

"And the driver."

"Who? Oh, him. Yes, well, Henry can call him on the car phone. Come on, let's go back to the office and we'll call Henry from there. Then I imagine he'll want you to go over to Lincoln's Inn and see him."

"I'd like to take a shower before I go and see anyone else," said Miles. "Would that be possible?"

"Of course," Roz said. "My father's office has a shower. Do you want to change? Do you have any clean clothes?"

"I have a clean shirt. Won't he mind?"

"Mind what?"

"Your father. Mind me using his shower."

"Oh," Roz said, and there was a wealth of sadness in her voice suddenly. "No, I'm afraid he can't mind. He's dead."

"I'm sorry," said Miles. "Recently?"

"Fairly recently. Back in May."

"Were you close?"

"In a way, yes," Roz said in tones that made it clear the subject was closed. "Come on, let's go. I can't wait to hear Henry's voice."

HENRY'S VOICE WAS irascible. "Well of course I was worried. Why on earth didn't you ring me earlier, Roz? Parsons has been waiting at Heathrow for over an hour. I thought Miles had done a bunk."

"You don't have to worry about him," said Roz, "he's not the bunking kind. He's upstairs having a shower. Shall I bring him over?"

"I think that would be best. But, Roz—"

"Yes, Henry?"

"I think I should talk to him alone. Preliminarily. If you don't mind."

"Really, Henry, what do you think I'm going to do? Abduct him? Offer him my body in return for his support and his share?"

"No, of course, not," Henry said irritably. "But I think in the interests of protocol . . . legal procedure . . ."

"All right, Henry. Protocol has it. I'll wait outside the door. Tell your secretary to get me a glass, would you?"

"What for?"

"So I can hold it to the wall and listen, of course. Why else?"

She sounded, Henry thought, unusually cheerful.

MICHAEL BROWNING SAT in his office on Madison Avenue and thought about Roz. He felt, deep within him, stirring through his outrage, a sudden sense of mild remorse. She did, after all, have a point. It was a pretty blunt one, but it was a point. His visit to Phaedria had not, he felt bound to admit to himself, been entirely innocent. He had not gone with a view to seducing her, but he did find her immensely attractive, and he had very much wanted to see her. On an adultery scale of one to ten, his behavior would certainly have rated a seven. With her cooperation, it would almost certainly have hit ten. Otherwise, he thought mournfully, drowning his fourth strong coffee of the day, he would have told Roz. No, he wouldn't. If Phaedria had been a sixty-five-year-old harridan, with crossed eyes and a wooden leg, Roz would have been jealous, because of who she was and because of the hold Phaedria had over her. As it was, with that hair and those eyes and that body—Michael wrenched his mind away from a contemplation of Phaedria's body with an effort and turned his attention back to Roz. Should he make a move? Hell, he'd made so many. It was always he who made them. She just waited, and took. And if he did call her and apologize, then what? Back on the merry-go-round, the eternal ding-dong of sharing her with that company of hers and her obsession with it. And sharing it certainly wasn't. It was one piece for him, and then around five thousand for the company. He'd had the rough end of that particular deal for years.

He wondered why and how he had stood it for so long. He supposed because he loved her. Had loved her. Did he still love her? He thought about her for a minute, saw her face as it was in the rare moments when she was relaxed and happy, with her white skin, her snapping green eyes, the heavy jaw that caused her so much anguish. He thought of being with her, of her swift, sharp mind, her salty humor, her capacity for lateral thought.

She was greedy, but her greed did not stop at money and power; it made her a desirable woman. Her physical appetites were considerable, she loved good food, she had a rare appreciation of fine wine— and could drink him under the table if she chose to—and her sexual prowess was remarkable. Michael had not known many women—in fact only perhaps one other, and she had been a whore from the Bronx—who could come to orgasm as many times and with such triumphant pleasure as could Roz.

But the price he paid for her was high. Too high. There was probably very little future in once again trying to stick the relationship together. The thought saddened him, grieved him, even. Roz had been the focus of his sexual and indeed his emotional thinking for so long, but it was probably better to leave it lying there, on the floor of the Algonquin, shattered, but at least dramatically, splendidly so, than go around patiently picking up all the endless tiny fragments and looking at them, endeavoring to see how they could be put back into a whole.

He thought of Phaedria suddenly, so different from Roz, and yet like her in some ways, with the same stubbornness, the same drive, the same courage. She was certainly not the gentle grieving young widow that the media had tried to turn her into. He admired her guts enormously. He admired a great deal about her. He wondered if they did indeed have any kind of future together. It was far too early to say. She might be—she undoubtedly was—sexily, divinely beautiful; she might be funny and interesting and original; but that did not necessarily make her into a woman he could love. What he did know was that he wanted to see her urgently, now, soon, more than anything in the world.

What was the time in California? Eight o'clock. She'd be having her breakfast. He picked up the phone, dialed the hotel, asked for her bungalow.

"Phaedria! Hi, it's me, Michael."

He heard her voice, low, relaxed, almost amused. "Hello. Why aren't you working? It's Monday morning."

"I know."

"Well?"

"I can't work."

"Why not?"

"I keep thinking of you."

"Well, that's ridiculous. You're supposed to be a tycoon. You can't be distracted that easily."

"I'm not distracted easily."

"Oh." He heard her thinking. Then: "Michael, I do think we shouldn't pursue this relationship at all." She gave it the heavy English, almost schoolmistressy emphasis.

"We don't have a relationship. I'm just trying to think what one would be like."

"Dangerous."

"Maybe. Well, I just thought, you're leaving there when? Friday?"

"Thursday."

"I didn't really complete my business in L.A. I might have to come back and have a couple more very urgent meetings. If I do, will you have dinner with me?"

"No."

"Lunch?"

"No."

"A glass of water?"

"No."

"Oh, God."

"Michael, listen, I—" She was silent.

"I'm listening."

"I just don't think—"

"I don't want you to think."

"But Roz—"

"Roz will never forgive either of us. We may as well make the most of it."

"But I have to work with her."

"You don't."

"Michael, of course I do."

"You could do something quite different."

"Really? Like what?"

"You could sell out and marry me."

"Oh, don't be absurd."

"That's not a very flattering response to a proposal."

"You know you didn't mean it."

"I might have."

There was a long silence.

"Phaedria, I'm coming out there. I've decided. I'll be in L.A. to-night. I'll be under your window at moonrise with a violin. You can turn me away if you like."

She laughed. She couldn't help it. "Oh, all right. I shouldn't say that, but all right."

"Bye, honeybunch."

"Good-bye, Michael."

She put the phone down, smiling, wondering where in the name of heaven, or hell for that matter, this was going to lead her. It rang again almost immediately. It was Father Kennedy.

"Ah," he said, "you are still here. I wondered if I could catch you."

"Yes, Father, I don't leave until Thursday."

"Ah, then, I'm glad I called. You asked me for a photograph of Mr. Dashwood?"

Phaedria's heart began to thump rather painfully. "Yes. Yes, I did."

"Well, I remembered. Of course I have one. It was taken at Miles's graduation. I took it myself. I found it last night, cleaning out my desk. Would you like to see it? It's a very nice picture of Miles as well."

"Yes, Father, I would," she said slowly. "I would really like to see it very much. Perhaps I could come down and get it this morning."

MILES CAME OUT of Henry Winterbourne's office a while later looking a little shaken.

"Henry!" Roz said. "The poor man's as white as a sheet. What on earth have you been doing to him?"

"He hasn't been doing anything to me," said Miles, mustering a smile. "Just breaking the news."

"And?"

"And I think I need a while to take it in. Suddenly I feel pretty tired."

"Look," Roz said. "Let's go back to Dover Street. There's a bed up in the penthouse; you can have a nap there if you want to. Meanwhile I'll get my secretary to book you into a hotel. Then you can make any calls or whatever you want to do."

"Okay," Miles said. "Thanks."

"Er, Roz, could I have a word?" said Henry. "About the contracts."

His rather long, solemn face distorted into a strange grimace, and

Roz suddenly realized he was trying to wink. With a great effort she nodded solemnly.

"Of course. Excuse us, will you, Miles?" She followed Henry into his office. "Now then, Henry, what do you think?"

"Well, he does seem to be an extremely nice young man, and I really have no doubt at all that he is indeed Miles Wilburn," said Henry. "He showed me his birth certificate and his passport and a letter from his college professor at Berkeley. His story about this Dashwood character is so extraordinary and so consistent with everything that Bill Wilburn said that it just has to be true, whatever it means. We now know a great deal about Miles, through the various stray ends picked up by your detective, and C.J."

"Oh yes," Roz said with a slightly sour expression. "C.J.'s detective work was very impressive. I'm surprised he shared it with you, since he seemed to be acting on Phaedria's behalf."

"Roz, it's in everybody's interest to get this thing sorted out," Henry said rather severely, stifling the memory of his early favoritism of Phaedria's cause. "C.J. felt we should pool our knowledge, and I think he was right. Especially with Lady Morell being away and so on."

"Quite," Roz said tersely. "Well, anyway, Henry, what happened just now, with Miles?"

"I told him simply that he had been left two percent of your father's company. And that on account of the extraordinary structure of the will, it was a controlling two percent. I thought that was quite enough for now. Of course, there isn't any more to be said anyway. And he hasn't been left any money as such. Oh, and I asked him again if he had any idea who your father was, if he was quite sure he had never met him, why he thought he could possibly have been left this—this legacy."

"And?"

"And of course he hadn't."

"Well," said Roz, "perhaps we shall all find out eventually."

"I think he's feeling a little shell-shocked just now."

"I expect he is, poor chap. Don't worry, I'll look after him."

GOING BACK TO Dover Street in the car, Miles said, "I feel like that guy in the fairy tale. You know, the one who was a frog until the princess kissed him and turned him into a prince. He must have felt pretty confused as well."

"Goodness," said Roz. "I hope Henry didn't kiss you."

Miles laughed. "No. But you know what I mean."

"I think I do. It's an extraordinary business, isn't it?"

"Sure is. I have to tell you my initial reaction is to just give it back."

"Is it, now?"

"Yeah. I don't want to get mixed up in some billion-dollar company. That just isn't *me*."

"Well, don't even think about giving it away," Roz said briskly. "At least sell it."

"Yeah, I hadn't thought of that," Miles said doubtfully.

"And then," Roz said carefully, "who would you sell it to?"

"I don't know. Who would you suggest?"

"Me of course," said Roz, carefully lighthearted.

He turned to look at her, not lighthearted at all, very, very serious. "Would you want it?"

"Of course."

"Why?"

"Well, because—oh, dear, Henry obviously hasn't explained things properly to you at all. That two percent would immediately give me the controlling interest in the company."

"Yes, he did explain that. Sort of. But why would you want that?"

"If you can't see that," Roz said, equally serious, "there's no point my trying to explain it. But anyway, much as I want it, I wouldn't dream of letting you hand it over just like that. Whatever you may hear about me in this company—and I do assure you, you will hear a great deal, not all of it, indeed very little of it, good—I do actually have a few scruples. I wouldn't dream of letting you hand over your two percent just like that. I would like you to sell it to me because I had persuaded you to for good sound commercial reasons, but I have no desire whatsoever to just walk away with it and leave you wondering why you let it go. Okay?"

"Okay," said Miles. He looked at her consideringly. "You're kind of an interesting person."

"Thank you."

"Tell me about the other one."

"Which other one?"

"The one who has the other forty-nine percent."

"Oh," Roz said, "Phaedria. The grieving widow."

"Sounds as if you don't like her very much."

"No," said Roz, "I don't. Maybe you should get someone else to tell you about her."

"So she's where?"

"She's in California. Taking an unconscionably long time to recover from having a baby."

"Why did she have it there?"

"Because she's a fool," Roz said.

"Oh, I don't know," Miles said easily. "I would think it's a pretty nice place to have a baby. I plan to bring my children up there."

"Do you, now? Do you plan to have a lot of children?" Roz asked, eager to draw the conversation away from Phaedria Morell.

"Yup. Like all only children, I wanted brothers and sisters. And like all only children, I want a large family of my own."

"I see. Is this large family imminent?"

"I don't think so," Miles said. "Candy—my girlfriend—is only eighteen. Her dad is pretty much against us getting married. He's a rich guy," he added. "He has a big business."

"Really. What's his name?"

"Mason McCall."

"Oh, yes," said Roz. "The candy bar king."

Miles looked at her with new respect. "You guys don't miss a trick, do you?"

"We have to know what other companies are doing."

When they got to Dover Street, a pale blue Rolls was standing outside.

"Goodness," Roz said. "News travels fast. That's my grandmother's car. She must have heard you've been found, and come to meet you."

She was right. Letitia was standing at Roz's desk, dressed in a cream silk suit, leafing happily through Roz's in-tray.

"Granny Letitia! How lovely to see you!" Roz said, kissing her fondly. "How are you?"

"Perfectly well, darling, thank you. I haven't seen as much of you as I would like, or of that great-granddaughter of mine." She looked at Roz critically. "You look very thin. And tired. You've been overworking."

Only Roz could have fully appreciated the wealth of meaning and double meaning in Letitia's voice; she smiled at her brilliantly. "Not really. You look wonderful. Whose suit?"

"Do you like it? Thank you, darling. Bruce Oldfield. Such a charming young man. Speaking of charming young men," she said, turning the full force of her violet eyes, her dazzling smile on Miles, "you must be Miles."

"I am," he said, looking at her bemusedly, holding out his hand. "It's a pleasure to meet you."

"Thank you. I am Letitia Morell. Founding grandmother of this company. So they finally found you. My goodness, there is so much we want to know, and you must be worn out, poor chap. And hungry,

I should think. Roz, why don't we take him to lunch, you and I? We could go to Langan's."

LUNCH WAS A great success. Letitia grilled Miles through the first course, about his childhood, his growing up in California, and in particular his days on the beach—"It sounds wonderful"—and then he grilled her through the second course about her days as a debutante, life in London between the wars, and the Prince of Wales with whom she claimed an ever closer acquaintance with every year that passed. Eventually they parted—Letitia reluctantly to First Street, Roz to the office, and Miles to his much-postponed sleep.

Miles let himself into the penthouse and walked into the little bedroom. He felt utterly and unaccustomedly exhausted. He supposed it was a combination of the long night flight, the champagne at lunch, and the considerable trauma of the morning.

This really was all something else. It was like some kind of a bad B movie. Billy hadn't been so far off when he had said something about him being Lord Fauntleroy. What a mob to get mixed up with. It was dynamite. There was that nice sexy bitch downstairs—nothing wrong with her, Miles thought easily, that a good screw and a bit of TLC wouldn't sort out; the funny old lawyer, straight out of Dickens; and the marvelous old lady. She was something else. He wanted to see a great deal more of her. And then there was the other one, the missing one, whom Roz was clearly dying to feed ground glass to three times a day before meals. What could she be like? The old lady was obviously very fond of her.

She was young—twenty-seven, they'd said—so either the old boy was still in good shape or she'd married him for his money. Probably the latter. That was obviously what Roz thought.

And he held the balance of power between them. The thought made Miles feel slightly sick. No wonder they'd wanted to find him. What on earth was he going to do? He had been speaking the truth when he told Roz he just wanted to give it all away again. The last thing on earth he wanted was to get mixed up in some power struggle. He didn't want to hold power, and he didn't want to assist anyone else to hold any. The prospect held about as much charm for him as joining a monastery. But he could see that even giving it away wouldn't be that simple. Whoever he gave it to, there would be trouble. Besides, Roz had a point. Why *give* it away?

No, the best thing would be to sell it and then go home to Candy and persuade old man Mason to let them get married. Roz would buy his share, that was for sure. He liked her, he thought she was really nice under that hard front of hers, and it would obviously help her. Why drag it out any longer?

God, this Julian Morell, whoever he was, must have been a mean old buzzard. Why would he screw all these people? And why involve him? Miles decided he really ought to wait until Lady Phaedria or whatever her name was came home, and talk to her as well. It was only fair.

He looked around. The room was bare, except for a bed, a coat stand, a cupboard, and a small bedside table.

There were a few photographs on the wall: an aerial view of a big house in the country and several pictures of horses. No people. He sat down on the bed, took off his jacket, slung it on the floor, looked around again.

His eyes fell on the bedside table. It had a couple of drawers in it. He opened the top one. It was empty. But in the second one he found a small silver frame. He took it out, turned it over and looked at the picture in it. For a moment the face in front of him meant nothing at all. Then his brain connected with what he saw; the picture first blurred, then clarified with extraordinary vividness. He stood up and slowly his eyes fixed on it, his mind a whirring, confused mess. He walked out of the penthouse and took the elevator down to Roz's office. She was talking on the phone and reading letters at the same time; she looked up at him, smiled, waved to him to sit down in the chair in front of her desk. Miles sat there looking alternately at her and at the photograph in his hand.

When she had finished talking she put down the phone and said, "What is it? Couldn't you sleep?"

"I haven't tried," Miles said. "Not yet. Look, Roz, I don't know what's going on around here, but why do you all keep saying you don't know Hugo Dashwood when there's a picture of him up in your dad's office?"

· 34 ·

FATHER KENNEDY WAS A LITTLE worried about Lady Morell. She seemed like such a fragile little thing, and seeing the photograph of Hugo Dashwood with Miles had obviously given her a big shock. She had tried very hard not to show him what a shock it was, had managed to smile and say what a nice picture, and it was wonderful to know what they both looked like at last, but she had turned very pale, and he had insisted she sit down and have a cup of tea before she left.

MICHAEL BROWNING ARRIVED at Phaedria's bungalow at six o'clock that evening. It was dark, and there was no light inside. He thought perhaps she might still be at the hospital and went to the desk to ask.

No, they said, Lady Morell was there; she had been there all afternoon. Perhaps she was asleep? Should they call her? No, Michael said, he would go himself and knock on the door; she was expecting him. Probably they were right and she was asleep.

He went back and knocked. Phaedria's voice answered. She sounded strained, odd. "Who is it?"

"It's the serenading team," he said. "Only we left our violins at home. Can we come in?"

The door opened. Phaedria stood before him, ashen. Her eyes were swollen, and there were deep shadows under them. She was shaking. "Oh, Michael," she said. "I'm glad you're here."

"Phaedria, what on earth is it? It's not—"

"No," she said, and there was just an echo of a smile on her stricken face. "No, Julia's fine."

"Then what is it?"

She walked through to the sitting room, picked up a photograph from the table. "Look."

He looked. "It's Julian. Who's that with him?"

"That's Miles."

"Oh. So Julian did know him. Nice-looking boy."

"Yes. But that's not the point. That isn't Julian. Well, it is, but it isn't."

"Phaedria, you're not making any sense."

"None of it makes any sense," she said, and there was a sob in her voice. "Well, no, that's not true. It's beginning to. This is Hugo Dashwood, Michael. Julian was Hugo Dashwood. He was obviously leading a completely double life. None of us knew about it."

ROZ FELT AS if she would never sleep again. She was possessed of a feverish, almost hysterical restlessness. Every time she felt her eyes closing she saw Miles looking at her over her father's photograph, and her mind snapped into frenzied activity again.

She wasn't quite sure what she felt: pain, confusion, disbelief, outrage. She felt as if everything that her life had been based on had been shot at and was steadily and relentlessly crumbling away underneath her. She had made Miles go over his story about Hugo Dashwood and the part he had played in his life a dozen times. There were still no clues as to why her father should have done such a thing. And how could he have kept it from them over all these years? His mother, his child, his wives, his mistresses—all of them had known him so little that he could perpetrate this deceit upon them? It was monstrous. Obscene.

How extraordinary, Roz thought, that Phaedria should have made the discovery on the same day, almost at the same time. Henry had phoned her to tell her about Miles's arrival in England and said she had been almost hysterical and had slammed the phone down. It was only when he phoned her the second time, to tell her about Hugo's identity, that she told him she had known; that had been the reason for her earlier distress. For the briefest moment Roz felt a flicker of sympathy for Phaedria; she suppressed it fiercely. Of them all she deserved the least sympathy over this. She had known Julian Morell for less than three years; she did not have a long, happy, private piece of history with him that she was now being forced to surrender as she realized there had been another life, and probably other loves, that she had no place in, no part of.

"What was he like?" Roz had kept saying endlessly to Miles. "What sort of person was he? Did you like him? What did he do? How did he talk? What did he say to you?"

And Miles, anxious not to make her pain worse, eager to reassure her, had begun to rewrite history. Hugo Dashwood had been very kind, very generous to his dad. He had helped his dad with his business a lot, his mother always said, and he had been very good to Miles's mother. He had visited her when she was dying. And of course

Hugo had been kind to him and his grandmother as well. His grandmother had really, really liked Mr. Dashwood, depended on him, looked to him for everything, and he had been good to her. She had talked to him much more often in the last few years than Miles had. Roz should talk to her.

And had he never even hinted of a family in England? Well, yes, he had, but it had not been this family, of course. He had told them —very little, very, very little—about a wife named Alice and two little boys, or maybe it was three.

Oh, God, thought Roz, was that family going to surface, too? Was that a real family or a second fantasy? Were they living somewhere, wondering what had become of their father, waiting for him to come home? The nightmare grew and grew as she thought about it, lived through it.

"Honestly," Miles had said to Roz, looking at her concernedly, his dark blue eyes full of sympathy, "I never did get to know him that well. He was my dad's friend, really. My dad's and my mom's. More my dad's. Well, that's what my mom said. She never seemed to like him especially. He made her a little nervous. Jumpy, you know? As far as I can remember, anyway. You have to remember I was only a kid when my mom died. It's a long time ago."

"Of course," Roz had said. "Oh, God, it's all so totally baffling. Why would he do such a thing? What did he gain? I just don't understand it."

Miles had looked at her. "Me neither," he said and then, anxious, eager to help: "Would you like me to call my grandmother? I warn you," he had added, "she doesn't make a lot of sense these days. I don't know what good it would do."

"No," Roz said, "no, I don't either. It would probably only upset her. I'll wait till C.J. gets here. He may have some idea what to do."

She didn't really have a great deal of faith in C.J. But he was family and he was better than nothing; she needed someone to help her through this. She longed passionately for Michael. He would know what to do, how to handle it. Where was the bastard, and why did it have to be now, of all times, that she had lost him?

And then suddenly, in the middle of her raging, she was assaulted by a thought so hideous, so malevolent that she experienced it as physical pain, a sick, awful pain, violent and sudden, like a crick in the neck, the crack of an elbow on a hard surface. She crushed it, raced away from it, wrenched her mind toward other things, other people; but it lay coiled up in her mind like some obscene monster, and occasionally, when she was least prepared for it, it would shift, stir, and threaten her again and again.

C.J. LOOKED DOWN at the gray depression beneath him that was Heathrow in November and wondered why on earth he had agreed to come back. Life had just begun to improve, to brighten, to simplify even. He was happy with Camilla, she made him feel appreciated, significant, calm, and those feelings were balm to his almost mortally wounded soul. He and Camilla had much in common; they were suited intellectually, emotionally, and much to C.J.'s surprise and pleasure, sexually. They had the same background, had been reared to the same upper-class American standards, attended similar schools, talked the same language in the same accent, understood the same jokes, shared the same values. They and their families, they discovered, had generations-back mutual friends. Had they been the same age they would have attended the same parties, gone to the same places on vacation, probably met, certainly have been attracted to each another, possibly even married.

PHAEDRIA FINALLY REACHED Regent's Park, exhausted, the following afternoon.

Julia had been very good and slept through most of the flight, waking only to feed and gaze sweetly around her, occasionally smiling her surprised, lopsided smile; nevertheless it was a relief to get her home and into the arms of her newly engaged nanny for a few hours.

Michael had seen them off at the L.A. airport; he had taken Phaedria in his arms and given her a huge bear hug.

"I don't dare kiss you even on your forehead," he said, looking at her tenderly, lovingly, his eyes nonetheless amused both at himself and at her for their entirely—as he put it—profligate restraint. "I would forget myself entirely and ravish you here and now right in front of Immigration. Now, take care of yourself, and call me if you need me."

"I will," she said. She felt she could have stayed there in his arms, safe, protected from the fears that filled her, for hours, days; she pulled back, looked at him, at his gloomily amused face, his restless dark eyes, interminably exploring her, his oddly hard, tough mouth —she had begun to dream of that mouth and what it could do to her —felt his warmth, his solid, comforting, caring warmth, and somehow managed to smile; but she felt chilled and totally bereft as she finally walked away from him.

All the way home she thought alternately of him and of Julian, her mind and emotions a jumble of hurt and fear, longing and confusion. It occurred to her suddenly, as she looked out at the endless blue beside and beyond her, that she had never met Michael, never been with him, under circumstances that were not extraordinary; when she had not been ill or frightened or grieving or shocked. And yet he managed unfailingly to make her feel calm, happy, safe, to make things seem hopeful and normal and, above all, interesting. He was very sexually attractive—very, very sexually attractive, she thought, wrenching her mind with an effort from a rather too vivid contemplation of what might have been—but, more unusually, he was emotionally exciting; he gave life, people, experiences, a new vividness and interest.

Well, it was not to be, she thought; she would just have to find them less vivid and interesting, and to suppress the ferocious feelings that roared through her body every time she even thought about him. He belonged to Roz, and even if she had been less afraid of Roz, less hostile to her, Phaedria would not have considered taking him away from her. The pain of seeing Camilla's head on the pillow of her bed, hers and Julian's, in New York, was still fresh and raw in her. She would not, could not, inflict that on anybody. Not even Roz. Moreover, just now Roz, probably even more than she, needed Michael. Even in her own considerable unhappiness, Phaedria shuddered at the thought of the hurt Roz must be enduring.

And there was another pain, equally fresh and raw, still in her, that she knew made it impossible for her to enter into emotional commitments. She had, with all their problems, their battles, the shortcomings of their relationship, loved Julian very much. He had been her first lover and her first real love, and he had died only six months earlier. She was still cautiously, painfully working her way through her grief—rekindled suddenly and horribly by this new trauma, and she was simply not ready to go forward into anything else.

Quite suddenly as she sat there, gazing blankly out of the window, a terrifying thought came to her unbidden, unwelcome. Straight from a nightmare, worse than a nightmare. So bad she had to get up, walk up and down the aisle for a while, then order a drink.

"No," she said to herself, half aloud. "No. It's not possible."

Her voice broke into the baby's sleep; she stirred, half opened her eyes, moved her tiny arms. Phaedria looked at her, and picked her up suddenly, holding her very tightly. "Oh, baby," she said, "what troubles we seem to have, you and I."

♦   ♦   ♦

"LETITIA? HELLO, IT'S Phaedria."

"Darling, how lovely to hear your voice. How are you, and when can I come and see you and meet that baby? I would have come out to see you in California, but my fool of a doctor said I shouldn't."

"Letitia, have you been ill?"

"Not seriously, darling, only the flu, but I did feel a bit tired after it. I told him the sunshine would do me good, but he didn't seem to see it that way."

"Letitia, you must take care of yourself. You do too much."

"I do far too little," Letitia said briskly. "That's half the trouble. I'm thinking of coming back to work full-time. Could you find me some little task, do you think? As accounts clerk or something?"

"I'm sure we could," said Phaedria. "It would be marvelous."

"Good. Well, maybe after Christmas. I'll come for an interview. Now then, when am I going to see you both?"

"Whenever you like. The baby is simply beautiful, Letitia, and she looks just like Julian."

"Oh, how wonderful. It's all too good to be true. Shall I come over in the morning? I expect you're tired now."

"I am a bit, but if you really want to, I'd love to see you now. I could send Pete."

"No, darling, I'm a little tired myself. I've had—well, a rather interesting conversation with Roz. About Julian."

"I know. That's really why I rang. To see if you were all right."

"Much more all right than you might think. Of course it was a shock, but you know, Phaedria, I had suspected something like this. Well, no, not suspected; that is putting it too strongly. But it certainly wasn't as surprising to me as it must have been to you."

"Really, Letitia? How extraordinary. Tell me why."

"Oh, I don't know. It seemed such a nonsense, his leaving that inheritance to a complete stranger. It had to be a kind of riddle. And most riddles have perfectly obvious answers after all."

"I suppose so."

"You see, he did have this passion for deceit. 'Secrecy' is perhaps a kinder word. He loved it even as a little boy. He used to go to such lengths to surprise me with birthday presents, things like that. And then there was his Resistance work in the war. He assumed at least two—three, I think—completely different identities. Separate papers, passports, everything. He adored it and he was brilliant at it. It's my guess this thing started as a sort of game, that he was bored one day and decided to see how far he could take it, and then it got out of hand, probably when this poor woman's husband died, and he was looking after her or keeping an eye on Miles. He had got rather close to them all, and it was just too late to say, 'Er, actually, I'm not who I said I was.' Do you see what I mean? And then of course"—her voice trailed away just slightly; and there was a short, painful silence—"there just might be another explanation, don't you think?"

"If you mean what I think you mean, no, I don't," Phaedria said quickly, determinedly, hearing in Letitia's quiet, almost detached tone the black nightmare that had first attacked her on the plane drawing nearer reality. "Not possibly. That couldn't be. It just couldn't."

"No, of course not," Letitia said. "No, obviously it couldn't. Well, perhaps we can talk about it all a bit more tomorrow. When I come and meet that baby. Now then," she said, deliberately changing her tone of voice, her mood, "you've heard about Miles, have you?"

"Well, yes—"

"I mean how deliciously handsome and charming he is?"

"I'm beginning to get the idea," Phaedria said, laughing, relieved to feel the nightmare fading again. "I shall meet him tomorrow, I imagine. Roz has whisked him off to Scotland so I can't steal a march on her and inveigle the shares away from him while she's not there. Poor Roz," she added. "I understand she's terribly upset."

"Yes, she is."

"I did try to phone her, but I missed her twice. I thought I'd ring her tonight at Garrylaig. She must see this as the ultimate betrayal. I mean, all this time she's thought that through all the relationships, all the wives, all the mistresses, she came first, that he loved her best, and now there's been this shadowy figure, this other life, all along."

"It's a pity Michael isn't here with her," Letitia said with a sigh. "I understand they've quarreled. Again. Now of all times. Well, I do hope they make it up. He really is the only man in the world who can handle her. She needs him terribly badly."

Phaedria wondered, as she put the phone down, if she had detected or merely imagined a slightly ominous note in Letitia's voice.

ELIZA TOOK THE news remarkably well.

"Nothing that old so-and-so did would surprise or shock me, darling," she said as she and Roz walked the castle grounds together. "If you told me he'd made off with the crown jewels or had personally murdered Lord Lucan, I would think it par for the course. I think it's all rather romantic. I just wish I'd known before, when he was alive. I could have teased him about it. You mustn't be too upset, Roz. He really was rather—well, odd. I know you loved him terribly, and if it's any comfort to you, I think you were the only person he really loved in return. I don't think this means you have to think he loved you any less."

"He must have quite loved Miles," Roz said soberly, "to have done this to us all."

"I don't think so. Quite the reverse. If he'd really loved him, he would have brought him out of the wardrobe or whatever the expression is, before. Good God, I— No, no, surely not. Probably not. Well—"

"Mummy, what on earth are you talking about?"

"Oh, I don't know," Eliza said, appearing to shake herself. "Just a thought. Take no notice, darling. My mind's wandering. Senility setting in. Miles is frightfully handsome, isn't he?" she said quickly. "And what a charmer. We could hardly have a more delightful pretender to the throne, could we?"

"No, not really," Roz said listlessly. "I'm sorry, Mummy, I simply can't accept this matter-of-fact view of yours. And Letitia's, it seems. C.J. phoned and says she's just fine. Says she's always suspected it or some such nonsense. I just see it as an awful betrayal."

"Oh, I think the will was a betrayal," said Eliza. "Don't get me wrong. But this double life business, well, it's just too ridiculous. Silly. You mustn't let it upset you too much." She looked at Roz's drawn, pale face and shadowed eyes. "How's Michael?"

"Fine," Roz said briefly. "Very busy."

"Really? I would have thought he would have flown over, with all this."

"Whyever should he? He has a business to look after. Why should a lot of nonsense like this have him rushing away from it?"

"He knows how much you loved your father. He wouldn't think it was nonsense. When is he coming over?"

"I don't know," Roz said irritably. "I really haven't discussed it with him."

Eliza gave her a probing look. "Have you quarreled again?"

"No. Well, in a way, yes."

"What about?"

"Oh, just about everything. I don't want to talk about it."

"Don't lose him, Roz. He's the right man for you."

"That's not what you said once," Roz said bitterly. "And I have a broken marriage to show for it."

"I know. I was wrong. Although I don't think I want to take the entire responsibility for your divorce onto my shoulders. But pride is a destructive thing, Roz. If this quarrel is even half your fault, you should apologize to Michael."

"It isn't," Roz said shortly, "and I'm not going to."

"All right, darling. Have it your own way. How's Phaedria?"

"I haven't the faintest idea," said Roz. "She only got back today."

"Ah," Eliza said, "so that's it. You were afraid she'd win Miles over to her side if you came up here alone. I did wonder."

"Don't be ridiculous," Roz said. "I just thought he might as well come and meet you instead of hanging around in London."

Eliza looked at her. "Which way do you think he's going to jump?"

"I don't know," Roz said wearily. "He doesn't want to jump at all. Just go home again to his girlfriend."

"Well, offer to buy him out and then he can go home."

"It's not as simple as that."

"Why not?"

"Because he knows he has to make a decision."

"Well, darling, I would have thought you were capable of leaning on him quite hard enough to persuade him. I would also have thought," she added, an expression that was half humorous, half shrewed, in her green eyes, "it might be quite a pleasure. Come along, darling, let's go in and have tea. I haven't told Peveril too much about all this yet. He already sees us as only a little better than the Borgias."

"Mummy, I don't think you should tell anyone about it," said Roz. "I don't want the gossip columns getting on to it. It would damage us all."

Eliza's large green eyes were widely candid. "Of course I won't, darling. Who would I tell?"

"Oh, nobody much. Just a few close, intimate friends—Nigel Dempster, Peter Langan, your friend Marigold Turner. No, Mummy, you really are not to talk about it. To anyone."

"So in that case, how do I explain who Miles is supposed be?" Eliza said crossly.

"An old friend of the family who's been mentioned in Daddy's will. It's taken us a while to track him down. Okay? We really cannot afford a major scandal about all this."

"Rosamund, whenever did I show any predilection for mixing myself up in major scandals?"

"Just about every week of your life so far," said Roz, looking at her mother with a mixture of exasperation and affection. "Come on, let's go in and have tea. I can't wait to see Peveril and Miles together."

"THEY WERE SOMETHING else," Miles said happily to Roz as they flew back to London in the company plane next morning. "I thought he was just the neatest old guy I ever met. I said I would ask him over to stay with us in California in the summer. He said he had always wanted to surf."

"Good God," said Roz, contemplating with great pleasure the vision of Peveril, complete with knicker and deerstalker hat, riding a board in the Malibu surf. "Can I come, too? I wouldn't miss that for anything."

"Sure," Miles said. "I'd really like that. And you could bring Miranda, too," he added. "She's a cute kid. Does she live up in Scotland all the time?"

"No, it's just that she was up there anyway. It's good for her, the air and so on, and with all this drama going on, I thought she and Nanny might as well stay for a while longer."

Miles looked at her curiously. She talked about and indeed behaved toward Miranda as if she were a small, none-too-familiar puppy. He had heard the English had a very odd attitude toward their children, first shutting them away in nurseries with starchy uniformed nannies, and then sending them off to school. It was obviously true.

"I guess she'll be off to boarding school soon," he said. Roz looked at him sharply, suspecting he was trying to put her down, but he smiled back at her with such transparent friendliness that she had to smile back.

"Not for a year or two," she said. "In fact, not till she's at least eleven."

"Did you go to boarding school?"

"Yes, I did. And I hated it."

"So why send her at all?"

"Well, because she has to go sometime," Roz said, looking at him as if he were querying the basis of the entire British constitution, "because it'll be good for her."

"It wasn't good for you."

"How do you know what was good or bad for me?" she said, quite crossly.

"Lots of things have been bad for you, I'd say," he said. "Otherwise you'd be happier."

"How do you know I'm not happy?"

"I feel it," he said. "I feel it and I see it."

"Well, that's just ridiculous."

"Why? Are you happy?"

"Well, not at the moment, no. Of course I'm not. I have a lot to be unhappy about."

"Like this business with your dad?"

"Yes, of course."

"Yeah, that's tough. I can see that. But before that were you happy?"

"Well, yes, of course I was."

"That's all right, then," he said, leaning back in the seat, looking out of the window.

Something about his air of complete relaxation and detachment irritated Roz. "Don't you believe me?"

"Not really."

"Why not?"

"You don't seem happy. Not to me. Of course I could be wrong."

"You are."

"Good," he said. "That's fine. You should know, I guess."

"Yes, I certainly should."

"Okay, I'm really glad."

He looked at her, his dark blue eyes examining her green ones, scanning her face, and smiled. "It's all right," he said, putting out his hand, covering hers with it. "You don't have to take any notice of me. I'm just a schmuck from California. I guess I don't understand you guys at all."

"No," Roz said, pulling her hand away, still irritated. "You don't."

"Okay," he said lazily. "Don't get uptight about it."

"I'm not uptight."

"You are, Roz," he said. "You're seriously uptight. But if you won't talk about it, then it has to stay your problem. If you don't want me to help, that's fine."

"And what," she said edgily, "do you think you could do to help?"

"I could do a lot," he said, his eyes caressing hers briefly, moving down, resting on her mouth.

Roz was silent for a while, digesting this, trying to suppress the conflicting emotions within her: irritation, misery, a desire at once to get closer to Miles and to keep her distance, and despite herself, the odd sense of physical disarray, of pleasant warm confusion he induced in her.

She looked at her watch. Only twenty minutes to go. Discretion won.

"It's very kind of you," she said, coolly courteous, "to be so concerned about me. But I really am perfectly all right. Or will be when this is over."

"Good," he said. "I'm really glad. I think I'll take a nap."

He smiled at her again, reached out in a tender, unexpected gesture and touched her cheek, and then closed his eyes and was asleep in seconds.

PHAEDRIA WAS JUST finishing her breakfast and concurrently giving Julia hers when the phone rang.

"Hi, darling. It's me."

She felt a rush of huge, bright pleasure, followed by the now familiar panic and unease.

"Aren't you speaking to me?" Michael asked. "Don't I get any kind of reward for having Franco wake me at five in the morning just so I could hear your voice? You're a hard woman, Lady Morell."

She laughed. "I'm sorry. I was surprised."

"Good. That was the idea. I plan to keep surprising you, catching you unawares. Eventually I plan to catch you so unawares you won't even know what you're doing or whether it's all right to be doing it. How are you?"

"I'm fine."

"Good. And what are you doing?"

"Feeding Julia."

"Oh, God," he said, "oh, God."

"What's the matter?"

"Nothing," he said. "Just having a little trouble with a particular part of my anatomy. Brought on by the image of Julia having her breakfast."

"Oh, Michael," she said, with a mixture of a laugh and a sigh in her voice. "Don't, please don't."

"Listen, honey, I'm trying not to. It isn't easy."

Phaedria gave up. "It's so nice to hear your voice."

"That's better. What are you going to do today?"

"I'm going to meet Miles."

"Ah. Where was he yesterday?"

"In Scotland," said Phaedria. "With Roz."

"Good Christ. She's not letting you get your hands on him, is she?"

" 'Fraid not."

"Will you promise to call me when you've finished with him?"

"Why?"

"Now, that is a ridiculous question. I can hardly believe you've asked it. Because I want to know what he's like. Because I want to know how you get along with him. Because I want to know what might be happening. Because I need to know how good-looking he is, in case I have to get jealous."

"Michael, please, please stop talking like this."

"Why?"

"You know why."

"I know why you think I should. I really don't know that I know. I have been giving our situation a great deal of thought, and I have come to a conclusion or two. Do you want to know what they are, or shall I stop donating half my income to the phone company and go back to sleep?"

Phaedria was silent, struggling with herself. Then she said, "Yes, I want to know."

"Okay. Here we go. I think you're terrific. I think you're clever and funny and beautiful. I love being with you. How am I doing?"

"All right."

"Only all right? For Christ's sake, Phaedria, here I am reciting a love letter across the Atlantic and all you can say is it's all right."

"Sorry. But you know—well, you know what I think."

"I plan to destroy your capacity to think. Can I go on?"

"All right."

"I want to go to bed with you."

"You can't. I've told you. Don't even think about it."

"Darling, I can't think about anything else."

"You have to. You have to think about Roz," she said.

"I've thought about Roz. Very hard."

"And?"

"I don't love her anymore."

"How do you know?" she said, her heart thudding so hard she could scarcely hear him.

"I just do. I did love her, very much. I loved a lot about her. But she killed it. Strangled it. It's dead."

"Michael, you can't fail her now. You just can't. She's so unhappy."

"Phaedria, I was unhappy lots of times. I was so unhappy, so lonely for her, I didn't know how to stand it. She didn't give a rat's ass. She said she did, but she didn't. All she ever cared about was that company and that father of hers, your husband. I beg your pardon, I don't mean to criticize him—"

"Please don't—"

"Sorry. I have to try to explain it, and he is crucial to the explanation. I spent years fighting him for Roz. It didn't stop when he died. Now I'm fighting him for you."

"No, you're not."

"Well, that's what it feels like. Okay, let's drop him. Let's get back to us."

"There isn't an us," she said, with such a huge effort it physically drained her.

"Phaedria, there should be. There has to be."

"There can't be."

"There will be. I swear it."

"Michael—"

"Phaedria, listen to me. Please, darling, please listen, for God's sake."

"I'm listening," she said, her resolve weakened by the urgency in his voice.

"Good. Because it's important. Very important." He was silent for a moment. Outside, she heard a car pull up. Pete, perhaps, back with the files she had sent for from the office.

"Phaedria, I know we have problems. Difficulties. I can see we have to take our time, tread carefully. But I can't go back to Roz now. I absolutely cannot." There was a pause. And a knock at the front door.

"Phaedria. I am seriously in love with you." Another pause. Voices.

"Phaedria, I think—no, for God's sake, I know, I want you to—"

"Good morning, Phaedria."

Phaedria slammed the phone down.

Roz was standing in the doorway.

"Good morning, Phaedria," Roz said again. "Please don't let me disturb your phone call. Was it important?"

"No," Phaedria said. "No, not at all. Good morning, Roz. How are you?"

"Very well, thank you. A little—tired, shall we say? So this is the baby."

"Yes."

"Very nice," Roz said, glancing dispassionately at Julia rather as if she were an ornament or a dress she didn't like the look of very much, but felt forced at least to acknowledge.

Phaedria looked at Roz steadily. She was pale but composed; she was wearing black, as she often did, with a scarlet scarf knotted around her shoulders. She looked dramatic, fierce, but not hostile. Indeed she was smiling faintly. "Well," she said, "welcome back to London."

"Thank you. Roz, I'm so sorry about the news—about your father. I did try to ring you several times, but—"

"I know you did," Roz said. "Thank you. I got the messages."

Phaedria stared at her, so effectively rebuffed she couldn't even speak.

"I—I think I'll take Julia upstairs," she said after a moment. "I'll ask Mrs. Hamlyn for coffee."

"Don't," Roz said. "I won't be here long."

"Well, I'd like some," Phaedria said firmly. "Excuse me for a moment."

She went upstairs, put the baby in her crib, and looked down at her for a while. Then, as if drawing strength from her, she stood up very straight and walked back downstairs.

Roz turned and looked at her, taking in the tanned skin, the glossy hair, the slender figure. "You look very well," she said. "But then, I suppose you would. You have just had what amounts to a very long holiday."

"In a way, yes."

"But you are fully recovered at last."

"I am fully recovered. It was Julia's health that kept me there, as you know. She was very frail."

"But she's well now?"

"Very well, thank you."

"And when are we to expect the pleasure of seeing you back at work?"

"Very soon," Phaedria said. "As soon as I have Julia settled. I'm looking forward to it."

"I daresay you are. You must have been bored and—lonely over there. Or weren't you?"

So that was it. A cold crawling chill invaded Phaedria's body; she felt sick. She swallowed hard and met Roz's eyes steadily. "Not really. I made friends. I had Julia. I was at the hospital most of the time."

"Good," said Roz, poisonously sweet, "and you had visitors, I believe?"

"Yes, I did. Several."

"Several?"

"Yes, several," Phaedria said steadily. "My father, of course."

"Of course."

"And Susan came, and C.J. and David Sassoon and your mother."

"So she did. How very thoroughly you have become a part of this family. Inveigled your way into it."

"Hardly inveigled," Phaedria said, meeting Roz's stormy eyes. "I did, after all, marry into it."

"You did. I tend to forget that. I somehow get the impression you do as well, from time to time."

"I don't know what you mean, I'm afraid," Phaedria said.

"Don't you?" Roz said. "Well, never mind. I believe Michael came to visit you?"

"Yes," Phaedria said. "Yes, he did. He came to see us."

"Us?"

"Yes, us. Me and the baby."

"How touching."

"It was very nice of him."

"Very. Extraordinarily nice. He stayed at your hotel, I believe?"

Phaedria had not realized she knew this. She swallowed again, hoping Roz wouldn't notice. "Yes, he did," she said.

"For two nights?"

"Yes."

"You slut," Roz said quietly.

"I beg your pardon?"

"I said you were a slut. My father has only been dead six months, that child of yours is only just born, and you start sleeping around with anyone who takes your fancy. Who else has been consoling you in your widowhood? C.J.? No, he hasn't got the balls. David Sassoon? You always did have the hots for him."

"Roz," Phaedria said, keeping her voice quiet with a huge effort, "please, could we stop this? I'm finding it grossly insulting. I can see that what's happened is difficult for you to accept, but nothing, absolutely nothing, happened between Michael and me."

"I don't find that hard to believe. I find it impossible."

Phaedria shrugged. "That's your problem."

"Is that all you have to say?"

"What else could there be?"

Roz was silent for a moment.

"I think you're lying," she said at last.

"You can think what you like," Phaedria said. "I really don't care. I do care, though"—and there was an icily warning edge to her voice—"if you share your thoughts with other people. I have not slept with Michael Browning, or indeed with anyone else. Nothing whatever happened between us, and that is the end of the matter. Have you talked to Michael about it?"

"Yes. He spun the same fairy story."

"Oh, Roz," said Phaedria, "it's not a fairy story. It's"—and her lips twitched, despite herself, into a half smile—"too unlikely to be untrue. Please, for all our sakes, take his word for it if you won't take mine. God, we have enough real problems, I would have thought, without manufacturing any more."

"Most of our problems," Roz said, "can be laid at your door. If you hadn't set out to trap my father, to worm your way into the company, to get your hands on his money, there would be no problems at all now."

"Roz, I did not trap your father."

"Oh, really? I suppose he fell madly and hopelessly in love with you and just swept you off your feet. And his money and his position meant nothing at all to you. Because if that's so, I don't quite understand why you can't just go away now and leave us alone, instead of hanging on for dear life, apparently totally set on getting your pound, or rather millions of pounds, of flesh. And anything else that might catch your fancy in the process."

"Roz, I'd like you to leave," said Phaedria. "I don't want to listen to any more of this."

"I don't suppose you do. Nobody else would say it, would they? They're all so besotted with you, so totally deceived by your innocent face and your little-girl ways, your grieving widow number. Well, I'm not. You make me want to throw up."

"Get out," Phaedria said, her eyes blazing. "Just get out. And shut up."

Roz looked at her consideringly. "All right," she said at last. "I'll go. I don't believe what you say but I can't prove that it's not true, so before you threaten me with slander action, you have my word I won't share my thoughts. For now." She looked at Phaedria very intently, the hatred in her eyes almost a physical force.

"Is there anything else you'd like to consider trying to take away from me?" she said. "First my father, then my birthright, and now my lover. Well, I do assure you there's something you are not going to get your hands on, Phaedria Blenheim, and that's Miles and his two percent."

"WELL," MILES SAID, "you certainly are a good-looking family."

He was standing in the doorway of the drawing room at Regent's Park; Phaedria had invited him to tea. Roz had gone straight to the office after her morning's visit to Phaedria and had consequently been unable to keep him under her eye any longer.

Phaedria inclined her head just slightly. "Thank you. I could return the compliment."

"Please do," he said, smiling. "A little flattery and I'm yours."

"Are you really?" She smiled. "Come in and sit down. Mrs. Hamlyn will bring tea in a minute."

"Thank you. So this is the famous baby?"

"This is."

"She's cute."

"Isn't she?"

"Of course," he said, "she has a head start on most of the human race, beginning her life in California."

"I do have to agree with you," Phaedria said with a sigh, looking out at the grayness of Regent's Park, the leaden sky, the dripping trees. "It seemed to me just the nicest place in the world. I was so happy there."

"Me, too." He sat down. "And I plan to go back there just as soon as I can."

"Do you really?"

"I really do. To Malibu. To the beach."

"My goodness," she said, "here you are, one of the most potentially powerful and rich young men in the world, and all you want to do is sit on a beach in California."

"Yes," he said. "Don't knock it."

"I'm not knocking it," she said. "I envy you. I think that kind of a life would be marvelous."

"You can go wherever you like," he said with simple logic, "can't you? You're not exactly too poor to spring for the plane fare."

"That's true. But I have—well, things to do."

"It's weird," he said, dropping the argument, "to hear myself described as powerful and rich. I've always been so hard up and so unpowerful."

She smiled at him. "The correct word is impotent."

"Yeah, well," he said, grinning back, "I'm not that. Thank heaven."

"Good," Phaedria said briskly. "That must be nice for someone."

"I hope so."

"You must feel you've strayed into some kind of bad dream," Phaedria said suddenly.

"Well," he said, "it's not all bad. But it is pretty strange. I really want to get back home soon, but I have some decisions to make first."

"Not really," said Phaedria. "Surely they can wait."

"Oh, no," he said, "I'd rather get it settled. Stay maybe a week or two and make up my mind. Then go home with a clear conscience."

"You won't even consider staying here and getting involved in the company?"

He looked at her and smiled into her eyes. Phaedria, who had not yet been on the receiving end of this particular experience, felt momentarily weak. She had no interest in Miles whatsoever, he was absolutely not the kind of man she found attractive, and yet at that moment, had he chosen, he could have trawled her into a fairly immoderate level of sexual interest.

"No," he said in answer to her question. "Not for a minute."

She was confused by him and by the tangle of her thoughts. "Sorry. Not for a minute what?"

He smiled again, aware of what he had done to her. "Not for a minute would I consider getting involved in the company."

"So what do you intend to do?"

"Sell out. Take the money and run. At first I thought I'd just run, but Roz said that was silly."

"Did she indeed?" Phaedria said thoughtfully. "That was very scrupulous of her."

"I think she is quite scrupulous," Miles said cheerfully, beaming at Mrs. Hamlyn who had come in with the tea tray. "Here, let me take that from you, ma'am."

Mrs. Hamlyn beamed back and rolled her eyes in a rather extraordinary way. Phaedria was momentarily alarmed; then she realized Mrs. Hamlyn was flirting with Miles.

"Thank you, Mrs. Hamlyn," she said briskly. "I'll ring if we want anything else."

"I wonder if Mr. Wilburn might like something more substantial to eat," said Mrs. Hamlyn. "That's not much of a tea there, not really."

"Oh, no, ma'am, thank you," Miles said, smiling at her again. "I had a huge lunch. But it's really kind of you to offer."

Mrs. Hamlyn rolled her eyes again and walked reluctantly to the door. "Well," she said hopefully, "there's plenty of food in the kitchen."

"Maybe another time," Miles said.

She looked up at him as if he had just suggested a weekend in Paris. "Maybe," she said with a last roll of her eyes, and then she was gone.

Phaedria looked at Miles and grinned. "You mustn't flirt with my female staff," she said.

"How about the males?" he said.

"Certainly not. Now then, come and have some tea and tell me again exactly what you want to do."

"What I really want to do is get married," Miles said.

"Anyone in particular?"

"Yes, my girlfriend. Candy McCall. She's eighteen."

"That's young," she said, "to get married. And how old are you, exactly? You look quite young to be getting married, too."

"Twenty-seven."

"Goodness. The same age as me."

"I'll bet no one told you you were too young to get married."

"Well, they did and they didn't," Phaedria said.

"I guess they said you were too young to marry—Sir Julian."

"Correct. They did. Miles, my husband—Hugo Dashwood, as you knew him—stepped in when your mother died, and took you on. Is that right?"

"Yes and no," Miles said carefully. "We didn't see a lot of him. Not until my dad died, anyway. Or rather until my mom got sick. Then he came to see her a lot."

"And—how do you remember him?"

"Well, he was very English, you know? A little formal. He was very generous and real good to my gran. She thought a lot of him."

Phaedria looked at him thoughtfully. "Does that mean you didn't?"

"Well, yes and no. He was very smart and all that. And it was real good of him to put me through college. I appreciated that. But we didn't have—well, a lot to say to each other."

"I'm surprised," Phaedria said, and meant it. "I would have thought you would."

"Why?"

"I'm not sure. I just would have thought you'd get on."

He smiled regretfully. "Sorry. No. Of course, the one thing I was really steamed about is all explained now."

"Which was?"

"I got mad because he wouldn't give me a job in one of his companies."

"I can't imagine you getting mad."

"I hardly ever do. But I was then."

"Well, as you say, it's explained now."

"Yup. I suppose it is."

"You studied math at college and graduated summa cum laude, someone said?"

"Yup."

"And you don't want to use that?"

"Nope. I just want to marry Candy, buy a nice house in Malibu, maybe get a boat."

He leaned back on the cushions, smiling at her. "I can see you all find that hard to understand. But I find it hard to understand the way you live. Working, worrying, fighting, as far as I can see. I mean Roz is a nice person. She could be so happy, you know, but she makes herself crazy worrying about where the next million's coming from."

"No, you're wrong," Phaedria said, adjusting with difficulty to the notion of Roz as a nice person—hadn't Michael said something similar a hundred years ago? "It has absolutely nothing to do with the next million. Or not a lot. It's about seeing something work and knowing it was you who made it work. It's very exciting."

"Uh-huh," Miles said.

"You and Roz aren't too fond of each other, I take it," he said suddenly.

"How do you know that?"

"I know she's jealous as hell of you. I know she thinks you're having an affair with her boyfriend."

"What!" said Phaedria. "She told you that?"

"Yeah, she did. More or less."

"Well, she's wrong."

"I told her she was wrong," he said, leaning back on the sofa, an expression of complacency on his face.

"Thank you," she said, amused. "That makes two of us, but I don't think she believed either of us. But how did you know it wasn't true?"

"It just didn't seem very likely."

"Why not? I'm intrigued. When you hadn't even met me. Or him, for that matter."

"I'm not sure. You'd just had a baby, and you were in a vulnerable position, weren't you?"

"Was I?"

"Well, yes. She'd been able to do what she liked here for a couple of months. You wouldn't have been so dumb as to upset her that much. She's pretty strong stuff, after all."

Phaedria looked at him in silence for a minute. "Miles," she said, "are you quite sure you don't want to be involved in the company? It seems to me you have a real feeling for office politics."

MILES WAS LYING on his huge bed at Claridge's, feeling lonely and trying to call Candy. He missed her and he missed home, and he had no idea what he was going to do about the situation he had landed in. He was also being assailed by a fear of such proportions, such complexity, that he could see that quite soon he was going to have to talk it over with someone or go mad. In the absence of somebody to talk to, he was trying to crush the fear, ignore it, push it to the bottom of his mind, but it went on rising up, ugly and threatening. In a desperate attempt to get away from it, he tried to occupy his mind with his dilemma.

As he saw it, he had three, maybe four choices. He could sell his share to Roz. He could sell it to Phaedria. He could offer them one percent each, which probably neither of them would accept. Or he could sell out to someone else altogether. Of all the choices, he most favored the last, because it would involve him in the least emotional trauma, but it would be an almost impossible burden to off-load. The sum of money involved—running into seven, possibly eight figures— would be considerable, but more significantly, perhaps, the buyer would have to be a person of quite extraordinary character, both personal and professional, hurling himself, as he would be, instantly into the eye of one of the most ferocious hurricanes in corporate history.

There was another option, of course, which was simply to go back to Candy and the beach and leave them all to it, but that would mean forfeiting the money. Miles reflected rather wistfully on the seven or eight figures. It was an awful lot of money. Too much. Too much for one person. Of course he could do good things with it, give lots away, to people like Father Kennedy and his grandmother and Little Ed and Larissa and the boys in the bars, but it would still leave a lot behind. He wondered if he shouldn't just go home without it. He had an uneasy feeling Candy wouldn't be too pleased. And it would land him right back in the same old situation, with him not being able to marry her and maybe doing awful dreary jobs like the one in the bank.

He remembered his conversation with Henry Winterbourne.

"You are a very rich young man," the lawyer had said. "You have been left a two percent share in this company, which is worth, at a modest estimate, four billion pounds. The other beneficiaries to the company fortune, Mrs. Emerson and Lady Morell, each hold forty-nine percent of the shares. I need hardly spell out the crucial role you have to play, whether you get involved with the company or not."

"No cash, no money, just on its own, with no strings?" Miles had asked hopefully.

"No cash," Henry said firmly. "If you want cash, you have to sell. Or become a salaried director of the company, which you are entitled to do."

"Jesus," Miles had said, "what a creep."

"I beg your pardon?" Henry had said, and Miles had apologized and changed the subject. It was all very scary.

PHAEDRIA SAT IN her white study in Hanover Terrace, trying to concentrate on the company reports, sheets of figures, financial forecasts, she had had brought from the office. Whatever else happened to her now, she had to get back to work. That was a clear, crucial need. It could wait no longer. She had to get back and she had to try to win; and in that case she needed to be absolutely on top of the situation in the company. It had been one hell of a day.

She went over it in her head as she began to tidy up the files. First had come Michael's phone call. God, why hadn't she been able to get hold of him? Where was he? She had phoned four, five times, to apologize, to explain why she had slammed the phone down, to tell him about Roz's visit. His secretary had just kept saying he was out, and Franco had exhibited his quite outstanding capacity for saying nothing at all. Well, she could try again tomorrow.

And then there had been the hideous visit from Roz and what she had said to her. It wasn't so much her words—Phaedria could have anticipated them—it had been her style of delivery, the burning hatred in her eyes, the ugly rawness in her voice.

Maybe she should duck out. Offer Miles some more of the company, sell out to Roz. Why not? What possible future waited for her in that writhing, albeit gilt-edged, can of worms?

Upstairs she heard Julia yelling lustily; there was certainly nothing fragile about her these days. She would fix herself a cup of warm milk —feeding a baby induced a desire for such childish pleasures—take herself up to the nursery, and meditate upon the advantages and possibilities of a new future away from Morell Industries.

Carrying her mug of milk, she walked into the nursery. The baby had worked herself into a fury and was kicking frantically, her small face red with rage, her fists flailing indignantly at the unsympathetic air. Phaedria smiled, put down her cup, and bent over, pulling back the covers, murmuring to Julia. She looked up at her mother, suddenly silent for a moment, and fixed her with a gaze of great intensity from her dark eyes. Julian's eyes. Julian's baby. His legacy to her, just as much as the money, the company, the nightmare. What of her father lay in this small, tough little creature? His brain, his charm, his capacity for survival? What would he have wished for her? What was due as his daughter?

Things suddenly became very clear to Phaedria. Julia was the heiress to this kingdom now as much as Roz was. She could have turned her back on it, walked away, on her own account, but she could not do it for Julia. That was not a decision she could or should make.

The company was Julia's inheritance, bequeathed to her, unknowingly, by her father; he would want it to be hers. She would never know her father, but she could know what he had done, what he had fought for and created, and through that she would learn much of him, appreciate his brilliance, his shrewdness, his toughness, his power. Phaedria could talk to her about him, show her photographs, make sure she knew and loved the people and things that he had known and loved. But the company, the heart of the company, was also the heart of Julian, a living manifestation of what he had been. And so Julia had to be part of it, too.

Well, she thought, stroking the small head, playing with the small frondlike fingers, feeling the strong, satisfying sensation of the hungry little mouth working at her breast, how did that alter the situation? Did it mean she could not, after all, walk away from it? Did it mean she had to battle on indefinitely? Probably, and it would be painful and wearisome, but at least now there seemed some sense in it all. And what of Miles's share? He had not even begun to understand the complexity of this situation even as it had stood. If she were to attempt to explain the factor of Julia into the equation, he would be still more confused. No, that was wrong, he would not be confused. Miles was not stupid: far from it. She felt for a moment the nightmare, the monster, surfacing again; she crushed it relentlessly down.

A thought suddenly roared through her brain; she sat frozen, still, turning it over. Would Miles sell his share to Julia? God, how neatly, how gloriously beautifully neatly that would resolve things. What was the sum Henry had mentioned? Eighty million. Could she raise that and buy the share on Julia's behalf? It was a great deal of money. It would mean selling many things—pictures, jewelry, houses—but she could probably do it. And what would the legal implications of the purchase be? As Julia's mother, she would, for all practical purposes, be in control. Roz would fight it to the death; Miles might not agree. But she could ask him. She could see what he thought.

She looked at her watch. It was nearly midnight. He would probably be asleep. Not the best time. She wanted his head clear when she talked to him. She would ring him in the morning. Maybe she should talk to Richard or Henry first. Richard Brookes. He would be more realistic about it, take a more practical view. It might be quite impossible. It might be against the law. But she couldn't really see why. She suddenly felt excited, exhilarated, her weariness forgotten. If only she could talk to someone. She looked down at the head now lolling blissfully relaxed against her and smiled. In time, Julia could fulfill that role for her. She would not be alone forever.

"Come along, little one," she said aloud. "You can't go to sleep yet. I have to change your nappy. And I have some news for you. Mummy has had an idea. . . ."

She was so engrossed in her thoughts and her task that it took her a long time to realize the phone was ringing. She picked up the nursery extension, a safety pin still in her mouth.

"Yes?" she said, her voice muffled.

Phaedria?" Michael Browning's voice came at her, disturbing her, delighting her, across the Atlantic, rougher, angrier than she had ever heard it. "Phaedria, I have called to say three things. One is that I love you. Two is that I intend to marry you. And three is that you are never, ever to hang up on me again."

· 35 ·

IT WAS CANDY WHO VOICED THE nightmare. Candy who took the dark, ugly shape from the recesses of their minds, shook it, held it up to the light, and ultimately managed to dispel it for all of them. Candy who was the only person sufficiently detached from it all to be able to face it and to wonder that they could not.

Miles had flown to Nassau ten days after he left, and Candy had met him, radiant with relief and delight to have him back.

"Hey," she said, "you look wonderful. Kind of tired and old, but wonderful."

Miles put his arm around her, looked down at her pretty freckled face, and moved his hand appreciatively down over her small, firm backside. "You feel wonderful," he said.

"Thanks. I missed you."

"I missed you, too. Do I really look tired and old?"

"Yeah." She looked at him consideringly. "But it kind of suits you. You look grown up. I love the clothes."

"Candy, I tell you, the stores in London are something else. You have to come and see them."

"Where'd you get that jacket?"

"In Harrods. It's by this guy called Armani. I got a whole load of stuff of his."

"What'd you get for me?"

"Oh, baby, just you wait and see what I got for you. Well, apart from this. This is the most important present." He looked around to make sure no one was watching, then took her small hand and pressed it over his erect penis, bulging at the fly of his mercifully baggy linen trousers. "This is what I really can't wait to give you."

"Well, I want the other things first," Candy said, smiling up at him. "Come on, let's get back to the hotel. Daddy's out till tonight, and Dolly has a new boyfriend. I think she might take off with him."

LATER, LYING BLISSFULLY sated beside him, her head cradled on his chest, the floor beside the bed covered with packages and bags from

Harrods and Harvey Nichols and Saint Laurent and Chanel, spilling silk shirts and satin lingerie and belts and bags and earrings and chains, she said, "Why did you come back so soon?"

"For this," he said, stroking her pubic mound, smiling as she squirmed against his hand, kissing the top of her golden head. "I couldn't stand not having you any longer."

"And?"

"And what?"

"Well, what was the other reason? This was a pretty expensive screw."

"Worth it, though."

"I guess you can afford it now."

"Not really," he said. "I won't have any cash at all until I sell my shares, but Henry Winterbourne arranged with the bank to make me a loan against the capital. So I do in a way."

"Good. So why did you come back? There must be women in London."

"There are," he said, "but not like you, and I needed to get away. It's pretty rarefied air over there. I needed time to think. I said originally I'd stay till I'd decided, but it was all really getting to me."

"Tell me about them. Maybe I can help."

He sighed. "It would be nice if you could. First there's Roz. She's really nice, but she's uptight as hell and incredibly frustrated."

"Hey," Candy said. "I don't like the sound of this. What does she look like?"

"She's pretty sexy," he said, patting her bottom fondly. "Not beautiful, exactly—well, not beautiful at all—but the most amazing figure. Very, very tall. She's really hot stuff."

"Uh-huh."

"I could do a lot with her. Then you should see her mother. She's nearly fifty, but she's really hot. She's married to this neat old guy. He's a lord, and he has a castle."

"A real castle?"

"Well, it sure as hell isn't made of cardboard. But anyway, Roz has a big share of the company. And then there's Phaedria, who was married to the Creep, as we now know. Jesus, what a bunch."

"Phaedria. That's a wild name. What's she like?"

"I'm not sure. She seems real nice, but you can't tell. She's beautiful too. She has the most incredible hair. And she has this little baby—"

"Is that the Creep's baby?"

"Yeah."

"That's sad for her."

"Yeah, it is. Well, anyway, she lives in this huge house in London, with God knows how many servants, and she has a few more houses scattered around the globe. And she's been having an affair—well, I think she might have been, anyway—with Roz's lover."

"God, Miles, this is better than Dallas."

"I know. And then there's Letitia, Roz's grandmother. Mother of the Creep. How she managed that I'll never know. She's a fun old lady. She's eighty-seven, and she's wild. She was nearly queen of England," he added.

"Queen of England? What, instead of Elizabeth?"

"No, instead of her mom. She had this huge affair with that old guy who used to live in the States, you know, the Duke of Windsor, and she almost married him."

"Oh, my God," said Candy. "This is really amazing. Can you imagine what the de Launays would say if they knew? So anyway, you have to choose between these two women? The sexy one and the one with the funny name?"

"Yeah. It's awesome. I can't make up my mind."

"Do you absolutely have to?"

"Well, there are options. I could not sell at all, but then we wouldn't get any of the money. I could sell to someone else, which I might do, because then I wouldn't have to decide. But God knows where I'd find someone with X zillion dollars who'd take this crew on."

"Er, how many zillion is it, Miles?"

"Don't ask."

"I have to ask."

"About eighty million."

"Shee-it."

"I know. Well, anyway, I could sell one percent to one of them, and keep the other. But then I'd still have to choose, so it wouldn't help me. God, it's awful. What do you think?"

Candy was silent, contemplating what eighty million dollars could do for her. Then she said, "I don't know, Miles. Which of them do you think needs it more?"

"I guess Roz, in a way. She's more desperate. But the old lady, Letitia—the almost-queen, you know—she said I should think real hard about it, because Phaedria has the baby, and so that makes a difference. I mean maybe she has more of a right to it. The other thing is that Roz hates Phaedria so much I think she'd kill her if she did get hold of it."

"Jesus," said Candy. "What a mess."

"I know. And it's such a mystery. I mean, why did it have to happen at all? Why did I have to be involved?"

She turned in the bed and looked up at him. "Seems pretty obvious to me."

"What do you mean?"

"Miles, I can't believe you haven't figured it out. You're not that dumb."

He looked at her, dreading what she was going to say, but at the same time longing to confront it, to get it over with. "Maybe I am. You tell me."

"It seems absolutely clear to me that you are Mr. Dashwood's son."

Miles was silent. Hearing it spoken, acknowledged as a possibility, made it feel just a little less dreadful, a lot more unlikely. He smiled uncertainly. "No, that is just dumb."

"It's not dumb, Miles. Why else would he have done such a thing?"

"I don't know. I just know my mom wouldn't have—couldn't have —Anyway, he would have said or she would have said—"

"What?"

"Oh, I don't know. But I do know that it is just absolutely impossible."

"Okay." She shrugged. "Have it your way. Seems possible to me. Shouldn't you at least—talk to them all about it?"

"Candy, I couldn't. I just couldn't. They're upset enough about it as it is."

"I'll bet they've thought of it. I'll bet you one of those eighty million they have."

"Well, maybe." He was silent, meditating on what she had just said. "Jesus, I can't think of anything more awful than being the Creep's son. My mom and him. Jeez, Candy, you just have to be wrong."

"And you never thought of it? Really?"

"Well," he said, with a rather shaky smile, "actually, I sort of did. But then I wouldn't let myself think any further."

"I'll bet you they all did the same. I really think you should talk to them about it."

"Maybe I will, when I get back."

She looked at him. She had never seen him so strained, so unhappy. She decided to change the subject, distract him.

"I have another idea."

"What's that?"

"If you went and worked for this company, you'd have some money, wouldn't you?"

"I guess so. But I don't intend to."

"Hang on. I mean, you'd be a rich guy that way, too. And you could keep your shares, and then you wouldn't have to choose."

"Candy, that is really dumb. I don't want to work for the company. It's awful there. Believe me. Anyway, I don't want to work for any company."

"Oh, all right." She sighed. "It just seemed like a good solution. And I'd like to live in London for a while."

"We could do that anyway, if you want to. But I am not going to work in that hellhole."

"Not even for a while? I'd kind of like being shacked up with a tycoon."

"Candy, I'm getting tired of this. Just shut up, will you? I'm not going to work there, okay?"

She looked up at him and smiled, then slithered slowly down in the bed, kissing, licking his chest, his stomach, and then with exquisite slowness and delicacy, began lapping at his penis with her tongue. She would change his mind. She always did. And this was one of the ways she did it.

ROZ WAS RIDING in the park when she had the idea. She had taken to riding early in the morning recently. It cleared her head for the day, made her feel better, and she loved horses. She had forgotten quite how much until she cantered along the Row the first morning, savoring the uniquely satisfying pleasure of feeling a powerful, well-schooled horse beneath her. She resolved to make the time to find a house in the country for weekends, and take possession of the horses her father had left her. It would be lovely for Miranda, too. She was nearly old enough to ride, and she was proving a tough, courageous little person. More of me than her father there, Roz thought with satisfaction.

Then she sighed and her heart dropped like lead to the bottom of her new riding boots. Any thought of the future led her to thoughts of Michael and thence into depression. She had not heard from him again, and she knew she would not. This time she had gone too far, abused their relationship, doubted his word, humiliated him publicly. She had decided with hindsight that probably he and Phaedria had been telling the literal truth; it would have been unlike him to have started what amounted to an adulterous affair without at least some kind of an early warning to her; and it would have been so crass, so insensitive to have started it with Phaedria of all people at this particular time in all their lives, that it really didn't bear close scrutiny.

And here it was, two weeks before Christmas, and they were still in the middle of this nightmare with no immediate hope of it being resolved. The more she thought about it, the better she got to know Miles, the more hopeless a prospect that seemed to be. He was so transparently nice and guileless, he wasn't going to be able to bear to pull a dirty trick, as he saw it, on either of them. What he really wanted was a small sum of money, nothing like the eighty million he was going to inherit, and to be left alone. Roz would gladly have given it to him, just handed it over, to put him out of his misery, but that wasn't going to solve anything for Phaedria and herself. Someone, somehow, had to break this deadlock before they all went mad. But how?

A thought suddenly came to Roz that was so petrifyingly obvious that she froze rigidly on her horse. He sensed her withdrawal, her sudden lack of empathy with him, and tossed his head, pulling at the bit. "Sorry, old thing," Roz said absently, reining him in, leaning down, patting his neck. "Sorry."

She walked him very slowly along the Row, her mind racing furiously. Suppose, just suppose, that someone else offered to buy Miles's share. An outside bidder. Someone nobody knew. Well, it was possible. Why shouldn't they? Nobody really knew about it at the moment, but someone *could* have heard. Miles would sell gladly. He couldn't wait to get back to California and shake the dust of the whole thing off his feet. And he wouldn't have to make any decision. He would be spared all the trauma, and he would simply get the money. It would be marvelous for him. Roz suddenly saw, very vividly, Miles's glorious heartbreaking smile, and smiled herself. She also found herself dwelling briefly on Miles as a man. She did find him horribly disturbing. It was his sexual self-confidence that got to her more than his charm or his looks, the way he so overtly put himself on the line, told her, quite frequently with a look, a smile, a remark, a touch, that he could, should she wish it, take her, please her, delight her. And the slight regret he always managed to convey each time she turned down his tacit, delicious invitations. Probably, she thought, if she did in fact accept one of them, he would be horrified, would close up, turn away, hurry home to Candy, and in her present state, with her own self-confidence at a low ebb, she was not about to put it to the test. Nevertheless, he remained there, in her subconscious and her sub-senses, a source of turbulence and odd pleasure. Keeping company with her fear. . . . So, if she presented him with an escape route in the form of a buyer for his share of the company, he would breathe a sigh of relief and escape. And the escape route could be so extremely anonymous—probably very formal, a small merchant bank or a consortium—that he would never dream of looking into it. He would simply, gratefully sell. At a very good price: Roz had no intention of depriving Miles of a cent of his due. And then, later on, the small merchant bank or consortium would be persuaded to sell its share back, for an even better price, to its rightful owner, the person who should have had it in the first place. Who was the true heir to the company? Who could run it with more skill, more understanding, more creativity, than anyone? The daughter of the founder. Rosamund Emerson. Née Morell.

MILES DECIDED HE would go and see the old lady; he liked Letitia the best. He wanted to hear more about her youth and how she had practically been engaged to the Prince of Wales, almost become queen of England. And she might be able to offer him some advice at the same time. Miles dialed Letitia's number, invited himself to dinner, dressed up in the new clothes he had bought the day before —dark gray wool suit from Gieves and Hawkes, a pale blue cotton shirt from Harvie & Hudson, and a splendid hand-embroidered red silk vest from S. Fisher in the Burlington Arcade—and then, looking heartbreakingly and romantically handsome, carrying a huge bouquet of pink sweetheart roses, set off on foot, in his new loafers from Wildsmith's of Prince's Arcade, to win Letitia's heart completely.

"Mrs. Morell," he said, lounging none too purposefully on her sofa, his long legs thrust out in front of him, "there's something we should all think about."

"Yes?"

"It may seem a bit upsetting for you." His blue eyes were wide, troubled. "But I really have to talk it through."

Letitia smiled. "Let me see if I can help you. Would it have anything to do with you and my son?"

"Yeah. Yes, it would."

"You think maybe you might be his son?"

He stared at her, very seriously at first. Then his expression slowly softened into relief and amusement. "You really are a great person. I thought you might have the vapors or something."

"I don't have the vapors very easily. Besides, why should I have the vapors at the thought of you being my grandson? It's a delightful thought. I agree, with certain complications attached."

"Yeah, well . . . . Anyway, yes, I do think that. That he might be my father. I hate the idea. I can't tell you how much I hate it, but—oh, I'm sorry, that sounded really rude."

"Not at all. You loved both your parents. They were obviously very special people. You want to belong to them."

"Yes. That's exactly right. It's nice of you to understand. But—well, it does seem to make some sense of it all. And I thought you might be able to help me find out how likely it was."

"I think I can. I shall have to talk to the others, though. Is that all right?"

"Of course."

"I have thought about it, too. In the end, however logical it might seem, I decided it was unlikely. You certainly don't look like Julian. But I'm sure we can establish the truth beyond any doubt if we really put our minds to it."

"All right. Thank you. I feel better already."

"Good," said Letitia, "I do too. Now, you pour yourself a glass of wine, and one for me. I got some California Chardonnay especially to make you feel at home, and I will ring Eliza. First of all, though, just tell me again when your birthday is."

"January second, 1958."

ELIZA ARRIVED THE following night for dinner, looking radiant and chic in a white damask jacket and brocade trousers, her silvery hair coiled up on top of her head.

"Where is Miles?" she said. "I hope I haven't gone to all this trouble for nothing."

"He's coming later," Letitia said. "I wanted to have a word with you first. Eliza, have you—that is, yes, of course you have, you must have done—have you thought that Miles might be . . ."

Her voice tailed off. Eliza looked at her in amusement, taking the glass of champagne she held out.

"That Miles is Julian's son?" she said. "Of course I've thought it. Straightaway. It seemed such an obvious solution. But I didn't want to worry anyone in case none of you had thought it, too. Yes, I've thought about it a lot."

"And? How do you feel about it? Does it upset you? And do you think it's possible?"

"Nothing Julian did has any power to hurt or worry me anymore. I think it's just ridiculous, the whole thing. But yes, I suppose it's very possible. Quite likely, in fact. What about you? Does it hurt you?"

"A bit." Letitia looked troubled and very old suddenly. "He's turning into more and more of a villain before my eyes. And I loved him so much."

"Oh, darling, don't be sad. Of course you loved him. He was worth loving. That doesn't change the fact that he was—well, difficult."

Letitia smiled a little weakly. "I think 'difficult' is a serious understatement. But all right, I'll accept that for now. I just do hope it's not true. But I think we have to try to find out. Miles has been worrying about it. And I daresay Roz and Phaedria have, too. And we've none of us said a word, afraid to frighten one another. Silly, really. It has to be faced."

"Yes. Anyway, what do you want me to do?"

"Well, obviously, darling, try to help me work out where Julian was in—let me see—in late March, early April, 1957, the year before Miles was born. Nobody else would know, with the possible exception of Camilla."

"Oh, God, I'd hate to have to ask her."

"Well, we may have to. We can get C.J. to do it."

"Of course. Well, let's think. March. March. He first went to the States in—when? Very early spring? No, it wasn't. It was actually the autumn before. So he was definitely spending most of his time there. My birthday is in April. I know he was home for that. I can remember being so pleased that he came back. Roz was only tiny. But that's the middle of April. And he was in America pretty solidly before that. Goodness, Letitia, I don't know. I don't seem to be able to help at all."

"I feel very much afraid we may be driven to Camilla," said Letitia darkly.

"YES? YES, THIS is Lady Morell. Who? Oh, yes, of course I'll take it. Michael? Hello, how are you? Good. Yes, of course I miss you. What? No, Michael, I can't come for Christmas. I'm sorry. I'd love to, but I can't. What? Well, because I've arranged to have my father down to Marriotts, and although I could easily tell him it's still June and put him off for several months, somebody else might notice. Yes, I do want to see you, terribly, but it can't be at Christmas. Sorry. Well, what about Roz? Don't you think she might hear about it? I just can't contemplate a showdown with her now, Michael, not with everything at fever pitch. Yes, I know you're at fever pitch, but you'll just have to wait. What? Well, of course you can wait. Try a cold shower or two. Anyway, what about Michael and Sharon? They won't be too pleased to find me beneath the tree on Christmas Eve. Nor will their mother. It's just a hopeless idea, I'm afraid. Lovely but hopeless. Anyway, I don't want to be away from Julia on her first Christmas. No, I know she won't know anything about it, but I will. God, Michael, just stop it, will you? I'm not coming. Yes, I know I'm a hard woman. What? Oh, now that just might be possible, I suppose. It would be so lovely. I wonder, I just wonder if I could. Do you think anyone would know? I suppose not. They'll all be staying up in Scotland for Hogmanay. You know, the Scottish New Year's Eve. Yes, I really think I could. Oh, it would be so exciting. No, I think I'll leave her behind. It'll only be two days or so, won't it? She's going off me now anyway. She's hit the bottle. I've gone down three whole sizes. Well, you may have preferred it, but that wasn't the object of the exercise. Yes, all right, I do promise. I'll book—no, on second thought you'd better do it. Book the flight right now. New Year's Eve. Early. Early as you can."

"CAN WE REALLY spend Christmas in London?" Candy's voice was ecstatic. "That sounds just wonderful."

"Sure," Miles said. "Just tell your father a good story, about staying with the Creep's mother or second cousin twice removed, and come. You'll like it."

"Where'll we stay?"

"It's nice here."

"Is that a fashionable hotel?"

"Really fashionable."

"Will I get to meet the women? And the queen grandmother?"

"Possibly. Don't see why not."

"Miles, you're the greatest."

"WHERE IS MRS. Emerson today?" asked Phaedria, halfway into her first full week back at work.

"She's away for a couple of days, Lady Morell. She's gone to Washington, to check out the office there, and the hotel. She'll be back on Monday."

"Good. Is Mr. Brookes in? Find out, will you, and ask him if he can lunch with me."

"Of course," Sarah Brownsmith said.

"Oh, and Sarah, give me a line, would you? I want to make a call."

"Yes, Lady Morell."

◆　　◆　　◆

"HELLO. IS DR. Friedman there?"

"No, she's away, I'm afraid. Who is it calling? Can I help?"

"I don't think so. No, thank you. This is Phaedria Morell. When might Dr. Friedman be back?"

"Not until mid-January at the earliest. She's visiting her sister in Australia."

"I see."

"Dr. Friedman said urgent matters could be relayed to her partner, Dr. Mortimer. Would you like his number?"

"No, really, this isn't urgent. I'll call Dr. Friedman in January. Thank you."

"C.J., IS THAT you?"

"Yes, Camilla. How are you this morning?"

"I'm fine, C.J. Missing you, of course. And looking forward to Christmas."

"I am, too, Camilla."

"Now then. I looked through my old appointment calendars. If it's any help to you, I can confirm that from early March right through to April we were all working flat out. Julian, Paul Baud, and myself. It was a crucial time. There was no way he could possibly have popped over to California then. All right? And the last few days of March we weren't even in the States. We were in Paris, with Paul Baud, looking at the stores there."

"Ah," said C.J. "Now, that's interesting. What about the week before that?"

"No, C.J., definitely not. I saw him every single day."

"Even on the weekend?"

"Yes, certainly the weekend," said Camilla with a touch of complacency in her voice. "We'd only just begun our relationship. Now, C.J., I have to go. I have an appointment with my analyst. See you in two weeks."

"ELIZA? THIS IS Letitia. Listen, we seem to have a watertight alibi for Julian. The early part of March he was very much in New York, with Camilla."

"Ah. Is she sure?"

"Yes. Apparently she has filed all her appointment books from birth," Letitia said.

"She would have. Sanctimonious bitch. Well, I suppose we should be grateful. All we have to worry about now is that first week in April.

Which could be crucial, I suppose. After that he was with me in London," said Eliza.

"Yes. I do feel awfully glad about it, I have to say."

"I think I do, too."

PHAEDRIA LEANED ACROSS the table earnestly toward Richard Brookes. He looked at her appreciatively.

"I need advice," she said.

"Ah. Of a legal nature?"

"Sort of."

"Legal nature is very precise, my dear Lady Morell. Sort-ofs don't have a huge place in it."

"I suppose not. But it isn't all that precise. It's quite difficult, really. But it struck me the other night that Julia is actually a most rightful heir. To the company and everything."

"Ah," he said. "I do not think legal precedent would bear you out. But please continue."

"The thing is that Julian didn't know about her. If he had, the will would have been very different."

"Possibly."

"Well, anyway, morally she has to have a claim, obviously."

"Possibly."

"And, well, I thought I might present this thought to Miles and offer to buy his share on her behalf. So that he wouldn't have to choose between me and Roz. He could solve the problem by letting Julia have his two percent. I think it might appeal to him."

"Hmm. It would clearly appeal to you."

"Well, of course it would appeal to me," Phaedria said irritably. "She's my child. I want her to have her rights. But she's also Julian's. He would have wanted her to inherit the company. Or a substantial share of it. What most appeals to me is getting this deadlock shifted."

"It wouldn't really, though, would it?" Richard was looking at her thoughtfully. "It wouldn't ease the day-to-day situation at all."

"No. Not yet. But at least Miles would be off the hook."

"Yes." He looked at her shrewdly. "Phaedria, have you ever considered the possibility that Miles might be . . ."

"What?" she said, her eyes full of panic. "Who?"

"Oh," he said, unable to continue in the face of her patent fear. "Oh, nothing. Nothing at all. Well, this plan of yours is certainly a possibility. Let's think about it a bit. You'd have to form a trust fund for Julia. To buy her share."

"Yes, I'd thought of that."

"And you'd have to raise a lot of money."

"I've thought about that, too. I can."

"Right. It would make Roz exceedingly angry."

"Richard, she couldn't be any angrier than she is already. At least this way she'd be kind of beaten. Impotent."

"I don't think Mrs. Emerson would ever be that."

"Well, you know what I mean."

"I do. Well, it's an interesting idea."

"Is it legal, though?"

"Oh, perfectly. As long as Miles knows what you're doing and agrees to it. You might well be right. It could be a huge relief for him. He might welcome it."

"So should I suggest it, do you think?"

"By all means, if you want to. Only perhaps you should imply that while he considers it, he ought not to talk to Roz about it. There is no great point in meeting trouble halfway. No, as I say, I do think it's an interesting idea. I see only one really big stumbling block."

"Roz?"

"No. Miles himself. I may be wrong, but I have a hunch that he may in the end decide to hang on to his legacy."

"Richard, you are absolutely wrong. All Miles wants is to get the hell out of here and lie on the beach with Candy McCall for the rest of his life, eating her daddy's candy bars. Believe me, I know."

"WELL, I THINK you're crazy," Candy said. She had arrived in London and was settling into Miles's suite at Claridge's with patent pleasure. "Just plain crazy. Just think, you could be a powerful businessman, and you're throwing it all away, just like that, without even thinking about it."

"Baby, I don't need to think about it. I told you I hate the idea."

"Of what? Money? Power? Success? Don't be silly, Miles. It would be great."

"I don't want power, and we can have the money. I just want you."

"Well," she said, looking at him, appraising him rather coolly, "I'm not sure I want a man who would turn down something so exciting."

"Candy, you don't know what you're saying."

"I do, Miles. I know exactly what I'm saying. You're clever and you're smart, and you've had a fantastic education and you've spent most of your life wasting your talent. I went along with it before, because there didn't seem any choice, but now there is. I think you should take this opportunity and make something of it."

He looked at her. "Candy, I can't. Not even for you. I just can't. I'm sorry. It's not for me."

"Well," she said, "you obviously don't love me at all."

"I do love you."

"You can't. Otherwise you'd at least consider doing what I ask."

"Candy, I can't and I won't."

"So you don't love me."

"I do. I swear I do."

"Prove it. Give it a try."

He looked at her as she stood there, her eyes filled with tears, her lips quivering. He thought of the secrets, the intricacies of her body, the glorious explorations and discoveries he had made within her; and he remembered her loyalty to him, how she had helped him, given him money, comforted him, reassured him, gone to Hugo's mail drop for him, lied to her father, stood by him when he had had absolutely nothing in the world to offer her, and he knew he couldn't let her down, couldn't leave her without at least seriously considering what she was asking him to do. He was angry, resentful, but he could see that he had to go along with her at least a little way.

"All right," he said with a sigh. "All right, I'll think about it. Seriously. I'll talk to them about it. For you."

"Oh, Miles," she said, throwing herself into his arms, kissing him, pressing herself against him. "Thank you. Thank you. I'm sure you won't regret it."

"Maybe not," he said, "but I'm afraid you might."

LETITIA WAS EATING her supper when she suddenly thought about the cars. She had been oddly moved by the fact that Julian had left them all to her with the exception of the Bugatti. It had been a gesture of faith in her, in their closeness, in his faith in her apparent immortality. They told a lot about Julian, those cars; about where he had been, what he had done. He had bought them all over the world. And the collection of logbooks Henry had handed to her after the reading of the will would chronicle it all. Why hadn't she thought about that before?

Letitia's heart was beating rather fast. She got up, walked through into her dining room, and unlocked the escritoire she had bought when she and Julian had moved into the house. The logbooks were all in an envelope in the top. She sat down rather abruptly and started thumbing through them. So many lovely machines, such a lot of care and attention and money lavished on them. And he had acquired them over such a long period of time. The 1910 Rolls. The Napier. The 1912 Chevrolet. The Delage. That was her own favorite. And, oh, the Bugatti. She shouldn't have the logbook for that. The Bugatti was Phaedria's. Or rather Julian's again now. Letitia's eyes blurred with tears as she remembered the keys placed so tenderly among the lilies on the coffin. She opened the tattered old book carefully. When had he bought the Bugatti—1957? Letitia's brain suddenly shot into overdrive. She leafed feverishly through the documents, the bills, the insurance certificates. And then her heart seemed quite to stop, and she sat staring down at the piece of paper in her hand.

She sat there for a long time, then walked back to the drawing room and picked up the telephone.

"Eliza? It's Letitia. Listen, I have some news. Nice news, I think, really. Julian was home that week before your birthday, the first week in April. He was at the car auction at Sotheby's. He bought the Bugatti."

"MILES," LETITIA SAID gently, "is there any possibility that your mother ever went to New York to visit Julian, do you think? Did she often go to New York?"

"No," he said, "absolutely not. My mom went to New York only once in her life and that was with my dad, oh, quite a while before I was born. She was always talking about it. She used to show me the pictures they took and the souvenirs she'd bought over and over again. She loved it. She said she would have given anything to go again, but it was really expensive. They didn't have much money, Mrs. Morell. I think you have to realize that. And anyway, my dad wouldn't have let her; he was possessive. Most of her relatives were in California, and she and my dad used to have real arguments if she wanted to go and visit them. He never let her. No, I'm really sure she could never have gone to New York on her own. It would have been like leaving my dad for good. If you know what I mean."

"Well, in that case," Letitia said, smiling at him radiantly, a great weight lifted from her own heart, "I think you need have no fear that you are not actually your own father's son. Julian was in New York at the beginning of March and in Paris for the last few days of March, the year before you were born. And in April he was in England. We can confirm all that."

"I hate to sound rude," said Miles, "but that really is terrific news. Thank you very much, Mrs. Morell."

"It's fairly terrific news for me, too, Miles. We are no nearer solving the mystery, of course, but it is still terrific news."

LETITIA SENT FOR Roz. She wanted to tell her herself, to have the pleasure of sharing the news. They had never discussed it, but she knew, from certain expressions in Roz's eyes, an avoidance of entering into any discussion about Miles, that she had thought of it, been afraid.

Roz came into the house at First Street late in the evening, after supper. She was wearing a long-sleeved leotard under a tight, short jersey skirt in dark beige from Alaia. It emphasized her breasts, flattered her lean, rangy body, made her legs, in black tights, look awesomely long.

"That's lovely, darling. You do look nice."

"Thank you. It is so nice to be able to wear short skirts again."

"You're very lucky to have those legs. You and Miles both look like racehorses."

Roz looked at her with the taut, edgy expression she wore whenever she felt threatened. "Does Miles have especially long legs? I've never noticed."

"Pretty long. Roz, tell me something—no, first let's have a drink. What do you want?"

"Perrier. I'm on the wagon till Christmas."

"Very commendable."

"Not really. I thought I was getting fat."

"Not terribly, darling. All right, help yourself. Now then," she said as Roz settled opposite her in the love seat. "I want to talk to you about Miles."

"What about him?" Roz said truculently.

"Well, I—and your mother, and indeed Miles himself—had all been worrying about something. I wondered if you had, too?"

"I can't think of anything." Roz swallowed. "I mean, there's lots to worry about, but I can't really imagine the same thing bothering us all."

"Can't you? Good. Then you've been spared a great many sleepless nights, which I have not. Can I tell you about it?"

"Of course." Roz was sitting very straight, her eyes fixed on her grandmother's face. She looked pale.

"Well, you see, I thought—we all thought—there might be an

explanation for your father leaving Miles that legacy which was fairly logical. Obvious, even."

"I can't think what."

"Can't you?"

Roz looked at her with her blank expression. "No."

Letitia laughed. "Sometimes you look exactly like your father. Well, anyway, what we all thought was that Miles might—well, might have been Julian's son."

"Oh." Roz tried to sound calm, disinterested, but her voice came out sounding rather shaky and weak. "How—how odd."

"Yes, well, it didn't seem that odd to us. Quite likely, really. At least it would have explained a lot. But obviously we had to check it out."

"I—I suppose so."

"Well—" The silence seemed very long. Roz was motionless; she put down her glass to conceal the fact that her hand was shaking. Letitia stood up, smiling at her. "Well, we were all wrong. Quite wrong. Your father was in New York and Paris during the relevant period. And then at home in London. I think that's probably quite good news, don't you?"

"I suppose it would be," Roz said, still sounding odd. "If you'd been worrying about it. Yes. Thank you for telling me, Granny Letitia."

There was another very long silence. Letitia went over to Roz and put her arms around her. Roz was smiling at her and crying at the same time.

"That's the thing I've been most afraid of," she said, "ever since I can remember, all my life."

·36·

MILES LISTENED CAREFULLY WHILE Roz told him of an extremely generous bid from a consortium in Zurich for his share of the company. He said he would think about it. Then he listened equally carefully while Phaedria outlined her idea that a trust fund should buy his share of the company on behalf of Julia. He said he would think about that, too. When he got back to Claridge's that night, Candy told him she had been to supper with Letitia, who thought it was a wonderful idea for Miles to join the company and had all kinds of interesting and exciting suggestions as to what he might do there. Miles listened carefully to Candy as well. He kept all these conversations to himself. He wanted time to think.

BOTH ROZ AND Phaedria invited him and Candy for Christmas, but they refused. They wanted to be alone together in London. They put their discussions on ice and had a pre-honeymoon. Miles took Candy shopping, and watched, smiling indulgently, as she fluttered like a dizzy, overexcited little bird from shop to shop, store to store, from Joseph to Brown's, Saint Laurent to Polo, Fortnum's to Harvey Nichols. They went to shows, to *Cats* and *Chorus Line* and *Evita* and *Another Country*, through which Candy slept and Miles sat bewitched. They ate their way around London, dressing up to dine at the Ritz, gazing at the celebrities in Langan's, picking their way through the chic, pretty dishes at L'Escargot, L'Etoile, the Caprice. Their favorite was the Ménage à Trois, which served only appetizers and desserts; one day they ate both lunch and supper there. And Candy liked the Great American Disaster; she said it made her feel at home.

On Christmas Eve they ate in style in the dining room at Claridge's: Miles wore his new dinner jacket, made for him at Dimi Major, and looked so wonderful that half the women in the room forgot what they had been saying to their escorts when he walked across it. He ordered pink champagne, presented Candy with a very large and vulgar diamond ring he had bought from Garrard's, officially proposed to her, and then said, "Come on, we're going to have a Christmas to remember." Which they did, never leaving their suite, ordering the occasional snack from room service, and exploring each other's bodies with a slow, lazy thoroughness and delight.

And all the time, the choices before him occupied Miles's mind with an increasing intensity. Two days after Christmas he left Candy in London, rented a car, and drove down to Marriotts to talk to Phaedria.

PHAEDRIA WAS VERY pleased to see him. She had found Christmas extremely depressing, alone with Julia, who had been fretful with a cold, and her father, who was excitedly occupied with a new subject, one of quite outstanding obscurity, even by his standards. She was Roswitha, a tenth-century German poet and nun, and Phaedria couldn't help feeling that even her father's loyalest followers might find it hard to feel enthusiastic over her.

Phaedria was guiltily ticking off the days to New Year's Eve, when Nanny Hudson, a large cozy soul, disdainfully referred to by Mrs. Hamlyn as Old Nanny Hudson, would arrive back from her holiday so she could take herself off to New York and Michael. Nobody except Nanny Hudson knew where she was going to be; her cover was a trip to the house on Eleuthera. She had explained to Nanny Hudson that it was very difficult for her to get away from the company and she needed a break, and that it was better for everyone to think she was somewhere other than where she actually was.

Nanny Hudson, who had not been born even the day before yesterday, was not entirely convinced by this explanation, but she was very fond of Phaedria, and so delighted with the prospect of having Julia to herself for a few days that she would have sworn the moon was blue and Phaedria had gone to have a personal look at it, in order to make sure nothing and nobody disturbed any of them.

Phaedria planned to fly out on the Concorde early on New Year's Eve and stay with Michael for forty-eight hours. Then to substantiate her alibi, she would fly down to Eleuthera for a couple of days— "Alone," she said firmly. "I had my honeymoon there; I can't go there with you, not yet"—and then back to London, crises, decisions, work.

MILES ARRIVED AT lunchtime; he was driving a perfectly horrendous Ford Escort in a particularly vile shade of blue. Phaedria laughed as he got out of it.

"Like your wheels," she said.

"A bit of real style there," he said, laughing back at her. "This is a nice place, Phaedria. I really like it."

"Good. Come in and have a drink. I'd suggest you meet my father but he's locked in his room with a German nun."

"I beg your pardon?"

"Well, she's not real. Or hasn't been for a thousand years. He's writing a book about her."

He shook his head at her, smiling. "You really are a wild family."

After lunch she walked him around the grounds and showed him the stables. "And this is the real love of my life," she said, leading him over to Grettisaga's stall. "Isn't she lovely?"

"She is," he said, carefully tactful. "I'm sure she is. I don't really know an awful lot about horses, nothing at all as a matter of fact, but she looks as if she has the right parts in the right places, a leg at each corner, that sort of thing."

"There's a book called that," she said, smiling at him. "It's by someone called Thelwell. Very funny."

"English funny or would it make me laugh?"

"Oh, dear," she said, "do we really not make you laugh?"

"Not often," he said, "but I'm learning to live with you."

"Good."

"How's Julia?"

"She's fine. Nancy's here."

"She's with Nancy?"

"The housekeeper." She spoke carelessly, casually; she had come totally to accept the fleet of people who saw to her, fed her, warmed her, cared for her wherever she went.

Miles looked at her shrewdly. "You like it all, don't you?"

"Like what?"

"Being rich. The life-style."

"I suppose so. I've got used to it."

"I suppose you have. I suppose I will, too. I haven't yet. I feel as if I'm at a party and soon I'll have to go home."

"But you want to go home, don't you?"

"You know what I mean."

"Yes, I do. Sorry. Anyway, what did you want to talk about?"

Her heart was thumping; had he made up his mind so quickly?

"Oh, you know, things."

"Tell me."

"Well, I've been thinking over your suggestion about buying my share for Julia. It's a neat idea. I like it. And you're right; probably she should have it. And it would kind of solve my problem. I wouldn't have to actually choose."

"No. But?"

"Two buts. It would still mean in effect that I'd gone against Roz. That you'd gotten control. In a way."

"No, Miles, it wouldn't. I've explained, there would be a trust fund with trustees. I still couldn't make big decisions about the company against Roz's wishes."

"No, but Roz would know that come Julia's eighteenth birthday—or eighth, probably, the way you people carry on—you and Julia could sweep the board. I don't feel comfortable about that."

Phaedria looked at him sharply. "You like Roz, don't you?"

"Yeah, I do. I really do. I think she's a bitch, but I like her. I think she's had a raw deal. Don't look at me like that; it's not your fault. I guess lots of it's her own, but it still hasn't been easy for her. Losing her dad twice over, losing the company probably, getting divorced, losing this guy of hers. He must be a real schmuck."

"Why?" Phaedria said carefully. She was beginning to find the conversation uncomfortable.

"He never even came over when she was feeling so bad. Never tried to understand what she was going through, never made allowances for her."

"Miles," Phaedria said carefully, "you may be a very perceptive person, but you don't know much about this particular situation. I don't think you should make judgments about it."

He shrugged, smiled at her. "Maybe I don't know much about it. All I'm saying is she's had a tough time and I don't want to make it tougher for her."

"Right. So you don't want to sell to Julia?"

"No. Well, not yet. I might someday, but not yet. I want to think a little longer. I just thought I should let you know."

"Well, thank you."

She was angry, disappointed. She walked faster, frowning into the cold air. Miles looked at her and smiled to himself. He put a hand on her arm. She shook it off. "Don't."

"I'm sorry. Can I ask you something?"

"Of course," she said, coolly distant.

"Did you screw Roz's boyfriend?"

Phaedria looked at him and rage suddenly swept over her. The crudeness, the insolence of the question on top of her earlier anger drove her beyond reason. She raised her hand and struck him hard across the face.

"How dare you!" she said. "How dare you. It is nothing, nothing to do with you. There is absolutely no reason why I should answer that question, particularly as I've told you before, but no, I did not, I did not screw him as you put it. I wanted to, I wanted to like hell, but I didn't. I wouldn't because I cared about what it would do to Roz. All right? Satisfied? You'd better go back to London right away, Miles. I can't see that we have a great deal to say to each other."

"Hey," he said, easily, catching her wrist, rubbing at his face cautiously with his other hand. "You have a real temper, don't you? I'm sorry. I didn't mean to upset you so much. I guess I shouldn't have said anything."

"No," said Phaedria, still breathing heavily, rage still pounding in her head. "No, you shouldn't. Now leave me alone." She shook her hand free, stood looking at him, flushed, her eyes blazing. He looked back at her, calm, relaxed, smiling slightly, and suddenly like a thunderbolt, shocking, unexpected, she felt a desperate lunge of desire, stood there, staring at him, fear and hunger in her eyes. He moved toward her, recognizing it, and put his hands up on her shoulders. For a brief brief moment she stood there, aching, throbbing for him, her eyes held in his. Then she leaned forward and kissed him hard, fiercely on the mouth, and as suddenly drew back as if he had hit her.

"Shit!" she said. "Shit. Leave me alone."

She started to run then, through the growing dark, down the hill, back to the safety of the grounds, the house. She ran upstairs to her bedroom, locked the door, lay on the bed, crying. She felt shocked, ashamed, horrified at herself. What was the matter with her? Was she some kind of whore, a slut as Roz had said, that she could have lain down on the hard ground and let one man take her there and then, when she was supposedly so much in love with another? What was it about that situation that had been so powerful? she wondered. What had made her feel that way? Was it just her own sexuality surfacing after so long, or was it that Miles with his rotten, powerful, arrogant beauty, had been too much for her? Partly perhaps, but there was something else, something gnawing away in her subconscious, some memory long buried, newly awoken.

Suddenly she knew what it was. It was the juxtaposition of anger and sex. And there had been a time when it had happened before. Here, in the country lane near Marriotts, in the middle of the night, when she had run away in the Bugatti and Julian had taken her, crudely, gloriously, wonderfully on the backseat of the car.

And there had been something about Miles in that moment on the downs, as he stood there looking at her, that had exactly brought it all back.

MILES, BEING MILES, put matters right fairly swiftly. He came up to her room, knocked on the door, said he had some tea for her and he really really wanted to talk to her. Reluctantly, shamefacedly, she opened the door, and he came in and sat on the bed, and said he was really sorry. He should never have asked the question. It was he who was the schmuck, not Michael, he said, and the best thing he could do was go back to California as soon as a plane could carry him. Maybe he should let Julia buy his shares, just to get matters settled, and what was a kiss between friends, which he hoped he and Phaedria were? She just shouldn't worry about anything; she worried too much, and she'd been through a tough time. She was overwrought and that made people behave very strangely. He said Candy did extremely strange things when she was overwrought and then could hardly remember them afterward. He could never remember them either, he said tactfully if illogically, and why didn't they have a drink and then he would be on his way.

He meant it all, too. He was not playacting; he was genuinely concerned for Phaedria and sorry he had hurt her, and he gave no more real thought to the kiss than if she had shaken his hand. His days on the beach and in the bedrooms of the hotels of Nassau had taught him to set a low value on sexual currency; it was good, it could be very good, it was fun, it made a relationship better, a day brighter, but it was not of any lasting importance or significance. What moved him about Candy was not really her eager, responsive body, but her loyal, brave little heart. He would have been prepared, as a last resort, to share the first, but never the second.

And so they sat, he and Phaedria, in the kitchen at Marriotts, and drank a bottle of champagne, and he told her that Candy was eager for him to join the company, work for it. What did Phaedria think about that? Phaedria said she thought it was a terrible idea, that he would loathe it, and he had said yes, he thought he probably would, too, but he had promised Candy to give it a try, or at least to see what everybody thought about it.

"I'll think about it, but I don't think you should do it," she said, relaxed by the champagne and their sudden closeness, leaning forward, kissing him in an entirely friendly manner on the cheek. "When I get back from New York next week, we can have lunch and discuss it properly."

She spoke without thinking and then suddenly realized what she had said, that she had told him she was going to New York, and looked at him wide-eyed in horror.

He saw it all, grasped the implication of what she had said, realized what it must mean to her that he knew. "It's all right," he said, smiling at her, reaching out, patting her hand in an almost fatherly way. "I won't say anything. I swear it."

She looked at him and half smiled back, pale, frightened, as amazed by his swift perception as she was distraught at what she had said.

"Come on," he said, refilling her glass. "You have to trust me. You can. Now forget it. I won't tell. And I'd love to have lunch with you in January. Okay? Now I have to go. Candy will be wondering what's happened to me."

"Of course," she said, struggling to relax, to smile. "I'll come and see you off. And thank you, Miles. For everything."

"That's okay."

On the front steps of Marriotts she kissed him again on the cheek.

"Give my love to Candy, Miles. Happy New Year. And—sorry about this afternoon."

"No, it was my fault. Just forget it. Happy New Year, Phaedria."

He drove up to London, turning the afternoon over and over in his mind, thinking about her. She was a far more complex person than she appeared. Sexy, too. He hadn't realized that at first. She didn't project sex like Roz did. She'd seemed rather cool, distant, despite her beauty. Well, she'd been through enough in the past year to turn anybody frigid.

And what, he wondered, trying vainly to urge the Ford Escort into a speed above sixty-nine, was she going to be doing in New York? And with whom? As if he didn't know.

"CANDY THINKS I should come and work for the company," Miles said to Roz, "hang on to my share. What do you think?"

"God," Roz said, "what an idea. I don't know, I wouldn't have thought you'd like it."

They were sitting by a roaring fire in the great hall of Garrylaig Castle, two days after he had visited Phaedria. Miles had phoned Roz to see if he could come up a day or two early for Hogmanay. Candy, he said, had had to go home early. Her stepmother had run off with her new toy boy, and her father was distraught.

"Have you—have you thought any more about that outside offer?" Roz asked.

"Yes, I have."

"And?"

"And I kind of like it. It would let me off the hook. But the one thing I can't understand is how it would be any good for you."

"It wouldn't," Roz said coolly. "That's surely not the idea anyway. It wasn't designed to be good for me. But it would at least break the stranglehold with Phaedria. And it's only two percent after all. Not a very powerful stake."

"Could grow though."

"How?"

"The consortium might work on one of you. Buy some more shares. Inveigle you on to their side."

"Not me. Her possibly."

"But, Roz, you'd still be at loggerheads with her. You still couldn't resolve anything."

"Of course we could. There'd still be a tie-breaking vote. Every time."

"I suppose so."

"And I think she'd weary of it anyway. She only wants to get control now because of me. She has no real interest in the company."

"What about Julia?"

"What about her?"

"Don't you think Phaedria might want some of it for her?"

"No. Why? Has she said anything to you about it?"

"No."

Roz looked at him sharply, trying to read his face, but she saw nothing in it at all. It was smooth, devoid of expression, his eyes totally blank. It unnerved her slightly, that look; it was so unlike Miles. It stirred unwelcome emotions, odd, placeless memories. She struggled to disentangle them, but couldn't.

Miles was talking again. "Tell me why you think me working for the company would be such a bad idea."

Roz thought fast. Maybe it wasn't an entirely bad idea, she thought. He was bound to tire of it fairly soon. In the meantime, she felt confident, she could draw him slowly, imperceptibly further toward her side. It would also be quite amusing. She would enjoy seeing Phaedria trounced slowly and agonizingly rather than in one swift, straight move. She could actually have enormous fun with the situation: a real live cat-and-mouse game. Besides, she enjoyed Miles's company enormously. The sexual attraction she felt toward him apart, he relaxed her, made her laugh, forget Michael, forget everything. It would be wonderful to have him around all the time. She had no intention of trying to seduce him sexually. It would be undignified; it would be politically inept. And besides, there was Candy. She had no stomach just now for any kind of sexual drama. But the fact remained that he charged everything up in a very agreeable way, made her feel good, alive, aware of herself. She enjoyed his company in the fullest possible sense; it would be the greatest fun to have him around the office.

"Why does Candy like the idea so much?" she asked, playing for time, time to think about it, to plan her answer more skillfully.

"I guess she likes the idea of being married to a tycoon. And her dad says if I'm working, you know, for you, then we could get married right away. She'd really like that."

"Wouldn't you?"

"Yeah, I would. I want to get married to her badly. But being married to her in London, and working, wasn't really what I had in mind."

She looked at him shrewdly. "It would depend, maybe, on what kind of work you did?"

"Yes. Candy was talking to Mrs. Morell—your grandmother, I mean—about it. She had some really wild ideas."

"Like what?" Roz said, slightly irritably. It was too bad of Letitia to think she could still interfere in the running of the company.

"Well, for instance, she thought I would like being involved in the stores. And maybe I would. I could just about take that, I guess. I like clothes and nice things."

"Yes," said Roz, looking at him as he lounged in front of the fire, his long long legs encased in Levi's, worn with brown knee-high leather boots, a dark green cashmere Polo from Ralph Lauren, a soft brown leather jacket. "You've learned your way round the London shops pretty fast, I must say."

"It isn't difficult."

"What other ideas did Letitia have?"

"She thought I might like working with the design guy. What's his name, David Somebody?"

"Ah," said Roz, "David Sassoon."

"Yeah, that's it. I took art in high school. I liked it."

"Yes, but with the greatest respect, Miles, you can't just walk into a very high-powered design setup and start making waves on the strength of a few school art lessons. Design is a very sophisticated business these days. You'd have to go to art school, learn what you were doing."

"Okay, okay," he said, smiling lazily at her. "No need to get all uptight. It was only an idea. Nobody's actually gone out and bought me a desk. I haven't even thought it all through yet."

"Sorry." She smiled at him with an effort. "It's just that it's a very complex business. I get upset when people imply it's simple."

"You get upset too easily," he said. "I keep telling you."

"Yes, well, I don't have that much to be happy about at the moment," she said.

"Oh, I don't know. You have a few pluses in your life."

"Like?"

"Well, you're not starving, are you? Not pushed for bucks?"

"No. No, of course not. But—"

"But money isn't everything. Is that what you were going to say?"

"Yes, I was."

"It isn't everything," he said with a sigh, "but it sure is a lot. You ask a few people who don't have any. See what they say."

"Yes, I know," she said. "Of course I'm very lucky in that way; we all are. But money doesn't, it really doesn't, buy happiness, contentment, love; it doesn't ease pain."

And to her horror she felt her eyes fill with tears.

"Come on," he said. "That's good. Cry. Cry and cry. Yell if you want to. Let it out."

"I can't," she said, smiling at him shakily, "not here. The others would hear."

"Okay. We'll go for a walk. Come on." He put out his hand, pulled her up. "Get your coat."

"Oh, this is ridiculous," she said, "going for a walk just so I can let out a primal scream or two."

"It isn't ridiculous at all. You need it. You don't have to scream. You can just talk it out if you want to."

"Oh, all right. Let's go for a walk. The dogs would like it."

They fetched coats and put on boots, and Peveril's three Labradors, who had been prancing excitedly round the great hall ever since they had first heard the magic word, "walk," followed them ecstatically into the woods.

"Now I feel silly," said Roz, brushing aside a small branch. "I can't cry now. You're watching me."

"You don't have to cry. You don't even have to talk. I keep telling you, I just want to help. This was the only way I could see just then."

"You are a nice person, Miles," she said, looking at him. "You really are. Why are you so nice?"

He shrugged. "Don't know. My mom and dad were pretty nice people. I guess that helps. My grandmother is real nice, too. I've had some very nice girlfriends. Plenty of people to set a good example."

Roz looked at him. "I know Granny Letitia talked to you about— about the possibility that my father was also yours. I was worried about that, too. I never told you, and I've never managed to talk to you about it since, but I was awfully glad that he wasn't. That it wasn't possible."

"Me, too. For lots of reasons."

"Yes."

He looked at her and grinned. "Wild, huh? Us being related. Brother and sister."

"Yes, well," Roz said shortly, "we're not."

"No."

He was suddenly very quiet, walking through the leaves, kicking them almost savagely.

"What is it, Miles?"

"Oh—oh, nothing."

"Now *you're* not letting things out. Come on, tell me. If you want to, that is."

He turned to her, and she saw his blue eyes were full of pain, that there were tears in them. She stepped toward him.

"Miles, what is it? Please tell me."

"Oh, well, I was just remembering, you know, the last time I ever saw my mother. She was in the hospital dying, and I remember thinking I couldn't stand it. I lay there on her bed in the hospital in her arms, and I just wanted to stay with her, to hold her hand and go with her wherever she was going, but I knew I couldn't. I was so unhappy and kind of scared. In the end she went to sleep and they came and told me I should leave, and I had to climb off the bed very gently, very carefully, and go without waking her, and that was the moment when she died for me. Actually she died the next day," he said, brushing the tears from his face, "but I never saw her again."

He sat down abruptly on the wet ground; Roz sat beside him. She put her arm around his shoulders, took one of his hands, rested her head against him.

"I know it's trite to say it," she said, "but I think I do know how you feel. And I'm so sorry. But at least you said good-bye to your mother. You were able to say everything you wanted to. That must be a comfort."

"Yes," he said, "yes, it is. They were happy days in a way, when she was dying. Can you imagine that?"

"Yes," said Roz, thinking of the nightmarish three days of her father's death as he lay in intensive care, an obscene mesh of wires and tubes in and around him, when she had stood and looked at him from outside the room, refusing to go in because Phaedria was there sitting beside him. "Yes, I think I can."

"Well," he said, "it was a long time ago. Mostly I don't mind anymore. Obviously."

"I'm very sorry if I made you unhappy. I wouldn't have done that for anything."

He turned and looked at her, took one of her hands and kissed it, then leaned forward and kissed her mouth, tenderly, gently, lovingly.

"You're a nice lady," he said. "You didn't make me unhappy. And I like you very much. Very, very much."

· 37 ·

"YOU LOOK TERRIBLE," MICHAEL said, holding Phaedria at arm's length, away from him. "I cannot believe how terrible you look."

He had been standing waiting for her by Customs; her heart had tipped over at the sight of him. She was struck forcibly, not for the first time, at the way he projected sexual power. He had an immense suppressed energy; he moved slowly, as if about to take off at great speed.

He had obviously made a great effort to look impressive for her; he had on a gray coat she had not seen before with a black velvet collar, his hair was neatly brushed, he was very freshly shaved, his tie was straight, his shirt uncrumpled. His dark eyes, exploring hers, exploring her, were tentative, tender, his mouth oddly soft and half smiling. He looked, she thought, almost cheerful.

"Thanks," she said. "You, on the other hand, look very nice. Did anyone tell you your face usually looks as if you had slept in it?"

"No, I don't think so. But if it's your phrase I like it. What have you been doing, for God's sake?"

"Throwing up," Phaedria said sheepishly.

"Dear God," he said, "if you continue to vomit every time we come close to each other, I'm not sure there's a future in this relationship. Come on, darling. Franco is outside with the car. Should I get some strong paper bags for you?"

"No," she said, smiling at him, thinking how, as always, he carried happiness in his wake. "No, I'm all right now."

"Good."

The mammoth black stretch waited by the curb. Franco was ignoring, with an earnest insolence, the harassment of a traffic cop. "Good heavens," said Phaedria, surveying the car's length, its tinted windows, its waving aerials, "you've brought your apartment with you."

"Yeah, there's a double bed and a Jacuzzi inside. Get in, darling, or we'll all be arrested."

She got in. "This is quite a car," she said.

"It gets me around."

"I don't understand why these things have two aerials."

"One's for the TV. Keeps me awake while I'm traveling. Franco, we'll go straight home."

"Sure thing, Mr. Browning."

They pulled away from the airport; she sat awkwardly, slightly apart from him, on the backseat, silent, looking out of the window. He looked at her, and his lips twitched.

"Are you going to tell me what's the matter or shall I tell you?"

She looked at him, startled. "Nothing's the matter."

"Of course there is. Otherwise you wouldn't be sitting over there like a frightened rabbit."

She smiled sheepishly. "Well, I—it's—"

He smiled at her. "Let me tell you. You're scared. Here we are, two people who hardly know each other, and fate has shacked us up together for two whole days and told us to get on with it. And among the things we have to get on with is a whole load of screwing. And you know I've been to bed a great many times with Roz, and I know you've been to bed a great many times with her father, and neither of us knows quite how we are going to handle it. Well, let me tell you, baby, I'm shit-scared, too."

"Oh, Michael," Phaedria said gratefully, crawling across the seat and into his arms, "how is it you always make everything absolutely all right?"

THEY WENT TO bed as soon as they got to the duplex. Michael said firmly, removing her coat, taking her hand, leading her up the stairs, that it was really the only thing to do. Get it over and done with. "We will deflower each other," he said very seriously, "and then we can start to enjoy ourselves."

"Good God," Phaedria said, standing still, looking around the black and white bedroom, at the massive circular bed with the battery of switches and lights set into the head, the arced video screen, the mirrored ceiling, the jungle of plants and brilliant tropical flowers all along one wall, the aquarium filled with dazzling sea fish built in all along another wall. "This is no place for a virgin."

"Don't you like it?" he said, and he looked so anxious, so near to hurt, so desperate that it should please her, that all her nervousness left her and she sat down on the bed, kicked off her shoes, and smiled up at him.

"I love it," she said, "and I think I'm going to love you."

Michael took off his jacket, his tie, his shoes, threw them on the floor, lay down on the bed, and pulled her close beside him. He took her in his arms and said, "Now let's just quit worrying. Let's just go with it."

There was a bad moment: after he had kissed her for so long and with such delicious slowness she felt as if she would scream if she couldn't have more of him; after he had removed her clothes and his and lain for a long time, just looking at her; after he had stroked her and smoothed her and played with her pubic hair and kissed and teased and sucked at her nipples; after she had, relieved at her own hunger, climbed onto him, lain there, rising and falling slowly onto him, feeling his penis silky hard against her clitoris, feeling the fire mount, heat, roar; after he had turned her suddenly, looked into her eyes, said her name over and over again; after he had moved down, kissing, teasing, caressing her with his tongue and she had lain, her eyes closed, thrusting herself at him, rhythmically, gently; after she had felt her whole body turned liquid, white hot, and he moved up again and slowly, tenderly sank into her. Then, suddenly then, a face swam into her consciousness, a pain-filled, frightened, dying face, and she tensed, tightened, froze. He drew away from her then at once, looked down at her, said, "Look at me, Phaedria. Don't think, don't think, just know that I love you."

And she opened her eyes again, looked into his different eyes, loving, concerned, patient eyes, and the moment was gone and she smiled and threw back her head, arched her body, drew him in, in, all the great longing urgency of him, and he groaned, cried out suddenly and came, clutching at her, and she was left, still suspended, alone, empty, and yet happy, oddly triumphant.

"Oh, God," he said after a moment, and there was a sob in his voice. "Oh, God, I would give the world for that not to have happened."

And no, she said, no, don't mind, don't. It doesn't matter, it more than doesn't matter, it was good, it was the right thing, I needed to wait, please don't be sad.

"Okay," he said, moving away from her, lying on his elbow, looking at her with a wealth of love. "We'll wait. But not for long. I promise you, not for long."

"NOW," HE SAID, after they had breakfasted on brioches and strawberries and orange juice laced with champagne, and coffee he had made himself with enormous care and exactness on his espresso machine, "now I think we should go out. I want to take you for a walk in the park, and then I want to take you to lunch at Le Cirque and then I want to bring you back here and make love to you again, and then I want to take you shopping and then I want to take you to tea at the Plaza, and then I want to make love to you again, and then I have tickets for *My One and Only*, and then I thought we could have supper at Un Deux Trois, and then we can come home and make love again, and we can see the New Year in in an absolutely outstanding, shattering, earth-moving, mind-blowing way. How does that grab you, as they used to say? If you trust me to deliver on that last part," he added soberly.

"I trust you utterly and it grabs me beautifully," Phaedria said, leaning forward, kissing him tenderly. "The only thing is it's an awful lot of eating. I shall get fat."

"No, you won't, as long as we keep screwing. Do you know how many calories a good screw uses up?"

"No, I don't think I do."

"Three hundred. At a modest estimate."

"Three hundred calories isn't really very much food."

"Then," he said, lifting his hand, stroking her cheek with infinite gentleness, "there will have to be still more screwing."

"PLEASE LET ME come to the Bahamas with you," he said.

"You can't," she said, "I don't think my body would survive it."

"I could leave your body alone."

"You wouldn't."

"You're right, I wouldn't."

They were lying in bed on the afternoon of New Year's Day; they had been skating at Rockefeller Center and had lunched off the street vendors' wagons on pretzels and knishes and cans of root beer. They had planned to go down to Chinatown, but Michael had suddenly looked at Phaedria as she sat in the cold sunshine, biting hungrily into her food, the light spangling her wild hair, and had felt a wave of longing for her so strong it caught his breath. He had reached out and touched her face, and without a word she had stood up and taken his hand and they had walked swiftly, urgently up Fifth Avenue to Michael's apartment building, into the elevator, and straight through the duplex to the bedroom. Then, facing each other, still not speaking, their eyes fixed on each other, they had torn off their clothes and fallen, hungrily, greedily onto each other and the bed.

Later he had gotten up while she was half asleep and made hot chocolate and brought it to her and had sat beside her, feeding her morsels of chocolate, occasionally bending to kiss her breasts.

"I like them better small," he said. "They were nice big, and I look forward to seeing them big again when we have our children, but right now I like them small."

"How many children are we going to have?" she asked.

"Oh, not too many. Around a dozen."

"Six of each?"

"No," he said, "twelve girls. Just like their mother."

"I love you," she said.

"I love you, too," he said. "Now, you see, I was right, wasn't I?"

"What about?"

"About us."

"Yes, I think you were. Was—" She hesitated. "Is—well, is the sex all right?"

"No," he said, smiling at her, into her eyes, "no, it isn't all right. It's lovely. Beautiful. You're very special."

"Really?"

"Really. Don't look so worried. When are you going to marry me?"

"Oh, Michael, I don't know," she said, suddenly anxious. "We have so much to resolve before I can think about that."

"What do we have to resolve?" he said, his voice light, but his face wary, watchful.

"You know what. The company. Miles. Roz. Everything."

"Roz and Miles I can see. The company I can't. You can just leave it. Come and live here with me. Forget all about it."

"I can't do that. I really can't."

"Why not, for Christ's sake?" he said and there was real anger in his voice. "Jesus, I spent years waiting to get Roz away from that thing. I don't intend to spend years more waiting for you. Just give it all up."

"No," she said, and her dark eyes were steady, in spite of a gripping fear. "No, I can't."

"Why the hell not?"

"Because Julian left it to me. Because I care about it. But most of all for Julia."

"Julia? What's she got to do with it?"

"A lot."

"How?"

"Michael, she's Julian's child. He didn't know about her, but if he had he would have wanted her to have it. All of it possibly. Certainly a lot. He probably wouldn't have played this bloody silly game with Miles and Roz and me."

"I think he would have. I think he would have had even more fun. Tangling you all up, making you trip over one another. God, I thought I'd finally gotten rid of the guy, but he's coming at me from the grave."

"I'm sorry."

"If you're sorry, Phaedria, prove it. Say you'll give it up. Come to New York. Marry me."

"I can't. I do love you, Michael, but I can't give up the company. Not yet. Maybe later, when it's settled, when I have a trust fund organized for Julia, when Miles has made up his mind, when the thing is running on a proper constructive basis, when Roz and I have a modus operandi, when—"

"Oh, no," he said. "No. I'm sorry, Phaedria, but I will not play second lead to that company. I will not."

"I don't understand you," she said.

"You don't understand? Dear God, how am I supposed to? Just what do you want me to do? Give everything up at this end, move over there, and sit around waiting for you to come home every night?"

"Of course not," she said. "Just wait. Just try to see my side of it."

"I'm sorry, but I can't deliver. I'm tired of waiting. And I don't see how you can let that tangle of power and intrigue get to you and keep you away from your own happiness."

"But if you'd only—"

"Maybe I do see," he said, and there was a heavy sadness in his voice. "I see that in your own way you are as greedy as Roz. And as selfish. I see that, like her, you want it all your way. You want my love your way. Well you can have my love Phaedria, but only my way."

"Which means?"

"You know what it means. You have to give up the company."

"I can't. I told you."

"Well, then," he said.

"Then what?"

"Then you may as well go. Go back to it. Now."

"Very well."

She got up silently, walked to the shower, dressed, packed her things. Put on her coat, stood facing him.

He was still naked on the bed, stricken, but yet angry. "Shall I have Franco take you to the airport?"

"Yes, please. It would be helpful."

"I hope," he said, with a huge sigh, pulling on his terry-cloth robe, walking over to the house telephone, buzzing Franco, "I hope you know what you're doing."

"I'm afraid I do," she said. "I am very, very sad, but I'm afraid I do."

◆　　◆　　◆

SHE HAD THOUGHT at first, as she sat, frozen with shock and disbelief in the car, amazed that happiness and love could turn so swiftly to pain and distancing, that she would go straight home, but she decided to go to Eleuthera after all. She needed time on her own, peace, a base to reflect from. And she felt instinctively that that house, that place, where she had been only once, and then much in love with Julian, was the natural one to be.

It was a fateful decision.

JULIA BECAME ILL around lunchtime on New Year's Day. She had had a cough ever since the beginning of Christmas, but suddenly it got worse. Her temperature began to climb; she was restless, fretful. Nanny Hudson, initially calm, began to worry. At tea time she sent for the doctor. He came at once, looked Julia over, listened to her small chest, and then put his stethoscope away, looking mildly worried.

"I really don't think there's much to worry about. She has a slight chest infection. I wouldn't take any notice at all, if it weren't for her history. I'll leave you some antibiotic to give her. Call me if she gets any worse."

Nanny Hudson, comforted, gave Julia the antibiotic, persuaded her to take her bottle, and put her to bed. She seemed calmer and went to sleep.

Two hours later, she woke up crying. She was extremely hot, coughing violently. Nanny Hudson phoned the doctor. He came back, examined the baby carefully again, and then said, "I wouldn't do this if her mother were here, but I think perhaps she should go to hospital. Just to be on the safe side. There's an excellent one in Eastbourne; you can be there in half an hour. I presume someone can drive you. I'm sure she'll be fine tomorrow, but it will be a better place for her, and you, to spend the night."

"All right, Dr. Spender," Nanny Hudson said, trying to fight down the fear that was rising in her. "If that's what you think, I would feel happier, too. Should I get Lady Morell home?"

"Where is she?"

"In New York."

"Hmm. I suppose you should tell her. She could get home very quickly if she wanted to, which I expect she would. Yes, give her a call."

Nanny Hudson, her hands trembling, dialed the number Phaedria had given her in New York. There was no reply. She packed a bag for

Julia and herself and tried again. Still no reply. Pete was waiting with the car. She decided to try again from the hospital.

MILES, ROZ, ELIZA, and Peveril were still celebrating the New Year.

Peveril had insisted on giving a party for Hogmanay in Miles's honor, and most of the county had come to the castle for champagne and Scottish reels, interspersed with the occasional Charleston from Letitia, and to see the New Year piped in. Miles had found the whole thing, particularly the reels, totally enchanting and had joined in with immense enthusiasm, insisting on borrowing a kilt from Peveril, which being rather too large for him, had fallen down in the middle of an eightsome reel. This had greatly added to the enjoyment of the women guests, and particularly as he had insisted on adhering strictly to Scottish male dress and not worn any underpants.

On the evening of New Year's Day they had gone to dinner with Peveril's sister and her husband thirty miles away, on the other side of the Sidlaw Hills. Letitia, reluctant to miss out on any fun, and still more reluctant to admit she was feeling her age, had still been forced to admit that a quiet evening on her own might be an attractive idea.

She had just settled down with her feet up and switched her television on when she heard the telephone. Monro, the butler, knocked on her door and said could she come to the phone; there was an urgent call for her.

It was Nanny Hudson, now at the hospital in Eastbourne. Julia's temperature was still rising, she seemed to be in considerable pain, and they were considering putting her in an oxygen tent. There was no reply to the number in New York Lady Morell had given her. Did Mrs. Morell have any idea where else she might be contactable?

"Oh, God," Letitia said. "Poor Phaedria. Poor child. If anything happens to that baby, I think she will kill herself. No, Nanny. I'm sorry, I don't. I thought she was in Eleuthera anyway."

"She will be tomorrow, madam, but not today. She should still be in New York, she specifically said that there would always be someone there to take messages, even if she was out for a while herself."

"Oh, Nanny, this is awful. How bad is the baby?"

"I don't know," Nanny Hudson said, and Letitia could hear the struggle to keep panic from invading her voice. "Quite bad. Her temperature is a hundred and four. I feel very, very worried."

"Is there a good doctor there? Oh, if only you were in London. If only I were in London."

"I think the staff here is excellent. The consultant pediatrician is on his way. But I think—well, I'm sure actually—that she may be developing pneumonia."

"Dear God. Nanny, stay there, keep calm. Oh, what nonsense I'm talking; you are far calmer than I. I will phone the house on Eleuthera and ask the houseman to meet Lady Morell at Nassau, in case she's on her way there now, and stop her traveling on to Eleuthera. That will save hours of time tomorrow, at least. Oh, God, and she could have been home in just a few hours from New York. This is terrible. Well, maybe she will come back tonight, still. I'll keep trying the number for you, if you like, and then you won't have to leave the baby. Nanny, let me know if there's any change, won't you? This is terrible."

She put the phone down and called the house at Turtle Cove. It was quite early in the day there. Jacintha, the housekeeper, said no, Lady Morell was not expected until the next day at lunchtime.

"Well, Jacintha, you must get Nelson to go to Nassau. Immediately. Wait for Lady Morell there. Tell her to go back to England. I will have a message left for her at the airport, of course, but to be on the safe side, I think Nelson should go as well."

"Yes, ma'am." Jacintha was sulky. She had been looking forward to a good New Year holiday with Nelson; they had planned a boat trip, and a bottle of champagne from Sir Julian's cellar. They thought of the house as more and more their own, now that visitors came so rarely and the master had gone. Still, a baby was a precious thing, and if Lady Morell's baby was ill, then she must be sent home at once. Although what she had been doing away without the baby, Jacintha could not imagine. They were strange folks, the rich English.

PHAEDRIA CAUGHT A flight to Nassau quite quickly. She could see it was going to mean spending the night there—there would be no connecting flight until next day—but she felt a compulsion to get away from New York. Strange how the city was haunted by unhappiness for her.

She began to come to on the plane, her emotions thawing into painful life. Michael's words kept coming back to her: "You are as selfish as Roz, as greedy as Roz. . . . Go, go now. I will not play second lead to that company."

Oh, God, what had she done? Why had she done it? Was it really greed, selfishness? No, no, she knew it wasn't. She had acted from a strong, almost primeval urge to protect her territory and her family.

Julian had bequeathed her the birthright of the company, and it was Julia's birthright; she had to safeguard it for her. That was all there was to it. And if she had to lose all that was personally dear to her to do it, then she would have to endure that. It seemed cruel, horribly cruel, that she should have to lose Michael and happiness when she had only just discovered both, but she honestly felt there was little option.

Thinking about Michael, what he had become to her in thirty-six short hours, pain almost overcame her, made her physically faint. He had brought her joy, laughter, tenderness, love; he had made her feel safe, peaceful, cared for, at ease. She could see, with a vivid clarity, all that her life could have become, all that she had deprived it of: and yet she had had, she knew, no choice at all. She had made a decision, although she had not known it—first, when she had married Julian, and then when she had borne his child—that she would become part of him and his life, and that life had included, indeed in large part consisted of, the company. And there could be no going back from it now.

IN A HOSPITAL thousands of miles away her baby fought death, drawing strength from where or what she did not know, but with a spirit that was a legacy from her father, who had lost his own battle, finally, and a mother who had a courage of her own, the full extent of which she had only just discovered.

LETITIA WAS STILL up, pacing the great hall, willing the phone to ring, when the others came back from the party, laughing, talking loudly, full of "did you see" and "wasn't she?" and "didn't he?"

"Granny Letitia, whatever is it?" Roz said, quickly taking in her grandmother's white face, her haunted eyes. "It isn't—it isn't—"

And no, said Letitia, swift to recognize a mother's permanent, painful anxiety. "No, it isn't Miranda. It's Julia; she's very ill, in an oxygen tent with pneumonia, and Phaedria is away and can't be contacted."

"Oh, Christ," Roz said, her hostility and outrage forgotten in a sudden, sweeping concern. "Why can't she be contacted? For heaven's sake, she must have left a number in case of an emergency. Why doesn't somebody ring it?"

"We have been ringing it," Letitia said patiently, "but she isn't there."

"Well, where is she, then? She's on Eleuthera, isn't she? It's not a big place; surely she can be found."

"No," Miles said, feeling he had to speak. "No, she isn't on Eleuthera; she's in New York."

"New York?" said Roz. "New York? What on earth is she doing in New York? Why did we all think . . ." Her voice trailed away into silence, and she looked first shocked, then angry, as she faced Miles. "How the hell did you know she was in New York, and why didn't you tell me?"

"Be quiet, Rosamund," Letitia said angrily. "Why shouldn't Phaedria be in New York, and what does it matter anyway? As a matter of fact, I knew she was there; Nanny Hudson told me. I've been ringing the number myself. That baby's life is in danger. All that matters is that, and that we find Phaedria. I'm shocked at you."

Roz ignored her. "What is this number in New York?"

"It's over there by the telephone. I was just going to try it again anyway."

Roz went over and looked at the piece of paper. But she didn't really need to. It was a number she felt was engraved on her heart.

THE PLANE LANDED on Nassau at ten o'clock local time. Phaedria didn't even bother to check whether there was a flight out to Eleuthera. All she wanted was to go to bed and to find a respite, however brief, from her pain. She had no baggage, only her overnight bag; she walked straight out of the airport and into a cab without ever seeing the message for her pinned to the board in the arrival hall, and she was also not to know that at that very moment, Nelson was desperately trying to find someone to pilot Julian's plane out of Eleuthera and into Nassau.

WHILE NANNY HUDSON sat helpless, terrified, by the oxygen hood, watching Julia wage her battle, Miles sat by Roz's huge four-poster bed as she wept endlessly, hopelessly, into her pillow.

"Roz, you just have to know two things. One is that I only found out by a freak chance. Two is that Phaedria didn't want you to know. I know she didn't, she wanted to spare you."

"Jesus Christ!" Roz lifted her face, ugly, swollen with crying and rage, from her pillow. "Why does everyone regard that bitch as some kind of a saint? If she'd wanted to spare me she could have left him alone in the first place. Just why don't you fuck off, Miles, and leave me alone?"

"Because it wouldn't do any good. Because you need company. Because I care about you."

"If you'd cared about me, you wouldn't have lied to me."

"Roz, I didn't lie to you. I simply didn't tell you Phaedria was going to New York."

"And how did you find out that she was going to New York? Some kind of psychic transmission, is that what you're trying to imply?"

"No, I'm not trying to imply anything. I'm telling you. I was talking to Phaedria, and she let it slip that she was going to New York. I promised her I wouldn't tell you. I feel bad now that I did."

"I'm sure you do. Whoever else gets hurt or let down, it mustn't be Phaedria. Oh, God, I hate her so much."

Roz's voice rose in a wail of rage and pain; she was drumming her feet on the bed.

Miles looked at her concernedly. "Roz, please don't."

"Why not?" She sat up suddenly and looked at him. "This is what you're always telling me I should do—let it all out. Let go. What's wrong with it, all of a sudden?"

"I don't know. I guess when her baby is so ill, it seems wrong to hate her so much."

"I was very, very sorry about her baby," Roz said. "When we first came in tonight, before I knew where she was, I was desperately sorry, I wanted to help, to find her."

"I know," said Miles. "I could see that you were. I know."

"But then I found out she was with Michael and I just couldn't feel anything but hate. I'm sorry. I'm obviously a bad person."

"No," he said, "just an unhappy one."

"Oh, shit," said Roz, "everything is so awful. Everything. I just can't cope with it all anymore."

"Of course you can," he said, "you're a fighter. You'll always cope."

"Do you think so?"

"I know so. I've told you before. I think you're terrific."

She looked at him and smiled a watery smile. "You don't know me," she said.

"Yes, I do. I think I know you better than most people, as a matter of fact. That's better; you're cooling off. Turn around and I'll massage your neck."

"Oh, Miles, no. Not now."

"Yeah, now. You need it now."

She looked at him, a long, considering look. "All right."

"You'll have to take that vest thing off."

"This vest thing is a silk T-shirt from Joseph."

"Who is this Joseph guy and what's he doing giving you T-shirts?"

Roz giggled. "Okay, I'll take it off. Just hang on a minute, I don't have anything on underneath. Let me get my robe." She went into the bathroom, came back wearing a silk kimono, and sat down on her bed with her back to Miles. He started working on her neck, stroking it, kneading it, pushing the tension out; Roz felt herself relax. "That's so nice."

"Good. Now your shoulders."

He slipped his hands under the robe, began working along the line of her shoulders, down her spine. Roz felt the almost familiar, dangerous lick of warmth through her body. She closed her eyes, put her head back, tried not to think. Miles moved over her shoulders, smoothing the skin above her breasts, then returned to her spine and gently, insidiously around the sides of her body.

"Miles," she said, half happy, half protesting. "You never did that before."

"You never were so upset before," he said calmly.

"Maybe not."

There was a silence while he worked on, his warm strong hands stroking her into an odd state: half excitement, half peace.

"Better?"

"Much."

He stopped suddenly, turned her around, looked at her very directly, his dark blue eyes smiling into her green ones.

"What would really help you," he said, almost conversationally, "is a good fuck."

Roz looked at him, shocked, amused, and most of all intensely aroused, emotionally and physically.

"Don't be ridiculous," she said with an effort.

"I'm not being ridiculous. It would."

"And I suppose," she said, in a hopeless attempt to defuse the situation and her emotions, "you think you should be the person to administer it."

"I sure do," he said and he smiled at her suddenly, his most dangerous, self-mocking, beguiling smile. "What's more I would really enjoy it. Wouldn't you?"

"No," she said, "no, not at all."

"You're lying," he said calmly, smiling again.

"Even if I am, you shouldn't even consider it. This is not the time or the place, and anyway, there's Candy."

"It is absolutely the time and the place, this is a bedroom, we have a soft bed, and Candy is thousands of miles away."

Roz looked at him thoughtfully, too amused to be anything but direct. "You really think it doesn't matter, don't you? To her, I mean."

"I really do. It doesn't."

"That is an extremely singular opinion."

"Maybe, but it's mine. That's what counts."

"Well, anyway, it would matter to me."

"Roz, it's not going to have to matter to you. Anyway, I'm not going to force myself on you. Although I think maybe I'd better go to bed. I want you pretty badly right now, and it's frustrating just sitting here, looking at you in that thing, with your tits half out. Good night, Roz."

He bent down and kissed her, lightly, gently, as he had in the woods, but all the emotions of the evening—the anxiety, the rage, the grief, the tension—swept through Roz and polarized into a frantic hunger. She lay back on the bed, her thin arms around his neck, her lips, her tongue working frantically on his. He kissed her back, hard, briefly, then disentangled himself from her and sat back on the bed looking at her.

"Have you changed your mind?" he said.

"Yes," said Roz, her voice very low.

Miles stood up. He pulled off his black tie, his dress shirt. His long body was still very brown, hard, lean. Roz lay there, looking at it, in silence; then she sat up on the bed and slipped off the robe, her eyes fixed on his.

Miles put out his hand, cupped one of her breasts, massaging the nipple gently with his thumb; then he bent and began to lick it, suck it. Roz moaned, took his head in her hands, pressing it to her; then she lay back again and sighed, a huge, long, shuddering sigh, smiling up at him.

"Take those trousers off, for God's sake," she said. "I've been thinking about this ever since I first set eyes on you, you beautiful bastard."

THE PEDIATRICIAN LOOKED down at Julia in the oxygen hood. She was still fighting for breath, her small chest heaving with the effort. The sun was streaming in at the windows; it was nearly seven o'clock.

"We have to move her to intensive care," he said.

Nanny Hudson looked up at him exhausted, so frightened now she could hardly think.

"Yes," she said, "yes, of course. Is she—is she worse?"

"She is certainly no better," he said, and sighed. "Do you want to come with her?"

"Yes, please. If I may. Oh, why did this have to happen when her mother was away?"

"It often does," he said. "I'm not sure why. They need their mothers, babies do. I've just spoken to her grandmother again. She's still trying to contact the mother. She seems to have totally disappeared."

PHAEDRIA, WHO HAD spent a wretched night at the Colonial Hotel in Nassau, finally got back to the airport at ten in the morning and checked into a flight to Eleuthera.

It was leaving in minutes; she shot through the comparatively informal passport control and ran out onto the tarmac toward the small yellow plane.

The pilot, a dazzling-looking young black woman, was waiting by the steps. She smiled at Phaedria. "Looks like you just made it, honey. Hurry up, now."

As the plane taxied down the runway, the clerk in passport control was receiving a serious dressing down from his superior, who had been alerted, a little late, that a Lady Morell had just checked onto the Eleuthera flight.

"It was urgent that we contact that lady, and what do you do? Let her by without a murmur. Now she's in the sky. Man, will we be in trouble."

"It's these new computers," said the clerk. "They cause a heap of trouble."

By the time the airport manager had worked out how acutely illogical this remark was, he had no energy left to be annoyed.

MILES WOKE UP in Roz's bed, wondering briefly where he was. He lay quietly, looking up at the curtains above his head, at the outline of the hills outside the window and then at Roz, her face peaceful, gentle in sleep, oddly unfamiliar.

He smiled to himself, thinking about her; she was a most complex creature. So angry, so tough, but with such a capacity to feel. And extraordinarily sensuous. Miles had spent a great many nights, and days, with a great many women, and he had never quite encountered such passion, such capacity for sexual pleasure, as he had found in Roz.

He had expected her to be hungry, ardent, had expected her to greet him, meet him as an equal; what he had not been prepared for was the way she entirely took the initiative, made love to him, used him, as if he were an object fashioned entirely for her delight.

She came, they both did, almost at once the first time, Roz lying beneath him, gasping, moaning, her long legs wrapped around him, her arms flung out, thrusting her body against him, around him, and he felt her as she climaxed in seemingly endless violent spasms. He drew back from her then, smiling into her eyes, kissing her tenderly, saying nothing, feeling the sweetness, the triumph of shared release, but Roz did not relax; she was violent, almost angry in her continuing need of him. She turned and lay on top of him and began to kiss him, slowly, intensely, and then moved down, licking, sucking, kissing his body, until she reached his penis. She took it in her mouth, working on it, determinedly, hungrily insistent, and then when he was ready for her, and tried to turn her, to enter her again, she said no, no, and it was almost a shout, a cry of triumph and she sat up, astride him, pulling him into her, drawing out her own climax, not allowing him his, retreating from him again and again, until finally he gave himself up to it and came, and she with him, not once but several times, and he could feel the waves growing stronger, more violent, greedier, each time. And still she wasn't satisfied; still she wanted more.

"You really are," he said, turning from her finally, desperate for rest, for sleep, "something else."

And now, he thought, now what? He was uneasily aware that what he felt for Roz, what he had shared with her through that wild night, was something unique in his experience. It went deeper, felt stronger, sweeter, than anything he had ever known. He shifted in the bed, trying to remember how he had felt when he had first slept with the other women he had really cared about, with Candy, with Joanna, and he knew perfectly well it had not been anything like this. Not sexually or—more alarmingly—emotionally. He felt, with Roz, a great closeness, a desire to care for her; a tenderness, he supposed it was, trying to analyze it. He felt tenderness toward Candy, too, but it was different; it was lighthearted, it felt less important. He also, in some strange way, felt responsible for and to Roz. Few people liked her and far fewer loved her. Trying rather alarmedly to decide which of the two emotions he felt, he decided it was neither one nor the other, but a strange heady amalgam of the two.

He decided it was just as well Candy was coming back to England soon. This situation could very easily get out of hand.

PHAEDRIA REACHED TURTLE Cove at two o'clock local time. She was exhausted. She had phoned the house repeatedly and got no reply and had had to get one of the appalling local taxis from the airport for the twenty-mile drive to the house. The one she took had its radiator needle jammed permanently on boiling, and a door hanging half off its hinges. The driver talked incessantly about his acute surprise that another year had come and gone. Phaedria tried to be courteous, but her head ached and she felt sick.

When she finally reached the house and walked into the cool hall with its whirring fans, it was deserted. She went to the kitchen; there was a meal on the table, left abandoned, Marie Celeste–like, on the table, a window hanging open. It seemed strange. Maybe they had got the days mixed up and were expecting her tomorrow. It didn't matter. She went through to the bedroom and pulled off her hot winter clothes. She climbed into one of the swimsuits she had left there, looking at the bed where she and Julian had celebrated their wedding, where she had lain sick with the sun and he had read to her. It had been a marvelous marriage, she thought, in the beginning. Despite what he had inflicted on her since, she had loved him very much.

Maybe that had been half the problem with Michael. That she had still been grieving, had not been ready. Part of her, part of her heart, was still with Julian. Well, it didn't matter now.

She sighed and walked out onto the veranda where they had eaten breakfast that first marvelous morning, after the snorkeling. She went down to the beach and slithered into the warm, silky sea. There was a conch shell by her foot; she ducked under the water and picked it up. It was small, its pink interior pale and marbled. She waded back to the beach and laid it on the silver-white sand.

What a lovely place this was. It made her feel peaceful, in spite of her unhappiness, whole again. She would not sell this, of all the houses, if she had to buy Miles out. She would rather sell Hanover Terrace. She needed Turtle Cove.

She swam strongly out to sea for a few minutes, then turned and trod water, looking at the shore. Suddenly she saw Jacintha waving at her frantically. Puzzled, worried, she swam back in.

"Whatever is it, Jacintha? What's the matter?"

"It's your baby, Lady Morell." She gave the stress on the first syllable of "Morell." "She's very, very ill." She sounded excited, important to be bringing such news. Phaedria nearly shook her.

"What is it? Where is she? Why didn't someone tell me?"

"We tried to tell you, Lady Morell, we couldn't find you. Nelson, he's in Nassau looking for you. You better phone old Mrs. Morell; she'll tell you all 'bout it. They been phoning you in New York and here all night."

"Oh, my God," Phaedria said, "it must be really serious if they've been looking for me that hard. Jacintha, what is the matter with her? What is it? Do you know?"

"I don't know, ma'am," said Jacintha, half enjoying the drama and her momentarily important role in it. "All I know your baby real sick. Like I said, you better phone old Mrs. Morell."

Phaedria raced over the sand, across the lawn, into the house, frantically dialed the number in Scotland. Letitia answered the phone.

"Letitia, it's Phaedria. What's happening? Please tell me. What's the matter with Julia? Who's with her? Where is she? What can I do?"

"Oh, Phaedria, thank God we found you. Julia's in hospital. In Eastbourne. Nanny Hudson is with her. Eliza has flown down to be with them both. We thought someone from the family should go."

"But what—what is it? Is it very serious?"

"Darling, it would be silly to tell you it's not. It's serious. She's got pneumonia. But she's—holding her own. And of course pneumonia isn't what it was. It still sounds very frightening, but with antibiotics it just isn't so bad. Phaedria? Phaedria, are you still there?"

"Yes," Phaedria said in a small, quiet voice. "I'm still here. Letitia, I don't know what to do. I won't be able to get home today. There aren't many flights out. I suppose I could get the company jet. The pilot is in New York."

"Thank God for that," Letitia said briskly. "He can be with you in a very few hours. You can get him to come and collect you. And, darling, don't despair. I'm sure, quite sure, Julia will be all right. Listen, why don't you talk to the doctor at the hospital? He'll be able to reassure you."

"Yes, I will. Give me his number. And do you think you could call the company pilot and ask him to ring me here? He's at the Intercontinental, New York. Thank God he's not in London. I just feel so . . ." Her voice trailed shakily away.

"Yes, of course I will. Now, you ring the doctor at Eastbourne and see what he says. I'll ring you back in about a quarter of an hour. All right?"

"All right, Letitia."

Phaedria put down the phone and frantically, desperately, dialed the number. She got through to the switchboard and asked for the pediatrician.

"I'm sorry; that number is busy at the moment. Will you hold?"

"No," she said, almost shouting down the phone. "No, I won't hold. I'm calling from the Bahamas. Will you put me through at once? It's very, very urgent. This is Lady Morell."

"I'm sorry," said the voice, coldly distasteful. "The line is busy. I can't interrupt. Will you hold, or will you call back?"

"Oh, God," said Phaedria. "Oh, God, I'll hold. No, wait. Put me through to intensive care."

"I'm afraid I can't do that," said the voice, colder than ever.

"Why not?"

"There is no line through to intensive care."

"But my baby is in there. Do you have any news of her? Can you at least tell me how she is?"

"Just a moment." The voice sounded just slightly more helpful. Phaedria waited, her head drumming with fear, her stomach a clenched knot. There was a long silence.

"Hello?" It was a man's voice.

"Hello, yes. Is this the pediatrician? I'm sorry, I don't have your name. This is Phaedria Morell."

"Lady Morell, yes. This is Dr. Peter Dugdale. Now, about your baby . . ."

"Yes? How is she?"

"Her condition is quite serious, Lady Morell. It would be wrong of me to pretend otherwise. But she is holding her own. I can't say more than that. Try not to worry," he added, in the voice of the dutifully sensitive. Phaedria bit her fist; she knew she mustn't scream, mustn't get too angry with him, antagonize him.

"I'll get there as soon as I can," she said when she had got control of her voice again.

Phaedria put the phone down. She looked out at the sea, the white sand, the palm trees, in disbelief. How could any place be so beautiful, so calm, when her life was an ugly, terrifying turmoil? If only the pilot would phone. Where was he, and how long would it take him to get her out of this awful, awful place? As she sat looking at the phone, willing it to ring, her head suddenly filled with a fresh horror. Roz had been in Scotland. She would have known about the whole thing. She would have heard that Phaedria was in New York, would probably have asked what the number was. There was no way, no way on God's earth that Roz would not know now that she had been in New York with Michael. And the awful irony was that she need never have known at all.

Phaedria rested her head on her arms and wept.

ROZ COULDN'T SLEEP the second night; she was haunted by thoughts of Phaedria, a battle raging in her between hatred and sympathy for her, and by thoughts of Miles. She had avoided him all day, half ashamed that they should have experienced such pleasure and happiness when Julia's life was suspended so perilously, half consumed with longing to see him, be with him, have him again. They had met at mealtimes, which had in any case been strained, distracted occasions, everyone jumping whenever the phone rang. She had gone to bed early, pleading a headache. Letitia looked at her sharply; Roz never had headaches, never went to bed early, never felt tired. She looked at her watch; it was two o'clock. She decided to go down to Peveril's library. She didn't feel like reading, but he had some magnificent first editions, of Thackeray, Trollope, Burns. It would be amusing to look at those. She got up, pulled on her robe, and went quietly down to the great hall and into the library.

She was engrossed in *The Eustace Diamonds* when the door opened quietly. Still half involved with the book, she turned around slowly. It was Miles.

"Hi. Couldn't you sleep? I guess we're all pretty strung out."

"Yes. I keep thinking about Julia."

"I kept thinking about you."

"Miles, I—I don't think we should carry on with this relationship. Not at all."

"Okay." He shrugged, smiling at her. "If that's what you want."

"Well, it's—it's not what I want. But I just feel things are complicated enough. And there's Candy." She stood up and turned away from him.

"Roz, I told you last night, she's three thousand miles away."

Roz felt a mild irritation. "I know she is now. But she won't always be. I don't want to play any more of those games. And somehow this doesn't seem quite the time for this kind of thing. Anyway, I don't like our relationship being reduced to a one-night stand."

"Do we have a relationship?"

She felt foolish, disadvantaged. "No, of course not. You misunderstood me."

"Sorry to hear it." He moved over, stood behind her, kissed her neck. "I was hoping we did."

"Miles, please don't."

"Why not?"

"I just told you why not."

"Oh, Roz," he said, "you're way too serious. And besides . . ." He was still behind her. He slipped his hands under her robe, moved them up to her breasts, started gently, tenderly massaging her nipples.

Roz felt a lick of fire shoot down in a white hot line to her abdomen, her vagina; she squirmed, pressing her buttocks back against him. They were almost the same height; she felt his penis hard, pressing against her; she felt dizzy, odd. She fought to retain some self-control. "Besides what?"

"You are just—well, sensational. I can't think about anything else." His hands moved down, pressing, massaging her stomach. His fingers began to probe her pubic mound, seeking out, reaching into her, finding her clitoris.

She put her head back against him and moaned. "Miles, please."

"Please what?"

"You know what." She turned around, took his head in her hands, kissed him savagely, pulled off her robe. He entered her as she stood there, his hands on her buttocks, holding her to him, pushing, urging her into an almost instant orgasm. Roz cried out, a wild, strange cry, oddly at variance with the sober quiet of the room.

THEY WERE WAITING for Phaedria outside the hospital—Eliza and Nanny Hudson, standing there. Phaedria nearly fell out of the car. "Eliza, Nanny, what is it? What's happened?"

Eliza looked at her, silent for a moment only, but to Phaedria it seemed like an hour, a week. Then she smiled. "Thank God you're here. Julia's all right. Phaedria. She's going to be all right, they think, but she needs you; she needs you so much. This is Dr. Dugdale. He's been marvelous. Come on." And she took Phaedria's hand and pulled her, after Dr. Dugdale, down the corridors, down the stairs, and into a side ward where Julia lay.

She was half asleep, breathing heavily, in her oxygen hood, restless, whimpering from time to time. As her mother came in she looked at her and opened her large dark eyes very wide, almost visibly relaxed, and smiled, a quiet, peaceful smile.

"Oh, Julia," Phaedria said. "Oh, Julia."

"She'll be all right now," Dr. Dugdale said.

LETITIA, BEAMING RADIANTLY, went to find Roz, who was lying rather uncharacteristically on her bed.

"Lovely, lovely news. Julia is going to be all right. She's much better. She has to stay in hospital for a few days, but she's all right. Phaedria's safely back with her. Poor girl, that must have been a terrible twenty-four hours."

"I'm glad," Roz said, "really glad. It's been a nightmare. I'm sorry I behaved so badly, Granny Letitia. I was distraught."

"That's all right, darling. I understood. Come and have some lunch. Where's Miles?"

"Talking to Peveril, I think. They get on really well. It's so funny. Miles is planning to take him to Malibu."

"Well, I don't think he'll be able to do that unless he promises to take your mother as well. So are you feeling better, darling?"

"Yes," Roz said, just a little too casually. "Much much better, thank you Letitia."

·38·

"SO WHAT HAVE YOU DECIDED TO do, Miles?"

Candy looked at him over the heap of bags in their room at Claridge's. She had come back tired and irritable after what had seemed like a very long week of trying to console her father on the loss of Dolly, trying to persuade him to go home to Chicago, to talk him into letting her marry Miles right away.

Miles looked at her thoughtfully. Easygoing as he was, he was beginning to find her nagging irritating. He was actually beginning to find her rather irritating altogether. She seemed shallow suddenly, uninteresting, lacking in emotion and depth. He knew it was unfair of him to think that way, that it was not Candy but he who had changed, but he couldn't help it. Still, something had to be settled. They couldn't live at Claridge's forever; it wasn't exactly cheap.

Roz's intelligent quirky mind kept intruding into his thoughts over Candy's prattle; her cool, amused green eyes looked at him when he was actually meeting Candy's Bambi-like blue ones; her greedy, outrageous body even invaded the bed as he lay caressing Candy's pert little breasts, bringing her to swift, easy orgasm. In the weeks she had been away he and Roz had been to bed together twice more, once in Scotland, once in London, drawn irresistibly, inevitably toward each other by the promise of an intensely powerful pleasure neither of them had ever known before. Each time they had agreed it should not happen again, and each time they had come laughingly together once more, saying why not, just once more? What harm could it do? It had to be good for them. It was fun, just pleasure, just the satisfaction of two exceptionally hearty appetites, and each time, as they parted again, they knew, without saying a word to each other, that it was rather more than that.

However, something had to be resolved, if not for Candy's sake, then for his own. And besides there was the question of money. The extremely generous loans Henry was arranging for him, on Roz and Phaedria's instructions, could not go on forever. He was getting going a monumental amount of money, by any standards. And he was growing weary of living at Claridge's and shopping. He didn't exactly want to work, but he didn't want to be idle in London, or indeed anywhere else in the world, except California.

But whatever he did or did not decide, he was not going to be pushed into it by anybody, least of all Candy. If there was one thing that turned Miles into an immovable object, it was the sense that an irresistible force was coming at him, hard, trying to carry him along with it, as Hugo Dashwood had discovered, to his cost, some years earlier.

Dark blue eyes met light with an expression of rare hostility.

"I haven't decided on anything yet," Miles said. "Stop bugging me, will you? Just leave me alone."

"MILES," ROZ SAID, sinking on to the chaise longue in the window of the Cheyne Walk drawing room, "are you any nearer to making a decision?"

"Nope," he said shortly. "Can I have a glass of wine?"

"Of course. Pour me one, will you?"

He poured two glasses from the chilled bottle and carried one over to her, careful not to touch her. The atmosphere between them now was so febrile that he knew if he so much as brushed her fingers with his they would be in bed in minutes.

"Thank you. Don't look so cross. It doesn't suit you. That's my prerogative."

"Sorry. This is all getting to me. And I'm homesick."

"Of course you are."

"I still kind of favor the consortium. It would let me off the hook. But I worry about the long-term effect on you. And Phaedria."

"Don't worry about me," Roz said darkly. "I can take care of myself. And don't worry about Phaedria. We have every evidence she can do the same."

"Yeah, I guess so. It seems kind of wrong selling out of the family."

"I think it's probably the best possible thing. Fresh blood and all that. The company is the nearest thing to incest this family will ever know."

"Maybe."

"What about working here?"

"Well," he said carefully, "I don't really know. I've kind of warmed toward the idea. It might be fun, just for a little while. And it would please Candy. But—well, she's pushing me real hard, and that makes me angry. And besides—" He looked at her.

"Yes?"

"I don't know if I could handle working with you all the time."

"I think it would be fun," Roz said.

"It would, I mean I'd like it in that way. But I think things might get out of hand pretty quickly."

"You mean we'd be screwing all the time?" Her expression was amused, confident.

"We'd be wanting to, I guess. And if I was married to Candy . . ." His voice trailed off.

"That would never do." She stood up, holding out her hand. "Right now you're not working for the company. And you're not married to Candy. This could be our very last chance. Shall we, Miles? For old times' sake?"

He took the hand, kissed the back of it, turned it over, kissed the palm. Then he looked at her and smiled.

"Yeah, okay. Just for old times' sake."

"MILES," SAID PHAEDRIA, "do you have any idea yet what you want to do?"

He had come to her office to have the promised lunch. He sat watching her while she sorted the files and papers on her desk into some sort of order, flicked idly through telephone messages, signed the letters Sarah had left for her. He thought how sad she looked, how thin and drawn.

"No," he said, "I don't have an idea. You're still keen on this trust fund thing?"

"Yes. Even more now." She spoke without thinking.

"Why?"

She flushed. "Oh, nothing."

"Did New York go wrong?"

He sounded so sympathetic, so genuinely concerned that she couldn't be cross. "Yes, I'm afraid it did. There—there isn't any future there, I'm afraid. So Julia's future seems more crucial than ever. Illogical in a way."

"I'm sorry."

"That must have been terrible for all of you," Phaedria said, "that awful day when she was so ill and they couldn't find me. I'm really, really sorry about it."

"I felt bad giving the game away."

"Did you?" She looked startled. "Miles, why? What happened?"

"Oh, I didn't fail you, not really. Only death would have dragged it out of me; I knew how much it mattered. But it seemed like death.

Or the threat of it. Julia's. I knew you'd care more about her than anything. So I told them. Anyway, Letitia already knew; Nanny Hudson had told her. But Roz learned it from me."

"Oh, God."

"Yeah, it was bad. But I calmed her down."

"You're very good for Roz. I've noticed."

"Maybe."

There was silence.

"Did she ever say anything to you?" he asked.

"No, nothing."

"Uh-huh. And is Julia really okay now?"

"She's fine. You'd never think she'd been ill. It's her mother who needs looking after. Come on, let's go and have lunch. Is Candy joining us?"

"No, Candy's sulking. She sulks a lot these days."

"Oh, Miles, I'm sorry."

"I am, too," he said.

AFTER LUNCH PHAEDRIA sat at her desk, looking out of the window. She still felt very unhappy. Her grief at the loss of Michael was more severe than she had expected it would be. Piled on the greater one for Julian, she found it almost unbearable.

Life had settled into a gray, rather lonely monotone. She worked all day and spent most evenings alone with Julia. It was what she wanted, but it didn't seem to be doing her any good.

She had half expected to hear from Michael, that he would call her, write maybe—although he always swore he was illiterate and could barely manage his name—to try to persuade her to change her mind. But there was silence. An awful, dead, final silence. She supposed that after all the years of battling with the company for Roz's soul, he simply could not contemplate starting all over again for hers. Sometimes she wondered if she had made an appalling mistake, wantonly tossed happiness out of the window and into Central Park that New Year's Day. Perhaps she was simply stubborn and greedy, rather than following the inexorable course Julian and Julia had set her on. But when she contemplated the alternative, she knew she wasn't. She couldn't be free of this monster until it had been tethered safely and was under her control once and for all. And that was still as far out of sight as ever.

She didn't think Miles was going to let her buy his shares. He kept saying he could see it was probably right, and then not taking it any further. He was either going to sell to the consortium, which even Richard now seemed to think was a good idea, or join the company. Candy was pushing him very hard in that direction. Phaedria couldn't decide whether it was a good idea or not. It would prolong the agony of division; he would be making decisions between her and Roz day by day, hour by hour, it could be acutely uncomfortable for all of them. On the other hand, he was such an agreeable conciliatory force that he would probably greatly alleviate the tension in the office. But it wouldn't, it couldn't last long. In the first place Roz would probably turn it sour, and in the second Miles would hate it. Or would he? Maybe he would like it. For someone who couldn't wait to spend the rest of his life on a California beach, Miles was taking an unconscionably long time to pack. She had been very impressed, too, when they had talked over lunch about what he might do, by a certain instinctive commercial grasp. He had an idea about establishing an offshoot of the cosmetic company in the fitness industry that had greatly impressed her. Phaedria fetched herself a glass of Perrier water from her fridge and tried to forget about Miles for a while and concentrate on company matters. But it was very difficult.

Apart from anything else, he did disturb her. It wasn't quite a sexual disturbance, although she had still not forgotten the passion she had felt that day after Christmas, and her shame at it afterward. It was an emotional one. There was something about him that reached out and touched her in some oddly familiar way. And yet she had never met anyone remotely like him in her life. It was probably because she was so lonely and fantasizing like some crazed old spinster.

Oh, God, what on earth was to become of her?

Phaedria suddenly remembered Dr. Friedman. It would be very nice to talk to her again. She would be back in London now. Maybe she could help her confront all her feelings about Miles and Michael as well as Julian. To come to terms finally with her grief. She hadn't talked to her since they had found Miles, made the discovery about Julian and Hugo Dashwood, since Julia had been born. Yes, she would go and see her.

She found Dr. Friedman's resolute impassiveness, her technique of meeting question with question, oddly comforting. She led you at your own pace into discovery rather than controlling you with it, and if you wanted to withdraw, to stand back, she allowed that, too.

She rang the number. Yes, Dr. Friedman was back, but very busy. Was it important?

"Could you tell her it's Phaedria Morell, and I'd be grateful for an appointment soon if she could manage it?"

The secretary went away and came back with the news that Dr.

Friedman would be delighted to see Lady Morell next Monday, first appointment of the day.

"Thank you," said Phaedria. "Thank you very much."

"WHERE HAVE YOU been?" screamed Candy as Miles walked into the suite at Claridge's at half past nine one evening. "Just where have you been?"

"Out," he said simply.

"Where out? Why not with me?"

"Because I had things to do that didn't concern you. Okay?"

"No. Not okay. I'm fed up and lonely, and I want to go home."

"Okay, go home."

She looked at him. "I think you're seeing someone else."

He shrugged. "Candy, you can think what you like."

"Well, are you?"

"I don't have to answer that."

"Miles, I can't tell you how sick of all this I am. Why don't you just make your rotten mind up?"

"I'll make my mind up when I'm good and ready, Candy. Right now I'm still thinking."

"About which of those bitches to give your lousy shares to?"

"Yeah. And whether to join the company."

"Holy shit!"

"It was your idea, Candy. Now I'm getting to like it. I told you you might regret it."

"YOU LOOK AWFUL," Roz said, looking at Miles across the bed.

"Thanks."

"No, you do. You've lost that marvelous Californian goldenness. You look like one of us."

"I'm beginning to feel like one of you. For the first time in my whole life I need a vacation."

"Maybe you should take a break."

"In California? Yeah, maybe I should." He reached out and wove his fingers lazily into her pubic hair. "Would you come with me?"

"I might. I just might."

"WELL," DR. FRIEDMAN said soberly. "You certainly have had a tough time. What's remarkable is not how bad you feel but that you've survived it so well. How's the baby now?"

"She's fine. She's beautiful."

"I'm sure she is." Dr. Friedman smiled. "Like all babies."

"No. Julia really is beautiful."

"Like all babies. I'm sorry, I'm being unkind."

"Dr. Friedman, do you think it was a mistake? Embarking on a new relationship before I had properly worked through the grief of losing Julian?"

"You never recover from real grief. So it's very much down to your capacity to handle it. How do you think your capacity is?"

"Quite good, I suppose. I seem to be tougher than I ever imagined."

"Well, then, maybe it wasn't too soon. How do you really feel about this man?"

"What do you mean?"

"Under the pain and the trauma of him being your stepdaughter's lover?"

"Having been."

"I'm sorry?"

"Having been her lover. The affair was quite over before I went to New York."

"But not when he came to see you, when he helped you through the discovery about your husband."

"No."

"But that was when you fell in love with him?"

"Yes. I suppose it was. But nothing—nothing happened. I wouldn't let it."

"No, and that was very well behaved of you. Nevertheless, the fact that he was not yours for the taking may have influenced your feelings."

"It might. But I really really do think I loved him."

"Loved? In the past tense?"

"Love. I think I still do. If he walked in now—"

"But you're not prepared to give up the company for him. Why do you think that is?"

"I feel I can't. Julian entrusted it to me, and he would have wanted it for Julia. I can't just sell out and walk away from it, give it up to Roz."

"He hardly entrusted you with it. Only half of it. Not quite half, in fact."

"No, but he meant me to have that. He could see it had grown important to me."

"Don't you think perhaps you are endowing him with motives he might never have felt?"

She thought carefully. "No. No, I don't, I think I knew him quite well."

"Did you? Well enough to realize that there was this other life going on?"

"No, all right. But maybe it wasn't an important life. Maybe it was quite trivial."

"Wouldn't he have told you about it if it had been trivial?"

"Perhaps." She sighed.

"And then there was the will. Miles."

"Yes." Her voice was very small.

"Listen, I'm not saying you're wrong. I'm saying be sure you're right before you throw all this happiness with Michael Browning away. That's all."

"Yes. All right. I'll try. Can I ask you some questions now?"

"You can."

"Did you—well, did you ever suspect that Julian was leading this second life?"

"What do you think? Does that seem likely? Think about it."

Phaedria sighed. "You really don't give much away, Dr. Friedman."

"Lady Morell, I'm trying to help you to know your husband. To help you through all this. I told you early on that if you really think, think about what he was, what you knew, you can still learn a lot about him."

"All right. But what should I think? I don't know in this case what to think."

"You should think about how much I did know. Quite a lot, we have established that. Given that information, how much more would he have—shall we say—imparted to me? He was a very secretive man, wasn't he?"

"Yes. Yes, he was. But clearly there were some things he had to share with someone. Things that were too painful, too frightening, too difficult. Otherwise he would never have come to you at all."

"Yes."

"So anything really painful—really important—"

"Yes?"

There was a long silence. Phaedria looked at Dr. Friedman. She suddenly heard the clock ticking, her own heart beating, a police car wailing past the window.

"You knew, didn't you? You knew it all?"

·39·

"I KNOW WHAT I'M GOING TO DO," Miles said.

He was lying on the beach at Malibu, salt and sun-streaked; his hair, shaggy from the sea, was full of sand, his eyes suddenly paler blue against his new tan. He had been out on his board for hours; Roz, finally weary of watching him, had been drinking beer and eating enchiladas at Alice's. When she saw him swoop in for the last time and fall exhausted onto the beach, she went down from the pier and walked over the sand to him.

"Was it good?"

He nodded, grinned wearily, ecstatically. "Great. I'd forgotten how great."

"What's it like? Try to tell me."

"Sex."

"Ah."

"Sex with the sun on you."

"Sounds good."

"Want to try?"

"Maybe tomorrow."

"I'll give you a lesson."

"You look tired."

"I am."

"I brought you a beer."

"Thanks." He drank it thirstily.

Roz looked at him. The sun was sinking now into the sudden dusk below the brilliant dark blue. Great streaks of orange shot through the sky, glanced off the sea. Miles' profile, sharply beautiful, was etched against the water.

"You do look amazing," Roz said simply.

He shrugged.

"You must know," she said, "how amazing you look."

"I suppose I do. It doesn't matter to me."

"It's like money, Miles. It would matter if you didn't have it."

"Maybe."

"Anyway, you use it."

"I do? How?"

She put out her hand, traced the lines of his face. "Seducing poor helpless maidens."

"And you."

"And me."

"I try not to."

"I don't believe you."

He turned and looked at her, drinking her in. She was already tanned; she wore a white T-shirt to protect her against the sun, a shocking pink bikini. Her nose, after two days, had freckled; her eyes with their brown flecks looked glassy green against her golden skin.

"You don't look so bad yourself," he said.

"Thank you."

"Oh, jeez, it's beautiful here. God, I love it. It makes such sense of everything."

That was when he told her what he had decided to do.

"THERE'S SOMETHING I haven't told you," Phaedria said. "Something I'd like to."

"What's that?" Dr. Friedman looked at her with the odd blend of concern and disinterest that Phaedria had come to rely on.

"At Christmas Miles came to see me. He said he wanted to talk to me about my suggestion that I should form a trust fund for Julia and buy him out."

"And?"

"We went for a walk. He was just talking. I started telling him things. He has that effect on you."

"What do you mean?"

"You tell him everything. Anything. He just makes you talk. I'm not sure why. He's the most nonjudgmental person I've ever met— apart from you," she added with a smile.

"Go on. Try me."

"Well, suddenly, he asked me if I'd slept with Michael Browning."

"And?"

"I got terribly angry."

"That isn't surprising."

"No, I know. But suddenly I was screaming at him, really yelling and—"

"Go on."

"Then I wanted to—to go to bed with him more than I'd ever wanted anything in my whole life. It was awful. At the same time as being so angry."

"Yes?"

"Don't you think that's odd?"

"Not in the least. Do you? Really? Anger and sex make very good bedfellows."

"Maybe. Well, anyway, that's only part of the story."

"So what happened?"

"I kissed him. Really kissed him."

"Was that all?"

"Yes. But I didn't want it to be all. I wanted to go on, there and then. It was awful."

"So what did you do?"

"I said something like, 'Oh, shit, leave me alone,' and I ran back to the house. I felt so ashamed."

"Why?"

Phaedria stared at her. "Because I was supposed to be in love with Michael. Grieving for Julian. And here I was just dying for sex, like some slut—that's what Roz called me once—with Miles."

"That's not very surprising."

"Isn't it?"

"Do you really think it is?"

"Yes, I do."

"Why?"

"Because it was so animallike, somehow. I mean, Miles is amazingly beautiful, but that's all. I'm not in the least in love with him."

"Don't you think that might have something to do with it?"

"What?"

"That he is so beautiful?"

"I don't know. Should it?"

"Of course." Margaret Friedman's face was calmly surprised. "Here you are, a normally sexed young woman, lonely, frustrated, waiting to go and be with your new lover, in a state of some—what shall we say—excitement? Tension? And here is Miles, quite exceptionally attractive, as far as I can make out, making you angry, talking about sex. Of course you're going to feel excited about him. To want him. I don't think you have to worry about that at all."

"Don't you?"

"No. Think about it. Do you?"

Phaedria thought. Then she shook her head. "I'm afraid I can't let myself off the hook that lightly. It was so strong, so violent, what I felt."

"Judge yourself harshly if you want to," said Margaret Friedman. "It's your prerogative. Why do you think your reaction to Miles was so violent?"

"I don't know," Phaedria said slowly. "It was more violent than anything I've ever felt for Michael, even. I don't often have sexual feelings as strong as that. Not really. It was—well, strange. Comparable with what I'd felt once for Julian."

"Really?"

"Yes. That was the strange thing. One night before we were married, Julian and I had a terrible fight. I left, in one of his priceless antique cars. He followed. He was so angry I thought he would kill me. And I was terribly angry, too. And we—we had sex, right in the middle of this fight, in the backseat of his car, in some lane at three o'clock in the morning, or whatever time it was. It was wonderful, but it was very violent. What I felt then was exactly how I felt for Miles that day. That violent. Strange. I couldn't stop thinking about it."

"How was Miles afterward?"

"Terrific. Really terrific. He just came and talked to me, told me not to worry, not to get upset. Said he was sorry for making me so angry. Completely defused the situation. He is such a nice person." She was silent for a while. Then she said, "There is something about Miles that gives me the strangest feeling."

"Yes? Can you analyze it?"

"I don't know. Let's see. He makes me feel warm, relaxed, kind of settled. He makes me laugh. He makes me see things kind of straight. But it's not just that. It's—" She was silent for a moment.

"Yes?" said Dr. Friedman patiently, watching her carefully.

"It's like being desperate for a drink. You know? Or—well, I've never taken any drugs, except a bit of pot at Oxford, but I imagine it's like being desperate for a fix. Something you've known and liked, needed, and then been deprived of."

"Yes?"

"Well, Miles is like that. Like a drink. A fix. A sort of familiar, predictable pleasure. Can you begin to understand what I mean?"

"Yes," Dr. Friedman said. "Yes, I can. Indeed I can."

THE NEXT DAY Miles took Roz all around the Los Angeles he knew and had grown up in. They drove along the Coast Highway into Santa Monica and walked out onto the pier. "I learned to skateboard down there," he said, pointing to the boardwalk, "and look, there, see, that's Big Dean's Muscle Inn. Muscle Beach was here then, not in Venice. We used to come here on Sundays, have lunch sometimes and go on the rides. They had the best swordfish steaks ever.

"Our house was down there," he said. "There was a road through there. It was called Appian Way. It's all gone now, in the name of progress. Come on, I'll show you my school."

They walked to the car and drove toward Santa Monica High.

"This town has a terrific history," he said. "Did you know James Dean lived in Santa Monica with his aunt?"

Roz laughed and said she did not.

"There it is," he said, pointing to the big brick building. "That's Santa Monica High School. I was so happy there. I had this really great girlfriend named Donna Palladini. She had the most amazing legs you ever saw."

"Better than mine?" Roz said jealously.

"Yup. Better than yours. She's probably married with six kids by now. Her husband's a lucky guy."

"If you're trying to spoil my day," said Roz, "you're doing a great job."

"I'm sorry. Come on, let's go have lunch on the beach in Venice."

They drove down to Venice, bought Cokes and hot dogs, and sat in the sun.

"Good God," Roz said, looking at the hippies, "it's still the sixties here."

"Yeah," Miles said. "I kind of like that."

"What, peace and love and all that?" she said, mocking him.

"Yes." He turned and looked at her very seriously.

They stayed there all afternoon, not saying much. Roz dozed in the hot sun and woke to find Miles hauling her to her feet.

"Now," he said, "the highlight of the tour. Mulholland Drive at sunset."

They drove up Santa Monica Boulevard with the top of the rented T-Bird down, looking at the tightly shuttered Rolls and Mercedes sedans that passed them, the women in their dark glasses and shoulder pads, the men in suits, chewing on cigars, the roller skaters, the joggers, all moving in a graceful coordinated pattern beneath the palm trees and the bright hot sky.

"Great place," Miles said happily. "Great place."

They turned left and up toward the hills; he took a few swift turns and drove into a high, twisty road. "This is it," he said. "You wait. Just you wait."

Abruptly the road snaked around to the right; on the left was a parking lot. He pulled in, drove toward the wall at the far edge and stopped.

"There," he said. "There it is. Take a look at that."

Roz took a look. Below them, curiously two dimensional in its effect, was the neat sprawl of Los Angeles, growing misty in the evening air, beyond that the silver-blue streak of the sea, and to either side the rolling, folded, velvety hills. The sky was turning bluish orange, pinkish gray clouds shot across it; the sun was dropping like a monster leaden fireball into the ocean.

"God," Roz said, "I do have to say that it is beautiful."

"It is, isn't it? Just beautiful."

"Now what do we do?" she asked, mildly amused by his rapture.

"We sit here and neck," he said, turning her face toward him. "That's what everybody comes here for."

LATER THAT NIGHT after they had dinner at Alice's and gone back to the house and made love and talked and made love again, Roz sat determinedly up in bed and switched on the light.

"Miles," she said, "I have something to tell you."

"Can't it wait? I'm kind of beat?"

"No, it can't wait. It's important. Sit up and listen."

He looked at her warily. "I hope you're not going to tell me you're pregnant."

"I'm not," she said. "Would you mind if I was?"

"Probably not. Go ahead. What is it?"

"Well—" Roz was not used to confessions. "Miles, this may make you very angry. Shocked, even. But I have to tell you. I just do."

"I'm listening."

"Oh, God, Miles, it's really bad."

"Can't be that bad."

"It's bad. You'll hate me."

"Try me."

"All right. Miles, the consortium. The Zurich consortium?"

"Yeah?"

"The one you've decided to sell to?"

"Yeah?"

"It's me. I dreamed it up. Laundered the bank account. Cooked the books. Planned to buy it back when you'd gone."

He looked at her in complete silence, his face expressionless, just studying her, contemplating her, as if she were some strange alien creature he had to familiarize himself with. Roz sat frozen, looking back at him, her gaze steady, waiting for dislike, mistrust, shock, to hit her. Then slowly, so slowly it was like the sun coming up through a deep thick mist, Miles smiled his glorious, joyous, beatific smile.

"I thought it was," he said.

◆　　◆　　◆

IT WAS LETITIA who put two and two together and came up with precisely four. She phoned Claridge's, wishing to invite Miles and Candy to dinner, and was told Mr. Wilburn had checked out.

Mildly surprised, she phoned Phaedria. "Darling, did you know Miles had gone?"

"Yes and no," Phaedria said carefully. "He was thoroughly fed up at the weekend. He'd been saying for weeks he wanted to go back to California. Maybe he and Candy simply left."

"Candy's still here. I spoke to her. Her father's with her. He's taking her back to Chicago."

"Good heavens. Well, Miles certainly didn't say anything about it to me. We had lunch last Thursday."

"Hmm," said Letitia. "Strange, I would say. Have you had any kind of decision from him?"

"Nothing. I'd begun to think I never would. I thought his next move would be into Julian's old office." She laughed a little too casually. "Maybe he's gone off to think."

"Maybe. I'll call Roz. She'll know. Thick as thieves, those two. It worries me sometimes."

"Why?" said Phaedria.

"I don't know. I really don't know."

Letitia phoned the house at Cheyne Walk. Mrs. Emerson was not at home, said the housekeeper. She had gone away for a few days.

"Good gracious," said Letitia, "this is very sudden."

"Yes, madam. She sent Miranda and Nanny up to Scotland. She said she had to go to America."

"Did she indeed?" Letitia said. "All right, Maria, thank you."

ROZ'S SECRETARY TOLD Phaedria that Mrs. Emerson was on a whistle-stop tour of some of the major hotels in the States and wouldn't be back until the following Wednesday. She had no numbers or addresses and no itinerary, but Mrs. Emerson called her every day for urgent messages, if Lady Morell wanted to leave one.

As Roz normally never went out so much as to get her hair cut without leaving contact numbers in triplicate and a maze of alternatives in the unlikely event of her not returning to the office within the hour, her behavior was as much out of character as if she had been found walking down Bond Street stark naked in the company of the Hare Krishna brethren.

Phaedria called Letitia and said she was beginning to think she was right, but did it really matter very much—feeling, indeed knowing, that somehow it did. Letitia replied, very much too lightly—also feeling that it probably mattered greatly—that of course it didn't matter; what they did was their own business, and none of them had any right to interfere.

But Letitia lay awake until the dawn broke, wide-eyed, distressed, wondering why she was so troubled by what was happening, and what she might be able to do about it. And Phaedria, after an equally sleepless night and without being entirely certain why, called Dr. Friedman and asked her for an urgent appointment.

"FOR YOUR PENANCE," Miles said to Roz, after breakfasting on a huge basket of strawberries and melons he had fetched early from the store for her, "you have to come and meet a very old friend of mine."

"I do hope she doesn't have amazing legs," said Roz, smiling at him.

"I've never seen his legs. They're always hidden beneath his long skirt."

"For God's sake, is he a transvestite?"

"He is not, and don't interrupt. And he has no idea at all what a screw might feel like. He is a man of God, and he was my grandmother's friend. My mother's, too," he added, more soberly. "I really want you to meet him."

"All right. I'll come."

He looked at her and leaned forward and kissed her. "You look different this morning."

"I feel different."

She did. For the first time in her entire life, she felt accepted and liked, loved, for what she was. Even with Michael she had never let her guard all the way down, had kept what she felt was the very worst of herself, the most devious, the most selfish, the most ruthless part, hidden. Miles had taken her in hand and with one careless, loving piece of acceptance turned her into a person as uncomplicatedly, as happily transparent, as he was. If he could take her as she was, then she could take herself. All her life she had felt the real Roz was valueless, not worth loving. Now suddenly someone infinitely important to her was telling her she was. She smiled back at him, radiant, shining with happiness.

"I love you, Miles."

FATHER KENNEDY WAS sitting in the sunshine, as he always did in the morning, dozing peacefully. He was a very old man suddenly. Miles, who had not seen him for four years, was shocked at how he had aged.

"Father Kennedy," he said, touching him lightly on the arm. "Good morning. How are you?"

The old man woke with a start. His faded blue eyes opened, alighted on Miles; his confusion cleared, and an expression of great joy came over his face.

"Miles! Miles Wilburn! This is a wonderful thing. How are you, Miles, and how is your grandmother? And what are you doing here?"

"I'm looking up old friends, Father. A great deal has happened to me."

"Well, now, I know quite a lot about that. I had a visit from young Lady Morell. So they did find you, after all, Miles. Is Mrs. Kelly all right? I miss her and our little chats very sadly."

"She's fine, Father, but very changed. She's—well, confused. I wanted to bring her back here, but I don't feel I should now. She is happy with Mrs. Galbraith in Nassau, and it would be wrong to disturb her. I'm going to see her next week."

"Then give her my best wishes. Oh, I would love to see her again. Maybe I can go down to Nassau one of these days, on a small vacation, and visit her."

"She'd like that, Father. And how are you?"

"I am very well, Miles. Lady Morell has been very good to me. She arranged for some money to come every month. It's a great help. She is an extremely nice person, wouldn't you say? Or haven't you met her?"

"Oh, I've met her, Father, I certainly have, and yes, she is an extremely nice person. Isn't she, Roz?"

Roz looked at Father Kennedy and then at Miles.

He grinned at her. "Go on, Roz," he said as if she were a small child. "Tell Father Kennedy what a nice person Phaedria is."

"Very nice," Roz said. The words were forced out, but she managed to smile. Dear God, she thought to herself, I have come a long way.

"And who is this?" Father Kennedy said, beaming at Roz. "Or am I not allowed to be introduced to her?"

"Of course. Forgive me. Father Kennedy, this is Roz Emerson. You'll be really surprised when I tell you who she is. Really, seriously surprised. You remember Mr. Dashwood?"

"Now, Miles, as if I would not remember Mr. Dashwood. He was such a good man," he said, turning to Roz, "so generous. He did so much for Miles and for Mrs. Kelly. Tell me, is all well with him, Miles?"

"Not exactly, Father. It's a very strange story. Could we maybe have some tea and I'll tell you all about it?"

"Of course. Now, what am I thinking of? Miles, you go and get the tea—you remember where the kitchen is—and I will talk to this young lady while you are gone. Come and sit down here, my dear, and tell me what you think of California."

"I think it's wonderful," Roz said. "Simply wonderful."

"So now, did you know Mr. Dashwood? Was he a friend of yours?"

"Well," said Roz, "in a way. He was my father."

"Your father?" the old man looked startled.

"Yes. But you see, we didn't know him as Hugo Dashwood."

"You didn't?"

"No. It's very complicated. Perhaps Miles should explain."

Miles came back with the tea. He put it down, sat on the grass beside Roz. Father Kennedy's old face was puzzled, troubled.

"Miles, you have to explain all this to me. I'm a foolish old man. I don't understand what Miss—"

"Roz."

"Roz is telling me. Are you saying that Mr. Dashwood was going under another name in England all the time?"

"That's right, Father. It sounds crazy, I know, but it's true. Like all the best facts, it's stranger than fiction. Only he wasn't going under another name in England. His name there was his real name—Julian Morell. That was the real person. Hugo Dashwood was a pseudonym. God knows why he used it. But he did."

"So Lady Morell is married to Mr. Dashwood? Have I got this right now?"

"Yes, I suppose so. Only she is not married to him anymore. He died."

"Died? Yes, of course. Lady Morell had recently been widowed. That's why she was looking for you, of course, because of the will."

"That's right, Father."

The old man turned to Roz. "I am sorry, my child. Sorry you have lost your father. Sorry to have been so tactless. You must forgive me. All that business with the other name, very upsetting, very difficult for you."

"Of course. Anyway, it was a while ago, I'm feeling much better now."

"Father Kennedy," said Miles, "the whole thing is still very mysterious. You might be able to help. Have you any idea, any idea at all, why Hugo Dashwood—that is, Julian Morell—should have left me a lot of money? A share in his company?"

Father Kennedy looked at them both. His mind was racing; he felt sick, trapped. He had to keep calm. He had to remember that he'd always told himself that Lee might have been mistaken, that the doctors might have been mistaken, that Dean and not Hugo Dashwood, or this Julian Morell, had been Miles's father.

He closed his eyes briefly, calling on the Almighty for aid; then he opened them again and smiled serenely at Miles.

"Well, now, Miles, he was very fond of you. You know that. And very generous to you. Putting you through college and everything. And when your parents died, he felt he had to take care of you, keep an eye on you. Your mother asked him to, and he promised. He took that promise very seriously. And kept it. And he was very proud of you, Miles. I think it is entirely to be expected that he should remember you in his will."

"I suppose so, Father. But it isn't just remembering. It's a lot—an awful lot—of money."

"Then I can only say I hope you will use it wisely, Miles. Money can be a terrible thing, if it is wrongly used."

"I'll try, Father. I'll take a page out of Phaedria's book and give some to you for a start."

"That would be extremely welcome, extremely. My goodness, the way we are going, this will shortly be the richest parish in the United States of America."

"Great. The money will be in good hands, that's for sure. But also, Father, can you think why he left me the money in such a roundabout way? Why not be more direct about it?"

"Miles, when you have lived as long as I have and seen as many things happen, you will not be surprised or even puzzled by anything at all. People do many strange things for many strange reasons, which are not for others to question and which seem perfectly good and sound to them at the time."

"I suppose so," said Miles. "Well anyway, it doesn't really matter too much. And something very good has come out of it."

"And what might that be?"

Miles reached out and took Roz's hand. "Roz and I have found each other."

A terrible fear had invaded the old man's heart. He sought desperately to make Miles dispel it.

"Yes, it is always a wonderful thing to find a new friend."

"Yeah, I guess that's so, but Roz and I are more than friends, Father. We're—well, maybe I shouldn't be telling you this, Father, in case you tell me I'm in mortal sin or something. I know in the eyes of the church it is a sin, but we're in love and we've been living together, and—well, Roz doesn't exactly know this yet, but I plan to marry her as soon as I can."

WHEN PHAEDRIA GOT into the office the next morning, tired and inexplicably sick at heart, Sarah Brownsmith was looking worried.

"I'm glad you're here, Lady Morell. Someone's been calling you from California. A man. He sounded quite old. With an Irish brogue."

"Father Kennedy," said Phaedria. "I wonder what he wants."

"He wants you to phone him. He sounded rather upset."

"Oh, dear. He's such a sweet old man. He was so kind to me. I wonder what's happened."

"Here's his number. It must be—let's see. Goodness, it's midnight there. It must be urgent."

"Yes," Phaedria said. "Yes, it must."

She phoned the number. "Father Kennedy? This is Phaedria Morell. Father, is something wrong?"

"It is, my child, it's terribly wrong. Or at least it might be."

"Whatever is it? Can I help? Please tell me."

"It's very difficult. I can only tell you a little. I would be breaking every kind of confidence to tell you more. But you are a sensitive and a clever girl, and perhaps you will know what to do."

"Father, you have to tell me what the matter is. Please. And I'll try to help."

"Very well. Today your friend Miles came to see me."

"Miles?"

"Miles. And he had a young lady with him."

Fear struck out at Phaedria. She sat up rigidly on her chair, trying to keep calm. "A young lady?"

"Yes. Her name is Roz. You know her, don't you?"

"I do. Yes."

"She is the daughter of your husband, who was my friend, Miles's friend, Hugo Dashwood."

"That's all right, Father. Go on, please."

"Well, Miles was telling me about the legacy and so on. It was very good of your husband, very good indeed, to leave him that money. But—well, Miles told me—and God forgive me, I didn't know what to say to him, so I said nothing, nothing at all—that he and Roz were in love and that they were going to get married."

"Married! Roz and Miles? Oh, Father, no, that can't be true."

"He told me himself, sitting here on the grass, holding her hand.

And they are a very nice young couple. But, Lady Morell, the marriage cannot be. It must not be. Now, you must not ask me why. I am not in a position to tell you, and besides that, I may be mistaken in my thinking. But for Miles's sake and for Roz's, you have to stop them marrying. Cohabiting, even. I suspect, and God forgive me if I am wrong, they are, they could be—they could well be in mortal sin."

"Father, I can't stop them marrying. They are grown people. I had no idea there was any question of it, none of us did, but if they want to marry, they will. Nobody, least of all I, can stop them."

"They must be stopped," he said. "They must."

He sounded so distressed that Phaedria felt frightened. "All right," she said, largely to soothe him. "All right, I will stop them. Somehow. I promise. Please don't worry, Father, I will talk to people here, to the family, and we will stop them."

"I DON'T THINK Father Kennedy was very pleased with your news," Roz said, laughing, as they drove away. "Poor old man, he looked terrible."

"Yes, he did," Miles said, looking thoughtful. "Really terrible. Shocked. I mean seriously shocked. I wonder why. Poor old man."

"Maybe he isn't well," said Roz. "He didn't look well."

"He didn't, did he? I'll drop in on him again tomorrow and see if he's all right. He might have a weak heart or something. The news may have had nothing to do with it. Or maybe he's just confused, like my grandmother."

"Maybe. Anyway, that was some proposal. Really romantic. You could have warned me."

"Oh," he said, smiling, "I have. Lots of times. If you'd been looking out for it."

"Maybe."

"Anyway, let me try to do it better." He stopped the car, pulled into a side road, and looked at her without moving, without smiling. "Roz," he said. "Roz, I love you. Please will you marry me?"

"Yes, Miles," she said. "Yes, I will."

"DR. FRIEDMAN, I really have to ask you some questions now, and you really have to answer them."

"Really? Why?" Dr. Friedman was as cool, as unruffled, as ever.

"Please stop asking me questions."

"It's the only way I can help you."

"I'm not so sure about that," said Phaedria. "But anyway, let me ask you one. Who is Miles? Do you know?"

"Don't you?"

"No. No, I don't."

"Are you sure?"

"Of course I'm sure."

"Think, Phaedria. Think hard. Don't run away from it."

"I don't know what you mean."

"Don't you?"

"No," she almost screamed the word. "Yes, yes, I do. Oh, God. I just hate this so much."

"You don't have to go on."

"I do. I do, though. You don't know . . ."

"Don't know what?"

"About Roz. And Miles."

"Roz and Miles?" For the first time Dr. Friedman reacted. Phaedria felt it, saw it. That told her everything. But still she turned from it.

"Yes. Roz and Miles. They want to—they're going to get married."

"Ah."

"So—"

"So, yes, we have to go on. Very well. And of course you know who Miles is, don't you?"

"Yes," Phaedria said, with a shuddering sob. "Yes, I do. He's Julian's son. Isn't he?"

"Yes. Yes, he is."

Tears filled Phaedria's eyes. She shivered suddenly, looked at Dr. Friedman almost fearfully. "Could I—could I have a drink?"

"Of course. What do you want? Brandy?"

"Yes, please. God—" She smiled, brushing the tears away. "I've had one this morning already. I'll be an alcoholic soon at this rate."

"There are worse things to be." She pressed her buzzer. "Joan, bring us two large brandies, will you? And some coffee. Now then"—she looked at Phaedria—"is it really so bad? For you? And didn't you—surely you realize this now—didn't you know all along?"

"Yes. No. You see we all wondered, obviously. We were bound to. But Letitia, his mother, you know—"

"Yes, I know."

"Letitia and Eliza, and Camilla. She's—"

"Yes, I know who Camilla is."

"Oh, God." Phaedria looked at her and managed to smile. "Is there anything about us you don't know? Well, we all checked out some dates, the time Julian would have had to be with Miles's mother. He wasn't. He was either in New York or in England."

"Phaedria, there's no doubt, I'm afraid. No doubt at all. Miles was obviously born either a little early or a little late. Which is the more likely, I wonder? Perhaps he will know."

"Perhaps."

"Well, is it really so bad, after all? For you?" she asked again.

"No, it's not so bad for me. But it's terrible, awful, for Roz. I just don't know how she'll bear it." Phaedria hesitated, then went on. "Father Kennedy, an old priest in Santa Monica who had known Miles and his parents ever since he was born, and who obviously knew about Julian being Miles's father, rang me, very distressed. Miles had been to see him with Roz. They told him they were going to get married. He told me I had to stop them."

"But he didn't tell you why?"

"No. Not in so many words. But I—well, I suppose I knew."

"Of course. The possibility must have occurred to you many times, despite the evidence of the dates: when you first heard about Miles in the will, when you first saw him, when you felt that very strong attraction for him. Well, you would. He is probably very like his father. You loved his father and you were very physically involved with him. And you said to me, something like Miles made you feel as if you'd had a fix of something you had known and liked and been deprived of. Well, of course he would."

"Yes, I suppose he would." She was relaxing now, calm with relief that it was over, out in the open.

"Is he very like his father?"

"Not at all, and yet terribly. He's straightforward and relaxed and blond and blue-eyed, so not at all. But then he's amazingly quick and intuitive and charming and makes you talk and talk, and he's very, very sexy, so yes, very like him. There is something about him, the eyes, I suppose, that is totally Julian. Even though they're the wrong color."

"I'm amazed none of you have worked it out before."

"Well, we did. I told you. But then—well, yes, you're right. Babies don't always come at the proper time. Look at Julia. Maybe he was early, like her. But then, you see, on the surface he is so very different from Julian. He couldn't act or look less like him. Could you"—she took a long drink of brandy—"could you tell me about it now? Have you always known?"

"Yes, for a long time. He first came to me when Lee had just died. He felt utterly miserable. It was a bad time altogether for him. Something had gone wrong for him here, something personal, some affair at this end as well. But I think he really loved Lee. Really loved her. She was obviously an extraordinary person. Very brave and lovely. And you see, he was unable to grieve openly. At all. So it became almost unbearable for him. That was what drove him to me. It was the only release. Otherwise it would have been an unthinkable thing for a man like him to do."

"I suppose so. Poor Julian."

"Yes. And then he was racked with guilt over Miles's father's suicide."

"Which was—because—"

"Well, yes. He found out. About Miles. Some fool doctor had told him he would never have been able to father a child. He put two and two together. That was tragic. Wicked."

"Poor Miles. We must keep that from him."

"If we can. And then, after Lee's death," Dr. Friedman went on, "Julian would have given anything to have been able to bring Miles out into the open, to tell everyone, to give him a home, his name. But he had promised Lee he would never do that, and besides it would have meant telling Miles. Very painful for a child. On top of his mother's death. So—more silence."

"Yes."

"The whole thing started as a bet with himself. Julian decided to pretend to be someone else and see if he could sustain the fiction for a bit. But he fell in love with Lee, made her pregnant, and the whole thing got out of hand."

"That's exactly what Letitia said must have happened."

"Do you think she knew too?" Dr. Friedman asked. "I mean really knew. Despite the dates."

"Perhaps. She was very worried about Roz and Miles."

"How do you think she'll cope with it all?"

"Oh, wonderfully," said Phaedria. "We don't have to worry about Letitia. She could fight World War Three single-handed."

"Good. From what you say of Roz, it sounds as if she may need to."

"So did he go on seeing you?" asked Phaedria. "Julian, I mean. All those years?"

"On and off. Yes. I think he became addicted to me."

"I can see why," Phaedria said with a half smile.

"He loved you very much," Dr. Friedman said suddenly. "Very much indeed. He said he had never felt anything quite like what he felt for you. He saw you truly as a new beginning."

"Oh, God," Phaedria said, and the tears started to flow again. "Oh, God, don't."

"Why not? It's important. It's good you should know that, surely?"

"Yes, but I wasn't a new beginning. If I was, I soon ended again. I behaved badly. I was selfish, difficult. Fooled around with someone. Oh, not really. But enough to make Julian angry and jealous."

"Phaedria, you mustn't be so hard on yourself. You were very young and you'd been thrown into an impossible situation. You tried. Julian did far worse things. Manipulating you and Roz. Sleeping with Camilla North."

"God, he told you all that?"

"Oh, yes, by the end of his life he was seriously mixed up. I was worried about him. I saw him very frequently."

"So what about the will? For God's sake, why did he do that to us all?"

"He was very angry with you. With you and Roz. I don't think he had any idea how difficult she made things for you. He felt you were both behaving very badly. At one point he really did think you were having an affair, and he made that will to punish you. Both of you. In a fit of dreadful rage. After he'd come to L.A. to find you. Remember?"

Phaedria nodded.

"And he'd seen Miles by then. Or heard from him anyway. He was quite determined to go and see him, tell him everything, urge him to come and join the family. He felt he'd be able to cope with the truth by then. Oh, of course he always meant to make another, more reasonable will, but he said doing that one had been therapeutic. He said he'd modify it when he'd told Miles and introduced him to the family. He thought he had plenty of time. Then I think when you found him in bed with Camilla North, and left him, he just forgot about it. He was so appalled at what he'd done. He just kept postponing remaking the will until something was resolved. It's a big thing, of course, making a will if you're as rich as he was. And the earlier one he'd made was before he'd met and married you, so he knew he couldn't revert to that."

Phaedria looked at her. "Why didn't you tell us all before? When you first heard he'd died? Or when I first came to see you? It would have saved so much unhappiness."

"If I'd known about Miles and Roz, believe me, I would have. But apart from that, I couldn't, Phaedria. I see my position as very like that of your friend Father Kennedy. I have to safeguard confidences."

"But Julian was dead. You wouldn't have been betraying him."

"I would have been betraying you if you hadn't been able to deal with it. I had to learn more about you. There was no rush. I couldn't keep you from the real pain. Of Julian's death and the will. And I knew you would work toward the discovery by yourself in time. I thought that was much better. I knew you had come to rely on me, would call on me if you really needed me."

"How did you know that?" said Phaedria, angry, hostile. "I might have done something desperate."

"No." Dr. Friedman was smiling into Phaedria's rage. "I could see you were very strong. I wasn't worried about you at all. Not seriously."

"Well, anyway," Phaedria said, still half angry, "what do I do now? Whom do I tell? Who tells Roz? And Miles? Oh, it's awful. Please tell me what to do."

"Well, you certainly shouldn't be the one to tell Roz. Who is she closest to?"

"Letitia." Phaedria spoke without hesitation.

"And you think Letitia could stand to do it?"

"Yes, I do. But maybe you should talk to her. I don't think I could bear to tell her."

"All right. Bring her to see me. Let me see—this evening, about six."

"Thank you. And how about Miles and Roz? We should get them home. The longer it goes on, the worse it will be."

"Yes. Can you contact them?"

"Father Kennedy might know where they're staying."

"Then ask him to get them to call Letitia."

"All right. What a nightmare."

"In a way," Dr. Friedman said. "But then, waking up from a nightmare is such a relief, isn't it?"

"I SUPPOSE," SAID Letitia, sitting very upright in Dr. Friedman's office, "that you are going to tell me that Miles is my grandson."

"Yes," Dr. Friedman said. "Yes, I am."

Letitia was silent for a while. Phaedria reached out and took her hand.

"Are you all right, Mrs. Morell?" Margaret Friedman asked.

"Oh, perfectly," Letitia said, brushing away a tear, smiling brightly, a trifle tremulously. "I suppose I knew all along. I suppose we all did. It was such a relief when we managed to persuade ourselves it was impossible. There was something, just something about him that was Julian."

"Yes," Phaedria said, "I felt it, too."

"Oh, darling," Letitia said, turning to her. "I was so hoping you would fall in love with Miles. That would have been so absolutely perfect. But I suppose life isn't like that."

"No," Dr. Friedman said. "Not often."

Letitia was silent for a while. "Poor Julian," she said. "Poor man. How dreadful to think he was so unhappy. So confused."

"Yes," Phaedria said, "that's what I feel. And so dreadful that I failed to de-confuse him. Make him able to tell me, to talk."

"You can't blame yourself for that," said Letitia. "You came into this very late. But I do have to blame myself. It's those old sins again, you see."

"Old sins?" Dr. Friedman said.

"Yes. It's an old Irish saying: 'Old sins cast long shadows.' I was talking to Phaedria about it the other day. An old sin of mine has cast a very long and dreadful shadow, I'm afraid."

And she dropped her head into her hands and began to weep.

"Letitia darling, don't, please don't cry," Phaedria said, putting her arms around her. "You are the lifeblood of this family, the person we turn to, the person all of us love. How can you talk about sin? You have done so much good for all of us; we couldn't survive without you."

"Yes, and so much harm too," Letitia said, taking the tissue Dr. Friedman was offering. "Thank you, my dear. I note you are not offering me any palliatives for my guilt."

"I don't ever blame or condone," Margaret Friedman said, smiling at her. "I have seen too much. I can only tell you that a person is many, many things, Mrs. Morell, and that genes and upbringing are only a part. We may take our children, warmly clothed and well fed, loved and cared for, to the crossroads, but then they become themselves, make their own way, take their own turnings. Your son did many good, brilliant things; he brought happiness and pleasure to countless people, and not just commercially. He made huge donations to charity, set up trust funds, founded research projects—well, you know as well as I. You do not sit complacently and take any credit for that; neither should you take the blame for the rest."

"Well," said Letitia, with a sigh, "I'm afraid I do. But thank you anyway. Now then," she said, visibly pulling herself together, "I suppose you want me to tell Roz?"

"Yes," Phaedria said. "Yes, I'm afraid we do."

ROZ AND MILES were lying on the lawn of the Malibu house when they saw Father Kennedy's elderly Ford lurching its way up the hill. They had just come back from the beach. Miles had been trying, without success, to teach Roz to surf.

"I don't know," he said, "if I can marry a woman who can't catch a wave."

"I'll learn," said Roz. She looked at him more seriously. "You won't mind about the company, will you, Miles?"

"What do you mean?"

"You won't mind me carrying on with it? Running it? Fighting for it?"

"Of course not. I don't care what you do, as long as you love me and make love to me and have a baby every year."

"Hmm. That might be hard to fit in. Could it be every two years?"

"No. Sorry. No way."

"All right."

"Seriously," he said, "for everybody's sake, but particularly yours, since you have to work with Phaedria, I think I should sell my share to a third party. A genuine one," he added with a grin. "If I let you have it now, it will amount to treachery. We have to live with Phaedria. And I think in the long run you'll have a more interesting, challenging, satisfactory time with someone else."

She looked at him. "Do you really think so?"

"Yes, I do."

"I hate the idea. I really do. You wouldn't consider staying on, working with us?"

"No," he said, "not now. Probably I never would have. It was an intriguing idea, playing store, drawing pictures, but it's not me, not really. Not what I want from life."

"What do you want from life?"

"You," he said, pulling her to him. "You. And this place. Nothing else. Nothing else at all."

Roz looked at him, and felt a huge, sweet wave of love engulf her, and at the same time a sense of such happiness, such peace, she could hardly bear it. "Oh God," she said, "I love you so much."

At that moment, Father Kennedy arrived.

ROZ SAT FACING Letitia on the sofa at First Street, her eyes stormy, her face set.

"I suppose," she said, "you're going to tell me I'm not to marry Miles. Well, it's nothing to do with you, and I shall marry who I like."

Letitia took a deep breath. "Roz, my darling, you cannot, simply cannot marry Miles."

"Why not?" Roz said, standing up, almost shouting. "Why the hell not?"

"Because he's your brother."

"Oh, God." Roz sat down again abruptly. "Oh, God."

She looked at Letitia, desperate, appealing; she was very white, very still. Then she laughed, a harsh, nervous laugh.

"But he's not. He can't be. You said so yourself. You're wrong. You have to be. How could he be? With those dates and everything."

"He is. Obviously we were wrong about the dates. Phaedria phoned Father Kennedy and talked to him before—before we talked to you. He remembered. He knew Miles from when he was tiny, baptized him, visited Lee in hospital when he was born. Miles was born more than three weeks late. It was quite a joke in the hospital. Their first ten-month pregnancy. Your father was obviously in California, just before—well, before he became involved with Camilla. He is Miles's father."

"I don't believe you."

"Roz, my darling, I am more sorry than I can ever say, but you have to believe me. It's true."

"Who told you? How did you find out?"

"Your father had been—seeing someone, a psychiatrist, for many years. She knew."

"No." It was a piteous cry, almost a wail. "Please, please no." She put out her hands as if to ward off a physical blow; her eyes were closed. "Please, Letitia, please, please tell me it's not true. That it might not be true. You were so sure before. I don't see why you can't be again. Please help me, Letitia, please."

"Darling, I can't."

"Who told you? How did you find out?"

"Phaedria told me."

"Phaedria! Oh, well it's not true!" There was a frantic look in her eyes as she scrabbled for rescue. "Phaedria made it up. She was so jealous of me, she hated me so much, she probably wants Miles for herself. Oh, Letitia, how could you be such a fool as to believe her?" She was smiling now, triumphant. "It's all just a fantasy of Phaedria's. It isn't true at all. Oh, thank God, thank God. How could you have ever believed her, Letitia? How?"

"Roz, I'm sorry. But you're wrong. Phaedria did not make it up. I have seen this psychiatrist, this Dr. Friedman, myself. It is undoubtedly true. Phaedria is desperate for you, quite desperate. And of course she doesn't want Miles."

"No," said Roz, "no, of course she doesn't. I forgot for a moment, she has my other lover, doesn't she? She stole him from me as she stole everything else—my father, the company—and now she's trying to stop me having Miles. Well, she won't. I won't let her. She won't."

She was hysterical suddenly, screaming, biting her fists, beating at the air with them. Letitia watched her in silence. After a while she crossed the room and sat by her, not even trying to calm her.

"Roz," she said, as the storm abated slightly and she could be heard, "you have to believe me. This has nothing to do with Phaedria. God knows I wish it were otherwise. But it isn't."

Roz looked at her quite suddenly and then fell against her grandmother, her head in her lap, weeping endlessly.

"Letitia, I can't bear it, I just can't bear it. For the first time, for the very first time in my whole life, I was happy. I never knew what it felt like before. It was like coming out into the sunshine from a cold, chill, dark place. I felt safe, peaceful. I can't go back in there, I can't. Don't make me, Letitia, don't make me, please."

Letitia sat stroking her hair, looking sadly over her head and thinking she would have given all she owned to have saved Roz this pain.

PHAEDRIA TOLD MILES. He took it badly. He was shocked.

"I don't know," he said, "that I can handle this. It's a lot of pain."

"Yes," said Phaedria, "yes, I know."

"I loved my dad," he said. "He was so good to me. We were all so happy, I thought. Now that's gone."

"No, it isn't."

"Yes," he said. "You're wrong. It is gone. It's been destroyed for me. As it was for them. Think what he must have gone through when he found out. Oh, God. That's why he killed himself, I suppose."

"Yes, I suppose."

"And my mother. How could she do that to him? And why did she have to tell him? Why couldn't she have kept it to herself?"

"She didn't tell him," Phaedria said quickly. "A doctor told him he could never have had children. He worked it out then. She never, ever told him. She never would have, I'm sure."

Miles looked up at her. His eyes were full of tears. "You don't think there could still be some mistake? That I could be my dad's kid? I mean, Letitia was so sure . . ."

He sounded like a child; Phaedria went over to him and put her arms around him. "Not sure enough, I'm afraid. No. I don't think there's a mistake," she said, "not from everything we know."

"I loved my mother so much," said Miles, his arms going around

Phaedria, his face buried in her hair. "So much. She was so pretty, such fun, she never did anything to make anyone sad, she was never angry; she was never down. I thought she was the most perfect person in the world. And now I know she wasn't. And I feel I've lost her all over again."

"No," Phaedria said. "No, you haven't. She was a lovely, lovely, brave, good person, Miles. From everything we've learned, we know she was. She made a mistake. Doesn't everyone? Sometimes? Haven't you? She spent the rest of her life trying to put it right. You know she did. It must have been terribly, terribly difficult, but she never gave in. Even when she was dying, she never gave in."

"No," he said, "that's true." A tear rolled down his face. "She said, even then, always, how good he was, my dad, how much she'd loved him, reminded me how happy we'd been. She left me that, that happiness."

"She was good," said Phaedria, "very good, I know she was. Very special."

"How do you know?"

"Well," she said, looking at him, smiling into his eyes, kissing his tear-streaked face, "she made you what you are."

"I HAVE TO give Roz my shares," Miles said to Phaedria and Letitia later that night. Roz was asleep, exhausted, heavily sedated. "She must have it."

"Of course," Phaedria said. "Of course she must. What will you do?"

"Oh," he said, "go home. To California. I don't even want the money. Just the house."

"Nonsense," said Letitia briskly, almost restored to herself by this sacrilege. "Of course you must have the money. You can't live on air."

"I can," he said, "almost."

"I'll tell you what we'll do," Letitia said. "We'll put the money in a trust fund for you. Nobody will touch it. Then if you ever need it, it will be there."

"Well," he said, "if you really think so."

"I do."

"I think," Phaedria said carefully, "it would be best if Eliza and Peveril never knew about all this. Don't you, Letitia?"

"Yes, darling, I do. Much better. How wise you are."

"Oh, God," said Phaedria. "I do hope Roz will be all right."

"She'll be all right." It was Miles. "She'll be fine."

They looked at him, both of them startled.

"Do you think so?" Phaedria asked.

"Yes, I do. I know so. She will be very unhappy for a while, but then she'll come back fighting. She'll have the company; she can do what she likes with it. That will be her salvation. It's all she needs for now, at any rate. Don't fuss over her too much. Just leave her alone."

"I think I'll sell her my share, too," Phaedria said, "now that it's all resolved. I don't want it anymore."

"Oh, I wouldn't give it all to her," Miles said. "Not if you care about her. A few fights, a little angst, will keep her going. Stir her up now and again, Phaedria. It will do her good."

She looked at him and laughed. "All right. But my heart won't be in it."

"Yes, it will. Think of Julia."

"She can have my share when she grows up."

"Yes, and fight Miranda for it."

"God. What a thought."

Miles stood up. "I'm going now."

They looked at him incredulously. "Where?"

"To the airport. I'm all packed; I booked a flight. I don't want to see Roz again. I couldn't stand it."

"Don't you want to tell her good-bye?" Phaedria asked.

"No. I couldn't. And there's no need. I'll always be there for her. And she knows that."

Letitia sighed. "You really love her, don't you?"

"Yes," he said. "I really do."

EPILOGUE

◆ ◆ ◆

PHAEDRIA HAD WRITTEN TO MICHAEL. A short, careful letter, explaining everything, saying that the company no longer mattered to her, had been taken out of her hands. Now that it was resolved, her share could safely go to Julia, in trust until she was of an age to know what she wanted to do with it. She did not say any more than that, except that she loved him, and she wished him well.

There was no reply to her letter. No phone call. Nothing. Just silence.

Weeks went by and she realized with an increasing dull misery that she had hurt and rejected him beyond anything he could be expected to forgive.

Life had reverted to some semblance of normality. Roz had come back, feisty, belligerent, spoiling for fights, but her old hostility to Phaedria had eased.

"I'm sorry," Phaedria had said to her that first day, and Roz had looked at her, her green eyes oddly soft, and said, "Yes, I know you are."

David Sassoon was paying court to Phaedria, lunching her, dining her, flattering her, trying to cajole her into bed; she resisted him rather weakly, struggling to persuade herself that she actually wanted to, and failing miserably.

C.J. and Camilla had married in a quiet ceremony in New York. Phaedria and Letitia had attended, with small Miranda, who had scowled at her new stepmother throughout in a manner so reminiscent of Roz that Letitia had been overcome with giggles and had to leave the room during the long, earnest speech delivered by Camilla's matron of honor.

Julia grew; she could sit up, laugh, scowl when thwarted, make noises that her doting mother knew were words. She was not exactly pretty; she had a rather ferocious little face. "A bit like Roz," said Eliza, looking at her one day. "Don't look at me like that, Phaedria. She is her half sister." She had dark curly hair like Phaedria's and very dark brown eyes like her father's.

Phaedria kept telling herself she was really very fortunate, but she didn't succeed in convincing herself in the least.

She was sitting in her office one June day, watching the rain pour past her window and wondering if a trip to Eleuthera might not be a nice idea when her internal phone rang. It was the new receptionist.

"Lady Morell, there's someone down here to see you. He won't give a name."

"Lorraine, you know I don't see anyone without an appointment, and certainly not if he won't give a name. Tell him he'll have to ring Sarah and fix a date."

"Lady Morell, he says he does have one important message for you. I don't know if it will make a difference. He says to tell you he's lost his raincoat."